KT-561-463

CHRISTOPHER
HOPE
My Mother's
Lovers

ATLANTIC BOOKS
LONDON

For Jasper

First published in Great Britain in hardback
in 2006 by Atlantic Books, an imprint of
Grove Atlantic Ltd.

This paperback edition published in 2007 by
Atlantic Books.

9 8 7 6 5 4 3 2

A CIP catalogue record for this book is available from the
British Library.

978 1 84354 383 1

Design by Lindsay Nash
Printed in Great Britain by
Clays Ltd, St Ives plc

Atlantic Books
An imprint of Grove Atlantic Ltd
Ormond House
26–27 Boswell Street
London WC1N 3JZ

'In Africa a thing is true at first light and a lie by noon.'

Ernest Hemingway

1   First Light

'They are trying to make Johannesburg respectable ... to
make us lose our sense of pride that our forebears were
a lot of roughnecks who knew nothing about culture and
who came here to look for gold.'

Herman Charles Bosman

I once asked my mother who my father had been.

We were shooting buffalo and, for the only time in her life, I reckon, she shot to miss. She turned her huge blue eyes on me – the rifle kicked hard, the .375 Mag H & H delivers close on forty pounds right into the shoulder – and said in her quietest voice: 'I haven't the faintest idea.' Then she handed the gun to me, her choice Holland & Holland, first made in 1912, always popular with big game hunters. She said: 'Your turn next. Remember, these beasts are tricky. Especially if you don't put him down. Captain Cornwallis Harris liked to remark that the buffalo will tramp you, kneel on you, sand-paper off your skin with his rough tongue, and then come back for another go.'

I didn't ask again.

Mind you, she told me, without my asking, that I'd been born under a thorn tree on the African plains while she had been 'with' (travelling with, sleeping with?) a white witch-doctor called Harry Huntley. He had taken her – heavily pregnant – into 'the bundu', the distant lonely veld, left her camped beneath a thorn tree and, armed only with a knife and a bag of salt, he'd gone off into the wilderness to hunt for wild bees and small game.

I always wondered: why small game, why not bloody big game? I had a very low opinion of Huntley, he seemed to me a wanker from the start.

Anyway, so her story went, it was under the thorn tree, alone, that she had given birth to her son, and he – I – might have died had her itinerant white witchdoctor not returned, and severed the umbilical cord with a whisk – get this – of his hunting knife.

My bundu birth sounded unreliable, but the bozo with the salt bag was all too typical. Africa has been chock with them. Soul-salvers, ravers, mystics, mendicants, dreamers from damp northern reaches of Europe in search of spiritual union with A-fri-ca!

Harry Huntley came directly from Leicester, and took to Africa rather as some men take to drink. He liked to go hunting elephant in Bechuanaland and his Tswana hunters apparently adored him: he went around barefoot, and lived rough in the veld on honey, roots and berries; he milked cobras which he kept in a sack; he took his water from the muddiest waterholes, and he slept at night among the roots of giant baobabs. It had been a career of feverish self-indulgence.

But, as I said, there has always been a lot of it about. You can trace a line from Harry Huntley back to David Livingstone. These guys all said the same things: they were in Africa to build railways, save souls, speed trade and/or end slavery. Popular pastimes, and useful dodges. Think of the funny hats, the odd habits, the ridiculous outfits, the bizarre wandering about in a fog of ignorance, all the while declaring they were lighting up the fucking place … Some wanted to be white gods; others went native and became *sangomas*, or rain-makers, or born-again bushmen, or praise-singers; others set about saving souls, along with black babies, lepers and the white rhino. But all of them, the slavers, the seers, the saints, the posturing white colonials had one thing in common: they took out a patent on 'their' Africa and flogged it as the one true original.

So I don't know why Huntley turned up in Africa, and I could not explain why someone like my mother should fall for a half-naked Limey from Leicester, wearing a leather skirt. She spoke English, German, Dutch, Afrikaans and Swahili. She could fly, ride, shoot – and knit. She could also box a bit: she went three rounds with Hemingway in a Mombasa gym, though as she'd say, 'He was pretty far gone by then.'

And yet she wandered into the bush with a crazy white witchdoctor.

But was Huntley my dad?

I never got the chance to ask him. Harry Huntley decided one day to swim the Orange River. Perhaps his old European education got the better of him, and he was copying Byron when he dived into the Hellespont. Perhaps he just felt like a dip. Anyway, halfway across the river Huntley got into difficulties, and was drowned.

Which of course meant even more stories grew up around the man: that he could run down lions, that he could talk to snakes, that he was a maker of rain and a sniffer-out of witches. Over the years, any number of devotees came to talk to my mother about Harry Huntley. Hollywood took movie options on one or other of the many books about him, books with titles like *The Bee Master*, *The Man Who Loved Lions*, quasi-religious tracts found on bookstore shelves marked 'African occult', and which bore about as much relation to the real Africa as soft porn did to real sex.

As to matters of paternity, then, I hadn't a clue, and my mother wasn't saying. I knew that during the last war she had risked three attempts at marriage but each time the pilot she'd been planning to marry was killed in action. She never made much of it except to say that the life expectancy of SAAF fighter pilots in the Western Desert was counted in weeks. Any of these men might have been my father. I had no way of knowing.

My birth certificate said I was born in Johannesburg, in 1944. Then again, my mother once confided that my 'paperwork' had taken 'a lot of getting hold of'. My baptismal certificate told me I had been christened in the Church of St Mary, Orange Grove, in 1945 (why the gap of a year I cannot imagine) and I was named Alexander Ignatius Healey. I was given my mother's surname, suggesting that I was born out of wedlock, though none of it proves that Huntley was my father.

Perhaps not surprisingly, then, I have always felt like a foundling, though my mother insisted that wasn't so, and that she was my legal, biological mother.

'But, my dear boy – don't I *look* like your ma?'

Nice one, that. As if by failing to spot the lineaments of motherhood, I had somehow failed the test of filial loyalty. Of course she didn't look like my mother. Not by a bloody mile. Ours was more of a compromise: she was my mother because she said so, and I was her son because I owned up to it, though not without misgivings.

Then there was my name.

'If you'd been a girl I'd have called you Alexandra, after the township. Alexander was as close as I could get... in your case.'

'What do mean... in my case?'

'Alex is a good name, don't you reckon? I learnt to box in Alex.'

Alexandra and Sophiatown, as it happened, in the 1930s. Her sparring partners were black guys hungry to punch their way to fame and freedom.

There it was. The features of her life made up a map of somewhere she said was Africa. But to me it was more mirror than map. I had to take on trust that just behind her, or over her shoulder, I might catch sight of the place itself. But it never really happened. Whenever I looked, the mirror was filled with her face.

And what a face ...

When I was a boy, she bought me comics on Saturday mornings, and I am ashamed to say I repaid her by seeing in her a faint but alarming resemblance, particularly in right profile, to Desparate Dan, the swaggering desperado with the mighty jaw. Although Desparate Dan had lots of sharp black stubble on his chin and my mother did not; at least, I don't think she did (though I have to say that sometimes *she seemed to*). Thus for me she summed up, though she did not mean to and he did, a kind of manliness.

Yet she was also entirely feminine, with a weakness for yellow cardigans and large leather handbags, and she loved turbans, except when she was on safari. No one, in my eyes, ever smoked a pipe so prettily, or clipped, lit and orchestrated a big cigar with such able-handed elegance. I think my ambivalent view of her was no more than a reflection of her astonishing range: she could be grave and tender, savage and subtle.

Our different ways of seeing each other went on widening all our lives and they showed in the distances between the places where we lived. I don't mean geographically, I mean temperamentally. We simply had very different ideas of home. My mother had always taken the grandest view of Africa; it was for her a shooting gallery, an endless sky, and she saw the European searchers, the Huntleys, Livingstones and others, as great presences, even great Africans. To me, people like Huntley, and the others who passed through our lives, were not mystics or miracle-workers, they were distinctly dodgy. I would not have bought a copper bangle or a slightly foxed bible from any of them.

I saw them as would-be actors constantly auditioning for parts in the great romance. Pallid players in search of themselves who only made sense when you thought of them as characters on a continent of their own scripting. Not Africa the place, not the groaning landmass where so many have been so betrayed by men in tunics, djellabas, and suits, who claimed to love the place, only to unleash the usual annihilation, but Africa the production, Africa the movie, Africa the road show.

My mother called this view banal and unworthy.

And what about her? She certainly had something of the theatricality. Except she didn't dress up and invent a new character; she played herself.

There was also her ambition. She was never particularly South African (that would have been far too modest), she never exhibited that limiting self-regard that marks South Africans, black and white, and leads them to see nothing else as real, and no one else as interesting. My mother wasn't to be confined to one bit of Africa, the lower leg of the continent; she took all of it as her birthright and loved it with a passion that was free of that yearning to merge that leads some people to tears (though the Huntley episode shows she was susceptible to moments of 'Jock of the Bushveld' hokum).

But, in the main, she was sound.

Take, for example, her attitude to wildlife, always a good way of telling a real African from a transplanted mythomaniac. Faced by the no longer teeming but still plentiful big game, her response was straightforward: she picked up her rifle, and shot something. Her admiration for Karen Blixen, whom she sometimes visited when she was a girl, had nothing to do with Blixen's love affair with the Kenyan highlands; it was more simply based:

'My God, could that woman kill lions!'

I went hunting with her only a few times. She was a good and patient teacher and I learnt a lot from her but it never really took. I was simply not gifted that way. She flew us to Livingstone in Northern Rhodesia, and then we drove into the bush. Buffalo don't hear or see too well but their sense of smell is exceptionally keen, and you stand more of a chance of getting in closer when you track a single animal rather than a herd. We stalked this single old bull most of the day, keeping well downwind. He had huge horns and fine bosses that made him look like some old-bufferish judge.

She was not amused by the comparison.

She was in her usual khaki shorts, and veldskoen, no socks, and a few rounds in the top pocket of her shirt. She talked as we walked.

'In the old days when we hunted there were lots of buffs, and you'd stalk them at night because they like to graze then, it being cooler. But one can't see in the dark. Problem! So what we did was to tie a bit of white cloth to the barrel of the

Mauser – we used 9.3 by 57s at the time – and the white cloth was a night-sight and direction finder. In daylight, we hunted as a group, say five or six guns; we'd stalk the herd from different directions and when the guns opened up, the danger was always that the herd might stampede and mow you down, so you had to blast away, hope to down the lead buff heading for you, then jump on his body and use it as a kind of shooting platform.'

Though I liked her warmth and her knowledge, the business did nothing for me. I understood the danger well enough. Buffalo are very strong, and they will circle back on their tracks to attack you; they can turn amazingly fast, and they will kill you as soon as look at you.

We got to within about fifty yards of the bull and she was breathing lightly as she sighted and said: 'OK, you go. Remember, you want to do as much damage as you can with your first shot. Never go for the head or the neck. Go for the boiler room, and if you're lucky you'll hit bone. It is very, very rare that you'll bring the buff down with a single shot so prepare the second; and remember he might run, then we'll have to follow. That's tricky.'

I was lucky: my shot broke his spine and put him down. She was pleased: 'One shot hardly ever does,' she said, again.

Afterwards we made stew from the buff's kneecaps – long cooking in an iron pot over the fire – and she talked of shooting and I talked of air temperature. That's what the bush did to me, it made me itch, it made me hot, it made me bored.

'There are no bloody fans in the veld,' she said.

'No, Ma. But there are methods.'

I told her about evaporative cooling. 'You soak a sheet and hang it in the breeze. Natural air-conditioning.'

'Where on earth did you get that from?'

'I read it in a book.'

'Oh, dear me,' she said. 'Air? I really wish you wouldn't.'

I liked reading about how you altered it and treated it. How you washed it clean, controlled impurities, moved it inside an enclosed space, governed its temperature. Most of all I liked the effect of my interest – so minor, so neutral, so innocent, so light – on people in a country where beer and blood and bullets flowed so easily. My interest in air sent people up the wall. Not only did it seem perverse, it was probably downright seditious.

In the old Cassell encyclopaedia my mother kept, I found the story of John Gorrie, and he became a kind of saint to me. Gorrie was a doctor and a scientist, born in Carolina: that in itself was magic – how far away was Carolina! As far away as I cared to dream. And if that were not enough, it turned out there were two Carolinas: North and South.

Gorrie trained as a doctor in New York. Then he moved to the Gulf coast and went to work in a town called Apalachicola, in Florida. I had never heard a name so beautiful, I said it over and over. But when I mentioned it at school people were very unimpressed, their faces darkened, they frowned – even quite intelligent people – and they said, 'What's that?' On hearing it was a town in Florida, in America, they often became angry, or even sarcastic. 'Oh, is it really. Florida, hey?'

My mother was the same: 'Apala— what? Honestly, Alexander, if I'd known what use you'd make of those old books, I'd have given them away to a jumble sale.'

The uses to which I put her books and which she so deplored had nothing much to do with information in the strictest sense of the word: for me reading was much more vital, more physical, more satisfying; it showed me how to escape. It got me out of the house, and out of the country, it got me as far as Apalachicola. How it rings – that name! – still …

In Apalachicola, John Gorrie treated malaria and yellow fever, though at the time no one could tell the difference; except that malaria began with terrible chills, shakes, and fever; it might come back again and again and sometimes it could kill. Far more mysterious was yellow fever, which only came once, and left you dead or alive. Yellow fever also began with the shivers and high temperatures, raging thirst, violent headaches, then awful pain in your back and legs. The next day you turned yellow as an old autumn leaf. Worst was the black vomit, a falling temperature and onset of the final coma.

Since it was widely believed that the terrible disease came from 'bad air' – *mal-aria* – desperate defences were thrown up to ward off the noxious effluvium: vinegar in your handkerchief, garlic on your shoes, sheets soaked in camphor, burning sulphur or gunpowder, and even firing cannons.

John Gorrie tried ice. He hung basins of the stuff over the patient's bed: cool air is heavier than hot air. It soothed, quite literally, the fevers of his patients. But ice was hard to come by – it had to be shipped in by boat from the lakes in the north – and that was when Gorrie had a revolutionary idea: he decided to build a machine to make ice.

In 1851, he applied for a patent on an ice-making machine. I knew the lines of his short application by heart and I could make my mother bellow simply by saying them out loud:

"'If the air were highly compressed, it would heat up by the energy of compression. If this compressed air were run through metal pipes cooled with water, and if this air cooled to the water temperature was expanded down to atmospheric pressure again, very low temperatures could be obtained, even low enough to freeze water in pans in a refrigerator box."'

Power for the compressor, Gorrie reckoned, could come from steam, water, wind-sails or, perhaps, horses. He got the temperature to drop by forcing gas to expand fast. Squeeze a gas and it heats up; relax the pressure and the gas expands, and as it does so it absorbs heat, and chills the space around it. Dr Gorrie's basic principle is the one most often used in refrigeration today; namely, cooling caused by the rapid expansion of gases.

He had a reverence for ice; he believed it cured fever. He was wrong about that. Mosquitoes caused malaria, not heat. But what made him a hero to me was that he wanted to alleviate the suffering of his patients, he wished to cool them, and to purify the 'bad air' that made them sick. Gorrie believed, in short, that reducing temperature would relieve suffering.

I was interested to know that, at the time, there were those who hated him, who believed that making ice was blasphemy. Gorrie had done what only God could do. He was vilified accordingly, and died young and broken-hearted.

I knew that in an important way he had been right. In my country we lived with bad air – with *mal-aria* – we had contracted the illness that was to lay all Africa low before long. We had the fevers, the sweats, the pain, the frenzy induced by infectious, highly poisonous ideas that were very much in the air: the purity of the blood, and the integrity of the tribe, group and nation. It led to madness and murder among us and it would lead to the same across Africa, as country after country came to independence. It might be called nationalism if that didn't sound too kind for a killer disease. The great disaster of our times.

My mother hadn't a trace of it, and I admired her for that. She sailed over it, she took no notice of boundaries, borders, divisions, races or tribes or nations: how could anything so stupid, so vulgar, so boring, so narrow be serious? Though she could adopt, for the moment – depending on where she was – particular people who embodied for her something of Africa. She took to Ituri pygmies, or leopard men, or even, because they had very briefly welcomed her father as one of their own, the Boers of the old South African republics. But she had no sense of clan or colour, only of friends or enemies. This was magnificent, in its way. But blind. As she saw the world, race never mattered. She simply wasn't interested in it. But as things turned out, it was interested in her.

I remember most clearly from the years when I could not have been more than five or six the piney tang of her flying boots, rubbed with waxy dubbin, the stuff used for saddles and holsters and gun-sleeves. I remember the smell of her pipe and the acrid bite of Boxer tobacco. Just back from somewhere, elsewhere, anywhere, she lay stretched out in her big wicker chair, the toes of her flying boots buffed to a gleam that reminded me of honey, fingering sweet shreds of tobacco from the small cotton bag with the drawstring neck, filling her pipe, black and slender, with a silver cap, clipped to a light silver chain, that snapped tight over the bowl when the tobacco glowed hot. My mother came in many versions. I sometimes thought of her as being like the sea: forever the same, forever altering. At other times I thought she looked like a man in a wig, rather like Jack Lemmon in *Some Like It Hot*. Only taller and bigger-bosomed, the recipient of a very successful sex change, with her hair in a centre parting, so it hung over her ears in a great scalloped but never entirely convincing curtain of chestnut curls.

Her long legs stuck out before her like stilts; she lay there breathing thick creamy smoke into the air, and at that point I'd be really pleased. Because she was there; because she was still, and not moving; because she was home; because we were together; because she had come back from wherever she had been: home from Mombasa or Lagos or Stanleyville. Come down from whatever altitude she'd been flying at; in Kenya or Nyasaland or South West Africa; back from whichever uncle she had been seeing just then – Uncle Hansie, Uncle Papadop or Uncle Bertie from Natal, who claimed to be a white Zulu.

Bertie had been one of the earliest of my uncles. He ran a big hotel in England; he'd made a lot of money and he believed that 'the Zulu nation' was as close as you got in modern times to the ancient Romans for 'fighting skills and stoic courage'. Why not become a white Swazi, or a white Xhosa? Well, because, for romantic hoteliers like Uncle Bertie, only certain tribes cut the mustard. One saw this whimsical fascination all over the damn place. In Kenya, it was the Masai who won hands down; in Arabia the Bedouin. For Uncle Bertie it was the Zulus.

He came out to Zululand back in the murky days of the mid-sixties when, if it wasn't bad enough living with crooks and criminals who liked to think of themselves as pioneering stock in this corner of Africa, we found ourselves groaning beneath the yoke of strait-laced puritans. We were used to dealing with rough villainy, but being ruled by guys with a sincere conviction that they were God's anointed was some-thing we had never experienced (and have never recovered from). But of course Uncle Bertie, being from England, knew sweet fuck-all about any of this. He knew only 'Africa'. Need I say more? The guys who ran our country liked Bertie, they liked his energy, his blindness, his attempts to be reasonable and rational. They also liked his take on the tribes. Didn't they think of themselves as an African tribe, albeit the one destined by the Good Lord to kick shit out of all other tribes? Well, then, what could be better than guys like Uncle Bertie wishing to join up to the Zulus?

Uncle Bertie was created a white Zulu by King Cyprian Bhekuzulu kaSolomon. His new name was Nqobizitha, which meant 'Conquer the Enemies'. When he came to visit in Jo'burg, he did a Zulu dance on the lawn by the dahlias. A plump, bare-chested hotelier in a leather dress and leopard-skin trimmings, paws dancing on his nipples, waving a knobkerrie...

'He's an idiot,' I told my mother.

'Don't let him hear you saying that, he won't let you play with his assegais,' she said. 'And it might be one of Bertie's places we're staying in next.'

It was. He bought a game farm in Natal and my mother used to go shooting there. On the wall, next to the Queen, he hung his certificate saying he'd been inducted into the Zulu nation.

We seemed to move just about every week to some new place or other, depending on my mother's flight plans, her hunting trips, or the uncle of the moment. We lived on farms or smallholdings in the Transvaal veld; we stayed for a while in neat and stony suburban bungalows; and in broad-shouldered Jo'burg mansions where immense lawns ran down to the distant white walls, and the sun on the mesh of the tall fence burnt diamonds in the baked rouge-red sand of the tennis court.

Looking back, I can't tell them apart, and they all – these passing homes – fused into our real home, the house in which we came to rest many years later, the house in Forest Town, up the road from the Zoo. Just as all my memories fused into these pictures of my mother, when she was at home and we were together.

On this occasion I remember she had just arrived back at the Grand Central Flying Club, taxied her Stinson into the hangar and driven home in the old Land Rover. My mother flew a variety of aircraft over the years, Piper and Beechcraft, but it was a Stinson Voyager, built in Wayne, Michigan, in 1947, that she kept longest. Four places for passengers, if you put in the two back seats, and loads of room if you didn't; a strong machine, able to lift around 700 pounds easily enough.

What she generally did when she headed out into Africa was to fly on conventional landing gear until Kenya where she'd put down on the rough landing strip belonging to some uncle or other, who happened to own a convenient dam or a stretch of water. Next day she'd swap conventional landing gear for a pair of floats, it meant she could put down on a piece of water anywhere she liked. And wherever she put down was hers.

I remember that particular homecoming so well because, unusually, she hadn't brought anyone back with her: no friends from the great bush that she flew over and into; no witch-doctors, no white hunters from Gabon or Congo or Kenya. This time it was just her and me, just us. I hugged her and she smelt of elsewhere: of campfires, cordite, pipe tobacco, boot polish and aircraft oil. Then I sat and watched her, and knew that she really and truly existed, and I hoped she'd never move again. I knew she would, of course; she was only resting; her way was not to stop but to be up and off, though for the moment you would never have thought so, seeing her lying back, the liquid shine on her toecaps, the ends of a lavender scarf offset by the woolly white edging of her flying jacket.

On the bookcase behind her, with its blue-shouldered, leather-bound Cassell's *Great Stories of the World*, there sat in its carved ivory frame the photograph of her father: an alert and yearning face, with a full moustache and a bold yet bruised look to his olive-dark eyes. And photos of Dr Schweitzer and Hemingway, as well as the façade of Muthaiga Club in Nairobi and a view of Mount Kilimanjaro, and all those people and places which – never distinguishing between locations and living beings – she called 'my old mates'. And because she never saw much difference between people and places, she would attach human feelings to different countries and ascribe geographical features to people: the Congo, she said once, 'has a shy, retiring nature; it's decidedly bashful...' And Hemingway was 'landlocked; always dreaming of having his own access to the sea'. For years I thought Hemingway was a country somewhere in Africa.

'Fighting a man, you have to protect your breasts. And Hem's arms were so damn long. But he didn't watch his middle, and I got in close and pecked away. We were about the same height, over six foot, though he had a big weight advantage. I would carry my left too low and he would dab away with his left and switch to the right. Hem was strong, of course. In a brawl in a bar he'd have murdered me, but in the ring you have space to move; he'd catch me on the chest, on the shoulders, in the ribs. His timing, though, was off. I would fall back, fall back; he'd like that; he'd come after me, and I'd back away, knowing he wanted to throw his right, then I'd step in and beat him to the punch. I'd hit him on the nose or mouth. Thing with him was he knew about boxers; he knew the stance, the talk, and he believed he was good. But he was an amateur. And so was I. But I worked out years ago with people like Ezekiel Dhlamini and Slugger Ntombi; they were the real thing.'

There was her picture of Hemingway wearing only a pair of shorts, with his hair shaved, burnt almost black by the sun, carrying a spear.

'He was going through his I-am-a-Wakamba-hunter stage. He liked to show himself off, did Hem. I felt sorry for Mary. What that woman went through!'

Hemingway decided that he needed an African wife and so he had found a girl among the Wakamba.

'Was he proud of Debba! He had this dream he would live with his "light" wife Mary and his "dark" wife, Debba, in a shamba, among the Wakamba. It's like old music-hall, isn't it?'

There was her picture of Hemingway when he did a stint as an honorary game warden with some Kikuyu as his troops. He is dressed in a uniform he designed himself, a lot of khaki and his broad '*Gott Mit Uns*' belt that he said he took off a dead German soldier, and he is being saluted by the troops.

'God, he loved dressing up.'

And so did they all. Where but Africa gave white men in fancy dress more kicks, more pleasure, or power? Only in Africa did they seriously impress; not so much by their talents or their morals, though God knows they liked to think that way. No, what impressed was their firepower, their murder rate; it was all such fun, it was all so easy, it was all so brilliant. And it went to their heads. Like their hats.

Then there were her fixed points of reference:

'My old dad ...'

'My old mates ...' (Those were my uncles, or her old hunting grounds.)

'My dear boy…' (That was me.)

Frankly, I didn't give a toss about her old mates. They got between us, they took her off; they were a pain in the arse.

And if you asked me what I didn't like about them I'd say they were so fucking stagy they hurt. Like the place itself. This was heresy, I knew that but it was no good muttering the magic mantra 'Africa', as if that helped. It did not. In my experience the mention of the word was either a bloody excuse, or a threat. The place should trade in the name and start again with a new one. I heard her use it so often I learnt not to buckle under its manipulative pressure. I took the view that whenever you heard someone say 'Africa', you'd best check the gun-safe and the security arrangements because the chances were someone somewhere was planning: to (a) take you for a ride; or (b) do you in.

So my old lady's mantra did nothing for me. She was always everywhere but home where I wanted her. This was around the time when she was travelling some two weeks out of every month; when a succession of nannies arrived to look after me, and then left, because my mother had found them new jobs, as nurses or saleswomen. She thought domestic service a mug's game, could not see the point of servants, and I'd no sooner got used to the cooking, the habits, the presence of the new Betty or Blessing or Ntembi than she'd be whisked away to be trained as a nurse, a needlewoman, a scientist, and my ma was damned pleased with herself for helping them to jump ship.

It went on like this until I got to be about ten or eleven, and learnt how to look after myself, how to make myself sand-wiches for school, how to boil an egg, and thank God we used no servants ever again but only a cleaning service called De Wet's Flying Dutchmen, pure white men in a white van.

Afrikaans men who cleaned the house and did the garden: tall sunburnt hairy moustachioed males in khaki shorts down on their knees, scrubbing the kitchen floor, weeding the garden and calling to each other: '*Ek sê, ou doosie, gooi ons die blerrie doek!*' ('Hey there, old cunty, toss us the rag.') It was their language which so affected Baldy, our grey parrot, and gave him his rich store of Afrikaans expletives, drawn from the household curses of those gruff male chars: Baldy loved to sing out: '*Die bliksemse seep is kak!*' ('This bloody soap is shit ...') and '*My jirre, maar die blerrie Hoover is opbefok ...*' ('Jesus, but this bloody Hoover is up-befucked.')

My ma's housekeeping arrangements had for years rattled the neighbours who flanked us: Mrs Terre'Blanche, Mrs Garfinkel, to the left and right; Mrs Smuts and Mrs Mason across the street. A pincer movement of fighting madams, my mother called them. But then she liked pissing off the neighbourhood. And it was pretty wild stuff, using a white male household cleaning service at a time when anyone patriotic and properly South African had two, three or four servants living in the back yard; and anyone who didn't was weird, if not downright bloody revolutionary.

She took no interest in my schooling. I was glad about that. Once she came to watch me playing cricket at school, still in her flying gear, and she leaned on the fence and lit her pipe. The other kids wondered out loud: 'Jesus Christ, who's *that*?'

For the life of me I didn't know what to say but honesty required a response and so I said she was, well, sort of ... my ma.

I was met with blank disbelief.

'Naw, it can't be! You fucking liar!'

And looking at her again, they had a point. But, then, if the tall figure at the fence wasn't my mother, just who the hell was she?

This was the time of our lion park, the first in the Transvaal. I think it was my old lady's riposte to Joy Adamson, whom she absolutely loathed:

'That bloody show-off ! One of those foreigners who come here and romanticise Africa. Born free, my eye! Let me tell you, dear boy, nothing and no one is born free; none of us is entitled to it; freedom's something you have to work to get and fight to keep.'

'Yes, Ma.'

'Don't you "yes, Ma" me.'

'No, Ma.'

Our lion park was to have been a money-spinner: my old lady's idea was to bring big game hunting to what she called 'the citizenry'. They were to pay twenty guineas for the guarantee of bagging a lion. She'd take the hunters out in her Landy and make sure they got what they paid for, a leonine trophy to stick on the wall right next to the flying ducks and the little wooden wall plaque that read: 'Everything I like is either immoral, illegal or fattening.'

It wasn't a bad idea. Even then, in the fifties, hunting in South Africa seldom meant big game. You needed to go north for that. Hunting more usually meant small game pursued by big men in bad shorts. My mother's idea was to make available to South Africans some of the pleasure she had on safari in Block 66 in Tanganyika, and the foothills of Mount Kilimanjaro.

She rented several thousand hectares outside Krugersdorp, already well stocked with springbuck, kudu and zebra. She talked to her pals in Arusha and shipped in half a dozen lions

– 'to test the market'. Her lions were black manes – a species long gone from South Africa – and they came from a terrain of thorn bush, colossal mats of blond grass, black lava fields and knife-edged sanseveria bushes, and she had them brought all the way down to the waving grasses of the flat highveld.

I was the gatekeeper. She dressed me in a khaki safari suit with the legend stitched in red letters on my back 'Healey's Hunts'. I sat in a plastic chair in front of the gate holding a canvas bag to collect what my ma called the 'spondulaks' from the grateful citizenry; she waited with the guns and the Land Rover. She used an old Mannlicher .256: 'nice and light for quick stuff', she said, meaning buck. For heavier stuff like buffalo and elephant, she used a .470.

What she hadn't counted on was the unwillingness, deep-set in South Africans, to pay for something they believed belonged to them. The South African hunter did not do licences, tents or sundowners or silver cups for bringing down the biggest buff. Unlike the guys in Kenya, he ate what he shot. If you wanted to shoot you went to your farm, or your several farms, or your sister's farm, and chased buck in a truck. South African hunting wasn't about safaris, or sex, or sport, or even style; the South African hunter did not mix with women, he did not use porters, and he despised those who did so. Paying to hunt was as bad as paying for sex: it was downright indecent, it was un-South African. Hunting was about guys, often in the backs of pick-ups, running down game; about being getting pissed on brandies and Coke, and throwing up under the thorn trees. It was about being proper South Africans. Proper South Africans were the last aristocrats; they owned the country. They did not pay at the gate. That sort of thing was for foreigners, faggots and females, which in the minds of the hunters in the back of the pick-up amounted to pretty much the same thing anyway.

My mother's hunting habits were different. She hunted in the Congo rainforests, in Uganda and Mozambique and Nyasaland. Her style was founded on the Kenyan model invented by rich Britons and richer Americans. Her idea of a safari had to do with blood, bullets, booze and sex: a silver service supper after a fine day at the salt lick. Good champagne whenever possible, because wines did not travel well. What she enjoyed, I suppose, were the prerogatives of birth and breeding. Her style had the marks that distinguished the old white hunters who worked in Central and East Africa: for whom hunting went with money and muscular snobbery; whose safaris starred barons, princes, presidents and film stars; who dreamt of night-time Africa in the bush as adventure: getting tiddly, or getting laid, under a fat buttery hunting moon, while beyond the circle of firelight the hyenas paced, yelping like traders on the floor of the bourse.

Thinking back, I see she wasn't wrong about bringing hunting to the citizenry but she was way ahead of her time. She set up what was to prove popular much later, what became known as canned hunts, where the victim – lion, buffalo, eland – was shepherded into the sights of some arsehole who bought a licence that guaranteed him one dead trophy. Healey's Hunts planned to offer 'salving spirits of Africa': rubdowns with aloe oil; she even talked of a line in cosmetics, 'Healey's Health and Beauty Lotions'. She foresaw the industry of 'lifestyle' lodges that would come in time to litter the South African bush. They stand there today, monuments to her idea that beat them to it by decades: 'wellness centres' and psychosomatic healing bomas, promising full-frontal African therapies like uplifting *ubuntu*, and all the attendant decor – hand-woven mosquito nets, canvas showers under the baobabs, healing baths in rooibos tea, or *buchu* brandy, along with 100 per cent genuine Zulu massage, ethnic bushveld cuisine, and all the free booze you can drink – at a mere thousand bucks a night.

Healey's Hunts folded after six weeks and was not mentioned again. I don't know what happened to our lions. But, then, I didn't know much about anything concerning my own life. Life, my life, all life, had a way of beginning in some past adventure of my mother's; and it continued like that until I went over the wall.

3

I once asked her how she came to be a flier and she said: 'I owe it all to dynamite.'

That was her stock answer to questions touching on matters she felt were too holy to be solved in a secular way. But as I pieced together the story, I got some idea of what she meant. Life was a matter of uplift. It was literally charged with propulsive power, primed to blow you sky-high and, in her case, keep you up there. Somehow, simply by being in and belonging to Africa, your adventures were legalised, and localised, and characterised by the successful use of high explosive. By blowing something up you said you owned it.

If she was used to being looked up to, it wasn't altogether surprising. Six-two in her socks – she knitted them herself – of warm grey wool. She had learnt to fly when she was eighteen, and never looked back; as a result, whenever she came back from wherever she had been, it always felt to me as if she had just dropped from the sky, which of course she had.

She always said that her old dad got her into the flying boats, and gave her a taste for altitude. I think being looked up to came naturally. She bestrode her world like the Queen of Sheba or Godzilla or Prester John: warrior queen, monster or male impersonator, who knows? And how many men loved her! Which was really odd, when you thought about it, since she always seemed to me too busy shooting things, or heading off somewhere new, to bother much about her desperate admirers, lost in the dust of her departures.

Now and then, 'just for fun', she flew me on low-level excursions over the dynamite factory at Modderfontein, on Jo'burg's eastern edge: the biggest in the world, if not the universe. She never failed to be impressed all over again by its capacity for destruction. My feeling was: so what? You fly over it, you look down, you see an expanse of roof; it was, after all, nothing more than a fucking factory.

'Why is it so important?'

'Why? How do you think we get at our gold? We drill deep shafts down through the rock; and to slice the rocky gold reef into getatable bits, we blast tunnels, or stopes, that stretch like branch lines, off the main shaft. Blasting takes lots of dynamite. Three million cases every year. Dynamite is what we do in Jo'burg. It's in our blood.'

She hoped that 'one day soon' I'd get my blasting certificate. When I said I didn't like explosives, her account of South African history, according to notable explosions, then followed:

'Eighteen ninety-six was an awful year. First came the Jameson Raid, followed by a plague of rinderpest that decimated every beast from here to the Zambezi. Then a brand-new ocean liner, the *Drummond Castle*, went down off the French coast. But most spectacular of all was the "Great Dynamite Explosion". It happened in Braamfontein on 19 February 1896. A train, loaded with fifty-five tons of dynamite, was left cooking in the highveld sun. It had been there for three days. A shunting engine happened to nudge the train and up it went, blasting a hole sixty yards wide and ninety feet deep, killed over a hundred, and injured two thousand. They had just begun to build Jo'burg, and then they blew it up. Par for the course, Alexander. Always remember how wedded we are to dynamite.'

Her idea of education, of a real qualification, was a licence to blow things up.

'My old dad got his blasting certificate when he was just sixteen. Fancy that! It was in the old Transvaal and the Kruger Volksraad passed a law that said no one but a white man could lay a stick of dynamite; only whites could load or drill or fire fuses. But this ran into the old South African problem. Blacks and Coloureds and Asians were good blasters. Coming up from the Kimberley diamond fields: hell, they could blow just as prettily as any white boy, and what's more, they blew for half the damn wage. Observe the old tableau: piety overwhelmed by greed. Why pay a stupid white boy a fiver a month to do what a clever black boy did better and cheaper? So how to stay pure while stiffing the mine owners who didn't give a toss for your race fantasies? Easy. Kruger's people lifted the race bar but they passed a law that only men with blasting tickets could use dynamite, and so ever afterwards, white men got the blasting tickets and black men carried the tools.'

I knew the lesson by heart. Getting rich was a messy business. Once upon a time, when Jo'burg was still a camp, anyone could buy some sticks, blast a hole in the reef and hope to get lucky. But singularity gave way to mass production, to control, to boredom and death.

My grandfather, Joe Healey, has come down to me in fine detail, preserved in the aspic of my mother's memories. She who forgot nothing and in whom details of the past lived on, in continual adjustment, concurrent with, and parallel to, the ongoing events of our own lives. She was a walking, talking almanac, detailing not only our family, but this country, and the mad, comic, tear-stained history of white settlement on this southern tip of Africa. Memories of the Boer War, the reef of gold, the damnable English, the bold fighting farmers of Smuts and Delarey and the talent of her dad for setting high explosives.

Joe Healey was a pioneer. Those pompous pricks forever banging on about 'the golden city' liked to say he came 'to make history'. In truth, along with all the riff-raff who swarmed on to the Rand at the end of the nineteenth century, Joe Healey came to make money, and very dodgy money at that. He came for gold and, very soon, that meant he had to pick up a gun.

'In the Boer War my old dad fought in the Irish Brigade.'

It sounded a grand name for the moustachioed ragamuffins in the picture she kept on her desk.

'My old dad blew up culverts with Major MacBride.'

She would lean on the word 'culverts' in that Jo'burg way, which lengthens the first and shortens the second syllable into a serrated knife-edge 'culll-vittz!' And then she'd add: 'Of course this was before John MacBride ever stepped out with Maude Gonne, or Willy Yeats was ever in the picture. They called my old dad "Spaghetti Joe" because when he laid a mine the explosion had the effect of knitting the railway line into tangles like spaghetti. He had the distinction of blowing up every railway culvert from Bloemfontein to the Vaal. The British' – she always spoke as if it had happened last week – 'wanted to wipe us off the face of the earth. The British saw us as barely human, cavemen, half-ape. A species headed for extinction – they wanted the heads of "Brother Boer" mounted on the clubroom wall. They came out for a spot of shooting, as if we were pheasants ...'

By 'us' she meant the Boers, the taciturn, stubborn, barely literate Dutch *paysans*. These were the guys with whom she passionately identified; they were 'our people'. But she seemed to me to care with the same passion she showed for saving threatened species, like the bongo and the white rhino. She cared, too, for the theatre of it, and, of course, the shooting.

'The Khakis would turn up at a farm and give us twenty minutes to carry what we could, and then they'd torch the place. They saw us as lice, as germs! They wanted to burn us out. To get back to the clean dream of an empty land with gold under foot. As a killing machine the British Army rivalled the Black Death; it carried off people night and day.'

Even though she'd been born sixteen years after the Boer War ended, and knew about it only from those stories she got from her father, it made no difference. She had been *there*, and the fact of her substantial presence during those cruelties meant that I was there too.

It was, I later saw, very Jo'burg, this inflatable history. It was the impulse of prospectors, dirt-poor miners, to pretend that everything you could name you owned. In the beginning, vocabulary was property. Even its present somewhat rumbling moniker – Johannesburg – was an afterthought; tarting up what had been a flat piece of nothing very much, first called Ferreira's Camp.

All that mattered was that under the feet of the lean and hungry diggers of Ferreira's Camp there ran deep rivers of gold in stone. And when you considered the charge sheet drawn up against our city, my old lady had a point. Many of the punters who dollied up Jo'burg into the gilded trollop with a pistol in her purse should have been locked up for causing grievous bodily harm, being drunk in charge of a lethal weapon, for perjury, fraud and for believing in casual killing as a form of moral persuasion. To some degree, of course, you could say that that was how things were done in this country, ever since the first settler splashed ashore and began booting the locals around. And you'd be dead right. But Jo'burg did it in spades.

From the instant in 1886, when the first seekers stubbed their toes on rocks veined with gold and realised that whole rivers of bullion lay frozen beneath their feet, Jo'burg was on the rise and has been ever since. A clutch of outlaws in Ferreira's Camp talked big, talked it up, talked it into what they wanted it to be; much as later on they floated their prize fights, their horse races, their brothels with a profligacy never before seen in southern Africa. 'Eldorado-on-the-Reef' and 'California-in-the-Veld', the 'Golden City', 'Egoli', miracle metropolis in the middle of nowhere where everyone was on the take and on the make and on the money, where diggers wore hats and called themselves gents, and girls in white gloves sipped tea in Ansteys and called themselves 'madam'.

It was Paul Kruger, appalled by its whores, conmen and dusty depravity, who called the town 'Sodom and Gomorrah' . Most Jo'burgers took that as a compliment. Ferreira's Camp grew into the greatest African city south of Cairo, whose gods were two: gold and the gun. What could you expect of a town conceived by vagrant remittance men? Not even a town, in truth, but a series of dusty claims and roped-off diggings. Men in hats, with shovels and spades in hand, and gold lust in their hearts. A happy-go-lucky sort of girl who flashed her gold-spangled knickers at every passing sucker.

On the walls of my mother's many bedrooms, transferred from house to house in our travels over the years, she hung photos her dad had taken of early Johannesburg. I saw the first of the wagons that arrived after the discovery of gold on what was called Witwatersrand; the first tents that went up in a louche settlement perched upon the greatest, deepest reef of gold in the world. Gold is the barbarous metal and these were barbarous men. They stand in my grandfather's pictures with their hats aslant. They stand beside the City and Suburban Mine back in 1887, the town just one year old, and they are already full of swagger; they have blasted the rock apart and a deep crack splits the earth and over the fissure they have rigged a pulley. Lowering a bucket down into the open hole, into the auriferous rocky womb, is a black man. The white men, muscular, debonair, are watching the black man working.

In Joe Healey may be found the route and pattern later followed by so many of us. Those who lived through the Boer War never got the hang of what happened after that; they believed in some weird way that this was a normal place where they could lead grown-up lives.

Dreaming of rich shipwreck upon the golden reef, Joe Healey came to Jo'burg in 1906. A town of tents, tin and unbaked Kimberley brick, home to more than 150,000 miners – one in three were white – and next to no women. Two stone buildings, both two stories tall: Consolidated Buildings and Corner House. In the beginning the diggers traded claims and shares in the street, and so did the whores. Then when the cash came in they built themselves a bourse, and they built themselves a brothel, and most folks never could tell the difference. The bourse has been a high-rise cathouse ever since. But those who made too much of the connection missed the spiritual dimensions; because buying stock was probably the only near-religious experience most Jo'burgers have ever had.

It was in Corner House, where my grandfather went to work. A courier hauling piles of paper scrip. In and out of the brothel, the bourse, the bar, running between buyers and sellers with paper promises to be redeemed or damned.

He got the hang of things pretty fast. Jo'burg was wild, the 'Rand' was booming, and it was made of the queerest set of people yet to gather in one corner of Africa and pretend they were living somewhere else. Like England or Ireland or Estonia or Russia. For among the Barnatos, Ecksteins, Rosenthals, Rose-Inneses, Bradleys, Paulings and Goldreichs, amongst Lithuanians and Limeys and Yanks were squadrons of Chinese imported into the mines. Much as van Riebeeck, when the Dutch first arrived in the Cape, shipped in hundreds of slaves from Malaysia, on the understanding that white men were in Africa to grow rich and all others were in Africa to work.

In Ferreira's Camp on the golden reef there were plenty of black guys around, but the Chinese worked longer hours for less pay, though there were complaints about the difficulty of learning their language. Nonetheless, Joe Healey managed a smattering of Mandarin, as well as Dutch, German, French, Russian and Swahili.

The city expanded in square blocks, in straight lines laid over the memories of old farms and fountains. The broad streets were named for the desperadoes who brokered the deals and salted the mines, who built mansions on Parktown Ridge, who lied and cheated and shot their way to fame: Eloff and Pritchard, Harrison and Jeppe. Rock-crushers, shaft sinkers, surveyors, conmen and notaries. Their temples were the mining houses – De Beers, Consolidated Gold, Anglo-American – and their saints were Rhodes, Barnato, Beit and Oppenheimer, whose sacred names we learnt as children when we directed our devotions towards the Stock Exchange in prayers hot and urgent: 'Our Rand-lords, who art in Hollard Street ... make us rich!'

My mother walked me through the early streets of the early town, much as she later walked me through the battlefields and concentration camps of the Boer War. Down Commissioner, the only street wide enough to turn a span of sixteen oxen, to the Turffontein races where Joe Healey, late of Kilkenny, without a farthing to his name, was soon racing his own thoroughbreds, to the Rand Club, corner of Commissioner and Harrison streets. The Club, along with the racecourse and cricket pitch, had been amongst the first things built: bullion, brothel, bourse, the unholy trinity that Jo'burg adored.

'The land for that bloody Rand Club, believe it or not, was given by Ikey Sonnenberg to that wicked magician, Cecil Rhodes. Given free, gratis and for nothing, in return for which, Rhodes founded the Rand Club and the Club spent the next hundred years keeping Jews out.

'Rhodes and Beit, and the other big goldbugs, bought out the small prospectors, and they built the biggest dynamite factory in the world and blasted tunnels through the rock to get to the specks of ore clutched in the rock. And let me tell you, it worked; they *were* the gold industry. But let me tell you, too, we paid for it. For every bit of ore we pulled out of the rock, a bit of brain ran out of our ears ... That's how it is here.'

'Here' was always Johannesburg; the only town between the Cape and Cairo worth thinking about. Any other place was a bit of a joke; and if it wasn't a joke, it was to be pitied. Jo'burg counted; it had treasure, height, danger and speed, the risk of sudden death. And the odd thing was she felt, we all did in a way, in these dark attributes a cause for civic pride.

'History? We don't have a history, really,' I remember her telling one of my many uncles. 'Just a police record.'

Ah, that 'we': not the royal 'we', not an editorial 'we', not a warm familial pronoun. No, hers was an imperial 'we' that reached beyond family pride, to gather into its brazen possessive stockade everything that made 'ours' not just the best town in Africa, but in the entire bloody world.

I'd argue.

'London?'

'Oh, please!'

'New York?'

'Nonsense.'

'Paris?'

'Do me a favour.'

'Shanghai?'

'You must be joking.'

Soon after the Great War ended Joe Healey married Millie Brokenshaw, the daughter of a Cornish tin-miner who came out to try his luck in the Kimberley diamond mines. Millie died in childbirth and left my grandfather with a little girl to bring up. When Kathleen was about twelve he parlayed his one and only talent, an intimate knowledge of how to blow up things, into a job and, even more important in Jo'burg, into a title – he got himself appointed Chief Explosives Officer for Corner House Investments.

It was quite a change. The boy who once went to war against those hated English who plotted and murdered to rob the Transvaal of its gold, now went on to adapt himself to the peace of Vereeniging – 'that hateful, horrid surrender' (my mother's words) – with which the Boer War ended by going to work for the very bastards – the goldbugs, the Rand-lords – who 'bankrolled' (my mother again) 'that smash and grab raid on the gold and diamonds of the Boer republics'.

It turned out to be a bright move. All over Africa there was buried treasure men wished to rip out of the ground. Mines were opening on the Rand, in Ndola and the Congo, and the mining houses loved high explosives. Joe Healey could blow anything: he could stash a charge in a stope with his eyes closed. It soon brought him money, three-piece suits, a pigskin briefcase, and lots of travel in the flying boats, carrying people and mail up and down the continent.

Yes, there were problems, disconsolate ex-Boers, angry blacks and a kind of missionary greed, together with an open worship of militant stupidity, but it was the new world, and everyone was, or would be, equal. Even the Catholic Irish …

Joe Healey really believed he was at home, though from the start all the indications were against it. He was in Africa and that made all the difference. He fought for the Boers who lost the war, but they won the peace. And when they came to own the entire country they had little use for Joe Healey, or for his belief in progress, in dynamite, in Johannesburg, in freedom, reason, in good sense.

'We'll sink our differences, or our differences will sink us,' said Joe Healey to his young daughter.

It sounded sensible, and modern and statesmanlike. But this was South Africa, the Boers were in charge, and such sentiments were baloney. All that the easy talk of freedom and good sense ever brought was better suits, turbans and flywhisks for the boss-men – and bigger shit for everyone else.

'We're cracked,' my mother said. 'We're the descendants of gold-crazed miners. With about as much taste or judgement as you'd expect. Everything's show. What do people want? They want a gold mine, six limos and a whacking mansion in the suburbs with an electric fence, a big pool and lots of guns. They want this from Soweto to Sandton; they all want it. Blacks and Whites and Asians and Coloureds and Chinese ... And they want it now. No one knows what he or she's supposed to be; everyone pretends like mad. One day you're a robber; next day you're a religious leader. It's not so strange. We're willing to try anything. You start off a cricketer or a drag queen, and pop up again as a traffic cop or a poet. And we don't have a problem with that. It's not strange. If you've a problem with that, you're *strange*. OK, yes?'

OK, no.

I had a problem with that. What I did, later, was a form of revolt most calculated to make my ma as mad as hell. She wanted guns and boots and the stuff that heats, detonates, goes off pop. She looked on our national predilection for hitting each other as just another way of staying in touch, and her heart softened. I wanted to throw up. So I went the other way, I went for the lightest and most insignificant and weightless of things. I came from a town where people would have had their

servants do their breathing for them, leaving them free to concentrate on masterly things, like gold, guns and talking up a
storm. I came from a place where we were ruled for ever by a
small bunch of demented bores who said they were the sons of
God, that their blood was washed in heaven and their skin
blessed by angels, and if anyone disagreed they would, happily
kick their fucking heads in, and frequently did so. Nothing
personal, just touching base.

These guys were opposed by another lot who felt that the
white guys who ran and ruined the country were so bad they
should, in the words of Louis Farrakhan, be killed and buried
and then dug up and killed all over again. And if you didn't
agree with either side, if you said what was needed was to cool
it down, not heat it up, you were nowhere. Or – as my ma said
– you had a problem.

Other mothers took their kids to churches or art galleries to improve their minds and souls; my ma used to fly me to the killing grounds of the Boer War. She hadn't been there but she loved fighting it all over again.

I liked flying with her; she was very calm, so calm she sometimes fell asleep. She wasn't completely asleep, more a waking doze; the plane used to climb and then descend gently, on autopilot, but it was still a weird feeling. I used to sit and watch the far-away koppies bobbing along the horizon. I didn't dare wake her and I didn't dare touch the controls.

She trained in a Gypsy Moth, when she was eighteen. She had her pilot's licence in 1938: one of the very few women in Africa to fly solo. And she wore, until quite late in life, what she called 'my old gear from the early days': a single-piece flying suit lined with quilt, and a sheepskin jacket. Her helmet and goggles became redundant, and always hung in the parlour beside the picture of Bamadodi, the Rain Queen. The helmet was lined with chamois leather and had rubber earpieces. Her goggles were of soft black leather with an elasticised headband. I used to put them on but my head never seemed big enough.

Come to think of it, that was a problem for much of my life, *vis-à-vis* my old lady. Nothing ever fitted ...

When we landed in the veld she always cut thick brush and piled it around the wheels because lions and particularly hyenas had been known to chew clean through the tyres.

On my tenth birthday, for 'a special treat', we had a day on a hill called Spionkop, where the Boers had slaughtered a great many British soldiers.

We took off from Grand Central Airport at dawn, having our *padkos* in a paper bag: two chicken sandwiches, a bottle of Lemos and two oranges. In those days you dressed to fly. My mother was splendid in sheepskin jacket, leather flying helmet and shining boots. I wore my grey woollen jersey, grey shorts and grey socks, as if I were going to school. Besides, she said, the place we were visiting was practically a cemetery. We dressed up when we went to lay fresh flowers on Grandpa Joe's grave in Westpark Cemetery, didn't we? Well then …

It took around five hours to Ladysmith, and bumping over the hot air lifting off the Drakensberg Mountains always made me queasy. Then the ride in the pale green Vauxhall, borrowed from the airport manager, who met us with all his mechanics and clerks in tow, white men in safari suits gawping, astonished and embarrassed, at this woman who flew herself around the place.

We crossed the Tugela River, driving on to the ferry, and I felt car-sick so I leaned out of the window of the Vauxhall and she said: 'You'll fall in and be carried off by a croc.'

I didn't worry in the least; I always felt as if I had, long before, fallen into something just as deep and brown and roaring as the Tugela, and been carried off, and I hadn't drowned yet. Mothers were what you drowned in. The Tugela was just a river and rivers I could handle.

Spionkop was a hard hill to climb, I had short legs, and my mother, her flying goggles tied to her waist, her big boots crunching smartly up the steep hillside, marched on and on, talking as we tramped.

'This is the position the Carolina commando took, dropping like flies when the British sharpshooters got amongst them: Reinecke, De Villiers and Tottie Krige, all coughing blood; bullets in the lungs. The English were up here, they held Spionkop for a while, yes; but we held Conical Hill, and Aloe Knoll. We were well dug in, and they were not; we got our big guns on them, and then it was easy. Easy!'

She scrabbled up on to the ridge from where the far-off peaks of green Natal stood up, like men surprised.

'At the end of it all, the English were retreating and we had the hill.'

She found a trench line, the seamed and ribbed sand where the Boer spades had dug, healed over like an old flesh wound. Her face darkened. 'Louis Botha gave his condolences to the British; they were allowed to bury their dead. It was that sort of war. They deepened the trenches where the soldiers had fallen and made them into a mass grave. Strange, isn't it? You move from blowing a man's face off to talking quietly about a decent resting place.'

Her eyes were always sharp; quick to spot things I didn't see, so scuffed and battered and at one with the dust and scrub in which they lay. But they sprang back into being for her. She would press into my hands hot metal mushrooms with the delighted exclamation, 'An English water bottle, very well preserved. And what's this? A tunic button.' She spat on the small flat piece of metal and rubbed it on her leather jacket.

'King's Royal Rifles ...' Sometimes she found things I regarded as more interesting treasures: small arrowheads, scrapers,
tiny ostrich-shell beads, faintly stippled with ochre; bushman-
ware, signs of the people who had been there thousands of
years before the great battle of 24 January 1900. I loved the flint
blades; they were neat, light and delicate. But these trifles
didn't count for her; they weren't real, like the gin bottles and
the shell casings and the spent bullets; like the soldiers who
fought a real battle in a real war. For her they were not ghosts,
they were real men fighting, the cries and screams of the dying
British troopers, the yells of defiant Boers, all of it, all of them,
still loudly alive.

'They lost over fifteen hundred here on this hill, but they
could afford it. We lost a fifth of that and it was too many.'

Listening to her lament as we straggled down the stony
koppie was like being asked to mourn the death of someone
you're told is close to you but whom you know, if at all, only as
a stranger. For her it was movement, history. For me, try as I
might, it seemed nothing had altered. She had a sense of
belonging. She was one with the fallen Boers, and their vanished Republics. Just as, much later, she had been one with
Koosie, when he was in hiding, and with the people she had
flown to Mozambique or Lesotho during the long granite
years of boredom and blood and racial madness, when the wild
regime killed what it would not countenance. Yet her hatred for
the insular lunatics who came to rule over us, and who claimed
to be the descendants of just these Boers, was rooted, per-
versely, in the defeat of the men who fought at Spionkop.

'We' fought like lions, but 'they' were too many. 'In the end,
they wore us down, burnt our farms, locked our women and

children behind wire in the concentration camps and we were forced to give in.'

For her those boys who fought at Spionkop had done something worth recording. To me they were just men I didn't know, and didn't care for. But we could agree on this: they were all around us still. The English who died that day rose from the dead and were present in those who came after them, wearing exactly their moustaches, using their loud voices; soldiers no longer, but sportsmen and farmers, ruddy men with big hands, with names like Dave or Clive or Geoff, who were something in a bank, or someone on the gold mines. And the Boers they had fought were also still with us: large, square, angry men with beards and names like Dawie and Gawie and Piet, who were now something in the fucking ruling classes.

For her the Boer War mattered because it ended badly. I had the feeling that it hadn't ended at all; it seemed to me that Dave and Clive and Geoff were still locked in a fight with Dawie and Gawie and Piet. The same battle with the same fighters; and if one side was ahead now, what did it matter? I was always overwhelmed by the stupidity of the long combat. But, boy, did I know all about it, my ma saw to that. Perhaps that was her at her truest: this expert acquaintance with death. In battle, or in the bush. Describing it, she'd touch the air, picking out the scenes as if they were figures in a tapestry.

'When MacBride's Irish Brigade were sent back home at the end of the war they asked my old dad if he wanted to ride along home with them, and he told them to stick it up their jumpers! After blowing up half the Transvaal with his dynamite, he reckoned he'd made enough of an impression on the place to call it home.'

'Home!' The word hummed in the tender nasal murmur she gave it, like a hymn or a spell against the evil one. 'Home!' she'd sing, and it would echo around the house.

We had a daguerreotype showing Paul Kruger, the Boer leader, leaning on the balcony of his house overlooking Lake Geneva: it had been done by a French sympathiser, and read: '*Le vieux Président regard avec des yeux nostalgiques, la vue du Lac Léman.*'

'After the war, my old dad stayed on. Never went back to Ireland. So we had the odd happenstance that Kruger was in Switzerland, living in exile, and your Irish grandfather was in Bloemfontein, living at home ...'

The daguerreotype was meant to make a person feel sad but it made me jealous. I thought Kruger a lucky bugger to be sitting beside Lac Léman. Home left me cold, but I didn't dare say so. Home was an odd place, where my mother never was; she was at home everywhere else in Africa.

We had a difference of opinion even then. I understood why she flew away; what I never quite understood was why she came back. 'Away' was so much more interesting than 'here'; that was something we could agree about. What we couldn't agree about, ever, was where it was best to be 'away'. Years later, in South East Asia, in Russia, in the old Yugoslavia, places that were home to me, I realised the difference between us: she was best 'at home', and I was at home 'away'. But I came to see that my travelling mimicked hers. We were made of the same stuff, like the earth and the moon; though our lives were worlds apart, I circled her, faintly visible but out of reach, and all our travelling – hers and mine – was really just time spent orbiting each other.

Her seductive power might be measured *in* the men who fell for her, though I have never had much luck in numbering my mother's lovers, or in deciding just what it was exactly that they fell for. Neither, I think, did they know themselves. After all, I was closer to her than any other man and all I can say is that she had a certain gravitational pull and when you fell, you fell towards her, crashed into her; unless, of course, you burnt up in her atmosphere, and were never heard of again.

When my mother was a young woman she went walking in the Magaliesberg, a range of mountains beyond Pretoria, famous for hunters, Boer rebels and ghosts. It was the summer of 1943, and she was in mourning as usual. I say 'as usual' because she had been almost married three times. She was just twenty when she got engaged to a fighter pilot; he was shot down. She tried again: her second fighter pilot went missing in action. Then she married a man who flew Lancaster bombers. It looked good for a while, then he crashed on take-off and she went from being almost married a lot to being almost widowed three times over.

She always said that nothing moderates grief like a long tramp. She climbed one of those hills so typical of the Magaliesberg, rock strewn in the afternoon sun, grey-green bush and the great silence. When she came to a village, thatched huts with mud walls painted with wavy lines, in green and blue and white, and triangles and zigzags in ochre and black, she asked for water. Though she did not know it, in that place she could not have asked for a more precious, a more sacred element.

She was taken before a proud woman with eyes like lakes of milk who sat on a wooden throne covered in lion skins; she

wore a leopard-skin cloak and all around her people scuffled in
the dust, and indicated that my mother should do the same.
When she asked why, they were shocked at the extent of her
ignorance. Didn't she know that she was in the presence of the
Rain Queen of the Magaliesberg, Bamadodi vi, monarch of
the mountains and ruler of the Lebalola people?

'Heavens, no! How was I supposed to know that? Boy, did I
get it wrong! I asked for water, and being a rain queen she
prepared to have the heavens open for me. Fancy that!'

The queens of the Lebalola had been making rain for centuries; and great chiefs like Shaka and Dingaan and Cetswayo
had paid them tribute. There were other rain queens, in other
parts, and they sometimes cured sickness in cattle or infertility
in women. However, the Rain Queen of the Lebalola was the
most ancient and the most orthodox of all the rainmakers.
Bamadodi vi did one thing only: she made rain, like her
mother and her ancestors before her.

The Queen summoned her counsellors, poured beer on the
ground from big black calabashes, and they proceeded to lick
up the liquid.

'This was Bama's way of getting ready to make rain, all her
councillors were bobbing about on their knees licking up the
beer. Their six long tongues, scuffing up the liquid, reminded
me of six red sausage dogs.'

'And then it poured?' I always asked.

'First she danced,' said my mother, 'then it came down in
buckets.'

My mother had been carrying her knitting; she had been
knitting a jersey for her dead fiancé who had been allergic to
machine-knits. The Queen was intrigued by her collection of
needles. Were they spears for stabbing enemies or ornaments

for beautifying the body? My mother was at liberty to demonstrate the use of these small spears upon the bodies of the Queen's counsellors. The counsellors, said my mother, stopped licking up the beer for a moment and stared at her with their tongues frozen between their lips like half-posted letters.

'These needles are made not to kill; they are to create,' said my mother, who had the gift of a ringing phrase when you least expected it. She held up her huge hands. 'I have to find work for these. And there is nothing you can do so beautifully with both hands – except perhaps to play the piano – so I knit.'

The Queen was intrigued. 'Show me.'

Then the counsellors went back to lapping up the spilt beer. My mother demonstrated a row of stitches; she used two big needles on a jersey and four small swift needles on a sock. Bamadodi asked my mother to show her three daughters how it was done and so she did. On several subsequent visits my mother gave the Queen's daughters knitting lessons, and ever afterwards Queen Bamadodi and my mother were friends.

And her tribe were great knitters. I have known experts claim that knitting was something the Rain Queens of the Magaliesberg got from British missionaries who tried – and failed – to covert them from their pagan ways. That was wrong: they got knitting from my mother. They learnt everything from garter and stocking stitch to cable stich. In later years, Queen Bama sometimes wore for her crown a wonderful woollen tower of green and sugary pinks and blazing yellows.

Ever afterwards, once or twice a year Queen Bamadodi would visit us in Forest Town. She never told us when she was coming and it was always a surprise to see the royal limousine outside the garden gate. She owned a Holden motorcar and that was incredibly exotic because it came from Australia. Queen Bamadodi always sat in the back, with her praise-singer beside her, and her chair-bearer doing the driving, and her throne roped to the roof-rack and covered with an ochre blanket. The first we knew of her visit was when her praise-singer, wearing monkey skins and leg rattles and carrying a whisk of jackal skin, would come up to our gate and sing out: 'Behold the great she-lion, the mother elephant of her tribe, the rainmaker blessed by God who makes the grass grow and the cattle fat and the rivers flush and the dry veld ooze like a young girl with full breasts of milk.'

And my mother would say, 'Heavens above! It's Bama, come for tea!'

Then the royal throne-bearer would come up the garden path into the house and set down the throne of fine yellow-wood, carved with jagged bolts of lightning, and then Bama and my mother sat down in the front room. The tea-tray was placed between them, covered in finest gauze against the flies; always the best tea service, Royal Doulton, peppermint-green porcelain with golden edges, and my mother thanking the Lord she'd baked her famous date loaf.

They'd sit and sip. And tell each other tales of looming disasters; somehow they frightened and calmed one another. The Rain Queen's praise-singer lay on the grass beside the garden gate, catching what shade he could from the lemon tree that grew beside the fence. The royal chauffeur dozed behind the wheel of the Holden.

I loved her visits. I loved Bamadodi because she kept the faith and she was fun. Her singleness of purpose I found admirable. She spent her life attempting the impossible – she wished to preserve the monarchy – and she danced to make rain. I loved her for simply going on being what she was, I admired the way she got over the difficulty of keeping faith in a godless world. I loved her for all the things she simply didn't attend to. She flew in the face of common sense; she didn't care about science, and she didn't practise accountancy. Or rugby. She did not care about the price of gold. What she did was to make rain.

Sometimes, by mysterious means, she made babies, and those babies were always girls because only women ruled the Lebalola people.

I was no more than about fifteen when she told me about her phantom lovers.

'My needs get seeded by spooks.'

'What sort of spooks?'

She looked at me a long time with her huge brown eyes.

'Alexander, if I knew that, they wouldn't be spooks. They wouldn't come in the night and seed my needs. And if they didn't seed my needs how would I have daughters? I don't see the spooks who call on me. I don't know who they are. It isn't important, so long as they remember their duty. The back door in the dark, and the seed. Afterwards, we do not speak of them.'

'What happens if you have boy babies?'

She lifted her huge eyebrows into her high forehead.

'We disown them.'

Queen Bama generally visited us in the summer, towards evening, a time when the highveld storms hit; and we never knew if the rain brought Bama or it was the other way around.

The neighbours were appalled. The sent a deputation to tell my mother that they hadn't settled in Johannesburg's northern suburbs to be serenaded by Johnny Witchdoctor. My mother sent back a note telling them to go and take a running jump. Other people, more dangerous, queried our Queen's credentials. They said she was a fake; said that there was only one true Rain Queen, and she lived much further north.

My mother said: 'Excuse *me*, our Bama makes rain all right. I've seen it, with my own two eyes. Besides, she's got a certificate.'

As the years passed, the Holden gave way to a succession of Toyotas. Queen Bama approved of the Japanese because though other countries boycotted us, the Japanese kept trading, and Queen Bama admired their sturdy conservatism and their freedom from moral scruple.

Very rarely, she brought her daughters whom I never knew as anything other than Princess One and Princess Two, who drank their tea with crooked little fingers and never said a word.

Sometimes Bama would bring her government certificate and, after my mother had made her usual protestations – 'Really, Bama, I don't know if I should. It's an official document' – she'd wash her hands and read it aloud:

'"This is to certify that her August Majesty, Queen Bamadodi vi, is recognised by the South African Weather Bureau as a professional meteorologist, and is qualified to practise as such within her Tribal Homeland."'

And then she'd say: 'My word, Bama, you must be so proud!'

Generally, rain interrupted tea. The sky came down like a lid. Then you heard a tentative bark of thunder a long way off, like a giant clearing his throat. The sky darkened to dead black, and bolts of lightning ripped it apart like shot silk. Each flash ended with a crack of thunder so loud it made you open and close your mouth to get your ears working again. The rain began drumming on the corrugated-iron roof. The praise-singer had run for the Holden and sat peering out of the misty window like a lost soul in the roar of water. Then, suddenly, the rain faltered and stopped, as if someone had switched it off. The sun was coming out, the heat bounced back, the grass was drying, the birds were in business, and the evening sky had turned to summer pink and gold. Only the water chugging in the storm drains and the salty, leathery aroma of the wet red dust told you the storm had been our way.

And Queen Bama sighed happily, and accepted another slice of date loaf, while the two princesses looked on with astonishment at the royal miracle.

You wanted to applaud.

The Stinson wasn't called the flying station wagon for nothing. It carried her guns and provisions, if she was hunting in Barotseland or with the Giriama tribesmen in the hardwood forests of Kilifi; and her evening clothes if she was planning to stop over in Nairobi at the Muthaiga Club. And since she flew with either conventional landing gear or floats, she could get to just about anywhere.

This blazing freedom to come and go on a whim and a wing. For her that was a kind of hallucinogen. The drug must be administered haphazardly if it is to lead to a sense of the strangeness of the new place that breaks down all the carefully assembled bits and pieces that make up the person you thought you were. In order to travel well, it is essential to be able to get seriously lost.

She did this brilliantly. Riding contradictions, swapping countries, roles, times made for a kind of cultural cross-dressing. On a typical day she would have got up that morning early, at home, in Johannesburg, and driven to Wemmer Pan, if she was flying on floats. Everything her eye fell on – from the traffic cop in his neo-Nazi gear, black cap, jodhpurs, glistening black leather boots, directing cars in Louis Botha Avenue, to the beggar who banged his mottled hands on her windscreen at a stop street in Orange Grove – was familiar. At the Pan she fired up the engine and headed north. After stopping to refuel on a dam at a friendly uncle's place, she'd be over the Limpopo, and several hours later, hundreds of miles north, she would put down on Lake Nyasa.

For some years she would spend the night in a lakeside village. Then, one day, she found out the witchdoctor had made a replica of her little yellow Stinson, right down to its floats, and was using it as powerful medicine. There was a shrine to her in the village.

'It's a bit much, finding you're a goddess,' she told me. 'The strain is tremendous. A deity is always on duty and it knocks the hell out of you. Everyone wanting something: cures, luck, children … No wonder the Greek gods just petered out. If people did a little more time as gods they'd be more considerate. It is a very great shock to have people always throwing themselves on your mercy, or trying to garland you with flowers, or bringing goats to your doorway and sacrificing them on the spot. You want to help but there's a limit. Though your followers don't see it that way. You're up against the believers and they will not take no for an answer. Resigning does no good. You stay divine. So I never went back to that village. I didn't know where to put my face.'

In the years after the Second World War, off and on, she would drop by the Schweitzer mission at Lambaréné in the Congo. Some time in the late forties she put her Stinson down on the Ogooué River, and a guy in a canoe poled her across to the island, where the port stood amongst palm trees, and she made her way to the tin-roofed hospital.

'I'd find Himself sitting down to supper. "Ah, Kathleen," he'd say, "I wish I'd known you were coming. I've almost run out of potassium, and sulphur and iodine …"'

'Then we'd have supper, and then he'd play some Bach on this mangy old piano which he battled to keep in tune, and he'd tell stories; he loved telling stories, though they always had a moral in the tail. People there called him *le grand docteur*. An inferiority complex was not one of his problems.

'He told me straight: "Sometimes, I fear, Kathleen, I am just plain Mr God."

'Well, he got a touch of sympathy from me. I knew all about that, once having been a bit of a goddess myself. And I must dispel a few myths about the old boy. Fact the first: Dr A. was a crusty old paternalist; he regarded Africans as untutored savages, but let's say in his favour that he saw them as *serious* savages, admirable savages. Savage was what he liked. It was his big thing. The many, many ways that Africans found to kill each other was one of the great fascinations of his life. Whether by poison, knives or witchcraft, he felt they did it so happily, so naturally they should be left alone to get on with it. We shouldn't interfere, except to ease suffering by medical science, like cure goitres, and ulcers, sleeping sickness and elephantiasis. For the rest, leave them alone! He didn't just like the idea of the noble savages; he believed you didn't get nobility to bloom by stamping on the savagery. If there was anything wrong with these children of nature, said Dr A., it was our presence. *Us*. You and me and the so-called civilised lot. Being in contact with the likes of us led them to blow money on booze, made them forget how to carve canoes, and start lusting after our salt, our tobacco and our shoes. He got furious with them for wanting these things.' She raised her eyes in that quizzical, startled little grimace which was as close as she ever came to irony. 'As if none of this happened back home, in darling little Europe … Anyway, he was a grand fellow – and we all have our blind spots, don't we?

'Fact the second: he was a racist with rigid ideas about discipline. He'd say about his beloved savages, he often called them that, "They must be shown that the tongue that speaks love may also lash them till they weep. *Nicht wahr?*" There was a lot of *nicht wahr*-ing in Schweitzer-talk. Mostly, in Lambaréné, he spoke French but he liked speaking German to me. Maybe because I was from South Africa, and since I said I wasn't English, therefore he assumed I must be semi-Dutch, or quasi-German, or something more or less Boer-ish.'

My mother's stories. My mother's friends …

Great stuff. Exactly what we wanted to hear. Probably all we *can* hear. This stream of images projected on my growing consciousness. Far-away foreigners all of whom seemed destined for stardom, because character was, ultimately, celluloid. Even as substantial a figure as Albert Schweitzer, snapped on my mother's box Brownie, in his white tropical suit, solar topee and walrus moustache, smiling from the buttery bamboo frame beside her bed, under the looping letters of his inscription: 'To my dear Kathleen, aviatrix, angel!' Even *'le grand docteur'* seems a dead ringer for someone who would one day play him in some cheesy movie – the saintly healer in a domed hat – and how odd that this impersonation would seem, ever afterwards, more real than the real thing.

But, then, whoever gave a toss for the real thing? It was sometimes said that conquest, colonies, empire, money and slaves were what the white invasion of Africa was for; but that is only half the story. Looking back, the entire absurd scramble for Africa seems one long trailer for Metro-Goldwyn-Mayer. All those busy soldiers who shot their way across the dark continent, those rogues, missionaries, explorers, white hunters, the Happy Valley lot and the Bwana Brigade, Boer and Brit and the fancy French botanists, aviators, miners, entrepreneurs, fakes, remittance men, red-necked adventurers from Ealing, Chepstow, Bremen and Bruges, who came to the Congo or the Cape, to Kenya or Nyasaland, Windhoek or Djibouti, whether they said they came to get rich, or get away from home, or the bailiffs, or to get to be king of somewhere: all of them were, in fact, no more than understudies; meat for the movies.

And because they – we – always had this feeling of redundancy, our true selves eaten away by the otherness of Africa, it made us noisy and muscular. We reached violently into the emptiness around us, in order to feel we were alive, accentuating our looks, passions, hatreds, cruelties in order to convince ourselves we hadn't been rubbed away to nothing. We wrote our names on mountains and rivers, talked ourselves up; in fact, did absolutely anything to keep away the feeling that we were lost in a place that did not hate us, but simply did not notice. We called it mastery. Worse, we even called it love.

The only things white men have ever done around the place are easily noted: they have shot something, or a great number of someone, or each other; kicked a lot of folks around; or died of some indigenous disease, as if copping it from malaria was a mission statement, or perishing of black-water fever showed your heart was in the right place.

But I digress. Let me say something about the men who lived in the tropical forest and transformed themselves into leopards. It was Dr A. who first brought the leopard men to the attention of an incredulous world, and when he told my mother about them, she said: 'Let's go and meet some,' and they did. Which is pretty odd when you think about it, this scary saint from the Congo and my old lady from Jo'burg, and their mutual liking for guys in costume who sliced up their neighbours in a fashion my mother loved to recount:

'Dr A. was a fund of good info; about how they sharpened their claws of steel, and how they made their bark camouflage, and how they filed their teeth! I loved it. It was so rich! Dr A. knew lots of leopard guys: the Anyoto of the Eastern Congo, the lion men in Tanganyika. He was very taken with these chaps ever since the thirties. In Ivory Coast, the boys come back from their initiation training in the forest and do the leopard dance in the village. And very fine it is too; a good deal of sinuosity, of arching the back, of growling. The outfits are superb, they don't go for gross realism, they go for "impressionistic renditions of what the soul of the leopard is felt to be". Quote unquote. They dress in bark, spotted black and yellow, and slink about growling and crouching and stalking and flinging themselves on their victims ...' She stiffened her large hands and the red nail polish on her long sharp nails gleamed in the lamplight. 'And while the victims scream blue murder the leopard men are carving them up with bladed knives, made into claws. Some simply stalk and pounce; some, like the leopard men of Lagos, also eat their victims.'

The hairs on my neck stood to attention.

'Didn't they even cook them?'

'Never. Kill, yes, but never cook: gobbled on the spot.'

'Why?'

'Whadyamean, why? Because leopards don't cook.'

'Yes, but is it true?'

'Is *what* true?' She always came down hard on '*what*'.

'Were they really leopards – or only pretend?'

'Some of it's true; some of it's pretend. They were like all of us humans, once upon a time, in the early days when we lived close to the animals, close to real life; when we were hunters and dreamers and murderers; when we didn't know if we were men dressed as animals or animals who were also people. You could say we were ani-men.'

It was Schweitzer who took her to meet some leopard men.

'I flew him up to northern Gabon, near Oyem, where they make a religion out of a plant called eboga. It's taken from the roots of a bush found in the forest that is ground, grated or dunked in water. It looks a bit like grated turnip. The people of Oyem took us into one of their chapels, which was really a hut built to one side of the compound. Because he was '*le grand docteur*' they were happy to let us sit in on a séance.

'We sat on the floor of the chapel, watching. Then one of the chaps, his name was Emana Ola, he talked us through the ceremony, in German. It was funny hearing Dr A. and Emana Ola chattering away in Deutsch, in a village in deepest Gabon, but, then, bits of northern Gabon were once the German Cameroons, so there you go. Emana Ola told us that after eating eboga God came to him and said that all strangers approaching the village who were not of his clan were witches in disguise, and must be killed for religious reasons. Dr A. said he didn't see why you should kill people for religious reasons. Emana Ola said there was an essential difference between white and black beliefs. Christians were always eating the body of God, so as to be joined with him. That was what the missionaries taught. But the sacred meal of eboga, which was Emana Ola's communion bread, opened the door of death and took him into the very presence of God, and of the ancestors.

'Now, of course, old Dr A. was not just a medical man, he was also a biblical scholar of note. But he was a Protestant and I could see that the idea of "eating God" had about it a Catholic taint he found somewhat disagreeable. Emana Ola asked us did we want to join the cult of Bwiti, and see God? And I said yes. The Doctor said no; he wasn't eating any drugs, thanks very much. So only I was inducted; I was called a popi, which means an initiate. Two people are set to look after you and they are called your mother and father. Their job is to watch you and decide just how much eboga they can stuff you with before you pass out or throw up. They walked me down a stream with someone playing the ngombi, which is an eight-stringed harp only used when you're doing Bwiti. By this time Dr A. had stomped off in a huff to smoke his pipe. Just as well because I was stripped to the buff; then I had to confess my sins, then I ate more eboga, then the priest rubbed me down with sacred bark from twelve sacred trees, then I was dressed in white and the priest tapped me several time on the head with the parasol fruit – that looks like an enormous phallus – and people joked about it. Then more eboga. Then I had a bit of a vision, I saw my father, my dear old dad, and he said to me: "How are you doing, sweetie?" So that was a bonus; but I did not see God, as I'd hoped, and then I passed out.

'I woke up feeling pretty groggy. Dr A. had told them I wanted to meet some leopard men and he was not going till I'd met them. Emana Ola said some of his best friends were leopard men and he'd give them a shout. About a dozen blokes turned up dressed to the nines. Claws and all. They did some prowling, growling and pouncing. Next, they climbed trees but frankly I have to say they did not look like leopards. Dr A. said it was not their outer physical likeness the leopard men sought to reproduce; they were spirit leopards. Anyway, they then got down from the trees and started practising little leaps and growling some more, and showing their teeth. Humans, of course, don't have fangs or a dewclaw and that's a letdown when you're trying to be a leopard, even a spirit leopard. Now the dewclaw of the leopard will scalp a man easy as winking. Slice his face off. These guys were not quite in that class. They had made claws from knives with hooked blades: five sharp pieces of metal protruding from grips that slipped over the fingers, rather like wooden gloves. Or razor-edged knuckle-dusters.

'But I did not scoff. I found their enthusiasm very pleasing. The good doctor, too; he kept nodding and saying "*sehr interessant*", and praising what he called the consistency of their spiritual impersonations. He reckoned that even if they had to work at it, the wounds left on their victims would have been a fair approximation of the damage done by real leopards after a good mauling.

'I must say I was struck by Dr A.'s inconsistencies, and bloody impressed at how little they bothered him. Dr A. puffed a pipe himself but he hated the tobacco habit he found amongst people in Gabon. But we always took along a box of American tobacco leaves and used a leaf at a time as money. Like banknotes. He'd peel off a leaf. It was dark, strong, poisonous stuff, but people loved it. So there we were, talking to Africans who got high on psychotropic drugs, saw visions and liked to murder people. Yet Dr A. was a puritan and a man who reverenced life. He believed in the living; he did not side with the dead. The leopard men were destroyers of life, if you took them seriously. They said they were killing witches, but, in fact, they were murdering innocent pedestrians. But Dr A. went along with it all, still finding it *"sehr interessant"* because, you see, for him they were noble savages, and he far preferred indigenous drug-addicts, dressed as big cats, out on a killing spree for genuine religious reasons, to those he saw as clever savages; educated Africans whom he saw as screwed-up versions of even more screwed-up Europeans ...'

No one said anything to my mother on the day she landed at Grand Central Airport with a passenger. A boy in the back seat and a large woman in flying goggles and a long lavender scarf, who looked like any other white madam travelling with her black servant. And besides, the boy wasn't wearing his gear, and you can't tell a leopard man just by looking at him. In the flesh he looked like any other cook or road sweeper.

When I asked her how she managed it, she said: 'Mrs Garfinkel has a gardener from Nyasaland, so why shouldn't I have a friend to stay? From Gabon?'

It seemed the little guy had a yearning to see Jo'burg. And even with Dr A.'s warnings about the poison of civilisation fresh in her mind, my mother, being in her way a sucker for rescue missions, flew him from real to urban jungle, for a taste of big city life.

He was called Nzong, and he was a lively bloke with very dark skin and beautiful hands. He lived with us in Forest Town for some weeks, and my ma got him to show me his stuff. His camouflage suit was a type of cloak made from tree bark, stippled in black and yellow paint. He tied it around his waist with a belt, and pulled it over his head to form a cowl. His tail was fixed to the belt.

We got on well, Nzong and me, even though we couldn't really speak to each other. I used to go and see him in his room in the back yard, and when I patted my tummy and chewed a bit, and he nodded, I knew he was hungry so I gave him half a loaf of bread and a Coke. He let me try on the body sheath and then he showed me how to spring like a leopard. I really liked his steel claws; and he let me wear them, though my ma said: 'For God's sake don't slash yourself, will you?' Then Nzong and I practised leopard leaps on the lawn with her looking on, and yelling: 'Arch your back, Alexander, and keep your eye on Nzong.'

He clapped his hands when I got it right, and I almost felt like a leopard. I knew that if I had a chance, in the forest, I'd also attack passers-by and tear them with my claws. It was what a decent leopard did. When Nzong was a leopard he was so good, or at least he was a good pretender. I could never be that good. I think it was because I never believed like he did.

But after a few days it palled for both of us. I didn't blame Nzong: when you get down to it, the leopard's repertoire is limited, and in a suburban garden especially so. As my ma said, for a real leopard man it was important to get in a kill fairly regularly, otherwise what was the point?

And so, by way of an outing, we took Nzong to the Zoo.

'It might make him feel at home,' said my ma.

At the Zoo, she bought us ice-cream cones and she promised us a ride on an elephant. We had a bit of trouble persuading the keeper to let Nzong up on to the elephant's back.

'No can do,' said the elephant-keeper. 'Black boys can't ride the elephant.'

My mother said: 'He's not a boy; he's a leopard man! All the way from the German Cameroons.'

The elephant-keeper took off his cap; he had a lot of blond hair and his cap, which was right by my nose, smelt of elephant. Men quite often took off their hats when they spoke to my mother.

'What's the Cameroons? I've never heard of there.'

My mother told him as if any clot knew the answer.

'It was a German colony in West Africa, on the Gulf of Guinea, extending northwards to Lake Chad. Then the British and French in the Great War won it. But some people in remote districts still went on speaking German for decades. This boy is one of them.'

'Is it, hey?' The elephant-keeper was not persuaded.

'Yes, it is.'

'Then make him say something in German.'

My mother spoke Nzong in Swahili; and he told the keeper:

'*Dummer Barbar – verfluchter schwarzer Dummkopf – Sie niedriger Form des Lebens.*'

The elephant-keeper was intrigued now. 'What's he say, hey?'

'He called you a stupid barbarian, a bloody black *domkop*, and an inferior form of life.'

'Hell's teeth.' The elephant-keeper was impressed. 'He's the real McCoy: a genuine bloody black kraut.'

And he let us up into the little wooden seat, high on the elephant's back, and off we swayed. Afterwards, we went to see the leopards, and I remember a big cage with an old tree in the middle of a dusty floor and on the white bald branches of the tree two leopards, their tails swinging. Nzong stared at the leopards, and he smiled.

'Thank heavens, Nzong's found some friends,' said my mother.

Nzong wanted to spend the night in the Zoo but my mother wouldn't have it.

'Only real animals can spend the night in the Zoo, Nzong, humans are forbidden.'

But she must have thought twice about this because she let him do it. After all, she said, Nzong was also a leopard man and he had a perfect right to spend the night among the animals. She bought him two more ice creams and a big bottle of ginger beer, in case he was hungry in the night; and we went home alone, and worried. When we went back next morning we found him sitting outside the leopards' cage; he'd eaten the ice creams and drunk the ginger beer and looked fine. The leopards didn't seem all that knocked out but maybe that was because he wasn't wearing his gear.

But Nzong grew even more broody and my ma saw things were getting difficult.

'He wants to be out and about. I do understand. It's what he does, where he comes from. If he wants to savage a passer-by, he's free to do so. Just to qualify as a leopard man you have to subsist in the forest on your own for eight weeks on whatever food you can kill yourself. But we can't have that in Forest Town. I have no idea whom he might kill and disembowel.'

She laid down restrictions: he was allowed to put on his leopard outfit only in daylight hours, only at home, on the lawn, where she could keep an eye on him. He wasn't to go into the street alone.

But she knew it was wrong and one day, without saying anything to me, she and he were gone. She flew Nzong back to the forests of Cameroon where he could pounce and slash to his heart's content.

It must have been a few months later that we went to see the film called *Tarzan and the Leopard Men* at the Lake Cinema in Parkview. In the red plush foyer there were posters everywhere, with pictures of guys in masks who leapt from trees and ate you up. There were also some pygmies. But they were fakes, like the leopard men were fakes. A poster said: 'From the Hellhole of the Congo – Come African Freaks and Marvels!'

I didn't like the film; I didn't like Tarzan, I didn't like the screaming – there was a lot of screaming – and I didn't want to watch any more so I went out and sat in the foyer, shaking a bit.

My old lady came looking for me: 'What's the matter? You scared?'

'No.'

'Well, then?'

'I don't like it.'

'Why not?'

'It's not real.'

She sat down and took my hand. 'Alexander. It's not meant to be real. This is just a film, a bioscope. Don't take it so seriously; it's only pretend.'

'I don't like pretend.'

My mother put her arms around me. 'Don't take it so personally.'

But I did take it personally. I missed Nzong. He wasn't a freak or a marvel, he was just a perfectly ordinary leopard boy who could kill and eat people, if he wanted. The actors on the screen weren't half as good, and yet everyone was supposed to go around saying how real and scary they were. Everyone but me. I didn't believe in pretend; that was my problem.

He would climb out of his little green Vauxhall at our gate, toddle up the slasto path to the front stoop where my mother sat cleaning her shotgun. A large bloke with a thick moustache, short brown hair, wearing a rather hairy sports jacket of biscuit-brown, with leather buttons. He was called Louis Labuschagne, known to his friends as 'Lappies', but to us he was just 'Oomie': little uncle.

He'd wink and move on. Or he'd slow down when he passed me, kneeling on the lawn, collecting snails for a penny a dozen.

'You've never seen me. Right?'

'Yes, sir.'

'I'm not here. I have never been here. Unnerstan'?'

'Yes, Oomie.'

He once told me: 'I have a very, very important job, Alex boy, only I can't tell you what it is. So when you see me, remember, I'm not here.'

Oddly enough, the man who wasn't there was to take on a lot more substance. I never thought the men who called at our place had any real life of their own; they were simply in orbit around my mother and assumed importance in relation to her. To begin with, Oomie was just another uncle and I had uncles like the garden had snails: there was Uncle Barrie, who travelled for Helena Rubinstein, and Uncle Jack, who was 'something in aluminium', Uncle Papadop from Rhodesia, and Uncle Hansie from South West Africa, any number of white hunters and one white Zulu. Each and every one of them passing strangers pretending to have real lives when what they really did was to buzz and bounce around my ma, like bees or rubber balls.

It took a long time before I could begin to see that sometimes these guys were what they said they were, men with jobs and backgrounds, lives and wives of their own, instead of being adornments my mother wore, until she wore them out. But of all my uncles I can truly say that Oomie surprised me most because I got the unexpected chance to see him in his real job. He sprang into view the way people did when they were truly alive, and not just mere blips on my personal radar that signalled heavy uncle traffic.

It was 1960, I was sixteen, and working weekends and holidays. My old lady believed in encouraging what she called 'the power of independent finance', by which she meant getting a job and looking after myself. 'See you anon', she'd say, before heading off for Kenya, Congo or Rhodesia, without leaving me any cash. She was very generous when she was flush, but paying for flying machines, she said again and again, 'costs a bomb'. So when I wasn't at school I took a variety of jobs. I did Saturday mornings selling hooch in a bottle store; I did Christmas at the OK Bazaars; I did Easter at Milner Park at the Rand Show on the instant soup stand, handing tiny scalding skinny plastic cups of the new miracle broth to passers-by. It was instant chicken noodle ... 'Brimming with goodness, made with reverence for all the old traditional farmhouse values ...' said the advertising posters. 'Just add water and stir.' We had never seen its like and it proved beyond doubt that Jo'burg was flying like a rocket into the future, no matter what anyone said or thought.

Easter, and I was, once again, on the soup stand at the Rand Show. It unfolded in a great jostling mix of men, beasts and machinery, in a vast space of tractors and ploughs and irriga-tion piping, and dozens of free brochures touting plastic sheeting, or miracle fertilisers or combine-harvesters; great gluey wads of glossy paper that small boys carried in tottering piles, hugged to their chests, salivating at the tang of these highly desirable slabs of totally free newsprint. There were exhibition halls, cattle-pens, fairground rides, and an illumi-nated concrete spike marked the centre of this great bazaar and was known as the Tower of Light. It was, I suppose, not much more than a cattle fair, plus diversionary swings and round-abouts, but it was run by men who called themselves 'gentlemen' farmers, and who made believe the gathering was some sort of Royal Show.

Like many of our delusions, this pretence was vital and consoling because it allowed us to believe, briefly (and briefly was better than bugger-all) that we were not, in fact, a path-etic rump of emasculated ninnies – English, Blacks, Jews, Catholics and foreigners of whatever stripe – all impotent, all ruled by bearded, bloody-minded Boers; big-necked blokes in khaki shorts who carried sjamboks; narrow, vicious puritans, who cared only for rugby, racial purity and being right; thugs who made the word 'farmer' the sort of word drunks in bars hurled at those they wished to insult. It let us pretend that we mattered; that we were not useless and despised casualties of history.

Pretending was what we did big time in Jo'burg: pretending was not just an art form, it was a fucking industry. We didn't just make mountains out of molehills; we made mountains out of mine-dumps. We were the pretending capital of the universe. We were a mining camp posing as an Anglican parish, prostitutes playing at parsons. We were greedy, grubby bandits, forever being caught with our hands in the till, and forever trying to make it look like we were putting the money back.

The Rand Easter Show, while 'agricultural', was not for Boers, at least, not in theory. The Rand Easter Show was for our sorts of farmers, jovial chaps with red cheeks and mutton-chop whiskers, who spoke English, and believed in fair play. They drove Austins and sent their sons to Oxford; Jo'burg's gentleman farmers, in hacking jackets and big red rosettes. It was our way of insisting, Look: there are English farmers, liberal farmers, too!

Things were particularly keyed up that Easter because the Show officials were preparing for a visit by the Prime Minister, Dr Hendrik Frensch Verwoerd, the man who more than any other was responsible for our deeply depraved and horribly boring obsession with racial purity and blood hygiene and religious strife.

The showgrounds at Milner Park had been named after Alfred, Lord Milner, the former High Commissioner to South Africa during the Boer War. Milner was a brutal dreamer whose visions of clean-limbed, poncy young English eunuchs ruling the world from the Thames to the Indus exceeded even those of Cecil John Rhodes in their poisonous perversion.

We had a bit of family connection, Milner and us. My grandfather, as a young bomb-maker in the Boer War, had wanted to assassinate Milner. It was 1901, the Boers gathered in Vereeniging were staring defeat in the face and had decided to sue for peace when my grandfather, who, like the rest of the Irish Brigade, violently rejected any idea of surrender to the British, came up with an idea. Lord Milner was being taken to Vereeniging by special train to discuss terms of surrender with the Boer generals, Botha, De Wet, Delarey and Jan Smuts. Well, then, why not blow his train to smithereens? My grandfather had even chosen the culvert. Alas, Jan Smuts scotched the idea with a remark that always pained my grandfather (who revered the Boer leader) for what he called 'its excess of Anglo-Saxon common sense'.

Smuts told him: 'You can't negotiate with a dead Milner.'

My grandfather was rather put out. 'And why ever not? You'll get more sense out of him dead.'

But Smuts prevailed, Milner lived, the Boers surrendered. Yet although they lost the war, ten short years later they won the country back from the British. And in 1910 they built upon the ruins of the old independent Boer republics a fantasy land in which all four provinces of the old South Africa were merged into a new Union of a new South Africa, an arrangement they called Paradise but which for just about everyone else turned into a dull and wretched prison where we would spend most of the next century.

It was to commemorate the fiftieth anniversary of that fateful union that Dr Verwoerd, evangelist of apartheid, sainted figure of segregation, was coming to speak at Milner Park. The irony of the visit – Apostle of Apartheid Addresses the English Philistines at the Poor Bastards' Invitation – had not gone unnoticed but, as usual, everyone had agreed not to make an issue of it.

I was on tea break when the loudspeakers strapped to the Tower of Light began announcing that the official opening of the Show by the Prime Minister was taking place in the Main Arena, and I wandered along to hear Verwoerd speak, moving through the crowds, feeling, as I always did at the Easter Show, that this must be what it was like to be in touch with the world, the movement and the bustle and life of it, cattle and tractors, irrigation piping and candy floss, turbines and roller-coasters, a kind of lively mess I believed made up the true world as it existed in other places, where many things happened at the same time to many people, and was not in the least like life in Johannesburg, which was a series of isolations, a Chinese box of interlocking vacuums, strong walls designed to keep out the wider world, and yet which held in precisely nothing.

Verwoerd was on a platform, with a lot of other VIPs, one hand in the pocket of his suit (double-breasted, black) plus red rosette. His cheeks were rosy and he had this lick of strong thick grey hair. The Chairman, Colonel Something-Or-Other, was thanking Verwoerd for coming, and got so carried away that when he'd finished thanking him, he thanked him again. On Verwoerd's right sat a guy I took to be just another farmer, and this guy kept putting his hand into the inside pocket of his jacket and taking it out again, as if checking his car keys or his wallet. I paid no attention to him, neither did anyone else.

What amazed me was that standing right behind Verwoerd was someone I knew very well: it was Oomie. And for a moment I couldn't for the life of me think what he was doing there.

The Prime Minister was very used to being thanked and he waited until the Colonel's speech had, at last, wound down into appreciative little smiles and winks, and then he took the mike. He began speaking in that high, rather strangled tone that always reminded me of a ventriloquist who threw his voice all right but lacked the dummy, and so his high-pitched mewl always seemed to be coming from someone else.

The farmers in hacking jackets were hoping for a miracle: to wit, that if they pretended to be good blokes, the Leader would pretend to be a civilised man and not mock and despise them as English nincompoops, silly liberals, heirs of the old enemy whom it was his duty to humiliate for starters, and then to destroy for keeps.

Verwoerd knew it was his duty to humiliate – for starters – and then to destroy – for keeps. His speech was suave; it snaked in and out between what were near-civilities and sardonic defiance. There were those, he said, who saw the 'Union' of South Africa – fifty years of it – as a triumph for 'the people'. But Union was a triumph only in so far as it had emasculated the hated British enemy. It had been a disaster for decent Boers everywhere who had inherited all the constraints and customs enforced by the old imperial enemy.

The farmers behind him on the platform looked at their brogues; trapped between deep embarrassment and furtive anger, alternately nodding and shaking their heads and trying like hell to pass both off as respectful agreement.

My eyes were on Oomie; what the hell was he doing here?

Verwoerd was getting to his brutal conclusion, his cheeks pink and white and shaking slightly with passion. His light blue eyes were blind. Fifty years of Union – his treble rose higher – under an English crown was a continuing insult to the thousands who died for the raped republics of the Transvaal and the Free State, and the sooner South Africa returned to its predestined divine status as a Nationalist Christian Boer republic run by Boers for Boers, the better ...

Then he sat down and all the farmers on the podium put on their shit-eating smiles and clapped. Good old Hendrik: he'd just kicked them in the balls yet again, and they were very, very grateful. Colonel Something got up and began to thank him all over again.

It was then that the guy who, earlier, had kept reaching into his pocket stood up and walked over to Dr Verwoerd, carrying what looked like a gun, except I knew it could not be a gun because if it was a gun, it might go off. The man called out nice and calm and polite, 'Dr Verwoerd?' as if he wanted to ask him the time, as if he wasn't quite sure if he had the right man, and then what I thought could not be a gun went off, and Dr Verwoerd sort of flinched. It was at precisely that moment that I realised why Oomie was on the platform; I knew why he never told me what he did. Oomie was a cop, a secret policeman, he was one of the Prime Minister's bodyguards.

The man with the gun then pushed it right up against Dr Verwoerd's ear, and it went off again, duller, softer this time, on account of it being right up hard against his ear, and Verwoerd fell over and began bleeding.

That was when Oomie also fell over, as if they'd rehearsed it, as if that had been the arrangement between them, and both of them lay there, and went on lying there. Except Oomie wasn't bleeding. Then Colonel Someone grabbed the pistol while other men began pulling the gunman off the stage, and when they got him down to the ground they picked him up and ran off with him because some in the crowd were obviously wanting to kill him. Sirens began screaming. So did the crowd. It was very South African now. Someone had tried to kill someone else, and a lot of other people wanted to kill someone, too. It was their turn, it was only natural, and it was only fair. The sirens got louder and then the white nose of an ambulance was pushing its way through the mêlée.

It was at this moment that Oomie, who had been lying down all the time, and who might have been dead, suddenly sat up.

He wasn't dead but it looked like Dr Verwoerd might be.

There were pistol shots that changed the world: there had been the Serb, Princip, at Sarajevo in 1914, and Lee Harvey Oswald in the Dallas Book Repository. For us there was 16 April 1960, when a man on the VIP stand at the Rand Easter Show turned politely towards the Prime Minister, and twice tried to blow his head off. And missed.

His shot echoed around Africa: it went on echoing, in the sounds of doors slamming in our faces, from the Limpopo to the Nile. From that shot onwards we would be confined to the southern tip of the continent, among our mad-as-hatters white brothers, where the master race awoke each day to bright boasts of their cleverness and innate nobility, and went to bed each night having obediently swallowed a dayful of lies. The results were not what anyone could have foreseen.

We measured the impact, or my mother did, by the refusal of the authorities to allow her to land in the Sudan. For the first time in her life she could not go as she wished in Africa; she was confined, as she put it, to bloody barracks, the white enclaves south of the Zambesi: Rhodesia, South West Africa, Portuguese East Africa. And the great journeys to Kenya; the dusty landing strips on distant farms from Dar es Salaam to the Belgian Congo; the rivers and lakes in a dozen countries where she could put down, cruising at just a few thousand feet, above the heads of hippo and the stalking lions, sunset over Lake Victoria, dawn in Khartoum: one after the other these places and pleasures were no longer open to her. I don't remember, as I grew older, that she travelled any less, but it got harder to do: she needed permissions, flight plans, papers, landing rights, bribes to fly into Central and East Africa, she couldn't drop into the Congo at will, at least not into the official aerodromes and familiar landing strips.

Though I didn't know it when I stood in the crowd that day in the Main Arena and listened to Verwoerd's speech, my mother was there, too, very close by. Between us was a throng of gentlemen farmers wearing moustaches and rosettes and looking like well-fed, well-dressed, very dead turkeys. I had thought she was in transit, in flight, in Addis Ababa or Zanzibar or Cairo.

All through my childhood I'd look up to the sky for a glimpse of my flying mother, and I pretended I could see her plane, a speeding point of energy. But I never quite got hold of her: she flew too fast for me. Later, I pictured her rather like the neutrino, a sub-atomic particle so small, so quick, so elusive that they tried to catch a glimpse of it passing right through the earth by placing measuring devices on the floor of mile-deep gold mines, and waited for a lucky strike. For years they never got so much as a sniff: the particles passed straight through whatever interceptors they used, and never left a trace. That was the way I thought of my ma, the human neutrino. She lived a life that could be predicted but not proven, and whenever you looked for her, you were too late. But eventually they got the neutrino: they saw its passing signs. It did exist. Ditto with my old lady. She sped across the continent, like some great galleon under full sail, always off somewhere, totally indifferent to the ocean of little silvery lives in the sea beneath her, or in the air above her. Living meant getting on. Getting stuck was for others, not for her.

Not being around was something for which she reproached me, after I'd left. She'd phone me, in some other world, in Hanoi or Vancouver or Siem Riep, her voice perplexed. 'Where are you, exactly? I never know where you are!' As if she did not for a moment realise that she was the model on which I based my ever-moving self.

On the day in question, 16 April 1960, I calculate that she must have been about twenty metres away, in that part of the crowd with a good view of the Prime Minister, the Chairman of the Witwatersrand Agricultural Society (how grandly silly was the title!) and Colonel Someone.

It is strange how knowledge comes to call. Mostly you get it from books, or neighbours or school; from sources more or less unexceptional. But there is an old tradition in my country that some important truths can also be delivered by bullet. Its essence goes like this: if you come across something or someone you don't like, then you shout; if that doesn't work then break something; and if the stupid bastards still refuse to be reasonable, start shooting. Gunfire-assisted learning is about as traditional down our way as rooibos tea or biltong or tsetse fly.

Certainly, this was my mother's view. I don't think she liked violence – in principle – but she was always perfectly unmoved by the amount of it that went on around her. It was all perfectly normal. It might have been bad for some, it might even have made her shiver, but she never dreamt of doing away with it because it was what people used to get things done. It was like dynamite; everyone she knew worked happily with dynamite, because this was Jo'burg, dynamite was what we did. Our family life was punctuated by explosions.

Dr Verwoerd lived; his recovery was, his doctors confirmed, amazing; it was, said his followers, miraculous. And Verwoerd now took upon himself the role of resurrected hero of his tribe, the death-defying deliverer of his people from the toils of Satan, for which read foreigners, Jews, Catholics, communists, homosexuals and, of course, the accursed 'English'. It is often thought that Verwoerd and his henchmen hated blacks: that is wrong – they hated everyone.

The would-be assassin, a certain David Pratt, was locked away in a mental home. His failure, to many, was not to have tried to kill the Prime Minister – everybody understood why he should have wanted to do that – but to get so close and then to miss twice.

South Africans have never believed, as the comforting old cliché goes, that violence changes nothing. We knew it changed everything, providing you got it right. Pratt's two bullets, fired from a .22 pistol, missed the brain. How do you shoot a man in the ear and miss his brain? Ask a South African; ask a liberal.

Then there was Oomie; he was a lot harder for us to deal with than Pratt. He presented more problems: problems of image, of race, of authority, of humour or the lack of it, of dignity and the need to keep it up, of the role of the police in what was constantly now being referred to as the 'new' South Africa, the Republic of South Africa. For the question was:

when he was supposed to be preserving the Prime Minister, had the silly mutt not perhaps simply passed out?

It was not permitted to speculate on this in public; the official line was that the Premier's bodyguard either:

1. Got down on the floor to consult with the PM on the right course of action.
2. Pulled the Prime Minister to the floor in order to protect him with his body.
3. Hit the deck as his training demanded, did the leopard roll and prepared to return fire.

No one said anything. There was nothing to be said. Whatever you felt about the cops, Oomie was a white man, and the day white men started running down white men, the end of the world was at hand.

People said power spoke to power but they did not know the half of it. In Africa power did not just speak to power, it nuzzled up and performed varieties of consensual solidarity so perverse they might be practised only with consenting tyrants.

After his fall Oomie still came to see us. I suspect we were just about the only people who would have him under their roof. He would turn up in his green Vauxhall and my mother always had a tray ready: fresh coffee and chocolate cake, because, she said, weeping sapped the energy. Oomie would take out his revolver and rehearse what had happened, showing us how he fell to the floor and did the leopard roll, as instruct-ed at police college, swearing he had been awake every moment he'd been on the floor. Super-aware, drawing a bead on the assassin, lining him up; and my ma would soothe him while he cried softly.

'Chin up,' she'd say. 'There are worse things.'

He never asked her what the worse things were. But, then, he seemed to think she didn't have political views. He was mistaken. She loathed anything that tied her down. Everyone was free to fly. She did not just believe it: she lived for nothing else.

If Oomie never asked, I did, and she gave me short shrift: 'Pass laws, jail terms, loss of land rights, curtailment of liberties, racial insanity, lethal boredom. In a world gone as mad as ours, a man who makes a mistake is rather endearingly human. If you hunt, you know anything can happen and anyone can have a weak moment. At least his behaviour was natural. In some ways, he was the only honest man on the platform that day, was my poor old Oomie.'

I was sixteen when Koosie came to live with us. Koosie told me that he was 'about' the same age. There was a lot I didn't know about Koosie because there was lot he didn't know about himself. He had attached himself to my mother at the airfield, where he had been living off scraps of food he got from the pilots and airfield staff, and he earned a few bob carrying bags to the planes.

My ma brought him home, as she did when someone she liked caught her eye; and that was how we came to grow up together for the next seven or eight years. It was an unusual set-up in the sixties. He was smaller than me; very thin and he had very big eyes. He always faded from sight whenever anyone from outside looked in on our lives.

He said he'd lost his parents. He sounded like he was still looking for them, as if they might turn up. He once had a house but it 'got taken'. I marvelled at this: how did someone 'take' your house?

Koosie got kind of cross, as if I'd said he was lying.

'I did have a house and it did get taken. I remember it.'

But I couldn't get it into my head.

'Who took it?'

'They came with bulldozers and they pushed it over.'

That haunted me: 'They pushed it over. Why did they push it over?'

He shrugged. 'Don't know. Then they took us away. We were removed.'

I didn't feel much for his lost parents. I lost my mother regularly and I'd learnt to get on with it. But to have the place that made you who you were pushed over, and carted away brick by brick. Then they removed you too …

Koosie did not live in our house but in the outside room. Instead of reducing him to some sort of servant status, it increased his standing, at least in my eyes; he was independent, he had his own roof over his own head and he was very good at looking after himself. When my ma forgot to leave enough food, Koosie picked up food at the Greek shop on the corner. I envied him, but I never felt guilty: he knew how to take care of himself and showed me, but he wore my clothes, rode my bike, read my books. Koosie taught me you could get by on half a loaf of bread and a Coke. He took me to Big Lou's place, the Golden Gate Fish Bar, for sixpence-worth of chips.

Big Lou's place was about a mile away, and we walked there. Big Lou had a round and heavy head, like a cannon-ball perched on a pyramid, a thick neck, big shoulders, he wore his white shirt open to the waist, he had lots of strong black hairs on his rocky chest, and immense hips.

He was a sight, like going to see a live volcano. Lou was always ready to blow his top. What a show he was; we could watch him for ages. Lou patting the pistol in his belt, shoved tightly among the folds of his tummy. Lou banging the chip basket on the lip of the fryer and reaching for the perforated jam tin that served as a salt cellar. Dumping the chips, glistening and steaming, on to a square bed of shiny white paper, which he had sliced with a huge carving knife. He made lovely parcels did Lou. One white sheet for the wrap, then a second slapped tight to seal. And the hot chips stung your fingertips right through the double wrap, and fumes of vinegar rose like a prayer. Sometimes he used his pistol as a paper-weight, barrel pointing at the customer.

Lou with his two queues, one black one white. But only one cash register, as Koosie pointed out. Lou with his bellowing voice when some black guy stepped out of line:

'You fucking black bastards, you want fucking chips, do you? You want hot patats? Fucking hell, you bloody wait till I nod at you 'cos nodding at you means you may step forward, but only when I nod at you 'cos that means I finished serving the boss, and only after I've served the boss do you get served, you mis-begotten fucking jungle bunnies, and if any of you so much as check me out the wrong way you'll get a slug in your thick fucking skull.'

And they laughed – the black queue laughed, a line of laugh-ers – they were really and truly amused, tickled, because, well – that was Lou; because he always talked like that. He was a roadshow; he was a riot.

The white queue didn't laugh when Lou started shouting. The line of whites looked the other way. They felt it was tacky, dangerous even to talk the way Big Lou did. After all, blacks were people too; no one liked to be called names. If you wanted to say things like that, then have the decency to say them in private. Lou was a bully and a big mouth and the white queue really wished he'd shut up; the white queue wished that the black queue would stop wriggling around and grinning when

Big Lou insulted them. It wasn't right and, besides, it didn't fool anyone; no one liked to be called a troop of fucking jungle bunnies; no one liked to have guns pointed at them and told to 'wipe that fucking grin off your face, or I'll blast it off', so why were they laughing at his vile language when all it did was to make them seem pathetic and make everyone else embarrassed? But that was the thing with the black queue: it never did what it should, or what was expected. No wonder there was separation; no wonder you had to have different queues: how were you going to mix with people who didn't know better than to encourage rampant racists like Lou to insult them?

Koosie grinned across the yard of green lino that separated us. He was very easy about it all. Not me. Lou terrified me, and he diverted me, but he never amused me ... I wondered about Koosie: did he get a kick out of Lou; did he *really*? I knew what he'd say afterwards as we sat licking vinegar off our fingers: 'That's life. Lou's a gas, and the chips are good.'

When my mother landed on us, it was like a storm at sea, exciting and disturbing while it was going on, but we were always pretty relieved once it had blown over, and she'd flown out of our lives again, back to the Niger Delta, or Uganda or the Rift Valley, into the other world we called 'wherever'.

'Where's Ma?' he'd say.

'Gone to wherever,' I'd say.

Our world was the house, the garden and the easy, never-explained, never-questioned friendship between us. Behind the split-pole fence that screened the house from the cars in Jan Smuts Avenue, two teenagers, living together for seven or eight years – till Koosie went missing.

'What we eating today?'

'What we got?'

'Eggs.'

'Good, let's have scrambled eggs.'

We lived, then, two boys in a house watched over by the pictures of my mother and her friends. Here she was drinking tempo, a strong beer, with tribesmen somewhere in Kenya; there she was standing beside her plane after scouting elephant; here she smiled on the set of *Mogambo*, flanked by Clark Gable and Ava Gardner, and one or other had scrawled, in what looked like lipstick, across the pearly grey sky behind her tousled hair: 'Darling Kate – Love from Us!!'

Koosie stopped going to school, and went back to work at the airport, or he did some gardening for the neighbouring missuses. It helped with getting in more money. He could not work at the OK Bazaars; he could not work in the bottle store on Saturday mornings; he could not even get into the Rand Easter Show. None of that was allowed. I earned quite good money; he earned next to nothing.

This was all perfectly normal; it would have seemed bizarre to the two of us if things had been any other way. We were simply two guys together. But I was growing up to be a white man; he was growing up to be a garden boy. Koosie stopped being real, stopped being seen, he was my shadow; he dogged my heels. Only I was real.

Behind the split-pole fence we washed our clothes and fixed the garden. De Wet's Flying Dutchmen came once a week and cleaned the house.

Outside the fence it was different. We walked down to the Zoo Lake together though we did not sit on the same bench; we did not go to the bioscope together; we travelled on the same red and cream double-decker bus up Jan Smuts Avenue, but Koosie would take the last seat upstairs, reserved for non-whites. I went to school each day; he went now and then; I took the bus; he rode his bike close on ten miles to school in Alexandra Township.

I could not take Koosie to my school: I could not talk of him there, not even to Jake Schevitz, my best friend. It would have made no sense. Even though Schevitz came to my house, even though he saw Koosie there, even though he took a relaxed view of my mother and our habits – even then – there was no way he could have seen that Koosie was as close to being what I never had: a brother.

Schevitz was the only guy I knew who looked at Koosie and me and saw nothing too worrying. 'Odd but consistent' he called my home circumstances. He meant me, alone at home, when my mother was somewhere else. Alone that is but for Baldy, our grey parrot, and De Wet's Flying Dutchmen. And, some time later, me and Koosie, two boys, one white, one black, living in a suburban house in Johannesburg. To take such oddities calmly, quietly, sensibly was a very remarkable thing in white-demented South Africa, which at the time was not really a country, not a society, but more of an armed gang: prodigiously perverted, wildly cruel, quite horribly hilarious. A gang glued together by not just an intense admiration of, and a raging thirst for, stupidity; who took it as a divine right, as a central plank of the national consciousness, to be not just dumber than just about anyone else on the planet, but to be very, very proud of it.

Schevitz and I used to wonder aloud just who got us started on this path and we blamed it on a bloke called Jan van Riebeeck, who arrived in the Cape with the ur-gang of Dutch freebooters, in the middle of the seventeenth century. The

Dutch grew a hedge, built a fort, shot anything and everything that came their way: all the normal colonial things. In some ways they were like all invaders from Alexander the Great to Julius Caesar to the Vikings: they thought murdering the natives was pretty much in order; they laid about them with vigour.

Let's face it, there are no pretty conquerors, but give me conquistadors, or Puritans dreaming of a shining city on a hill. Give me Romans, Turks, Vikings: anyone but fucking book-keepers, ledger-clerks and smarmy parsons with guns.

Here was the trick: they were going to turn black man's sweat into white man's gold at the stroke of a whip. They set the tone. The founding fathers of white civilisation on the southern tip of Africa were going to strike it rich by doing nothing. And the Dutch did a lot of nothing: they built no roads or schools or bridges, they played no music, they com-posed no poems, they began no newspapers, they dreamt no dreams; instead, they sat around on their capacious rear ends and sent for slaves to do their living for them. They hadn't been in the Cape three minutes before there were more slaves than freemen. What was the Cape of Good Hope became the Cape of Slaves – you couldn't move for slaves – and that was OK because white men didn't move, that's what they had black men for. Move themselves, move the world.

Later, old van Riebeeck, a Dutch functionary hungry for gold, was canonised. He would not have known himself. He never wanted to be stuck in the Cape, at the toe of Africa, under a sawn-off mountain, surrounded by a lot of Hottentots. But they made him into this patriot. They gave him a noble brow, chestnut hair and sober mien, and put his face on the money. There were statues. An ambitious upstart, who couldn't wait to get the hell out to somewhere serious, stood on prominent plinths all over the damn place.

What was the effect of this sort of monumental brazen bloody nerve? It made you mad, yes, and sad, yes, perhaps precisely because it was sad it induced in Schevitz and me a kind of raging hilarity. You laughed because you couldn't stand it, really.

My mother wanted Koosie to love Africa in a way I guess she felt I did not. That's to say: her way, her Africa. She lay back in her chair and told us stories about how she'd been attacked by elephants and leopards, but it was the hyena that scared her to death. She once woke up with one in her tent, staring down at her. She took us to shoot elephant in Mozambique. She said she could see Koosie was a natural hunter. She showed him how to use the big shotgun; they tracked an old bull and had him side-on. She showed him how to aim for a point about a third up from the belly and a little behind the front legs. The aim being to send a bullet through the heart and smash a leg at the same time; to kill as quickly as possible.

He fired, he missed and the bull was gone.

'Never mind, there'll be lots of chances. Is there anything you'd specially like to shoot, Koosie?'

He nodded.

'Lion, buffalo, eland?'

'People.' said Koosie. 'There are some people I'd like to shoot.'

Just how differently Koosie and I saw things became apparent slowly. We had been on a trip with my mother to the Congo. We stayed with a small band of Efe in their village, which was called Baudouin, after the Belgian King. (This was when the Belgians ran the Congo and ordered European names for everything, before Mobutu took over and ordered African names for everything.) The Efe were very kind: they put us up in a hut in the middle of Baudouin, and all the kids came to stare at us. From the thatched roof of the hut dangled drying fish, and three thick white buffalo horns.

My mother was off all day hunting. Koosie and I saw a lot of the kids who took us into the forest and showed us how to play *mangola*, a kind of pygmy draughts, except you used dried seeds for counters, and made four rows in the red earth and moved the seeds along the little furrows. They showed us elephants' prints in the mud, and taught us to eat yellow mushrooms called *lobololo*. The Efe kids had French names – Mathieu and Lucien and Marta – which made them sound very foreign, and they sang a lot and warned us that certain orchids should never be touched or the rains would wash them away, and tree branches would tumble on their heads. They had a hundred taboos in the forest but we were safe, they said. Being *muzungu*, white men.

'I am not a bloody *muzungu!*' Koosie said. 'I am as black as you.'

But they didn't think so.

The kids sang almost all the time, and they smoked a lot of dagga; they got drunk on banana wine, they told long stories about witches. Koosie, I think, was at first bored, and then really rather cross. I didn't know why.

My mother said he was a city boy and country irritated him. I think now it was not just that they didn't see him as one of them, it was that Efe kids were incurably and utterly themselves and yet they were million miles from Koosie. That's when I felt the difference: it was seeing Africa as it looked to him and it had nothing to do with my mother or me. The pygmies failed him; they weren't the Africans he wanted them to be. They named their villages after their waterholes, when they didn't call them after Belgian kings; they ate fried manioc and chicken. The Efe had no real sense of money; their lives were one long exchange. Koosie gave up his penknife and got back smoked elephant meat and it made him throw up. He was impatient with the way the Efe leaned on the forest, like it was some sort of mixture of god and garden and guardian and lover. He was impatient with their self-defeating ways. When my mother told us that the BaBudu pygmies used nets, and nets were much more useful in hunting game, he wanted to know why the Efe stuck to their bows.

Koosie got impatient with the Efe the way the first Dutch settlers under van Riebeeck got impatient with the Hottentots for drifting here and there; and with the Bushmen for always stealing. He got impatient in the way the British got impatient with the Boers for being dogged, illiterate Calvinists. He got impatient in the way whites got impatient with blacks because they simply refused to be, well, more like us; and, when I look back now, I see he got impatient in the way that blacks were going to get impatient with us.

It was a sign but I could not read the signs.

Koosie read a lot of poetry; he read Tennyson and Charles Causley and Henty and Auden. He wanted to be a poet, but more than that: he wanted to write about flowers. Now, that was wild. Flowers? Us? He found a set of old botanical sketches amongst my mother's books.

'This is the Cape pansy, sometimes called "little bonnet", or "lion-mouth". Look, it has leaves like narrow teeth.'

He showed me his stuff; he read it to me and I can still remember lines of it:

'The white-eyed lobelia is watching me.'

It was the peacefulness and the unexpectedness of these interests I found so beguiling. In a violent land I'd never met anyone so easily taken with quiet and pretty things. I thought, imagine telling Big Lou about this. Flowers … He'd pick up his gun, he'd say, 'You're writing … what? Stay away from fucking flowers, you spastic jungle bunny, or I'll let so much daylight through you that daisies is what you'll be fucking well pushing up.'

> I look into the dark soft mouth of the petunia
> And something tells me it has only good thoughts;
> And will never betray me,
> Or dream of cutting its own throat.

That was the way it started for Koosie, with flowers and poems and amusement. That wasn't how it ended, but, then, it never is; in this country nothing ends easily. Maybe nothing ends.

Koosie was destined for resistance on a grand scale. I should have seen it when he grinned at me from the other queue in Big Lou's place. I should have seen it when he took me on those Sunday trips to the city.

The town centre at weekends was an empty tomb; the city that ran on high octane all week long dropped dead each Sunday. From Saturday lunchtime Jo'burg began to empty, and by five everyone had left. No one lived there; whites didn't want to and blacks weren't allowed to. The white guys went back to the deepest suburbs and prepared to do what they did on Sunday: nothing. They went into a coma, because that was the law; nothing moved on Sunday, and if anything did, the cops would want to know why. No trams ran, no shops opened, no one smiled if they could help it.

And the black shadows that served the white city also went home, to the dusty townships, somewhere out of sight; and the town, so wild and loud all week long, became some vast and vacant set for a movie that never got made. The streets ran like rivers of grey between the ghostly canyons. On Commissioner and Anderson, on Plein and Jeppe, what you heard wasn't just silence, it was the sigh of the dying, of life passing. Nothing moved outside the Library Gardens except a scrap of newspaper, or a single pigeon pecking at a cardboard ice-cream cup.

Sunday in Jo'burg: the day of the dead.

That's when Koosie showed me something rather special. We'd walk from our house: it took about an hour. We'd head down to somewhere central, like Commissioner Street, and then we'd wait. Not for long.

'Look,' said Koosie. 'It's a Ford Fairlane.'

The lead limo was the bridal car and it carried newly-weds from the forbidden townships. Following the Fairlane came a

Skyline in apple green with a retractable canvas roof, its white-walled tyres painted up so bright they glowed in the shadows of the skyscrapers. Studebaker Hawk, Hudson Hornet and Chev Corvette, in shades of caramel and plum, shining like heaven, filled to the brim with revellers, sitting on the bonnet and doorframes; men wearing fedoras and cuff-links, spats and buttonholes and women in tight skirts with sheeny nylon knees. Flash limos, zoot suits, spats, saucy little veils; wedding guests come to king and queen it for a few hours in the Sunday city. It was worth the walk and the wait, to sit on the pavement and watch the weddings go by, jazzing up the brain-dead city.

'You seen *Street with No Name?*' Koosie asked me.

'No.'

'Well, go.'

I did, alone of course. Koosie wasn't allowed in our cinemas. And saw Richard Widmark, alias 'Styles', in his belted overcoat, taking deep lingering sniffs from his benzedrine inhaler, and biting deep into his apple.

I reckoned they got it just about right, the showboys cruising down Harrison or Jorrissen or Jeppe in a Caddie red as cherries, red as blood, or Lincoln Continentals that looked like they were carved from whipped cream, with the hood back, ivory leather seats, silver trim. Koosie knew them all: the Russians, the Americans, the Gestapo, the Berliners; all the *tsotsi* hoods who dressed in belted macs, like Widmark, walked like Cagney, and talked like Humphrey Bogart. They were gangsters, real or aspirational, sure. But, then, who wasn't? What was crime to you was constitutional development to someone else. The guys in far-away Pretoria who ran our lives were just another gang pretending to be a government.

The township *tsotsis* floating by in their Chevys and Lincolns were in love with style and flair and angle and rhythm and irreverence; they knew – better than politicians, better than the truisms of all the parties in our lamentable land – that it was precisely *not* solidity but lightness, not uniformity but oddity and angle and colour that were the real true rebellion. The wild wedding parties jazzing up the death-grey streets were a slap in the face of the disapproving day.

I finished school; I got a job. Koosie never finished school because he never really began. He did a few things like caddy-ing or gardening. He found it hard to get work but it didn't worry him because his work was already chosen. He was going to resist. Koosie was increasingly obsessed. And, in a strange way, increasingly dull. Koosie, the flower poet, had been so radical it took the breath away. The kid who showed me the wild carnival of limos sailing down the death-grey Sunday streets, or talked of the wise-eyed petunia – who showed in such things a bravery that stopped the heart – was subdued. The adrenalin rush of the struggle tamped down rebellion. Revolution watered no flowers. Delight gave way to serious-ness, and seriousness led to obedience. Koosie did not just join the movement, he took holy orders in some sort of semi-divine congregation of heroes, a communion of latter-day saints and saviours.

I was also increasingly obsessed. I learnt that the Hungarian parliament had used ice taken from a lake as the way of cooling the building. I learnt that the Persians, as far back as 400 BC, built huge subterranean refrigerators with walls many metres thick, insulated from heat transfer with a mortar mixed from clay, goat hair and egg whites.

I can date the moment when I knew Koosie was off on some track that was not mine. He was just back from somewhere. He didn't say where, I didn't ask. We were sitting in the front parlour.

'Big Lou got drilled. Did you hear?' He laughed.

I didn't like the sound of his laugh.

'One night last week.' Koosie big eyes blinking, his voice rising. 'Lou was leaning on the counter – y'know how he leaned on one elbow – and in walked this little black guy, I mean tiny. Two bricks and a tickey high. Doesn't join a queue. Walks right up the counter. He's so short he can hardly get his nose over the counter but he's got this very big gat in his fist. He doesn't say anything. Lou says, "And what do you want, my old China?" He doesn't say anything. Lou says, "Well, if you can't find your tongue, fuck off outa here." Guy still doesn't say anything, just looks; eyes just above the counter, like croc's eyes just above the waterline; and then he drills Lou. Plumb centre. And Lou, he's heavy, so he sags to the right, so it looks like he's going for his own gun, but he's not, he's dropping under his own weight. But the little guy drills him again, this one in the chest … then he walks out. Lou was dead before he hit the floor.'

Listening to him, I heard amusement and shock, I heard anger, I heard admiration. Part of me understood the admiration – here was this little black guy who waltzes in and shoots the ogre of the Golden Gate.

Or, as Koosie put it: 'Not bad for a fucking jungle bunny.'

I was sorry, not for Lou – it was pretty amazing someone hadn't shot him years before – but because part of what we were had been blasted away. That, of course, was the whole point. After all, what had Pratt tried and failed to do when he pushed the pistol into Verwoerd's ear? Pratt fluffed it. But the magical black midget had turned in a virtuoso performance and Koosie felt good about it, and he was angry that I didn't. We no longer saw things the same way. How could we? The exigencies were so different, his anger was so great, and the times so violent.

We were hot, too hot by far.

I wanted to know why killing Lou was good but all he could tell me was that it was necessary. I thought that was old news. Koosie wanted me to stop thinking, stop remembering what we were, say nothing about the idiocy of blood certainties. His comrades were on the side 'of history'. I said history was an orgy of murder interpersed with moralising crap designed to make monsters look good.

'Your history, maybe,' said Koosie.

For me, the really interesting thing about the little guy was the novelty of his method. We did not know why he'd killed Lou. What set him apart, though, made him so different from the ham-handed guys we were, was his efficiency. He was economical, quick and deft; he preached no sermon, he started no political party, he did what he came to do and simply vanished. He was not a proto-revolutionary, not a freedom fighter; but he was perhaps an anarchist, an improviser, even an artist.

'Shooting him was the best.' Koosie came back to it often.

'For what?'

'For freedom.'

'Freedom's another fairy-tale we tell ourselves before going out and shooting someone.'

'You're soft, Alex.'

From there on out we split. It was painful, deep and permanent. Because we shared the same house it was impossible not to know what the other was doing. Koosie was deep into the revolution. I was building models of wind catchers. Wind catchers were like funnels, or V-shaped towers, mounted on the roof of a building. They might face in one direction, and drive air downward, or they might swing like a windmill. This downwash of cool air was a steady, clean form of air-conditioning. If I positioned the funnel over a basin of water, I found temperatures fell astonishingly. Koosie would stand in front of one of my beautiful creations and ask why I was wasting my time.

'Well, if you want cool clean air you can get a slave with a tree branch to wave it over your head, or you can open the back door of your cave, hut or hovel, or you can wash and dry the air we breathe.'

'Things are wild, mad, necessary... and you're blowing air ...?'

So there it was. I thought history – the new one that Koosie was all for – looked dismayingly like it had last bloody time round.

The seventies saw the start of the killing years. The cops, the security agents, the spies, the strategists of the regime were very effective, and those who said or did the wrong thing got hit again and again.

It had to be said – though no one did – that Koosie's comrades were not very effective. In fact, for a liberation movement formed before the fucking Chinese Communist Party, they were amazingly duff. No one on Koosie's side ever took out a cop with the coolness of the midget killer who knocked off Big

Lou. Koosie's people, if they resembled anyone, looked alarmingly like that great double act I been lucky enough to witness at Milner Park: the Pratt and Oomie Show, who between them failed either to shoot or save Verwoerd.

That's where my ma came in. The security cops were deep inside every liberation movement: there were arrests, assassinations, betrayals, confessions, and fuck-ups, and that meant there was a queue of guys very keen to get the hell out to neighbouring havens in Lesotho or Botswana or Zambia.

Koosie made a pitch perfectly calculated to win her over. He offered her a chance to serve the cause, and his talk of it reminded me of someone who had found his family, who had signed on to salvation.

'What we need is a guy with a plane, a bloke without any tie to any political group. We need a man the cops would never dream was running people out of the country. Someone a bit odd, who is always going here or there in Africa.'

My mother didn't blink. ' Then I'm your man. I'll do it, but not for the cause, whatever that is. I'll do it for the fun.'

She would check into a posh hotel, like the Carlton, under a false name, and in the morning she would go down to the lobby, wearing a different coloured blouse, according to instructions. She would carry a copy of *Le Monde* or *La Stampa* each day for a week, and if no one showed up she would go home.

When the plan failed she'd be scathing about her handlers. 'Job's off. Waste of bloody time. This lot can't tell their arses from their elbows. I tell you the liberation movement is totally useless!'

But she kept on doing it.

When the job was on, someone, usually a woman, would walk into the lobby and sit down next to her and slip her a note with a phone number. My mother would walk to a phone booth and call the number and she'd be directed to another hotel. There she'd meet the person planning to skip the country. She would file flight plans for the Kruger Park if she was heading for Mozambique, or the Free State if it was Lesotho. Then she'd spend time in these diversionary base camps to make it look legal. On the day arranged, the customer would get to the agreed airfield and my old lady would be waiting. Once over the border, she usually put the plane down on a dirt road and ditched her passenger. She'd fly flew back to her camp in the Kruger and go game spotting for a few days. I guess she must have helped a dozen or more people to slip the net and make it to Maputo, Francistown, Addis Ababa or Lusaka.

She was pulled in twice by the cops for questioning; she was in solitary for fifty-six days, but they noted the size of her biceps, and they told themselves that anyone who went hunting in South West, made her own biltong and shook your hand so hard she crushed your fucking fingers – 'I kid you not, *ou maat*' – wasn't the type to help fucking black commie bastards jump the borders. She was a good bloke; she was the very essence of the rough, tough white pioneer.

Her cover was so good because in many ways it was so real.

They called her 'the aunty who flies'.

Koosie was the very last man my ma flew to safety. He'd been detained twice, spent 146 days in solitary confinement, and was under house arrest in Soweto when she sprang him. She flew him to Maputo.

That was the last I saw of him for a long time. I heard he went to Addis afterwards, then London. He was wedded, as they say, to 'the struggle'. As for me, well, I was wedded to wind catchers but it didn't stop me getting married twice, and divorced, in fairly quick succession.

It would not be true to say – well, not exactly true – that my mother sank my marriages; and yet to Benita Freeman, in the late seventies, and then to Maxine Vermeulen, in the eighties, she proved damned well fatal.

When I think back to her impact it was pretty amazing, considering that she was hardly ever there. But like the Gulf Stream, or the lunar tug, it was the effect she had. In the seventies she was flying political fugitives to Addis Ababa, or Maseru, or Francistown. In the eighties she was hunting in the Congo; but in one way or another she was always around: 'like something in the wind', as Benita once said.

Benita and her breasts go round in my head like an old song.

Benita had been a beauty queen. Miss Transvaal in 1971 and then Miss Orange Free State two years in a row, a record that has never been equalled and now never will be, names of places having changed. At twenty-seven she retired from beauty competitions, went into cosmetics as Benita Freeman Beauty and hit the jackpot. She patented a line of cosmetics called Juvenescence, and she had corporate headquarters off Oxford Road, a Bentley and a staff of thirty.

Her left breast was marginally larger than her right. Her pale, chalk-smooth complexion was enriched by a speckling of tiny auburn freckles that spread over the bridge of her nose like shapely sugar ants. I remember her use of the word 'para-mour', especially the way her lip curled so prettily when she said it.

I was what I heard my mother once pretty fairly describe as a salesman of sorts. I couldn't have put it better myself. My job was desultory but my product was vital, exceptionally light-weight and widely available and, in its natural untreated state, entirely free. So a salesman of sorts summed me up pretty well.

Benita was good about my ethereal career. What she could not live with was my mother, or what my mother did. Was it my mother as hunter, pilot, explorer that she found so difficult? No, in fact, it was my old lady as bar-room brawler. Along with the broad shoulders, big muscles and huge hands that the secu-rity police had found so compelling, my ma also had – after a few drinks – the joshing manner you see when white guys get pissed in a Saturday night bar and pick fights over questions of rugby, or revolution, all of them vital male preoccupations in my home town. My mother drunk, or even slightly tipsy, had a mean streak in her.

Benita might have ignored this; our fault line was never really social, it was racial. It wasn't that she objected to Ma's views; it was my old lady's unabashed blindness that got to her. I don't think my mother distinguished between black and white. She was in no way liberal, she simply overlooked race, rather as a monarch ignored intrinsic differences of rank among her subjects. She was grandly blind.

I have to say I understood Benita's concern. If you did not know where you stood on race you did not know where you were. After all, white South Africans were trained from the womb, from the very first embryonic bundle of natal cells, to register in the minutest degree the difference that more, or less, melanin made to the complexion. So super-aware were we of racial rankings that, at every quiver on the skin-colour scale, our ultra-sensitive sensors rang out like fucking church bells.

Not so my ma. She carried on regardless, treating people as if they were like her, or would be if they were incredibly lucky. Or like everyone else, when, quite plainly, they were not. You could go to jail for thinking like that. Her blindness was not simply unusual, it was scary, it was illegal, it was offensive, it was provocative, and it was unwise.

It simply wasn't, in words Benita used a lot, 'very nice'.

Benita believed that if she tried very hard, it would be possible to live in a world that was 'quiet'. How much yearning she packed into that word. One where she could be like 'proper' people, who lived in places like Stockholm, and walked their dogs and drank their coffee in peace; instead of being trapped on a continent that bled all over the place, where at any moment some damned thing came flying in. That wasn't even a place, it was a problem that constantly challenged your right to exist, that mocked every attempt you made to impress yourself on an indifferent, endless land that by its sheer bloody otherness made you uncomfortable, continually reminding you that, actually, you had no standing, no worth, no place here! That the only way you could be seen was by standing on the shoulders of someone else. That you were even less real than some character in a novel; hell, you weren't worth the paper you were written on.

Then, too, the other difficulty was that my mother did not keep servants. It was not from her point of view a principled stand, it was plain good sense.

'I'm sorry, I've tried, but what for? What do they do? I just don't see their point.'

For Benita servants were not necessarily there to do anything in particular. They were there to stand between you and the raw life beyond; they were there so that, as a proper white person, you knew who you were: a Lord of the Universe. But the trick only worked if everyone played the game, and that meant you took up your lordly duties and they went off to clean the bath or cook dinner or mind the kids. We were superior only if they were servile. And vice versa. Anyone who didn't keep servants was letting the side down.

Benita and I led a normal life: we had a black manservant called Francis: and Benita dressed him in a white tunic and a red sash and she always rang a little brass bell to summon Francis from the kitchen where our cook, Emily, saw to things; just as, in our large green garden, two strong men, Nicodemus and Good Man, made things grow. I had never in my life used a pick, mowed a lawn, washed a dish or carried a parcel. This was all perfectly, effortlessly normal. Our lives were lived on one single premise: people like us didn't do anything; we were done unto. The only finger my wife ever lifted was to close the windows as we waited on Francis to serve the roast lamb because, as she liked to warn: 'This is Africa, and something might fly in.'

Well, my mother flew in, and kept on bloody well flying in. Wanting Benita to fly out with her, to the Congo, to Kenya; wanting to give her boxing lessons.

Then there were my uncles.

'Your mother takes lovers the way other people take hot showers,' said Benita. 'I mean, just who does she think she is?'

I hadn't the faintest idea who she was, and that was the trouble.

Benita talked casually of my ma's 'love affairs'. But I'd been exposed all my life to men who floated through our lives like motes of dust in a shaft of bright sunlight and love never seemed to be in it. Some few stayed with me – her liaisons with, say, Oomie, or Uncle Papadop – but the rest drifted away and I thought of them no more.

Benita would say: 'Surely you knew they were sleeping with her?'

And, yes, I suppose I realised in a vague way that they might have been sleeping with her; but not for the life of me could I imagine that, therefore, she was sleeping with *them*. That was to think of my mother as something other than a gale or a thunderstorm.

Benita persisted. 'If she didn't care for them, why did she do it?'

Again, I didn't know. Perhaps she did care, but not much, and not especially. At best, I think she cared for certain ways of being human – yes – but for the most part she seemed utterly careless about beings who happened to be human.

Benita was embarrassed; she said it wasn't 'nice' for someone of my mother's age to 'flaunt' strings of 'paramours'.

The reason for this delicacy wasn't natural fastidiousness, but the usual problem: race. The old and firm belief widespread in our country amongst the whites that to reveal your desires, to brandish your sexuality, to own up to your passions was, somehow, to lower yourself 'to the level of the Bantu'.

Benita never used the words 'black' or 'African', words not just politically subversive, but crass. They stirred up trouble and so sensible people preferred 'Bantu' because it gave them a way of not talking about things they knew they had to talk about but which always ended in fights and tears, thus preventing people from getting on, in life or business, as ordinary, sensible, reasonable – above all – normal, for Christ's sake, people wanted to do.

I said to her once, 'Hang on a mo', have you listened to yourself? Just listened to the bloody sound it makes? It's not just meaningless, it's silly. One Bantu, two Bantu … I'd rather be called a kaffir.'

'I have never, ever, ever …' She couldn't complete her sentence.

'Never? I've been called a white kaffir so often it doesn't touch sides.'

'When?'

'When? You mean, when not? It's the sort of thing guys say when they don't like your driving or your face or your manner, like, "Hey, what's with you? You fucking white kaffir!"'

'I have never, and I will never, use that horrible word.'

So there it was. The word was all around us, you could not escape it but you could prefer not to hear it. As South Africans we were separated not by class but by degrees of auditory embarrassment brought on by certain sounds. Sonic triggers. The long owl shriek 'oooooo' in Bantu did for me; I wanted to hide under the bloody table, I wanted to run screaming from the room. And it was the whirring, lip-shivering curl of the final 'firrrrrrr' in 'kaffir' that did it for Benita.

One day, Benita ran off with a small ginger-haired country and western singer called Frikkie La Page, the 'Boer Caruso' …

She wrote in her parting note:

'Your mother has gone native and I just don't want to be near her any more. I am very sorry, but it's her or me ...'

I tore up her note, I made myself a cup of rooibos tea, I took a hot bath, I listened to the radio, I lay in the warm water and remembered vaguely that a bath is good place to die – if you slit your wrists, death comes in a drowsy darkening of the warm water. They played an ad for chocolate milk-flavouring powder, spoken by a man with a phoney Dutch accent: he urged us to try 'Bensdorp's Chocolate Shprinkle-Shpread...' and it seemed sad and soothing all at once.

I had some sympathy for Benita's dilemma – my mother was impossible, yes – but Benita had been wrong about the native bit. My mother did not 'go native' – that suggests a distance travelled – my mother was native from the word go. Benita wanted a kind of niceness founded upon a version of gentility, a world where native meant *Bantooo* and everything was normal. Instead, we all lived in a place, and in a way, where no one had a clue what normal was; and nothing was ever nice.

When she heard about our break my mother offered to track down Frikkie, and wallop him, and I had a lot of trouble talking her out of it. It was not something I wanted: my wife leaves me for another man and my mother beats him up!

I said: 'Thanks ma, but no.'

'Hell, I only offered because I love you.'

If Benita was 'nice', then I guess I married Maxine some years later because she wasn't. Tall, with very blue eyes. A rather wonderful forehead, broad and calm. Tiny, pink, pursed lips. Maxine taught speech and drama at the University and you might have taken her for some artsy-craftsy, airy-fairy type but you'd have been wrong: she was very tough, as I was to find out, and the finding out of it changed my life for ever.

Maxine was so far ahead of the radical academic crowd – mostly Marxists, Trots or Stalinists – that she was almost out of sight. Generally, our intellectuals lived by proxy; they were like long-range radio receivers; their inspiration, their books, their films and their language, their Marx and Fanon and Gramsci, their *New Statesman* and their *African Communist*, their pamphlets, posters, slogans and songs came from far away, picked up as faint signals mixed in with lots of static, from that great store of all that was vibrant, admirable, exciting, persuasive, the place we called 'overseas', or more often 'the outside world'. If ideas didn't come from there they were not worth knowing, and if you didn't know that then neither were you.

Maxine had a cousin who worked with a group of animal rights activists in England. They were written up in *Country Life* because they broke into mink farms, cut the fences and set the animals free. They were so radical they didn't have posters or pamphlets or books; they communicated by code. Maxine had a thing, not so much about mink but about what they stood for. She formed with some friends a radical group called Animals Against Apartheid.

When I look back now I see that Benita and Maxine, in every way different people, had this in common: both wanted the place where they were to be more like the places they dreamt about. For Benita it was somewhere careful and clean and white and quiet – like Sweden. For Maxine it was the Essex marshes, and guys in duffel-coats running about misty fields, liberating mink.

Maxine didn't keep servants, and she didn't give a damn what my mother did with other people; that was good.

It was animals that came between them.

My mother called Maxine a 'fauna freak' because Animals Against Apartheid – AAP – picketed zoos and abattoirs on the basis that animals were segregated behind wire, imprisoned and killed, much as blacks were corralled behind the wire of townships and homelands.

Maxine called my mother a murderer.

It was the trips to the Congo that got to my wife and, in particular, a group of friends among the Wambuti pygmies whom my mother visited up that way. The Wambuti and, in particular, the Efe, a people who hunt with bow and arrow, had been in the family almost as long as the bloody Boers. We'd known the Congo pygmies ever since my grandfather befriended Sir Harry Johnston, the hunter who spend a lot of time in the old Belgian Congo chasing giant gorillas and butterflies and pygmies; he believed that somewhere on the flanks of Ruwenzori, high in the Mountains of the Moon, or deep in the jungles of the Semlik valley, he would discover some extant dinosaur or specimen of early man.

Instead, what he had found was the okapi, a preposterous creature somewhere between a horse, a zebra and a buck, known to the Wambuti – though no one paid any attention – as *ndumba*, but renamed in honour of its gun-toting pursuer Sir Harry Johnston (*Ocapia Johnstonia*).

Pictures of the pygmies first came my way in a series of films given to my grandfather by T. Alexander Barnes who had filmed them on what he always called his 'kine'. His jerky grey films showed the Wambuti in the Ituri forests, wearing loincloths of woven leaves, smiling at the camera and tucking into their salt, which they adored. Mr Barnes referred to them as 'forest dwarfs', and he knew for a fact that the Wambuti were the missing link: 'the ape was all there, up to the hair, which was discernible in some cases over the entire body of the dwarfs ...'

My ma had been hunting okapi in the forests for years, and since no one knew the okapi better than the Wambuti, they were her guides. Her mates were a married couple from the Efe tribe, called Bara and Buti. These were their new names, taken after President Mobutu decreed in 1972 that all the old Christian and European names of the country, its towns and cities and its people, should be dropped and proper African names substituted. So the President, Joe Desiré Mobutu, became 'Mobuto Sese Seko Kuku NgBendu wa ZaBanga', which roughly translates into 'the all-powerful warrior who, because of his inflexible will to win, will go from conquest to conquest leaving fire in his wake'. A finer description, word for word, of just about every oppressive measure taken against Africans by their blasted rulers it would be difficult to invent.

And Alphonse and Desirée became Bara and Buti.

'Really good little guys,' said my mother.

Quite why it was the Congo trips that so appalled Maxine, when my mother at the time was constantly visiting Lebanese diamond merchants, Rhodesian farmers, German visionaries, white hunters in Kenya and black leopard men in Gabon, I can't say, and considering the nature of those times, you might have thought that anyone actually living among people in the Congo would have impressed the political activists as pretty bloody progressive. But, then, our radical spirits were never interested in Africa's other places; they were interested, as Maxine was, in principles. Maxine had never been anywhere in Africa but she had views.

I watched Maxine and my mother with despair. I loved my wife, and I loved my mother, but in the way you love the sea. Something you want to sit beside but prefer not to be cast adrift upon. I loved Maxine for her soft flesh and the way she cried in her sleep and the outpouring of her vulva when we made love, an almost embarrassing wetness. To be honest, I loved Maxine for her pussy; the trouble was Maxine had principles and principles won over pussy any day.

My mother had been everywhere, and she did not have views. The pygmies of the Ituri were simply friends, family, and trackers. She took strangers and rendered them into blood relatives … as if it had been meant this way, as if everyone did it.

Maxine said: 'The Congo? Sounds like a cop-out to me.'

My mother said: 'Animals Against Apartheid? More like Arseholes Against Apartheid, if you ask me.'

Maxine said sweetly: 'Tell me how it feels to be a professional killer.'

My mother raised her steely brows. 'Pretty good. I'm off tomorrow.'

It was Maxine's turn to be scornful. 'Why the Congo? What's there? The struggle's here.'

'You struggle,' said my ma. 'I'm going after okapi with the Wambuti. I may bring a few home with me.'

'Okapi?'

'Pygmies.'

'You mean you'd bring pygmies home?'

'Why not? For a bit of R&R.'

'Kathleen, that just perpetuates the pattern.'

'Pattern, what are you talking about? What pattern?'

'Hunting animals, hunting people. It exploits living beings for profit or pleasure.'

'I don't perpetuate the pattern: I'd say it perpetuates me. I've hunted with everyone from Karen Blixen to Gregory Peck and I'm proud of it. What does hunting have to do with racialism?'

'They're much the same, Kathleen. We keep our blacks the way some people keep mink.'

'I don't keep blacks. I don't keep mink either. I've never seen a mink.'

'Not you personally, and not mink *per se*. But there are people who breed mink in captivity, and kill them to make furs for stupid rich women.'

My mother was amazed. 'Where do they do this?'

'In Essex.'

'In Essex!'

Oh, the loathing, the stupefaction she put into the word.

A week later my mother called. 'Come and meet my friends.'

Maxine said: 'I'm not going. If she's got pygmies with her I'll freak. She just scoops them up and carries them off like … groceries …'

'Don't come, then, if it upsets you. There is always an element of provocation when she does these things.'

'Provocation! Listen, this is not provocation, this is open warfare. Of course I'm coming. I can fight, too.'

My mother was on the stoop, in a cane chair; puffing at her pipe and sitting at her feet were two small people. She reached over and tapped each in turn with her pipe stem. Her friends were tiny, around four feet tall. Above the garden walls there stretched five feet of fine wire.

'Meet Buti and Bara. They have the run of the garden.'

Buti and Bara were wearing only a few leaves around their middles, and smoking pipes stuffed with what I knew to be

marijuana. Their pot bellies hung over the edges of their loincloths and they followed my mother everywhere, like cats. She
spoke Swahili to them and they laughed a lot, but they were
very, very thin. I loved their trumpets, which they carved from
ivory and wore slung over their shoulders.

Maxine had no time for trumpets.

'First you shoot what they eat, and then you collect them
like dolls!'

My mother was unmoved. 'These aren't dolls, they're complete killers, these guys. Good for them, too. Killing is the thing
never to be lost sight of. There is a lot of it about. The slavers
did it to the tribes, the tribes did it to each other, the white settlers did it to their black servants, and their black peons did it
right back to their colonial bosses, the Belgians, when they took
over the Congo and chased them to hell and gone. And
absolutely everyone did it to the animals, and in the forests the
Wambuti get the sharp end of the stick from just about every
tribe around … I'm doing them a favour. I bring them here for
a bit of peace. I give them the freedom of my garden. Free
chicken and all the salt they can eat. They adore salt.'

Maxine was out of her league. You don't fight whirlwinds,
earthquakes, tidal waves. If you're wise you take to your heels.
I was used to my mother's friends, and her finds, her prey, her
passions, her memories: they were part of the way it was with
us, something no one else could understand.

Maxine said: 'What is the chicken mesh for?'

'To make sure they stay in the damn garden.'

Maxine was appalled.

'It's like a chicken coop.'

'Better a coop than a bird that's flown. Without the chicken mesh these two would be over that wall in a trice and into the traffic, and they wouldn't last three minutes in the traffic.'

Maxine appealed to me. 'You've got to make her understand, Alexander. She cannot keep people locked in her garden, like ornamental peacocks.'

'These little buggers will eat anything,' said my mother, beaming at Buti and Bara. 'I have to keep a sharp eye on them. Given half a chance they might *slag* a bloody cat, or something. Think what Madams Terre'Blanche, Garfinkel, Smuts and Mason will say to that! One butchered pet on the fire.'

Instead of cats, she gave them chicken to roast over open fires and salt from a large blue can of Cerebos, which she replaced every few days. They called her 'Bibi', which amused me because it means 'the wife' or 'the married woman'; and they seemed happy to stay in the garden, eating chicken drumsticks and smoking their long pipes.

'I gave them some dagga. They can't do without it,' said my mother.

It was absolutely fine until the night someone broke into the garden and cut a great hole in the chicken wire and the Wambuti were 'liberated', according to Maxine, or 'fled for their bloody lives', if you listened to my mother.

'And,' she added grimly, 'that's what they do to mink, I believe, in Essex! Set the little bastards free to screw up the countryside.'

Bara and Buti didn't flee very far. They headed straight into the nearby and much larger gardens of Madams Terre'Blanche, Garfinkel, Mason and Smuts, and went to ground. The pygmies of the Ituri forest spend their lives in hiding; they are complete experts in vanishing. They climb, they burrow, they creep into the tiniest hiding places, and five acres of Johannesburg gardens made vanishing easy among blue gums and loquat trees and mulberries.

But if Bara and Buti stayed next to invisible, you could hear them: they hunted with music and it was the music that woke the neighbours. When they hunt at night the pygmies of the Ituri call to each other like birds, and they use their ivory trumpets to produce a sound not unlike pan pipes. It is very sweet and utterly unforgettable, a low fluting, soft and lovely in the night, and far, most beautifully far, from the usual Jo'burg symphony of dogs, screams, gunshots and sirens ...

The first casualty was our old parrot, Baldy but as my ma said, you could not blame them: the Wambuti had a passion for the grey African parrot. We suspected they had slipped into the house and taken him away. We never found so much as a feather. After that, being adaptable, they made do with doves, mossies, wagtails and took their chickens live.

My mother said: 'Well, as long as it's only our stuff they poach, fine. But I have my doubts about that. If things get sticky I may have to call you.'

It didn't take long. One morning, Mrs Garfinkel was confronted by the pelt of her pet Alsatian, Domitian, swinging, salted and dry, from the branch of a mulberry tree. Luckily, she told everyone what everyone usually told everyone under these circumstances, namely that some bloody natives must have killed poor Domitian. One kept large dogs in order to savage natives, and it was inevitable that natives sometimes savaged dogs. It was in the nature of things.

My mother phoned me. 'I need you to sling some weight.'

We parked the Land Rover outside the garden gate. Then we climbed into the Garfinkels' big garden. She carried a small blowgun with a tiny flashlight strapped to the underside of the smooth bamboo barrel: an old hunting trick she used when she went after leopard at night.

She sprinkled a trail of salt from the rose bushes to the mulberry tree where she planted a fat bag of Cerebos. When Bara and Buti smelt the bait and crept towards it, she picked them off, one by one, with a brace of beautifully judged darts loaded with tranquilliser. The .04 calibre blowgun was a fine and silent weapon: the darts moved at anything up to 300 feet per second. They ran, of course, which made the drug all the more effective. We found them sleeping like babies.

'Little buggers!' said my ma, as we carried Bara and Buti to the Land Rover. 'They won't bloody stir till they're home again.'

At the airfield she sighed as we strapped them into the passenger seats.

'I do wish you'd have a word with that wife of yours, Alexander. This could have turned out very hairy.'

She taxied out and took off into the vast night sky. I watched until her lights vanished. The Voyager hit speeds of around 115 mph. She would be in Kenya by dawn, then into Stanleyville the next day. No problems.

That was the last I saw of her for a while. She stayed for several weeks in the Congo, hunting bongo.

I didn't have a word with my wife. I left people to think what they thought. Maxine believed she had freed the Wambuti from colonial oppression. Mrs Garfinkel grieved for Domitian, done to death by wandering natives. 'They probably make hats from the poor boy's fur,' she said with a shiver …

And so it was that I went away. It was a race for life. Maxine thought I had run off with someone. She was right: I went off with myself. No more mink, no mother, no more militants of any stripe. Both of them thought I was mad. Why abroad, when there was all of Africa still to see?

From then on out, I kept moving, and from then on out, my mother tracked me. It was a game, it was a hunting safari, it was a lifetime's career, seeing how far I could get before she found a way of pulling me back, trapping me, turning me round for home.

11   The Cuban Crisis

'Strange he is, my son, whom I have awaited like a lover.
Strange to me like a captive in a foreign country...'
'Monologue of a Mother', *D. H. Lawrence*

I had been upriver for several days on the *Mistress of Mandalay*, an old paddleboat turned steamer that plied the Irawaddy between Rangoon and Mandalay. Her owners were replacing the air-con system in her six cabins. We were heading for Bagan, once called Pagan.

Burma was special. Here was a land suspended between names: Burma/Myanmar; suspended between Buddhism and brutalism. A most unmilitary land, misruled by generals, where omnipotence resided in a bloke known as 'Secretary One', and his picture was everywhere.

In Burma you learnt to breathe the right way. In Burma you got arrested for talking, or for joking, or for no reason at all. And why not? When your existence depended entirely on the say-so, or otherwise, of the earnest bespectacled godlings whose mug-shots appeared, like men in wanted posters, on the front page of the *The New Light of Myanmar* (known to its readers as *The Nightmare of Myanmar*). The generals were shown 'vigorously' inspecting pig-slurry facilities and saluting each other frequently. Cruel, dull and preposterous; perfect specimens of the gargoyle effect of huge power upon pompous pricks.

The idea that language should be reasonable or clear or fair or gentle is a sustainable delusion only in places where the cops won't shoot you, or lock you up, for using certain words. There are signs of power madness only the victims know. Places where all words are forms of force, a means of getting your way. Where the right to talk is actually a kind of tyranny. The tongue in jackboots. Places where the boss owns the words, and you don't, and won't be getting permission to use them any time soon; and as a result people use fewer words and more signs: a sigh, a shrug, a twitch to an eyebrow has everyone telling you to keep your damn voice down. Free speech is as much a government decision as, say, free health care. In fact, in some places, and Burma was amongst the most interesting examples, keeping your voice down *was* about the only medical help on offer. Speaking out could seriously damage your health. And learning to breathe correctly – internal air-con – was the right breathing in sticky circumstances.

I loved Myanmar/Burma so much I'd almost forgotten where I came from – certainly I'd forgotten *whom* I came from. I didn't have to think about home, or her, or bloody South Africa with its poisonous insanities – I could look instead at an Asian madhouse, gentled by a Buddhist temperament, as sweet and slow-flowing as the lovely Irawaddy, with its clouds of white moths floating beside the boat, like prayers in the moonlight.

In Bagan we tied up against a muddy bank and I clambered up the steep stone steps and walked through old town, where medieval Buddhist stupas litter the baking plain like mushrooms after the monsoon. The painted figures of the guardian spirits of the town stood on either side of the ancient city gate; they were endearingly named Mrs Golden Fish and Mr Handsome. Besides the Buddha, who was supreme, and as a way complementing his perfection, imperturbable and subliminal, the Nats, more human and wilder guardians spirits of hearth and home, were also revered.

Once upon a time, in my country, people also worshipped beings called Nats, but our godlings were white, puritanical, sex-fearing bores who brought nothing to us but tears and bloodshed. This did not in any way dilute the worship of their followers who were once as numerous as the stupas upon the baking plain of Pagan, but recently they had all melted away as if they never were. A miracle!

I prayed to the Nats of Bagan: 'Mrs Golden Fish and Mr Handsome: keep me from drear dread spirits whose self-importance weighs on us all like lead. Torment the rulers of this land and infest their dreams with demons ...'

In New Bagan town I tagged along behind a long caravan of well-wishers, celebrating the approaching novitiate of two small boys, about to be enrolled as monks. The rich parents led a procession of dancers, archers, handmaidens, cannons, musicians and a pantomime elephant made of black velvet with very white tusks, and bringing up the rear, someone carrying a sign: 'Video now available! Manchester United v. Arsenal.'

At the Bagan Hotel, I was handed a fax. It had been following me for almost ten days, having gone first to my suppliers in New York, from where it had been sent on to Bagan and waited for me while I was on the Irawaddy. I sat outside my room, a cold Myanmar draught beer in hand. The fax was from Jake Schevitz and, brief though it was, it crackled with his sharp dry bark.

Alexsy boy, I had your old lady round here and she has in tow this little dark bloke – with a Latin look. She must have at least half a bloody century on Don Juan. She tells

me they want to get married. Alex lad, I'm worried. You're
going to have to do something …

Yours in the bowels of Christ,
Jake S.

I liked the 'bowels of Christ' bit.

Jacob 'Jake' Schevitz always was a mordant bugger. As a Jew at a Catholic school he learned to drive, he liked to say, on both sides of the road. He knew all our prayers by heart; he was – his word again – 'ambidextrous'. That had always been his edge. He took what was known and settled and assumed and threw it right back in your face.

Schevitz at about fourteen: ears sticking out of a sharp, foxy face, a mind like a flick-knife. Schevitz at thirty: one of the finest attack lawyers ever bred. Defended just about everyone who came up against the ranters running the country. A man with a cause. He'd reckoned the old regime to be about as close to Nazis as we were ever going to get, and he'd fought them tooth and nail. If you got banged up by the security cops, you turned to Schevitz; if your kid fell out of a ten-storey window while in police custody, you turned to Schevitz; if your friend died in the back of cop van and they said he hit his head while attacking an officer, and the tame police doctor confirmed it, you turned to Schevitz. Relentlessly affable, but utterly merciless in court, he ripped police evidence to shreds and reduced state witnesses to tears.

That was Schevitz in his glory, saving the weak from state hooligans. Schevitz, who raised cash for black lawyers, who got aid for detainees in solitary; who began the Legal Outreach Bureau, who himself spent a week in solitary for refusing to testify at Koosie's trial on explosives charges. Schevitz, whom the pundits and the prophets agreed was sure to be appointed, in some better fairer, never-again-to-care-about-skin-colour administration of a wholly new South Africa, a Supreme Court Judge or even – why not? – Minister of Justice ...

Ah, but that was then ...

There hung over Schevitz now a whiff of chagrin. More than a whiff: unhappiness seeped from him like damp. Schevitz had changed – 'evolved' was his word – from lead attack-dog in the days of the old regime to crusty critic of the new guys who governed our rainbow nation; and at the end of said many-hued illusion you were likely to find, Schevitz would growl, not a pot of gold but 'a bloody can of worms'.

Things weren't what they used to be, but Schevitz was, and it hurt. He simply couldn't come to terms with what had happened. And he wasn't alone. There were lots like him. Dismissed, disdained. And it knocked them sideways, though somewhere deep inside they all knew they shouldn't have felt quite so groggy because it wasn't the first damn time they'd been floored. They had been here before, flat on their backs, out for the count.

The fate of people like Schevitz, people like us, had been to live through two revolutions. The first happened back in 1948.

Schevitz once said to me: 'When the race-crazies won back in 1948, people, decent people – dare I say it, democrats – wrung their hands and said to them, "Gosh, chaps, this is a political reversal, isn't it?" And the new bosses said, "Fuck you, buddy. We don't do reversals; this is revolution." And we said, "For the moment. You're the government and we're the opposition ... that's democratic, isn't it? But it could change, next time round." And they said, "It's democratic, all right, that's why it won't change. There is no next time; we're here to stay. You guys think we're low-life Neanderthals who live in caves. Well, welcome to the new world. Caveman is king-pin, and you guys are seriously fucked."

'Having been seriously fucked once before,' said Schevitz, 'we should have seen it coming. But we never did. We sleep-walked into the punches, our eyes shut, our chins out. Last time round, it was race-crazies obsessed with the colour of your skin. Calvinists with chips on both shoulders; tribalists who said we were the luckiest little country on God's earth and they'd fuck up anyone who had the nerve to disagree for being left-leaning, whining, pinko-Yiddish, Commie defeatists.'

Quite so. The white regime that took over in mid-century had loathed Schevitz. Oh, what a ding-dong battle it had been! What terrific fun war can be when the bad are so proud to be so, and the angels are on your team.

Now we had new rulers, end-of-the-century revolutionaries. And they were truly good; they were so holy it ached; they weren't a political party, they were saints come down to earth to save the country. They were nationalists, true, but they were nice, caring, fair-minded, nationalists.

And yet – here was the rub – they also hated Schevitz, and for much the same reasons as the old lot. Worse, they despised him – what did he offer that they couldn't do without? A clapped-out, wishy-washy liberalism from another time and another culture. But they didn't fight him; they didn't see the point of fighting him; in fact, they didn't see the point of *him* – period.

So Schevitz was put out to grass. Retired. Kicked into touch. And everything he stood for, everything he did and loved and believed in, was suddenly old hat. He went overnight, poor

Schevvy, from radical firebrand, and hero of the struggle, to yesterday's leftovers: pale, male and past it. Worse still, in a country now more than ever obsessed with the colour of your fucking skin, he was white. Those thus colour-coded were no longer seen as living entities, but as walking footnotes or crumbling ruins. So: no more fights, no more glory; just sobriety, respect, oblivion. These were Schevitz's pickings after the years of fire.

And maybe this was what it had to get down to. Maybe Schevitz stood for those of us who, however much we may have amounted to in the past, were fatally maimed because whatever we appeared to be never really constituted our essence. Whatever camouflage we wore – and it was true some of us gave astonishingly realistic impressions of being accountants or doctors or lawyers – something was amiss.

It is right to say that we white guys are not simply proud of our ignorance, we're fiercely protective of it. Secondly, because we have been forced for so long to live at several removes from reality, encouraged at every turn to believe in our superior status, we have learnt to act out several lives at the same time, parallel lives. We have a genius, almost, for swapping individual existences for others, and taking them on more or less simultaneously, and with relief. Because it is precisely by entering into other roles, which serve as a mask for our own, that we can tell ourselves that we are not alone. Loneliness is the real horror of the people from which I come. And being other people, simultaneously, almost makes up for have no true life of our own.

What a crew: no Fausts us! We sold our souls for no great stakes. Fakes. We didn't even rise to the rank of real bastards. We just pretended to be real. Sometimes we got within millimetres of being what we said we were – bank managers, or soap salesmen or mining magnates – but we never really pulled it off. For a profoundly important reason: because the sole role assigned to white South Africans was to go around being white. Nothing else counted. Though we would have denied it angrily, we would have threatened violence had anyone persisted in saying so, yet we knew it was true: we knew it because we carried off being anything else so awkwardly. White, then, wasn't a colour, it was a destiny. A full-time occupation. It gave us status, wealth, power; it gave us cooks, gardeners, nannies … helots.

And you took it very, very seriously. That's what added *gravitas* to your dealings with the man who made your garden or the woman who cooked your food.

Yet you needed to differentiate yourself; to show you were not like the other lot – your Afrikaans compatriots who kicked people around and decided everything, from whom you might not marry, to what you could not read, to when you might hold a raffle or a jumble sale. You, *per contra*, were decent, tolerant, fair.

And indeed there was a difference but it wasn't one of morality, it was one of power. They had it; you did not. You were helplessly weak, no one cared what you said and no one asked your opinion. And so you dived ever deeper into disguise. It was necessary to keep up appearances, not only as a teacher, a doctor, a plumber; it was even more necessary to kid yourself that a niche of your own could be found, a saner world where people went to church on Sunday and called the minister Vicar, where the rule of law was taken for granted and judges handed down valid verdicts.

But we never really pulled it off; we inherited too much inhibition from our English forebears to act with the conviction that so distinguished those red-hot nationalists who ran our world. And who ran right over us.

Schevitz had been handed his redundancy papers not once but twice, and he now wanted to hit back. And he reacted to his decline with a show of force – he was, after all, South African. Ask him if he got depressed at what was happening all around him in 'the new-sarth-effrica', and he would round on you, fighting mad.

'What sort of question's that, hey? You fucking crazy? Listen, I am happy, I am *very* happy. I think this is the best bloody country in the world, all right? Show me the country that doesn't have problems. Sheez, man, just because a guy points to certain problems doesn't mean he's unhappy. It just means he's got questions. What's wrong with that? Hey, hey, hey?'

And on he would go, spitting fury. 'Fucking hell! I mean, what are you saying, hey? Of course I'm bloody happy!'

So happy he wanted to hit someone in the face.

I tore up the fax. I ordered another beer. I knew my mother had done a number on Schevitz: her plan was to reach out through him to me.

I could hear his question as he looked over her latest lover. 'Does Alex know about this?'

And I heard her immediate reply.

'Certainly not, and I'll rely on you not to breathe a word.'

I remembered how, in the seventies, we used to go and see George Adamson, in the Kora National Park in Northern Kenya. He had a fine campfire trick, did George. We'd be in the middle of nowhere and he'd pull a piece of venison off the flames, douse the lights and toss the meat into the bush, then he'd turn on a torch and there were seven pairs of eyes shining back at us.

'It's a race,' said George. 'It's us they want but the meat will do.'

My mother had stared into the dark, wondered where I was, and thrown a bit of Schevitz my way.

'You're going to have to do something ...' he had written.

But there was nothing to do. She was as impervious as a veld fire, as a column of army ants. This was not about sorting her out; it was about sorting me out. She was after me: the calls had been multiplying, she planned to round me up and bring me home. But she was too good a hunter to underrate her quarry. She had often talked of how her old friend, Eddie Blaine, paid for forgetting that. They were hunting up in the Masai Mara. Eddie hit a buffalo with three good shots and was sure he'd done enough damage; so when the buff turned and vanished into the bush, Eddie went in after it. When he didn't come back, my ma went looking for him and found Eddie, a mass of fraying flesh and torn clothes, with the furious buff stamping and pawing the body. She killed the buff with a shot through the brain. Then she took a good look and found that Eddie's first bullet had gone in at the shoulder but ever so slightly high, and he'd followed it with a second, marginally low. Good shooting but not near good enough. His third was a beauty: the heavy round from Eddie's .470 had gone into the head, kept moving and exited at the end of the ribcage.

'That buffalo', she said, 'was dead – but he didn't know it, and there is nothing more dangerous ...'

Always in her telling of the tale there was mourning and pain for poor Eddie. I always felt for the buff. But I couldn't to say that to her. She would have taken it as a blow against her own person, against her role as a mother, a role in which she was magnificently, unforgettably bad.

I had been abroad for over twenty years, with infrequent visits home, and on my travels I had grown used to my mother's cry that echoed down the phone line across vast stretches of the globe that, I was pleased to know, safely separated us.

'You're selling air – where?'

That is what I did: I sold air. I sold the compressors, the pipes, the coolants, the fans, the pumps and the systems for putting it where you wanted it, when you wanted it, at the temperature you wanted it. I could blow hot, and I could blow cool; myself, I preferred cool. Coming from where I do, it was second nature, selling air. I did not really see it as a job. It came easily to someone who grew up where I had, where more air was routinely spent on bluster, bluff, and bombast than any place I knew. All I did was to parlay a past into a future.

Ever since I'd left Africa in the eighties, after what I think of as the 'Maxine and the pygmies' episode, I'd kept moving. I think I was in search of home, of a sort. Anyway, I'd found places where the smell of hypocrisy was so strong, the absurdity of power so wonderfully brazen, that I knew immediately where I was. Across South East Asia; in Vietnam and Laos and Cambodia, I had encountered all the old fragrances, all the things I had detested when I lived with them in my own place, and newly found, how they filled me with fierce, cold delight.

It seemed to me that the world was, roughly, divided in two. There were the settled and colder northern regions, vast oceans of air, pretty much inert air; and there were islands of turbulence where the passage of air took precedence over everything, moving through the diaphragm, over the vocal chords, out into the open in the form of shouts, screams, orders, cheers, sighs, edicts, trumpetings. Places where there were a few favoured very big, very bad wolves who got to huff and puff and blow everyone down – and there were lots of little pigs whose job it was to get eaten.

Hate, as it were, always exhaled. It was the compressed air that drove the tribe. And it was a fact everywhere to be noted that people who behaved nobly under tyranny, once free of it, often behaved as badly as their old oppressors. Indeed, it might be said that in a tyranny the victims must concentrate every-thing on the struggle to stay alive, and so they neglect their desires to harm those weaker or stranger than themselves; and it is only when the tyrant is removed that their natural feelings bubble to the surface and one-time victims turn out to be as cruel and stupid as the oafs who once kicked them about.

In Burma I had reached that point of stasis that good travel induces: I had nearly forgotten where I came from, and I didn't care where I was heading. The great easy swell of the Irawaddy under the boat soothed and quietened my heart. I was no one, travelling through nowhere. I sold air, yes, but I sometimes felt, though I'd never say so, it was more than a job. It was a kind of calling.

I mean, think about it: David Livingstone wanted to bring, as he put it, commerce and Christianity to Africa, in order to alleviate the benighted lives of those he found there. So did I, in a way – my mission was put an air-conditioner in every home, to bring cool refreshment to sticky, overheated lives. I worked for two small American suppliers and we had a good relationship, based on two stipulations: I did not travel to America and I did not carry a cellphone. Fixed-line phone or e-mail was quite enough for reaching me.

One of my suppliers, a man called Hiram, once said to me: 'But if you had a cell, contact would be easier.'

And I had to explain: 'I don't want it easier.'

So then, on the news of this latest maternal caper, 'Keep moving,' I told myself. 'She's getting close.' I didn't give myself much of a chance, mind you. She was on my trail. I did what any sensible son would have done under the circumstances: I confirmed my flight for Malaysia. I had meetings in Merlaka, and I planned to be there.

Besides, I knew all about my mother's Cuban.

I had met him on my last visit home, a few months earlier. They were in the little parlour, just off the sitting room, overlooking the front garden, drinking tea and eating freshly baked date loaf; there was a bottle of rum on the tea tray.

It was a signal honour, to entertain him in the parlour, because no one but the Rain Queen was received there. It was a custom that went back to the early years of Queen Bama's unexpected visits. In those days, before the security walls went up, we had no front fence, and the Queen was able to keep an eye on her Holden Imperial, which would be parked outside the garden gate, with the royal chauffeur dozing behind the wheel.

He was in Queen Bama's chair, sipping rum.

My mother said: 'First things first, dear boy. I want to you to meet a very special friend of mine. This is Dr Mendoza.'

'Is pleased.' And Mendoza shook my hand.

'*Muy buen!*' My mother grinned. 'He's teaching me a bit of Spanish. He doesn't speak very much English – do you, Raoul?'

She must have had fifty years on the Cuban. In his fax, Schevitz had remarked on the discrepancy between their ages. Far more striking, when I saw them together for the first time, was the disparity in size. She loomed over him. She was so tall and solid. Mendoza was small, neat and debonair. But what struck me most was her evident delight in the man.

'Isn't he the sweetest thing?'

She smoothed his curls, and he caught her hand in his and kissed it.

'Where did you find him, Ma?'

'I got him from Papadop. He phoned a while back, and said he'd collected this Cuban, and he was in a bit of trouble and could he give him to me?'

Papadop was one of my oldest uncles. When I was a boy and my mother was still flying in and out of Africa, we used to go and stay with Papadopolous in his house in Mount Darwin, a small town north of what was then Salisbury, where he sold farm equipment from a shop under a huge jacaranda. He was a big dark man with a big square solid body, and in those days he drove a Hudson Hornet with a two tiny dachshunds dangling from the rear-view mirror. I called him Papadop and the name stuck.

He came to Africa from Athens, an orphan, a skinny, hungry boy, and like a lot of Greeks he ran a corner shop down the road in Parkview, and that's where my mother met him. But he tired of it. What was the point of being put into these straitjackets that South Africans were so crazy about? If you were Portuguese you sold vegetables, if you were Greek you ran the café on the street corner, if you were black you did hard labour and if you were a white South African you did bugger all.

'The bloody Dutchman only thinks about blacks and the English only think about games with balls. What a bunch of palookas!'

So he cleared out, went up north to Rhodesia, where folks didn't bamboozle themselves with who was, or was not, white. And he sold tractors and irrigating systems in Mount Darwin.

He became a Rhodesian; it was, he used to say, 'my middle

period'. In the life before that he had been Greek; he called this his 'primary period'. Later he became a Zimbabwean; he called it 'my final period'. He was proud of all his periods; he was proud of everything he had done in Africa. Papadop was a fierce patriot.

'Where do you keep this Cuban?' my mother wanted to know when he phoned.

'Kathleen, I'll tell you when I see you. You'll like him. He's a nice boy.'

Two days later he turned up at her place in Forest Town. Papadop arrived in his Datsun, with those skinny number-plates they go for in Zimbabwe, and he had this guy with him.

Papadop told her: 'He's called Raoul.'

My mother shook his hand. 'Will he have some tea?'

'Have you got any rum, Kathleen? They like rum, do Cubans – isn't it, my boykie?'

And the Cuban nodded, like a good dog.

Then they all sat in the little front parlour, drinking tea spiked with a slug of Blue Bay Jamaican rum, and Raoul wolfed down my mother's date loaf.

'Where did you find him?' my mother wanted to know.

'He found me.' Papadop patted the Cuban on his black curls. 'Didn't you, sonny? We are good mates.'

'How did you get him over the border?'

'I popped him in the boot and covered him with a blanket.'

'How'd he breathe, Papadop?'

'I drilled some holes.'

'Heavens above.'

'Not too many, mind. Bloody holes breed rust and my jalopy's on her last legs.'

'In the old days I could have flown him out.'

'In the old days, Kathleen, this would never have happened. Anyway, it was no sweat. The border is bloody chaos. At Beit Bridge crossing point you wait a coupla hours; they check your papers; you drive through, they don't really care. Not if you're in a car. Beit Bridge is also clogged with truckers. They wait maybe a few weeks. Then there are the guys on foot: traders, hawkers and guys on the hustle, looking to buy hard currency, or maybe smuggling drugs into SA, or they're carrying empty bags or paraffin tins or bottles, so they can fill up on the other side then go home and flog the stuff. Then there are the crooks, the *guma-guma*. These guys are seriously bad news: they'd stick a knife into you or shoot your head off, given a chance. They like to hijack motorists from down south. White patsies from the Republic are easy meat. Everyone knows most South Africans, they've never been in Africa before, they're not just wet behind the ears, they have litre bottles of the stuff swinging from their earlobes. The *guma-guma* puts on a peaked cap, pretends to be Customs, and sticks these SA tourists for whatever they got. The South Africans got cops and troops watching the *guma-guma* but no one can stop the traffic in paraffin or people or guns: they're the oil in the machine of corruption run from the top by Big Brother Bob, our beloved leader.'

My mother poured the Cuban another shot. 'Does he speak English?'

'Watch this,' Papadop lifted his teacup. 'Hey, Raoul – viva Cuba!'

'Viva Cuba.' Raoul lifted his cup.

'Viva Castro!' said Papadop.

'Viva Castro!' said Raoul, and then he added, 'Die – bastard!'

Papadop gave a shout of laughter. 'Isn't that great, Kathleen? He hates Castro. Who wouldn't? This boy arrives in Harare fresh out of Havana; first thing they do is they take away his passport, and they send him to Mount Darwin to be the doctor. But our hospital there, it's been closed for months; we have no medicines, no dressings and no light bulbs. Zilch! Raoul opens the hospital; he does what he can; he's a great doctor. Each month he's paid 300 dollars US by our great and good government. But he doesn't get to keep it. He has to take the dosh to Harare and hand it over to his embassy. Hard currency, you see. I got sorry for the guy. He'd come over to me of an evening, we'd have a drink, and I'd give him a steak and a beer. Then one day he says he's not going back. Ever. Isn't that right, Raoul?'

The Cuban nodded hard. 'I run away. I kill myself. I never go back.'

Papadop patted him on the shoulder. 'Don't you fuss, boy. I said to him, run you can't, boykie! Did you look at your shoes? You won't get far in bladdy plastic slippers. This is Africa. So I took him out to the river, where I got my fishing shack. I left him some condensed milk and corn-flakes and some oranges. He thought he was in heaven, poor little guy. Sure enough, next day the cops came by my house, looking for a Cuban. "What Cuban?" I say. Then the Cubans sent some goons from Harare to suss him out. They sniffed around town but Raoul was safe out by the river.'

I knew Papadop's fishing shack on the Musengezi River. There was more to the Musengezi than fishing. Papadop felt about the Musengezi the way Indians felt about the Ganges:

it was a holy river. He fished it, drank from it and swam in it. Though he like to remind people that it hadn't been so long ago that crocs made swimming impossible.

Papadop used to tell me the story of the first white man in Mount Darwin, a guy he called 'the Port' or that 'little Porto palooka, the priest blokie'.

This man had been a Portuguese Jesuit called Silveria, who had landed at Sofala in 1560, in what is now Mozambique.

'This guy was a go-getter. Inside no time he'd met King Monomatapa who liked the little Port and wanted to give him gold and cattle and female slaves. But Silveria said, "Thanks but no thanks, not for me." He didn't want gold or stuff like that: he was preaching the word of God. Anyway, Silveria wandered on towards what is now Zimbabwe, and he came to what is now Mount Darwin, and he met the chief of the place, who was an OK guy, except he worshipped crocodiles and sold people to the Arab slavers. Silveria tells the chief that he's way out of line in the God department: the croc is an ugly beast with lots of teeth and is not suitable for worship. But Jesus, on the other hand, is a God you can rely on. And the chief sees the light and says: "OK. No more crocs for me. Me and the wives and the tribe will shun the crocs and pray to Jesus." So it is all looking wonderful for Silveria.

'But you know how it is in Africa – always close the windows, or something flies in. Well, something flew in all right. There were these Arabs, right? The ones who sold slaves. They'd sold slaves for ever. If you stopped an Arab in Africa in those days and asked, "What d'you do?", chances are he'd have said, "I flog slaves; how many d'you want?" It was business. Anyway, all of a sudden the slavers see this Porto priest is screwing up business, telling every chief he meets, "No more slaves." Well, you can imagine what they felt about that. So they go to the chief and they tell him, "Listen, chiefie baby, this Porto priest, he's bad news, he's bad *muti*; he's a witch, a wizard. The holy crocodiles are very, very angry because you've dropped them for the Jesus god. But the crocs are prepared to do a deal: come back to your senses and they'll reward you." Anyway, the chief buys it. And when Silveria thinks everything is fine the chief gives a sign and his guys strangle the poor Port. Then they throw his body into the Musengezi to say sorry to the sacred crocodiles.

'Isn't it one of the saddest things in Africa: the bullshit local people swallow from smart-arse invaders? Yours truly included? Anyway, I kept the Cuban down in my shack on the river until the cops and the Cubans got really heavy. And then I had to get him out.'

'What will we do with him?' my mother said.

'I was hoping you'd tell me. I can't keep him. Things are not what they were up my way ... you know, hey?'

When Papadop first went to Mount Darwin, in the fifties, it was a lively town. There were English farmers, there were Greek families who ran the garage and the general store, there were banks, hotels, shops and a community hall. My mother was still flying safaris north of Salisbury. Sometimes we used to stay with Papadopolous on his little farm with lots of new tractors dotted about under huge trees.

Then came Rhodesia's declaration of independence, and the bush war of the sixties and seventies. Farmers and guerrillas fought and killed each other. The community hall became the soldiers' billet where the women's association served hot soup.

After the war, Papadop stayed on. He didn't like the war, and he didn't like the bone-headed men who ran the Smith rebellion. He became a citizen of the new Zimbabwe, even joined the ruling party. He spoke perfect Shona, he was elected comrade mayor of Mount Darwin, and he took tea with Robert Mugabe – twice.

'Perfectly gentle, pleasant bloke. He didn't seem like a blasted commie at all, more like a country gentleman. He wanted to talk about cricket. Balls, balls, and more balls. I said to him: "I do not know, I do not care a bugger, about balls. But I see a lot of changes in Mount Darwin, Mr Prime Minister – and I think now is the time to consolidate."'

But the changes kept coming. The Greeks went next, then the bank, the garage, and the hospital closed. The white farmers who had once considered Mount Darwin part of Europe, and saw blacks as servants or savages, packed up and left. They were replaced by black farmers, who saw whites as a form of vermin. Papadop ran for mayor again and lost. The community centre closed, the country club became a brothel, but the ex-comrade mayor remained in his house under the jacaranda.

'I am the last white man in Mount Darwin,' Papadop liked saying, with a mixture of pride and sorrow. 'Or I was, last time I looked. Then this Cuban came along. I want to help, but I can't keep him, Kathleen.'

'So you want me to keep him?'

'The way I see it, there's a million refugees from Zim hanging out in Jo'burg. What's another one – among friends? Maybe he could ask for political asylum? What's sure is he's out, and he'd better stay out. If anyone catches him it's tickets for Raoul. They'd pack him off back to Havana, or feed him to the crocs.'

So she kept him. The Cuban with the curls wasn't someone she took as family; he was exotic. He needed special care. She found him Spanish videos and CDs; she brought home canned chilli con carne from the supermarket because she reckoned he'd like it. He didn't go out because people might be looking for him. He stayed in the house all day, watching soap operas, and my mother took care of him in her hunter's way. I'd seen it with Nzong, and with Bara and Buti. She took in not waifs or strays, she took in quarry: those she would also have been quite capable of shooting in other contexts. But even I could see there was something special about Raoul. Maybe it was just that he was the first non-African to have touched her.

Soon enough he was an obsession.

'If only I were younger I'd have driven out to Grand Central, fired up the Piper and headed for Maputo.'

But she knew in her heart that, even if she hadn't hung up her flying helmet, it was a hopeless dream. Mozambique, in the days when she'd been flying in refugees, had been a haven where they fought the regimes of white southern Africa, and dreamt of freedom.

'Now they really are free they don't want rebels.'

She also toyed with the idea of Lesotho – another bolt-hole for guys on the run, in the good-bad years – only to reject it.

'Most Sotho hate us now, ever since we invaded them and they burnt down all our banks. Poor Raoul would be picked up in two ticks.'

I told her plainly: 'You can't keep him, Ma.'

'I'll come up with a plan, you wait and see.'

She had driven her old Land Rover to the tall skyscraper in Commissioner Street. First trip up in the lift she didn't get out; she rode the lift all the way down again to give herself time to check the bit of paper on which she had written Koosie's African names.

He wasn't just renamed, he was relaunched was our Koosie. After the long years in exile, after the decades of struggle, he'd come home in 1993, and a year later he'd been elected a member of parliament in the democratic government. Next, he was 're-deployed' in the Black Empowerment sector, and sent to head up an outfit monitoring what was called 'transformation in the media', which meant making sure more black editors, copywriters and TV presenters made it into the mainstream.

The air was hushed when she stepped out of the lift on the twentieth floor. The large brass letters above the entrance to the executive suite read: 'The Media Marketing Council'. Through the glass walls of the reception area all of central Johannesburg showed clear: skyscrapers, mine-dumps, and in the distance the skinny Television Tower, like the strangulated hat of some minor deity.

She adjusted her tall blue turban and told the coiffed and beautiful receptionist with firm, clear confidence:

'I've come to see the Director, Mr Sithembile Nkosi.'

'*Dr* Nkosi,' the receptionist said.

'That put me in my place. This kid looked at me, in my turban and smock, as if I were something the cat had dragged in. Some mad old bird in a funny hat. And then, when she showed me into his office, I quite forgot what I was supposed to call him.' My mother gave her delightful bashful giggle, in which was contained girlish embarrassment and guilty delight. 'I said, "Hello Koosie" – and the girl looked around the room, trying to work out who the heck I was talking to.'

Koosie's new name kept pace with the new developments but, then, so too had his old name. In the old days being a black boy called Koosie was quite a smart move, a token of esteem for the Boer ruling class. In fact, Koosie's new name wasn't all that new. His name had always been Nkosi but it got Dutchified, to Koosie. In the new era it was a loser. You could not have a veteran of the fight for freedom wearing a tag that identified him an Afrikaans farm boy. So out went 'Koosie' and in came Dr Sithembile Nkosi, Director of the Media Marketing Council.

In many ways that was fair enough; all of us had been many people, impersonators from birth. All of us had led several lives. So what was one more mask? Koosie had already been a whole lot of things: orphan, domestic servant, gardener, prisoner, poet, refugee, freedom fighter, black radical and then, after the new dispensation, a man of importance.

So when Koosie and his friends came to be the Power, they went straight on pretending, the poor bastards, that the past had been mad but the future was sane and they were the future and soon – ah, very soon – true things would happen.

Koosie hadn't turned a hair when she fluffed his name; he

took her hand and drew her into the room, closed the door, sat her down, and offered her tea from a big silver teapot on a big silver tray.

And so the scene was set, a scene to be remembered or denied, cut or kept. I could see them, in the big office, with the tea tray. The big tall old woman in the blue turban; the elegant, thin ('too damn thin!') black man, our friend who-was-not-Koosie. It played out the way it always did in Africa, when white met black. It took on this quality of show and shimmer. We were shadows always dreaming of growing into real people, aching to put on flesh, to mean what we said, to feel we belonged, that we had true weight in this place, when we knew we never have had. For all you might say about the long, long misunderstanding between white and black in Africa is that neither side ever seemed to find the other.

'He was still our Koosie – but different.'

I knew what she meant. I used to see him when I was back in town and I never got used to the change either. Once he had been full of dangerous flash, lighting up the dead afternoons when he and I went to watch the weddings go by. Now that he'd become Dr Nkosi, he was slower and even a bit ponderous, and filled with what I can only call a spirit of reflective melancholy, as if he couldn't quite figure out exactly how he came to be where he was, a respected exec in a fine dark blue suit, and a red tie and a brand-new BMW. He was the very opposite of Schevitz who was sad because he never got to where he wanted to be. Koosie struck me as sad because he had arrived.

'I knew it wasn't going to be easy, but I thought of poor Raoul and I had to try,' said my mother.

•

Koosie poured tea, offered biscuits and then he asked her how he could help.

'I have this Cuban,' she said.

Koosie put down his cup. 'What sort of Cuban?'

'Well, I suppose he's just an ordinary Cuban, a common-or-garden Cuban.'

'Where does he come from, your Cuban?'

'Havana, I believe.'

'But after that?'

'From Zim. He was a doctor there.'

Koosie poured her another cup. He stirred his tea, round and round, saying nothing, till my mother lost patience.

'What difference does it make where he comes from?'

Koosie put his cup down and counted off the points on his fingers.

'One, he's here illegally: he jumped the border; he has no papers. Two, he skipped Zim while on assignment for the Cuban government. Three, he is living in your house while he's on the run.'

My mother said: 'Just a tick. Am I listening to the Koosie I know? Who used to live in my back yard? Am I sitting opposite a man who fought to be free? Who got locked up by the police? Who went into exile? Yes, my Cuban is on the run. He needs help. Like we helped each other. '

'Yes, Kathleen, we helped each other. And I'll never forget.' Koosie came round his big desk, and put his hand on her shoulder. 'But we were in the struggle then.'

'So is he.'

'We were fighting an illegal regime.'

'What do you think Raoul is doing? He's got out of Zimbabwe. One of the worst hell-holes in Africa.'

Koosie winced. 'What do you think I can do?'

'Talk to your friends in the Home Affairs Office, Koosie. Get me papers for the man.'

Koosie shook his head. 'What are you saying, Kathleen? Home Affairs has got illegal immigrants coming out of its ears. If I tell Home Affairs about your Cuban they'll have cops round at your place in two shakes of a duck's tail. They'll have you up in court for harbouring an illegal immigrant, a political defector.'

My mother put down her cup, she wiped her lips, she got up from her chair and she walked to the door.

'What would you have said if I'd quoted the law to you when the cops were on your tail?'

'I told you, that was an illegal regime.'

'So is Bob Mugabe's.'

Koosie sighed. 'That's a matter of opinion. And, anyway, it's not just Mugabe. Between you and me, I don't care a damn about Mugabe. But we've got our Cubans, too. Doctors working in the countryside. The Cubans, they loan us these medics on condition we return them – every last one of them. But these crazy guys sometimes bugger off, they fraternise, they fall in love with some local girl, and then she says I want to marry my Cuban. Next, they ask to stay here. And we can't have that.'

'Won't have it, you mean.'

'Yes. Because if we did, they'd all be doing it! We have to take a firm line.'

'What sort of firm line do you take with your Cubans?'

'If they run away, we send them home.'

'I don't believe this. Guys in fear of their lives come to you and you send them home! Why the hell do you do that?'

'Because it's the only way. Say yes to one, and who knows how many more will be queuing up?'

Koosie said he was sorry, and so did she. She called him Dr Nkosi, very pointedly, but the point was pretty damn hard to make because he *was* Dr Nkosi, or at least he was giving a pretty fine impression of being so. They were on different sides of the fence. It made her sad.

I had been noticing for some time my mother's sadness. It was new, like the walls she put up around the house, and the security gates, and the closed-circuit camera. What this sadness consisted of it was difficult to say. It was like a perfume and it changed according to the emotions, the internal temperature, of the wearer. We might be forced to choose from a very limited range of brands but we wore our particular scent of melancholy in our own way; that was why no two sad people ever smelt the same.

My mother's sadness was expressed very originally. She put it this way on one of my visits: 'There is no news any more.'

I don't know if she drew this impression from the TV or the papers. It was hardly likely to have been either. She had never taken much interest in news before the great changes. Each time I went back to Jo'burg, and that was several times each year, she'd mention the lack of news.

I asked her: what news did she mean?

She answered: 'Hah! You have no idea! If you had an inkling of what's happening …'

She'd be sitting in her blue Dralon chair, knitting on her lap. Behind her on the wall was the picture of her old friend, the Rain Queen, who still dropped by from time to time. The two women had a taste for catastrophe, yet they got on because their demons were different. Each succeeded in calming, or at least dampening down, the other's nightmares.

The Rain Queen was in trouble and it took bewildering forms. It called itself scientific and it did not like her traditional ways. It came in the form of cocky young men in baseball caps who disliked the certificate and its links to the old regime. The young men whispered words like 'a sell-out' and 'old-fashioned'. They said whatever a rain dance might once have stood for, it was not in the spirit of the new Africa.

Queen Bama had seen them off.

'I chased them away with my whip, I beat them with my knobkerrie. Fools! Africa is *desert*. Africa is *drought*! In Africa you please the gods. Do not throw out the rainmaker with the washing-up water. We must respect. Respect, Kathleen! Even the Boers knew respect. They pray for rain.'

She was in a fight for her life and it made her touchy. The modern young men were insolent; they were calling the shots now; enough of royal privilege, of floods and queens, of the rain dance. Clean, free water for all. That is what they wanted, in every house, in every village, in every life, in every pail. And they asked a question that drove her wild. What was she *for*?

Again she had reached for her stick.

'Young dogs!' she said, 'I made them run!'

My mother, so fearless in the bush, began to react to the wildness of the streets, and the kill rate. Once, she'd have ignored it. Serene and impervious. But in her eighties, she seemed to falter. It was then that she built the security wall around the house, topped it with electrified wire, and had a closed-circuit camera watching the garden gate. Now the first she knew of a royal visit was when the gate buzzer sounded and Queen Bama's liquid eyes stared at her from the TV monitor.

She and Bama had known each other so long, understood each other so well, that they sat there, drank their tea and sighed. For a long time I did not know what it was that was getting to them; then, later I began to understand. They felt sidelined: when they looked in the mirror their redundancy looked back.

Perhaps that is what happens when there has been a revolution; perhaps the markers, the patterns of everyday life, are rudely changed and everything that has fed your waking dreams dries up. Perhaps that is what my mother meant when she said there was no news any more.

Life was a very bad, very violent B-movie.

For want of news, the two friends upped their diet of catastrophe. That, at least, was a familiar staple. A story they came back to again and again was the one about the men locked in the fridge. It had happened months before: a meat truck had been hijacked. No surprise there; hijackings were not news. But this had a twist because there were six men on the truck: loaders, porters, humpers of the frozen carcasses. The hijackers drove the truck to Alexandra Township, ordered the men to offload the meat, then locked them in the huge fridge and made off.

The captives made desperate attempts to prise open the door with meat hooks. They left the gouging of their nails in the ice that caked the walls for all to see when the truck doors were opened by the police. Six men, three black and three white, froze slowly to death in the locked truck.

The symmetry horrified the two women; but something about it satisfied them, too. Since the racial mix was so perfectly weighted, the pain could be shared equally. In a time of trouble, when the world as they knew it had suddenly stopped existing, then anything, however dark, that confirmed the worst at least confirmed something. My mother saw in the murders signs of what happened when you destroyed established order. The Rain Queen saw it as an omen of what happened when jumped-up young men in baseball caps took over the country, and spat on the ancient beliefs.

My mother added drama to the tragedy by imagining what had happened, as if her feeling for the suffering men somehow made things better for her: 'Just think, Alexander, scratching your nails on the walls till your fingers bleed.' My mother emphasised her pain by feeling her way into the pain of others. 'Poor, poor men. Can't you just see it?'

Plainly, she thought I could not see it. I had disqualified myself from feeling what tragedies racked the country by living abroad.

My mother looked at her hands. 'What is happening to us, Bama?'

'Please, you tell me, Kathleen.'

My mother reached for the teapot. 'Search me, Bama. Search me.'

Then there was the dancing. Of an evening, behind windows she blacked out, in what had once been the servant's room behind the garage, Raoul taught her to mambo. Her movements were good but she was no longer quick on her feet. 'I do the stately version,' she said.

Raoul told her she did just great. '*Hecho muy bien, Kataleen!*' He would clap and snap his fingers and call out when she got going: '*Mambo, qué rico el mambo!*'

She loved it.

'Raoul says mambo is an African word meaning a conversation with the gods. It's a fusion of African rhythm and European style. Isn't that something?'

'You can't keep him, Ma.'

'I'll come up with a plan, you wait and see.'

The day I was due to fly back to Asia, she told me she had taken a volunteer's job at a home for disabled children, a place called the Sunbeam Shelter. I think she hoped it would provide cover if she were seen to be going off to work every day, while Raoul hunkered down in the old servant's room in the back yard, where she joined him after sunset, and they put on their music and mambo'd together.

'He says I move wonderfully.'

'I'm pleased, Ma. Really pleased. But what will you do with him?'

'Don't quite know – yet. But he makes me feel good. It's like old times. Before I was grounded. When I lived high on the wing.'

She laughed her old throaty rumble in the girlish way she had when she was 'tickled', the way she always sounded when she was younger and less sad, before she was unable to sail away as she chose, to any place that took her fancy. Grounded by age, by the wars that had shut off whole regions of Africa where she had flown all her life, without permission or passports, dropping the little float-plane down on any decent stretch of water. Forty or fifty years before, when Africa was wide open, and when her presence at any place of her choosing, anywhere on the continent, was something she regarded as entirely natural. When people travelled in Portuguese East and West Africa, in Nyasaland and Uganda, to Zanzibar and the Congo, South West Africa and the Spanish Sahara as easily as winking. Before South Africa severed links with its neighbours, then with reality, and retreated into an underground bunker of its own making; and before 'her' Africa went to war with itself.

I made her promise to stay in the room behind the garage when Raoul gave her mambo lessons.

'You think I'll be raided? Surely not! This is the new South Africa: the cops don't raid you any more. Don't you worry about us! I'll work out something. Something … elegant.'

'I don't want you to frighten the neighbours.'

That tickled her. She had always frightened the neighbours.

I was in Merlaka, staying at the New Renaissance Hotel.

Each day I started with coffee in the ornate lobby, sitting in a large leather armchair with the *New Straits Times*. The sound system would be pumping out Haydn or early rock 'n' roll. Everything came with muzak in Malaysia. I found an 'advertorial' for chicken soup, in pill form, known as Brand's Essence of Chicken, developed, it was claimed, in the kitchens of Buckingham Palace to cheer and comfort George IV. Property developers in KL were selling the rising rich luxury homes whose marble lounges contained recessed areas called 'conversation pits'; several employment agencies were offering a 'reliable maid', with a free replacement 'if she runs away'.

Malaysia was authoritarian, deeply and unprettily nationalistic. Malaysia had done what aspiring modern despotisms do: it had ensured that democracy was good for you by using it to cement the Great Leader in place, and keep him there. Running the show was a bunch of men who thought with their blood, zealots who did as they liked, while everyone else did as they were told. An empire of agitated air, noisy with menacing talk about 'the nation', 'the chosen', 'the sons of the soil': a jet stream of pomposities so super-heated you could hang-glide across the country on the thermals.

Malaysia wanted cooling off, and that was good for business. But it was odd, when I thought about it. Places like Malaysia were said, just a few years before, to be on the downside of history, to be in need of help if they were to manage to become decent liberal places in the little time left before history, already pronounced to be at an end in the West, closed down everywhere. History was hot no longer: it was very cool. Tolerance and democracy were coming to a tyranny near you; despots would retire their secret police, close up their jail cells, and pension off their hangmen. Countries once deemed 'backward' would be moving forward. Victims everywhere would flock to the polls and vote for freedom. And it would not take long because history was in a hurry to see to it that places like Malaysia sweetened up and dropped the tribalism of the favoured few.

But all that was long ago, before September 11, 2001, when those planes flew into the Towers in far-away New York. And now, instead of tight little tyrannies looking odd and old-fashioned – soon, poor dears, to catch up with the sweet enlightened, tolerant world – suddenly, tribal hatred and racial warfare looked like pretty sensible projects. Suddenly Malaysia wasn't left behind at all: not a damn, it was postively futuristic. Because in this craven new world, we were all tribalists, and that talk about tolerance turned out to be so much sentimental crap. Might was not just right, it was sensible, it was reasonable. It was progressive. Internecine wasn't nice but it was necessary when the other guys were worse. Stripped of sustaining pieties, we were our old murderous selves again. When plane came to tower, sweet talk dissolved in blood, and there was no one who wasn't happy to be twice as homicidal as the guys next door.

That's how it had always been in Merlaka. A port city, dubious, dreamy, shimmering in the hazy heat of the grey-green Malaccan Straits, where pirates waited, and on some of the islands separatist Islamists kidnapped foreigners. It used to be called Malacca, it used to be Dutch, then British, and it was always semi-Chinese, with some ex-Tamils thrown in for good measure. Now it was run by one more prevailing tribe, which, like all the others, called itself the chosen one. History hung over Merlaka like a troubled dream. Merlaka had been so many things it wasn't sure what it was supposed to be any longer.

It's odd that deeply and cruelly colonised cities, capitals built to the glory of the guys who kicked your head in, once they get their freedom, hardly ever achieve greatness. They become, instead, interesting and rather charming exercises in somewhat doubtful nostalgia, living on their memories, with occasional spurts of 'development', made in a frantic attempt to be modern. But it is done without any great sense of conviction, as if people know that what once made them important, powerful and worth fighting and dying for had gone away and wasn't coming back.

Each day I was happy getting lost; walking beside the muddy Merlaka River, or crossing into Jonker Street, where the antique dealers worked, and wandering among the old colonial shop fronts and the fine houses where the rich Chinese merchants once lived. I spent time in the shop of Mr Wah Aik. He made red silk brocade shoes for Chinese women who'd had their feet bound as children. The shoes were about three inches long. The pain, said the shoemaker, was great, at least until the bones were broken. He showed me pictures of the feet after binding, compressed to points: they looked like delicate pigs' trotters. Women did it, he told me, because men liked it, and one came out of Wah Aik's shop thinking of love, pain and tiny feet, erotic, irresistible in China for thousands of years.

I passed a doorway where there leaned an enormous billowy coffin the colour of toffee, ornamented with buttery swags of brass. The Chin Chin Longevity Shop made not coffins but kites, and the old kite maker was sitting cross-legged on the floor, splitting reeds. There were box kites and bird kites swinging in the rafters overhead; a young woman was rocking a baby in a hammock in the corner; over the road a few pallid tourists piled out of coaches marked 'Batik Tours', blinking in the immense early sun.

I made Merlaka my own with all the spurious sincerity of a traveller who really calls no place home, and so was in the habit of burrowing beneath the surface of a town and pulling it over him like a blanket, of thinking idly, happily: I could settle here – a sentiment entirely true though strongest, I noticed, just as I was about to leave.

The magic was working: I had almost forgotten where I was from. I'd stop for a beer or buy the occasional trinket, a teapot in the shape of a small boy riding a water buffalo, painted in deep bamboo greens and tans. I found a fat chuckling money Buddha sculpted, unusually, from pink resin. He leant back on his bursting sacks of golden sovereigns, his perfect paunch shining from the touch of a thousand hopeful fingers that, over the decades, had rubbed it for luck.

I had spent an afternoon walking around the old colonial town centre, a few streets painted a rusty red, woeful and uneasy amid the bustle of modern Merlaka, rather as if this slice of the past had been quarantined off. Here I found the old British Club, prim and straitened, like an elderly maiden aunt marooned in some Eastern bazaar. Christchurch Cathedral, built by the Dutch and, like so much of Merlaka, taken over by the British, was no longer a place of worship but simply a boxy building devoted to a foreign cult no one in Merlaka knew much about.

In the old Dutch Town Hall, the Stadthuys, I stopped before a portrait in oils. I looked up at it and I knew him instantly, the way you know someone whose face is on the paper money in your country. I stood looking at this burgher with his chestnut beard and his lace collar and his air of imperturbable gravity – the rock-like self-importance of these rulers was truly sublime – and I found it hard to not to break into wild laughter. There he hung: Jan van Riebeeck. He had been, in the seventeenth century, the first governor of the Cape of Good Hope and the guy Schevitz and I had decided long ago was at the root of all the rot.

You simply could not get away from the bastards.

The Cape hadn't been much of a posting at the time. A flat-topped mountain and a bay, in the back end of nowhere. Van Riebeeck planted a vegetable patch, built a fort, shot lots of natives and got the hell out. He moved 'East', said our history books. Well, now I knew where. He had gone on to become governor of Malacca from 1662 to 1665. Malacca had what the Dutch craved: it had riches, it had gold, it had the East at its feet and you could smell the spices on the breeze.

I reckoned Malacca got off pretty lightly. All that remained of van Riebeeck, in his Eastern manifestation, was this daub of paint in a dim room. We were still recovering from the damage he did in South Africa. That was the thing with national heroes: whether they were on the banknotes or the wanted posters turned out to be a matter of timing.

The room was darkening and losing the last of the afternoon light. Even the shadows seemed heavy. Dark beams overhead, dark wooden window-frames, black and white tiles on the floor, solid wooden chests ranged against the walls. I knew lugubrious rooms like this; hell, I might have been in Cape Town.

Cape Town! God, how the heart sank.

'A dowdy little madam of a town with a bloody hill slap bang in the middle,' said my mother once.

I looked at van Riebeeck and he looked at me, and I got the message. We were playing Sudden Death, that was clear. I had been put on notice; things were closing in. There is something alarming in finding that you have moved as far as the tip of Asia, only to end up facing the man whose dull but rapacious yearnings charged generations of pebble-hearted creeps with saving Africa for Western Christian civilisation. And why was it that this man, who had such crushing weight in Africa, here in this dim room seemed nothing more than a passing accident of history, just another pale, fatuous functionary on the make?

I think it had to do with power. The Portuguese, the Chinese, the Dutch, the British in Malaysia were powerful, yes, but somehow never insistent, and so the poison of their presence was less toxic than it was in Africa; from the peaks of their pride they looked down on the people of Asia but never did they assume they did not exist. In Africa they saw nothing human; they stripped it of its people, polished them off, not just with guns and germs but also by truly and honestly doubting they ever were truly alive, and so they became nothing. And once this mental genocide was done, they could populate the empty space with figments of their fancy; and shoot, collect, whip, steal and destroy what they wished. As a result,

Africa was still depopulated, vacant even today of easy, natural, ordinary people – and filled with fevered ghosts clamouring to be born again as human beings.

Africa …

For my mother it was a word she used without the least trace of embarrassment – as if she owned it, lived and was one with it. And I knew I should really feel as easily and as naturally about her. After all, wasn't that what love was? Instead, the feeling I had towards her was too hot, unbalanced and so fever-ish, like a bout of malaria. I felt that the word 'love' should be approached with considerable caution, in particular when coupled with Africa – keep an eye on the gun-belt all the while – because it often meant a kind of murder.

And as for being the son of my mother, well, that was an accident; maternal was not her mode. She was more like some mad aunt best kept locked in the attic, until she broke out, got drunk, took off her clothes, ran riot. She was what I loved – and also all I most wished to get away from. Whenever I thought of her, I was appalled. I think I had felt that way all my life. And I knew now, with van Riebeeck peering at me in the gloom, that the more distance I put between us, the better.

But I knew, too, it was never far enough. The further away I got, soon enough, sure as shooting, I'd find her waiting round the next corner. I'd arrive, anonymous, in some hot and torrid frontier town where no one had ever heard of me and the next thing I knew, over the hill with a warrant for my arrest and extradition, galloped the pursuing posse of my past.

But I wasn't handing myself over yet. There was an early morning express train to Kuala Lumpur and I would be on it.

All the way from Merlaka I shared a compartment with a cop and a prisoner in handcuffs, who was reading a book. Both were small brown quiet men. The policeman was called Bashir, his prisoner was named Affendi, and they seemed the best of friends. Affendi was handcuffed and Bashir had to pour him a glass of water, help with the sweet chilli prawn cakes we all shared, and take him down the corridor when he needed a pee.

'The poor chap is of unsound mind, and he's awaiting trial. He's been awaiting it for a few years now: ten in all. He's almost what we'd call a forgotten prisoner. I can see you're shocked but, on the other hand, if he weren't awaiting trial, he'd be in the condemned cell, waiting to be hanged. He stabbed a tourist in the Cameron Highlands some time ago. Do you know the Camerons, sir?'

I knew the Camerons. It was there that the mist came down like a veil and played games with the mock-Tudor fronts of the fake English hotels; where the Kosy Korner Teashop sold blowpipes, along with bacon and egg breakfasts, and in the pretty cottage gardens the jungle began where the well-kept English lawn ended. It was there my friend, Jimmy Li Fu had his hotel, The Gloucester, which offered the 'Best of British

Cuisine': Beef Wellington and Spotted Dick and Bubble and Squeak; boarding-school fare transformed by Jimmy's hands into the strange and alien cuisine of inscrutable, far-away Albion.

Bashir was taking Affendi to KL, 'so this high-end mind doc can check his mental health. And, then if found to be sane, he will certainly be hanged, as soon as possible.'

He repeated this often as if it might make up for the years the prisoner had been forgotten.

Affendi was deep into a North London novel, the sort you see a lot of on the London Underground, by writers with names like that sound like suburbs – Pawnsley or Gormlee – tales of girl trouble on the Archway Road, or high jinks in Kentish Town. Affendi was reading *All My Loving* and its cover showed Buddy Holly, owlish specs shining like twin moons rising over a grainy view of Hornsey High Street.

Not perhaps the sort of thing you expect to see in the manacled hands of a prisoner between jails and, quite possibly, on his way to the gallows. Then again, such joshing tales were, like the mock-Tudor English lodges in the jungles of the Camerons, strangely exotic, if not downright sultry, in the right place. They spoke of a world that was expensively dull, and safely grey, where no one ever starved or died of heatstroke or dengue fever, where horror never happened – and if it did, someone would demand an urgent enquiry – where the shadow of the hangman never fell.

Bashir and I played dominoes. Affendi read swiftly, eagerly, lost in romantic Hornsey, the chink of his handcuffs as he turned the pages the only sound. And the train ran on towards KL, and life or death. Outside our windows, in dusty village lanes, half-naked kids, their thin legs thudding in the dust, chased shrieking chickens, an old sport in Malaysian villages; and the hot chilli of the prawn cakes pulsed in my throat.

It was good to be moving, good to be free at times like this. The happy ache that came of knowing you were alive in a foreign place, and richly lost. Where none of your rules apply, where nothing you know is of any use.

The old Central Rail Station in the middle of KL was built by the British in the ornate, overheated style of their great cathedrals to steel and steam. It was a Moorish vision, designed by an architect who dreamt he was in Granada. The old station was all minarets and spires decked out as something from the Arabian Nights. No Disney designer could have matched it for sheer nuttiness and bloody arrogance. It took the great cartoonists of colonial times to pull it off. Birmingham dreaming it was the Alhambra. St Pancras in the middle of Asia.

The area around the station was electric with the static left behind by the great imperial star, long since exploded; it crackled with currents of an improbable past. The ghosts of the old imperialists didn't just walk around the old railway station, they held fucking demonstrations.

And it reminded me of my mother, that station, though she would have hated the comparison. She was, also, in many ways, built by the British: she was tall, she was alarmingly exotic and, when placed in the African landscape, she was a gigantic temple to strange gods. It was uncanny.

At a stall under the great roof, Affendi, Bashir and I lunched on samosas and coffee. Affendi ate, lifting both manacled hands to his mouth, but he made a bit of a mess and Bashir wiped the flakes of pastry off his upper lip, tenderly, as a mother might. We all hugged each other goodbye. I don't know why we felt so bound, so close.

Jimmy Li Fu was waiting for me. He'd parked his new Toyota next door to the cricket pitch.

'Welcome, welcome, Alex. We'll to go your hotel first and then get some good coffee at the First Cup.'

'What's new in KL, Jimmy?'

Jimmy smiled, his narrow brown face with its pointed nose reminding me, again, of a very elegant wasp. Despite the smile he looked slightly put out. 'Nothing – I am happy to say – nothing at all.'

I first saw Jimmy Li Fu in the teahouse of the Victoria and Albert Butterfly Farm, up in the Cameron Highlands. It was a light and spacious place because caging butterflies was a delicate thing. He was at the back of the teahouse, sitting at a long trestle table, with a very slim silent young Chinese woman, his mobile on his ear, drinking Coke. He caught my eye because the front of the room was packed with a party of Americans touring the tea plantations, and they looked heavy. It wasn't the tourists' fault but they were in the wrong place. By comparison with their solidity Jimmy was private, austere. As thin as a finger, and very brown, and we'd been – friends is too odd a word – useful allies ever since. Jimmy sometimes gave me the impression he subsisted on nothing but air and excitement.

I knew more about him now. I knew now that day at the Butterfly Farm he had been on the phone to his bookie in Singapore. I knew the woman with him was one of his 'workers'. I knew Jimmy to be of that indeterminate category best described in Asia, in neutral tones, as 'a businessman ...'

If you looked at him in some sort of boring way, Jimmy was dodgy – a gambler, a brothel-keeper, a hotelier, a chef. As a boy he'd been a member of a particularly vicious Chinese triad. He had the triad emblem of red dragons tattooed on his right arm. But to bring the deadly pragmatism of the settled world to bear on Jimmy was an exercise as cruel and as stupid as chasing after the pretty, fluttering confections that looped around the plastic cages of the Victoria and Albert with a meat cleaver – and as little likely to catch the essence of the man.

Jimmy was a lost soul. He came from what I'd call the marginalities, small ethnic slivers who lived far from whatever race or country or nation or tribe or group or gene pool gave them identity, and for whom even 'lived' was a tricky word; say rather they had found a way of uneasily co-existing among much larger groups of racial purists who barely tolerated them (good); did not tolerate them (bearable); or threw them out (tricky).

Jimmy drove me to the Federal Hotel where I dumped my bag, and then we dropped in at the First Cup, a coffee shop in the B&B Plaza, slap bang in the middle of The Golden Triangle, but far enough way from the Petronas Towers to be civilised. The rich young kids of KL shopped a lot, and the B&B Plaza was a hot spot for shoppers who watched the world go by from the terrace of the First Cup.

We hadn't been there five minutes when the riots started.

Jimmy Li Fu said: 'Students. They're demonstrating against ISA, the Internal Security Act, which gets people locked up very easily, and keeps them locked up. These people don't like the government, they don't like the Prime Minister; they don't like anything.'

There were cops everywhere. They sealed off the café and the shops and the street, and began chasing the students towards big red trucks, mounted with water cannon. The metal shutters were down at Kwang's, the Authorised Money Changer. The girls at the Heavenly Massage Parlour had stopped working. The blinds were drawn in the windows of Dr Gigi and the Fong and Goh Dental Surgery. The only people out in the open were tourists in big shorts and waist-wallets.

The cops manning the water cannon tested their range by firing at the First Cup which had a deflective shield formed by the curved roof of the taxi rank across the way, which is very useful when the cops are aiming powerful jets of water at you.

Behind us, in the Plaza, the shopkeepers had visions of their customers suddenly turning into looters, so they dropped the steel grilles over the exits and if any shoppers were still inside it was too bad. Minutes earlier the rich kids had been guests at Sweet Polly's Department Store; now they were prisoners. They stuck their hands through the bars, waving and making a muffled lowing sound, like milk calves torn from the udder. Those who'd made it out of the shopping centre before the grilles came down grabbed the remaining tables, put down their Gucci bags, ordered coffee and watched the riot.

Native to each culture are the means used by the police for assaulting the citizenry. Riots have their own geography and physics, and the number of ways you may be attacked are varied and compelling. Where I came from we were chased by men with leather whips, sjamboks, made, if you were a stickler for tradition, from rhino hide, but cowhide would do. Sometimes the cops fired birdshot. This was painful but not usually fatal, and it was better than rubber bullets, or plastic rounds, or tear gas – we called it tear smoke.

The cops of KL wore black and carried long canes and when they lashed out they reminded me of the Irish Christian Brothers who schooled me. Lifting and bringing down a stick on someone's back or legs is a violent gesture: it distorts the body, starting with a flexing of the calf on the pivot of the ankle, like a golfer, a rising shoulder and a forward darting downward movement as the bamboo comes down on the flesh of the victim. You can read in the twisting body of the attacker an expression of happiness. Hitting another person – striking the target repeatedly with a fist, a foot, a stick until it runs away or falls down – has a naturalness about it that suggests it must have been one of the earliest hominid's pleasures.

The rioters, young and quick, dodged the cops by running into doorways. The cops didn't get the chance to do this often, and they were not going to be cheated. They looked around and spotted the tourists. There were lots of them. In the season of Asian slump and uncertainty, travel agents had been selling Malaysia hard. It was hot, cheap, safe, familiar enough to appeal to British and Australian travellers of a certain age: Malaysia had Worcester Sauce and Guinness, and to call the police you dialled 999.

Well, someone had dialled 999 but when the cops arrived they weren't nice English bobbies at all, they didn't smile and call you ma'am. They were nippy and vicious and wore shiny body armour that made them look like menacing beetles. The tourists were easy game. Even as they were beaten, even as they flinched when the truncheons slapped home, I could feel their outrage, their sense of shame. This was happening to them! The knowledge outstripped their pain. They'd got up that morning and had the buffet breakfast; and they expected the day to unfold as the schedule said it would. That was their

right as sober, solid citizens from some of the most privileged
societies the world had ever known, swathed, mothballed,
counselled by state officials, whose only duty was to see they
were safe, happy, pensioned, healthy. Now, without warning,
they were overweight, clumsy, pale-skinned targets, ridiculous
in Bermudas and money-belts, being chased by sprightly
dervishes with sticks and hoses who wanted to hurt them ...

In the thick of it all, Jimmy's mobile began cheeping. He listened for a moment and then said: 'It's for you.'

I stared at him. 'Who knows where I am?'

'They know where I am – the whole of KL knows you're
with Jimmy Li. Take the phone, Alexander.'

My mother's voice echoed down the line, much as it had
echoed down the years of my life. The phone, in her hands, was
an instrument perfectly adapted to expressing sharp emotion
but giving nothing away, wearing all those verbal colours that
made up her characteristic acoustic camouflage: disdain.

'What is all that noise? Where on earth are you?'

'I'm in Malaysia, Ma.'

'May-laseeeya!'

What consternation she put into the word. If I'd said I was
spending the weekend in Sodom and Gomorrah she could not
have sounded more offended.

'I phoned the number you gave me, and I got some hotel and
they said to call this number. Are you busy right now? What's
going on there?'

'How are you, Ma?'

'I'm fine – but I was fired from the Shelter.'

'Why were you fired?'

'I hugged the kids.'

'They fired you for hugging kids?'

'I couldn't help it, Alexander. I simply had to put my arms around them; I loved them. And they liked it. But the powers that be were not best pleased and they said hugging kids was not policy. They couldn't keep me. So my friend Cindy said, "Well, Kathleen, if that's the way they feel, I am going with you." And she did! Resigned on the spot, without so much as a kiss my foot. Imagine that, dear boy. And Cindy has a lot more at stake than I have, what with her own child in the Shelter.'

'Ma, what have you done with Raoul?'

'Hidden him.'

'Hidden him where?'

'Where they'll never think of looking. Tell you when I see you.'

'Ma, Jake Schevitz faxed me. He says you went to see him.'

I could hear her snort.

'Fat lot of good it did me. What a total *woes* that man has turned out to be. I had a lovely plan, but all I got from Jake was one damn reason after another why it couldn't be done. Imagine if I'd gone to him in the old days with Nelson Mandela and wanted to hide him; would Jake have told me it couldn't be done? What on earth is that noise, Alexander?'

I didn't want to tell her. I said to myself she wouldn't wish to know. If she'd phoned halfway across the globe only to find I had gone and got myself caught up in a riot, she'd have been furious. She'd have said: 'Well, really; if you must do that sort of thing, we have perfectly good riots of our own, right here in Africa. You don't have to go all the way to Malaysia.'

A boy with blood in his hair was walking in circles. A plump tourist knocked over by water cannon was sitting in the road, wiping her face with her skirt.

'So what now, Ma?'

She sighed. 'He's gone, he's safe, but I miss him. He was fun. By the way, I have to have some tests; doctor says it's important.'

Suddenly I was listening hard, as she had intended.

'What sort of tests, Ma?'

She lowered her voice. 'I've been bleeding … I won't mention from where – not on the public phone. Anyway, I called the doctor when I discovered the you-know-what. I had a bath, I did my hair and I climbed into my old Landy and drove off to see him. Doctor says I have to go to hospital, so I am.'

'When, Ma?'

'Right now. When I put the phone down. I'm checking into Fourways Clinic, a private hospital out on the William Nicol Highway in the far northern suburbs. You wouldn't know it, darling, it was after your time. Father Phil from my parish is visiting priest there. Isn't that lucky? I don't think you know Father Phil, he was also after your time.'

The cops were driving the tourists towards the water cannon. An elderly man in short grey socks and sandals was trying to cover his head with his camera case, and the cops beat him about the buttocks. I saw three women running with their handbags flapping, then the water hit them between the breasts and knocked them down.

'I'll come home, Ma.'

'You'll do nothing of the kind! I wouldn't dream of it. I'll be out of hospital and right as rain in no time. Where did you say you were?'

When I told her again, she said: 'Well, I never! Goodbye, darling, I must go now.'

My mother hated using the telephone to say anything important, and she only phoned to communicate rage or alarm.

For her to have tracked me down was her way of being as alarming as possible. It was a rare thing, a long-distance call, it would have cost her dearly, and it meant that this trip to the hospital was a serious business. Finding me in Malaysia would have further lowered her opinion of the shocking, indeed the scandalous unreliability of the telephone: it cost a fortune and took you to very strange places where you had no wish to be.

Jimmy snapped shut his phone and dropped it with his smooth elegance into his top pocket.

'You should get one of these. People could reach you.'

'I don't want to be reached.'

'Bad news?'

'My mother: she's not well; she's on her way into hospital. I'll have to go home.'

We watched a small policeman kicking a large student who had fallen over and was trying to cover his face, but the policeman tore his hands away, wanting particularly to kick him in the mouth.

Jimmy said: 'I am shocked, Alexander. This does not happen in KL.'

What shocked him was not the boot slamming – with a sound not unlike a dry cough – into the broken mouth of the man on the ground but the riot itself. The water cannon bowled over a small clutch of tourists who fell down, like this was some fairground sport and they were having fun, and they skidded along on their haunches, screaming.

Jimmy was tutting to himself: 'Dearie me. Best to keep out of the water. It's got something chemical in it. Sticks to the skin like mad. Get a touch of that water and you're itching for days.'

·

That night we dined at the Coliseum, a reassuring shabby restaurant in old KL, a place British rubber planters once made their own and on which they had left their distinctive brand of overdone, steak-and-kidney exoticism. Jimmy presided at the bar, on the stool they reserved for him, calling for more gins. The bar was dark and warm and rich and filled with the sort of dust I think of as past particles of those who once used and loved it.

It gave him a boost to lean up against the bar and buy me gin and tonics and pretend for a while that since I spoke English he could lord it over an itinerant Brit because long ago the British had put him down for being 'a blooming chink'. Jimmy's thin face grew stony when he thought back to those times.

If it comforted him, I didn't mind. But the British were no longer the enemy and hadn't been for decades. Their influence lingered in Malaysia, where it lingered on at all, as a slightly gamy, strangely perverse, overheated kind of jungle Anglicanism. It was the Bumiputra, the regular certified pure Malays, the sons of the soil, who were the masters now and they had long ago drawn Jimmy's sting, had cut off his balls and told him, 'If you want to fill you purse, fine. But keep your mouth shut and never forget you're nobody.'

Jimmy did more than he was told, he 'loved' the Prime Minister. God help him, this sardonic, clever man had done the deal that turned his brains to soup; he had sat up and begged and in exchange he was permitted to hover around the place like the harmless house ghost, who did deals, who might loom large in the Chinese community; and he might be rich but what good was gold to ghosts? It bought influence, race-horses, whores and security. But it did not buy belonging. He was not of the tribe, he did not belong to the sons of the soil, he had influence but no power, he had cash and no substance.

'May the Prime Minister live a hundred years,' Jimmy Li Fu lifted his gin.

'Why, Jimmy, why?'

'What do you think will happen to Chinese like me, if the government falls?'

'Chinese, like me': the cry of all small communities that existed, like the Straits Chinese from which Jimmy came, on sufferance, by permission, at the pleasure of bigger, not very friendly hosts.

A perfect phrase for expressing the rights of a parasite. If you imagined the tribe as a wasps' nest, then Jimmy was a certified drone. He was allowed just one thing: to be rich, to use his influence in his narrow world but never to have the slightest say in the way his world was controlled. As long as he obeyed the rule, he might hoard as much treasure as his sharp little proboscis could carry without bursting. But if he ever so much as dreamt of stepping out of character, they would inflict on him a punishment so cruel he shivered to think of it: *they would send him home*. Home was another country where he was even more of a foreigner than he was in Malaysia. Jimmy was Straits Chinese by extraction and that meant he was generations removed from his motherland across the water.

A line of visitors stopped at our table – Chinese guys who owed him favours, then a Malay cop and his girlfriend. They paid their respects, received Jimmy's crooked yellow smile of benediction. They did not linger; they visited him the way people visit a lucky shrine, paid compliments and stored up, they hoped, good luck. Of Jimmy's slightly sinister authority there was no doubt, and I imagine he used it and enjoyed it in just about the same way he did the power that came from belonging to the triad he ran with as a boy: in much the way he saluted the Prime Minister. Politically he bought protection from whoever ran the place to keep his rackets safe. Just as we had always done.

When I was a child in the Transvaal, I visited a uranium works and was given a tiny little pellet of yellow mud they said was uranium: I kept it in a blue matchbox like a pet mouse, and took it out and looked at it from time to time. I liked the purity of the yellow, and when I think back now I wonder if it really was uranium, and thus radioactive, and dangerous. That's what Jimmy Li Fu reminded me of, and when I stopped off to see him in KL I never spent long; I didn't really want to expose myself to whatever rays he was giving off.

'So, Alex, when will you go?'

'Tomorrow, if I can get on a plane.'

'Where will you go to?'

'Johannesburg, that's home.'

'Jo-han-nes-burg? Good to know you're from somewhere.'

It was an old joke between us. He was Malaysian, I was African, but only in a manner of speaking. These alibis could be stripped away any time, and Jimmy would be turned back into a blooming Chink just like I could have my African name stripped away and turned into just another interloper from bloody Europe.

'We're from nowhere, we two,' Jimmy liked to say. 'And it will be held against us. Chinese like us.'

Now he looked at me and said slowly, carefully, like he was trying it out:

'Nel-son Man-de-la ...'

He meant well, I know it. But it didn't really touch the sides. A country that otherwise you know nothing about can sometimes be known exhaustively through one individual. One size fits all. You said the word and you were off the hook. It was like saying 'Mother Teresa' – and bingo! You're done with Calcutta. I didn't find this disconcerting. On the contrary, I liked it because it relieved me of the fatuous burden of guilt and knowledge and the even more ridiculous South African notion, once prevalent, that everyone knew all about the place: in the past, because the people there were so nasty; and nowadays because they're so nice.

Jimmy said again: 'Nel-son Man-dela.'

He did it to show that he knew and cared about where I was from. In fact, like many in South East Asia, he knew very little about South Africa, and cared not at all. African countries, all African countries, were populated by wild creatures, and South Africa's saving grace was to have strong brand recognition in this superman who had emerged by magic from the chaos and become a lucky charm, a mantra, the intoning of whose name brought calm and order and dignity to a dark place.

It was a kind gesture, offered in the hope I might like the sound of it. It made us the sort of friends that only people like us could get to be. What we were, when you got right down to it, was closer than family. We were tribe, Jimmy and me; we were joined at the fucking hip, and what connected 'Chinese like us' was this: we knew that home wasn't ever any place left behind; it was always some place you were on the way to, always somewhere ahead.

My Lufthansa jet entered African airspace above Morocco, then passed over Cairo and began following the Nile south over Egypt, and on to the Sudan. The 747 traced almost exactly the route that the old Empire Flying Boats, in the thirties, flew from London, across Europe, and down Africa to Durban. The great Sunderlands of Imperial Airways could fly only by day, and they kept low, like fat ducks, sitting steady at fifteen hundred feet, looking down on Africa, while Africa looked up. Lovely fun for the gorgeous few, souls gifted with the rarest of freedoms: the right to go where they pleased. Those who flew to Africa to farm or fish or run countries six times the size of England left Dover and flew over France and Switzerland and Italy, but it was when they cleared the European mainland and sailed over Africa that reality fell behind.

When Joe Healey wished to take his little daughter along for the ride, who was to object? The gold mines were rich beyond speaking. A burly Irishman in a blue suit and a panama hat, his dynamite sticks in an attaché case which 'he arranged under our seat', said my mother.

'The detonators he kept in a gunnysack. Many was the time we played blackjack using the attaché case for the table when we took the boat.'

'His job as Chief Explosives Officer took him to Northern Rhodesia, or Angola, or the Congo, and once to Egypt. I remember we put down in Wadi Halfa. You could go to places in the thirties and forties and fifties that have been off limits now for half a century.

'From Egypt the Boat flew on across the Mediterranean, towards Crete, touched Europe over Italy, the Swiss Alps, France, the Channel and then, at last, England.

'But we flew into Africa, always. Never beyond. It was ... heavenly. The craft were plump, they floated in air; they were truly water creatures. Whales with wings! The captain was a qualified seaman! They also were proper boats. Ocean liners aloft. You could play a game of deck quoits – in flight! – while all of Africa unscrolled at your feet. They catered, dear boy, to those with expensive tastes.'

She recalled very exactly her old excitements: the man with a turban who rang the bell for departure in Wadi Halfa; the tartan curtains in the observation lounge; the mellow Cunard voices of the stewards; the dark green leather seats; the Blue Grass perfume, 'available in dollops, quite free in the ladies' restroom. I just helped myself ...'

An Empire Flying Boat did not follow the spine of Africa. Instead, it veered east so it might begin, like a great skimming stone, to lake-hop its way down the length of the east coast. From Cairo the flight path led to Khartoum, and the plane put down at Gordon's Knee. And then on to steamy Malakal, and along the Upper Nile to Jubba in the Sudan and, if time allowed, a short detour over the Murchison Falls before touch-down at Port Bell, the big craft ploughing two hissing furrows on the dark waters of Lake Victoria and the night stop in Kampala. Next day to Mombasa, then Dar Es Salaam, and the night stop in Beira, a tawny, steamy sea-front, a taste of Portugal, prawns peri-peri and Chianti, speciality of the Imperial Airways guest-house.

The boats flew low enough for the passengers to count crocodiles on the banks of the Zambezi, low enough to spot tickbirds between a buffalo's horns. Pressing their noses to the shop window of Africa, letting their eyes fall wherever they chose. And why not? It was all theirs and it was all free.

And then the big craft dropping her nose and swooping down to hit the water, the airframe shouting and shuddering in the hissing foam as they taxied to a stop in the huge, hot, ticking silence. The obedient launch nosing out from the landing stage. On the Zambezi they sent a launch to chase away the hippos. Then the kind boatman with the strong arms helped her down, and she chugged across the water to the lodge for the night. It might be Lake Nyasa, or Livingstone in Northern Rhodesia, where the Victoria Falls raised in the sky its great fists of spray. Or the Kisumu Hotel on Lake Victoria, for a hot bath and dinner: starched napkins so stiff she cracked them open like slices of cardboard, waiters in white tunics and bright red sashes, silver service, candlelight, and Africa muttering outside the windows, a nearby lion as loud as an air-raid siren, while she tucked into roast beef and Yorkshire pudding.

Next morning, up at the crack of dawn, bound for Lourenço Marques, then into South African airspace, flying down the dark green sweltering coast of Northern Natal to Durban, over the Bluff, banking above the big hotels on South Beach for touchdown on the Indian Ocean, taxiing noisily into the Imperial Airways moorings at Congella.

'Can you feel the freedom?'

These flights across Africa were celestial board games played by people called Rodney and Felicity and Millicent and Roy, who put away the board at night, folded it up and forgot it, because terrific fun though it was to play the game, floating like gods above an exotic zoo, it wasn't real. Or rather it only became worth something when you touched down, and reality only began and ended while you were there, making the place exist by your presence.

Of course it was the nature of settlers to be cut off and to grow into mutant beings. But it seemed the destiny of these arrivistes to be the oddest mixture, assembled according to no known recipe, to be a kind of pale hallucinogenic mould or fungus that grows in the dark and thrives for unclear reasons in unlikely spots, and then vanishes.

My friend Koosie once said that the smell of defeat hung over us. And I asked who he meant – the whites, the English? – he opened his big brown eyes really wide, he stroked his tiny pointy beard, he snapped the brim of his fedora, he flicked a speck of dust off the wide blue lapel of his fancy pinstripe suit, and he said: 'Check me out. Take a deep breath, be ready for deep shock. Do I look white? Do I sound English? Listen, baby, I said "us". I meant the whole horrible crew. The most stuck, the most narrow, the most cut-off provincial palookas on the planet. You, me and everyone else is who I mean. Every man, woman and child. South Africans. That's *us*. Excuse me while I spit. Seen nothing, been nowhere, and, heee! so proud of it!'

It was the best compliment I ever got from Koosie. The nice bit was the '*us*'.

.

I had a German beside me, a big, very pink man, reading Rilke and drinking brandy and Coke. He told me he was from Namibia; his name was Dieter and he owned a big ranch near Luderitz, which the government was talking of confiscating.

'They say I'm an absentee landlord. Maybe they'll take it away. Maybe they're bluffing. Namibia is not easy farming country. *Ja*, I own a lot of land but you need more and more land for a farm that is to make money. That's the bottom line. If they want, they can give my land to poor blacks. But they will stay poor. And it's thieving. What's the good of that?'

I could see the good of that: when foreigners, aliens, incomers have robbed you blind for centuries, you want some of your own back. It's not nice but when has getting your own back ever been nice?

Dieter said: 'Do you know much about Namibia?'

I said: 'Nothing about Namibia; but I knew German South West Africa pretty well once...'

He looked faintly embarrassed. 'German South West? I haven't heard it called that for a long, long time.'

I said: 'Where do you live, Dieter?'

'I live in Hamburg.'

'Where were you born?'

'Windhoek.'

'So what does that make you?'

He was surprised. 'I'm Namibian.' He took out his passport. 'Look.'

There was something depressing about having to show your passport to prove who you were.

I said: 'I don't think you can be a Namibian.'

He took this as fighting talk. 'Why can't I?'

'Because you're not African; only Africans can be Namibians.'

He said: 'We've got a good constitution. It says anyone can be Namibian.'

I said: 'Honorary Namibian, just maybe. That's about the best you can be. Party's over, so are we.'

He was hurt, so he made the speech that began: 'But I belong here ...' and went on – and on.

Large white men telling you with tears in their eyes how much they love Africa; it's a cloying, it's crap, and, worse still, they mean it. There is also usually anger buried in this claim, maybe because these lovers know that the beloved doesn't give a toss, never thinks of them, and may well loathe the sight and smell of them.

'On the other hand,' Dieter went on, 'you can't blame them for hating us. We Germans in Namibia, we don't have such a good record. They're touchy. Very touchy. I don't blame them, not at all; we have been very, very bad. In the old South West Africa, it was a killing ground. Look at what we did to the Hereros in 1904. Our troops, under General Lothar von Trotha, they shot tens of thousands of them. There, in the Waterberg. Well then, what can we expect? We killed; they died. Now they're the boss and we must pay.'

It was true. But that didn't make it, any of it, less awful, or Dieter's mewling any less sickening. He didn't need to explain who 'we' and 'they' were. Of the horrible passage of whites through Africa there was no doubt. It did not matter whether they were British or Belgians or French or Germans, the pattern was the same: contempt followed by mass murder. We had moved from the era when foreign Europeans shot locals at will to the time when white Africans spend their time apologising. Homicide to homilies, rope to repentance.

But it came too late. Worse, it came from the wrong people. Those who did the damage never felt the lash of hatred from their newly liberated serfs, never indeed ever came close to imagining that they were not wonderfully bright, kindly, superior beings appointed to rule over savage children, to correct them where possible, and shoot them when necessary. Never failing to affirm, as they caressed their whips or oiled their guns, how much they adored Africa … while Africa went on hating them, and since that hatred needed a target, we were it. What whites were left would carry the can. Like the Anglo-Irish, we had gone into other lands and stayed, settled, almost believed we were at home; and like them we were wrong: wrong people, wrong time, wrong place.

Among the pictures in my mother's knitting basket was one of her old dad. After the Boer War, and long before he had become Chief Explosives Officer for Corner House Investments, my grandfather, at a loss to know what to do next, joined the British South Africa Police. They were a kind of African Mounties. He is seen in pith helmet and puttees, carrying a Lee–Enfield, posing on the battlement of a great stone pile called Namutomi, a mock-medieval castle, with stone turrets and towers, erected in the bush by Germans with baronial delusions, dreaming of Bavaria and mad King Ludwig. The South Africans captured the castle in 1915 in the invasion of German South-West, and my grandpa is on his horse, wearing a long dust coat, and a bandolier and his high-domed solar helmet that makes him look like a smiling shuttlecock. He was there because of talk of insurrection amongst the defeated farmers whom he had fought beside all through the

Anglo-Boer war. But of course (and herein you may read the entire mad saga of the white man's walkabout in tropical Africa) under that funny hat there was a considerable killer who learned his trade in the first modern war that set the tone of conflict in our time – when peasant farmers took on the greatest army on earth.

And a story.

I believe – you could not have had a mother like mine without believing it – that nothing became the Boers as much as the way they fought to right that wrong. And nothing, before or after that event, ever breathed so much as a hint that they might be capable of such heroism. Until they chose to take on the British Empire, they had been the usual hooligans, oozing the usual bloody stupidity.

'Give us jobs, not work' was their cry. 'Proper jobs, jobs that let us do nothing but sit here feeling superior.'

But they did it: they went to war and they damn near pulled it off. Only the slow deaths of their wives and children in British concentration camps made them see at last that their enemy was prepared to wipe out the entire tribe if that was what it took, and decreed a painful surrender. And so there arrived the next 'new' South Africa. This time round, it was led by Jan Smuts, and the 'new' Boer leaders who would march us into a fairer future, at the point of a gun if it came to that. Which it did. The 'bitter-ender' Boers who had never accepted the new South Africa saw their chance when the Great War began, and dreamt of revolting. Last time around they had lost by a whisker. Now they would drive the hated enemy from the beloved country. And everything would be the same once more, only better!

The bitter-ender Boers had a prophet, Niklaas van Rensburg, and he took a peek into the future, and foresaw the end of the British Empire in the looming clash with Germany.

'Fight the damned khakis, kill them, and freedom is ours,' the Prophet told the rebels. 'The hated imperialists will crumble to dust and the glorious destiny of the Boers will flower once more.'

The Germans agreed with the Prophet but they took a higher tone. They told the Boer rebels that the *zeitgeist* was with them; history was working through them to destroy the oppressor.

This was their plan, so hopeless it makes me weep: while the accursed English were busy fighting the Germans, the Boer rebels would rise up and seize back their lost republics and the freedoms stolen from them. The Transvaal and the Free State would be theirs once more.

Was there ever a people with such a gift for thumping, self-destroying bullshit? It sounded terrific, until you thought it through for about a split second. The glorious destiny of the Boers, in the main, consisted of sitting on their backsides, on their distant farms, drinking coffee, bestirring themselves once in a blue moon, just enough to kick their black serfs. But now they rose in rebellion, and South West Africa became the cockpit of war. The British destroyed their free republics, robbed them of gold and diamonds. Now they would strike back. For a while raw joy surged: they had guns in their hands once more.

And everything conspired to ensure they fucked up.

This time round these farmers weren't facing the British: they were riding into war against fighters from the same tribe, they were fighting brothers, born-again modern Boers, who ran the government, the army and the country. They were fighting the 'new' South Africa.

Such was the insanity of our people that among these ruined sharecroppers, these bedraggled fighters, there were those loopy enough to believe that they could fight and win the Boer War a dozen years after it had been lost.

Although the men who ran the 'new' South Africa were not British, they were now firmly on the side of the Empire, tolerance, democracy and liberal values. They might once have been great Boer leaders but now they were determined to be statesmen; and they were not in the least sentimental about rebels. My grandfather's old comrades-in-arms, Jan Smuts and Louis Botha, were not going to dally with a bunch of bearded backwoodsmen who didn't realise that times had changed. Like all hot converts to a faith they once loathed, these New Men were more merciless than the old enemy when challenged by traitors. A rebel was a rebel, and a rebellion must be put down.

And so it was that Joe Healey went to fight the very men for whose cause he'd once blown up culverts in the veld. He may have dynamited every railway bridge in the Free State for the Boer cause, but he had no illusions about these dour, disapproving, sly, cruel, left-behind stepchildren of the trek.

Ah, South Africa … what sublime idiocy …

My mother also kept in her knitting basket, amongst the needles and balls of wool, a photo of her father with the prophet van Rensburg. The Prophet's beard is long and white; he has a blind stare and a sallow, seamed face. My grandfather is dapper; his moustache is spruce. Both men hold out stubby lengths of wood in front of their chests, each with a crosspiece, like the hilt of a sword. The two men are playing a Boer sport called *kennetjie*, using a length of broomstick as the bat, on which is balanced a small piece of wood that serves as the 'ball'. What you do in *kennetjie* is to loft the chip of wood into the air and see how far you can hammer it with your club.

That's more or less what happened to the renegade Boers of South West. This was South Africa, history did not reveal itself without a police escort, and the sort of *geist* that inhabited our *zeit* you wouldn't want to meet in a dark alley. Lives counted as little as scraps of wood, and what history did with the rebels was to toss them into the air, heft its truncheon and knock them clean out of the yard.

In the early 1950s we flew to South West Africa every week. I must have been about seven or eight, and we stayed with Uncle Hansie. Uncle Hansie built a *Schloss* in the desert, a mini-version of Namutomi, and he was the representative for Porsche in Windhoek. Though only in his thirties, Hansie was greying prematurely but elegantly. He had a silver beard, silver hair, silver suit, silver car. Uncle Hansie would accompany himself at the piano while he sang 'Die Schöne Müllerin', and my mother would be very taken, and slap him hard on the back when he finished, so that his monocle dropped from his eye like a fat, surprised tear.

Uncle Hansie was for me the closest thing to Europe I had come across, his dark oak dressers stuffed with books, gilt lettering on their blue spines – Goethe, Schiller and Thomas Mann. Uncle Hansie was the only man I knew who proudly kept, on the walls of his bedroom, a row of perhaps a dozen pictures of young women wearing no clothes at all, and seemed quite unashamed of it, and who was married to a Herero princess.

Another uncle; another airfield; another thread in the family tapestry; another ludicrous episode in the lives of the whites who went to Africa and, monumentally, got it wrong.

Did I know Namibia? Did I ever.

What do you say to those who have never been much further than Hamburg or Windhoek?

They were drawing down the blinds and putting on the movie. This was the old route of the flying boats, more or less, but we were about six miles high, in a cabin pressurised and slumberous, and outside the portholes the frozen dark rushed at us, like the future. And Dieter, the Namibian, slept, his book cradled in his lap.

The movie screens in the cabin flickered with the smiles and cries of a pretty actress pretending to be a poor unmarried *chocolatière*, with a pretty child to support; pretty girl falls in love with a pretty young man pretending to be a gypsy, on a pretty film set pretending to be France. It all had not just the gloss of artificiality – that would have been merely tiresome – but the brazen gleam of Hollywood happiness, the desirable lie that everyone will, sooner or later, simply have to believe. And it beamed this one-eyed fascism into the brains of the slumbering hundreds, belted to their seats, eyes and mouths open, like dead mackerel in the blue half-light of the flying tube.

Outside my window there was nothing to see but the dark. We did not need to see where we were going. What did it matter? We knew where we were heading; it said so on our tickets – Johannesburg – and we shot towards it like a bullet.

Flying into Jo'burg, the swimming pools hit you first: thousands of blue eyes winking eerily out of the dun, dry veld. Then a sheaf of skyscrapers ringed by mine-dumps, yellow hills of pulverised rock that once held the gold Jo'burg hugged to its stony heart. At the outer edges of the sprawl were tell-tale smudges, so well hidden below the smoke of a thousand cooking fires that only a forensic racist – of the kind we were all raised to be – could identify them as the foot and finger and heart prints of those who built and worked this town: row upon row of tiny brick boxes that were the townships, squatter camps and shanty towns where most Johannesburgers were hidden.

We banked over Soweto, home to the heroes who fought for freedom but from where – Koosie told me – anyone who could run was leaving as fast as their pay cheques allowed, heading for the green and shaded ghettos of the northern suburbs whose names echoed the identity crises of those who told themselves how truly African they were: Killarney and Sandton, Rosebank and Morningside, Houghton, Blairgowrie and Rivonia … Once upon a time, the swanking mansions in these wooded enclaves had been exclusively home to those who called themselves 'Eur-pee-ons' or 'Wharts' …

Beside me, Dieter yawned, stretched, closed his Rilke and said, 'Af-ri-ca!' Then he went off to the bathroom, and came back wearing khaki shorts and bush jacket.

What was it about landing on the continent that addled the brain?

Af-ri-ca!

Those must be the emptiest three syllables ever coined. A menacing prayer that passed for patriotism from Cape to Cairo, the sort that said: if you love the place, reach out and hit someone.

The queue was long; the passport officers at the far-away desk were slow. Dieter yawned once more, he stretched, he smiled, and he wrapped his arms around – nothing. 'Good to be home,' he said. Again, the urge to exude, to expand, to flow outwards, to embrace the warm body of Mother Africa. It was powerful, this urge to merge – it had been like that perhaps since the first white man set the first white foot on the continent. Indeed, maybe most white life in Africa was down to footwork; white feet walked from one end of the continent to the other, stamping new names on a place that already had plenty of its own, and then white feet kicked the natives around.

In the days of the crazies, Johannesburg Airport had been one of the prime misery holes; famously, prodigiously gloomy; the departure lounge commanded by surly white officials: a place from which a thousand exiles flew out on one-way exit permits, stripped of their passports, never expecting to return.

The big thing long ago was to drive to the airport on Sundays to watch the planes taking off. Most of everything else was forbidden. It was Jo'burg's way of desecrating the Sabbath.

Guys sitting up on the airport roof for hours. Watching the big craft taxiing out for the sheer exhilaration of knowing they were going somewhere when everything else insisted we were going nowhere, and when it felt like just about everything else was banned.

Then, for a short while, after the former owners of the country retired, the airport was a joy. A new army of black officials had arisen, and blotted out the memories of the past. Black passport control, customs officers, cops: all the new people buzzed; it was utterly charming.

But the strain of autonomy got too much. Tempers shortened, the shine of the new dulled into indifference, a feeling of 'Well, if this is freedom, now what?' When it became apparent that the answer to that was 'Nothing more, just much of the same', tempers grew shorter still.

Dieter was ahead of me. At the desk he handed over his passport and the immigration officer showed how little she liked him, in the way she turned the pages, in the frown that ruffled her clear forehead, in the careful way she touched the lapels of her crisp white blouse. She scorned him and she showed it and it made him flustered. He spoke very good English but he could not understand what she was saying, or rather why she was mumbling into the air, a foot away from his right ear.

What took place between them was not just a dialogue of the deaf between a German man in khaki and a petite black woman in gold shoulder flashes, but the dance of the blind. She talked right past him; she wanted to know how long he was staying in South Africa, she wanted to see his ticket for Windhoek, and his return ticket.

Dieter kept saying, 'Zorry? Zorry?' and cupping his hand to his ear as if to capture at least a few of the words she tossed in his direction. Because he really was sorry: sorry he could not understand her accented English; sorry she was giving him uphill; sorry that a man with love in his heart and Af-ri-ca! on his lips, a farm in Namibia and a perfectly good passport should be treated in this way.

Dieter saw himself as a regular guy who paid his taxes and kept a flat in Hamburg. But to the passport officer there was so much wrong with him she barely knew where to start. He was a throwback to the bad old days. He was too sure of himself. He had property and money and had spent many years in Africa. She saw him for what his passport said he was: Namibian. Other whites who passed before the officer came from Germany and Spain and Italy: real countries, proper countries, countries they would go home to. They weren't pretending to be at home in Africa; they didn't wear safari suits and present the passports of neighbouring states; they did not belong the class of pale, aging orphans who called themselves Zimbabweans or Kenyans or Congolese but were quite clearly some inferior form of settler trash, not merely redundant but probably dead broke, adrift in a black continent. Frankly, they were an embarrassment.

There were probably further reasons for her disdain: South Africa was a hot destination for people fleeing their own fucked-up countries, guys forever trying to jump the border illegally; and that included whites from Zimbabwe and Namibia.

So she didn't like him, any more than she liked visitors from the Congo or Chad or Guinea, or any of the no-hopers from north of the Limpopo. It was pretty clear from where I was standing that she didn't like her job either.

Dieter was still saying 'Zorry? Zorry?' when, suddenly, like a gale that stops blowing, she abruptly lost interest, and waved him through with a long, lingering yawn.

He took it personally, I could see that by the way he went off reproachfully towards the luggage carousels, every so often throwing an angry look at the officer's impervious back, looking for all the world like a rejected and angry lover.

But, then, what did he expect? He'd landed in the new Jo'burg; if the old depressed the hell out of you, the new took off the top of your head. Arrive anywhere in South Africa after the granite years of racial obsession and chances are you'd step into a place recently vacated by officious lunatics.

At the luggage carousel Dieter was talking to himself. 'Fucking stupid black bitch,' he was saying as he hauled his Louis Vuitton bags off the conveyor and dumped them on a trolley.

I could see Dieter was getting the hang of it again. He was remembering where he was. I said goodbye with a lighter heart. By the time he hit Windhoek he'd be just about his old self.

I walked out into the concourse, brushing off a posse of porters, noticing how architecture and advertising have now become the way to give South African life the face-lift everyone wants to see, a kindly, 'we love each other' look. Advertising at Jo'burg International tells every new arrival how we are in this happy land where people of every shade and hue and gender, the gifted and the disabled, meet, mix, make love, drink beer and talk all day long on our cellphones; devoted to becoming caring, confident, competitive sports stars.

The girl at the Hertz desk, round, vivacious and dressed in bright yellow, like a lively lemon, opened her mouth and spoke to me in what must be one of the queerest accents in the world: pure Jo'burgundian. The tone came from the small space left when the tongue was lifted towards the back of the palate, squeezing and releasing the words with a twang that reverberated in the nasal passages in a distinctive whine that foreigners found excruciating, but which, if you were born in this town, was deeply moving.

The Hertz girl said simply: 'Hullo, howzit? And where d'you get in from, then, hey?'

'Malaysia.'

'Ma-a-la-aysheeaah!'

It was my mother, all over again, her incredulous, faintly irritable what-where-above-all-*why*? melody. It was strange how these things affected you: suddenly, I wanted to weep. Suddenly I was home.

The Hertz girl lifted her hand with the keys in it, like a benediction, and she said in her quavery singsong: 'Have a great stay, enjoy your day, take care ...'

The blessing of a car-hire company was not much to go on, but this was Jo'burg and under the circumstances I'd take anything I could get. In the shadows of the parking garage I sat for a moment in my rented red City Golf, smelling of leather, wax, plastic and, faintly, of the lavender fragrance used to wipe the dashboard, and I thought, Why move? I'd happily stay, right here, safely cocooned. It was the temptation that always accompanies the beginning of a journey, the deliciously subversive demon that whispers, 'Well, then, why not turn back now and never start at all? Climb out of the car, go back inside the airport, take a plane out of here, and never be heard of again. Get out, go back, but above all, don't go on.'

But I was back now, and I had to pretend to be part of the place. That's the traveller's paradox. When you don't belong anywhere, you're forever putting down shallow but precious roots. No one digs in as fast as true, homeless wanderers. Drop them anywhere and it's not two minutes before they're pitching a tent, setting up shop, acting like they've been there for ever. They're incorrigible settlers: they'll settle for anywhere, or for anyone, the way lost children want to tie up with any apparently benign adult who happens along.

I drove out into the sunshine, air bright with that jagged highveld glitter. I drove towards the preposterous skyline that is Jo'burg, Joeys, Jewburg, Egoli, Josi, J-town, Gauteng ... not so much names as aliases. The four-lane highway wound towards central Jo'burg. The locals called it Death Road. Lined with factories, shopping malls, rubber factories and, here and there, the hard-baked, biscuit-blond hairy shoulders of an old mine-dump. The road from the airport was littered with low-browed slit-eyed concrete bunkers, built in the seventies and eighties, when the old fascist regime and its business lackeys loved penitential office parks.

Our god, though, was not business: he was bullion, buried dark and deep, but always there when you went looking for him. My grandfather had blasted him out of the surface rock. Now you dropped nearly two miles underground in search of the plunging reef, plummeting after him: taking two lifts, plummeting 11,000 feet in just eight minutes, to land in Hades, tiny passages, slime lapping your ankles, temperature up to 115 degrees, and rising, kept just about bearable by piping in miles of iced slush, and huge air-con plants. You cannot have gold without air-con: a fact that did me no harm at all in the years I sold systems to the mines. I would make the pilgrimage, rather like my granddad did except he set charges, turned up the heat to force the great god to show his face. Mine was a secular mission, I went into the underworld to cool things down. You are locked in a cramped oven, crawling on your belly, two miles of rock overhead until, in the torchlight at the end of the tunnel, a slash of red paint says, yes, hallelujah! The scream of the drills biting into the rock, the squeak of the thigh-high boots the miners wear. This stone held what you sought. Here you would set your charges, blow open the rocky tabernacle that held the sacred spirit then winch eight tons of debris to the surface, crush it and scour it with cyanide, all to win an ounce of ore.

Every year cost more blood for less bullion: once this town mined over two-thirds of all the gold in the world; now it was down to one-fifth, and you found it where it was deeper and darker and hotter – three miles down was the latest thinking, if we could keep the air-con going and the iced water pumping.

To this deity we were fiercely loyal, and gave our souls.

When I was growing up the mine-dumps rose above the city, bright yellow hills looming above the slime dams, depositories of the cyanide sludge discarded after the gold had been pulverised from the ore-rich rock. The dumps were local landmarks; they were the only hills we had. Scrubby grass like fierce stubble grew over their crests. For decades no one gave them a second thought. Then some bright spark reckoned there must still be some gold in all that sand, tiny scraps of ore they hadn't extracted first time round, so they began carting them away and rummaging through the sand a second time.

Each time I came back, there were fewer gold mines and more casinos.

When I'd lived in Jo'burg, there had been rules to stifle anything that moved. From raffles to reproduction. Everything was off limits. Except rugby and race phobia. If you had to ask, the answer was almost certainly 'No'. We were locked inside a mad preacher's tent, called white South Africa, and what was remarkable – no, horrible! – was what happened in the tent. Nothing happened. Zilch, *nada*, *niks*. And no one wanted anything to happen. Happenings were subversive. Happenings happened somewhere else. Happenings were the fault of crazies, blacks, Jews, commies, pinkos.

In other places when you get too many rules you sometimes get lively disobedience. Not here. South Africa was rare in that as a country it was both dead in the head and inert below the waist. Whites were so timid, so abject, so gutted by years of the old fascist rubbish, they asked permission before passing water.

Two BMW convertibles, red and blue, left and right, came screaming past me, neck and neck, hoods back, hitting two hundred, and I swear one guy had a mobile phone glued to his ear. The Jo'burg earring. They called it 'dicing', this high-speed racing. Dicing with death. The ultimate game of chance. It was, I suppose, the new equality, this risk-taking, and whether you did it on the roulette tables or the roads, it was still very Jo'burg. In this city, playing sudden death wasn't a game, it was a serious career move. It was like playing the stock exchange; casinos just had better-looking brokers.

Jo'burg was proud of its new casinos. But, then, people who made this town have always had an identity crisis, they never knew which to build first: pleasure palaces or police stations. Were they going be screwed or arrested? Jo'burg suffered from the urban equivalent of bi-polar depression, swinging endlessly between a lust for fun and the desire to lock people up for having a good time. It resembled the greedy king who was punished for his love of gold by having molten metal poured down his throat. The difference was that the king died; Jo'burg swallowed all the gold you could pour down its gullet, but came back for more. Jo'burg did not have a destiny, it didn't have an identity; it did impersonations. For a while it got ideas about being a financial centre. It was going to be London in Africa; then, for a while, after democracy arrived, and hawkers took over the streets, it dreamt of being an African city; but Jo'burgers who had never been anywhere in Africa now got to take a look at places like Lagos or Harare and the idea died: why go from gilded bordello to fly-blown wreck? But, at last, with the coming of the casinos, it believed it had discovered its true vocation: Las Vegas in the veld.

I dropped down the exit ramp into Motortown, past the old Carlton Centre. To build the place in the late sixties, they had to excavate a fifteen-acre hole. Those razzle-dazzle boys, the mining houses, put up the money and gave the place its semi-religious aura. The papers ran all the usual wanking headlines: 'SA Leads World In Big Holes'... 'First Kimberley, Now Jo'burg!' Jo'burgers told each other they dug holes faster and deeper than anyone in the world. The Carlton hole was big enough to swallow the Empire State Building (if melted down). The tower that rose from it was fifty storeys high, the tallest concrete building in the world. It contained shops, restaurants, pavement cafés, movie houses, an ice rink and a hotel so luxurious only the super-rich could afford its silver cutlery and linen napkins.

I drove past the hulk of the Carlton, Jo'burg's own *Titanic*, sunk for years now and unable any longer to disguise its profound lumpish ugliness. All that energy, that wealth, that chutzpah reduced to an island of dereliction; the hotel shuttered; the ice rink melted; the silver cutlery sold off; and even the pistol-toting guards who used to accompany what few brave guests still came to the Carlton on daring shopping expeditions in downtown Jo'burg, long since laid off. An eerie wreck of a place: beggars, hawkers and the homeless seethed around the deserted tower. It was now just another of those tall buildings left behind when the rich moved northwards to the gated suburbs, leaving behind a shell-shocked city, all the landmarks still in place: the Standard Bank Building, City Hall, Park Station. The city centre still went through the motions, working by day, but eerily empty after hours.

Across the Queen Elizabeth Bridge and into Braamfontein, the news headlines flapping on the billboards sang old, remembered songs.

Paraplegic Kids Mugged
Corpse Applies for Pension
Puppy Milo Breathes His Last

The peculiar blend of the horrid and the humdrum, a bluesy fatalism that was very Jo'burg. The words changed, never the tunes.

I was home.

Fourways Clinic was large and cool and hushed, with blue-tinted windows, palms and a parking lot glossy with fancy coupés. At the desk they asked me to wait because my mother was seeing her minister.

A few minutes later I was directed down a short broad corridor smelling of beeswax. A large priest in a short cassock that showed his grey flannels was walking toward me, talking to the ward sister. He was white, dressed in black, she was black, dressed in blue, and both were round and big, like boulders. Now they rolled down the corridor towards the lifts where I sat with my back to the Coke machine. He reminded me of a wrestler. It was the way his hair was cut, the big muscles in his neck. He wore around his neck a red stole edged with gold and carried a small silver box. I guessed it had held the host, which meant he had been giving my mother the last sacrament. He was shockingly young. My mother had been a sucker for air force pilots in the war, and in later life she took to priests – maybe because they combined spiritual authority and uniforms.

He tossed the stole over his shoulder like a scarf and shook my hand.

'I know all about you. I'm an old friend, Father Phil. I'll be along again to see your mom a little later. God bless!'

The ward sister said to me, 'You're waiting to see your mother. Go along, then.'

She was in a ward with two other women, and lay propped up on two stiff white pillows, a TV monitor overhead. Her white hair spread out on the white pillow made her face stand out as if cut from stone, her chin square and firm, her blue eyes bright. The blue and the white gave her a vaguely nautical look, like some old sail-boat laid up in dry dock. She looked well – strong even – and it was really only her hands, bunched into fists, still beside her, and somehow smaller than I remembered them to be, that spoke of declining physical power and, perhaps, of pain.

A notice at the foot of the bed warned: 'Nil By Mouth'.

She blinked hard and looked at me the way she did when I showed up, pleased to see me but certain I must be in trouble or I wouldn't have been there. If I wasn't in trouble, well, I soon would be.

'Good golly. What on earth's happened?'

She raised her eyebrows at the two women on either side of her as if to say that, well, one had sons, they wandered off to some very strange places and they returned without warning and what was one to do?

I said, 'Hullo, Ma,' and bent down and kissed her.

We sat for a while, holding hands, and then she threw this daggery look at the two silent women – 'Just reminding you,' the look said, ' that this boy is capable of anything, but don't blame me, and don't say I didn't warn you.'

She said, faintly, accusingly, 'I thought you were away, somewhere far away.'

'I was in Malaysia.'

She looked at her two friends and raised her eyebrows and coughed, embarrassed at this confession. The next question she did not speak, she signalled.

'Well, if you were in Malaysia, what are you doing here?'

'I was headed this way, so I stopped to see you.'

She said: 'This is Mrs Blum and Mrs van Niekerk; they have been very nice to me. This is my boy. He goes off at the drop of a hat.'

Mrs Blum's powdery skin was creamy and her hair was bright gold. Mrs van Niekerk was smooth as caramel and her hair was hidden beneath a bandage. Mrs Blum was brown and Mrs van Niekerk was white; they both wore pink nightdresses and had an air about them – something funereal. Or let's just say that they knew why they were there. I had left – left my mother and my country – and since my mother had no one of her own to watch over her, they'd taken the job and they felt slightly aggrieved that this Johnny-come-lately had turned up and claimed her, just like that, out of the blue. They had seen it all before. They knew all about vagrant children. Who didn't? All over the country were aging parents whose children had gone away to far-flung places.

Of course, this was not new, there had always been exiles. But the number had built steadily in the years I'd been travelling, and the diaspora could be divided into different layers.

There were, to begin with, what you might call the ur-exiles – most of them white guys who got the hell out in the twenties and thirties because the place was narrow, boring and distant, and legged it to Europe; lost their flat accents, turned into refined English poets or fascists or scientists or ballet dancers.

Then there were the exiles-of-shame who left in the fifties

and sixties, who had gone into such deep cover that all traces of a connection with the land they'd left had been hidden. I'd be in Bolton or Slough and – bloody hell – there was a Bloemfontein lawyer, or a Cape poet, so deeply embedded among the natives that no one guessed where they came from. And they weren't saying either: the fear of being outed as one of the new Nazis was there.

Then came the angry exiles of the seventies, guys who hung about under grey European skies: Pan-Africanists, Marxists and Nationalists, wating for the revolution to happen, who might have given up had they not been kick-started back into life and hope in the mid-seventies by the angry young kids who got out after the Soweto uprising, kids who loathed the effete old revolutionary guard, and got them off their arses.

Most of these had gone home in 1994; home to the ministerial job, the mansion and the Merc.

But oddly enough when the old regime collapsed, a wave of new migration began. Young men. Being pale and male in the new South Africa was a loser's ticket. You were not wanted on the voyage. But abroad was cool: better dough, bigger cars, more fun, zero guilt and no one hitting on you for your colour.

Most of those leaving were professionals: doctors, lawyers, engineers, nurses, and teachers. Entire snowy towns in Canada were serviced by Afrikaans medics on the run, who worshipped at their own Dutch Reformed Church and said 'Jislaik!' when surprised, and ate *melktert* after the *braaivleis* – even when the mercury dropped to 30 below. Others settled in colonies in Australia, around cities like Perth, occasionally pining for cold Castle beer and dreaming of Mrs Ball's Chutney. London and the Home Counties were thick with them; they colonised entire neighbourhoods, implanted *boerewors* in deepest

England, and Tassenburg wine; sticks of black biltong swung like fly papers in butchers' windows in Chiswick and Ealing.

These new expats were intensely patriotic, and unlikely ever to return. The flowing green of the new national flag flashed from their car bumpers, and medallions bearing the face of Nelson Mandela swung from their car keys. They talked loudly on the Tube, alarmed the locals by going barefoot in public places, and became misty-eyed when they heard '*Nkosi Sikelel'y i Afrika*'.

One thing drew them back home, unexpectedly, briefly, from Birmingham and Boston and Azerbaijan, blinking in the dazzling highveld sun, slightly sheepish, slightly guilty, slightly – let's face it – foreign. They came back when a mother sickened, or a father died; they came back *in extremis*. For a last-in-a-lifetime visit.

So, no, it wasn't Mrs van Niekerk and Mrs Blum who were the angels of death; it was people like me.

Mrs van Niekerk put her hand on my arm. 'I want to tell you how very, very proud we are of your mom. There is a dreadful nursing sister who thinks she's the bally bee's knees; doesn't she, Kathleen? She's been awful to us. But your mom told her where to get off.'

'And she called your mom a stupid white bitch,' said Mrs Blum.

'I thought she was going to take a swing at Kathleen, she was so cross!' said Mrs van Niekerk.

'We are proud of your mom,' said Mrs Blum. 'Kathleen is a person we have got to know very well.'

My mother had that light in her eyes that told me she had been making waves somewhere and it had done her good. But before I could ask her what it was, a nurse arrived and I caught sight of the trolley outside the door. This time it was a white nurse and the air was heavy with a sense of what had gone before.

'Time for theatre, Mrs Healey,' said the nurse in soft tones that were kind and apologetic.

My mother nodded, then she sighed. We all waited, uncomfortably. At such moments the predominant mood was one of fear mixed in with embarrassment at all that could not be said. Just as I was wondering if I'd ever talk to her again, she found her voice.

'Just a tick.' She gave her old smile of hellish delight. 'D'you remember my wig?'

'Yes, Ma, I remember. From Monrovia.'

'Yes. Well, one day I may want you to give that wig to Koosie. Would you do that?'

'Of course.'

'He's been phoning me: wanting to make amends, I think. Or to save me from jail. I guess I scared the daylights out of him.'

'You did the same to Jake Schevitz.'

My mother sniffed slowly. The degree of disdain in that long intake of breath was deep.

'Poor old Schevitz. What a fall was there: a burnt-out firebrand. A wet, a *woes*, a schlemiel! I wanted something very simple, very elegant. You would have thought I'd asked for the earth.'

She looked straight at Mrs van Niekerk and Mrs Blum and said simply: 'I wanted to get married, to a young doctor. From Havana.'

Perhaps then it began to dawn on these new friends that Kathleen was, after all, not someone they knew at all.

She had us all now, even the nurse.

'We bought a ring, my Cuban boy and I. We took it with us when we went to see Schevitz. But instead of helping, he read me the riot act. Can you imagine? Fat lot of good he was. If I'd wanted a sermon, Alexander, I'd have gone to see Father Phil.'

She turned on the nurse. 'Now, my dear, I am ready.' She gave her pantomime aunt pout. 'Into thy capable hands does this old biddy commend her ridiculous body.'

I sat in the waiting room, an open space at the end of a corridor, between the lifts and the Coke machine, and studied the notice-board to which was pinned a tourism poster that used a montage of zebras, Zulus and Table Mountain to push the line: 'South Africa – the World in One Country'.

To the left of the lift doors someone had stuck a handwritten notice ending in a line of formal capitals: 'It has come to our attention that certain staff are failing to meet their roster times. If this continues, fines will be levied on latecomers. YOU WILL PAY THESE FINES!'

I wondered about those capitals, the tone of the warning. It sounded like bluster, couched in new words which made everyone equal: no sex, no colour, please – we're new South Africans ... But I knew who was talking to whom. The writer of this warning wasn't at all sure that 'they' would pay the fines. Maybe 'they'd' tell him to bugger off. And there was nothing anyone was going to do about it because these days 'they' ran the show.

Of course, there were always some who bored on about common sense and logic. Who decided – God save us – to be sensible; who said some things would stay the same because they had to; who insisted that there were facts, and facts would not yield to political manipulation; that two and two always made four, and germs spread disease. These methodical madmen said that if you ran a hospital you ensured the staff turned up on time, made the beds, washed the patients, opened the operating theatre punctually.

Plain facts, inexorable logic. Such rules stood to reason, and they had nothing whatever to do with skin colour and they would be followed. But this was South Africa: nothing followed and *everything* had to do with skin colour. If you were black or Asian or mixed race or white, you brought with you your colour, your historical baggage, yourself.

I guess about two hours passed in these reflections, then, suddenly, the matron in crisp blue and white came in and asked me to see the surgeon.

There is comfort in quiet professionalism. The surgeon was a small shy man who managed to communicate his helpless distress at knowing the facts but being unable to do more. He did not waste time, he did not equivocate.

'The cancer is very large, very aggressive. All we can really do is to make her comfortable. We're putting her in a private ward. You can see her when she wakes.'

I knew she was dying and he left it open to me to say so or to ask him to confirm it, and he would have done so. But I didn't need to ask.

The matron walked me back to the waiting room and I asked her about the trouble between my mother and one of her nurses.

She did not flinch. 'One of our nurses was changing your mother's dressings and your mother called her "my girl", and told her not to be clumsy. The nurse responded in an unprofessional manner.'

'What did she say?'

'She said she wasn't a servant. If your mother spoke to her like that she could change her dressings herself. At least, that was the gist of it.'

Not quite. I could hear her. 'Can't you be a bit more careful, you silly woman!'

And the silly woman would have said, 'Who are you to talk to me like that? You stupid white bitch.'

I never knew my mother pay a smidgen of attention to skin colour, but she didn't pull her punches, and she never hesitated to attack. And my ma would have said: 'If I wasn't feeling bad, I'd knock you over, my girl.'

She wouldn't have been bluffing either.

The matron said carefully, 'I want to apologise for the behaviour of the nurse.'

'I'm sorry, too. My mother can be sharp.'

'Your mother is ill, she's our patient. The nurse was rude. Your mother is in our care; it's a question of being professional. We do not allow rudeness to patients.'

We looked at each other. We were speaking for the people we came from. We were, at the same time, putting aside the fact that she was black and I was white. We didn't believe saying sorry changed anything, but we apologised anyway. The situation required smoothing falsities. Nurses shall be professional at all times no matter what the provocation. Put that in capitals and pin it to the notice-board beside the lifts, and it still rang false. Then again, knowing something wasn't true generally meant we had to start believing it.

It was towards early evening that she began coming round. She didn't open her eyes but she suddenly said: 'Give me your mitt.'

We sat there for a long time, holding hands. She'd try to say something but the anaesthetic kept knocking her back. Her breathing was heavy, her hand easily covered mine, and I saw in the V between her thumb and forefinger a vein pulsing fiercely. A transparent bag filled with clear liquid was suspended over the bed; a tube ran into her arm and skipped to the tune of her pulse.

Then she seemed to wake because she said, suddenly, clearly, with this fine smile: '*Hecho muy bien, Kataleen!*' And I knew she was dancing in the back room to Raoul's mambo music...

I put my lips close to her ear. 'What did you do with him, Ma?'

She opened her eyes and looked at me as if she wasn't really sure who I was.

I said: 'It's me, Ma.'

'Yes,' she said, 'I think it is.' But she didn't sound too sure.

'Where is the Cuban, Ma?'

She opened her eyes wide and her grip on my hand was strong. Then she began to talk, slowly, clearly, with such pleasure, interrupting herself now and then to shake her head or laugh or sigh. But mostly to laugh. It wasn't so much that she was telling me: she was telling herself the story because it thrilled her.

'When Koosie turned me down, I was flummoxed. Then I had a thought, a tiny thought. I remembered something Papadop said when he brought Raoul to me. He said there were millions of Zimbos around Jo'burg without proper papers. And there were lots more who had the correct stuff. So I asked myself where in Jo'burg a person might get hold of the correct stuff and the answer had to be Hillbrow, because you can get just about anything else you want in Hillbrow: girls, guns, gold. So I got in the car, and in Kotze Street, outside a chicken roastery, I saw this guy. He had about four cellphones round his neck as well as a lot of gold chains, and red trainers, and a white shell suit, and he was leaning up against the wall. I just had a feeling about him so I asked him where I could buy some ID papers for a friend. Just like that, straight to the point, no beating about the bush. I didn't even bother to keep my voice down.

'Such a charming guy, even if his clothes were a bit odd. He told me his name was Chinaza – it means "God answers my prayer" in Igbo – how about that! He came from a place called Ogbelle in the Niger Delta. What a surprise. I've flown that Delta more times than I can remember. Snails the size of soup plates, and lots of red snapper. Big fish eaters, the Delta people. They call it bush up there but it's really rainforest; waterways, swamps; sometimes the mangroves can hang two hundred feet above the floor of forest: they're like cliffs on either side of the wings when you drop down to land. It was a tricky thing, putting down on water. I liked to sight on the fishermen in their dugouts for depth reference but I often landed a bit long and had to use reverse pitch to pull up.

'Chinaza told me that fish was not what most people lived off today in the Delta. It was all oil up there now; big orange flares burning day and night, helicopters and oilrigs. Lashings of money in the Delta but no work. So he came south, and hit Joeys. He explained he didn't actually do identities. He did stimulants and substances. Any kind of powder I cared to purchase. But if I was after paper, not powder, I needed a paper man.

'Chinaza took me to a house in Yeoville, to another Nigerian, with lovely brown eyes. He was a top paper man. And so courteous. "Your wish is my delight," he told me. He had helped hundreds of people. All I had to decide was did I want to borrow or marry? Or did I want a "Newborn"? If I borrowed, that meant I got the use of the personal particulars of a living person. He'd arrange to marry Raoul off to some genuine South African without, of course, her knowing the first thing about it. Or, if I liked, he could give him a new name, a new life, and make him a Newborn.

'Well, I didn't want to borrow, and I didn't like the idea of Raoul being married, even if his wife would never know. So I went for the Newborn option. But I also wanted him to stay a doctor. This country needs doctors. No problem, says the paper man. I can make him whatever you like: doctor, lawyer, professor, whatever the client wants. He needed four passport photographs, five grand in small denominations, notes no bigger than fifty bucks, a new name and date of birth. And if I told him which medical school I'd like my friend to have attended he'd throw in a perfectly good diploma, ready framed ...

'Such service!' She squeezed my hand. 'Don't you love free enterprise, don't you love the energy of immigrants?'

She photographed Raoul, stuffed the cash into an envelope, and went back to Yeoville. One week later, her Cuban had his papers: his driving licence, his birth certificate and his passport. Raoul Mendoza vanished into plain view. She had turned her Cuban medic into a new South African, with a very traditional name, an Afrikaans name. He became Dr Cornelius du Toit.

'His friends will call him Connie, you can be sure of that. Letting him go wasn't easy but it was best, for him. He's free. I opened the cage and let him fly.'

And he had flown to freedom, like many thousands of others – Armenians, Russians, Thais, Mozambicans, Zimbabweans, Congolese, Syrians, Chinese, Arabs – all busily buying, acquiring, assuming, stealing or borrowing. In a word, achieving citizenship. It was only right, when you thought about it. It was really the fulfilment of a very great lack. After all, there had never been any true South Africans: right from the starting whistle the term was no more than a convenient form of shorthand, when it had not been a sentence of exclusion. It was a nationality so baggy, so amorphous, and so phoney, it was ready made to fit just about anyone who tried it on. It was made to be stolen, or borrowed.

I reckoned Raoul would be OK. How could he fail? These Newborns, so recently transformed into South Africans, were likely to wear their new identities with more assurance and authority, ease and enjoyment than any of the bloody indigenes – white or black – who really hadn't the first idea what it meant to be anything.

I was pleased, though, she had made him Afrikaans. To turn him into one of the former racial rulers was a master stroke. If she was going to give him a start in life in the new South Africa, the last thing a decent Cuban needed was a whole lot of liberal angst and ineffectual grief. We – this dwindling band of fugitives – were leftovers from the silly idea that parts of the world were improved by mere Anglo-Saxon presence. This had been not only sentimental but shortsighted. What counted was what always counted for all invaders, settlers and colonists, if they were not to be wiped away for ever like some invasion of pubic lice – firepower: it secured their presence and their loot and their legitimacy.

But of all the invaders our lot seemed to have been the scrapings. Not for us the clear directive: 'Tell you what, go out to X, exterminate the natives, inherit the land like the Yanks, or the Ozzies, and you'll be laughing.'

No, for us it was more like, 'You lot are bloody useless, can't find work, can't feed yourselves, can't cross the street unaided. So here's a free passage to Africa – where you can pretend to be important.'

So we off we went, and the rest was history. We became marooned ex-sailors or failed farmers in a place where we were not prepared to work, or kill, with sufficient energy. We were never even a tribe: the best we managed was a kind of B-team. The sort of people who'd rather be murdered in our beds than make them ourselves.

The story of Raoul's transformation into Connie had tired her. Her eyes were still closed, and she hummed a snatch of a tune I recognised as '*La Faroana*'.

'Promise me something, dear boy.' She was twisting the sheet with her free hand.

'What is it, Ma?' I took her other hand.

'I've fixed things.'

'What things?'

'All my things. Everything's fixed – but you make sure. Will you?' Her grip on my hand was urgent, almost frantic.

'Make sure of what, Ma?'

'I need you to find them.'

Her breathing was ragged. I did not know who 'they' were so I said, hoping to make her feel easier, 'I'll find them.'

It seemed to be the right thing because she let go my hand, tried – and failed – to snap her fingers, and then said softly: '*Mambo, qué rico el mambo!*'

Her breathing was more and more difficult. She seemed to be choking. I wanted to tell someone, so I stood up very quietly and had got almost to the door when she suddenly opened her eyes and looked at me, as if this was the first time she'd seen me.

'I thought you were in … Malaysia?'

I went back to her. I tried to sound easy, 'I was, Ma, but I had to pass this way so I stopped in to see you.'

This time I knew it was me she saw. But her surprise sprang, I rather think, not from my sudden turning up – she was pleased, yes – but from her own success.

She was fighting to speak and yet I heard the contentment in her reaction.

'Lordy, Lordy, how you get about!'

I found the duty nurse and told her abut the choking and she asked me to wait in the corridor. The faint nightlights ran like blue glowing mushrooms down the passages; the doors to the wards opened and closed with a swish. I studied the patient lists pasted to the glass windows of the night matron's cubicle. The VIPs were identified by initials only: Prince X from Zululand was in post-op; His Excellency, President of Y, and

His Excellency, Prime Minister of X, were to have nil by mouth; a Lebanese named Khoury, a diamond dealer described as Zairean, was in for observation; and his bodyguard had requested vegetarian meals; my mother was listed as Ms Healey – Kathleen, PILOT. I liked that.

When I was allowed back into her room she was deeply asleep and they had put an oxygen mask on her. The bag above her bed began to turn pink. When the night sister put her head around the door I pointed to it.

She said softly, gently: 'It's blood; it means her kidneys are failing.'

The oxygen eased her breathing. She seemed almost fine. Her size, her solid bulk under the blankets, the peace of her sleep, all of it flew in the face of what I knew. The bag above the bed was a warning flag, darkening all the time. From the road outside came the rush of traffic and, further off, police sirens; familiar Jo'burg night music. Her breathing was steady. I leaned back in the chair and closed my eyes for what I thought was no more than a moment, and when I opened them, her eyes were open, too. It was very quiet in the room and the bag was filled with deepest red.

I called the night nurse, who came and checked her pulse and sighed and said: 'You've been very good; I am so sorry.'

I looked down at the bed and saw my mother, unchanged. But what I saw, too, was the gap, the place where she no longer was, and it was immense. It ran not just from one end of my life to the other, it reached from the tip of Africa to Egypt, from Zanzibar to Mombasa. It was as hard to think of her as dead as it was to think of clouds passing away, or of dead air. It was like seeing Gulliver pinned to earth. Pinned down only at the

edges, like some enormous kite, or the pelt of some great
animal, pegged to the far corners of the continent where she
touched ground; at those points where her friends, her quarrels,
her landing strips pulled her to earth. But mostly she stayed
aloft, her life was spent high, the billowing spread of her sailing
overhead.

The night sister said: 'This is painful, but I am going to do
something now.'

She lifted my mother's hands and slid the rings from her
fingers. Then she opened the drawer of her bedside table and
took out her glasses, her purse, two strings of pearls and a
prayer book, and gave them to me.

'We prefer not to leave these here. I think you should take
them with you, keep them safe.'

It was one of those things I heard often enough. A belief
expressed rarely in public, perhaps only in deepest privacy, or *in
extremis*. A statement that both speaker and audience understood would be absolutely denied if reported or challenged.
The night nurse, who was black, spoke to me as a professional, telling me in the code of the place that if the rings, the cash,
the pearls remained when the staff came for my mother's body,
when they took her down to the morgue, these things might
vanish. This was another truth she was sad about but there it
was. People were not well paid and it was best not to leave
temptation in their way. Her statement answered the question
I did not ask: did that mean they would rob the dead? Damn
right they would. Hatred and anger, poverty and a lack of
power, the arrogance of rich white bastards who ran the world
and ruined the continent conferred the right to rob them blind,
alive or dead. The old advertising slogan beloved of South

African tourism that boasted of South Africa – 'The world in one country' – was just a word short of being dead right: we were the world war in one country.

III   Last Rites

'Life is life and fun is fun but it's all so quiet
when the goldfish die.'
Bror Blixen

I drove home as dawn was breaking slow and pink over the East Rand, a sky of crisp highveld colours so delicate that you do not so much see them but taste them, running your tongue over the cool grey edge of the early breeze and the damp red earth. In this quiet time, the city glinted like dodgy jewels in an outstretched palm, or those fake watches hawkers flashed on crowded streets. Like all the contraband that made this town.

I swung up past Sandton Centre, through Illovo, then Rosebank. On the pavements, in wooden hutches, night sentries were knocking off, stamping on their fires, shaking out their blankets at the foot of the high walls that hid the houses from the world. No town had built more walls or built them better. Tall, beautiful walls of brick, terracotta, plaster, of dressed stone and steel; tipped with spikes or high-voltage wire, studded with closed-circuit cameras, bright with the hoardings of rapid response teams, flying paramedics, neighbourhood watch and guard dog patrols ...

The roads were empty, briefly free at this early hour from the anxieties of the armed hijack. Usually, this was a matter of pistol-toting thugs demanding the keys to your car. And then shooting you, lest you identify them. This was not only callous but unnecessary as the inability of the police to catch hijackers was almost as legendary as the robberies themselves. Hijacking happened so often that only celebrity victims made news: a well-known chef shot and paralysed; a neurosurgeon abducted and murdered. The boss of a gold mining company gunned down and left to free-wheel down the road till his Merc hit an overhead bridge, and someone reported what looked like an accident.

The early headlines were on the lampposts, singing the songs that made the music of the place: that morning it was a real lulu ...

'School Hall Stolen'.

I drove up Jan Smuts Avenue and turned into Forest Town. It took me some time to locate the right keys in the bunch I had found in her purse. The house was quiet and dark. I walked in through the porch where my mother used to have tea with the Rain Queen. In the sitting room, on the old stinkwood desk, sat the collection, in blue leather covers and gilt letters, of Cassell's *Great Stories of the World*. There were three small snaps of me as a child of about two, sitting in a small car, my hair done up in a kiss-curl; at ten, I was pointing a toy rifle at the sky. At around twelve I was seen with my first kill: a gemsbok in the Kalahari. My foot rests proudly on the dead buck's skull much as a boy might rest his foot on a ball. There were no other hunting pictures of me; I lost interest after that. I preferred Cassell's *Great Stories* and I grew up in other lands, on other terms. That never pleased her much; she had little patience with bookish people.

'Africa', she liked to declare, 'does not need readers.'

I went over to the map of Livingstone's journeys, traced in

rashes of red stipple which always reminded her of 'a lost ant stumbling round several big drops of water'. The big drops of water were the Great Lakes, a favourite destination when she was still flying: Lake Victoria, Lake Albert, Lake Edward.

Below the lakes were these lines from Livingstone's journals, copied out in green ink in my mother's looping script: 'There is no law of nations here. The weakest goes to the wall.'

On the floor beside her desk was a wooden box: about nine inches wide, and a foot deep. Someone had addressed the box in bold black ink:

> *To: Prof. R.A. Dart*
> *Dept of Anatomy,*
> *Medical School,*
> *Hospital Hill,*
> *Johannesburg.*
> *Contents: Skull*

The other sides of the box carried a warning:

> *Contents Very Fragile*
> *Handle With Care*
> *Stow Away From Boilers*

She told me that this was the very box that once held the skull of Mrs Ples, 'an Australopithecus lady who lived near Jo'burg about two and a half million years ago, probably a close relative, far closer to us than the apes.'

The box she used for housing her collection of Congolese stabbing spears.

On her desk was a letter from her old friend from the Kenya hunts, 'Testa' the Argentinian. Testalozzi had been such a hit with the women in Nairobi, and had hunted more of Africa than any man. Testa hunted the two Rhodesias, Kenya, the Sudan, Bechuanaland and Barotseland, where he specialised in black-maned lions. He married an Italian contessa, only to witness his mother-in-law taken by a croc in the Zambezi, and he finally cleared out when rebels in Chad hit his camps and killed his trackers, his dogs and his wife. He now ran an African safari park in the American west and wrote long sweet letters of which this was the last:

'Africa has stolen my heart and buried it in the African bush as surely as Livingstone's was – except that Livingstone was dead before it happened and mine was buried still beating…'

Bamadodi, the Rain Queen, proud on a wooden throne, in one of her wildly coloured knitted crowns, bright zigzags of pink and green. The photo was inscribed: 'To Kathleen, from her friend Bama.' Hemingway with a shotgun; Schweitzer in a pith helmet; various smiling moustachioed pilots standing beside Hurricanes and Spitfires and Lancasters; and assorted uncles: Uncle Hansie from South West and Uncle Dickie from Kenya, Uncle Bertie with assegai, Uncle Papadop, Uncle Manny from Nyasaland; and the twin uncles Ronald and Rupert from Uganda; my mother in flying helmet and goggles and scarf at the controls of her Stinson, somewhere over Africa.

And the many pictures of a hunting life, taken in the 1940s and 1950s. Each location had been noted and ranged from the Kalahari to the Congo. My mother beside a buffalo, elephant, bongo, duiker or lion she had just shot. Her face grave and reposed she sat astride a huge croc, a river behind her, rifle across her knees. Or fording a river with a string of porters.

Here she was towering beside a tiny pygmy in the Ituri forest ...

There was something haunting about these pictures of the kill, something primal but also absurd: the small live hunter, the big dead beast; and to stand, as she did, looking neither greedy nor silly nor bloody, but simply sedate, required a degree of unselfconsciousness that the world had long ago lost.

My mother after a kill is a being in a state of happy repose. She is no longer thinking of the hunt, she is happy to have done what she planned and now she is ready to be off again. Somewhere, out of the picture, her plane waits to lift her up and away. She cares utterly, passionately for the sport of the moment, but when the hunt's over she will not give it another thought.

Grainy, creased, fading snapshots, yet I could see quite easily the muscle of her forearm. She was colossal but feminine to a fault, a wisp of dark hair blown free of her pith helmet, which she would not tuck back but kept out of her eyes by every so often giving it a little puff of air, which made it fly up on to her scalp and lie for a while before beginning to fall once more.

And from the locations of these safaris you could have drawn another map, which would have said as much about my mother's Africa as her map of Livingstone's ant-like wanderings around the Great Lakes. He was propelled further and deeper – into what? For Livingstone, said rational people later, looking back at his feverish wandering, the goals were Christian conversion, commercial opportunity and potential colonies for England. But, really, to me his travels seemed the wanderings of a lost man, grimly going mad.

What propelled my old lady, I rather think, must have been the feeling of immense space. Venturing into it, crossing it, looking down on it, spotting game from the air or simply finding a suitable landing strip or a sufficiently long stretch of water to land a float-plane. Above all and everything the feeling that it was empty and all of it belonged to her. Every one of the countries she had felt at home in was something else now, and all the people in the pictures were dead or displaced. And the space had never been empty. One had to allow for the possibility that her travels had been an even greater folly than Livingstone's.

Maybe white incomers were condemned to redraw the map of Africa in their own likenesses; the punishment for having it all their way was the obligation to reinvent it. From their very first arrival some demon blinded them to the real place and made them believe in their empty maps. Africa for them was, literally, Africa *à la carte*. Perhaps that was why, when asked where she was at home, my mother puzzled over the question. She knew what she was: she was a South African from the Witwatersrand, the daughter of a settler. She regarded Jo'burg as her city and the greatest metropolis south of Cairo. But all her life it seemed to me she resisted the suffocating trap of that identity. Resisted, yes, but I did not believe she escaped it, because where we came from identity was destiny.

In one of the few formal photographs on the wall she sat in front of a group of women dressed in white robes with green sashes. Everyone is smiling, but stiffly posed, like a class photo. These were the Zoo Lake Zionists, a local choir. Back in the bad old days, the black choir had not been permitted to sing in the Zoo Lake grounds since they were reserved for whites only, and so the ladies rehearsed in our back garden on Sunday afternoons, and elected my mother their life-long patron for letting them do so – until the cops closed us down after an anonymous complaint. Anonymous, though everyone in the street knew it came from our neighbours, Mrs Terre'Blanche, Garfinkel, Smuts and Mason, in the form of an unsigned note pushed under the door of Parkview police station.

The note read: 'Mrs Healey's got a bunch of Bantus in her garden – every Sunday – yelling their heads off …'

She received an official summons, a fussy piece of creamy paper commanding her to appear in court for 'for disturbing the peace by permitting a Bantu Vocal Assembly to foregather on suburban premises in contravention of the health and safety regulations of the City of Johannesburg'.

She had it framed. This document was a beautiful case of the bullshit that passed in those days for meaning. If you translated 'foregather', it meant in Jo'burgese 'a fucking bunch of fucking blacks is fucking cluttering up the fucking back yard and fucking yelling their fucking heads off'. But 'foregather' went down on paper because no one ever wrote the way they talked, any more than they ever said what they meant. The phrase 'health and safety' was another flashy number meant to pump up self-esteem, but it had nothing to do with hygiene or security: it referred to the divine right which not only permitted but encouraged whites to use any means – boots, guns, dogs, jails – to keep blacks down and out of sight. As for the 'City of Johannesburg', that fatuity rang oddly in a mining town recently descended from a mess of threadbare diggers' tents and vermin-ridden shanties inhabited by hucksters, whores and highwaymen. But, then, the actual words Jo'burgers used, when they used words at all, were so curt, so ball-breakingly stupid, so in thrall to muscle and might, that no one has ever had the heart or the guts to reproduce the few dozen grunts, cuffs and bellows that passed for the everyday patois of this town, preferring instead the florid lies and airy legalese of my mother's creamy summons.

The signs of her departure a few days earlier, after she had phoned me in Kuala Lumpur, were evident: her bedroom neat with its water-colour of Stanleyville, the masks from Guinea and the kudu skin on the polished Oregon pine floor. And in the bathroom, her nylons hung neatly to drip-dry over the bath. Everything of her was there but herself.

My bedroom was untouched. She must have known I'd come home: the bed was made. Someone had been working in the house and garden, I could see that. Life is so sad that sometimes you can't help smiling. What option did you have?

I made myself a cup of coffee and went back to the living room and sat down in the blue rocker, facing the blank TV. Her chair. The house empty made an even stronger statement than it had done when my mother was alive, when she'd be sitting in her blue Dralon chair, with her knitting on her lap. On the wall, the Rain Queen watched me with dark and beautiful eyes.

And on a hook, right next to the Queen – a fall of bright orange foam – she had hung the wig. You might say she died dreaming of wigs. Not your normal hairpiece, the sort of thing you would see in some hairdresser's salon or theatre, but a Day-Glo blood-orange fright-wig of the sort kids wear at Hallowe'en. This one had belonged to a kid – with an AK 47 almost as tall as he was, who fought in Liberia, in the children's army of a man called Prince Johnson. His picture was on the wall next to the wig. He leans on his gun, like a staff. He is about fourteen, perhaps, and his eyes are red-rimmed, and it's not camera flash. Oddest of all, he is wearing a wedding dress.

I was in Hanoi at the time the picture had been taken. It was 1991 – June – and very hot. I was staying at a hotel called Le Colonial, not far from Hoan Kiem Lake, and I had been spending time at the Ho Chi Minh Mausoleum where they were thinking of renewing the air-con in the chamber of the little mummy who lay there, his wispy beard making him look rather like a blanched prawn.

One day when I got back to my hotel, the desk clerk gave me a message, scribbled on a piece of hotel notepaper.

'Off to rainforest – back soon – Ma.'

She didn't say which rainforest; I thought, at first, she must have meant the Congo because I knew she was particularly concerned about her friends. In the early 1990s the civil war in eastern sections of Zaire had got bad, and some soldiers, convinced the pygmies were magical non-humans, had taken to eating them.

Rainforests are not easy places and yet I knew she would have gone alone. She was by then at least seventy-five, and the news was alarming.

That was the idea.

Did I do anything about it? Certainly not: there was nothing I could do when my mother reached out towards that visionary destination she called 'Africa'. This sort of thing happened increasingly as she got older and I roamed further. But this was one of the most compelling of her messages I received, as I kept moving around the world.

My mother's hunting techniques were based on shooting large game. She was at heart an elephant hunter and elephants are sociable beasts and move in groups, usually an old bull and plenty of females. African elephants stand some thirteen feet high and weigh anything up to six tons. They don't see too well but they have a very acute sense of smell and fine hearing. So keeping downwind is essential; the slightest deviation will mean they get your scent, even up to half a mile away. They are also very smart; perhaps, with the exception of ourselves, the most intelligent animals we hunt. Elephants will come to each other's aid: most hunters killed by an elephant are killed not by the animal they're hunting but by an ally who has waded into the fight. It is always dangerous. You also need to get up close: forty yards or less.

The classic kill of an elephant is the brain shot but it is difficult and best left to professionals. Always take your first few elephants with a heart shot was my mother's advice.

The brain of the elephant, though about twice the size of a human's, is deeply buried in bone and spongy protective cartilage anywhere up to two feet thick, and a shot from a small-bore rifle that misses will simply result in the elephant bolting, not much the worse for wear. The wound will heal pretty quickly, too. There is also the risk that if you're using a high-velocity gun, say a .375 or a .404, your bullet, instead of travelling straight along its ordained path, may strike some obstruction and alter direction and hit something, or someone, on the far side of your target.

As my mother liked to remind me: 'I've seen men shot, fifty yards on the far side of the elephant, by a bullet that changed its mind …'

She also liked to point out that bulls are particularly tricky. Because even when well hit, they can stay on their feet. 'I once put three .700 nitro bullets into a big bull up in Northern

Rhodesia, and they were damn good shots, and he still wouldn't go down.'

Quite so.

When on my trail, and within range, she alternated shoot-ing strategies: sometimes she tried for the brain; sometimes she went for the heart. The rainforest caper, when I was in Hanoi, was a head shot. She knew it would intrigue me. Even more than it worried me. She knew I'd want to know why she was in a rainforest, and which one she was in. She wanted me to care, she wanted me to share her excitement, her sense of adventure, her hunting talents; she wanted me to be *there*.

I wasn't. I resisted and rejected it. I thought her love of the place, of Africa, was absolutely, inextricably tied to various forms of murder, large and small, and I did not see it as a sacred vision, a cause, or a victim to be saved. Neither did I see all of it as a natural extension of my own back yard. And I thought of those who did as willing collaborators in the killing game.

This scepticism led to differences between us, which were not resolved. It has been suggested to me that the succession of lovers my mother took over the years was an attempt to make up for the love she never had from me. There might be some-thing in that. But what we get back to, as always, is this: you've only to look at the direction of the links between my mother and her lovers to know that they needed her, not the other way around.

And this was the case with the boy who was to become the youngest of her far-flung adorers. Was there anyone not bowled over? Because she loomed so large, she felt so close. It was an optical and an emotional illusion. Her lovers longed to cross the gulf of their own yearning. Distance was essential to admiration.

As it turned out, it wasn't the Congo, or the pygmies, that had taken her off. It was the Liberian rainforest she had in mind, and she got there via Sierra Leone. In the old days she'd have flown herself but this time she took a commercial flight to Freetown and then rented a four-wheel drive and headed over the border into the Guinean rainforest and on to Sinoe County, South Eastern Liberia.

But when I learnt this it didn't much help because I knew she no longer hunted. At seventy-five she could not be sure of her aim.

'Always shoot for the spot – never at the whole animal – as any professional will tell you. And I don't see too clearly, and my hands shake.'

What then took her to Sinoe?

I guess it was the preservationist in her. Like many hunters, she believed passionately in shooting animals, and she believed just as strongly in seeing animals prosper: it's a difficult position to maintain but one she held with her usual equanimity, as she did with positions that had what she felt were real African dimensions.

Sinoe was where she'd once hunted bongo and elephant back in the fifties and sixties, when she'd known the late President Tubman, of whom she had fond memories.

'He was a crook, but he was a gentleman crook. When he died, things fell apart. Liberia was founded by freed slaves from America, who had no sooner been freed than they enslaved every local Liberian they could find. Naturally the locals rebelled.'

I'll say.

President Tubman died in hospital, and after that things went downhill fast. His successor, President Tolbert, was murdered by Master Sergeant Samuel Doe, who became President until Prince Johnson killed him. And from then on, everyone tried to kill everyone else.

It was into this mess that my mother had stepped. Her concern for wildlife in Sinoe was misplaced. At that time Liberians were so given over to human slaughter that the animals came off OK. But the fighting was another matter, and she had to leave the rainforest, only to find there was no way back into Sierra Leone. So she pushed on towards the capital, Monrovia, on roads choked with refugees and corpses and soldiers hopped out of their minds on whatever they could find. She was planning to get a ship out.

It was outside Monrovia, a place called Chocolate City, that she met the Small Boys' Unit headed by a kid called Washington. Roosevelt Washington was about fourteen, or so he thought. Two-Ton Terror was his *nom de guerre* and he was dressed in shorts, a filthy Bob Marley T-shirt and a bright orange wig. He carried the usual AK 47 slung over his shoulders in the manner of a broomstick or a spear.

'Always approach an AK butt side on,' said my mother, in one of those pieces of advice I hoped never to need.

Washington and his 'battalion' of skinny, highly armed, hungry kids mobbed my mother when they saw she had a camera.

'Take me, take me,' they kept yelling.

Washington's nails were painted ivory and worn long.

'Why ivory?' she asked.

'Because it goes with my dress,' said Washington.

'You wear a dress?'

'Yes ma'am, I fight in a dress.'

He went off and came back wearing a wedding dress and his orange wig; he also carried a small handbag.

And that was how she photographed him.

'They were smashed,' she recalled later. 'They had been drinking cane powder, which is fermented sugarcane juice spiked with gunpowder.'

That's what accounted for the red-eye in the boy in her picture.

The boys were fighting for Prince Johnson and they were commanded by a guy known as the Bare-Assed Brigadier because all he wore were sneakers when he led the boys into action.

'When I met the Brigadier he was properly dressed, and quite open about this methods. He told me: "Before leading my troops into battle, we would get drunk and drugged up, sacrifice a local teenager, drink their blood, then strip down to our shoes and go into battle wearing colourful wigs and carrying dainty purses we'd looted from civilians. We'd slaughter anyone we saw, chop their heads off and use them as soccer balls. We were nude, fearless, drunk and homicidal. We killed hundreds of people, so many I lost count."

'It took some getting used to, dear boy. I read somewhere that he became a preacher later, did Brigadier Bare Ass.'

When Prince Johnson killed President Doe he had the events videoed. Copies were being hawked by the boys on the road to Monrovia, and Washington said it was known locally as 'With or Without Pepper Sauce'. Did she want to buy one? All proceeds to the Small Boys' Unit.

The video came home, along with the fright-wig. It makes difficult viewing.

Doe is naked to the waist. Tied up and badly beaten, he begs Prince to loosen the ropes. Prince Johnson sits back while his face is mopped by a female aide and pulls at his beer. Then one of Doe's ears is hacked off.

In the video you see Johnson expanding in importance. Heating up. Whoever wants power must fill space and grow heavy and important and obtuse. He puts on suits and turbans, tunics and swords, and then rolls over and crushes the poor sods beneath him …

In Africa, it wasn't that the emperor had no clothes; quite the contrary: he was the only one wearing any.

Prince Johnson always denied he'd actually murdered Doe. He told a journalist who approached him later, with all the right degree of reverence and horror modern political power demands:

'I captured the late President Doe and held him until he was pronounced dead. I still say he committed suicide.'

The terrifying respect that rode on the title 'the late President Doe' was one of the most grisly features of failed leadership across Africa. The 'late Pres' in this case having been captured and tortured, remained a man to respect, and talk of with care, even when you had cut off his ears and eaten them. Or did Prince Johnson force Doe to eat his own ears, and his balls – as Washington insisted – 'with or without pepper sauce'? That was the question the red-eyed troops of the Small Boys' Units of Chocolate City asked, and to which there was no answer. But, of course, to look for answers in the execution of the late President Doe was to mistake its purpose.

I saw later just how far ahead of its time that film was. It looked ahead to when we would become consumers of cruelty. Once again, Africa has showed the way. From the first hominid sucking marrow from the splintered tibia of his neighbour to the latest reality TV. It was not about providing answers; it was about providing a new form of entertainment: murdering a real man in real time in front of the cameras. And where Liberia led, the world sooner or later was sure to follow. Earless Samuel Doe, bleeding everywhere, and dying on camera, told us that the gap between showing and doing, between cinematography and killing, was shrinking fast, and the day was coming when the murder and the movie would be much the same thing, with or without pepper sauce.

She had left the back yard as it was, overgrown and remote, but there under a loquat tree, in what used to be called a servant's room, I came across him.

He said: 'My name is Noddy, sir, and you are Mr Alex.'

Clarity is helpful when you're mourning. Death is a loss, yes, but it is very confusing: you're cut off from someone you relied upon; the anchor has gone and you drift. You are the one who is lost.

His name was really Uthlabati, and it meant 'Man of Red Earth', but he preferred his other name.

He said: 'I work for the madams, sir. I am Noddy of the Five Madams. Madams Healey, Terr'Blanche, Garfinkel, Smuts and Mason. I do their gardens and I live at your house.'

I hadn't heard the term 'madam' for some time. It was a throwback to the old days and that, too, was comforting. He would have been Noddy of the Five Madams only when my mother was alive.

'She isn't here any more. She passed away this morning.'

'I know, sir.'

It was an expression of sympathy; it was also, I rather felt, a declaration of firm intent.

'Madam said you would want me to work for you.'

When I was a child, in one of many, many houses where we camped, we found a man living in the garage, and my mother kept him on.

'What else could I do? He came with the house.'

Now her house was mine. And so was the man under the loquat tree, and he turned out to be one of her revolutionary bequests that were to change so many lives. She had gone but I had taken her place. That made me the fifth madam.

Strange how things turn round: we become like our parents when we get older but we don't get older till they're dead.

The funeral was set for three, on a Wednesday afternoon, blue, and shining, and I was early. Rosebank Catholic Church, on the corner of Tyrwhitt and Keyes avenues, was a broad blond building with a soaring façade, and a police station across the road. There was a sex shop on the corner: Lucky Lovers, 'Everyone's Favourite Adult Entertainment Emporium'. It sold inflatable Miss South Africas (in 'all shades of our randy rainbow nation') and genuine rhino-hide whips ('taste the sting of Africa!'). A small thicket of penis enhancers decorated the window.

I parked outside the police station. Close by I could hear the girls of the Convent of Mercy singing the *Salve Regina*, much as my mother would once have done long ago in her convent in Boksburg, where her old dad had installed her when his trips to distant parts of the continent took him away for weeks at a time, and he couldn't keep a sharp eye on her.

On the hot tarmac yard of the cop-shop, a sergeant was briefing a line of rookies on the art of shooting to kill. Several ladies of the Zoo Lake Zionists' Choir, in black skirts and white blouses and silver stars, were sitting patiently on the kerb. I hugged Nandi and Rebecca and Makania and Grace. Someone put his arm around my shoulder. It was Schevitz, wearing a dark blue suit and a red tie.

No more than a month had passed since I'd picked up his fax in Bagan, and everything had altered: the Cuban was gone, so was my mother, and I could see from his face that he felt he'd failed her when she came to see him with her marriage proposal. His mouth, always slightly droopy, worked in a way that suggested grief but came out as rage.

'I'm sorry, Alex, boy.'

'Me, too.'

'I wanted to say: she came to see me just last week. Said nothing about our little falling out, and asked me to fix up her will. I didn't need to do much. It was all down on paper, neat as a pin. I shoved in the legal bits, had it witnessed and registered. Being your old lady, it has, let's call them "aspects". I'll explain when I hand it over. Can I drop by?'

'Any time.'

'I should've helped her with the Cuban crisis, and I didn't.'

'Don't take it hard. She saved him herself in her own crazy way.'

He wasn't hearing me. What came next was what always came next: fighting talk.

'I got it wrong, or I started out from the wrong place: thinking what was right for the law. I should've remembered it's humans that count in this place, the law is just rubbish, man! She knew that; I forgot that. She was on the side of human beings. Just because things have changed doesn't mean we forget who we were, and what we believed, and become other people. They say we should be reasonable and sensible and adapt; they say we must fit in with the latest dictates of the latest bunch of gonzos who've taken over this country. That isn't just shameful – horribly shameful – it's plain wrong. "We" won: that's their argument. So we're supposed to roll over and die. So what if they won! Does it make them right? Did it make the Bolsheviks right? Or the ayatollahs in Iran? It doesn't make them right! I'm pleased you're home, Alex, because I want to talk to you about the politics of power in our country.'

I didn't really want to talk about anything of the sort at my mother's funeral. I was glad when Father Phil came over, a Nike bag slung over his shoulders.

'Will you speak today?'

'I wouldn't know what to say.'

'If you don't mind, I'd like to say something. Your mom was … noble.' He held up his Nike bag. 'Now, I'd better shuffle along to the vestry and change into my togs.'

A small pale lady with a vague look came over and shook my hand.

'I'm Miss Dewar, your organist.'

She was calm and comforting, a professional who had done these things many times.

'I take it you'd want a mix of music, in the main?'

'Yes, please.'

'Your mother was a wonder. Such carriage. Shall we say a Catholic hymn or two? Some Bach? And something African? The Zionist ladies are going to do "Swing Low, Sweet Chariot" and "By the Rivers of Babylon".'

'Thank you.'

'Come along, ladies,' trilled Miss Dewar to the Zoo Lake Zionists, who stood up, brushed down their skirts and followed her into the church.

'Carriage', 'noble': good words, if a trifle ponderous. They missed, somehow, her essence. There was something about the way my mother held herself. Always tall, always straight. If I were to add another term it would be imperious, almost, but not quite, to the point of being overweening: it was a matter of bearing. Like some great schooner she skimmed over life, over lovers, over family, over Africa.

I would also add that she had no maternal instinct I ever saw. Now she was gone I faced a puzzle. I had to do my best to live up to the expectations of being, as it were, my mother's sole surviving child. But I felt a fraud. I didn't truly connect myself with the woman we had come to bury: Kathleen Mary Healey. I carried her name, she had brought me up, she called herself my mother, and allowed the world to believe so. And yet there was something lacking between us. Even assuming that DNA tests confirmed that I was her son, it was also, and nonetheless, a learnt connection, a role I had had to grow into. I loved her, in a helpless headlong way, as did the elderly men now turning up in numbers outside the church, some in berets and some in wheelchairs and some on the arms of nurses. The truth was I hadn't the faintest idea who she was. She pretended to be my mother and I pretended to be her son. In the end we both believed it, sort of.

Being lifted now with gentle care from the back of a new Mercedes SUV with Namibian plates was Uncle Hansie; and doing the heavy lifting was a tall Herero woman in tribal costume, and a diamond bracelet, and what looked like Gucci bag and shoes, who said to me: 'I am Veseveete. Please accept my condolences on your great loss.'

Uncle Hansie, more silvered than ever by the decades, smiled as Veseveete strapped him into his wheelchair. 'She speaks English, German and Herero, and it shocks the hell out of our political masters that she lives with me. Because we Germans once massacred Hereros, they believe it's wrong for blacks to speak our language. Alexander, the world is filled with fools. Veseveete is my last mistress. My last duchess. D'you know what Veseveete means in Herero? It means "Let them die for the good of the liberation..." It commemorates the guerrilla war when parents gave their kids warrior names. Good revolutionaries always toss their kids into the bonfire of their good intentions. There is no crueller parent than a loving revolutionary. When Veseveete was five she was flown to a camp in East Germany to be trained as a little guerrilla. Then the Berlin Wall collapsed and, suddenly, in the old East Germany no one liked blackies any more. So they packed teenagers like her on a plane and flew her back to Windhoek. After ten years away they couldn't find her parents so there was a sort of auction for these unclaimed kids, and I bid for her. She was sixteen. Let me be honest: I liked her breasts, she liked my castle.'

'How is the castle, Uncle Hansie?'

He laughed. 'I am invited by the government to consider selling it to them. Willing seller, willing buyer. The invitation was delivered by five policemen with AK 47s.'

'Come on now, Hansie,' said the splendid Veseveete. 'You know that sort of talk will only upset you.' And she pushed him into the church.

'Goodbye, dear boy,' called Uncle Hansie. 'Your mother was a wonder. God bless her!'

Papadop was just pulling up in his old Datsun. Like him the car looked tired, out of date, out of luck. What struck me again and again about the whites of Africa, those still there, was how they'd aged, how little glamour was left. Once Africa was a doddle: now it was a mug's game.

He wept a little when he hugged me. 'I'm just this minute down from Zim. I miss her, boy. She was one of the best fellows I ever met.' Stooping close to my ear he whispered: 'D'you know what she did with our Cuban?'

'I do, Papadop. It was brilliant. Tell you later.'

'What's the seating plan?'

'You're in the front pew; it's for family.'

I watched him shuffle, sighing, into the church. The loss of good friends robs us of life.

I looked out for the Rain Queen; I was sure Bamadodi would come. Of my mother's feelings towards men I knew very little, but I knew she loved Queen Bama.

A hearse was turning at the corner of Tyrwhitt and Keyes, passing Lucky Lovers. The white-winged emblem was stark on the waxed black doors of the slinky limo: 'Doves' it said. It was one of my mother's old jokes: 'Storks brought you into the world; let Doves take you out.' The coffin was barely visible, lost under a foaming mound of flowers rising to the roof of the car.

I had run funeral notices in the *Star* and the *Sowetan*, asking that friends consider making a donation to Sunbeam Shelter, rather than send flowers. This had been done with malice aforethought: it seemed to me that by pelting those unimaginative creeps with unsolicited cash, I might piss them off as much as my mother's habit of hugging kids had done. My reasoning was this: an excessive and unexpected outflow of generosity was something they found hard to handle; fine, let them choke on unsolicited dough. But looking at the mountain of wreaths in the back of the hearse, it seemed no one had taken any notice.

Two black undertakers in morning suits were climbing out of the hearse.

'Excuse me, sir. You are the bereaved?'

'I am.'

'Mrs Kathleen Healey, late of Forest Town, she was your mom?'

'She was.'

'Thank you, sir; we must check.'

They began unpacking the great hill of flowers covering the casket and putting them on the roof.

'Sorry, sir. They're supposed to go on the roof to begin with. But we can't put them on the roof. Not while we're driving,' said the first undertaker.

'Why not?'

He seemed surprised at my question.

'Then what happens when we stop at the lights?'

'What happens?'

'We lose them. They can strip a car inside a few minutes.'

'People steal flowers from a *hearse*?'

'Sir, they'd steal the brass handles off the coffin, if you gave them a chance. *Eish*! This is Jo'burg.'

The second undertaker nodded hard. 'That's right. Over in Alex, sometimes they steal the coffin from the grave. They dig them up, and sell them second-hand.' He lifted up to his chin a huge bunch of lily of the valley: his face peered over the wall of waxy purity like some clerical imp in a dog-collar. 'You don't know about the slimmer's scam?'

'I don't.'

The convent choir in the school next to the church began singing the *Salve Regina* in high treble voices that sent shivers down my spine. Across the road in the yard of the police station the instructor teaching rookies how to shoot to kill was yelling at his men: ' Nummer wan! Never go into a crime scene without back-up. Nummer twooo! Remember: body shot beats brain shot, hands down!'

And so it was: while the police sergeant talked body shots and the convent girls praised the Queen of Heaven, the men from Doves told me of the slimmer's scam, and they were not mocking, not cynical, but carefully explanatory; they took me for a foreigner, and they wanted to talk about their city, about its habits and customs.

'What happens, sir, is like this: you find someone with slimmer's, right?' Undertaker One measured between his open hands, so close the palms almost touched. 'Someone thin, thin, thin. Like this, but who's got a bit of time to go, right? If they're too thin, then it's no good.'

'Unless you put them in a fat suit,' said Undertaker Two. 'And not everyone's got a fat suit; fat suits don't grow on trees.'

'This is how they do it,' Undertaker One continued, having allowed the point about fat suits to sink in. 'You take your slimmer to the hairdresser and you buy her new clothes and get her to look almost OK. And then you send her on a shopping spree to buy everything, everything, everything you tell her. On credit. Furniture, TV, you name it. And when it's delivered, you pack it in a lorry, pay her good bucks for food money, beer money, fun money – whatever – and you tell her: "Have a good time, enjoy yourself" and then off you go and you flog the stuff chop-chop. When the shops send in the bailiffs to repossess, it's all gone, it's walked: fridge, carpets, Hoover … all gone.'

'So has the slimmer,' said Undertaker Two. '*Eish!*' He laughed in praise, in admiration, in disbelief. 'No one to arrest, no one to blame. That's the slimmer's scam.'

Into their voices there crept that note of astonished horrified pride this town inspired in its citizens.

The undertaker's men assembled a little trolley. 'We're taking Mom inside now, sir. Can you please stand here and watch the florals?'

I was watching the florals when a woman came over to me, with the controlled totter of a woman on very high heels, in a very tight skirt. She was somewhere in her late twenties, I reckoned, with dark hair and a complexion of pure honey. Her eyes were green and her fingers ringless. She was dressed more for a wedding than a funeral. A low-slung pink blouse, a very frilly hat. She rested one hand on the head of a boy of about seven. He had fairish hair and a flattish nose and a flattish face and I knew before I saw the slanting eyes that this was a Down's child. He carried a tennis racket, which he swished from side to side, and she had to watch him carefully, or he might have swatted a number of mourners.

'I'm Cindy,' she said. 'I worked with your mom at Sunbeam Shelter. This is Benny.'

The boy had the biggest smile I ever saw and he held on to my fingers after we'd finished shaking hands and he said: 'You play tennis?'

'I do.'

'Oh, let's!' Benny tugged my hand.

'Not now, darling,' said his mother. 'First, we're going to say goodbye to Kathleen.'

'Where's Kathleen gone?' asked Benny

'To Heaven,' said his mother firmly. 'Accompanied by clouds of angels.'

'Don't you mean crowds?' asked the second undertaker, loading wreaths on to the trolley.

'No, I mean clouds,' said Cindy with the air of a woman who knows her own mind. 'Kathleen hated crowds. Look at all the lovely flowers!'

'I asked people not to send flowers. I asked them to make donations to the Shelter. Looks like no one paid attention.'

She looked at me kindly. 'I'm sure they paid attention. Maybe they also wanted to give flowers.'

'I thought donations were best, even though they fired her.'

'I know. I worked there, too.'

'Yes. And when she was fired, she told me that you went, too.'

'I had to. She was my friend and what they did was bad.'

'Why did they fire her?'

Cindy screwed up her nose and shook her head. She had a beautifully balanced head, sitting on a shaft of neck. Very, very neat was Cindy.

'I think she had this effect on the kids. I think the management did not know what to make of it. Voluntary helpers had special tasks – like washing the kids, drawing, singing, painting – but your mom didn't do any of that. She'd start OK but inside two minutes there'd be this love-fest going on. They'd sit on her lap and cry or laugh or just sit, and she'd tell them stories. The permanent staff couldn't deal with it.'

'Why? What was so bad about it that they got rid of her? I simply don't get it. Actually, the whole business baffles me. I don't know why she did it anyway. My mother was not the sort to go around hugging anyone.'

'Perhaps she felt she had to. I don't know what the chemistry was, but you'd find her and some kid hugging the life out of each other. It happened all the time. It was like she never had any babies of her own and these kids had never had a mother.'

She looked at me reflectively, as if somehow along the road I had failed to provide my mother with the sort of huggable heaven she'd found in Sunbeam Shelter.

A chauffeur-driven BMW was pulling up and out of it got my old friend, Koosie. He looked elegant, if very thin. His tie was dark blue, his suit black, his chauffeur was white.

'Sad day, Alex.'

I said to Cindy, 'This is my friend, Koosie, Dr Nkosi, as he now is. I can't get used to it.'

Koosie shook her hand and said, as much to her as to me: 'There's a lot he can't get used to. It's something that maybe runs in the family.'

'I have a philosophical problem', I said, 'with forced change.'

Koosie said to Cindy: 'He means a political problem. About freedom.'

We stood there; it wasn't the time to quibble. Koosie and I fell out because he took a view of the world that I rejected. He was in power now, or close to it, and that messed things up. Worst of all was what it did to words. The big talk that followed liberation played hell with all the good old words. People talked of freedom when they really meant power. Power was what counted. And hot air.

Koosie said: 'I went into politics; Alex went into air-con.'

It was just as well the undertakers came back then with the empty trolley.

'We'll take the florals now. Thanks, sir.'

Koosie said: 'I'm sure your ma told you about our meeting.'

'She did.'

'What did she do with the Cuban?'

'He's fine.'

'I won't ask what that means. You tell me about it some time?'

'Sure.'

'Come and see me.'

'I don't feel good in government offices.'

'I'm not working right now. See me at home. In Soweto.'

'I've never been to Soweto,' said Cindy.

Koosie shrugged. 'That's OK. It's normal. About ninety per cent of people have never been to a township. But Alex here, he was named after one. Ask him to tell you about it. No – better – get him to bring you when you come to see me.'

'Can we please go and see Kathleen now?' Benny asked.

Cindy and Benny and I walked down the aisle towards the coffin, which was set on the third step of the altar, banked with flowers and patrolled by Father Phil in his emerald-green togs looking like a kind of holy scrum-half.

The organist was playing '*Panis Angelicus*', 'Bread of Angels', a curiously appropriate hymn. The outer skin of Rosebank Church was a golden biscuit colour but inside it was a lime-green meringue; the light filtering through the stained-glass windows was filled with motes of dust that seemed to sway in time to the organ. The Zoo Lake Zionists took over from the organist and gave us 'Swing Low, Sweet Chariot'.

'Where's Kathleen?' asked Benny.

Cindy didn't answer.

'Is she in the box?'

'Yes, Benny,' said his mother. He didn't look like he believed her and I didn't blame him.

Benny was right to be sceptical. My mother had been an escape artist. The coffin on the altar under its weight of

cellophane, crêpe bows, notes, ribbons, lilies and orchids was
like the pillow stuffed under the blankets by the prisoner who
has fled his cell: a decoy designed to buy time.

My grandfather once said about her:

'Kathleen was like the wind. Tie her down with baling wire
and she'd slip the knot like a lubricated rabbit.'

'Lubricated', I said, 'means drunk.'

He said, 'It does, when used of me. Then it means drunk,
plastered, slammed. When used of your mother, it means slip-
pery, gone in a flash, like greased lightning.'

From first to last my mother proved him right; and now, one
more time, she'd slipped the knot. She was off and she didn't
know where she was going. Neither did I: she hadn't filed a
flight plan.

Benny said: 'Why's she in that box?'

'Don't point,' said his mother.

'Why?'

'It's rude. Look at these pretty flowers. Shall we look at the
flowers?' said Cindy.

There were wreaths from the ANC: 'With deep appreciation … Kathleen – Who Flew Many Comrades to Safety'.
There were flowers sent via Interflora by uncles in Kenya and
Umhlanga Rocks and America and Scotland. There were
wreaths signed Siegfried and Llewellyn and Boetie, from men
who wrote their messages in shaky ballpoint: 'Gone but Never
Forgotten' and 'Flying High In My Heart' and '*Rus in Vrede
Ouus*' and '*Hamba gahle*'. There were also tributes signed with
the sorts of names people used when they wrote letters to
the papers, denouncing the rape of babies and/or the lousy
pronunciation of radio announcers: pseudonyms like 'Zulu
Warrior', 'Lover-Boy' and 'Oscar–Romeo'.

I said, to myself really: 'Why don't they sign their names?'

Cindy raised an eyebrow. 'Secret admirers? Could be, hey?'

'But pen names on funeral wreaths?'

'*Ja*, well, no. But this isn't the sort of place anyone just comes out and says what they think. For ages no one signed his name to anything if he could avoid it. Where, if you asked the President a question at an election meeting, he sent the secret police round. Even today, when the President hears that rivals want his job, he calls in the secret service to suss them out. Not long ago, even reading things could be tricky. Everyone's been hiding for so long it's like a habit.'

'It still strikes me as pretty odd. A grown man signs himself "Love-Lorn of Cyrildene" on a bunch of lily of the valley, which he sends to a dead woman, and everyone nods and says, oh *ja*, that's how it is.'

Cindy shrugged. 'That is how it is.'

When I saw the ring of white roses with the simple message '*Hey Mambo!*', and I knew the Cuban had seen the funeral notice.

Even in her absence, there was more to my mother than most people dreamt of: she was large, she opened spaces, and the sheer range of mourners in Rosebank Church that day testified to a most unSouth-African breadth. In the front pew reserved for family I sat with Koosie and Jake Schevitz, Uncle Hansie and his mistress, Cindy and Benny, Papadop, who wept easily and quietly, and Noddy, the gardener, who came in last of all, and carried a Tyrolean hat with a rainbow feather.

And that mix was a pretty faint selection of the sort of wild richness she had relished all her life: a politician from Soweto, a Jewish lawyer, a German aristocrat, his Herero mistress, as well as an ex-Greek, a Jo'burg dolly-bird, with a sweet and ruffled-looking boy who kept pointing up to the dust floating through the candy-coloured light from the stained glass windows and saying: 'Look, it's clouds of angels!'

Behind us sat Mozambicans, Zimbabweans, Kenyans and Malawians; blokes who once farmed in Africa, then took the gap and headed 'Down South', leaving behind the ranches and fisheries, safaris, mission schools, forests and farms they once called their own, and loved to distraction.

How many of her friends found their way that day! There were even a few of the last old white hunters still in Africa, those who hadn't gone off to the States to open safari parks, where African buffalo and white rhino wandered under the American sun. There was 'Scrubber' Atkinson, who had once killed a leopard with a knife and had half of his face ripped off by the leopard's dewclaw and now wore a kind of highway-man's mask over his mouth which he lifted only to eat and drink; and old 'Slapper' Dewey, the gypsy hunter who, in his teens during the thirties, went hunting with the Prince of Wales; and 'Tick-Bite' Tallinger, who was said to have had an affair with Grace Kelly when she came out to film with Clark Gable; and Big Bill Bruma, who shot his brother by mistake when the bullet carried straight through the lion and out the other side.

Old friends from Stanleyville, and Salisbury, and Lourenço Marques; wraiths and shadows of their once huge selves, from town and countries that were, like them, sad phantoms. Once so sure of themselves, so secure, so effortlessly superior, so rich, so ruddy, so stolid it seemed nothing would ever shift them.

When I was a kid my mother used to take me the Muthaiga Club in Nairobi. I would sit in front of the fireplace and eat oxtail soup and listen to the hunting talk. The words: '*Na Kupa Hati M'Zuri*' were carved above the fireplace.

MAY GOOD FORTUNE FIND YOU ALWAYS ...

The high-pitched, reedy, lisping English voices calling for more champagne, talking guns.

'I was out near Makindu station, with Frenchy Du Preez. I had my .375 and I went for a brainer. Hit the buff well, but a touch high because he came at us like a bloody locomotive. Next thing: blam! Frenchy's big .500 blasts, right next to my ear, and the buff goes down like an oak, not two feet from me.

'Careless, Alfie, very careless ...' was all that bloody Frog said. Talk about *sang* bloody *froid*!'

My mother once pointed out that, before independence, whites hunted widely across Africa; after independence, whites were widely hunted, and often shot. Odd how many died violently.

And she'd reel them off: John Alexander, Dian Fossey, George and Joy Adamson ...

And she'd say: 'At least they're dead, and not living on, like Beryl.'

She meant Beryl Markham whom she'd met when she was a girl and kept up with during all those years, after Karen and Bror Blixen and that world faded. She used to drop in on Beryl in Nairobi, now an old woman in a small concrete house, drinking gin and orange at a terrific rate, and trying to remember the places where she'd once flown; taking out a rusted tin box with her flight maps, and the bush air strips, to chart the great solo flight she'd once made across the Atlantic.

'Beryl keeps being robbed. The last time landed her in hospital with a cracked skull. Alone, you see, and old. But all she wanted to know was had I flown recently to Mara-Mara or to Oloitokitok?'

Among the mourners, too, that day, were some who still lived where they'd always lived, and had flown down to Jo'burg for her funeral: the Africa lovers, the big talkers, the 'I am devoted to the continent and I'll fucking knock your head off if you don't love it too' brigade. There was Rex Thistledown from the Kenyan Highlands, one of the few white ranchers still going in Kikuyuland, son of old Nicky Thistledown who used to hunt with my mother, drink with Hemingway and whore with Bror Blixen. Rex, the poor bastard, was what so many once wild and improper white settlers had been reduced to: good causes and keeping quiet. Rex was into ecology now, saving elephants on his 50,000 highland acres, and saving his acres from the Kikuyu tribesmen who persisted in believing his land belonged to them, and had started invading it, waving pictures of Robert Gabriel Mugabe, a continental hero ever since he'd started booting white settlers out of Zim. In the fifties, Rex's dad, Sir Nicky, known as the nabob of Nairobi, once rode his horse into the club with a naked blonde over the saddle and drank a stirrup-cup to the cheers of assembled diners. By contrast, Rex drove an old Range Rover, didn't drink and, like lots of Kenyans, he kept a farm in South Africa, as a kind of insurance against the day the Kikuyu finally won, and kicked him off the land.

Behind us there was a row of ancient chaps in their blue blazers, their rheumy eyes blinking back tears, all of them lovers of my mother, all of them lost in an Africa they had not bargained for, narrowed and angry and young and hostile. But one person who didn't pitch that day – and it surprised me – was Queen Bama.

Father Phil was in the pulpit.

'We come to say goodbye to Kathleen, a towering woman who changed lives, who flew and fished and hunted; who did not just aim for the stars, she was one. Conservationist, Africanist, a woman with the poise of a fashion model. A woman whose innate warmth was like some great and good campfire; a woman from this town who was made of the treasure of this town, a heart of gold … a mother who had children reaching out to her; and hunters toasting her around the campfire. I am sad she is not here; I miss her deeply. She shone so brightly that to mourn her too deeply, to grieve too greatly, is natural enough, but I for one would rather celebrate her amazing life.'

It was rum. Very. Here was a man dressed like a Christmas tree and speaking by common consent, rather well. Cindy was weeping. It was exactly what we always do at such times, run the fancy stuff alongside the real stuff. Standing up in the pulpit, in his Erin-green togs, talking nonsense about my mother, was one of the last of her lovers. The priestly role in Africa was about as odd as the ruffian's, the entrepreneur's and the explorer's. The same love of dressing up, the do-goodery; the desire Africa inflicts on otherwise intelligent people to go around succouring the weak, saving the sick, and alternately seducing and savaging the same. All in the name of 'love'.

Next to me, Papadop shifted and wept. Papadop, who used to tell me about Father Silverio, the poor little Porto palooka four centuries before, who sat by the waters of the Musengezi River, just as Papadop had done, as the Cuban did, as I had done. Silveria was the first white man in Mount Darwin, just as poor Papadop, a thoroughly fucked by now ex-Greek ex-South African, ex-Zimbabwean ex-everything, was today the last.

It was amazing how these things connected up. Everything joined and converged: Father Phil, the sad figure of Papadop slumped in the pew, the Cuban's wreath. The Cuban whom Papadop hid in his hut beside the Musengezi, the river into which the first white man in Mount Darwin had been tossed to appease the crocodile gods.

My mother had never recognised this Africa. She had simply sailed over the top of it, and so made good her escape. Believing you could be who you were, disdaining even to regard colour; she did Africa without doing race. But those she left behind were finding that option wasn't available any more, despite the lies, the sweet talk, the high hopes: we were saddled with the skin we wore.

Amazing and terrible to face it, after half a century of thinking of nothing but colour, tribe, blood and race; and swearing that whatever happened in the future, we would never do it again. Not only were we doing it again; it was the only game in town.

When I left the church, I found Queen Bamadodi's praise-singer waiting for me across the road, outside the sex shop. He was in full regalia and he was shifting from leg to leg. Maybe he figured the shop offered a neutral backdrop. Clearly, he didn't feel too relaxed, turning up in knee-rattles and monkey tails at a Christian funeral.

He had not come in the royal limo; he was there by taxi, a packed minibus waiting for him across the road. He was wearing a Swatch and for some reason this troubled me. A modish Swiss timepiece on the wrist of an old royal retainer who has to use a taxi ... Things must be bad for Queen Bama.

Only his greeting still had the rich old ring.

'I bring you blessings from the great cloud of plenitude, she who makes the rivers run and waters the world. She without whom all would be desert and dust. The great udder of heaven embraces the son of Kathleen and asks him to visit her in the Great Place.'

I felt sorry for him. He had to get a cab back home to the Magaliesberg, and he knew he'd better arrive with news the Rain Queen wanted to hear. I understood and appreciated the honour I was being accorded yet I did not want to go. It made no sense. The Rain Queen did not entertain men, she did not have sons, she did not care for husbands and, whichever way you looked at it, I was a man, and a white man to boot.

But she was part of my family.

The praise-singer was anxious to be off; his taxi hooted.

I said I'd come.

He was relieved: 'There will be feasting and rejoicing in the Queen's Great Place.' Then he thought it over, and said, carefully: 'There will be rejoicing. Look, I have marked the way.' And he gave me a tourist map, which read: 'Welcome to the Magical Magaliesberg, in the Platinum Province. A Bird Watchers' Paradise.'

Then he consulted his Swatch, and shoved off.

IV   Golden City Blues

'I am not defenceless; I have a Lüger in my locker.'
West with the Night, Beryl Markham

22

I saw no one for some weeks after the funeral except for the gardener. In the time I lived in my mother's house in Forest Town I had no better friend or companion than the Red Earth Man. Nothing I said persuaded him that Noddy was a poor substitute for his real name. He was Noddy – Noddy of the Five Madams – and it did not bother him one bit.

In the afternoons I'd walk in the Zoo. When I was little my mother took me riding on the elephant, swaying in the wooden seat, high up on his back. She held tight to the brass bar. She said the world looked better from an elephant's back. Afterwards, we visited the lions and she'd point and say, 'Golly, just *look* at those teeth.' Then we'd wander over to the monkey cages and watch people feeding peanuts to the chimps. People would be yelling and throwing and pointing and jigging up and down; sometimes they threw orange peel, which the monkeys caught and could not eat.

'Honestly, how cruel can you get?' my mother said. 'I really can't tell which side of the bars the monkeys are on, can you?'

You need time and some space to mourn.

There had been changes at the Zoo. The elephants still took kids for rides and the lions were as yellow as ever. But the cages had gone. The animals lived in enclosures dotted about with trees and veld grass and waterholes. A deep trench kept people further away from the chimps, so they couldn't throw nuts at the chimps. Down the road a bit, across a moat filled with clean green water, lived a gorilla.

Things take you in strange ways when you're grieving. I began hanging around the gorilla. I felt the way neglected kids feel: they cling to the nearest friendly stranger. It's not real love. It's replacement therapy. They don't want you really; they want their mothers. You aren't her and they know you aren't, but you'll do to hang on to till what they've lost comes back.

They didn't have a gorilla in the old days but my mother would have liked him. She had a great sense of wonder, and a fine sense of fear. The two went together, which is why she thrilled to see the lions' teeth. The gorilla had a whole environment to play in; he had trees with old car tyres swinging from their branches, and a hill built of fake rocks with a little cave halfway up where he could rest from the hot sun. A ramp led up the back of the fake hill and entered the gorilla's cave. This was the keeper's entrance. The gorilla's name was written on a big sign over his enclosure: 'Rwandan Gorilla, Origin Kigali'. Just that: pretty bald, pretty lonely, take-it-or-leave-it sort of stuff.

One day Noddy asked if he could come with me to the Zoo and it became a regular outing, two guys taking a walk. He showed me pictures of his wife. She looked young, perhaps twenty-five, with that burnished glow of young Matabele women.

'She is called Beauty, Mr Alex, and I have two kids with her. My sons are Joshua and Sipho and they are at school and the fees must be paid each month.'

He showed me pictures of Joshua and Sipho. Bright and shining faces, in school ties and crisp white shirts. His sons were happy at the school. It was run by a good principal, 'one of our best men'. He said this with unusual force, as if I was going to argue with him.

'My wife, she works in the school. Some days each week, in the office of the principal himself. He's a first-class fellow.'

Like many migrant workers, Noddy had no papers. If he was picked up he'd be jailed and deported. I couldn't see it happening because I couldn't see Noddy in jail; it was hard to think of Noddy doing anything that warranted it. He was simply too decent a man, too responsible, too caring of his wife Beauty and his two boys. He was so solid that, next to him, I felt like a vagrant, a gypsy.

'Jo'burg people don't like immigrants, they don't like me. I am not from here, sir. I am foreign from Matabeleland, I go there twice a year. Where are you foreign from?'

'I am foreign from South Africa.'

'But where is your home?'

I tapped the ground with my toe. 'This is my home.'

He thought about that and I saw he got my drift. Not all of us feel at home at home.

'It is hard to be a traveller.'

'Why is that, Noddy?'

'A traveller loses all he leaves behind.'

He was homesick, like all of us. He had left home and headed down to Jo'burg for the same reason that anyone ever came to Jo'burg: for the loot. He did piece-work in five gardens six days a week; it paid a fair cash wage and he sent most of it home to his family in Matabeleland.

If I liked anything in particular about Noddy it was his wide range. He was many things. Travel, distance, other places, other worlds, and other ways: these things are very hard for

Johannesburgers to live with. They take offence. Jo'burgers
believe their city to be the very hub, the navel of the world.
They think it is like New York or Chicago. It's not, of course.
If it is like any American city, in its sprawl, its smog, its money,
its drive-by shootings, then it is remotely like Los Angeles.
But tell people that and they think you're putting them down.
Very few of them have even been to these American cities but
that never stopped a Jo'burger knowing what was what. And
telling you.

Noddy didn't like the government of Zimbabwe. He talked
politics with me, he talked easily, he didn't have any of the
brittle concern about sounding the right way that so gets to
people down South.

'They sent the Korean killers, the Fifth Brigade, they
murdered our people and threw their bodies down old mine-
shafts.'

Noddy noticed how the clothes of the people killed in those
shafts were mingled with bits of bone.

'It's a miracle, Mr Alex. Our clothes last longer than our
bodies. Ha, it makes me sad.'

When I think back now I know we were useful to each
other. Without him, I would have been even more lonely. I was
back in a city that had been my own and I found I wasn't really
there any more. I felt like one of those shades in the underworld, anxious, plaintive, always wanting news of the real
world. So the flesh-and-blood guy I found in the back-yard
room was a gift. We had more in common with each other
than we did with those we should have been closest to. I got his
company, and in exchange he got a free room; that was very
important to him, the room. Without it, he would have been
forced to rent a room in Alexandra Township, a tiny shed

carved out of someone's garage. And having to pay through the nose for the privilege. He wrinkled his forehead; Alex was too bad, too dangerous, too much drink, too many guns. He would get lost in Alex.

I see now that Noddy was very kind to me. He knew I was adrift, he knew I was lost. He knew that too many years on the road had addled my brains; and, especially, he knew I was hurting. We were foreign natives in a strange city and foreign natives had to look out for each other. He had travelled, he knew a man can live in more than one place, and if he does he will be more than one person. And that's all right.

Back home in Matabeleland Noddy was a landowner: he had his own farm, he raised cattle and goats, he had peach and apricot orchards. He was in every sense a man of substance, a fact very hard to square with the piece-work gardener in his grey trousers and his T-shirt. He had about him weightiness, a gravitas quite out of keeping with his size, his little hands and his neat feet. Solid, reliable, these were the things that struck you about Noddy, even if he was barely five feet tall and so fragile he looked as if the wind would knock him over. He had standards, ideals; a man of quality, he did all the things you're supposed to do to get on. In another, better world he would have been helping to run his country.

We were two foreign natives talking about China and Iceland and Montenegro and he liked that because it made him not seem too far away from all he knew and loved, his farm with its fruit trees, his wife Beauty, his boys.

For day-to-day work in the garden Noddy wore grey flannels and a white T-shirt. The T-shirt showed an Alp and the Swiss flag, and read 'Gstaad, my Love'. On Sundays he went to the Methodist church over in Parktown North; he wore a dark blue pinstripe suit and black shoes, and his hat, a beautiful dark brown shapely confection with a generous brim and a black hatband. Riding athwart the hatband was a brilliant pheasant feather – a jaunty cockade. What we had in common was that home lay behind us. What I got from him was a sense of relief that things did not have to be the same, always and everywhere – which is what death insists on. He gave me other ways of being, he stood out against death, he was good in bereavement. Death is monotone, unalterable, it reduces us to bone and bits of clothing. It is the ultimate application of force. Death is radical that way, it threatens your own life and so you seek reassurance. Noddy reassured me because there were so many versions of the man. He was never monotone, he was many-sided. He was versatile. Noddy in the week, Noddy on Sundays, grandest of all, Noddy, country squire.

Only the feather in his hat pointed to some other life that was garish, noisy, fast and loose. It is not too much to say that when he wore that hat both lives were on show: one down-to-earth, dependable; the other floating and brash.

He liked fine feathers. And he loved the costume museum across the road that had been created by the Bernberg sisters. I could still remember when I was a boy seeing the sisters walking out in the afternoons to catch the bus to dancing classes. They wore white stockings and ballet pumps and must have been in their seventies. My mother watched them with scorn. 'What do they think they look like?', she would say. 'Who do they think they are?'

The tiny Bernberg sisters always dressed to kill. Sometimes they were 1920s flappers; sometimes vamps, in short black skirts and white stockings and flat shoes and berets or cloche hats. When they held hands at the bus stop, which was right outside their house, they looked like very old little girls dressed up for a party. They were a splash of colour in an otherwise dull street, dancing birds of paradise in Forest Town.

When the sisters died they left their house and their fashion collection to the city of Johannesburg. The rooms were filled with costumes of the eighteenth, nineteenth and twentieth centuries. The models stood in glass showcases wearing Voortrekker shawls, or slinky cocktail numbers from the 1930s. There were national costumes from a dozen countries. There were even examples of the great Parisian couturiers like Coco Chanel. The Bernbergs had cherished what in Jo'burg did not rate: the pretty, the delicate and the foreign.

Noddy liked it that I knew nothing about gardens and he decided to teach me odd things from time to time. 'Removing the buds on your dahlias gives better blooms, Mr Alex.' He set the tines of two sharp garden forks at the neck of a dahlia plant so that they locked around its throat like fingers.

'Dahlia tubers should be lifted from the ground – like this. It stops you breaking their necks.'

I didn't much care for dahlias, but there it was. I didn't plan to learn to raise dahlia tubers without breaking their necks.

Now and then, so strongly it shook me, I felt that Noddy was the key to something vital, if only I could see it. He could not tell me; he could only hope I saw it. I did not. I fell into the worst sort of provincialism; he was the country I could never quite grasp the reality of, so I doubted its reality. I tried to understand him by referring only to myself.

Noddy saved his money in the Natal Building Society and his book was fat and neat and shiny and tied with two elastic bands in a red rubber cross. He showed it to me, cupping it in the cradle of his fingers, rather in the way the tines of the two forks intermeshed when he lifted the dahlia tubers. Here were his wages; here was the monthly sum he sent home to his wife.

We talked of climate and customs and politics. Was it very cold in England, or very dangerous in America? Did they also hate foreigners in other countries?

Noddy would stand at the great apes' enclosure and read off the description: 'Rwandan Gorilla, Origin Kigali'. There was an air of grief about that gorilla. So it felt to us. He came from many miles north, from mountains and forest, to this penitentiary beside the war museum that is the Jo'burg Zoo.

'He is also a foreign native, Mr Alex.'

Sometimes he sighed and I knew he was thinking of his boys who went to school at St Aloysius where his wife Beauty worked in the office of the principal who was a first-class fellow.

Jake Schevitz eased himself into the blue Dralon chair, and he gave me the crooked smile I knew so well. Behind his head was Livingstone's water-colour sketch of Victoria Falls; the path that snaked up to the Falls was inked in royal blue and it seemed, from where I sat, to grow out of Schevitz's left ear.

'It must be strange, to be here without her.'

'It's the emptiness. It feels like I've been living all my life next to some huge engine. A turbine. Or a waterfall. A bloody Victoria Falls so loud, so monstrous, I couldn't hear myself think. And now suddenly it has been switched off; and the silence is harder to deal with.'

Schevitz got up and came over and put his arm around my shoulders.

'You going to stay on?'

'Yes. At least until I make sure everyone gets what she left them. I promised her that.'

'Well, don't be a stranger. Give me a bell, we'll hit a few pubs.'

I said I would but I could see he didn't really believe me, and I could see, too, that he was relieved. Jake Schevitz might have been an old friend, but I had been away a long time and he no longer knew what to say to me. I wasn't who I had been. My being-awayness had emptied me of the stuff that made recognisable South Africans: brawn, blood, beer, BMWs, ballistics, balls, as well as any amount of passionate bullshit. It had ruined me for flesh-and-blood company. I was living in my mother's house but to Schevitz I was more ethereal than she was. She might be dead but I was the real ghost.

Jake handed me a heavy buff envelope. On the envelope was typed in capitals: 'Last Will and Testament of Kathleen Mary Healey'.

'Keep your head down, Alexsy boy. It's loaded. Hand-grenades from heaven. She had a helluvuh sense of humour, your old lady. She's parcelled out her stuff in such a way that it's either exactly what you might have liked, or the last thing you'd ever want. For instance, I get her Spanish dictionary and grammar books and *Spanish for Early Learners*. Lest I forget I stood between her and happy marriage to a toy-boy defector half a century younger than her.

I began to see what she had meant in those last moments when she had extracted from me the promise to see to all her 'things'. Her bequests had been chosen with a certain Olympian piquancy. The pairing of gift and recipient calculated to keep her smiling in the after-life. Schevitz got the Spanish dictionaries; I got Noddy, the house and garden.

And that was just the start.

Cindy September inherited her flying jacket, boots, leather helmet and goggles. I phoned her and she explained, as one might a visitor from another planet, where she lived.

'D'you know Sheerhaven?'

I did not.

'Well, for sure you know Lonehill?'

Cindy's sonic history vibrated down the phone line. Her long 'a's deepening into '*j-a-a-r*'; her short 'a's fading into flat – 'flet'– 'e's. Her constant use of 'ut' to express surprise or solidarity: 'Uzzzut, hey?' Each note a marker, a flag, an identity. The places out of which we evolved had been scratched on the way we spoke, in much the way slave-shackles rubbed raw the wrists of the prisoners they encumbered. We were what we sounded, until we sounded different.

She was incredulous when I said no again, but she was game.

'Y'know Halfway House?'

'I do.'

'OK. *Ja* … Let's see then. *Ut's* easy to find … if you know how to get on to the William Nicol Highway. That's where your mom was in the clinic. OK? Get on the William Nicol, and just keep going. Don't branch right for Halfway House when you hit Buffalo Belle's.'

'What's that?'

She laughed, short and, I thought, slightly bitter. 'You don't know *thet* either? Everyone knows Buffalo Belle's. You can't miss *ut*. Anyway, you don't want to stop there, that's for bloody sure. Aim for Monte Casino.'

'Monte Casino?'

'A ginormous bloody place, like an Eyetalian town. Couple of k's after *thet*, make a left and you're there. Big gates; lotsaguards. You'll see a Woolworth's smack bang opposite the gate. If you see a Checkers opposite the gate, you're at the wrong gate. Woollie's *uz* the smart end. Ask for me when you get to the gate. See you now-now.'

When I met Cindy at my mother's funeral I'd have said she was probably from somewhere down in the Cape. Mixed race, 'Coloured'. But listening to her on the phone, I'd have put her down as white Jo'burgundian, northern suburbs, possibly Jewish.

Wrong on both counts.

I was driving out into the flat veld of the northern reaches, where the names of walled, gated and guarded suburbs – Fourways, Lonehill, Halfway House – spoke up for what they were: border outposts on Jo'burg's long march north, its rush to leave behind its other older self among abandoned skyscrapers and shrinking mine-dumps. Jo'burg was on the move and it was taking the city with it. Shiny shopping malls stood shoulder to shoulder with glossy auto show-windows stuffed with mouth-watering new models, glinting and winking at the drivers stuck in the endless traffic jams in much the way whores patrolled for trade on street corners: hoiking their skirts and flashing their pants at passing punters.

Do it with product; do it with pussy. Same difference, as they said around here.

I kept hearing Cindy's voice as I drove. 'Woollie's *uz* the smart end ...'

Somehow, the entire fucking history of the country was lodged in that phrase.

I'd grown up in what I believed was the 'real' Johannesburg of years gone by, when there was nothing north of Sandton and Fourways on the map, it simply didn't rate: a stretch of nothing between Krugersdorp and Pretoria. Well, it wasn't nothing any more.

The flat stretches north of Johannesburg were pullulating with intense termitic activity. I was in a solid line of very slow-moving traffic; expensive traffic: 4x4s and Mercs and BMWs, stuck in a jam tailing back all the way to the outskirts of the old Jo'burg. There was new world fervour, giant cranes and tiny workers swarming over the rising walls and roofs of what were becoming walled estates, stockaded cluster suburbs. Pinned to the walls of these gated refuges 'For Sale' signs showed grainy photographs of estate agents, etched into the metal: Evaleigh and Trompie and Charlotta were happy to flog you the padded cell of your dreams in the fortified cluster villages where everyone lived safe, certified lives.

The melancholy faces reminded me of something I could not for the moment quite identify.

Everywhere bulldozers rolled forward on great rubber knees, preparing the ground for yet more temples anointed with the names of faint yet still magical European memory: Mon Plaisir and Ma Provence, La Capri, Tuscan Heights, Tuscany Towers, Casa Tuscana, Linga Longa, Le Mistral, Verona Heights and Aquitainia ...

Then, rising out of the flat veld, I saw it: a russet fortress with turrets and battlements. Monte Casino. I remembered there had been a famous battle fought by South African troops against the Germans in a place of that name but I did not imagine for a moment that whoever built this giant gambling joint, masquerading as a castle in Italy, had in mind a far-off battle in a war no one remembered. No, this piece of mountainous kitsch was about the new South Africa, increasingly, also, a giant casino and clip joint that totted up its assets in poker chips.

Next thing I saw was a ranch house, an arch of entangled cowboy hats and lariats, surmounted by a pair of big neon horns, and the legend: 'Buffalo Belle's – Love's Our Life-Style!' Cindy had been right. You couldn't miss it.

A few minutes on and I came to a set of steel gates, a guard-house and, yes, Woolworth's across the road. I'd hit Sheerhaven; the smart end. The double wall that looped around the estate reminded me of the old barrier between East and West Berlin, fifteen feet high and topped with electric fencing.

A discreet notice at the front gate advised: 'Attention. There is enough power in this fence to cause fatal injury.'

The CCTV cameras looked me over; the guards asked my name and business, then they signed me in and phoned Cindy who said: 'Oh, hi, Alex. Glad you found *ut*. Just tell the gate you want Beauchamp Drive.'

Beauchamp Drive lay on the other side of Hampstead Ponds and below Berkshire Meadows. Cindy's house was a three-storey villa, all columns and colonnades, with windows above the huge portico that reminded me of the White House. Two life-sized copper cranes stood on the lawn; a pink Porsche was parked out front; the garden walls were painted in Ndebele zigzags of green and black.

Cindy wore white jeans and a top of gilded silk and her dark hair was piled high. It was good to see her.

Sheerhaven was built around the golf course, and it was, Cindy told me matter-of-factly, metre for metre, the priciest real estate in town, and the most closely guarded. There were armed patrols and a lethal fence; infra-red sensors were buried below the wall to stop anyone thinking of tunnelling, and there was constant TV surveillance. There was no crime in Sheerhaven, no robbery, no rape, no riots. There were also no shops, no bank, no restaurants, in fact no hustle or bustle at all. I got the feeling nothing moved, except by arrangement.

Cindy said, 'Dead right. No one is in this place who should not be in here.'

'What if you need stuff?'

'We've got Woollie's. Anything else we want gets brought in. Don't smile, I'm serious.'

'It's unreal.'

'Maybe. But we don't want reality here; we pay big bucks to make sure it doesn't come near us.'

It was my first experience of paradox in Cindy: she was sharp, quick, shrewd, unsentimental and unimpressed by much of the tinsel that so excites Jo'burgers. And yet she loved every last tacky bit of it.

She took my hand. 'Like to look around a fairy-tale house that goes with a fairy-tale life? Come see.'

She was open, affectionate, and I found her deeply appealing. In half an hour I had felt the temperature of the water in her coral-pink pool, I had seen her bedroom, with its little pathway made of resin cobbles with roses buried inside the cobbles; I had reviewed pink fairy-lights that twinkled from the plastic bough that leaned over her heart-shaped bed. I had admired her pink and green Venetian mirror that made the two of us look like mischievous leprechauns in her candy-floss cavern. I had approved of the lamps built of clunky African bracelets, and the tall African pots, and the two stressed yellowwood giraffes standing a metre tall, supporting on their heads a shelf displaying big books about the Masai, Jackie Kennedy and the latest hottest designer game lodges in Kenya.

'OK. Now we can make a little tour of Sheerhaven. It might be interesting for someone like you ...' she gave me a sideways grin I was soon to know as a sign of Cindy entering sardonic mode '... who's never seen our premier lifestyle suburb.'

We went walking, and Cindy reminded me just how rare this was. The sun shone bright on Waverley Villas and Tunbridge, on Wessex Weald and the Devonshire Downs. A long, rather graceful silver pipe, lifted high on great silver stanchions, a conduit I took to be some sort of viaduct, ran high above our heads, the fairway, the river and the rooftops. Sheerhaven's villas ranged across the architectural spectrum, from African Zen to Spanish haciendas, to French Provincial to New England; each bulking large on surprisingly small plots of land. The owners built right up to the edges of their allotted space, creating a strained and almost stifled look, at odds with the broad empty streets and the landscaped public spaces. What passing traffic I saw was made up of small, politely painted vans dashing hither and thither: 'The Flower Fairy', 'Darling Domestics', 'Hephzibah's Antiques' ... For the rest the streets were eerily empty but for the occasional black maid pushing a stroller and young kids piloting electric golf carts. On a low hill overlooking the golf course stood a large and tumbling shanty town of corrugated-iron huts and wooden hovels. Cindy saw me looking at it and she was amused.

'Our sister settlement, our face in the mirror, that's Donkergat, "Dark Hole", the squatter camp, or "informal settlement", they call it. Close by, isn't it, hey? Right in our faces. Reminds us we're related.' She was truly delighted. 'Very Jo'burg. Lest we forget.'

'Related, but behind your wall.'

'Sure. Related, but not terrorised. That's what all this is for. We live in Sheerhaven the way people used to live: with our doors open, and our kids safe, and the sun in our faces. But you only get as much of paradise as you pay for.'

Nowadays, the colour of your money was what counted; and the quality of your security. Jo'burg had gone back to core values. Whoever could stump up the bucks was welcome in the sated, gated suburbs, where road-booms shut out intruders and algae-sucking hoses called Kreepy-Krawlies chugged across the swimming-pool floor; where the high-voltage current humming in the razor wire that topped the beautiful walls sang the song of safety. A world of Lamborghinis, gunfire and sirens, where the panic button brought you instant armed response patrols and the hotline got you the 24/7 Medivac chopper. And where, even if God wasn't in his heaven, at least the sentry was on the gate. Where – on paper at least – life was perfect. On paper. But, then, perfection in this town was always paper-based, and paper-thin, and papered over with dummy shares, fake title deeds, IOUs and dodgy treasure maps.

That was Cindy's take on locking yourself away in a fortress in the veld. You bolted the doors, paid the guards, unleashed the dogs and called it heaven. Wellness within the walls: phoney, but blissful. Cindy knew that in no far-off blessed time did anyone live safe with the sun in their faces and their kids free to come and go. Time, in our terms, being measured from the moment van Riebeeck's boot hit the beach in the Cape and he began shooting Hottentots. The war had gone on since then with peace talks that lasted just long enough for the belligerents to reload. But so what? You proceeded by proclamation; you said things were bloody marvellous even when they terrified you because our terror was more bloody marvellous than the mundanity of others; and you locked up, or duffed up, anyone who disagreed. You invested time and energy creating a past that led flawlessly up to the present creation of yourself. Declared it to be the real true you; and then did it all over again. Everyone did it but no one did it better than Jo'burgers. You might have thought, if you didn't understand the enormous benefits of self-invention, that ours was a patch of veld where murder was as common as dirt; rape was rife, where the poor starved and women were attacked, often fatally, by their partners, more often than anywhere else on the planet. Cindy knew that but ignored it. A bit of steadfast denial and it was easily fixed. You just slapped in a tall wall, an electric fence, an armed patrol and – bingo – welcome to Sheerhaven, welcome to the premier lifestyle!

I rubbed it in a little. 'In what you call "the old days", people also built a Berlin wall around the bedroom. Everyone lived in daily expectation that the servants were swiping the booze, and gangs of burglars lurked in the sanitary lanes that ran between the houses, or plotted in the servants' rooms behind the houses, waiting to hit your place and clear you out of soap and silver. Everyone compared designs of burglar bars. Did you use grilles or slats or mesh? And in your choice of domestic chain mail, did you like circles or rectangles or graceful art nouveau flourishes? Did you rivet them, weld them, or bolt them? Did they spread like a grille across the space or did they spring free of the wall in wavy lines? Did they come in tasteful shades of pastel to match the face brick? These were hot questions, even then, and the pistol sat in the sock drawer, just as it does now, except now they have his and hers. What's the difference, at heart?'

She grinned. 'Something pretty crucial. We take anyone at all into the stockade. In the old days they ran a fence between people. We don't.'

'You do walls.'

'Honey, this is Jo'burg: everyone does walls between us and the outside. But inside Sheerhaven, we're totally open to anyone at all. Black, white, pink: anyone who can fork out several million bucks. The new black billionaires are really just Jo'burgers at heart: they don't want to be revolutionaries; they want to be Rand-lords … stinking rich and safe as houses. That's how it was, that's how it is. Shall we go home and have a drink?'

She carried a tray of drinks into the back garden that ran down to a stream with its view of the main fairway, off to our right. The great silver pipe soared overhead, catching the sun rather beautifully, and we sat there and drank gins and tonics.

'What's that for? Does it carry water?'

'*Thet*,' said Cindy almost proudly, 'is a sewage pipe. Weird, hey?' She clearly enjoyed my surprise. 'It takes ours, and it takes theirs, from Donkergat next door. It's our link with the outside world: our only link.'

It was quite a thought, the stuff flushed down the costly Italian-tiled toilets of Sheerhaven merging with the sewage from the even more prized – because rare – plumbed-in lavatories of Donkergat (which made do for the most part with the old bucket system). A wondrous, characteristic twinning, signified in an elegant viaduct that shimmered in the heavens above Highgate Ponds and Hampstead Heath, Cheltenham Close and Cheam Crescent, sweeping over the green fairway and the bowling club: a pipe in the sky so rich and elegant and really rather lovely, and full of shit.

'I have something my mother gave to you.'

I fetched the stuff from my car. As I was handing them over I was uncomfortably aware what a sad bundle other people's old clothes can be.

'Her pilot's gear.'

I had wrapped the flying boots and helmet and goggles in the sheepskin jacket. 'Don't look like much but they were hers and she left them to you in her will.'

Cindy held up the flying jacket; it was much too big for her. Then she picked up the flying boots. They did what boots do when made of soft leather – they buckled, and caved in.

She hugged me, and then she hugged me again, and she said, 'Thank you, thank you! Dear, dear Kathleen. I loved your mom.'

Cindy in her tenderness and her reverence made me feel sad and pleased and somehow wanting. I felt she knew more about my mother than I did; but, then, who didn't?

Cindy said: 'I've been thinking about your question: why did Kathleen hug the kids? I'd have to say it was unqualified love.'

'I'm sorry but I don't think so. Love isn't something she knew about, not love for people, at any rate. She was commanding, stubborn, arrogant, successful, passionate and because of, or maybe despite of, this, there were people who loved her. Fine. But I'm not sure if she ever loved any of them.'

She gave me the close look she'd given me at the funeral.

'It's maybe an obvious thing to say, but I think that what love is depends on what you want, or need. She was getting something when she worked with the kids. If you get what you need from someone, that's a kind of love. Even if they don't know they're giving it to you.'

'That's double Dutch.'

She shook her head. 'It isn't. You can feel love even if the person you're aiming at isn't consciously giving it to you.'

'But where is it coming from?'

'From here.' She touched her chest. 'You get it precisely because you're the one giving it. There isn't any perfect love. Something is love if it's love to you.'

'What is it to you?'

'Something that gets me out of a hole. Two people have done it for me: my mom, and my husband. Ex-husband, I mean. Bloody useful, let me tell you, if you come from where I do. No one – repeat, no one – would want to get stuck where I was. So I ask myself, what hole did it get your mom out of, loving the kids? I don't know but maybe it was something she never had from anyone else? And if you turn the question around and ask, what did the kids get from your mom? I can tell you some of it: warmth. You should've seen her with the kids; they adored her. My Benny thought she was the best thing ever. He'd climb into her lap, she'd fold him in her arms and they'd sit there, rocking … just that, no more.'

'Where is Benny now?'

'At the Shelter. When I quit, I just couldn't take him out. He loves it so much. He spends the day and I collect him around five. Want to ride with me later to fetch him?'

Cindy drove a Porsche, bubblegum pink, with black leather seats, which reminded me strongly of some sort of lingerie, a silly, sexy, powerful car that seemed absolutely right. It went with the territory, the extraordinary world of Cindy September.

'I sell property in these.' Cindy waved a hand at the fortified, look-alike, cluster communities that dotted the veld for as far as I could see. 'They're wannabe Sheerhavens. Only they don't cost the earth. But then again, they don't do paradise quite so well. I'll show you.'

She drove into Tuscany Towers, flashing her pass at the guard at the gate. It was a tight conglomeration of small ochre townhouses, each with a square of lawn and a braai area. 'Here's where the youngies start. Bladdy small. No privacy whatever. You can hear a fly land on the roof; but very, very popular with the first-homers. Not *too* pricey but you still get your gates, your walls, your guards, your instant armed response service, your peace of mind. Just because it has an Eyetalian name doesn't mean you're limited. Styles are what we call African-eclectic, which basically means French Provincial, African fusion and African Zen, as well as ethnic bush style – bush means thatch. But Tuscan is tops. Tuscan is over everything like a rash. I flog teeny little hutlets as "Genuine Tuscan-

African" – Tuscany isn't a country, it's a lifestyle. The youngies love it for a few years and then they go.'

'Where do they go?'

She blinked her surprise at me. 'Into bigger clusters. I told you, we're not selling houses, we're selling lifestyle. It's secure, it's comfortable. It's all the rage. As opposed…' she giggled '… to death style. They get the clubhouse, the braai area, the pool, floodlit tennis court, kids' playground and giant TV, so everyone can get together on weekends and watch the rugby.'

'Don't they ever go out?'

'You mean to work?'

'No, just for the hell of it.'

'Not if they can help it. Out is where they work; out is the world. Out is what you want to forget at the end of the day and over the weekends. Out is dangerous. They don't want out; they want in. Maybe they'll drive to the gym for a workout, or the shopping centre. But mostly they have it all here: some of the blocks have eateries, laundrettes. And there are plenty of pizza places outside the walls that'll deliver.'

'Do they walk?'

'Good God!' As if for reassurance, Cindy opened the glove compartment, reached inside and touched the pearl-handled butt of her pistol.

'No one, but no one in their right minds walks in Jo'burg.'

We left behind the thousands of little hutch-homes; the great crowded emptiness of Fourways and Lonehill and drove back to the city, the skyline where worlds met and collided and the minibus taxis darted, stopped, cut in, stalled and never stopped hooting.

'Rather hooting than shooting,' Cindy said. 'We have taxi wars here. I've ducked for cover in this road more than once.'

Cindy had a delightful way of emphasising disaster, leaning back and placing her fingers under her chin, which had the effect of lifting her almost perfect nose. I wondered briefly if she had had plastic surgery. The sharp corners of her dark hair would swing down till they brushed the tips of her ear lobes. Her green eyes were bright when she said terrible things. In her laugh there was a mix of pride and helpless delight at the unique terrors of her home town.

'When women got together in the old days, they used to ask, "Who's your gynae?"'

She looked at me to see if I was impressed, amused, shocked. I wasn't any of these – but I enjoyed the music, an old familiar tune; dark, bluesy and very Jo'burg, I could hear the rising tones, up and up the voice would go till it hit the long 'e' in 'gyneee', and in the sudden silence that followed I'd see those last 'ee's hanging in the air. The Jo'burg twang knows no modulation; it takes off and keeps climbing until it peaks and there it hangs like a naked trapeze artist – *ee-ee-ee*...

'And now?'

'Now they'll say: "What calibre you carrying, doll?" It's got worse since freedom. It seems another world where, once upon a time, people slept with their windows open because they liked feeling the wind in their faces. Democratic freedom has brought personal terror. One person, one prison.'

Keeping out of harm's way was as old as the city but listening to Cindy I got the impression it had become an entire career. It consumed, exasperated and exhausted her; strategies for survival filled her waking hours. I had already had pointed out to me my lack of qualifications for saying anything about Jo'burg. I lived elsewhere, wherever that was. She asked in passing about Hanoi, Laos, Thailand, Siberia, America, but always with a slight scepticism, as if either she had trouble believing they existed, or she could not quite understand why anyone should bother to be there. It was a scepticism like my mother's: it did not doubt the existence of these unseen foreign places but it was quizzical about what made them interesting when, fuck *ut* – as Cindy would say – all around you was the real thing. This city, this weird, made-over mining camp, treasure trove, killing ground … ripped-up town of demented rip-off artists.

'*Lissen*,' said Cindy. 'Crime's so bad, even Rwandan refugees are leaving …'

Like a lot of Jo'burgers, she felt that if you left town for long enough, you lost all recollection of the unique textures that made the place so terrifyingly special. In my experience, just the opposite took place: it was amongst those who had lived in Jo'burg and never left that the returning traveller found real amnesia. Johannesburgers had no sense of the past, perhaps because if they kept on remembering they would go mad, perhaps because the present is so all-absorbingly wild. Or, when they do remember things, it is often because they wish to highlight, with perverse pleasure, what a falling-off there has been. The outside world and its crises are irrelevant – meaningless wars and quarrels. The only questions that matter run along the old parallel black and white lines, despite all the talk of love and unity. From the hungry majority: 'How do I get fed?' From the lucky minority: 'How do I not get shot?'

OK. But what I didn't understand was – if it had always been a bit like that, what made it so different now?

Cindy nibbled her fingernail. 'I guess I'd say: murder. More of it. People are into it in a big way. Anyone, at any time. All of us, any of us. That's why I'm bloody glad I live in Sheerhaven.

And so would you, so would anyone be if they came from where I come from.'

As we drove, she told me a depressing, unexceptional tale, common from coast to coast. She'd been born in a place called Blaukrans, a dirt-poor settlement out among the slime dams, in the shadow of the mine-dumps; a ghetto for despised, in-between, neither white nor black people, who were at home nowhere and loved by no one. Everyone else – blacks, whites, Asians – at least knew, as Cindy put it, 'who the hell they were, even if they didn't have a bloody clue where they came from. But us, we were no one and nowhere.'

The Coloureds of Blaukrans, descendants of Malay slaves or German mercenaries, Dutch sailors and English renegades, or Khoi people or San Bushmen, or all of them, were disparaged by their Indian neighbours, loathed by their black neighbours and ignored by their white overlords.

So far, so utterly ordinary. She came from not just the other side of the tracks, but the other side of the universe. She told me about herself with that steely enjoyment with which so many people have learnt to disguise the considerable pain of growing up another colour in another world.

'We were so far from being anyone we were outa sight! We were called Coloureds or Browns or Mixed Race people or Hottentots or Kleurling or Klonkies or Goffles, or whatever name got fixed to us. But, in the beginning, when we arrived in the Cape, I think we were slaves. September was a slave name. I could have been October or November or December. Same difference, isn't *ut*?'

I nodded. 'The guys who ran the Cape were not exactly bursting with ideas. They called their slaves by whatever name came to mind. Months were an old standby. Days of the week. Monday to Friday.'

She laughed. 'Cindy ... Friday: I like that!'

Leaving the Cape for the Reef and heading up to Jo'burg, that had been the one bit of good fortune her mom ever had. In Jo'burg she met the man who became Cindy's father, and it was downhill all the way after that. The Septembers lived at number 24 Paradise Street. Her old man had hawked vegetables and hit the bottle as well as his wife and his kids. She had two brothers: one fell into the cooking fire and was burnt to death; the other peddled dagga, and was killed by the cops.

Her mother had been the one to resist: her mother remembered; she hankered back to the Cape, which became, in retrospect, a great, good place. It was not surprising. In the hard Transvaal, where all that counted was the gun, the whip and the boot, the Cape took on aspects of paradise.

'It was balls, when you think about it,' Cindy said, 'but I don't blame my mom. Longing to be back home. In the Cape she'd been to college, she qualified as a bookkeeper. Her big stroke of luck was to land a job keeping the books in the local Dutch Reformed Church in our township. Coloured branch, of course, but what the hell, it was a job. My mom kept us going. My mom got me to school, and after school she got me a job in Motortown. It was my mom who made me. It was 1989, I was sixteen. "Take your wages, rent a room in Hillbrow," said my ma. She cried but she made me promise: "Never come back." And I promised, and so I never did.'

'Never?'

'Never. Later, I heard that she died and I felt bad but I said to myself she'd have died glad. She got me out of there. I had that job in Motortown, it was a new life, a new me: I was out in the world. By the nineties, the old ways were breaking down. They didn't, like, hold your colour against you. They never noticed mine much anyway. You know what they called "trying for white"? Well, I didn't even have to try. I just was.'

It was familiar, and amazing. I thought of myself, of Koosie, of Noddy, of Bama, all of us marked by the places we came from. Maybe we escaped them. But we never denied what made us. Cindy had to unmake her home and she didn't have bulldozers to knock it down, like Koosie's place was knocked down in Sophiatown. She had to demolish her old life herself and start again.

'Would you do something for me? Would you show me where you grew up?'

She was astonished. 'I've known guys who wanted to go to bed with me. But no one ever asked me to show him where I come from.'

'It depends what excites you.'

'You are weird. But sure, we can go; we're in no rush. Benny won't be out till five.'

The city lulled and infuriated. We were in Orange Grove. No oranges, no grove. Small yellow-brick villas behind broad-bellied burglar bars, old cars rusting among the weeds in the front yards. Cindy's small, square, confident hands on the wheel of the Porsche ...

I got more reading the walls than I ever did from the papers. Parables, sermons, eye-candy ... 'Booze Brothers', 'Geffin and Garfunkel – Attorneys', 'Mtshali and van der Merwe', 'Tuxedo Tavern', 'Tombstone Memorials – Lifetime Guarantee', 'Ace

Guns and Acme Gold'. Then we were passing 'Nussbaum's Kosher Butcher', 'The Doll House Road House', 'Zuma's Teeth Whitening Clinic', 'Harry's Hair Relaxation Parlour'. And across the road from a yeshiva: 'Kalashnikov Security', on whose white-washed wall some street-wise physician had scrawled a prescription for our paranoia: 'One settler – one Prozac'.

'Like it?' Cindy asked.

'I love it. I grew up right here; this is one of the many parts of town where we lived. I went to school down the road.'

She looked like she didn't believe me. As if someone who spent so much time so far away couldn't really come from here.

We picked up the elevated highway that looped around the city, like a lariat, and headed south into the smudgy edges of the great sprawl. Where no one ever went if they could help it.

Number 24 Paradise Street turned out to be a building of yellow face brick. Left to gather damp on the tired lawn, old mattresses sprouted mould like huge cabbages. You might have thought there was not much to steal and yet the sun was bright on the burglar bars behind the broken window-panes. Cindy was horrified. Three black guys in woolly Rasta hats sat on the low wall: great colours, lovely needlework, my mother and Bama would have loved them, but they did not look very friendly. One of them slowly lifted his arm, sighted and made to pull the trigger.

Cindy said: 'Oh, great! So much for freedom.'

'It is a long way you've come. Out as a clerk, back in a Porsche.'

She responded by gunning the engine. 'Yeah. I made it. I'm a target now, like everyone else. That's what is making me nervous. This car is begging to be done over. Seen enough?'

I nodded.

'Good. Let's go.'

We screeched out of Paradise Street, swung hard into the main avenue, only to be stopped by a red light. Three beggars surrounded us, their reflections swirling in the high gloss of the Porsche's bonnet. One guy was the colour of rust, and wore an old grey hat without a crown that was kept up by his ears, and he carried a piece of brown cardboard on which there was written in green chalk: 'White, poor, honest and hungry. No food for family. Please help.' There was a cripple, who made an attempt to clean our windscreen with one hand, rubbing with his sleeve until it was really smeary. In the other hand he held a cellphone. The third beggar was a child; he stood just at Cindy's window and stared at her. She said, 'Fuck this! Fuck it! Why do they do this? I work! You work! Why should I run the gauntlet? Bastards or billionaires, that's all we seem to produce … What a fucking country!'

The light flashed green, she put her foot down, and the cripple fell away. The child leaned forward and withdrew, like a bullfighter making a particularly dangerous pass, as close as he could get to the razor point of the bull's horn as the wing-mirror passed within millimetres of his nose.

On the highway she sighed. 'I'm sorry, but they freak me out. We've got enough stress around here. I just have to look at street people and I do my nut. I want to get out of the car and injure someone! Isn't that awful? But I do, because I'm think-ing it's me or them. D'you know what my nightmare is? Listen, this is it. Right? I'm stopped at a robot, and some guy sticks a gun in my eye and throws me out of the car and drives off with Benny still in the back. It's happened, you know. A mother gets hijacked, and her baby starts crying and the hijacker throws it out. Now, let's go fetch Benny, and let's drive the long way round and I'll talk to you like a Dutch auntie. Do you wanna hear Cindy's rules for staying alive? They're on the internet.' And as if this conferred sacred status, she chanted them for me like a poem, or a prayer:

1. Be alert and save yourself from murder, rape, assault, robbery and hijacking.
2. Be especially careful at night, at stop streets, at red lights, in heavy traffic, at tollgates on all national roads.
3. If stopped by the police, where possible do not stop but drive to a police station or phone 10111. Hijackers like to play at being cops.
4. If you break down, do not stop, never leave the car, drive on your tyre rims to somewhere safe.
5. If you see someone in distress beside the road, *do not stop*.
6. On arriving home, drive slowly past your house, go round the block, twice, especially at night.
7. Kill the radio before driving into your house. Listen hard. Look carefully.
8. If hijacked or held up, do not make any sudden movements.
9. Undo your safety belt before driving into your driveway in case you are held up, and loosen your safety belt in case a sudden movement makes the hijacker think you have a weapon.
10. At such moments, do not reach for your cellphone.
11. Keep looking your hijacker in the eye. It soothes him. Try to remember what he looks like.
12. Co-operate or die.

'That's it. Remember them: they may save your life. Why're you smiling?'

'It's thinking about you on Paradise Street. It's something about the unconscious poetry of names.'

'Poetry! Do me a favour!'

She didn't have to add what I began to learn was her usual signifier: 'This is Jo'burg.' I heard it in her voice. Life was too fierce, too fast, too deadly for poetry. In general, I was to discover, Cindy was withering about anything that distracted from the one serious question: how to stay alive? She was particularly scathing about 'artsy-fartsy stuff', which she regarded as little more than a dishonest diversion from the acid of 'real' life. Artsy-fartsy stuff, said Cindy, was 'unreal', even 'sickmaking'. I'd never heard it put like that before; the accepted view was that art was for faggots or foreigners or women. Cindy seemed to feel it was also bad for your health.

I asked what was wrong with painting or poetry or ballet.

'There's just something in the air that's against it. Don't ask me why; there just is. Something won't let it be a natural thing. I guess it's OK in, like, other places. But here, not. This isn't Mozart country; this is murder and robbery country. *Ut's* ball games, big talk and beating-people-up country. People who go arty go down; they fall into little cliques; they go around sniffing each other's droppings. It's kind of grubby.'

'And murder and robbery are clean and up-front?'

She shrugged. 'You come from overseas. It's not the same there.'

'Cindy, I come from here. I lived in this town longer than you.'

'I don't say I approve of murder, I just say it comes naturally: lots of people do it. It's in the air. But, yes, you're right. When I see Paradise Street I know I have come a long way and, like I said, I owe it to my mom first of all, and after that I suppose I owe it to Andy. That's my ex. Andy Andreotti. I was a receptionist in Motortown, and he came in to buy a new Alfa

Romeo. He seemed pretty geared up. He was manager at the Bank of Naples. Soon we were going out. He never asked where I came from, he never asked to see Paradise Street, he never imagined for a moment that I wasn't what he thought I was: a nice girl from the northern suburbs. And that was fine by me. He was pretty crazy about me but, even better, he seemed to think I was, like, perfectly normal.' She gave her high, quick, disbelieving laugh. 'I remember thinking, I've made it! I thought my mom would have been really proud.

'Andy took me to Sun City, and that's where he asked me to marry him and, of course, I said yes. And so that's how I got to be the other half of a classy Jo'burg couple. We had a house in Fourways, a Jacuzzi, armed response, his and hers pistols – the whole bladdy tutti. We drove matching Alfas; we bought a farm in the Lowveld; we sailed on the Vaal. I did the lot: the book club, the BMW, lunches at Baldassar's in Rosebank or Carlucci's in Hyde Park. My friends were called Melissa and Sharon. Not bad, hey. It's amazing how quickly you pick it up. I ended up as Mrs Andy Andreotti in Fourways. A *twenny-four* carat, genuine Jo'burg princess. Isn't that absolutely fucking amazing?'

It was, and I said so.

'Even more amazing is this.' Again she laughed at her luck but also at some genuine discovery she'd made. 'When I think of Andy now, I realise that people like me are more fashionable than people like him. Isn't *ut*, hey? D'you know what I mean?'

'I don't think I do.'

'Well, people like Andy, whole gangs of them, are such utter dorks. I mean, now. They weren't then but they are now. Sort of out of date. Anyway, did Andy fuck up! Did he ever. But I can say, really, honestly, *troooly* I'm grateful to Andy, like I'm grateful to my mom; except my mom was a saint and a martyr, while Andy was an arsehole from the start. From when Benny was just born. You could see straight away Benny was different. He was slow to move, slow to crawl: he's not co-ordinated. All Andy could think of saying was, "But he won't be a sportsman ..." That's Andy for you. That's my luck.'

It didn't sound like luck to me.

'But it is, it is! If he hadn't been such an arsehole, I'd still be married to him. And then where'd I be? Probably where he is.'

'Where's that?'

'He's in jail right now. Ten years.'

'Gosh.'

'Yes, well, like I said: he's an arsehole. But then again, don't feel sorry for him. Andy thought ten years was cheap at the price.'

'What was the price?'

'Everything he had, and then some. It was around about 1998, the new age, the age of freedom. We'd been married around three years. Buffalo Belle's had just opened. It was a brothel, right? Except they didn't call it that. Libido Lounge, they said. A parking lot the size of a rugby pitch, gaming tables, six bars burnished in brass and chrome, big screens showing reruns of old rugby matches, water-features, mudbaths, saunas, massage. They had Japanese koi in the pond; they had private suites named after the big five, the trophy game you always hoped to see in the wild, these suites with names like Buffalo Bay, Elephant's Walk, Lion's Den. All the other game-park crap.

'But it was a whorehouse, purpose-built for guys looking for a bit of fun after a lifetime in government-issue concrete codpieces. At long last, white men could fuck for freedom. Andy started going there. The girls waited at the bar. Prices went as high as a thousand bucks a trick. They shipped the girls in. They had Cambodians and Romanians and Russians and Thais. As it happens, the cops are after those girls right now. They're illegal immigrants. The papers are full of it. Foreign competition. The local sex workers bitch that they're losing out to cheap imports. Part of me thinks they should leave the girls alone. If enough dickheads want to get screwed by foreign fluff, so what?

'Anyway, that's where Andy met Mona-Lize. She wore a white negligee over a white G-string, and long white boots. They checked into the Leopard's Lair and he found to his amazement that she was priced at the lower end of the scale: 500 a trick. Andy wasn't only surprised, he was really angry: Mona-Lize with her blonde hair, blue eyes, white negligee, was the most beautiful woman he'd ever seen. How could she price herself so low?

'Mona-Lize liked that. She liked Andy for seeing it, and for saying so. For being understanding. She said it was cheap labour, it was immigrants, it was globalisation, and it was all those tarts from Taiwan, Estonia and Prague ... But she was local and local was – as they say – "lekker".

'And Andy lapped it up. He wasn't just a dork, he was a patriotic dork. In fact, Mona-Lize was more local than Andy knew. In real life, as if anyone gives a monkey's about real life, her name was Mary, from Blairgowrie. She was married to a Romanian called Mimicu, had two kids by him and then thought she deserved better, so she decided to up her household allowance by working a night-time shift at Buffalo Belle's ... So Mary Mimicu from Blairgowrie got to be Mona-Lize of the Leopard's Lair.

'He didn't just love her. He wanted to make up to her for the stupidity of all South African men who paid to fuck tarts from overseas. He wanted her to have what she needed, and Mona-Lize needed a lot. For starters Andy bought her a diamond ring, a BMW, an entire fucking tank of Japanese koi. Mona-Lize loved it; she said Andy was a born hunter.

'That's when I heard about it. He just told me one day there was someone else and he wanted a divorce. It was pretty horrible; I had Benny to think of. Anyway, we got a divorce, I got a settlement, I kept the house and Andy went back to Mona-Lize.

'The divorce cost him a bomb; suddenly Andy was short and Mona-Lize didn't like men who were short. So what did my ex-dork do? He began lifting large amounts from the trust accounts at the Bank of Naples. Then he set about making up for being short. He bought her a mansion in Wendywood for a million, a Rolex gold watch, he got through another quarter of a million in pretty trinkets, he paid for her to have her face lifted and her boobs done. In six months he blew three million bucks.

'But Andy, remember, was an arsehole. Worse, he began to have, well, pangs. He was not a thief by nature. It weighed on him, taking the money from the Bank of Naples, and he did something you do not do in Jo'burg: he began to fret. He told Mona-Lize how unhappy he was and why he was unhappy. Mona-Lize became very unhappy, too. She had always thought it had been his money. Now here he was, telling her that the money he'd spent on her was stolen. How was she supposed to feel about that? How could he do this to her? What right did he have to feel bad about it? What about what she was feeling? All right, then, if he was going to feel bad about it, then he should give back the money. Andy said he couldn't do that: he'd taken too much. Well, then, said Mona-Lize, do the decent thing, go tell the Bank of Naples what you've done …

'Andy said he wanted to do the decent thing but he didn't want to go to jail. So you know what? Mona-Lize did the decent thing for him. She got into her BMW and went along to the Bank of Naples and told them what Andy had done. He was arrested; he got ten years.'

'Did the bank get its cash back?'

'Some of it. They got back the house in Wendywood. But how do you reclaim on a face-lift and a boob job? In court it turned out that Mona-Lize had begun to suss out that Andy might be a diminishing asset long before he did. So she had begun to diversify. On the nights she wasn't seeing Andy, she was running ads in the personal column of the *Star*: "Sex Kitten Seeks Lions and Tigers for Rough and Tumble. Strictest Confidence; all Major Credit Cards Accepted."'

Cindy laughed aloud. 'What a woman! Wasted in a knocking shop. She should have run a gold mine. Maybe she did, when you think how much cash Andy shovelled her way. Anyway, she did me a favour, too. Andy went to jail. I was free and I went into real estate. Thank you, Mona-Lize!'

What a town! The headlines wired to the lampposts sang out the edgy, bitter, banal news of the day, so familiar, so wild:

Raped Baby's Mother Arrested
Toddler Shot Dead in Bed
Two Burn in Shack
Boks Crush Aussies

'Your eyes are all glazed,' said Cindy. 'Are you on something?'

'Yeah. I get high on home.'

'Well, sober up, buddy, I need you: I didn't just bring you along for the ride. Fetching the kids has got harder since guys began mugging the moms who came to fetch them.'

'You're not serious. In broad daylight?'

Again I saw on her face that look of horrified pride. 'Sure. Daylight never stopped anyone. Nice, hey? You're pretty encumbered with a kid who can't walk, or something. So they wait here … Smart thinking.'

'Bloody hell!'

'Welcome to Jo'burg.'

Sunbeam Shelter was once the home of a great and rich Rand-lord – a red-tiled fortress up on Parktown Ridge, built of hand-cut yellow Jo'burg stone, and big lawns running down to the electric fence. I watched Cindy teetering across the road in her snakeskin backless high heels to join the knot of mothers, and nannies in crisp white tunics, and kids in wheelchairs, kids in leg-irons.

She came back with Benny. His round face, the full skin, made him look younger than his eight years.

Cindy told him: 'You remember Alex. He's Kathleen's son.'

Benny looked at me as if I was much too old to be anyone's son.

'Where's Kathleen?'

'Kathleen's in heaven, Benny, darling. Remember, we said goodbye to Kathleen in Rosebank,' Cindy told him.

'When's she coming back?'

She looked at me. 'What do I say to that?'

'She's not coming back, Benny,' I said.

'Why?'

'Because she likes it where she is.'

Benny looked a little crestfallen but he took it well enough. He said: 'Will you stay and play tennis with me?'

Cindy looked at me. 'Would you?'

'Sure.'

She turned to the boy. 'OK. But just for a bit and then it's bath-time for you, my fellow.'

Playing tennis with Benny meant batting the ball to and fro, but he'd only use his backhand. He was obsessive about certain movements, certain ways of standing. All the time we played he sang: 'One man went to mow, went to mow a meadow.'

It was very relaxing. Cindy came out to watch. 'Try your forehand,' she said.

'No, I won't,' he said.

'He gets, like, fixated,' she said by way of apologising.

'Don't worry, so do I.'

I watched her bathing him. He took particular pleasure in kicking, long sinuous thrusts of his stubby legs, as if he were pushing them into stirrups or silk pyjamas, or soft leather riding boots. It was beautiful. Benny, so ungainly in the air, was so easy in water. He loved, I think, the sudden lightness of his cumbersome body which was too solid in air; he liked having something to kick against, he liked the feeling of getting somewhere because for Benny getting anywhere was pretty hard going. It was different in water: then he might go somewhere as a fish. He was made for life underwater, a mer-boy, sentenced to live in another medium.

Driving home that evening I saw again the pale faces on the estate agents' signboards outside the walled townships and I knew what they had reminded me of. In Serbia, during the tribal wars that followed the end of Tito's reign, I spent time in a town called Pec, fixing air-con in the local Offices for Security and Co-operation in Europe. A very hopeful sign it was, too, in a town on the brink of war, filled with Serbs and ethnic Albanians who loathed each other. But, then, installing air-con is always a serene thing to do: it supposes calm; it assumes life will be stable for a while; it promises that there is a world in which simple things like comfort win out over killing. But that didn't happen in Pec. People didn't want to be cool; they wanted to kill.

In Serbia, the dead were remembered in photographs on lampposts or tacked to trees. Flimsy memorials to the departed. The faces of the estate agents on the 'For Sale' signs outside Sheerhaven and its sister stockades reminded me of those guides to the land of the lately deceased.

I knew such refuges were the future, they were what everyone wanted. It was a very South African way of cheating those who wished to end your life. You checked into one of these electrified mausoleums and pretended to be dead.

What had Cindy said? 'One person, one prison …'

Once, it had been the state that had locked us away in the narrow cells of skin colour. Now we were free and we didn't need anyone to lock us up. Give us the bars and we'd do it ourselves.

Later that night Noddy knocked on my door. He had been weeping. I thought the cops had picked him up. Looking back now, I should have known something like that would not have rattled Noddy. Arrest, however awkward, was social, it went together with the benefits of a civil society, with rules and lawyers and bail and law courts, things that Noddy – the farmer, the landowner, the man of property – approved and supported. Arrest would have not done this to him. The man on my doorstep was going to pieces.

We went through to the dining room and sat down at the table. I waited for him to tell me what he had come to talk to me about but it soon became clear that he wasn't going to do that; he reached over to the pot of snapdragons on the window-sill and began pulling the drooping heads off the flowers.

'This is snapdragon wilt, Mr Alex. There is no cure.'

Then from his back pocket he took a letter, opened it and gave it to me. It was written in pencil on a sheet of lined paper and it was very short and it had all the ornate flourish of a letter penned by a scribe.

'Greetings, my brother,' it began, 'I have to inform you that your wife and mother of your children, Beauty, has been found to be carrying the child of another – to wit the principal of St Aloysius School, and I write to ask you, my brother, to take such steps as are necessary without the least delay. I am, my brother, your brother, Johnson.'

Noddy looked at me. 'A woman who does this thing, who carries the child of another man – when she is married – must not stay any more under her husband's roof.'

'Where does she go?'

'She must be sent back to her father's house. It is our custom. My brother says she cannot be my wife. I do not know what is best. I asked the others, "Tell me what I must do." The others have said their thoughts to me.'

He had been canvassing his madams. Pulling out the letter, watching them as they read it. Just as he was watching me.

I thought it was mad and wrong to go round from house to house, asking other people to decide the fate of his wife and family. I gave him back his letter.

'Noddy, where will Beauty go?'

'My madams all say the same thing. "Take her back," they say. "Forgive her," they say. "Shame, poor woman," they say. "Think of your sons, Noddy."' He sighed and he pushed the letter back into his pocket. 'I hear what my madams say. All women say the same. But my brother says: make her go. It is our custom. What do you say?'

'What about your boys? How will Joshua and Sipho managed if their mother is gone?'

He didn't want questions, he wanted answers. He said again, hopelessly: 'It is our custom. I must go there. I will go by train.'

'I'll get you the ticket.'

He inclined his head. Like someone accepting a jail sentence.

I have never made travel arrangements with less joy. We could not talk about where he was going because it wasn't travel in the sense that we knew it; duty and sadness took him back to Matabeleland. He packed his brown suitcase with the brass clasps, he wore his best Sunday suit, and his hat. Set for disaster, or joy, we look the same. I drove him to Park Station and he waved goodbye to me from the train window, as if he were going on holiday.

Her guns went to Oomie: the .505 Gibb, her favourite elephant gun; the .416 Rigby; the .375 Magnum Holland & Holland; and a Mannlicher .256 that she preferred for lighter game.

But Oomie had vanished without trace. Just as he had 'gone to ground' (my mother's kindly phrase) when the shots from David Pratt's pistol rang out forty years before, now he seemed to have done it again. I had to consider that he might be dead, but somehow I reckoned my old lady must have had a shrewd idea that he was still around when she left him her guns.

I tried the Johannesburg Central Police Station, from where, in the old days, when it was called John Vorster Square, Oomie and his mates had made their prisoners beg for mercy or concocted ingenious accidents whereby they died, after slipping on bars of soap in the showers, or falling from high windows. But this was the new South Africa and, apart from looking at me rather strangely, the new cops had no note or memory of the former secret policeman who had once been assigned to guard the one-time Prime Minister and who hit the deck with such alacrity at the Rand Easter Show all those years before.

They weren't covering up for the guy. I don't think their memories went back to the sixties. If anyone was responsible for expunging all traces of the former detective sergeant, in the secret detail assigned to guard the Premier, it had been Oomie's old colleagues who simply had not known what to do with the strange case of the recumbent bodyguard. (How instantly he'd dropped to the floor that day!) How embarrassing, how ridiculous ... Faced by unpalatable facts, they did what they had done when faced by unpalatable people: they abolished them.

I ran ads in the *Star*, the *Cape Times*, the *Natal Mercury* ...

If Mr Louis 'Lappies' Labuschagne, formerly of the South African Police Service, and a friend of the late Mrs Kathleen Healey of Forest Town, Johannesburg, would contact her son, at the address or phone number given below, he may hear something to his advantage.

A few days later I got a letter, special delivery, from the Nelson Mandela Retirement Village, Umbilo, Durban.

Dear Mr Alex Healey,

I am the man you are looking for. I am the old friend of your mom's. I am in a home in Durban. If you would phone me some time we could arrange to a get-together.

Yours sincerely,
Louis Labuschagne (Det-Sergeant, SAPS – Retd)

The Nelson Mandela Retirement Village and Frail Care Facility – 'Celebrating Our Diversity' – was a complex of neat sturdy thatched rondavels, with only slightly less security fencing than Sheerhaven. I had taken the precaution of parking the Land Rover around the corner. I didn't want to have to explain to the armed guards at the gate why I was carrying enough firepower to start a small war.

Once inside the grounds I realised that the difference between Cindy's golden citadel, or the neo-Tuscan barracks where the 'youngies' spent their lives, and this modest old-age home was minimal. All such retreats represented the final destination for those who had once reigned supreme in South Africa; a supremacy that had some just claim to be called the most stupid in history, but no matter. All were heading for what looked, and felt, like early retirement.

The man who came to meet me at the reception desk was wearing white shorts and a matching belted tunic, buttoned down the middle, reaching below the hips. It was that old standby, the safari suit. Where had all the safari suits gone? One upon a time, entire phalanxes of servants ironed late into the night to keep regiments of men in crisply creased uniform, a uniform they wore with brisk aggression, like a badge of honour. The safari suit came in white, slate-grey, electric blue and khaki, a favourite shade. The tunic was worn open at the neck in a deep V, showing a patch of chest hair. The knees were exposed, and below them you wore long thick woollen socks and brothel creepers, if you were English, or veldskoen, if you were Afrikaans. There was always more of the pharmacy than the veld about the safari suit. Something strangely antiseptic, the perfect costume for shaven-headed fascists.

He patted me on the back. 'Alex, man, it's good to see you again!'

There seemed no comparison whatever between the dark, restless, taciturn Oomie who used once to call on my ma and this rather gentle old gnome. Small, fine-featured, with a sweet, rather sleepy smile. White hair, white beard, white eyebrows, his skin smoothly milky. Even Oomie's safari suit was cream and for some reason I found that rather moving. Strange how these things take you.

'We'll go sit in the lounge,' said Oomie. 'Have some coffee.'

The lounge was a large room with parquet flooring and lots of green leather armchairs, with a picture of Mandela on the wall, smiling down on us. At a couple of tables, people were playing cards. Other people were sitting staring ahead of them. Every so often a nurse would come in and turn them round a bit, or coax them to have a cup of tea. A couple of elderly ladies were ranged in front of an enormous TV, which was running a very violent American gangster movie. One guy kept smashing his gun into another guy's face. The old ladies watching did not move. When I was growing up TV was forbidden, like everything else that might frighten the voters. Then when TV finally arrived in 1976, someone made a bulk buy of B-grade stuff, and every set showed what seemed to be the same clip over and over again, for ever after. In bars, hotels, filling stations and corner shops you saw some guy who kept smashing his gun into someone else's face. It is very standard stuff. Hitting had always been our way of staying in touch.

Oomie sat me down in one of the green leather chairs and offered me coffee and fruit cake. I said no; to eat was somehow to take part in the submarine gloom of the room. Give him the stuff, I thought, and get the hell out.

But Oomie wasn't to be rushed. He seemed strangely comfortable, as if he felt good inside his skin, as if he'd made peace with whomever there was to make peace with.

'Sorry your mom passed away. She was a wonderful, wonderful woman.'

I said, 'Listen, Oomie, she wanted you to have something.

That's why I tracked you down. It's not money, or anything, it's — ' I stopped. How did I describe a personal armoury? 'It's more … personal.'

'*Ag* no,' he said. 'I'm very, very touched Kathleen remembered me.'

'She remembered everyone. I'm just not sure if she remembered them the way they wanted to be remembered.'

'Your mom had a hellavah sense of humour.'

'Did she? Sometimes I wished I knew my mother the way others did.'

'*Ja*, she used to say to me, "Oomie, we must laugh at our little peccadilloes, there will be time later to be saints." Only your mom would call them peccadilloes.'

She had been very forgiving of Oomie's little lapse, his failure of timing. In fact, it had endeared her to him far more than it would have done had he blasted back at Pratt the instant the silly fellow let fly at Verwoerd. But at the same time I couldn't help feeling that coming from someone who had never, so far as I knew, failed to shoot when the moment demanded, or the target offered itself, there was something especially perverse in her bequest to Oomie, something faintly ominous. A man who couldn't handle a gun gets left her entire arsenal.

Oomie said again: 'A wonderful woman. You must be very proud, Alex.'

He had tears in his eyes. I never did know what to do with what felt to me like excessive emotion. It frightened me, this welling liquid. And it didn't feel right. My ma died as she had lived, doing exactly what she wanted. There was nothing sad about her; there was much that seemed to me shocking, outrageous and even cruel.

I said: 'So what you been doing, Oomie?'

'Long story, Alex. After the SAPS, I couldn't get no work, *ja*. But then I got a break: I heard they was looking for securi-ty people over at Sheba Sands. So I goes along and I meets this guy, Barrie Gluhnik. You know him?'

Who didn't? Gluhnik was a typical white South African; that's to say his family came from somewhere else, from Poland or Russia or Argentina or England, no one was quite sure, and it didn't matter. The family Gluhnik had come to this country, like many before them, hoping to get very rich, kick a lot of black ass and never work again.

But it hadn't panned out. Gluhnik had grown up poor in the southern suburbs of Jo'burg; he'd been in his time a wrestler, a bouncer, a water-diviner; he was burly, quick-witted and barely literate. Like many whites, if men like Gluhnik thought there was anything wrong with apartheid, it was that there wasn't a whole fucking lot more of it ... But successful entrepreneurs soon learnt that backing the status quo never stopped you making a buck by beating the system. And Gluhnik found a way to do it.

Gluhnik saw that the price white guys were obliged to pay for a guarantee of lifelong superiority plus servants was large amounts of boredom. They sold their right to excitement (except on the rugby field or the rifle range) to a clique of rabid fundamentalists who branded any form of sexual expression theologically unsound because it offended God, or politically seditious because it offended them. In short, Gluhnik saw that most whites signed up to the dictum: 'A normal South African is a neutered South African.'

Barrie Gluhnik's first breakthrough was to see that, although they may have signed up to it, they didn't exactly like it. Having sworn off gambling, illicit sex and inter-racial mingling, there was a real itch for gambling, illicit sex and inter-racial mingling. His moment of illumination he summed up in a phrase: 'If you want an orgasm, go abroad.' So Gluhnik, in the 1960s, started an outfit called Pussycat Tours. Each week a planeload of punters took off from Jo'burg for Amsterdam and its red-light district, to Las Vegas and its gaming tables, to Hamburg and the girls in the Reeperbahn.

Pussycat Tours was a smash hit. But a planeload of blokes in safari suits does not make a very big market. If only Germany and Holland and Las Vegas were not so far away, if only abroad was closer to home ...

I recalled reading an interview with Gluhnik who told of the moment when the answer came to him. 'It had been', Gluhnik told this interviewer, 'like a flash, like a vision. Like that doll had at Lourdes. Or St Paul, when he was heading down Damascus way on his camel, and blam! Know what I mean?'

His idea was simple. Why fly clients halfway round the world to do what they could do in our own back yard? South Africa was, in fact, littered with foreign countries. We had more foreign countries than we knew what to do with. All over the damn place the regime had created black homelands, with their own flags and presidents.

'OK,' said Gluhnik, 'if they are sovereign countries, why can't they have sovereign casinos, and sovereign bordellos, and sovereign striptease?'

That's when Gluhnik knew he had it made. He would create pleasure palaces in the bare veld where red-blooded South Africans could do whatever they did abroad – without leaving home. In the country down the road, or next door. Or over the hill. Sheba's Secret was the first of the great pleasure domes;

then the Solomon Sands, then the Monomatapo Majestic rose like mirages in the bone-dry veld of dirt-poor black reserves. They offered golf, girls, fruit machines and chorus lines, flown in from London and Vegas. There was striptease, mud wrestling and books, movies and musicals banned in South Africa. Sex across the colour bar was as easy as calling room service. And all just a couple of hours' drive from the gloomy Calvinist dungeon-state of white South Africa.

I said: 'Of course I know who he is.'

'Well,' says Lappies, 'Barrie Gluhnik looked over my CV and he says to me, "OK, Detective Sergeant, I'll tell you what. I see from your CV that you were security for Dr Verwoerd, and I remember from the papers there was, let's say, a little falling-out when the nutter Pratt took a pot-shot at the PM. I also know there's some that say you took a dive. But I say I think you did a good thing: you took cover, so as better to think about your next move. Now, I like a guy who thinks, Lappies, because the world is going more and more towards blokes what can use their heads. The days of goons is gone. There's always room for shooting, I got nothing against shooting, Lappies. There will always be shooting. But these are not the sixties any more, these are the seventies. The country's changing. We got a thinking Prime Minister now. We're gonna need *thinking* security. I've had the privilege of meeting Mr John Vorster and I want to tell you he's a true gent. Between you, me and the gatepost, I never liked Verwoerd. Too rigid. And a fucking immigrant to boot. But Vorster's different. He's gonna press ahead with these homelands, where blacks can stay blacks, but he wants them to be happy blacks. He wants them to love their homelands and I, Barry Gluhnik, help them to do just that: they work in my palaces as security, maids, caddies, guides, cleaners. People who never had a job before. The PM is very appreciative of that. Very. Let me tell you, I believe one day John Vorster will play golf with Gary Player on one of my championship courses. At the Solomon Sands, or the Sheba. How about that?"

'He must have seen the look on my face, 'cause he said: "I know, I know, you're thinking this guy's loony! The Prime Minister's never going to come to the Solomon Sands when the Soloman Sands is just one big casino and knocking shop, where everybody watches dirty shows, and sleeps with black girls, like they cannot do back home. Well, let me tell you, Lappies, I have a dream, just like that bladdy Martin Luther whatever he's called, over there in the States. I'll tell you my dream, Lappies. My palaces are just the start. One day, instead of people having to leave home to do what they want, they're gonna be able to do it at home! And when that happens everyone will see that Barrie Gluhnik wasn't just about gambling and girlie-shows and golf. Barrie Gluhnik was about freedom! He saw that when everyone is free to gamble all day, screw whoever they like and at the end of the day have a round of golf – and do it at home! – then we'll have a new South Africa. That's when they'll put up statues to me, like Winston Churchill, or Simon Bolivar. It'll be 'Barrie Gluhnik, Liberator'! What do you think, Lappies?"

'And I said: "Sorry, Mr Gluhnik, but as you're asking me, I think you're fucking crazy. It'll never happen."

'And he said, "You look after security, Lappies, and leave the vision stuff to me."

'So I did. I worked for Mr Gluhnik till I retired.'

Again, the watering of the eyes. 'And, you know, he was right. Today, we are like that. You don't need to go to the Solomon

Sands any more; you don't need to drive to the country next door to be free: you can be free, and do whatever you like, right here, at home.' Lappies looked up at the picture of Mandela. 'Mr Gluhnik saw it coming. The new South Africa. Hell, I'd put him right up there with Madiba.'

You had to hand it to these guys. From security cop ready to kill to weepy Mandela devotee. At the drop of a hat. I had no doubt he meant it. He would have hung Gluhnik next to Mandela, just as once he would have put Verwoerd there. Hell, he would have put Attila the Hun up there, if it kept the gods happy.

Across the room a nurse was feeding an old woman. The woman was thin and her skin was like silk tightly stretched, so smooth and shining. She had trouble chewing so the nurse was moving her jaws up and down. But she could barely swallow, so the nurse, who was big and black and young, massaged her neck after helping her to masticate, rubbing her neck the way a farmer will massage a goose's neck when he pours grain down its throat to enlarge its liver, from which one day he will make good *foie gras* ... Feeding the patient like this was the nurse's professional duty; but it was also a contest of wills. The old lady did not want to eat. I could see her trying to break free from the fingers clamped around her jaw, but the nurse was not going to relax her grip until the patient opened her mouth and took another bite. She did. Then the massaging of the neck began again and the old lady swallowed painfully, the nurse nodded and smiled, brightly, encouragingly, and implacably.

'You will eat your biscuit; you will swallow your food ...'

I remembered my mother in hospital. I remembered the warning to errant staff who had broken the rules:

'You will pay these fines ...'

My mother had died fighting the nurse, and the nurse had kicked back. For all the sweet talk about racial amity, there was a war going on, and it had hotted up since the end of hostilities had been proclaimed. In truth, there was no peace, there wasn't even a ceasefire. There was more anger, more killing and more hatred. We pretended more desperately. We lied to ourselves more fiercely. Like Oomie, we mutated.

Oomie looked so peaceful, so relieved, because he had made the leap of faith and ceased to think. His brain had turned to a watery mush. Verwoerd, Vorster, Gluhnik, Mandela ...

The place gave me the creeps. All the elderly residents were white; all the staff were black, and young. And it seemed to me that this was the way most whites were heading, straight into old-age homes, with smiling leaders, any leader, looking down benignly upon their last days. Out of the frying pan and into frail care; and pretty damn good riddance most of the country, the young country, would say.

Oomie saw me looking at Mandela and he said: 'A great man.'

'Yeah. That's why he had to be locked up all that time.'

'We didn't know.'

'Didn't know what, Oomie?'

'What was going on.'

'Balls. Everyone knew what was going on. It wasn't possible not to know. Everyone knew about it. People dying, being shot, vanishing, being kicked to death, thrown in jail, being assassinated, shadowed, spied on and blown to bits by parcel bombs. It was in the air, it was in the papers, day after day.'

'In the English papers,' said Oomie, 'but for us that was all just propaganda.'

'Come on, Oomie, be serious. You were amongst the guys who made sure what was going on kept going on.'

'Not me,' he said with complete conviction.

'But you were at the heart of the machine that made this happen.'

'How so?'

'*Because you were there.*'

'I never killed anyone, I never beat people to death, I never tortured them, or shot them and burnt them and buried them in the veld.'

I was wasting my time. You could travel the country and never find anyone who had loved and supported the old regime, the old gang, the old ways. It was a fucking miracle. Everyone had turned into Oomie. Or maybe Oomie had turned into everyone.

Just as bad was the suspicion that maybe this was the way to go. It wasn't just expediency, it was good sense, reasonable, necessary, even – God help us – kind.

'Shall we go get the stuff from my car?'

In the street he seemed nervous. 'You left your car outside, in the street? You're bladdy lucky you haven't been robbed.'

I opened the boot and we looked down at the guns. 'That's why I parked out here. I didn't know what the guards would say to this lot.'

'Jissss,' said Oomie, the air hissing between his teeth. 'There's a bladdy lot of them, isn't it?'

'She was a professional hunter; she needed a lot of guns. Heavy, medium and light gauge.'

'Hell, man, what'd she think I was going to do with all that?'

Go down shooting?

I didn't say it. Why hit Oomie where maybe it still hurt?

And, yes, her armoury was impressive. But then again, when you thought about it, my mother had done a lot of shooting, a lot of killing. In fact, she was, in her way, a big-hearted mass murderer. That was, in a profound way, her *point*.

'Look, if the guns are a problem, tell me, and I'll just close the boot and take them back.'

'No, I'll keep them. They're from Kathleen. She wanted me to have them. It's just that I don't know how we'll get them inside, to my room. We can't just like walk past the desk carrying a load of shotguns. Maybe I could ask a favour? You drive around the corner, where you can't be seen from the desk, and you take out the guns and pass them over the wall. I'll be on the other side and I'll stick them behind the flowers. Then you come inside and help me get them to my room. How's that?'

That's what we did. I lifted the guns over the wall. Oomie hid them behind the dahlias, and then we collected them and took them to his room. It was a modest room with a cupboard, a table, a single bed with a blue candlewick counterpane. On the table was a picture of Oomie and Barrie Gluhnik. The cupboard was too small for the guns so we stowed them under his bed.

Oomie fetched a bottle of Klipdrift brandy from the bathroom.

'Can I give you one for the road?'

'Sure.'

He poured two shots of brandy and lifted his glass. 'Here's to your mom, God rest her soul.'

Again, his eyes filled with tears. What was it about Durban that induced these displays of emotion? I reckoned Alan Paton started the rot with *Cry, the Beloved Country*. Ever since then people have gone weepy each time someone remembered how bloody awful we had been. It has never done a blind bit of good. Oomie wept for my mother, but he also wept for himself. It was a powerful magic and I wished very much that some of it might touch me but it never had. I didn't in my heart feel in the least sorry for my mother. I felt sad that she was gone. I felt unsettled and abandoned, too. Her going had been, like all her departures, on her own terms and at her own pace, and in her own way.

No, if I did feel sympathy for anyone, it was for Oomie. He had been at a loss when he looked at the weapons. He felt uncomfortable to be faced by this gift – enough firepower to blow away a dozen prime ministers …

'What'll you do with the guns?'

He drained the last of his brandy. 'Hell, I don't know. But I'll think of something. Suppose I could always blow my brains out. Isn't it, hey?'

Still, maybe he'd been right about Gluhnik. Because of all those who'd been sure they knew how things would be in the new South Africa, when peace came and the future arrived, if you took a punt on Alan Paton or Gandhi, or Jan Smuts, or Hendrik Verwoerd, or Nelson Mandela, I think you'd have to say Barrie Gluhnik came in an easy winner.

Noddy turned up in Forest Town one night, dressed as he had been when I saw him off: Sunday best, the feather rampant. I put my arm around his shoulders, took his case and told him how glad I was to see him.

He couldn't say anything. He went to his room, hung up his suit and put away his hat. Next morning he was in the garden wearing his old pants and his T-shirt, and the day after that he was back with his other madams. I couldn't pull out the *Times*

Atlas and get him to show me exactly where he had been, and make him feel better about being someone who lived a lot of the time away from home, just as he had helped me to feel better about being a gypsy.

He seemed to be walking in his sleep. He'd been home and home had crumbled to dust. He was bereft. But I could do nothing to help him in his bereavement the way he'd helped me in mine. I knew he had listened to his brother, he had told Beauty to go. Joshua and Sipho could not go back to St Aloysius and the headmaster who had impregnated their mother. That was not possible. And they could not stay at home without a mother while he worked down south. So he had boarded the boys at his brother's place. They went now to a farm school three days a week. A bad school.

Maybe I should have said something that night he'd asked me about Beauty. But how could I advise a man whether or not to put away his wife? And what difference would it have made? Which way would I have gone? I had added my voice to those of his other madams and told him to be kind, to forgive. But I reckoned that in his shoes I was much more likely to have done what he did.

Anyway, it was eating him up.

He bought a blue overall with the legend: 'Executive Horticultural Assistant' in red stitching across the back. In place of his sober blue church suit, he bought himself as flashy a number as I'd ever seen. It was cream silk. It had golden buttons; it had a certain elegance; the vents of the jacket were lovely to look at; the turn-ups fell beautifully on his new brown and white golf shoes.

He had always been a tiny, dainty man but now he seemed to be shrinking, drying up from the inside. It was as if he had decided to be everything he hated before, as if his gravitas, the responsibility that he'd worked so hard for, was horrible to him now and he was going to squander it, ruin it, and ruin himself. Before he was always sober, now he was forever tanked; before he was solid, now he was flighty. Before he was Noddy, the farmer from Matabeleland; now he was wrecked. But showy.

He kept nothing of his old self. Certainly nothing of our friendship. Gone was the steady measured life in his back-yard room. We didn't talk or walk. He didn't come with me to the Zoo, or the costume museum. He didn't attempt to remedy my deficiencies in the garden. Gone was the sober suit on Sundays; gone was weekly trip to bank his wages, carrying the building society book, so comforting and fat in its red rubber bands. It was cash now for everything.

He had a new friend, one of the guys who worked down the road. His name was Jake and he lived in Alexandra and I didn't like him much. On Friday nights, Jake took Noddy to the she-beens in Alex, both in their sharpest suits. He'd be back much later completely smashed. Saturdays they'd wander down to the bottle store and come back with paper bags full of bottles and sit in Noddy's room and sink the stuff like there was no tomorrow.

Everyone was changing but Noddy wasn't built for it. Anyway, he was more interesting when still in his original form. And the least interesting of all was to evolve into a Jo'burg boykie, dress in his cream suit and hit the shebeens with Jake; everything dedicated to reflecting the brilliance, the cock and strut, the shimmer of the feather in his hat.

Noddy was undergoing some kind of internal collapse: a decline from the solid man from Matabeleland, who had weight and substance and reality, to the small, brittle made-up Jo'burg wise guy.

It was closer to self-mutilation. It was not natural organic change but obligatory metamorphosis, a kind of plastic surgery of the soul. The only question was: did you do it to yourself, or did it happen anyway? Let's call it identity trauma in an age of change.

Where does a whale keep its heart?

That was the question my mother asked me once.

I'd been about thirteen and we were walking along the beach in Durban, where we were spending a week's holiday, and we came across two Southern Right whales stranded high on the sand. It appeared that several attempts had been made to pull them back into the sea. Harnesses had been draped over their enormous bodies and, here and there, the ropes had cut deep into skin and blubber.

Near them, in a deck chair, there was posted a skinny white guy, burnt mahogany by the Durban sun, a tiny tennis visor on his mottled bald head and a big box of Westminster 50s in his breast pocket. He was there to keep out blacks, Indians and Coloureds who might have had the nerve to try sitting on sand assigned to others. He was angry now, as only a white functionary could be who suddenly had to deal with the unexpected, and improvise.

'Fucken,' said the deck-chair man.

'Fucken what?' asked my mother, helpfully.

He was not happy, the deck-chair man. In reply he jerked his tennis visor towards the whales.

I saw some kids playing on the whales, scampering up a black and shining shoulder, skipping around the encrusted barnacles, then sliding down again, as if the whales were giant beach toys, huge, inflated inner tyres.

'Fucken people, that's what.'

Such were the crowds of the curious that however often he shooed them away, as one might clouds of flies, the next thing they were back.

Worse, they were 'mixed'. What contributed to the anarchy was the fact that, although people knew they were not permitted on beaches other than those colour-coded to their racial grouping, there was nothing in the law that said you could not go down to the sea and look at two beached whales. The whales were bigger than the beach laws. Besides, the sightseers were not swimming or sunbathing or eating ice creams – all expressly forbidden – they were gawping at two giant fish.

'I got coolies, kaffirs and klonkies ... I got bladdy liquorice all-sorts ... Now, I don't give a toss about these bladdy whales, but that's not nice, is it? Using them as a kids' playground? Taking rides? Some people, they come with knives and cut off whole pieces!'

'It's horrible. They should be put out of their misery,' my mother said.

'Sure thing, lady. But what d'you want me to do? Hit them on the head? I spend the whole bladdy day keeping the fucken people off the bladdy whales. I didn't ask to do it. I get paid to see to the chairs, and the chairs is all I get paid to see to. And keeping the wrong people off the beach. Not off the whales.'

My mother said as we walked away: 'Why didn't I bring my rifles?'

'Do you know how to shoot a whale?'

'I'd find out.'

'Where would you shoot a whale?'

'Head. I suppose. That's where I'd shoot an elephant. I don't know about a heart shot. Where does a whale keep its heart?'

I considered that. The whale had a very large head and so, I assumed, a very large brain. But I did not know where whales kept their hearts. How many shots would you need?

'Ma, I don't think you could just walk on the beach and shoot those whales. They harpoon whales, don't they?'

'What does it matter how you do it? To leave them lying here is a crime.'

The next day the word went out that the authorities had a plan for the humane disposal of the whales. We went down to the beach, and found hundreds already waiting. The deck-chair man seemed to have given up and gone home. The sand had already banked up on the seaward side of the creatures and the smell was strong. They had trucks, a crane and a man in a white coat and lots of municipal workers. There were cops with loud-hailers and we were pushed back some fifty yards or more from the whales.

Supervised by the guy in the white coat, workers cut into the heads of the whales with flensing knives. Then small charges of dynamite were set into the cranial spaces and, with a meaty boom, their brains were blown out. My mother could not resist nudging me. 'See? Head shot.' The cranes lifted the mighty remains on to flat-bed trucks and the headless bodies were taken away to be turned, it was said, into animal feed.

'Next time, save the whales – and blow up the bystanders,' muttered my mother.

Looking back now, through the long lens of memory, I saw her and Queen Bama, sitting in the little parlour, sipping tea and shuddering at the world. Far away and fading fast. And I thought of those whales. Washed up and waiting for someone to come along and dynamite them to kingdom come.

I did not know where Noddy was going, but he was off somewhere, that was sure, and I missed him already. He was one of the few friends I had made since coming home.

Except maybe for Cindy, and so I phoned her and asked her to come over. I had a problem, I said, a problem with staff.

Noddy was forking over the sweet-pea patch, wearing his blue overall with its 'Executive Horticultural Assistant' tag, when I took her over to him.

'Noddy, I want you to meet Cindy; she's a friend of mine.'

He stopped digging and gave her his shy smile. 'Hello, madam.' Then, spitting on his hands, he picked up the big garden fork and went back to his work.

We went inside. Through the windows we could see him working with a furious concentration that made me sad.

Cindy said: 'Noddy? Is that really his name?'

'Noddy of the Five Madams. He insists. But his real name is Uthlabati, which means "Red Earth Man".'

'Where did you find him?'

'He was here when I came. He has the back-yard room.'

Cindy watched him 'He's not a happy bunny.'

'No.'

'Live-in staff are bad news. Very. Most people use the agencies now. You don't need live-in. You ship in who you want; ship 'em out end of day. No drama that way.'

'But don't lots of people still have live-in staff?'

'Yeah, but mostly old-school types. Or they're just plain lonely. The kids have left for Detroit, or Calgary, or wherever.

The house is too big, too empty. So they cling to their staff. Bribe them, pet them, cosy up to them, buy them cars, send them on holidays, even adopt their kids – anything to keep them sweet. It can be useful. You pass it off as proof of what a great rainbow person you are, but it hides the truth: you're shit scared of being left alone so paying the maid's kid to study medicine or rocket science looks good. And maybe it'll keep you safe from burglars, rapists and guys keen to bop you over the head one dark night.'

'Does it?'

'Sometimes. And then again, sometimes it's your staff that does the bopping. You like the guy, don't you?'

'He's from somewhere else. He's like me: a traveller.'

'Yes. But there must be more.'

'I like him, and I let him down. He came to me for help when his wife ran off with some guy and I didn't help. He's been really torn up by it.'

Her pretty face softened for a moment. 'I can relate to that. Happened to me with Andy. Happened to you with your mom.'

'Please, don't give me the Oedipal stuff.'

'Your mom always felt you ran off; she spent her life trying to get you back. She told me so.'

'Listen, she ran off with an entire regiment of guys. She ran off with a bloody continent. She went her way and I went mine.'

'She ached for you to come back, Alex. She wept for you.'

'Are we talking about the same person?' I didn't recognise my mother in the woman she was talking about.

'Yes, she said you only understood things looking back.'

Maybe that was right. Maybe that was what I was lacking.

I couldn't see how to go about making myself into the sort of person who would be recognised here, in Africa, or who could see what others really were. But there was no 'really', just as there was no 'nice'. Only constant refashioning, method-acting your new role until you became what you played.

As I took from the house, one after the next, those things my mother wished her inheritors to have, as I saw the house emptying, I'd hoped to get closer to doing the sensible thing: to sell up and head out. Once I'd tracked down the last of the beneficiaries, I'd be off. That's what I told myself. But I had the uncomfortable feeling that I was lying to myself and it wasn't just unfinished business that kept me stuck in Forest Town: it was something in me. I wasn't finished.

For reasons I could not explain, Noddy was important even as he went down the tubes. There was something about his transformation that I failed to understand and bitterly regretted. Uthlabati, the man of red earth, the man of quality, was on his way to becoming a parody of a flash guy around town. And yet maybe precisely because he was altering so disastrously it meant he got closer to the way to be than I ever had. I kept feeling there was something he was trying to tell me, something my old lady had in mind when she left him to me, along with the house.

'So what do I do about him?'

She gave a little shrug. 'Why don't you fire him?'

'It's too late: he's fired me, that's my problem.'

She put her hand on my arm, then she put her arm around my shoulders and like that we walked to her car. I could feel Noddy behind us, watching, forking over the earth, driving the shining tines deep into the dark red earth.

Cindy said: 'Listen. There's a big bash, Saturday night, at the Prester John's Palace, in Sandton. Fourways Rotary is giving a dinner in aid of Sunbeam Shelter. Not my usual thing, but it's a duty, really. Would you like to come with?'

'With?'

'With me. As, like, my partner.'

'It's been a while since anyone asked me to a party.'

She looked at me steadily. 'Does that mean yes?'

'Thank you. It does.'

She gave her dazzling smile. 'Nothing to thank me for, you may hate it. It may be very, very ordinary. Pick you up around seven.'

She was dead on time, wearing an off-the-shoulder black dress with a neckline whose diving descent between her breasts reminded me of a fast ski run. Her hands were deft on the wheel and she talked and laughed and did her Jo'burg riff as we drove, stabbing the air with her forefinger, a perfect pink nail driving downward as if to tear the air apart and make it bleed. Always this immense emphasis. Noddy had used the same force to drive the garden fork into the sweet-pea patch. I lived in a world of agitated air. Angry interrogation, pronouncement, edict, threat: these were the ways the country talked to itself. What a perfect opportunity for the missionary who wished to teach easier breathing.

But it would have been silly to try. They did not want it; there was no discussion, there was declamation: you shouted, or took a shot at something...

The evening headlines were on the street; blocky black capitals on shiny white posters, wired to the lampposts:

Racism Row Hits Rugby
100-Year-Old Granny Eats Baby
Motorist, Hijacker Die in Shootout
Residents Stone Rapist
Rand Lurches Lower

Cindy was talking hold-ups with the same happy passion with which she'd taught me her rules for staying alive.

'Armed heists, cash-in-transits: they're so bloody well organised, so frequent, you wonder why these gangs aren't running the country.'

'Maybe they are.'

'Yah, and if they aren't maybe they should ... hey? If you're going to be ruled by gangsters, at least let them be pros. Better all round.'

One of my mother's delights had been flying over the Serengeti, skimming so low she could hear the drumming hooves of the stampeding zebra. Cindy got high enumerating the advantages of the secure parking. She gave a rave to the facilities offered by Prester John's Palace and Casino.

'I mean, it's essential. Izzzuntut?'

'Is it?'

'Sure. Who'd go out otherwise? It's like sex, hey? If you're not relaxed, you can't perform. Isn't it? If you don't feel safe, you can't spend. If you're not happy, you won't come. Given the schlep of just getting there, Christ almighty, the last thing some hotel or shopping mall or casino wants is for you to be shot dead in the parking lot. It pays to keep the punter alive. Know what I mean?'

I knew what she meant but marvelled all the same.

'You'll see how good it is at this place we're going to tonight. You're out of your car and into the lobby without looking over your shoulder. Mind you, they learnt the hard way. At the start Prester John's had this idea of transparency, right? When they built the place everything was see-through. Crystal, glass, Perspex: desk, walls, shop fronts, the works. That way they thought nobody could sneak up on them. You could see right through the lobby into the shopping mall on the other side. But the morning after it opened an armoured car drives smack through the plate-glass doors and into the lobby. Four guys with machine-guns jump out, shoot the desk clerk and rob every single shop in about thirty minutes flat. Nobody could do anything but watch. They called it "the see-through heist". The place hadn't been open twenty-four hours and they got hit. It set some sort of record.

'Boy, have we or have we not got talent? These gangs have a structure. On the ground they use "spotters" to case the joint before the hit. Then there are stealers, who hijack the get-away vehicles used for the heist. Then drivers. And then the shooters, who do the hit. They use heavy stuff, often AK 47s, and wear body armour, and send a lot of lead around the place and scare the shit out of everyone. Even if you've got big security. Even if the cops arrive in minutes, what are they going to do? Shoot back and kill passers-by? Anyway, half the time the cops are outgunned. In the effective armed heist we lead the world. One person, one vote, one AK 47. What a town!'

She laughed that high trill in which were mixed pain and pride; true amusement with a sharp edge of hysteria. Could you be proud to be scared? You could if you were Cindy.

That was one of the best things the town did to those who

lived there. When they got to the other side of all the big talk and the bullshit, people took a dark delight in being sinner, shyster, seducer; in being down so deep they had nowhere left to go but up. And how were you going to con everyone else if you couldn't do a pretty good job on yourself? But after telling yourself things had never been better, bigger, richer, safer, fairer, then came the flash of honesty that grubbed in the dirt and the dark, like moles, and came up with what you said was gold. But moles were blind, weren't they?

The Prester John's Palace was a cliff-face of bland stone glittering with glass and marble trimmings, standing in a grid of streets with women's names like Alice and Maud. Within its brightly lit cells, people ceaselessly shopped. The tower held within it the Prester John. We turned into the parking lot and dropped steeply down into the basement, our tyres squealing softly as we descended.

Four levels down, a flunkey dressed in powdered wig and white silk stockings stepped forward, as if expecting us. Cindy handed him her keys, and he all but kissed her hand. We walked out of the garage and into the hotel lobby set about with fountains, finished in black and pink marble. The whole place was hung with banners and posters shaped like hearts, each one pierced by a thorny arrow and inset with the photograph of a child.

'Prester John Loves Sunbeams', said the banners floating in the vast lobby.

'Our Little Angels', said the posters.

The staff wore golden 'Sunbeam' halos with jagged edges.

'Well, what do you reckon?' said Cindy. 'Nicely over the top, or what?'

'I'm impressed.'

'That's the spirit,' said Cindy. 'This just might be fun.'

We stepped into the glass lift and drifted skywards. The lift shaft had been lined in thick pink plush. It felt as if we were travelling up through a very deep throat, fleshy and gleaming. We passed lounge after lounge where thick-necked men in smooth, costly suits sat over drinks in spaces so large they shrank to the size of lonely midgets. The fountains reached roofwards like watery palm trees.

The African Renaissance Room was a domed penthouse built to evoke a giant beehive, or traditional tribal hut, in vaguely Zulu manner. The expansive floor area was broken here and there by rectangles of neatly raked pebbles, and Japanese paper screens. It was a style, Cindy told me, known on the cluster estates as 'Neo-Fusion' or 'Afro-Zen'. The great windows looked down to the highway far below where long lines of Saturday night thrill-hunters, each car chained to the next by the bright links of its headlights, headed for the fruit machines and gaming tables in clubs called The Erogenous Zone and Flagrante Delicto, for an evening of lap-dancing and karoake. In the middle of the dance floor, a raised canvas square with roped borders was rather puzzling.

Cindy looked at it. 'What do you reckon?'

'Of the dance floor? I've been here before.'

Oh, had I ever been there before! What I felt was the shock of the deeply familiar. Laid out before me, in the Renaissance Room of the Prester John's Palace, was an event I knew deep in my marrow. This was, with small variations, what I'd known thirty years before. Maybe it was *foie gras* and not chicken in a basket, maybe it was twenty-year-old Chivas Regal and not brandy and Coke, Martinis and not port and lemon, maybe it was black tie and five hundred bucks, and it wasn't in the church hall, it was a high in the glassy eaves of the Prester John's Palace, corner of Alice and Maud Streets, Sandton – but it was the same damn thing come back to haunt me. I had one foot planted in Vegas and the other buried in the back yard. Thirty years after I left Jo'burg I was back at a fucking dinner dance.

Moving on.

People in this town were continually kidding themselves they had moved on. In fact, what we, our tribe, the last pale speakers of English in Africa, did not do – *ever* – was move on. What we did was to sink into retirement, obscurity. The young in New Zealand, the old on Zimmer frames or taking refuge on residential golfing estates, checking share prices, cruising to the Maldives, or fixing nostalgic school reunions where men called Harry ask for news of Merle, last seen in Rhodesia in 1954, and before that head girl at Parktown High…

Not moving but drowning.

We inhabited a universe whose essence could be summed up in the single word 'more'. We went to bed dreaming of more Mercedes, and woke up dreaming of more mansions on the coast. Our former serfs seemed to have hit on a way of destroying their old tormentors by giving them what they wanted – *more* – opening their mouths and pouring it in, making sure they swallowed it, like the nurse did, her fingers massaging the throat of the old woman in Oomie's retirement home. More! Shovelling down our gullets the treasure that would choke us.

'No, not the dance floor,' said Cindy. 'I meant the ring.'

·

'I don't know. That, I must say, is new. Kickboxing? Mud wrestling?'

She gave her helpless, happy, despairing laugh. 'Oh, my God! Let's find our table. Whatever it's for, I'd like to be sitting down when I find out.'

Large round tables covered in creamy linen were liquid with silver and crystal. Our table was beside the dance floor. There were flowers and pink place cards and a crowd of people hitting the scotch. Our table companions were reasonably tanked, and talked about themselves with the openness of Jo'burgers meeting for the first time. In a few minutes you knew where they worked, what they believed and where they played golf.

To my right sat Sharalee and Duane, who were in advertising and marketing. To Cindy's left sat Lindiwe and Tembi, in matching gold and black tunics. Lindiwe was with the Ministry of Health; Tembi headed up a black empowerment outfit called Afri-One.

Sitting opposite them was a merchant banker called Jacobus; he sold what he called 'financial instruments'. His wife, Monique, helped small businesses to cross the divide between the old, cold South Africa and the new, warm fiefdom of the future.

Beside them sat Rupert and Petronella, a couple of leathery throwbacks. Rupert once headed up the Farmers Bank. Petronella, solid as steel under her green silk gown, her face sitting high and proud of her immense bosom, was a lifelong trustee of Sunbeam Shelter. The sunburnt folds of their faces were stitched into smooth seams rather like crocodile-skin handbags. They embodied a type: ruddy-faced men; women with rasping voices who had once had it all for the taking –

sun, smoke, whisky. Their coterie had once run state banks and nationalised industries. They'd got out when the former regime collapsed, fortunes intact, and now did very little: some charity work, a lot of golf. They'd washed up in comfortable retirement, wrecked but rich.

Also there – corn-blond hair, and a rumbustious manner – was Willem. And on the other side of Cindy a guy called Dikene. Their wives, Nicoleen, white, slim and svelte, and Tanzi in black, ebony and ivory, like two piano keys. They talked babies. Willem and Dikene talked money. Willem was in construction. Dikene had been a youth leader in 'a local party structure' until, said Willem, 'as CEO, I decided to bring him on board'. In doing so he had made Dikene a millionaire. In return, Dikene had sweetened Willem's image among the new masters of the universe by altering his alias from what Willem happily described as 'exploiter, racist and Boer bastard' into what Dikene called 'a forward-looking element within the new democratic structures'.

It was hard to think of Willem, so exuberantly what he had always been – a noisy bully with a big bank balance – as an 'element' in the ' structures' of anything except his sport-bound world. But words were the paint needed to tart up old models, and words came cheap and were mutually advantageous. The cosy swap Willem and Dikene had pulled off had nothing new in it. The pattern had been fine-honed over the decades by the Dutch, then by the British, then by the Boers, then by Afrikaner nationalists so recently departed. In those days, heavy men like Willem (except then he would have been among the supplicatory classes and spoken English) with interests in cement, or steel, or gold, would have palled up with men just like Dikene (he would have been an Afrikaans power-broker) and cut a deal.

It was called 'mutual co-operation' then; it was called 'transformation' now; but whichever you named it, everyone agreed that this time round it was genuinely new. There had never been anything like it before. Right? Forget the past, forget what the world was, or you were. Embrace forgetfulness, dissolve your doubts, and don't listen to anyone who said things were not a thousand times better. Forgetfulness wasn't just useful, it was patriotic. Denial wasn't a fault, it was a career move.

For this was our destiny, we the pale ones, we the ridiculous ones, who had neither the gall of our old masters, who knew that murder was better than prevarication and power was more perfect than any principle, nor the authenticity of our new rulers because they can say what we never could, except when lying through our many pieces of fatuous headgear. They can say they know who they are. We never even get close.

Those around our table, huddling close to what they hoped were the new renewable forms of power, skimmed across a glittering surface, gold ring on one ear, cellphone tacked to the other, telling themselves, 'We've changed, we've changed, we've changed, we're moving on, we are new, we are free, a liberated, tolerant tribe, with DVDs in our BMWs, anti-hijack satellite trackers in our 4x4s, winners in the racial rainbow stakes...'

It looked like being quite an evening.

Supper was served. There was smoked salmon and venison. The wines were good. The waitresses, in short black skirts, white aprons and mob-caps, moved between the tables, but I had the feeling some moved very slowly, unsurely, and others held hands. And their eyes were strangely still.

Cindy whispered, 'Do you think those girls are what I think they are? The ones that bump about a bit between the tables?'

I said – not quite believing it myself – that I thought they were.

Cindy let out a long breath and raised her eyes to heaven. 'God Almighty.'

Petronella, across the table, caught her look. 'You noticed, hey?'

Cindy nodded sweetly. 'You're using blind girls as waitresses?'

'Not all. Some of them can see a bit. Each unsighted girl has a helper, like her seeing eyes. At first we thought they could use their dogs but Prester John's management said no dogs in the dining area. So we got in seeing girls, too. There are eighteen waitresses altogether. Nine from St Thomas's School for the Blind and nine from the Orange Grove Orphanage,' said Petronella briskly. 'Fourways Rotary believes very strongly in helping the disabled.'

'*Ag*, shame!' said Nicoleen. 'Blind girls, and girls who got no moms or dads. Working for kids in Sunbeam Shelter. That's so cute.'

In a way they were. Most of them in their teens, peachy-fresh in their maids' outfits, flushed and nervous as they reached to clear plates and glasses and serve fresh courses.

Lindiwe from the Health Ministry was talking about ramps. 'Government wants to improve access for everyone: the handi-capped, as well as women, and kids, too. Government says participation at all levels is the aim.' She took a large bite of venison. 'That means more ramps!'

'Ramps?' asked Jacobus.

'Lots more ramps,' said Lindiwe. 'Government has a national plan to install ramps outside all government buildings and to make a plan to employ quotas of disabled people in all government departments. But government can't do it all. Government looks to private enterprise. Government hopes all stakeholders will come to the party.'

'I think it's wonderful, letting people participate,' said Monique, who helped people bridge the transition between old and new South Africa. 'I think it's fabulous. It's just a pity that those who make change happen in our country don't get the recognition they deserve.'

At about ten o'clock, over coffee and liqueurs, the lights in the Renaissance Room dimmed and bright spots flooded the boxing ring, which had small flickering neon hearts hanging from the ropes. A girl in a golden cloak dipped under the ropes and stood in corner of the ring. A man in a silver cloak took up a position in the opposite corner. A second woman in silver and second man in gold now entered the ring: four cloaked figures in the four corners of the ring, where the pink neon hearts flicked on and off. Ravel's *Boléro* started up and with a simultaneous flourish, rather like that which waiters use to lift the lids of silver salvers, all four people in the ring removed their cloaks and stood there, wearing nothing but a coating of oil, brief thongs and ballet slippers.

A man and woman moved now to the centre of the ring, grappled, and began to mime, in detail, positions from the Kama Sutra, while the other couple waited at the end of their ropes. It was something between tag wrestling and a live sex show.

This beat the hell out of anything I might have imagined. Judging by the way Cindy reached for my hand and squeezed it, I think even she was pretty shaken. This was, after all, as I kept trying remind myself, a fundraiser run by solid citizens on behalf of a school for kids with special needs. But, then, as Cindy never tired of telling me, this was also Jo'burg.

The Renaissance Room was very quiet. I guessed that even old hands were pretty awed by what was playing out in the ring. The only sounds were the occasional chink of glasses when one of the sighted waitresses blundered into something. To the blind waitresses the dark was no problem, but it made things hard for their orphan helpers.

In the spotlit ring each dancer, or partner, replaced the other until, in a loud finale, all four people joined in a palpitating foursome of backs, bottoms and body oil, a choreographed group orgy, and everyone clapped and whistled.

There was pistachio ice cream for dessert with a lychee sauce. I sat there in a little buzz of happiness. I had just seen simulated sex in a boxing ring in front of a room full of Rotarians.

I could admit it now, Cindy had me on toast. I thought I knew Jo'burg. I was wrong. I understood then her helpless awe when confronted by the inventiveness and grotesquery of local life. A-I kooks; alpha lunatics. You couldn't have told anyone about what I'd just seen: they would not have believed it. I struggled to believe it myself.

A waitress squeezed her way past the back of Rupert's chair and he turned appreciatively and said in a clear voice, 'Nice little backsides they got, hey?'

Petronella spoke to him from on high, as if she were some ocean liner hailing an errant leisure craft: 'Rupert, man, don't let's have any nonsense, hey!'

'*Ag* man, I'm just looking.'

'Looking never stops there,' said his wife.

And it didn't stop there, with the pistachio ice cream and people back on the dance floor, because, what with the wine and the floor-show sending a charge though the crowded room, things got hotter, and it was the waitresses who felt it first. A hand lay lightly on a passing hip; at the next table a big man with a beard pulled a girl on to his lap. Somewhere someone was crying. At our table, Duane planted a kiss on the nape of a waitress who had bent to clear his plate, and a small blonde girl who made the mistake of reaching past the old leathery crocodile straightened suddenly with a little scream, and ran away, tripping as she did so and sending her tray crashing to the floor. And all around me women were saying, loudly, accusingly: '*Ag* shame, man!'

Someone took the mike then and said he had a 'Very Important Announcement', but wild cheers drowned him. 'Please, folks, please, folks,' he kept saying, until at last they let him speak. 'We're getting reports of some folks preventing the girls from approaching the tables.' (Applause) 'Now, it's been a lovely evening, guys.' (Cries of 'Yes! Yes!') 'Let's not spoil it. Play the ball, not the man.' (Laughter) 'Our waitresses have done a sterling job here tonight and they want to get home to bed.' (Laughter/cheers) 'So folks, may I ask you to take your partners for a last dance…'

They all danced, and then they all sang the national anthem. It sounded pretty good, too, and quite covered up the sound of the sobbing that went on softly somewhere out of sight.

•

In the car Cindy said: 'Well?'

'A complete triumph.'

She glanced across at me and said in the straight way of hers, 'Do you want me to take you back?'

I thought about it, about the empty house, about Noddy, brooding in the back-yard room.

'I don't have much to go back to.'

'That's what I reckoned,' she said, and swung the car towards Midrand and Sheerhaven. It was past midnight, the traffic had thinned, and the pavements were deserted. Only the lost, the dangerous and homeless walked after dark.

We stopped at the lights where Sandton Drive hit William Nicol; the headlines read: 'Ten Shot Dead in Bed.'

A huge triangular neon sign mounted on a traffic island flashed its message in the night: 'Say Hello to Safe Sex or Say Goodbye to Life.'

Later, she lay back with her eyes closed, her dark hair spread on the snowy pillow, the tip of her nose pointed directly at the angel blowing a trumpet which she had painted on the ceiling, a blonde angel with flesh like butter, borrowed from Rubens, and a pretty face borrowed from her son, Benny.

With her clothes off, stretched out, there was something entrancing about her symmetries, the way she lay perfectly horizontally, and pointed: her nose at the angel, her nipples at the overhead light, a fluffy affair of pink satin; her toes, smoothed with a soft nail varnish, aiming at the mirror on the wall opposite the bed, a scalloped mirror of gold frame and bevelled glass in which, for the past hour, Cindy had been riding. Making love, for her, was rather like making off on some far trip. She worked softly, slowly, with little circular movements of her pelvis, her eyes shut, a lock of hair over her eyes, a look of peaceful intense concentration. The mirror gave back its brazen view, her firm brown breasts rising and falling above my softer, older body as she built and built and rode herself to climax.

Then there was Cindy ridden, someone else again: stretched out, letting her head fall back over the base of the bed, her strong brown to my pale, mothy white. Her dark hair trailing, her eyes open, expectant, as if I should take her somewhere; as if, by watching and hoping, by some miracle, she should not end up where she had started.

v Mutant Strains

'Wapiganapo tembo nyasi huumia.'
'When elephants fight the grass gets hurt.'
Swahili proverb

28

Cindy and I had a thing going, though precisely what it was neither of us knew, or much cared. I asked her, just once, what she saw in me.

'I see your mother in you.' Enjoying my bewilderment, she added, 'And, for that matter, so does Benny.'

She was so clear about it that all I could manage was 'Really?'

'Sure. That's why he likes you.'

Cindy took me as one takes a trip, a slug of booze, a whack of something mind-bending: for respite, relief, escape, recreation; yes, in order, for a while, to think of something else, to be someone else.

Her hair, cut to a point over each cheekbone, reminded me of the tips of black palm fronds. Her short, sturdy body, her short perfect shirt, her high backless heels, her slightly chunky calves, big leather bag, her poise on those high heels, her air of someone always being perfectly turned out even though she also always seemed to have thrown her clothes on at the last moment, always in a hurry, always late. Yet all of her always arrived together.

Cindy was the most accomplished actress and make-up artist. It was her ability to become the woman she played that fascinated me. I had been in awe of Maxine, and her passion, but she was, in our terms, very familiar. Cindy came trailing all sorts of recognisable signs that tied her to this place, to Africa, yet so much of her was strange and new. I'd never met anyone so fiercely original. I think I fell in love with her in much the way uncounted uncles had fallen in love with my mother, and for very similar reasons. The intensity of her vision of herself and her city and her life. My mother escaped skywards, reaching across the continent from Cape to Cairo, but that had been in another era when the rulers of all had automatic overflying rights. You could say my mother never had her feet on the ground (she would have been the first to agree). Her feeling about Africa was that it actually encouraged her to leap over it in her seven-league boots. A version, indeed, of the boots she had left to Cindy. They were far too big, that was clear from the start, and the contrast in the way they saw their worlds was also vastly different. Kathleen Healey's was the view from the clouds. Her Africa was airy, free, and endless.

Cindy was an insider. Her country a was a tightly guarded stockade, a Tuscan villa set in an English close; copper storks on the lawn, fat golfers shuffling over the fairway, electric fencing and infra-red sensors buried deep in the earth to stop the tunnellers; it was a pink Porsche, sudden death at the traffic lights. It was, at the same time, utterly of the place; and about as far away from 'Africa' as she could get. It was about being somewhere else.

Cindy, too, like my former wife, Benita, had never in her life met or mixed with Africans. Cindy lived among millions of darker-skinned people but it did not mean she saw them, knew them or credited them with any sort of existence except as a shadowy presence: benevolent when it washed dishes, wicked when it erupted in fury and kicked someone's head in.

To some degree they both shared a view of Africa as an island, midway between mundanity and mayhem. Just as the Dutch have reclaimed precious land from the sea, privileged South Africans have turned back the tides of Africa by building dykes, beautiful walls, fences, barricades, built them not just of bricks and razor wire but of strategic ignorance.

The differences between Cindy and Benita became terribly clear when you knew where they came from. Benita was once vaguely 'British'. Cindy would have been called 'Coloured', or 'mixed race', 'brown Afrikaner', mulatto, or some other ugly designation. In the recent, even more cracked terminology of our new times, some insisted she be called 'black'. But in truth, and in life, she was as far from being black or African or native, as Benita was from being British. Benita believed or imagined that she possessed a real provenance: she came from somewhere and, much more importantly, she come from *someone*; she belonged to a long and honourable line of Anglo-Saxon adventurers who had headed off for foreign parts and called them home. Or so she said. But people like Benita were ghosts. She called herself 'African' but it never convinced anyone; not even her, I think. People like Benita had to pretend to belong, pretend to be normal, pretend to be alive.

Cindy didn't know who her progenitors had been and, for a long time, if she had known she wouldn't have said a word about it. She knew, so ran the common wisdom, that people like her did not exist till Dutch settlers slept with slaves, or Hottentots, or anyone else in convenient chains, and then, appalled by their own faces in the mirror, denied any resemblance. People like

Cindy were walking warnings of what happened when you crossed the racial borders marked out by our rulers from the very first moment white met black in Southern Africa, and unbuckled his belt or reached for his rifle.

But while all claims to identity had been a boast, or a lie, it had been the 'Coloureds' who were forced to live out the cruellest fictions.

Cindy was a ghost, pretending to be a Jo'burg princess. The one-time 'Coloured' girl from a dusty township was now the mistress of Sheerhaven, with her Porsche and her Gucci bag and her stunning impersonation of a Jo'burg dolly-bird, as svelte as they come this side of Sandton, living in a sphincter-tight security in a villa in Beauchamp Drive, in what she called '*absolute bladdy luxury*'.

You'd have sworn she was straight out of Parkview and Saxonwold and Sandton, Sandhurst and Rivonia. A good school, followed by a couple of years on a fine arts degree. She was the epitome of the Jo'burg 'kugel', those warrior matrons, or Armani maidens, named for round doughy sweetmeats, so delicious and so dangerous, stuffed with raisins, and razor-blades.

Every stroke of this portrait was made up as she went along. And she didn't pretend it was anything else, she was proud to be what she'd turned herself into. That was the advantage of being forced to lead many lives: sometimes you hit one that suited you, one you could pass off as your very own. She was a lovely creation, and she'd done it all herself: a true queen in a camp full of con artists.

What I did not realise – not for a while – was that she might decide to do it all over again.

The only time Cindy showed any sympathy for her ex-husband was when she told me that Benny was not just a Down's boy, he was also slightly autistic.

'That really finished off Andy. He used to say he could deal with the other things because we knew what to expect. I mean how Benny looked, the rounder face, and the fact that he was slow, that he didn't grow as fast as other kids, and the way he had a smaller mouth and the way his tongue stuck out. It still does. Maybe he could have taken that. But then there were Benny's fixations. He will only sit on a special chair in one place at one time. He switches every light in the room on and off exactly six times. He carries the tennis racket with him everywhere. It's a toy and a friend and security blanket. He goes to bed with that racket. When I changed my car from the Porsche to a Merc, he went bananas. I had to go get the old car back.'

Benny was her joy and her terror. He was, I suppose, not only her child but also the child in her. Because of his slow and dreamy way, because of his fixations – with small round objects, golf balls, plum tomatoes, marbles, which he would twirl between finger and thumb for hours at a time, and his distant but affectionate way of hugging her, or me, or the cushions on the settee, or the table leg, with equal passion – he had an unearthly remoteness you simply could not penetrate. He would, occasionally, abruptly, affectionately, reach out to you; but you could not reach into him.

Watching Benny was like watching a creature in a perpetual state of preparing to be, to come out into the world. And though he always seemed on the brink of doing so, Benny never emerged: he was away in his own space, and love might look in, but it could not step inside. It pained her terribly; she tried but she could not reach into him. He was sometimes perfectly loving, but only on his own terms. He hugged and kissed her, but he hugged and kissed me, too, and anything else that took not his heart but his inner eye – he tried to hug the Porsche – his love simply went equally in all directions.

'Oh, hi, Alex,' was all he said one morning, when he found me in bed with his mother. 'Have you seen my golf ball?'

'You left it in the fridge, with the tomatoes,' said Cindy.

Benny nodded. 'Good, it keeps fresher that way, doesn't it?' And climbed into bed with us.

He said to his mother, 'Why have you got no pyjamas on?'

'Because I'm as warm as toast.'

Benny drew back the sheets and looked hard at her naked body. 'You do not look like toast to me. You look like … an orange …'

'Why an orange?'

'Because you got all little grooves in your skin, just like an orange.'

'Those are goose-bumps,' said his mother, who found Benny's dreamy stare, so deep and yet so blind, very disconcerting.

'Why did you got them?'

'Because I'm cold.'

'You said you was warm as toast.'

She firmly drew the sheets around her. 'I was, until you took the blankets off.'

'An orange,' Benny repeated, 'a blood orange.' He turned to me. 'And you look like a clothes peg.'

'Now we know what we look like and it's quite a combo,' said Cindy, 'the blood orange and the clothes peg.'

·

It might have been worse. We were a peculiar couple. Perhaps alliance better described us. No: on balance, 'act' is the better word. A fine double act. She played the Jo'burg princess; I was the visiting hick from abroad. Our oddity came not just from the difference in our ages but also from many oceans of otherness between her past and mine. It didn't matter because we pretended so. That was not hard to do. We had been many other people, in many other places, before landing the parts we were playing now.

To her friends she introduced me as, 'This is Alex; he's from overseas.'

It was the best disguise I could have had. They talked, her friends – Dean and Sharon, Lindalee and Tristram, Lionel and Hephzibah, Izzie and Bopi – above and around and across me. Sometimes they asked me what I did and I said I travelled and sold air-con, and that did what it always did: my profession faded immediately as a topic of conversation. How many times had I been grateful for its vanishing qualities.

Travel: that got them more interested.

'Where to?' they asked.

'Cambodia, Burma. Malaysia ...'

They nodded vaguely, their faces relaxed; lands of no importance.

'It's just so hard to get a handle on, being in those places,' said Cindy.

That was fine by me. It was like those near-death experiences where the patient, apparently unconscious, hears and sees what is going on around him, while doctors and nurses talk about him as if he wasn't there. It was like being Lazarus; except that people actually saw Lazarus when he came out of the tomb, restored to life. I was more like one of the ghosts in

Virgil's Hades, pale and bloodless and not merely ethereal but clueless. I said something of the sort once, and Sharon wanted to know where Hades was.

'It's where souls go after we die. It's what the Greeks and Romans called the underworld.'

'I knew it couldn't be northern suburbs, or I'd have heard of it,' she said.

29

To Koosie went my mother's old flight plans, escape routes and Washington's fright-wig. The routes she flew were detailed in her large round hand on yellowing pages of lined foolscap and preserved in plastic envelopes. An aerial diary of desperate, often dangerous escapes; fake flight plans she'd filed with the authorities, as well as the real routes flown; dozens of risky trips to remote bush strips and secret airfields in Zambia, Lesotho and Tanzania. Notes of mechanical problems: 'compression down/cylinder/50 over 80 psi...' A fat dossier of charts, diagrams, fuel estimates, weather forecasts, times of arrival, payloads.

When I told Cindy I was going to Soweto to see Koosie, she remembered him instantly.

'The thin guy in the limo at Kathleen's funeral? Can I come? He said I could. Only... what do I wear?'

'Whatever you feel comfortable in.'

'One thing's for sure: I won't feel comfortable in whatever I feel comfortable in.'

On a bright blue Thursday morning, I picked her up in my old lady's Land Rover. Not that I reckoned her pink Porsche wasn't just the job for Soweto, but it simply wasn't the sort of car I'd have felt comfortable in.

She wore a white T-shirt, a pair of denim jeans so snug they seemed painted on, a broad belt of fake snakeskin with a silver buckle the size of a soup plate. Between her breasts, reminiscent of presidential heads carved into Mount Rushmore, smiled the bearded, slightly podgy face of the young Nelson Mandela, bought, I guessed, from the hot boutique in Rosebank where Steve Biko and Bram Fischer and Hector Pieterson had moved from being martyrs to fashion idols, from torture cells to T-shirts, for a generation unborn when they died.

'Whadya think?' she asked me. 'Here I am, armed to the teeth. Do I have what it takes?'

'You look wonderful.'

'But do I look right?'

'Who knows what's right for Soweto; I'd say you're perfect-ly pitched. I'd say you're exactly on the money, I'd say that's remarkable, for someone who has never been there. Must be osmosis.'

'Os-*what*?'

'Never mind. You look great.'

Cindy had also dressed with certain anxiety and I sympa-thised. What do you wear when you're heading off the planet, into intergalactic space; how will the aliens receive you? But her instincts, as always, were sound, because Soweto was as much an invention as she was. The journey alone that we made that morning, from Sheerhaven to Soweto, was at once so wild and so humdrum that only the paranoid could take it in their stride. We moved, in a forty-minute drive, from the gilded northern ghettos to the smoky dormitory town, south-west of the city. We'd traversed galaxies.

Soweto was a puzzle. What it was depended on who was asking the question. Sometimes it was Jo'burg's sister city, sometimes a revolutionary bastion. Its real name, South Western Townships, spoke of banal anonymity lurking just below the sexy acronym. It was never planned as more than a dumping ground for those kicked out of real places. It was, and it wasn't, a city. It was Jo'burg's guilty secret, where the city walled off its workers and told them they were in heaven. Miles of brick bungalows in the spreading veld, under the cooling towers of the power station which, so the legend went, supplied electricity only to Johannesburg. Just as Soweto existed only to supply workers to the city of gold. Even the numbers of those who lived in Soweto was subject to doubt and manipulation; was it one, two or three million? The answer varied, depending upon whom you asked. But since the riots of 1976, followed by the shootings, riots and sieges of the eighties, and the election of 1994 that brought Mandela to power, everything had changed. People said so in the strangled way that warned you not to ask what had changed, or they'd take a poke at you.

After 1994, increasingly, those who could, got the hell out, headed for the other places, for the real 'suburbs' in the 'real' Jo'burg. Places like Houghton and Morningside for those with the bucks; high-rise slums like Hillbrow and Yeoville for the stragglers.

I hadn't been back for years. Last time I'd seen Soweto my mother had been flying blokes out of the country; there had been armoured cars on the dirt roads and blood in the dust. Soweto, when I knew it, had been a dusty dormitory of modest brick houses roofed in corrugated iron, stretching away for miles, with some pockets of conspicuous affluence. As far as I could see, so it was still. The cops and the armoured cars had gone, but it seemed Soweto had been asleep for decades. I knew it wasn't so: the country had been turned upside down.

But everything I saw and heard and smelt was so the way it had been that it was hard not to feel shocked by the unchanging familiar blur of it.

Koosie was still in the small house in Diepkloof where he'd always lived, only the black Mercedes under the blue striped awning was a sign of status.

He opened the door himself. 'Hey, Alex, good to see you back here again after all these years.' He gave me a hug. 'Hey, that's good. It's been too long.' He felt thin, frail almost, his bones small under the good blue wool.

'You remember Cindy?'

'Sure? Kathleen's funeral. Don't be shy, Cindy. Come in, come in! Welcome to Soweto. I like your shirt, and that belt.'

She melted; you could see it. That they took to each other was not surprising. They were the made-over people, the changelings: Dr Sithembile Nkosi and Ms Cindy September, in their starring roles. I was a fly on the wall and, probably, in the ointment, the man from nowhere. Just as Cindy had dressed for Koosie and the township, he had dressed for her, the rich blue suit, the careful cuffs; dressed for his status as an arrived man, but dressed also, I had the odd feeling, for disguise, to stabilise himself before meeting us.

'Let's have coffee, or a drink, or something, and then I'll take you on Dr Nkosi's Eyeball-to-Eyeball Tour. Show you over the place, top to bottom. You'll like Soweto; and Soweto will like you.'

Cindy said: 'That'd be fabulous ... If doesn't take too much of your time.'

'I got time,' Koosie said carefully. 'I haven't been into the office in months. In fact, in fact, not since your ma came to see me. I've been on sick leave.'

I said: 'Nothing serious?'

'Bit of this, bit of that. I'm much better. Got a new doctor who isn't trying to kill me.'

He laughed, and we laughed, as if it was natural that your doctor should try to kill you. As if killing you was what doctors did.

I gave him the flight plans and the maps in the big plastic envelope.

'Kathleen left these to you in her will.'

Koosie took the envelope. 'Escape routes. That says it in one, doesn't it? Your mom always had a sharp sense of humour, isn't it, hey?' He turned to Cindy. 'Kathleen used to fly people out of the country. She was wonderful. She was a true friend.'

He put the envelope down as if he wasn't quite sure what to do with it, then he smiled his thin, clever smile.

'What's the wig?'

'It's a fright-wig. It belonged to a boy soldier called Washington, up in Liberia. A souvenir of a friendship.'

Koosie shook his head. 'Boy soldier! Your ma never missed a trick, did she? That guy, where did she hide him, finally?'

Cindy said: 'What guy?'

Koosie said: 'She was hiding a Cuban doctor who skipped from Zim.'

'Was she?' Cindy shook her head in affectionate admiration at the oddity of her friend. 'She was truly something else, your mom. What did she do with him?'

I said: 'Mambo, among other things. He was teaching her.'

'Oh, my God, to mambo!' She was laughing helplessly and shaking her head and half crying all at once. 'Where's he now, this guy who was teaching her to … mambo?'

'All I can tell you is that she went out and got him a new

identity. Bought it. Apparently, it isn't difficult to do, if you know the right people. There's an army of new South Africans and my old lady's Cuban joined the ranks. Apparently, it's a fucking growth industry.'

Koosie told Cindy: 'She came to see me about her Cuban. She wanted me to help and I turned her down.' He tapped the plastic package. 'That's why I got left this: evidence of our old adventures. It says she helped others. And me. Then I let her down. And the wig says it, too; I was a boy soldier once. But I had forgotten it. That's what all these presents mean. That I forget I was a rebel. Except it wasn't like that.'

I said: 'Wasn't it?'

'I tried to tell your mom: those days are gone! I didn't forget, I just grew up. What we did then we can't do now.'

'For God's sake, Koosie. The guy was a refugee from Castro's Cuba. Castro locks people up. Castro's a creep. But for you Castro's legal because he's a socialist brother.'

'Alex, the guy was on the run. He had absconded from a country where he was contracted to work. He was in South Africa illegally.'

'What's this legal shit, Koosie? Fact is, legal is what you decide it is. Legal is what suits, when you say it suits. Once upon a time you guys legged it across the border, and that was good and legal. But a Cuban medic who goes AWOL, he's a criminal and should be locked up. Even though he's running from the despot on our own doorstep, Bob Mugabe. But Mugabe's legal, hey? Because he's an African brother. So your party props him up, just like the old regime propped up the old white Rhodesia. For the same reasons.'

'I find it damn offensive for you to compare our democratic

government with the old apartheid regime. If it wasn't for our revolution, you would not be free.'

'Koosie, let's be straight. There was no revolution. As a liberation movement your lot were complete bloody wankers, from start to finish. What actually happened was that your people and the last lot cut a deal. The guys with the guns, and the guys with even more guns, they carved up power between them. That left people like me, and the Cuban, and anyone who wasn't one of your guys or their guys, absolutely bloody nowhere.'

Koosie was angry. 'If it hadn't been that we were so damn magnanimous, you lot would have been in the dock for war crimes. Like the Nazis at Nuremberg.'

'Guys, guys, guys,' said Cindy, taking our arms and leading us out to the car. 'Where's that tour you promised me?'

We took his car. Cindy sat next to Koosie who began an expert, loving, funny, sometimes scathing, and altogether riveting performance, emphasising his points with wide sweeps of his arm, like a conductor encouraging an orchestra to deepen and enrich the sound, painting his town in all its moods and all its originality.

Koosie giving his eyeball-to-eyeball tour was Koosie at his best. None of the earnest moralising that seemed to have become the other side of his nature, nothing of Koosie the party loyalist. He was sardonic, sharp, unsentimental. And he loved the place the way you love a dangerous kid. He told us house prices were on the up; and guys no longer got thrown out of trains on their way to work; and crazy folks didn't open fire from the windows of Zulu hostels, well, they hadn't for a while.

Touch wood. And the taxi wars had quietened down so he did not wake to the sound of AK 47s ... And with each deadpan line he'd glance to see if he got the reaction he wanted; and he did. Cindy's face mirrored all the joy and terror and delicious awe of the first-time visitor to a legendary scary place. He was, for a while, the old Koosie, the guy who took to me to downtown Jo'burg on Saturdays to watch the weddings go by. The boy I grew up with, my brother, and my friend.

'This suburb where I live is called Diepkloof. It comes in two versions. Like a lot of things. The Diepkloof you see here is a bunch of little houses, each with a shack or a garage or lean-to in the tiny back yard, and this gets rented out. The lodgers in the back room get no water or light. Rents are *very* expensive but people will take anything ... because they can't get any place to live. Only in Soweto do you get middle classes who are pretty poor, but who're also slum landlords at the same time.'

The houses began to expand now into mini-mansions, bulky, brick palaces with front gardens and real garages, and no shacks in the back yard.

'Here is the other Diepkloof, where you find our upper classes. Mostly bank managers, drug dealers, and so on. They keep BMWs in their garages, not tenants. You'll notice there are no burglar bars or watchdogs. Or walls. This is a low-crime area. No one steals. Because if you do, you're dead.'

We passed the hospital. 'This is the Chris Hani Baragwanath Hospital. Biggest hospital in the southern hemisphere. Hani was a friend of mine. Poor Chris, leader of our army, fighter and communist, gunned in his suburban driveway by two white fanatics just before the 1994 election. The hospital can be dicey sometimes. Doctors hijacked, even gunned down as they left work. Couldn't have that. Bad for morale. It's safer now than a few months back. They've beefed up security at the front gates.'

Cindy swallowed hard. She was hooked; Koosie's delivery kept the concentration level high.

Next up was the lost car pound, where hundreds of vehicles waited like stray pets behind the wire for owners to reclaim them. Recovered from hijacks and hold-ups; retrieved before they could be driven over the borders, into Mozambique or Zimbabwe, or disappeared into a local chop-shop, a kind of oxyacetylene abattoir, where a few deft strokes of the welder's torch reduced desirable models to their lucrative body parts.

'If you lose your car,' said Koosie to Cindy, 'come look for it here … or right next door, at the cop-shop. Sometimes the cops bring them here.'

'Good.' It was the first word Cindy had spoken since we set off.

'Not really. It can be unlucky.' He smiled. 'Our cops do a big trade in spares. You might get your car back, missing just about everything.'

Past the school, where a couple of men had shot a teacher the week before; and on to the great taxi rank, where hundreds of mini-vans waited, rumbling and steaming, ready to run to anywhere in Africa, from downtown Jo'burg to Lusaka, or Cairo.

'It's a long wait, so the drivers grab some sleep, or they do a bit of dagga. No wonder when they hit the road at three in the morning they're not always in a good mood.'

The real pleasure of his tour was in Koosie's performance; and Cindy's face.

She said: 'How poor are really poor people?'

Koosie touched Cindy's sleeve. 'Let's go to Mandela Village.'

Mandela Village was a slum of small wooden and plastic and tin shacks, with rutted dirt paths between the houses. We met Daisy, who had four small kids and a husband in town, looking for work. The shack was small and clean and terribly empty of everything but babies' blankets and cooking pots. The floor was hard earth. The walls were papered with Sunlight soap wrappers and looked wildly bright. It had been home to Daisy for eight years. The whole impression was of order and patience, and Daisy herself exuded a dignified despair.

'I hope things get better for you,' Cindy told her.

Daisy simply sighed and shook her head, too polite to contradict.

Outside on the street, Cindy said: 'I'd like to go back and give her something. But I feel bad about giving her money.'

'Go back and do it,' Koosie said. 'She has no electricity, no running water except a stand tap or two, no job. Daisy is the sort of person we promised to help, nearly ten years ago, but the cheque's still in the post. Then we'll go on to the "shrine".'

This was a granite circle and a large parking area: the Hector Pieterson Memorial. Within the granite circle there was reproduced in all its grainy horror the image of the dying boy being carried by another boy, like a sacrifice, an offering, into the guns of the police. The boy seen carrying Pieterson that day was called Mbuyisa Makhulu, and he disappeared after that march and was never seen again. He almost certainly died at one of the camps where cops like Oomie had been based.

'The shrine,' said Koosie. 'Remember the day – 16 June 1976 – when schoolchildren with no weapons of any kind took on the state.'

What made the 16 June uprising so remarkable was its single-minded simplicity. Kids still in school were ordered to learn Afrikaans. Being ruled, beaten, mocked, used and hated by murderous and stupid persecutors was something they had withstood as best they could for what must have seemed like for ever. But this was too much: they would not be forced to speak the tongue of the enemy. They said no, and they marched into the guns.

The children's revolt belonged to them: it had nothing to do with the liberation movements. A true rebellion, so amazing it was still not fully comprehended and was now increasingly hard to recall in all its blood and bitterness. Now it was patchily commemorated in a public holiday, and served as an occasion for self-serving speeches by tired functionaries and rambling monologues far removed from the spirit of that spontaneous, leaderless revolt.

As the spirit diminished, the shrine deteriorated.

We struggled to find parking; the big coaches were depositing French, German and British tourists. It had always been foreigners who went to Soweto, to see it for themselves, to visit the memorial to Hector Pieterson and the schoolchildren's revolt.

'We have a way of turning tragedy into a tourist trap.'

Koosie waved his hands to embrace the touts waiting around the flower-beds: hawkers of bad American rap and elderly editions of African verse, cellphones clipped to their belts.

'These guys like passing themselves off to foreign visitors as the heirs of the children's revolt.' Koosie shook his head. 'It doesn't work: foreigners know racist American rap when they hear it.'

I said: 'Mark a place as sacred, elevate it into a site of pilgrimage and you get touts and hawkers making a quick buck. Selling the saint's dandruff. The virgin's sacred unicorn. It happens at Lenin's tomb in Moscow; it happens in Bernadette's grotto in Lourdes. It never stays pristine.'

'Why not? Why the crap?' Koosie asked. 'Why not some … respect?'

'It doesn't stay pure because, probably, it was never pure in the first place. It's getting towards thirty years since this boy was shot. He's a hero; but he's also a draw. Maybe it's a sign of normality. Messy, meaningless, commercial normality.'

'Then I don't want it; it's too soon.'

'I know what you mean,' said Cindy. 'You want things to stay, like, pure. Pristine.'

'I do. That's the word, "pristine".'

'Like it ought to be,' said Cindy.

I said: 'Making things like they ought to be is what did the damage. To us. To the country. I hate it. It's brought us nothing but blood.'

'Alex doesn't understand,' said Koosie kindly, with an edge of mockery in his affection.

'That's what I tell him,' said Cindy.

Koosie and Cindy smiled the smile of fellow conspirators who knew at a deeper level than visitors, than strangers, what constituted reality because they lived in a place they have never left, a place called 'home'; who felt they knew it, loved it, fought for it, owned it. Who made their personal geography into morality? Who believed that if things were not right they must be made so?

'Keep telling him,' said Koosie.

I left it there: it was enough that they got on; enough that Koosie talked more easily to her than to me; enough that Cindy was beside herself with pleasure. I got this shiver at the back of the neck, this hollow in my middle, this terrible falling feeling, because those who will do anything to keep things 'pristine' generally mean what they say. All forms of perfection seemed to cost a lot of lives.

We pulled up next at a very ordinary little villa and Koosie said:

'Nelson Mandela's old house. It is not so very remarkable, is it? Do you want to see inside?'

'Yes, please,' said Cindy.

'I'll stay here,' I said. 'You go with Koosie.'

Cindy said, upset, even a little shocked: 'You don't want to see Mandela's house?'

'It's a fake.'

'I don't believe it. It can't beeee,' Cindy wailed.

'Well, not a fake, exactly. More a reconstruction,' said Koosie delicately. 'The original house, that was destroyed.'

'Who by, the police?'

Koosie paused carefully. 'No. It was the neighbours.'

'Why did they do that?' She was appalled.

'When Mandela was in jail on Robben Island, Winnie lived here; this is where she kept her football team. You know, the kids she sent to mess up people. This is where those kids got locked up at night and some of them didn't come out again. The stories out of this place were not good. They were disturbing for the neighbours. Maybe the screams, too. One day the neighbours here, they burnt the house down.'

Cindy didn't say anything.

Koosie took her arm. 'It's called a Museum of the Revolution now, and it will cost us a couple of bucks at the door.'

I watched them go in. He held her arm and she looked up at him. Teacher and pupil. Koosie was good, he was sound, but there was something not right with him. Cindy's ignorance was deep and sincere . She knew no history, of her own, of her country, of its past. Didn't know, didn't want to know. The kids who'd been held in the Mandela house had been guilty of not being as they ought to be. Not pristine. The fatal flaw. But Cindy didn't know a damn thing about what had happened to them. The nature of what she did not know was embarrassing, and normal, and even, perhaps, admirable. After all, Cindy was emphatically part of the new; and part of that was not needing to know about the past. She knew where to shop, what to do to protect herself against robbery, rape, hijacking … what more did she need? And if she did need to know, then someone would supply. Koosie was showing her Soweto, much as the poor schmuck, her husband, Andy Andreotti, had shown her Sun City. Come to think of it, though they served very different purposes in the wild cavalcade of South African life, each place was as horrendous and as unreal as the other.

When they came out, Cindy was crying. I thought it must be that she was so moved by what she'd seen in the house, and what she'd learnt of the tragic struggle of Sowetans. Though a moment's thought would have told me that Cindy did not cry over politics. And politics would not explain why she kept putting her arms around Koosie and hugging him. He looked abashed, uneasy at all this attention, as if he hadn't meant to stir up this emotion.

We drove back to his place without speaking. Cindy was behind us and she had trouble stifling her sobs.

When we got back to his place Koosie didn't ask us in. He thanked me again for my mother's gift to him. Standing outside his house, in his blue suit, the sun glinting on his gold cuff-links, he waved us goodbye with the big plastic envelope that held her old flight plans and the escape routes, upon which, in another age, many lives had depended.

We were back in northern Jo'burg, riding through streets lined with tall walls, razor wire and sentry boxes, when she said:

'I'm sorry I made a fuss back there. But it really got to me.'

'Soweto?'

'No, not Soweto. I liked Soweto.'

I must have looked blank because she said: 'I got an inkling inside five minutes of meeting him. It isn't just that he's thin, it's the look. There is a definite look, and once you know it, you don't mistake it. I've seen it before. And then, when we went for our little walk around the Mandela house, he told me. Straight out. He made it a bit of a joke; he said he couldn't tell you because it took a South African to understand.'

'Understand what?'

'Six months ago he tested positive for HIV.'

I did not know what to say.

'When he was diagnosed he was with a private doctor who prescribed ARVs. Antiretrovirals. He was lucky. Most people don't get them. He started taking the ARVs, but then he stopped.'

'Why did he stop?'

'He says Aids is a syndrome and a syndrome isn't a disease. He said his problem might be due to a whole lot of factors. Diet, genetics, spiritual malfunction. There are other treatments, other solutions. And he is exploring them: his phrase again.'

'But he knows he's ill.'

'He says he hasn't been well. He does not say he has Aids. And even if he did, he takes the line taken by a lot of powerful people here, right up to the President, that antiretrovirals don't help with Aids. That is, like, the party line. Official. Aids is not Aids, it's something else. It's TB, bad nutrition, malaria, it's a lot of local diseases, alone or in combination. Aids is a syndrome. ARVs, the drugs that fight it, are a conspiracy by Western drug companies to plunder sick people. And to poison Africans. ARVs – so goes the line – are more dangerous than the disease itself, which may not be the disease they say it is anyway. Koosie believes he can lick this thing without drugs. If he eats the right food and believes the right people. He's incredibly determined to do the right thing.'

Loyalty was what Koosie had always had. For Koosie, the Movement was not just his family, it was his church, it was his supreme guide. It had happened, this conversion, shortly before the shooting of Big Lou. In Koosie's religious scheme of things, the tiny killer who shot Big Lou was some sort of divine messenger sent to reinforce that faith. It was a faith he would die for, or kill for. He held his own life cheap when the divine adjudicator demanded obedience. Oh, yes, Koosie was loyal. Pristine. And I might have said dangerous, bone-headed, lamentable, principled and deranged; almost as crazy as all the other oafs who had ruled over us. Though I didn't say so.

We pulled up at a red light. On the traffic island sat a small tow truck with a logo on the driver's door that read: 'Harry's Cash and Carry'.

Cindy said: 'See that stubby little blue pick-up swinging a hook, parked on the traffic island. They call them happy hookers. Those pick-ups work the streets, just like girls on the game. Except these vultures are after road-kill. They listen in on police radio frequencies to catch news of a smash and head for the carnage. First come, first served. There are fights. They pay the cops kickbacks for early warning. But sometimes business is slow so be careful at crossings like this when it's wet. And after dark. Because when business is slow, the happy hookers like to sweeten the odds: they may reset the lights, or spread oil on the road after rain.'

'Nice guys.'

'It's a job.'

'I'll remember.'

'Good. Might save your life.'

I said: 'What's going to happen to Koosie?'

'Without the ARVs he'll die.'

'And this new doctor he talked to us about? The one who isn't killing him?'

'He's seeing a traditional healer. A *sangoma*. She's giving him some sort of special *muti* and he swears it's doing him good.'

I was unsure of what sort of response was required, or fitting, in the face of so much dying. Saving one's life was pretty problematical right now. The value placed upon any individual existence seemed to be not only sharply diminished but caring about it at all seemed to smack of intolerable elitism.

Soweto itself was marked by it; everywhere in the country was marked by it. The Pieterson memorial stood for heroic death, freely faced; the Mandela house remembered the death of children by torture; Koosie, thin, elegant, angry, smiling, wanted to dodge death by – what? Syndrome? But, then, what Koosie feared more than death was unbelief. Salvation lay in cleaving to the party line; in a land where the line was long ago shot to ribbons, and the party was a fractious band of avaricious fat cats fighting for position and power, Koosie remained a true believer. A kind of saint.

The Land Rover drifted along, through Craighall, Sandton, and on towards Four Ways and Lone Hill and Sheerhaven. I went with the flow, serenaded by the day's dark blues:

Crowds Stone Suspect
Uncle Rapes 6-yr-old
SA Tops Travel Poll
Gold Up
Eleven Cows Hacked with Pangas
Gold Down
Drugs Don't Cut Aids – Minister …

30

I wasn't in Forest Town much after that. It was too sad; just me and the wraith of my mother and an ectoplasmic Noddy, who went on living in the back-yard room and haunting the garden: remote, shadowy and unapproachable.

When I did go back to the house, it was with Benny, carrying his tennis racket. He loved looking at the pictures of the animals my mother had shot, and the mounted kudu heads, the leopard-skin rugs; he loved the picture of my mother with Baldy the grey parrot on her shoulder. He was sentenced to look always for things that made sense to him in a world where making sense was an ordeal. He was impervious to change and fiercely dependent on routine. And so we did the same things, in the same order, each time we visited my house. After turning all the lights on and off in precise patterns, we looked at photographs. I had to tell him in exactly the same words the story of how Baldy learned swearwords from the Flying Dutchmen who came to clean the house, when Koosie and I were boys. He was particularly fascinated by the pictures of Bara and Buti, the rainforest pygmies, and hearing how they stalked, and ate, old Baldy.

The way Bara was shown sticking his tongue out fascinated Benny. He always stuck his tongue out of his rather small round mouth, just as he was always smoothing the soft straight hair over the fold of skin at the back of his neck with small square hands on which his small fingers had just one joint, instead of the usual two.

'What does parrot taste like?' Benny would ask, holding his racket to his face and pressing the strings against his lips. With the racket strings breaking up into fleshy cubes the soft skin of his face, he looked like some odd little animal imprisoned in a hutch.

'Like fire-crackers and old shoes,' I always said.

'Do his feathers stick in your throat?'

'For a week and a half, at least.'

Cindy told me that he was so cemented into routines that Benny would take a trip with his classmates from the Sunbeam Shelter but when they got to the park or the cinema, or the museum, Benny stayed right where he was. Only when the bus was back at the Shelter would he agree to leave his seat, and then only in the correct order. He went last of all.

I took to spending the rest of my time in Sheerhaven, as a kind of honorary resident. The guards at the gate no longer asked my business; they knew the car, and they nodded me through. And once inside the walls, under the great silver sewer in the sky, I felt I'd migrated to some strange, quiet country. Maybe that is what it was, and it made a sort of sense: after all, if people lived parallel lives, they needed parallel worlds in which to live them. The rich no longer needed to move to other countries. They could build their own.

And there was Cindy. I hadn't decided what to do yet, and she didn't ask, and I was grateful. I had bequests to deliver; I still had to find Papadop and I had to see Queen Bama, and until I'd done what I'd undertaken to do, I was content to stay.

Being with Cindy was a bit like being at some non-stop late-night party where you feel, despite the fact that you're having a great time, that for some reason you can't quite put your finger on – perhaps it's your age, or the decor or the music – something doesn't quite fit.

On the other hand, what did? This was Jo'burg. Nothing fitted.

And then there was Koosie.

'You and Koosie are as close as that.' Cindy snipped her forefinger and index finger together. 'And yet you're at daggers drawn.'

'Maybe it comes of being almost brothers once.'

'He needs you now.'

'No, he doesn't need me. But I think he needs you. I think you remind him of my mother.'

She looked pleased. 'Really? That's a lovely thing to say.'

I didn't pay much attention then. Later on, I wished I'd thought harder about what I'd said, and why I'd said it.

'He was your friend first. Will you come with me?'

It was true enough. But what I did not say and she would not have understood was that the friendship had foundered long ago. After Koosie's conversion to the Cause, and to the anger I had first seen, but not understood, when Big Lou was shot.

'He won't thank me.'

She came over and kissed me. 'You're weird. D'you know that?'

'I know it.'

'So will you come?'

•

We got into a routine. Three days a week we'd drive from Sheerhaven, drop Benny at the Shelter and head on out to Soweto, and stay maybe an hour. We did not so much talk as listen because Koosie was growing weaker, he was in pain and it made him short-tempered and insistent, about everything. He was still losing weight and he complained of headaches. He insisted he was getting better, that he was responding well to the *muti* he'd got from the traditional healer. She was seeing him each morning and she was working marvels. He would be better soon. We never saw the healer but we saw her roots and powders beside his bed.

A few weeks later he was suffering hot and swollen feet. Increasingly often he wasn't up before noon. We went late in the day, and we cut the visiting time to thirty minutes. He tired so easily and he would nod off in the middle of a sentence ...

Then suddenly, without any sort of preamble, he announced that he was on new medication. And he had another 'health adviser'.

It was a strange term to use.

'What happened to the traditional healer?' Cindy asked.

Koosie shrugged his thin shoulders as if he could not be bothered to think back.

'She's not around any more. She moved on.'

'And the medicine she gave you, the special *muti*?' Cindy asked.

'I stopped taking that. It didn't agree with me.'

One morning, we found him sitting at his kitchen table drinking tea with a visitor, a sturdy, quiet, pale woman called Millie Loubser. She came from Brakpan, on the outskirts of town, and ran a garden-care business with her sons, when she wasn't helping people with Koosie's symptoms. It was hard to believe that a man like Koosie would be content to swallow large pink capsules from a bottle marked 'Celestial Solution', but swallow them he did. They were boosting his immune system, as Millie Loubser promised they would; he could feel it.

'She's a miracle worker.'

Koosie indeed looked good; he seemed stronger, he was almost his old self again, and he owed it all to her and her treatment.

'She turned up, like a gift from God. I opened the door and there she was. She looked at me, deeply, oh, so deeply, like she saw into my soul, and she said: "Do you want to live?" And I said yes.'

Millie Loubser diagnosed him as suffering from what she called 'immune imbalance', leaning into the syllables as if they were the name of some pop song or dance movement. Imm—une Imm—balance...

'He's stronger every day, thank the Lord. I prayed for him to be spared, to live his life in and for the Lord. I've had patients far worse than this gentleman, and they're healthy today.'

As we were driving home Cindy said: 'The woman is a bloody fraud.'

She was, too; but what were we to do about it? Koosie believed in this pleasant charlatan, and that was the end of it, for the moment.

'Look at me!' Koosie would say each day. 'Aren't I better?'

And for a while he was. He religiously took the capsules three times a day, after meals, until he could not longer keep his meals down.

Cindy challenged Loubser. 'What qualifications do you have for treating someone like Koosie?'

Millie Loubser gave her a sweet smile. 'I had a favourite sister and she died of cancer, and the pain I felt was terrible. I am treating over a hundred people today, they come to me because I help them.'

'At how much a throw?'

Millie Loubser was unperturbed. 'One hundred rand for a week's supply of Celestial Solution.'

'You are a fraud; you take dying people for a ride.'

'If I take anything, I take their suffering into my heart. I ask God to ease the pain of people like Dr Nkosi: I pray for him to be spared.'

'You charge him a hundred bucks for a pack of pills. You're a fucking shyster, a blooming harpy, a vampire ...'

Millie Loubser looked at the furious Cindy and said simply: 'I forgive you, girlie. In your anger and pain you know not what you say. I will pray for you, too.'

'Pray for me, and I'll kick your teeth in,' Cindy said.

Millie Loubser did not stay to have her teeth kicked in. Koosie suddenly stopped taking her pills and, like the traditional healer, Millie Loubser no longer came to the house.

'I feel better without her,' said Koosie.

It became an exercise in helplessness, a drive to the now familiar streets of Diepkloof, there to sit and watch the cruel decline of a vibrant man. It was made worse by having to see the disease killing him and to feel we were being forced to attend some sort of religious seance. But the alternative was to stop visiting. So we had learnt to reduce ourselves, in the face of Koosie's remorseless emaciation. Cindy wore no make-up, she chose clothes that hid her flesh, masked her evident health, that would not seem an insult to the stick-thin man with the shining eyes.

We were the visiting party, the sympathisers, the people who wanted to help but could not. Cindy was very affected by her feelings of helplessness.

Coming home from Soweto of an evening, we would pass Buffalo Belle's and, it seemed, there was trouble. Women in white cowboy boots and stetsons, wearing very short skirts and carrying placards – 'No To Foreign Sex-Workers' – lobbied motorists at the stoplights. Their breasts fell forward into the driver's window when they leaned into the car and asked you to sign their petition to keep the joint open.

It was not sex for sale that got everyone so worked up. It was the girls selling the sex, the émigré paperless whores from Bulgaria, Cambodia, Burma and Estonia. The girls about whom Mona-Lize became so exercised. Taking jobs away from perfectly good local tarts. What did a girl from, say, the Hmong hill tribes of Vietnam know about the libido of the home-grown male? About golf? Or rugby?

'Keep lust local,' said these angry girls. 'Keep pussy patriotic.'

It went on for some weeks. The papers began to pick up on these protests – if rather gingerly – in headlines like 'Fourways Sex-Workers Forum on the March'. Headlines were always wordier when political correctness kicked in, and never did it kick in faster than in matters of sex.

Why not 'Whores Get Mad!'?

Too close to the bone; too un-South African.

We were travelling between the dying man and the protesting girls. I was struck again by the mischievous, if not malicious, juxtaposition of tragedy and comedy that South

African street life did so effortlessly. Cindy called Millie Loubser a joke. Yes, she was, if you could bear to laugh. And it did not stop there. We moved daily from the bedside of a dying man to the bordellos of the northern reaches and home to eerily, superbly sterile Sheerhaven. It was all perfectly ordinary. All in a day's drive.

In the following month, Koosie was in hospital twice: he had a bout of meningitis, and he also developed pneumonia. But he wasn't daunted; indeed, he put up with these illnesses almost cheerfully, with a sense of relief. They were identifiable, proven, curable; and he recovered.

That is to say he did not die. He came home from hospital, his bones poking up against his skin. He stared at us with hot eyes. They had given him a catheter; he was wearing nappies and he had full-time nursing care.

Dr Toodt was Dutch. She simply turned up, just as the others had done.

Dr Toodt said: 'I am a medical doctor, a trained chemist, and a researcher with many years of experience. I plan to treat this patient with micro-nutrients. I am here at the request of the Ministry of Health. They sent me and they trust me; and they know I can help Comrade Nkosi.'

To be 'sent', to be 'trusted', to be 'known': the sacred trinity of success.

She had an open, square face with strong, well-defined bones, and a very square jaw; and best of all, she was qualified. It seemed she specialised in cases of Koosie's sort. He was suffering from severe dietary deficiencies that had undermined his immune system.

Angela Toodt had developed a dietary supplement called the

African Antidote; it was composed of carrot, garlic, beetroot, lemon juice, yoghurt, banana, and *mielie-meal*, bolstered by various anti-oxidants, as well as grape seeds, lychee flesh, and extracts of the African potato. She was sure of everything. 'I belong to Africa,' she told us when Cindy asked about life in Holland, and I had the impression that what she really meant was that Africa belonged to her.

We were getting like Koosie, clutching at straws, and, for a while, we were very pleased to see Dr Toodt at his bedside.

Koosie took the medicine, when he could keep it down, and sometimes he seemed to brighten, and then he would call me to his bedside, obsessed with finding the missing Cuban. Our earlier argument over what was 'legal' was forgotten. In his increasingly confused mind, it was as if finding the Cuban would not only repair the damage done by his rejection of my mother when she went to see him but, somehow, by regularising the refugee medic, he would be making a kind of recompense that might count well with those spirits in whose power it was to see him live or die.

'Time for your treatment, Dr Nkosi,' said Angela Toodt.

Cindy confronted her one morning.

'Why don't you put him on antiretrovirals?'

Angela Toodt looked at her calmly, as if this was a question she had been expecting and which it was possible, but only just, to answer with a modicum of civility.

'He doesn't need them, he doesn't want them, he would not take them if I gave them to him.'

It was chilling, watching this determined woman keeping African indigenous healing, Western science and the exigencies of Leninist discipline all in some sort of balance. She stood not just for the powers of the land but for health and sense and political probity: a woman who espoused by the belief that micro-nutrients, potato, garlic and lots of vitamins were making Koosie much better when, plainly, Koosie was dying.

We knew it, and he knew it.

'Find him,' Koosie would beg, 'and I'll fix it. Then he doesn't have to live his life as someone else. He can be himself again.'

'Koosie, I'll try. But please don't worry.'

Cindy also felt I should find Raoul. He had been the last man with whom my mother associated. Curious, how the Cuban worked on people. Schevitz had been just as insistent I should do something about him.

Koosie was comatose for long periods now. Cindy sat with him, holding his hand; I'd walk up and down the street. Dr Toodt continued to administer her diet of micro-nutrients and vitamins intravenously, and she saw an improvement.

She sent off regular blood samples for testing and confronted the results with grim equanimity. Koosie's immune system was now so weak it was prey to any passing opportunist infection.

We were watching death by ideology. Koosie was dying, persisting in saying that he was not ill, in line with party dogma. Both the physician and the dying patient were driven by principle, and Cindy and I were powerless to do anything but look on, excluded as we had been from what the principal actors considered the miraculous 'African Antidote'.

Cindy again challenged Angela Toodt. 'If you had what he has, would you take antiretrovirals?'

'I would not. They are toxic and they do not work.'

'The virus is killing him!'

'There is no virus,' said Angela Toodt.

But there were, nonetheless, signs of resistance from the patient himself. Not from Koosie the party member, but from Koosie the human being. He found it harder and harder to keep going, and this somewhat irked Dr Toodt who, though she never said so, gave the impression that he was not really trying hard enough; and what he was not trying hard enough to achieve had touched a metaphysical plane. It was no longer a question of illness: it was a matter of faith. Koosie was barely alive. Even Dr Toodt knew it. What mattered now was that he should achieve a good death.

We would return from Soweto to Sheerhaven wretched and depressed.

Then, one evening, the protesting cow-girls were gone, the sprawling ranchero stood dull and lifeless, the neon lariat on the roof was cold, a large lock hung on the gates. Instead, we saw police cars and a hovering helicopter. We were too exhausted to do more than note it in passing and wonder what was going on.

The answer came on the evening news. Belle's had been raided by the Aliens Investigation Unit. The cameras showed a group of women herded like frightened sheep into the street. They wouldn't show their faces: crouching on the pavement in the TV lights, legs bare, holding their handbags over their heads like hats. I remembered seeing on one of the last marches of the Fourways Sex-Workers Forum outside Buffalo Belle's, aimed at exposing the foreign competition, how they lifted their skimpy shirts to show, pinned to their panties coloured like the national flag, the slogan: 'Proudly South African!' The foreigners were a mixed bag: they came from Bangkok, Bucharest, Moscow. According to the report, the girls had been charged and then released on bail into the care of the medical officer serving the establishment and who was, it seemed, the only bona fide South African in the place.

There was a shot of him: he smiled a little bashfully at the camera; he wore a grey safari suit and large spectacles. He looked very convincing, and you would have said he was typically South African, if you hadn't once met him in another incarnation, in another life, when he lived in the back-yard room of your house, danced the mambo with your mother and was called Dr Raoul Mendoza.

I never knew whether it would have made Koosie feel better to know we'd found my mother's Cuban. Probably not. He was too weak by then to have done much about it and, anyway, I wondered what anyone could have done about it. Koosie's analysis of the position as he'd given it to my mother was correct. If you bought his line on legality, it mattered to Koosie that Raoul would be who he was. But why? Who in their right minds wanted to be who they were? Dr Mendoza was dead; long live Dr du Toit, physician to a group of foreign female refugees, who wanted as much as he did to be anyone in the world but themselves.

Our Cuban had been transformed into something so close to the real thing no one would ever be able to tell the difference. From where I stood it looked to me like Raoul was fine. Hell, he was better adapted and adjusted than I was. Dr Cornelius du Toit no doubt had all the features that testified to his new estate: the BMW, a gun safe, a swimming pool, and plenty of staff, behind a tall wall where he talked rugby and threw another chop on the barbecue with all the assurance of one born to braai.

·

The next day, when we went back to Diepkloof, the house was empty, Koosie was gone and so was Dr Toodt. We went over to the hospital and there they told us Dr Nkosi had died during the night.

Cindy said to me: 'Dr Toodt would have written the death certificate, wouldn't she?'

'She would.'

'What's the bet it says meningitis or pneumonia? Poor Koosie. She gets to say what he died of, she gets to tidy it up.'

I saw what she meant. How he died or why he died were beside the point. It was not the virus that killed him. He would have been struck down by a confirmed, observable, legitimate disease: malaria or TB or pneumonia, or 'acquired immuno-suppression'. His would have been a good end. Dr Toodt would have made sure of that. Yes, poor Koosie. Not only fictional lives, you also got imaginary deaths. Someone, some-where a long way away once said history was written by the winners. Not here it wasn't; here it was written by whoever made out the death certificates.

The Party arranged his funeral. We drove to the marquee, pitched on a football field. There were flags and speeches and songs; there were invocations of Koosie's past and his service to the cause and the struggle, there was praise for his loyalty, and his courage. There was no word spoken of his illness, and it was possible that many of those present were under the impression that he had not died at all but that he'd gone into quiet retirement, beside the sea perhaps, or somewhere in the country.

Then we followed the hearse to the graveyard and Koosie was laid to rest, and then six young men on motorbikes did a series of wheelies beside the grave, revving the big machines and kicking up clouds of red dust that made some of the guests cough and splutter, though they took it in good part and joined in the applause for the motorbike riders.

Back at the marquee, the sit-down meal was catered by La Rochelle Fine French Foods, the funeral DJ played Kwaito hits, and soon the party was swinging.

Cindy said: 'It's more like a wedding, isn't it?'

She was right: what started as a funeral became a kind of party. I kept remembering how, when we were boys together, brothers together, Koosie had taken me on Sunday afternoons into the hollow centre of the empty city to watch the gorgeous brides and grooms perched up on the back seats of the big Lincoln Continentals. What they were doing, in the face of blind immovable stupidity, was showing a bit of flash, having a bit of fun. I had the feeling Koosie might have liked the send-off he got.

Cindy said, 'I think maybe it's like a party because it happens so often. Because of the kill rate of the virus, because there are just so many funerals. People must spend almost every Saturday in a graveyard. Watching family and friends being buried. You can only take so much grief. So you begin to jazz things up. Like making a good show of it. Going out with a bang. Because that's the best you can do.'

Maybe so. But it was strange. The funeral wasn't just a party. Matters of status were involved. It had a kind of glossy format. It felt almost – if you forgot for the moment why you were there – like a religious revival. Koosie wasn't dead, he was elsewhere; there was no death, there was only dancing; there was no virus, there was only vitamin deficiency. So you took the tablets, took your partner, took courage, and danced at the edge of the grave till you dropped.

So we danced, too, Cindy and I.

'It's a pretty weird party, even so.'

'Weird is where we begin,' said Cindy.

31

To Queen Bama: her knitting patterns, her collection of needles, in bamboo, metal, rosewood; her crochet hooks; her magnetic case for metal needles and her big pencil box for wooden and plastic needles; her wools, remnants of yarns – merino, silk, and several balls of 10-ply wool in bright yellow and cerise, once destined to become a huge and serpentine scarf. All the other bits and bobs a knitter needs were in a small linen bag that closed with a bone button: things like needle-sizers, shawl closures, scissors and thimbles. In an old tin that had once held golden syrup she kept bobbins, buttons, blocking pins, stitch holders and a box of plastic point protectors in lime green and flesh pink, with which she always carefully capped her metal needles.

I was carrying all this out to the car when Noddy came to me. He faced me, his manner polite, distant.

'I have a woman who may stay with me.'

'Good,' I said. 'Very good.'

'I'm telling you because it's your room and I must know if that's good with you.'

'You can have whoever you like.'

I was really pleased; maybe a girlfriend would make things easier. The man facing me in his blue overall, with the ridiculous job title he'd stitched in red across his back, was not Noddy, as I knew him. I missed my friend and I wanted him back.

I found my way to Lebalola country using the map in the pamphlet about the pleasures of the Platinum Province, handed to me by the Rain Queen's praise-singer at my mother's funeral. I had never been to visit Queen Bama *in situ* before, and all I had to go on was my mother's account of her first visit, sixty years earlier. On that occasion the Queen sat on her yellowwood throne, wearing a leopard-skin cloak, in front of her Great Place, flanked by courtiers and counsellors.

Her Great Place was situated on a hill known as Heaven's Tip and it was not particularly impressive. It looked like many hillsides in the Magaliesberg, a lunar loneliness, scattered with rusty boulders and dusty green scrub. I parked and walked up the hill. I found the village in the last of the light. Maybe thirty huts around a baked-earth compound, empty but for a few thin dogs and a couple of dripping stand-taps. Some of the huts had TV aerials above their thatched roofs. In the smoky evening among the huts, without a clue where to go, I heard her calling me.

'Welcome, Alexander, son of Kathleen, to the land of the Lebalola, to the country of Queen Bamadodi.'

I had thought I'd remembered the Rain Queen in every detail. A big woman, almost as tall as my mother, with an easy step. The little gnome who called to me, sitting on the stoop of an orange brick bungalow with a corrugated-iron roof, seemed a long way from the powerful woman I remembered; except, perhaps, for a smouldering, melancholy anger. She wore no cloak trimmed with leopard-skin; she was sitting in a Lay-Z-Boy recliner chair of what looked like yellow leatherette, rather patched. There was no court; there was no praise-singer; there was only, from somewhere behind us in one of the huts, a radio pumping out rap music.

Queen Bama said: 'We are in mourning for those who have gone. You cry for your mother who has gone to the Lord, and I cry for my daughter; she died a few days ago.'

I didn't know what to say.

'I had three daughters; two have died already. Before. And yesterday the last who was my eldest, she also died.'

She waited a moment and then she said: 'If the Queen has no daughters, as I have now no daughters, another girl has to be chosen.'

I didn't ask the question but she felt it in the air between us.

'But what will she find, the new Queen of the Lebalola, the one who comes after me? What kingdom will she come into?'

Around us, pressing close, the night was velvet, smelling of dust and dung and Africa. The rest of the people of the village, it seemed, were in front of the box, watching the usual Hollywood shoot-ups. Queen Bama stiffened in her Lay-Z-Boy recliner at the sound of repeated gunfire.

'Once, we took water from the river and we kept water in the calabash. Once, it was precious, it came from the sky, and we knew what it was to thirst. Then those boys, the new boys, from the government, they came here, and they said: "We will change things, we will give water to a million people, we will send water into the taps and people will drink and wash."

'And I chased them away with a sjambok; I hit them and hit them some more. But now, see, they have done what they said. We have a pipe and tap where once we had only the river below the hill. Oh, they were very happy! They laughed and said: "Yes, Queen Bama, things have changed and we have changed them."

'And again I took my sjambok then and I ran at them and I beat them and beat them till they cried and they ran away and they were shouting: "You may beat us, Queen Bama, but we are right."

She leaned over and spat on the ground. 'They are dogs. They are fools, they are liars. They put in their pipes and their taps and they say this is better. Where does it come from, the water that flows in the taps? From heaven! And where will it come from when the heavens give no more?'

There was no feast that night. Queen Bama and I ate a little chicken and rice from a tin, and she poured me a very strong brandy with a little water, and then I slept in a hut with two plastic chairs and a skinny metal bed.

In the morning, when I went to say goodbye, she was sitting in her Lay-Z-Boy, holding a heavy knobkerrie, and on the stoop in front of her were several rows of what looked like large bedsocks, or the soft nose-cones of woollen rockets, or very big tea-cosies, some with a pink or green tassels at their tips. Queen Bama took up a knobkerrie and began turning over the items at her feet.

'What are these, Queen Bama?'

She got up from her chair and with her knobkerrie she lifted up a woollen tower, knitted in pink and peppermint zigzags, crowned by a bright green pom-pom.

'Have you not heard, Alexander? Do they not have it far away? In places overseas? The slimming sickness that men have brought to my people; as men bring dangerous things. The sickness that took away the daughters of Bamadodi?'

'The doctors came from the hospital and they showed us little socks. And they said: "Women of Lebalola, these socks guard against the sickness. Show your men. When they come to you, show them how they must wear them."

'And we said: "Yes, these socks are well to wear but see how small they are. They fit on a finger." And so they told us to make big, big ones of wool and to take them to all the villages to show people.'

She held up the knobkerrie with its knitted candy-coloured condom bright in the early morning sun. Even here, in the large-scale production of teaching materials to be used in combating the Aids virus, the natural genius of the Lebalola knitters had reproduced on woollen condoms the patterns painted on the walls of their mud huts: the zigzags of lightning, the bright metal blue of the highveld sky and the black and grey undulating lines of the laden rainclouds.

I knew then how Queen Bama's daughters had died; I knew the sickness was rife amongst the Lebalola.

Queen Bama looked at me. 'What are we going to do?'

She asked me, just as she had once asked my mother, but I couldn't answer, like my mother, 'Search me, Bama,' and reach for the mint-green Royal Doulton teapot and the date loaf. And we couldn't hug each other and shake our heads, women together, appalled by the cruelty of the world. I wasn't my mother, I was only my mother's son.

Tears ran down her cheeks and into the dust; and the next thing I was crying, too.

She stopped first. She sniffed, straightened her shoulders, shuffled her feet, rocked her hips, and then she danced.

She had been the relief of my childhood. She had flown in the face of all the lethal cannons of customary boredom aimed at me. She did not – magnificently did not – do anything that everywhere passed for being 'normal'. She had always been – gloriously, stubbornly, madly – herself. The Bama I had known since I was a boy, and this was why I had always loved her. What she stood for was full rivers, irrigation, fat cows and dams aslop with chocolate water. What she knew was that much of Africa was desert and the desert was gaining. Queen Bama knew that water was more than H_2O; she knew there were cycles, seasons, rhythms, and unless they were observed with love and respect, they would die; and when they died, more of Africa would die, of disrespect, of neglect, of thirst.

I had to smile, and seeing this she danced harder, and I was with her, all the way. I even laughed. So did she, though it was more like a groan. We laughed, it was terrible, yes, but what were the alternatives? The woollen towers, castles, hoods and sheaths standing erect? The loss of those we loved; the mocking young men? The implacable virus?

Or the Rain Queen, on a dry summer evening, dancing a preferred world?

This wasn't a repeat performance of her triumphs in our garden: the sky remained blue and the confident note of the birds said rain wasn't coming. But she wasn't dancing for rain. She was dancing for me. For herself. Shaking her stick with its woollen hood and its ridiculous pom-pom at the empty sky.

'Young dogs,' said Queen Bama. 'I made them run.'

I was glad she had beaten her tormentors. It was an entirely splendid thing to have done. She was always splendid in her clear-sightedness. If the young men prevailed then all the trees in Africa, and then all the trees in the world, would be cut down, and in their place the young men would bring us beach umbrellas; they would be our forests.

She got things running. That was what she was for. She was for storms, for endless ooze, for the not-dry, for the unstuck, for the flow.

I drove down the hillside; the ancient rusty red rocks baked in the morning sun, the scrubby bushes were bunched like fists. Nothing had changed for thousands of years, but everything had altered. I'd seen the Rain Queen in full flood. No single thing I'd done had so cheered me since I stepped off the plane and went to my mother's bedside. Things were looking up.

When I arrived back at the gates of Sheerhaven the guards did not wave me through. I was handed a note. It was from Cindy and said simply:

'Gone to hospital. Ask security how to get there. Come quickly!'

32

She was in the waiting room, sitting in the corner, her arms folded and her face very white, her head pressed back against the wall, barely breathing. When I asked her what had happened, she told me; but she told me like she didn't believe it, like she was begging me to say it wasn't so, that there had been some mistake, that she was talking nonsense.

'Benny's in the theatre. They're operating now.'

'Operating?'

'To try and get the bullet out.'

Then she lay down, put her head in my lap and tried not to sob too much or too loudly. It was awful. I had no clear idea what had happened. Benny seemed too young and too small to have anything to do with bullets. But 'bullet' was what she said, and since it was all I had to go on, I said to myself, to stop thinking the worst, that if Benny had been in some sort of shooting, then at least he was in very good hands. No doctors outside a war zone had seen more gunshot wounds than the medics who held the line in this city, and who had Benny on the operating table.

We sat in the little waiting room for what seemed like hours until the surgeon came out and said faintly, warmly, 'We've removed the bullet, Mrs September. We're all in the laps of the gods now. You can see him for a few minutes.'

They had Benny rigged up to lots of monitors, his round smooth face faintly flushed on the pillow, his left side swathed in a dressing. Cindy bent over and kissed him and stroked his hair. But then they were busy around him again, and we had to go back to the waiting room.

Cindy didn't cry but she did tremble now and then, and said often, and without conviction: 'There's nothing to do but wait.'

Even that was too consoling. We had not waited more than an hour when they came to tell us they were very sorry.

We walked back into the ward and he looked just the same, except he was no longer rigged up and the people around him were gone. He was very small and very alone.

I held Cindy's hands; they were like ice.

'Poor, poor little boy,' she said.

This was something Cindy knew, something she had prepared for. She carried a gun, she knew the risks, she rehearsed in her mind again and again exactly the sort of scenario that had turned horribly real. She had taught me her rules of the road for staying alive and – it was hard but it had to be faced – she had taken some dark sardonic pleasure in the very brutality this town so feared, and secretly liked, condemned and extolled; she shared in the belief that Jo'burg was more than just bad: it was magnificently lethal.

But nothing had prepared her for this.

They said she should sleep in the hospital that night but she wouldn't. She was shaking; the idea of sleeping under the same roof as Benny filled her with horror. At the same time, she could not leave him. And yet she refused to go back to Sheerhaven, and her empty house. Could not stay. Could not go.

I said maybe it would be better if she came home with me,

and she said yes. As if this lifted from her a great weight, as if this was not a desertion of her beloved child but an awful compromise that she could live with, when she did not care whether she lived or not.

'I think I'll feel better somewhere else.'

It was not so much a statement as a prayer.

When we got back I knew she had been right: my house was cold and almost indifferent. There was relief in that. Having stood empty for some months, it had that slightly reproachful air neglected houses give out when their owners go missing. But it was nothing to her, and it was vacant, though a faint light burnt behind Noddy's window in the room in the back yard, and I wondered, briefly, if his woman had arrived.

I put her in my mother's room, beneath the gaze of Dr Schweitzer and Hemingway. Lions, kudu, okapi, dik-dik, springbuck, bongos – shot long ago and mounted on the dark wooden walls – looked down with liquid eyes. I helped her out of her clothes and found one of my mother's nightdresses, in white cotton. It was too big and made her look very small and very vulnerable and even paler than she was.

I gave her the sedative the doctor had said she should have, and she swallowed the capsules like a child. And then she asked me:

'What am I going to do now?'

It sounded like a sensible question, and any sort of sense was desirable in a world broken in madness. But it wasn't a question I could answer. It also assumed things could be done; it assumed an 'I' who functioned; it assumed a modicum of sense, and of security; it assumed a moment, a present, a 'now' in which one might *want* to do something; and I was not sure about any of that. A small boy had been shot to death and the world had not stopped in its turning, or cried out.

I lifted the blankets and helped her into bed.

'I'll need things from … the other place.' She could not bring herself to mention the name of Sheerhaven.

'Later. Leave it till later.'

'Yeah, later.' She nodded and closed her eyes. 'No hurry now, is there?'

Later was no better, no relief. Later was just when we knew what had happened. Later we traced the route the bus took that day, wondering again and again at the wild stupidity of it. We gave it a form, a beginning, middle, end … even though what had happened had no sense or form. What it did have was a grim logic: the thing Cindy knew about, guarded herself against, constantly talked of, fantasised over and had been so clever to avoid, suddenly sought her out, homed in and struck her like a grief-seeking missile.

Later we went over it, moment by moment, name by name. Cindy could think of nothing else, as if in explication some consolation might be found. The conventional wisdom at such times was that talking somehow helped. But it made things worse. And yet we went on talking and it never got any better.

The story we shaped was brief, unexceptional and without mercy.

The kids from Sunbeam Shelter had climbed that morning into their bus for one of their weekly outings, this time to the Zoo. It was a white Mercedes minibus that carried the exhortation, painted in big blue letters across the sliding door, 'Be Happy – Africa!' It had been specially adapted to carry wheelchairs, and had been donated by a spice merchant who blazoned his wares in tongues of forked flame along the side of the bus: 'Peck's Pimento – The Pepper Peter Piper Picked!'

In the roomy blue leather recesses of the bus rode four children, and one teacher named Muriel Makanya, who was in the rear seat. A six-year-old called Sammie leaned against Muriel's broad brown bosom. He had had polio and wore iron callipers on both legs, and a heavy boot. In the seat ahead of Sammie and Muriel sat Annie. She had been born blind, and was singing to herself. One seat ahead of her sat Benny in his chosen place. In the front of the bus, close to the door because it was always difficult to get her out of the vehicle, a paraplegic girl called Precious was in her wheelchair, which was anchored in the aisle, directly behind the driver, Josephus.

The bus was sailing down Jan Smuts Avenue, which dips steeply as it passes through Forest Town, and motorists usually put on speed as they approached the dip, in a Gadarene charge to the bottom of the hill.

Everyone on the bus was absorbed and happy, each with his own thoughts or his own game or his own song.

Up in the front, Precious was singing, 'We're off to see the Wild West Show, the elephant and the kangaroo-oo-oo-oo ...' helped by Josephus, the driver, one hand on the wheel while he conducted with the other.

Annie was listening to Benny who was calling out, as he always did when they made these trips: 'There's a car and there's another car and there's a bus, and there's a lamppost.'

Hardly riveting stuff, but Annie was riveted.

Muriel was singing to Sammie a Zulu lullaby about a baboon that stole a baby and ran off: '*Thula, Mama, Thula ...*'

I knew every inch of the route they took on that bright high-veld morning. I'd made the trip to the Zoo a thousand times: with my mother, with Koosie, with Nzong, the leopard boy, and later with Noddy. The kids would have passed my house in Forest Town and two blocks further down the bus turned right and set off down broad and tree-rich Saxonwold Drive, which curves around the southern edge of the Zoo, making for the entrance that lies close by.

It was then that a small saloon car – Josephus thought it was an Opel Corsa – moved to the middle of the road dead ahead of the bus, slowed suddenly, and stopped. Josephus had to brake hard and, as he did so, a large blue truck drew in tight behind and trapped the Mercedes. Two men got out of the Opel, guns in hand, and told Josephus to open the door, which he did, and they climbed into the bus.

What you had next was the typical, deeply insane encounter that pretty much passed for normal in this part of the world. The guys with guns had no other ambition that to hijack the vehicle. To them it wasn't a bus, it was a prize, it was a Mercedes, and they assumed that this glitzy high-powered cost-a-bomb bus was filled with cost-a-bomb people: sleek white male golfers, or rugby players, or salesmen, or rich stupid tourists in South Africa to see animals, and thus, all of them, not just easy game but deserving victims, folks who had too much anyway and got it from folks who had too little, and were suitable targets for a little bit of retributive Robin Hoodery.

But, instead, as Muriel Makanya the teacher, hugging the whimpering Sammie to her chest, told the two hijackers loudly, fiercely: 'These are special children, with special needs, and they can't just get off, like you say, just because you say get off!' Her voice trembling between fury and fear as she stared straight at the round black eyes of the men's pistols.

And as if to emphasise how special these children were, one of them, a little black girl strapped in a wheelchair, continued to sing, 'Never mind the weather, so long as we're together, we're off to see the Wild West Show', even though Josephus the driver was no longer conducting and was standing trembling on the pavement with a gun to his head.

The gunman on the bus realised this was not, then, your normal hijacking, where people did what you told them to do or they got shot. This one you had to work for. So he pocketed his weapon, reached forward and lifted the wheelchair containing Precious, and backed down the steps with his heavy burden, put the wheelchair down on the pavement while Precious sang through it all, of the elephant 'and the kangaroo-oo-oo...'

Now the aisle was clear, and the man got back on the bus, pointed his gun at Muriel and said: 'Off!'

Muriel carried Sammie slowly down the aisle, and his dangling steel callipers clanged on the seats in the hot silence.

'Is this the Zoo, Muriel?' Sammie said, and Muriel said: 'Yes, Sammie, this is the Zoo, this is where we get off.'

Hearing this, blind Annie obediently got up out of her seat and, guided by the sounds of Sammie's callipers hitting the metal floor, she came down the aisle to the exit. Josephus, moving very slowly so as not to give the impression to the nervous hijackers that he was threatening them in any way, helped her down the stops on to the pavement.

That left just Benny, sitting a long way back in his seat, watching but not moving.

This relative success in disposing of most of these unexpected problems had done the gunman's nerves no good. He was faced by a small boy with a moony grin, staring back at him, as if he had just recognised his best friend.

'Get off.'

'Hullo,' said Benny.

'Get off!' said the gunman, into whose barked repetition of this phrase there had crept a note of raw panic. And his panic sharpened when his partner climbed behind the wheel and started up the engine.

'Let's go!' yelled the driver.

'Get off!' the gunman yelled again. He was almost in tears now.

'Hullo, Baldy,' said Benny.

The gunman was not bald. But, then, Benny wasn't thinking of him, he was almost certainly thinking of my mother's grey parrot, the one that Bara and Buti had eaten, the bird that tasted of old shoes. No, the man was not bald and he did not look like a bird, so who knows what the connection was in Benny's highly original mind. Maybe he thought the gunman sounded like a parrot. Whatever it was, Muriel Makanya, who saw it all, was perfectly clear that it was now that the gunman came down the aisle and began pulling Benny out of his seat.

That was not a good idea: nothing ever moved Benny from his place. He changed in an instant from a smiling boy into a kicking, scratching ball of fury. He fought the gunman every step of the way, screaming and grabbing at any rail or strap, anything that prevented the gunman from getting him to the door of the bus, which had begun to pull away from the kerb.

'Leave the boy!' Muriel banged on the window, terrified that they were taking Benny with them. But a moment later he fell, or was tossed, on to the pavement, and the Mercedes accelerated and vanished around the curve of Saxonwold Drive. Neither Muriel nor Josephus could be sure whether it was before or after Benny fell that they heard the shot.

The cops picked up Benny's killers inside an hour, standing beside the road, hitching. Bloody useless as hijackers, they had stalled the bus, and were no better at thumbing a lift. Their names were Unathi and Brightman, and they were both sixteen years old. Street kids, hustlers. Unathi, it turned out, was HIV positive and Brightman had a crack habit. They were also orphans, or at any rate without parents. Inept, deprived kids who didn't steal the bus because they wanted it but because there was a commission out on a good new Mercedes from the men who supplied customers in Mozambique, which was often the way it was done. Hijack by appointment, it was called in the trade. The hijackers claimed they had thrown Benny down the steps because he was slow. Not because they wished to kill him. They had dumped their pistols before the cops got them. Both denied shooting the boy; both were charged with murder.

33

Cindy would not go back to Sheerhaven, and she asked if I would mind if she looked through my mother's wardrobe to see if there was something 'more' she could wear. I have never forgotten that 'more'. She rummaged around and managed to find some stuff that just about fitted her, and she altered pants and blouses on my mother's old black Singer machine.

I suppose I'd just assumed her stay at my place was temporary and that eventually she'd want to go home to Sheerhaven. But it soon became clear that, as far as she was concerned, she didn't live there any more. She found herself on the other side of some ditch she did not know she'd jumped, shaken but alive, and hating herself for it. What had been her immediate past, like last week, yesterday, a few hours before, suddenly accelerated, so that what had been actually very close to her, just yesterday, felt like ages ago and faded as she watched. It was not the lightness of being that brought nausea, it was the feeling that all her belonging and belief, in that place and that time, with all the indications that this love for this person was real and lasting, were false. She'd woken up and found what had been closest to her, most precious to her, was rushing away at the speed of light. She did not only feel sad and weak, she felt betrayed; but she had the horrible feeling that she was, somehow, also the traitor.

In the time when she first stayed with me, after what we simply referred to as 'it', I hoped she might recuperate; as if she were a patient getting over a very painful operation, learning to get out of bed and walk a bit. She was so skittish, so fragile and tremulous. I told myself what you always say in the circumstances: that she had been shockingly wounded; that she wasn't herself; that she would get better. I waited for a sign that something of her raw suffering had eased a bit.

She asked me to make the funeral arrangements.

'At Rosebank Church. Like your mom.'

So that is what we did. Father Phil conducted the service. Doves made the arrangements. Cindy altered an old dress-suit of my mother's and looked very like an undertaker herself. She and I were alone in the front pew because she had refused even to tell her ex-husband about Benny. All the kids from the Shelter came along and that was good. And Precious, representing the kids who had been on the bus with Benny, laid a wreath of lily of the valley on the tiny casket on the altar steps. But we were a small congregation, easily outnumbered by the reporters who turned up.

There was a kid with a stiff wave of gelled hair, in a white suit, and a blonde in black, and several guys in jeans, with cellphones, and I knew they were having trouble working out what demeanour to affect, and what the fuck to do with their cellphones. I felt rather sorry for them, blinking rather shyly in the bright bars of green and pink lights thrown through the windows of Rosebank Church. They had been sent by their papers to cover the obsequies of the young victim whose passing has been recorded in headlines like 'Slow Boy Blown Away' or 'Sick Kid Slain' and 'Thugs Plug Toddler'. The papers were facing an impossible task. Expected to register, and condemn, and celebrate the violent cavalcade they paraded past the horrified eyes of the their readers: the rapes and muggings, hijackings and bank heists. And catering to what was pretty much the other urgent need set in the South African soul: the desire to see sporting opponents getting their faces kicked in, to read about bloody murder, big tits and good batting, and not necessarily in that order. But expected to keep paying at least lip service to the usual pieties about peace and harmony and pots of gold at both ends of the rainbow.

Benny, then, was big news. Even in a country where more people were killed by their neighbours than any other place on earth – except maybe Guatemala – where murder, so went the dark joke, was just a way of life. Where death by gunshot was democratic and almost equally available to all, whether you lived in a walled villa in a gated suburb or a wooden shack in a squatter camp. Where most murders rated less space than the stock exchange prices, Benny's death – the boy who was too slow to move – propelled his story into that terrible book of mythic murders, right up there alongside accounts of men who believed raping babies was a cure for Aids; or the farmer who dragged his workers behind his truck until the skin peeled off their bones; or the six men locked in the freezer van, whose scrabbling nails bleeding on the icy steel door so haunted my mother and Queen Bama...

One Sunday paper went so far as to split its front page. On the left was a picture of school kids visiting Jo'burg for a sports competition, grinning young guys in face-paint, beneath the banner headline: 'A Feast of Schoolboy Rugby'.

The right-hand half of the page showed the abandoned

white Mercedes minibus, under the headline: 'Sick Boy Tossed From Bus'.

There were angry editorials about the inhumanity of people who would drag a disabled child from a vehicle and, when he would not move fast enough, shoot him dead. There were sermons preached against our propensity to kill; there were anguished questions asked about a people who, in the first flush of their freedom from a murderous tyranny, seemed bent on destroying each other, more wantonly, more cruelly, and more frequently than ever.

Another Sunday paper, in that peculiarly sticky-sweet prose that characterised officially approved public debate, compared Benny with Elvis Presley. The argument was complicated: much in the way blacks and whites could enjoy Presley's music, as a symbol of their shared emotions, he being famously described a 'white Negro', so the nation might come together by seeing the murder of Benny both as a crime – shocking and savage and reprehensible – yet also as a lesson, and an opportunity. Whites were forever whining about crime and yet, to some, their complaints were really a kind of coded race hatred, because blacks were robbed, raped and killed far more often than anyone else. However, Benny straddled the race divide. The child of a mixed marriage, he was neither white nor black but both, or, as one columnist put it, stretching wildly for accuracy, 'pale-black'. This put his fate into a broader, and more desirable, context. It showed that inexplicable cruelty could happen to anyone, 'irrespective of colour, class, creed, gender or disability'… The lesson of Benny, the editorialists declared, was that we must 'pull together, sink our differences, level the playing field, and consult all relevant structures, stake-holders and role players ...' Benny, it was said, must be seen as a bridge.

To my alarm, Cindy seemed to take heart from this self-serving crap.

'Maybe he *can* be a bridge?'

I said, 'Why stop at Benny the bridge, why not the book of Benny? Why not the entire fucking Bible of Benny?'

She was hurt. 'But, Alex, Benny the bridge, it's only a metaphor; it speaks for what we can't say. It's really rather touching.'

Benny – the metaphor.

At Cindy's request, Benny's ashes were interred alongside my mother's, in the wall of the Garden of Remembrance at Rosebank Church. Later, we went back to the house in Forest Town – my house, my mother's house – as if this for her was the most natural thing in the world. As if she were coming home.

34

Although Cindy in no way resembled my mother, there were links, and they grew all the more evident in the weeks we lived side by side in the house in Forest Town. I didn't feel it was mimicry; it was a more a form of crusading approval, with something reckless about it.

'Your mother was number one. I really admired her. To the uttermost, to the nth degree.'

Cindy was trying on one of my mother's blue turbans.

'I mean, this is a woman who knew what she wanted; this is a woman who didn't let anyone give her uphill, hey? Who didn't take any bullshit—'

'I think you have to wind the turban the other way.'

'Show me.'

She stood in front of the mirror while I wound the bright blue sash around her small pale forehead, higher and higher, until she looked rather like Nefertiti.

I said: 'Cindy, I don't know about this mix and match business.'

'Oh, why not, hey? I'm only trying a few things.'

'I know, but it's a bit like walking into a charity shop and trying on the hats.'

'Whajamean?' Her anguished query rose to a note of high

keening: *me-e-e-ennnn*? 'Your mom wouldn't have minded. Your mom was a most generous person.'

Cindy had begun to wear more and more items from my mother's wardrobe: a yellow cardigan, a white blouse, a pair of old dungarees. She looked rather interesting in faded khaki bush jackets, jodhpurs, old jeans, velvet smoking jackets. All were rather mannish and gave her an elfin appeal; a little girl dressing up in her dad's clothes.

She wore her own shoes but that was because my mother had such big feet, just as she had very large hands. I got the feeling that she wasn't so much trying to wear her clothes as much as trying my mother on, getting the feel of her. There was, of course, a terrific disparity: my mother had been almost a foot taller, and much broader. Cindy could not wear her flying boots, and she could not have handled any of her heavy guns; she did not fly. Yet what she could do was to select samples, much as someone prospecting for gold takes samples of rock and tests it for signs of the auriferous seam that says: 'Here be riches.'

Cindy sat for hours carefully cleaning the glass frames that held the maps of Livingstone's travels. She marvelled at the photographs of Schweitzer and Bror Blixen; of Hemingway in shorts and sweatshirt, gloved up, facing my mother in her breast-protector. She pored over the weighty, leather-backed albums of black and white snaps showing my old lady stalking leopard, taxi-ing down the runway of some long-ago bush strip in some unnamed African colony, rafting rapids, fording rivers, posing beside the huge and wide-eyed head of a dead buffalo, picnicking, drinking, camping; my mother smiling, beside men of every type and height and moustache and rifle.

She was like some sort of refugee, someone in transit. It was not that she went backwards or forwards; no, I'd say she was going round and round, sinking deeper and deeper into her new role. There were parallels for this sort of biological camouflage. A little creature like the rabbit flea, being small and needy, has learnt that the price of staying alive in a lethal world is to bury itself in some bigger, warmer, body, and so it has adapted accordingly. The rabbit flea has surrendered its reproductive cycle to its host. The hormones of the rabbit govern the season when its invader has babies. The little bloodsucker gets pregnant only when mummy bunny gets broody.

That is what Cindy did, though she did it in such subtle ways that it took me some time to realise what was going on. She got broody, she took on things, she took things *in*; and she was full of something I did not see until it had grown too large to stop. I don't blame myself for not seeing what was going on; I don't think Cindy did either.

Perhaps, too, it was also a form of distraction, this dressing up in someone else's clothes. By shedding her former life and becoming someone else, something of the horror of Benny's death was eased in Cindy. She never spoke of him but by moving all the time deeper into my mother's wardrobe, someone who had known – and hugged – Benny, as she had known and hugged all the kids in the Shelter, was perhaps a way of clothing her wound in borrowed dressings. She seemed to be reaching into the immense amplitude that was my mother. The individual bits of clothing were not important: she used them as charms, or fetishes. Or relics.

There was also something bloody ridiculous about it. Here was this tiny Jo'burg kugel waltzing around in cardigans, turbans, bush-hats and the silk scarves my mother liked to knot at her throat when she took off for somewhere fun, like

Tanganyika. But I wasn't going to question it. She had gone through something so terrible there was nothing to say, and no comfort to be given. Benny was dead, in a way she had almost predicted. Her worst terror had come to call. It made her vulnerable and, yes, in its dreadful finality, and in her endurance, it made her unreachable.

We were lovers no longer, we were not sleeping together, we were merely occupying my mother's house; we might have been lodgers leading adjacent lives or some couple who had long since stopped coupling. We ate together, we talked, and we co-existed. I got the breakfast and later I went walking. She read my mother's books; she watched the old ciné films of the Waturi pygmies. At night she wanted stories about my mother, her life and her lovers. She began to tidy and dust and make some order in the accumulated souvenirs of a lifetime. Like the costume museum across the road, where the Bernberg sisters had lived.

My mother became the subject of our suppertime conversations; Cindy would look up over the angel fish, or the pasta, and say:

'Tell me about her time with Hemingway; tell me what she thought of Schweitzer; tell me about the leopard men ...'

Cindy picked up my mother's old pipe, and stuck it between her teeth.

'Tell me what tobacco she smoked.'

'It was called Boxer tobacco. Strong black stuff. It came in a white cotton bag, with a drawstring neck.'

'Will you buy me some, hey?'

I found a bag of Boxer, showed her how to fill the pipe, lit it for her and watched her blow creamy smoke around the room.

'I puff but I can't inhale. No way!'

'Just as well, that stuff's lethal. Cindy, why are you walking around in my ma's kit?'

She blew smoke at Livingstone's maps on the wall. 'I like to feel close, that's why. You don't seem to miss her.'

I didn't like the question, or the tone. Cindy could dress herself up as much as she liked, but I wasn't going to partner her to the fancy-dress ball.

'Of course I miss her.'

'Oh, *ja*, how much?'

'I don't know how to answer that.'

'Well, do you miss her more now that she's not here any more?'

'Listen; in the first place, I missed her even when she was here, when she was alive.'

She took the pipe from her mouth and slowly knocked out the tobacco in a back mahogany ashtray, carved to resemble an elephant carrying a maharajah. Then she spat out a few crumbs of tobacco that had travelled down the stem of the pipe, and made a face at the bitter burning on the tip of her tongue.

'There is something I'd better tell you. I'm going back to work.'

'Back to selling houses?'

She shook her head. 'No. I've signed up at the Sunbeam Shelter. Don't look so amazed. I start tomorrow morning.' She enjoyed my astonishment. Watching me steadily, her green eyes limpid in her clever, pretty face, under the great crown of turban. 'I wanted to do something for Benny. I reckoned this is what he knew, the school – and the kids.'

She said it with the utmost simplicity. Why then did I feel it was an excessive movement towards making things right? Making them … 'pristine'. There is, of course, nothing to be said when someone tells you that they have been moved by love and devotion to give themselves over to good works.

So she began working again at Sunbeam Shelter, setting off each morning in the old Land Rover, riding up the hill to the big house. I wondered if she was hugging the kids but I didn't want to ask: I had an idea what she'd say.

Cindy, once so irreverent, so deliciously wry, had gone the way of the heart. Some terrifying power had taken Benny from her. How was she to soften her anguish? She would not rail, she would submit. She was reaching out and taking into herself that which had swallowed up her son. She was repositioning herself for her life after Benny; in the house of my mother; in the role – dare I say it – of my mother, setting out to embrace 'Africa'.

Something, incidentally, that my mother never did. She took it by the throat, yes, but she never, ever saw Africa as morally improving. For the simple reason that she saw no reason for moral improvement, because things, and that included herself and her world, were quite perfect as they were, thank you very much. Yet when she died she tore a hole in our lives, and it was that loss which Cindy had found a way of repairing.

It was increasingly odd. Exactly who were these people living in my house? Cindy was someone else, Noddy was certainly someone else. Only I was the same and that was no great help. It was clear that I lacked a crucial ability: the gift of change. Others shuffled off their skins and became new people; it was like living in a fairy-tale, where I was the only grown-up, the only non-believer. It was not that I didn't aspire to the same magic – I did – but I simply could not see how to make it happen.

Noddy's friend who came to live in his room turned out to be a languorous young woman called Nonsuma, and he appeared to have as little as possible to do with her. Mostly, she sat outside Noddy's room in the sun, or she did a bit of washing and hung it on the line very slowly. I got the feeling Nonsuma didn't mean anything in herself, she was just another milestone on his road to perdition. Very soon she began to put on weight, and she made Noddy look even smaller.

He had always looked tiny but solid; now he looked just tiny. The only confidence he allowed himself now was at the week-end when he headed into the townships, spry and glittering in his golden suit and the rainbow wave of the feather in his hat.

And then, from one day to the next, Noddy and Nonsuma were gone.

But he had left behind every last thing he owned: his old grey flannels, his Gstaad T-shirt, his blue overall, his old dark blue Sunday suit and his golden shebeen suit. His building society book was there, still in its red rubber bands, and it showed Noddy's savings: he was several thousand bucks in credit. The letter his brother had written him, telling him the terrible news about Beauty: everything that went to make him the man he been left with me. To me. Everything of himself, except his true self, and his hat. The hat was gone, too, along with its owner.

I packed all his gear in his suitcases: cardboard in a tartan pattern and cheap locks, which he had used when he travelled between his gardens in Jo'burg and his farm and family in Matabeleland. You never know, I thought, he might come back. But I wasn't counting on it.

•

I spent a lot of time in the afternoons wandering around the Zoo. I liked the polar bear. There had always been a polar bear when I was a kid, and he had seemed normal, just another of the many exotic species behind bars. Even though he was thousands of miles from where he lived, he belonged, because he was in the Zoo. That great, shaggy, rather dusty creature lived in a cage and reminded me of a giant furry phantom. They sprayed him with water from time to time to alleviate the heat from sharp highveld sun, and his cage always stank of fish. He struck me as lonely. He would push his paws through the bars and hang on for dear life. Or that's the way it looked. The new guy was in a glassed-in arctic habitat, at the right temperature, and he would stand quietly with his arms wrapped around his waist, like a man trying to warm up.

Remembering that bear, I had an explanation of my mother's extreme attachment to the children at Sunbeam Shelter. It wasn't about hugging them. It was herself she was warming. She was ill, she felt in danger of being swept away, and she needed someone to hold on to, so she put her arms around the kids. Maybe, like the polar bear, her situation was absurd. After a lifetime of doing and flying and being in Africa, she had come, as had her friend Queen Bama, to the recognition that she had got it all wrong, and everywhere about her she saw dissolution, the terrible onrush of time. A hurricane had torn past her and she took hold of whatever might save her from being blown away.

One day I was in the garden, looking at the lavender. The sky was that uncertain gold you see only on the highveld. It was about five in the afternoon and the grass, which I had recently mown, smelt of the shaded afternoons of my boyhood when the touch of grass on your bare soles spelt freedom and relief.

I heard the plane very low overhead. It was a Cessna and it circled over the house a couple of times, then soared up into the sky and then came in low over the telephone wires, and the birds sprang up, complaining.

When Cindy got in that evening she sat back in my mother's old leather chair, she put her feet up and I saw she was wearing a new pair of flying boots. Those at least were her own.

'I thought I'd surprise you. Did you know who it was?'

'Instantly. When did you get your licence?'

'I've been learning for weeks now. Today I made my first solo flight as a qualified pilot and I decided on a fly past to mark the event. Did you think of your mom?'

'In fact, no. If I was reminded of anyone, it was of a guy called Bob Mistry. D'you ever hear of him?'

She shook her head. 'Tell me.'

'Mistry was in the Congo in the old days, a journalist working for UPI. He had two things going for him: he could fly and he could use a film camera. That's what got him to the Congo where my ma met him. Mistry was amongst the first TV reporters in the Congo when it blew up in the sixties. He covered the rapes, the killings, the assassination of Patrice Lumumba. She took Bob Mistry hunting okapi with her, and she introduced him to her Wambuti friends. He wasn't a bad shot but what worked against Bob in the bush was his extreme fastidiousness. He was a dapper man, he loved wearing white, and he had a sleek brown moustache, neat little feet, pert little buttocks. He was so sleek and he combed his black hair over his head in a wave, like it was built of shellac. He looked to me a bit like an intelligent seal in a suit. Anyway, Mistry was crazy about my mother, and she liked him, I think.'

'Did she love him?'

Again the question. Really strange, that question. Delivered by a woman wearing my mother's yellow cardigan, smoking my mother's pipe, sitting in my mother's chair.

'I've tried to explain this before. I'm not sure if she ever loved anyone. A lot of men loved her, and a lot of them she devoured.'

'Go on.'

'When she'd finished hunting okapi, she'd done the Congo for a bit, and she'd done Bob Mistry. Only he didn't understand. He dropped everything and came down to Jo'burg. Now, my ma, when in another place, had no time and precious little recollection of what or whom she'd left behind. She didn't just go off the man, she couldn't quite remember who he was. But he kept turning up: at parties and picnics and airfields. Everywhere she looked, there was Mistry, with his white shoes and his shining moustache, pleading to be reunited, and appalled that my mother didn't seem to know, or care, who the hell he was. She lost patience – she never had much – and she told him if he kept pestering her, she'd kick his balls in. Mistry was pretty downcast, and that's why he did something so completely odd I've still not quite worked out why he chose it. So potentially messy. It was so out of character in such a prissy, contained man.'

She looked triumphant: 'He tried to kill himself?'

'Not quite. In fact, he tried to kill her. You looked surprised. But it was a smart move on his part. You see, if he'd tried to kill himself, my old lady would not have been very impressed. But trying to wipe her out, that was the sort of thing that gave her a lift. And then there was the way he set about it. Bob called up late one night and I took the call: she wouldn't speak to him. I told him what she said, which was to drop dead. Mistry sounded quite pleased, something I found puzzling. I realised later that the call had been a blind: he was making sure she was home. What Bob did then was to get seriously drunk, climb into his Cessna – rather like the one you were flying – and take off, leaving no flight plan. In those days my ma and I were living on the top floor of a three-storey block of flats called Fawn Glen, in Parkwood. Mistry flew over the building at around three in the morning when we were fast asleep; he took a bead on our flat, and flew his plane smack into the top storey.'

'Are you serious?'

'Totally. I've often thought of him since those planes smashed into the Twin Towers in New York. Our block was a lot smaller and a lot tougher. Those thirties blocks were built to last and, anyway, being pretty pissed, Mistry hit the wrong fucking flat. The one right next door. He didn't knock down the building, he didn't harm us, but he did kill the elderly couple next door, and himself.

'What did she say, your mom? Was she impressed?'

'Up to a point. She liked the fact he'd got off his arse and tried to wipe her out, but she thought him an idiot for missing the target.'

'Why are you telling me, Alex? Is there some kind of moral point here? Is it because I buzzed you? Is it because maybe you think I want to do to you what Mistry wanted to do to your mother?'

It was my turn to shake my head.

'This isn't a story, this is a factual account of something that really happened. That's why it sounds so weird. Bob Mistry's failure to kill my mother isn't really what it's about. It is about the people he did kill. It turned out that the elderly couple next door were old friends of Mistry's. The guy had been the bureau chief at UPI when he was starting out: Bob Mistry killed the man who made his career.'

'And what conclusion do you draw from this?'

'None. I don't do conclusions, and I don't do morals. It was just something that happened, and I'm aghast at the oddity of life, and death.' I looked at her. 'I don't do mothers either.'

'Tell me, Alex, tell me truly. Did you love Kathleen?'

'I think I did, when I didn't want to bump her off. A bit like Bob Mistry.'

'Bump her off?'

'Push her over a cliff. Something like that. Look, it's precisely because I did love her that there were times I'd have cheerfully strangled her. I loved her the way I love the southeaster that cuts your ears off, I loved her like I do the lightning that kills people on the highveld. I loved her the way I love diving very deep into clear water and lying there down at the bottom till my lungs are about to pop and I can feel myself passing out, but it's so big and peaceful and cool down there I don't want to surface ever, but I know if I don't come up for air, I'll die. That's how I loved her, like you love something that is big and wonderful and appalling; but often, very, very often, you just wish it would fucking well stop!'

'Why do you think your mother hugged the kids?'

'I don't know.'

'I told you what I think. I think it was an outpouring of love, she couldn't help herself. You're so suspicious of love you can't see it.'

'I think you're dead wrong. It assumes she had some sort of feeling for kids. Let me tell you that she was wholly lacking in maternal feelings. If I had to compare her with any other animal, any other species, I'd go for the cheetah. The cheetah makes sure she looks after her brood for just as long as she has to, until the cubs are functioning, and then she's off. Another mate, another litter, another life. Never looks back.'

35

On my mother's desk, between the pictures of Schweitzer and Hemingway, there now appeared photos of two young black boys, unsmiling. I knew who they were, I had been at the trial, I had heard them sentenced to twenty years. Unathi, wearing a white T-shirt, and Brightman in a black turtle-neck sweater.

Also new was the headed notepaper on her desk, heavy white bond with the embossed letterhead: 'The Benny September Memorial Trust'. Its directors were Cindy September and Jacob Schevitz.

This was a perfectly logical continuation of Cindy's new role – my mother's house, her gear, and now her lawyer. I don't think Cindy and I said more than good morning to each other after that. I went to see Schevitz and he told me what was going on.

'The Benny September Memorial Trust is dedicated to helping kids like Unathi and Brightman to realise their full potential as citizens of the new South Africa.' He saw my face and sighed. 'Hey, Alex, lay off. It's not my idea, this foundation. All I'm doing is setting it up for her.'

I think Schevitz probably found her visit even more per-plexing than the time my ma hit him with her Cuban. Cindy was wearing a pair of my old lady's jodhpurs, a pink silk blouse, and her eyes were lovely. And, then, too, he felt he had failed my mother and he did not want to fail Cindy.

She told him: 'I think of them.'

He had not given her an easy ride. 'Why do you think of them?'

'Because they're so young!'

'Old enough to hijack a school bus, old enough to carry guns, old enough to use them.'

'Yes, but you know their history. Aids orphans, left to fend for themselves, then the move to Jo'burg, then the need to keep body and soul together.'

'Yes, then the guns, then the killing ...'

'I know. But their faces haunt me. Where do you think they are? Can I go and visit them?' Cindy had asked him.

Schevitz told me this pretty matter-of-factly. 'Before you go off pop, let me tell you it also worries the hell out of me. But it's her choice; she wants it like this. Imagine, you commemorate the brutal killing of your only son by trying to help his killers. And whether you or I agree or not, it is, well, remarkable.'

'Yeah. Remarkable. Maybe we could start blaming Benny for being the boy he was, on the wrong bus at the wrong time, and being so slow, and so these guys were forced to shoot him. Maybe that's the next step, Schevvy: getting Benny back, to stand up and say he's really sorry, to apologise to these poor killers for being so unhelpful. Maybe that would be most remarkable of all; maybe since Benny can't say it himself, being dead and all, you could say it for him, stand up and say: "Unathi and Brightman are innocent, OK; and Benny's to blame."'

Schevitz said: 'Look, the love and tenderness thing towards these guys, the selflessness thing, is a bit much. I told her that. But you gotta think of the alternatives. You could say she was a shining example of forgiveness.'

'You could say that Benny was innocent kid who got murdered – and he deserved better than this crap.'

Schevitz stuck it out. 'You could say that she is taking an impossible situation, one that's full of pain and suffering, and changing it.'

'Go on say it: transforming it.'

'I didn't say that, you did.'

'You're right. I'm sorry I said that. It was a low blow.'

It was true. The old Schevitz had never gone in for that sort of crap, though it seemed he was skirting pretty close to it now. Transformation, the old Schevitz had once remarked, was about changing yesterday's blood into tomorrow's Mercedes Benz. But that had been before he fell into the arms of Cindy, and into the sticky, stifling web of culturally acceptable newspeak about what 'role players' and 'stakeholders' were 'bringing to the party' …

Schevitz said: 'She's the one who lost her kid; frankly, Alex, she's entitled to do any damn thing she wants about that. You haven't any business being less forgiving than her. Or angrier than her. And anyway, what are the alternatives? To be stuck in bitterness or to move on?'

'It's not about alternatives. Alternatives are exactly what are not available under what we might call the Cindy scenario. Alternatives imply choice and different versions and the hope of freedom; none of same are on offer here. There is only the authorised version of some very horrible facts. Those facts are now going to be shoved around till they come out looking different. What we have here is maybe the only story of this country: forms of force passing themselves off as freedom. The kind of freedom that says if you don't let me do what's good for you, I'll shove your face in.'

'Alex, I can see why you don't stay here. You've got nothing good to say about the place.'

'Fuck you, Schevvy.'

'OK, Alex. Let's leave it there, OK?'

Schevitz was a good guy, an honest guy, and he had never gone in for bullshit on a vast scale. Now he was ashamed, but I saw something else and it hit me like a locomotive. Schevitz was along for the ride. To ease what remorse he clearly felt at not helping my ma when he had the chance. But also because, after years of bitterness in the political wilderness, he was back where he had once been happy, fighting the good fight, being of service. I do not mean he championed the little killers of a small boy who didn't move fast enough: Schevitz might be making a fool of himself for love, perhaps, but he was no sentimentalist. No, the old dream had hooked Schevitz one more time, as it had done years before when he fought the good fight against the bastards who ran our world. After years of being out of it, a ridiculous old white liberal put out to grass, suddenly Schevitz had a cause again. The Benny September Memorial Trust ... Cindy's new deal.

And who could gainsay her? After all, as Schevitz had pointed out, it was her suffering, her child, her idea to make contact with his killers, her choice to forgive. Her right to do so. It didn't matter how it looked to me or to anybody else. It wasn't really our business. What was more, her way was consonant with so much that was morally uplifting as well as politically desirable in a country in which hatred between whites and blacks was always and everywhere. The way she had put aside her own anguish by bringing hope and consolation to those who did not deserve it was magnificent.

Why, then, did I find it so appalling? Noble, perhaps, but even so I recoiled before Cindy's selflessness. I also saw that what Cindy felt was not really perverse. If she had made herself over from the poor girl out of Blaukrans into the northern suburbs Jo'burg princess, she could do it again, and change herself into this saintly figure of forgiveness.

Brightman and Unathi were held in a detention centre for juveniles in the Limpopo Province, near a town called Polakwane. There was an airport at Polakwane and whenever she got permission, she and Schevitz flew to see 'the boys'. Cindy bought them books and baked them cakes and wrote them long letters on lilac paper in her sloping hand. She announced her five-year plan to rehabilitate them with the same degree of enthusiasm and passion that she'd once taught me the rules for staying alive on the road, or given me the low-down on Jo'burg as it really was.

That Cindy no longer existed; she had been too unserious, too flighty, too much of the 'old South Africa'. The new Cindy was earnest, repetitive, long-winded, well meaning and deeply, even fatally, confused. But she had the great gift of being able to believe every word she said, which meant she was perfectly suited to the times.

Her five-year plan was to win permission to visit 'the boys' once a month, and 'to win their trust'. That desire was nauseating, she knew it, but she didn't care to hide it, she simply repeated it when I winced. There was also an appeal in preparation. Next, in the fullness of time, she hoped to persuade the authorities to allow Unathi and Brightman out on parole so they could come home with her.

She had no doubt where home was, and I faced hard decisions. What was left of the place that had once been mine, of the mother who had given birth to me, and of the stories that she had told me, and what they said about who I was, who she was? Because the longer the 'new' Cindy lived there, the more the 'old' life was covered in the exciting revised customs and plans of the incomers. Cindy was colonising the space, and doing it for the best of motives.

I was living, then, in my mother's house, with someone who seemed increasingly to be not her double but her successor; and the more fully she filled that role, the more pointless staying on seemed to be. I felt what I guess my mother had been feeling in a world of brutal change.

The question now was: what was I to do? I knew I could go back to what was an ephemeral but useful job: the supply of cooler air in overheated spaces. Indeed, the more I thought about it, the more useful a job seemed it to be, in its modesty, its ability to clean, wash, steady the air we breathed.

The new Cindy not only had right on her side, she had the future on her side. And I was a hopeless reactionary. Because I preferred the house as it was; I preferred Noddy and Queen Bama; I preferred the leopard men and the Wambuti pygmies to this new version of events. And as sure as hell I preferred my mother to Cindy's version of her.

And yet both repelled me: my mother's high indifference to everything she flew over; and Cindy in emotional meltdown. When I considered what Cindy had melted down from, the smart cookie who flogged real estate, whose life revolved around big bucks, the right BMW, cash in the bank and a pistol in the glove compartment, to the Mother Teresa of the juvenile correctional facilities …

Worse, I had to face the fact that she was on to something; she was immersing herself in the way things were, and had to be. And you did that or you stayed out in the cold.

It wasn't about humility or acceptance, not really. It was about what it was always about: it was about winning, it was about power; it was about moral elevation; and as soon as anyone claimed the high moral ground in Africa – you could put money on this – the more certainly and more cruelly it pressed down on the heads of the poor. What had Cindy found in the cupboard of my mother but the entire fucking outfit suitable for the high moral ground, after some slight adaptation, right down to the boots and right up to the fucking hat, or should I say turban?

There seemed nothing to keep me any longer, and very little chance of ever working out the two crucial mysteries that plagued me: why my mother hugged those kids; and why it was that Noddy still meant so much when he had finished with me. Why I still felt he pointed towards something vital, if only I could work out what the hell it was. I told myself, relieved to find some excuse for staying on, that I could not leave just yet. I had two last bequests still unfulfilled. The mambo music was meant to go to Raoul Mendoza. Having seen what it took to turn him into a happy, well-settled South African, I saw no need to blow his cover.

And then there was Papadop.

36

To Papadop went her Livingstone relics: these included one of the explorer's own route maps, tracing his prodigious treks to and fro across sub-Saharan Africa; a sketch of the Victoria Falls, with Livingstone's careful measurements in his clear hand: '1860 yards wide – 310 feet deep ...' As if accuracy of this sort was a way of affixing certainty to a bewildering encounter with an Africa so resistant to good sense, so ungrateful to missionaries, explorers, soldiers, traders, visionaries. And yet so responsive, then as now, to the gimcracks and gewgaws given by invaders to chiefs and head honchos, those absurd big men whose role has been to soak and suppress their people, and to shaft their continent.

Also among her relics was a brass-bound mirror Livingstone had given to a chief in Ujiji, whose grandson in turn had given it to my mother, taking it from a glass cabinet in which he kept other memorabilia of the doctor: razors, beads, several iron spoons, one copper jug, a brass tray, a single-bladed penknife, a snuff box imprinted with the head of Queen Victoria, and a red and blue accordion that wheezed a bit but still worked. The chief had kept Livingstone's mirror in a cabinet of curiosities in order to study, my mother told me, 'in a state of permanent perplexity', the habits and customs of the early white invaders.

It was the perfect emblem of that invasion. Whoever looked into Livingstone's mirror found the face they wanted: their own.

There was also a sepia print of the old mango tree, which was said to mark the spot where Livingstone and Stanley met in Ujiji in 1871. Beneath it was a big stone identifying the site as 'The White Man's Tree'.

There was Livingstone's famous cap, with the blue crown and red band, which my ma had always insisted was the very one he tipped to Stanley. But then again, Livingstone's caps were not all that rare. He had lots of them made for him by Starkey's of Bond Street. It was an essential prop in a long career, as distinct a trade mark as Charlie Chaplin's bowler. Behind the legend of the missionary, the liberator of slaves, the explorer, geographer, the namer of mountains and waterfalls, the dour Scot who came to personify Africa to all the Anglo-Saxon world, was the other Livingstone, the mendicant trouper, proud, stubborn, cruelly uncaring of his wife and children, an actor never upstaged, with a fine line in hats.

I'd seen another of these caps displayed by the Royal Geographical Society in London; they swore theirs was one Livingstone doffed to Stanley. Questions of authenticity go to the heart of things in the long and violent poker game that is Africa. Who's faking it, and who's lying to whom? Those were the only questions worth asking.

I called Papadop's number in Mount Darwin, and I got someone on the line whose voice I didn't know.

'Papadopolous, he is not here.'

'When will he be back?'

There was a pause. 'Never.'

'Never?'

'He is not coming back.'

'Do you mean he's moved?'

'Yes.'

'Do you know where he's moved to?'

'No.'

'And what has happened to his place?'

'It is not his place; it is my place now.'

I got it then. I had heard of the seizure of white-owned farms by hopped-up young men claiming to be old soldiers of the liberation wars they were far too young to have fought. But somehow I never thought of Papadop as a farmer. He had stopped farming long ago, when he went into selling agricultural machinery. He owned land in Mount Darwin, stretching all the way to the river, where he had his fishing shack, but it never crossed my mind that someone would take his home, his land. And besides, Papadop was no ordinary white settler: he was a Zimbabwean citizen; a member of the ruling party; he spoke the language; he had been for years comrade mayor of the town.

I missed Noddy all over again. He was someone I could have talked to about this. For most people, Zimbabwe barely existed, or, if it did, it was that little place 'up north', formerly known as Rhodesia, famous for the Victoria Falls and bugger all else, run by a despot who kept stealing farms and locking up anyone who stepped out of line. Much as the crazy white despot who'd run Rhodesia had done, with the same support from our old 'white-is-right' gang of desperadoes as the current tyrant got from our new 'black-is-better' regime. And for much the same reasons: the big bully up north might be a bastard, but he was our bastard; he wasn't just kin, he was skin-kin.

I phoned everyone I could think of in Zim. The so-called war vets were on the rampage, some guy called Hitler Hunzvi was wrecking farms, people were dying. No one knew anything about Mount Darwin. Papadop seemed to have disappeared without trace.

Then I got lucky. I called one of the commercial farmers' unions which tried to keep track of their dispossessed members, and they gave me a lead. Word was he was no longer in Zim at all. It was thought he was across the border, living near a little town in north-eastern Mozambique called Chimoio. Getting there was not easy. I would need to fly from Jo'burg to Beira on the east coast, rent a car and head out into the country.

Beira airport was small and comfortable and the first thing I noticed was the marked lack of aggression. Everyone smiled. It was worrying. I paid seven dollars airport tax, I got my passport stamped and then I rented a small Toyota. When I told the girl I was heading for Chimoio, she smiled and said gently: 'Try to stay on marked routes all the time: there are uncleared land-mines up that way.'

I left behind the muddy, sludgy sea off Beira. The road was empty and fleecy clouds hung low in a coppery-blue sky. Travelling in this way always frees the mind. I was alone in a landscape of dark green bush and rich red earth and here and there a small, bourgeois, poignant Portuguese villa, stuck in the past, tin roof, paint-flaked shutters and shady veranda. Abandoned, suddenly, when independence came in 1975. Anywhere else these empty houses of the old Portuguese set-tlers would have been vandalised, or cannibalised, or turned into precarious squats. But they waited among the banana plants and the thorn trees, forlorn, deserted on the far shore of a vanished world.

After the Portuguese fled, civil war began: another of those cruel local wars, fought by proxies of the bigger powers. After sixteen years of fighting, a million dead, six million displaced, and most Mozambicans were living on under a dollar a day.

There would be landmines, said the car-hire girl. Of course! There must be landmines. But landmines did not compete in kill rate with a human carrying a Kalashnikov, and what was so extraordinary, on the road out of Beira, in a country ruined by strife, and as poor as any on earth, for someone fresh out of Jo'burg, was the deep peace and easy air of the place. Looking at the map, I saw that if I had kept travelling on up the coast from Beira I would have come to Quelimane, the port where Livingstone setttled for a while and became British consul. And here I was, on yet another bloody missionary venture into the interior, carrying in my pack some of the very trinkets Livingstone had handed out on his wanderings in this country. Except that Livingstone was there when the show began, when Africa opened like a brilliant and lavish production dedicated to 'commerce and Christianity and the suppression of slavery'. It was the greatest show on earth and Livingstone the first of its impresarios.

I was there to search for survivors, for whoever was left when the show closed and the circus headed out of town. A lost tribe of one.

Chimoio was sleepy and dusty. An old helicopter, probably brought down in the war, sat in someone's back yard like some giant toy. The bar in the middle of town was admirably named the Plymouth Arms. It was simply and ruggedly built: a concrete floor under a corrugated-iron roof, and a generous, shady stoop. A huge Union flag was painted on the back wall.

It was run by a Mozambican called Cecelia who wore denim hot pants and saw to it the booze kept flowing to her thirsty customers, half a dozen very large white men in khaki shorts who were knocking it back like there was no tomorrow.

I ordered a beer and asked Cecelia about Papadop.

Her English was pretty, oiled with the soft liquids of her own Portuguese. 'I know him. Big, dark, crazy old man. I know him. He comes here for a drink, for ice. He calls everyone "bastards".'

'Yeah, that sounds about right. Where do I find him?'

She sketched directions on the back of a paper napkin.

'Fifteen, maybe twenty kilometres. Hard country. Stay on the track and you'll find him. Look for a tent on a hill.'

She caught the look in my eyes and waved a hand at the men drinking behind me. 'Zimbos.'

'Zimbos?'

Cecelia's smile showed white, even teeth. 'Yeah. In Chimoio we have got Zimbos, Ports and Pongos, but Zimbos are ...' She lifted a finger like a pistol and trained it on her right temple.

'Why's that, Cecelia?'

'Because they come here from Zim with ...' she joined thumb and forefinger in a neat O '... *nada em tudo*: nothing. And they kill themselves.'

'How do they kill themselves?'

'It's the malaria. Or too much work.' She flicked her dark eyes towards the big men at their table that was carpeted in litre bottles of lager. 'Or too much of mine. If they wish to kill themselves, for me it is better when they do it with mine.'

She had a point.

The sweltering land I drove through was lush, but empty. Fine farming country, yet left alone, aching to sprout. Everywhere there was this feeling of something waiting to happen. Fifteen kilometres out of town, I spotted a tent on the crest of a hill. I had to manoeuvre up a track so rocky I left the car and walked the rest of the way.

He was sitting on a stone outside his tent, old Rhodesian army issue, with his back to me, staring out towards the low hills on the horizon. In the gentle valley below him was an enormous and beautiful field of young tobacco plants.

I said: 'How you doing, Papadop?'

He turned and stared, then he got up slowly, wiping sweat from his forehead with the brim of his floppy khaki hat.

'Bloody hell – Alex!'

For the next few hours we sat outside his tent and drank brandies and Cokes, and he told me in his flat, rhythmic drawl the story of how his world had fallen to pieces.

'I got this first Section 5 – like a warning, notice, order, whatever the fuck it's called – it said my farm was listed. Listed for expropriation. I was being evicted. I thought, they can't be serious. I hadn't farmed that land in twenty years. I'm not a farmer; I buy and sell machinery. I tore up the letter and had a word to the party boss in Darwin and he said I had nothing to worry about, an old comrade like me. Three months later, I got another Section 5. This time I went to see a lawyer in Harare and he said we would lodge an objection to the eviction order. Weekend after that, I went fishing, stayed a few days at the shack, and when I got back I found my land had been pegged, divided up, and there were people settled all over the place. About forty families camped on my land. I told the bastards to bugger off. They told me to get lost – and if I didn't clear off they'd kill me. "Come and try," I said. A month later I got another order – a Section 7 – it said I had forty-five days to vacate. So I went back to the lawyer and he went to court to try and stop it. I also went to see the DA, another old friend, and I asked for help. The DA looked into my eyes and said he'd do anything he could. I knew he meant it and I also knew he couldn't do a bloody thing. Next morning the guys camped on my land stole my tractors, and my borehole pump. They told me again to leave or they'd take me out. I don't want to sound like I had it so hard. Everyone was getting invaded, beaten, robbed. I mean, at least I wasn't murdered. But I was alone and if I'd been taken out no one would have noticed. Other farmers had rigged up a support network; they kept in touch by radio, phone; they had patrols; they had family. Hell, I didn't even have a security fence. What for? I was home, wasn't I? But these guys had pangas, and they weren't kidding. "I can't just pack up and leave. It's been forty years," I said. "Go, or die," they said. I went to the cops and told them I was being threatened; they were very polite and said they'd come over and take care of it. But they never pitched.

'A few nights later, the squatters lit fires in the garden; they were dancing and singing. My own staff took off; they were too scared to stay. I tried to phone the cops but the line was cut. I sat up with a shotgun, but the guys in the garden knew I'd fall asleep sooner or later. Frankly, I was fucked. So, around midnight, I packed up some food, some clothes, my passport, some booze and loaded the Nissan *bakkie*. And then I waited. When first light came and I knew the bastards would be getting some kip, I opened the barn doors, climbed into the *bakkie* and put my foot flat on the floor. I hit the farm gate at about forty k's and tore right through it before they could rub the sleep out of their eyes. You know, Alex, when I landed in Darwin, back in 1963, I was carrying more than when I fucking left.' Papadop laughed. 'Bloody funny, isn't it, hey?'

'Not really.'

'*Ja*, well, no, maybe not; that's why I'm laughing. What else can you do?' Papadop poured us more brandy. 'Sorry about no ice in the Coke. I always stock up on ice at the Plymouth Arms when I go into town, but I got nothing to keep it bloody cold, you see, except a cool-bag. As soon as I earn some bucks from that …' he waved towards his field of tobacco '… a fridge is first on my list.'

I reckoned it was a long list. He had next to nothing: his tent, a sleeping bag, a shaving mirror, a few clothes and an old Nissan truck. Yet the man exuded a kind of weary relief. Anywhere was better than home was the way he put it. 'I've been in Moz five months now, and I'm winning.' By scrounging what he needed from neighbours he'd planted his first tobacco crop. He had been down with malaria a couple of times, 'It's bloody endemic here. But they got good Chinese *muti* at the hospital. Couple of shots, and you sweat it out. Shit, man, I tell you malaria's manageable; Mugabe isn't. I love it here. I go down on my knees and thank God for my lease.'

'You don't own this land?'

Papadop enjoyed explaining: it appealed to his sense of the ridiculous. There were some verbal adjustments that needed to be made. Mozambique clung poignantly to old Marxist ideas, and all land belonged to the state. New farmers, said Papadop, could not buy land but they could lease a patch for fifty years.

He was seventy-four, his black hair streaked with grey, but he was full of plans. The soil was rich, the rains good, water plentiful, and the local labour force was 'wonderful'.

'They'd steal the milk outa your coffee if you didn't keep an eye on them, but really nice people.'

He spoke no Portuguese but his Shona was better than his English.

'After all, we're just down the fucking road from Zim. Head on up the road and you're *en route* for Harare. All the guys in these parts speak or understand Shona.'

There were around two dozen Zimbos farming around Chimoio, said Papadop.

'The woman over at the Plymouth Arms, she talked of Ports and Pongos. Who are they?'

'Ports are Portuguese who've come back to Mozambique to farm, or whatever. Pongos are Brits who turn up, as Brits do, in odd places like this. We've even got a few Boers here from South Africa. But it's us Zimbos or ex-Zimbos who're making stuff grow. Or putting in some dairy herds, or farming flowers.'

It made a kind of twisted sense. Mozambique needed skilled technicians, which farmers were, and the old colonist bosses needed a leg-up. Put them together and bingo! Except that the Zimbos were not colonists, they were – or they had been – citizens. Until suddenly they weren't. They were homeless, stateless, unmentionable.

'I'm not allowed to call myself a "farmer" 'cause that has, well, layers of meaning. Back in Zim, it means settler, and settler means white. So here I'm not a farmer; they call us "investors". But it's being white, that's the bugger, Alex. It really is.'

Being white in Zim endangered your health; all it did in Moz, said Papadop, was to cramp your mobility a bit. Official thinking had it that hard-drinking Zimbos in the bush would gang together and begin behaving badly. And it might look like the bad old days. So the Mozambicans had taken a leaf from old ethno-fascist South Africa which always believed tribe trumped all other considerations: it was a wheeze called 'influx control' that Mozambique used to limit the numbers of white Zimbos in any one area.

However, these restrictions aside, the visitors might plough, sow, reap and sell to their hearts' content.

And it worked. Zimbos, Pongos, Brits, Ports and Boers raised cattle, fish and flowers. They swapped tractors, begged capital, sold themselves to the big tobacco companies; they hustled, schemed and grafted. They got legless at Cecelia's pub. They lived under tents, in shacks, they took over deserted Portuguese villas, they camped in caravans or in half-built ranches on remote hills.

It was admirable, and it was weird; they were doing what their great-grandparents had done, making a home in Africa. They were boisterous, big-mouthed and rude: in a word, they were pioneers. All over again.

In Africa, what passed as a new dawn was as often as not just the old dawn repackaged. I remembered how Papadop had hated the old racial divisions as practised down south, the boxed-in mind and manners of the apartheid state; how he'd settled in a free country, Southern Rhodesia, and acclimatised. Then did it all again in a free country called Zimbabwe. And now here he was, once again, on a hillside in Marxist Mozambique ...

'Right back where I fucking well began: the bastards!'

'What or who do you feel you are now, Papadop?'

'Buggered if I know. When I came to South Africa I was a

Greek; then I moved to Darwin and I was Rhodesian; then I was a Zimbabwean. I thought I'd die a Zimbabwean.' He chuckled. 'Come to think of it, I damn nearly did!'

'So what'll you do?'

He scratched his head and reached for the brandy. 'Keep going.'

'Forward?'

'No, Alex. Not forward. There is no forward for me. Keep on, that's all. It's over for me. But here I can at least pretend.'

'Pretend what?'

'Pretend to be liked, pretend to be home. When I first came to Africa there was British Nyasaland, German South West Africa, Portuguese Zambesia, Northern and Southern Rhodesia, French Equatorial Africa; the Spanish Sahara, Belgian Congo, Italians in Abyssinia, Germans in Cameroon. Some guys even dreamt of a new Israel – in Uganda. That was the time of the visitors: Asians, Chinese, Russians, Lebanese diamond dealers, Belgian priests, French colonials, British polo players, Ports, Germans, Rhodies... Zimbos. Odds and sods from the world over. Where are they now? Or, where are we?' He showed his good, strong teeth. 'I think it's over, the whole adventure. Finished. And soon it will reach down south.'

'It's started. There are South African expats from Detroit to Vancouver. You even get them in Greece. Could you go back to being Greek?'

He laughed again and shook his head, 'Man, I can't even remember being Greek. My trouble is I love Africa, and that's a very bad mistake because she does not love me.'

'But you're still here, Papadop.'

He shook his head. 'Some of me, maybe. Pretending to belong, pretending to be a pioneer. Can't be done. It doesn't really work. It could work, maybe, if I came at it from some utterly strange direction. Maybe you gotta die, and come back as someone else? Even then, I'd stay very, very close to the ground, so I didn't cast a big shadow. Look at me. Look where I am now. A little patch of rented land, a few tobacco plants. I'm not really a farmer, not a Zimbo, not a settler. If I went up the road an hour or two I'd hit the Zim border. I can just about see from here the land I left, but it isn't home any more. And I think maybe it never was.'

He did not suggest I stay and I would not have wished it. I'd found him, I'd done what I'd wanted, he was still alive, and that was good to know. He walked me down to my car, and I gave him the stuff.

'My ma wanted you to have these.'

Papadop examined the map showing Livingstone's journey from coast to coast; he laughed at the rusty sound of the accordion; Livingstone's cap fascinated him. He kept turning it around in his hands. But he also looked a bit perplexed. He rubbed his jaw in the way I always remembered and which, for some reason, I found very moving.

'Bloody hell, man, is it the very thing?'

'She thought so.'

'It's not that I'm not very grateful, Alex boy, but I don't know quite what to do with them. You see how I live.' He waved his hands at the tent, his camp fire, the empty land that reached to the smudgy hills on the horizon.

I said: 'Yeah, I see.' He hugged me and I climbed into the car.

I couldn't turn the Toyota so I backed slowly down the hill. He watched me; a bulky man on a hillside in Mozambique, waving me on encouragingly with the cap until I'd bounced and scraped my way to the road. When I looked back he'd put on the cap and was watching me. It suited him, that cap; you could say it fitted.

After their famous meeting under the old mango tree, Livingstone went on to die a hero and a saint, and Stanley went on to seriously fuck up the Congo. Both were vividly remembered. Papadop was not going to be remembered. Except by me. Perhaps that was the real sign of change. Whites who came to Africa once strove for remembrance; now all they ask is to be forgotten and forgiven. Or ignored. Like Jimmy Li Fu in far-away Malaysia, thanking God that the government tolerated him, and did not send him 'home'.

I drove down Jan Smuts Avenue, and parked outside the house. I unlocked the security gate. The lights in the house were on and I heard music from the living room. It was '*Mambo Italiano*', then '*Freeway Mambo*', and then, as I stood there in the garden, it was '*Besame Mucho*', and I heard a man say, '*Hecho muy bien, Seendie!*'

I knew many things all at once.

The last of my mother's lovers had found each other. Or at least a way of life that suited the circumstances. In my mother's house that very finished South African, Dr Cornelius du Toit, could pretend for a while to be a refugee again, a Latino on the lam, daring, wild, exciting. And Cindy could pretend to be my mother.

My mother had felt the wind blowing and held on to the kids. Papadop, too. The kids made a pretty insubstantial anchor and so did Papadop's ridiculous lease but nonetheless he clung to it, in his tent, on the rich red hillside of a foreign land. Hung on for dear life.

The music stopped and started again. Again, I knew the tune. They were dancing now to '*La Faroana*', and I heard Raoul clap, and snap his fingers, and call out when she got going: '*Mambo, qué rico el mambo!*'

I knew, too, that this latest development left me free to leave. But I kept walking.

You gotta die, and come back again as someone else ...

So what changed?

As you might expect, everything and not much. I still went to the Zoo and stood in front of the gorilla. I remembered that Alexander Barnes, who roamed across the Congo with his 'kine', and whose jerky films of the Waturi pygmies, those 'forest dwarfs', lit up my boyhood, had a particular weakness for shooting any animal at all, but killing gorillas was amongst his favourite forms of slaughter. He gave my mother a picture of a rare Kivu gorilla he had shot in the Virunga Mountains. The gorilla looked alive, seated on the grass, his eyes open, his mouth gaping, his arms raised above his head: you needed to look carefully to see they were roped by the wrists to an overhead branch. Next to the rare gorilla was his servant, identified on the photograph as 'the boy Swalim'. He was a man of about forty, a tiny figure in a buttoned white tunic, sitting beside the great ape, to give a sense of human scale.

I went most days to the Bernberg Museum, though it opened now for just three mornings a week. It was a sign of the times. The present Jo'burg City Council was not the one to which the sisters left their house. The new council was strapped for cash. It had other priorities. A museum of European fashion did not accord with the spirit of the new council, which wanted to put its money into break-dancing.

People who wanted old Eurocentric stuff, like couture and ballet, could pay for it themselves.

To begin with I think Cindy was a little perplexed to find me among the flower-beds, mowing the lawn, weeding. But she got over it. After all, everything was sort of back to normal. My mother's house again had an owner, and a gardener in the back room. After a few weeks no one looked at me twice.

One evening, about six months later, I was in the garden. The light softened and lay gently on the grass, the colours that had burnt out in the midday sun came flooding back and everything turned gentle and flowed and I could forget Jo'burg was flat stony veld set about with mine-dumps. I had the sprinkler going on the lawn, the grass smelt of water and earth, when looping over the electrified fence topping the security walls came the evening paper. It landed with a thud in the concrete path: the Johannesburg *Star*. I could read the headline: 'Jo'burg to Get a Thousand More Cops!' Lying beside the paper was Noddy's hat. The feather caught the sun, all its rainbow colours shimmering.

I kept the handsome Tyrolean hat on the hook on the wall in his old room, waiting for him. Sometimes I used to go and look at it, so silly, so lost. A hat without a head. I knew what it was to exist cut off from the vital reality that makes us make sense to ourselves. Without the person of Noddy to give this hat a body, an Africa to carry it off in, it remained marooned. Something similar was facing me. Get ahead of the game, or fuck off out of here, said the voice of sharp Jo'burg wisdom. Grab hold of things, or get lost.

Cindy knew that. Almost every day there was a new move.

She was on her way: Dr du Toit came at night, moonlighting, literally. Upstanding general practitioner of impeccable credentials by day, mambo dancer by moonlight, and the man who taught her the difficult rhythms of that most tricky dance. Cindy perhaps taught him those things he most needed to understand: like the meaning of *ubuntu*; and empowerment and stakeholders and what a role player was.

So I did as Papadop suggested: I kept my head down, kept myself to myself. I wasn't an air-conditioning salesman, I wasn't a white South African, I wasn't a gun owner, I wasn't interested in politics, or the price of gold, and I had no intention of making myself known to anyone.

I have very little in my room. A bed, a hat, a box. The box is the one we always believed once held the skull of Mrs Ples. I like to think of her as one of the first in these parts to have got the hang of things, to have known she was transitional, destined to pass away, but who give rise to some hair-raising descendants, alarming super-hominids of which Jo'burgers are still the primal example. It all began here; what a sobering thought. My mother had been quite right: this town doesn't have a history, it has a police record. Or would, if only there were some cosmic cops around. As it is, I'd take Cindy's advice: 'If stopped by the police, do not stop...'

I kept an eye on Cindy, in the way we like to think the spirits of the departed keep watch over the living world. At least, I liked to think so. Cindy said this haunting freaked her out, but I had to correct her. I was no ghost, I was simply the gardener, I lived in the room assigned to the gardener.

I didn't shout the odds. Neither did I assume too much authority, even on my chosen patch; after all, my knowledge was minimal, the little I'd picked up from Noddy. I had to teach myself a lot before I could tell the difference between a poor man's orchid (Schizanthus) and a cupid's dart (Catananche). But I knew how to lift dahlia tubers without breaking their necks. And I bought wilt-resistant snapdragons.

Dear Reader,

Welcome to the world of Fairley Terrace's Ten Houses, the Somerset setting for my new series of sagas about the families who live in one of the rows of mining cottages, and the effect which a local colliery disaster has on this close-knit community.

This series was inspired by a real-life disaster just a few miles from Radstock where I was born and grew up, and also the tales my own father told me of his days as a carting boy.

It's been a huge pleasure to write about my much-loved home and the triumphs and tragedies and joys and sorrows of the characters I've created.

I do hope you will enjoy *All the Dark Secrets*, and will want to come back to visit the families of Fairley Terrace with me again in the next books in the series – I have many stories I'm looking forward to telling!

I love to hear from my readers so do visit me on Facebook www.facebook.com/JennieFeltonAuthor or on Twitter @Jennie_Felton where I share my latest news!

Love,

Jennie x

By Jennie Felton

The Families of Fairley Terrace Sagas
All the Dark Secrets

JENNIE FELTON

All the Dark Secrets

headline

First published in Great Britain in 2014 by
HEADLINE PUBLISHING GROUP

First published in paperback in 2015 by
HEADLINE PUBLISHING GROUP

8

Cataloguing in Publication Data is available from the British Library

ISBN 978 1 4722 0984 9

Typeset in Calisto by Avon DataSet Ltd,
Bidford-on-Avon, Warwickshire

Printed and bound by CPI Group (UK) Ltd, Croydon CR0 4YY

HEADLINE PUBLISHING GROUP
An Hachette UK Company
338 Euston Road
London NW1 3BH

www.headline.co.uk
www.hachette.co.uk

For my darling husband Terry
1936–2013

Acknowledgements

When I'm writing a book there is always some new avenue to explore about which I know nothing! This time it was the making of stained-glass windows. And I couldn't have done it without the help of a dear friend, Richard Jones. Richard's father did actually make a stained-glass window for a cathedral in New York in the 1920s, which gave me the idea. As a hobby Richard followed in his father's footsteps. He explained the process to me, showed me round his workshop, and loaned me a manual which had belonged to his father. Due to ill health, he was unable to check what I had written and sadly has since passed away, so while I hope I have not made any blunders, if I have they are entirely down to me. RIP, dear Richard.

So many people play a part in bringing a book to publication that listing them all would be a bit like an overlong Oscar acceptance speech, so I'll simply say a huge thank-you to everyone at Headline. I must make special mention, though, of my lovely editor, Kate Byrne. And many thanks too to Sheila Crowley, my agent, and her assistant Rebecca Ritchie, who is never more than a phone call or an email away.

Last but not least, my heartfelt thanks to my wonderful family and friends who have been there for me throughout a very difficult year. I love you all.

Historical Note

'In this grave are deposited the remains of the twelve undermentioned sufferers all of whom were killed at Wells Way Coal Works on 8th November 1839 by snapping of the rope as they were on the point of descending into the pit. The rope was generally believed to have been maliciously cut.'

So reads the inscription on a gravestone in a churchyard in the Somerset coalfield near to my home, and it provided the inspiration for the terrible accident which is the catalyst for my story.

Though of course what I have written is all fiction, this disaster was all too real.

I have, however, used a certain amount of poetic license in my story, which begins in 1895. By this time the hemp rope hudges had long been replaced by four-deck cages. However, I have explained that the owner of Shepton Fields, my fictional pit, was a penny-pinching coal master who did not want to invest in his mine. I hope readers will bear with me on this – and enjoy the story!

Don't go down in the mine, Dad
Dreams very often come true

Robert Donnelly and Will Geddes

Prologue

Something terrible was going to happen. Maggie knew it. One minute she was walking hand in hand with Jack in the dew-fresh meadow, watching the grey morning sky streak pink above the dark skyline, listening to the dawn chorus of the birds and loving the scents of summer; the next she was so afraid she could scarcely breathe. The feeling of oppression and dread was all around her in a suffocating cloud, and inside her too, tightening her chest and chilling her to the marrow. Her fingers tightened on Jack's, but when she turned towards him, looking for comfort, she saw that it wasn't Jack at all, but her father, Paddy. And Frank Rogers, who lived a few doors away from them, was there too, taking her other hand. Frank Rogers? Why was Frank here? She didn't understand. It made no sense, and the confusion added to the terrible feeling of foreboding, bringing her to the edge of panic.

Maggie's footsteps faltered and she came to an abrupt halt, but the hands holding hers pulled her on.

'Come on, my girl, we'll be late.'

'No! Dad – no! Stop! Please . . . You mustn't . . .'

But it was no good. Her father ignored her pleas, dragging her on along the path worn by many feet through the knee-deep grass.

'No, Dad, no!'

And then, quite suddenly, the ground was giving way beneath her, and she was falling. No, not falling, plummeting into inky blackness. She tried to scream, but no sound came; it was trapped somewhere deep inside her. There was a sharp, fetid smell in her nostrils and a rush of cold air against her hot cheeks, but she couldn't breathe. Every vestige of breath was being forced out of her lungs, and terror was coursing through her in an icy tide. Falling, falling, faster, faster; dear God, would it never stop?

It was the violence of the jolt that woke her. For a moment, Maggie lay motionless, feeling the rapid beating of her heart beneath her ribs and staring into the darkness until her breath came easier and the terror began to recede a little.

A dream. That was all it had been. A dream – well, a nightmare really. But it had been so real! And the horror of it was with her still, binding her tightly like a fly caught in a spider's web. She sat up, swinging her legs over the edge of the bed. She didn't want to risk going back to sleep in case the dream began again. She padded across her tiny bedroom and drew back the curtains, letting moonlight flood in. Outside, it was illuminating the very fields she had been walking through in her dream, and beyond them, the great black carbuncle that was the colliery waste tip – the batch, as they called it. Though it was a warm summer night, Maggie shivered, and the shiver was not just because she was suddenly cold, but because the terrible sense of oppression was still enveloping her, just as it had in the dream.

All very well to try and tell herself it was nothing, just a shadow of something that hadn't been real. All very well to scoff and pretend it meant nothing. Maggie didn't like it when she got a feeling such as this one, different from normal apprehension because there was no solid reason for it. Almost inevitably it was the precursor of something bad. Ever since she was a little girl she'd known that. A sick feeling in her stomach at the thought of going to school and there'd almost certainly be trouble of some kind; childish trouble, maybe, but something to upset her day. One summer, she hadn't wanted to ride on the back of the hay wagon as she usually loved to do; she'd felt that awful shadow of dread as Ewart and Walter, her older brothers, had pulled her up on to the bales of hay. And sure enough, the wagon had rolled into a rut in the ground, and two or three bales broke free and fell, taking the children with them. Walter had broken his leg, and walked with a limp to this day. So it had gone on over the years: not a frequent occurrence but one that was reliable enough to alarm her when the dark foreboding overcame her.

Maggie had never told anyone about it; she didn't even want to acknowledge that somehow she could foresee the future. In any case, she wasn't seeing, exactly, just feeling a distress that wasn't yet justified. But this . . . this was far worse than anything she had ever experienced before. It wasn't just the terror of the dream, though, that was still making her shudder, even though she was now wide awake. It was the dense black fog that had closed in around her, and the dreadful weight inside her, making her feel sick with dread. As she stood at the window, the moon disappeared behind a cloud and the whole vista before her went dark, as if a light had gone out. Maggie shivered again. Should she tell someone this time? But tell them what? That she'd dreamed she was falling? Nothing too unusual in that. That Jack had turned into her father and Frank Rogers had been there too? Nothing unusual in that either. Everyone knew that dreams made no sense. No, it was this weight of oppression that was really frightening her, but if she told anyone about that, they'd just say it was left over from the nightmare, and perhaps they would be right.

Reluctantly Maggie dragged herself back to bed and pulled the woollen blanket of crocheted squares up to her chin. But it was a long while before she could bring herself to close her eyes, and even longer before she fell into a fitful doze. She didn't dream any more that night, but when she woke next morning, the feeling of foreboding was still with her.

She must forget about it, she told herself. It was nothing but the aftermath of a horrible dream. And even if it wasn't, there wasn't a thing she could do to avert whatever it was that was going to happen.

Chapter One

June 1895

'Hey, look, it's the rag man! Billy the rag-and-bone man!'

'Where'd you get yer coat, Billy? Off Farmer Barton's scarecrow?'

The jeering youths were squatting collier fashion against the rough stone wall of the outbuildings that backed Fairley Terrace – or, as it was known locally – the Ten Houses. Billy Donovan had seen them there as soon as he came out of the back door of number six, and his heart had plummeted in his skinny chest.

His tormentors were the bigger – and older – lads who worked with him at Shepton Fields Colliery – fourteen and fifteen to his twelve. As far as they were concerned, he was fair game; they called him a sissy because he still worked on the screens in the pit yard whilst they were 'carting boys' underground, and they looked down on him for being one of the Donovans, the poorest family in the rank and, in their eyes, nothing but scum. Billy wished he didn't have to walk right past them, but there was no way he could avoid it, not unless he wanted a good hiding from his father. He glared resentfully at the quart jug in his hand. Paddy Donovan had told him to take it down to the snug of the Prince of Wales and get it filled with best bitter. And when he wanted a drink, Paddy Donovan was not a man to cross.

'Hey, Billy! Billy the Didiky!'

Billy lowered his head, staring at the ground and plodding on. It wasn't the first time he'd been called a didicoy, as the locals referred to gypsies. He longed to yell at the lads that he wasn't a didicoy, that his father was Irish and had only come over to England because there was no work to be had in Dublin, but he knew better. It would only make things worse if they saw they were getting to him. Fury rose like bile in his throat. How he hated them! Not that that would worry them much. But one day – one day he'd get his own back. Just let them wait – he'd show them!

'Hey, look, Billy's off to the boozer!' That was Frank Rogers, who lived at number two, a big, thickset lad with a puggy nose and a loud, jeering voice. 'Gonna make you big and strong, is it, Billy? That'll be the day!'

'Naw, it's for old Paddy to get tipsy again. He oughta get you a decent pair of trousers afore he spends it on beer.' That was Charlie Oglethorpe, at fifteen, the oldest of the lads.

'Shut up!' Billy muttered.

'What's that you said?' Charlie snarled.

A hobnailed boot shot out right in front of Billy, and he cannoned forward, landing with a sickening thud on his hands and knees, the quart jug shooting from his hand as he tried to save himself.

'Have a good trip, Billy,' Frank Rogers laughed.

The jug had rolled towards the youths; they leapt to their feet, and Dick Riddle, who fancied himself as a footballer, got a steel-capped toe underneath it and gave it a nifty flick.

'To you, Frank!'

To Billy's horror, the youths began kicking the jug one to the other. He scrambled to his feet. His hands were grazed and bleeding and his neck hurt, but he scarcely noticed. If the beer jug got dented, he'd be for the high jump and no mistake!

'Give it here! Hey, don't do that! Give it here!' he begged.

His tormentors ignored him, kicking the jug about enthusiastically. Then Frank Rogers dived to pick it up, waving it in front of Billy's face, taunting him.

'Want yer jug, Billy? Come and get it, then!'

Billy threw himself at Frank, skinny arms flailing wildly; Frank twisted away. Billy made a grab at Frank's shirt, and the thin fabric ripped thread from thread beneath his skinny fingers.

'You tore me shirt, you little bugger!' Frank threw the jug down, diving for Billy instead. They went down in a heap, Frank pounding the smaller boy furiously, Billy scrabbling helplessly. Charlie and Dick stood by, yelling encouragement.

'Give him a good hiding, Frank!'

'Kick his brains out – if he's got any!'

Frank was sitting on top of him now, his full weight pressing down on Billy's stomach, whilst he banged the smaller boy's head on the hard ground. Billy was seeing stars, and he could scarcely breathe. If he thought at all, it was that his last moment had come.

The commotion of the fight carried clearly through the open door into the little scullery of number six, where Maggie Donovan was blacking her boots ready for work next day. Maggie always blacked her boots on a Sunday evening – the rest of the week they had to make do with a lick and a promise, just a quick wipe over with a duster to keep them looking respectable enough to meet the high standards of Mrs Augusta Freeman, owner of the drapery shop in High Compton where Maggie was a sales assistant.

'I expect my girls to be smart at all times,' Mrs Freeman had said when she had taken Maggie on as an apprentice. 'A slovenly appearance is the outward sign of a slovenly mind, and will not be tolerated.'

Her small, beady eyes had gleamed behind her wire-rimmed spectacles as they swept critically over Maggie, seeking the shortcomings she had expected in a Donovan, and finding none. Maggie's high-necked blouse was as pristine white as only a blue bag in the washing water could make it, and perfectly pressed, her dark skirt the very picture of modesty, and the tiny posy of silky rosebuds pinned on the waistband showed style and imagination, both qualities that would prove an advantage in a draper's assistant. But all the same . . .

'I also expect a willingness to work hard, an ability to learn, and, most importantly of all, courtesy to the customers,' Augusta said sternly. 'The customer is always right, no matter how much you think they might be inconveniencing you.'

'I know,' Maggie had said. 'I won't let you down, Mrs Freeman, I promise.'

That had been five years ago. Now Maggie was a fully fledged assistant in the drapery shop, and was even helping to train up Cathy Small, the newest apprentice. She'd done very well for herself – for a Donovan – everyone agreed.

Maggie paused now in the cleaning of her boots, blue eyes narrowing as she heard the commotion. A fight – there was no mistaking it. And Billy had just this minute gone out to fetch her father's beer.

She dumped shoe brush and boot on the oilcloth-covered cupboard that served as a worktop and hurried to the door, looking along the rank. Yes, it was a fight, and as she had feared, Billy was involved. She couldn't see much of him because that great galumphing Frank Rogers was sitting astride him, but she'd know his carroty hair anywhere. And it was plain he was getting the worst of it, as usual. Why did those bullies have to pick on him all the time?

Maggie shook her head in disgust and set off up the rank to intervene. It wouldn't help Billy in the long run, but she couldn't stand by and watch her little brother taking a beating from those thugs.

'Hoi!' she yelled loudly as she approached them. 'What d'you think you're doing?'

For answer, Frank Rogers banged Billy's head on the ground again.

The Irish was up in Maggie now. Abandoning all pretence of dignity, she ran the last few yards to reach the fighting boys, grabbed hold of Frank's collar and gave it a hearty tug so that his shirt buttons popped all at once. His head jerked round, surprise and outrage written all over his rather red face.

'Stop that this minute!' Maggie ordered furiously. 'Leave our Billy alone and pick on someone your own size, you bully.'

For a moment she thought he was going to defy her and let into Billy again. Then he thought better of it. He'd had his fun, and there would be plenty of other times to knock seven bells out of Billy when his sister wasn't there standing over them like an avenging angel. He gave the boy one last punch, just to show he wasn't really afraid of Maggie, and let him go.

'Bloody Donovans!' he muttered as he got to his feet, trying to button his torn shirt, which was now also open to the waist.

Maggie was anxious that the boys might have really hurt her brother, but she knew if she showed concern it would only give them more ammunition to taunt him as a sissy. 'Come on, our Billy, get up from there,' she said sharply. 'Look at the state of you! And isn't that our jug over there by the wall?'

None of the lads dared touch it again, right under Maggie's

baleful eye. She might be a Donovan too, but they had a healthy respect for her sharp tongue, and anyway, she was a grown woman. As a rule, lads didn't give cheek to grown women – especially ones as pretty as Maggie. She rescued the jug and thrust it at Billy.

'You'd better go and get this filled up before our dad comes out and gives you what for,' she told him. Then, turning to the other lads: 'And if there's any more trouble from you lot tonight, you'll have me to answer to.'

With that she turned and headed back towards number six.

'Billy the baby!' Frank hissed at Billy, who had started off in the direction of the Prince of Wales but had stopped to mop at his bloody nose with a rag that had once been the tail of a shirt but now did service as a handkerchief. 'You won't always have your sister there to save your bacon. Next time . . . just you wait!'

Billy felt sick, not just from the beating, but from fear for the future. Frank was right – there would be plenty more episodes like this one. He lived in the same rank as his tormentors, worked at the same pit. There was no escaping them and there never would be.

Unless he could get away to Yorkshire, like his two older brothers, Ewart and Walter. Hope flared in him briefly, then flickered and died. Yorkshire was likely just as full of bullies as Somerset, and they'd pick on him too. Everybody picked on him and always had. Even his own father. Paddy had no time for him and wasn't afraid to show it.

Billy trudged painfully along the rank, fighting back tears. Resentment and hatred for his tormentors was like bitter bile in his mouth, mingling with the salty taste of his own blood. Oh, if only he could think of a way to get back at all of them. Just give him a chance and he'd show them he wasn't the useless lummox they all thought him. But how he'd ever get that chance he didn't as yet have the first idea.

'What's going on?'

Rose Donovan, Maggie's mother, was at the back door, peering out anxiously. Truth to tell, Rose's permanent expression was one of anxiety, and not without reason. Life had dealt her a bad hand. She had once been a pretty girl with a fine head of curly chestnut hair, which Maggie had inherited, and a neat figure, and she had caught the eye of plenty of lads who would have made her a far better husband than Paddy Donovan had. But from the moment he had arrived in High Compton in search of work, she had wanted no one but him. She had fallen head over heels for his swarthy good looks – dark hair, and eyes as blue as sapphires – his powerful physique, and the wonderful Irish brogue that was so different to the Somerset drawl she was accustomed to and sounded so much more romantic to her ears.

Rose had lost her head as well as her heart and allowed Paddy liberties no decent girl should allow a young man. But at least he had married her when she had found out that there was a baby on the way – well, wouldn't her father have taken the double-barrelled shotgun he used for shooting pigeons and rabbits to Paddy if he had not?

And then her troubles had started.

To begin with there was his gambling. Paddy fancied a bet on the horses and often passed a betting slip to the bookie's runner who hung around outside the Prince of Wales pub, but though he was sure he was picking a winner, more often than not he lost. 'The bookie always wins in the end,' Rose's father used to say, and he was right.

Then there was his drinking. Rose had known that Paddy liked a drink, it had been part of his charm, but there was nothing charming about him when he got roaring drunk on a Saturday, spending half the wages that had been doled out to him before he even got it home. There was nothing charming about him when he yelled at her for not having a meal ready for him on the table, or a copper full of water hot enough for his liking when he wanted his bath. And there was certainly nothing charming about him when he turned on her and beat her.

The black eyes he gave her were the worst; she could hide the bruises on her arms under long sleeves and grit her teeth against the pain in her ribs so that nobody knew how much every breath hurt her. But the black eyes she could not hide, and no matter what stories she made up to excuse them, she knew the neighbours could see right through them to the shameful truth.

The first time Paddy had hit her was when Maggie was just a little girl, and truth to tell, Rose hadn't been able to find it in her to blame him. It was no more than she deserved, she'd thought, as she burned with guilt and shame for what she'd done. What husband wouldn't be driven to lash out under the circumstances? But after that first time, it had happened again and again, year after year, whenever he was angry with her, whenever he was drunk, whenever she fell foul of his quick temper and surly moods.

He didn't often hit her these days, and never when Maggie was about. He seemed to have a respect for his daughter that he never showed anyone else, certainly not Billy, and not even Ewart and Walter, his two elder sons. When they'd lived at home they'd tried to intervene too, but they had only been given a good hiding for their trouble. All Rose's sons took after her in build, and Paddy, who scorned them for it, could have beaten any of them senseless with a hand tied behind his back if they'd tried to take him on.

It was because of Paddy that Ewart and Walter had gone off

to work in Yorkshire, Rose felt sure. They said it was because the work was easier there than in the narrow, faulted Somerset seams, but Rose knew that wasn't the real reason. They had wanted to get away from their violent father and the stigma that attached to them for being his sons. They had wanted to be able to bring home their wages and not have him take half off them to buy more drink, or back some 'sure-fire winner'. And Billy would do the same, she thought, just as soon as he was old enough. She couldn't blame them, but she did blame Paddy for depriving her of her children.

And not only her living children, either, but the ones she had lost for ever, too. Three miscarriages she had endured, one of them certainly because Paddy had punched her in the stomach when she was seven months gone. And then there was little Alice, dead of the fever. If they hadn't been so poor because of Paddy's drinking and gambling, maybe she could have afforded the doctor's bills and Alice would be alive today. Ten years old she'd be now, but to Rose she would always be fourteen months, with a big gummy smile, toddling unsteadily on her plump little legs. The memory of Alice was an ache in Rose's heart that never went away.

Nowadays Rose was just a shadow of the girl she had once been. Her once pretty face was thin and lined, with a defeated look to it. The harshness of her life had taken its toll on her small frame, making her scrawny, and she was always exhausted. She took in washing to help make ends meet, so her hands were red and puffy, and in winter, long, painful cracks opened on her fingertips and never healed until summer came. Now, just to make things worse, she was pregnant again. She'd thought all that was behind her; the prospect of going through it again was a constant worry that weighed in her stomach just as the baby soon would.

She stood in the doorway now, arms wrapped around her sunken chest, fingers plucking nervously at the blouse that years of careful laundering had made thin as a bee's wing, as Maggie flounced back along the rank.

'What's going on? What's the matter now?'

'Oh, just those louts picking on our Billy again,' Maggie said crossly. 'I gave them a piece of my mind, but a fat lot of good that will do.'

'What's that?' Paddy appeared in the scullery, on his way out to have a smoke while he waited for his jug of beer.

'Our Billy,' Rose told him. 'Them boys have been picking on him again.'

Paddy grunted, surly and impatient as he always was where Billy was concerned. 'It's time he learned to stand up for himself.'

'That's easier said than done, Dad,' Maggie retorted. 'They're twice his size, all of them.'

'And he's just a sissy!' Paddy said scornfully. 'Our Ewart was no bigger at his age, but he could give as good as he got. He didn't get picked on, our Ewart, and woe betide the bugger who tried.'

Maggie said nothing, but she knew he was right. Ewart had been like a little terrier, gouging and fighting dirty if needs be. But Billy wasn't Ewart, and never would be. As Rose had said to her once, Billy was different to the others.

'I've got to get these boots cleaned,' she said, picking up the brush from where she'd left it. 'Jack's calling for me later on, and I expect we shall go out for a walk.'

'Oh, that's nice,' Rose said automatically, but her heart sank a little.

Though it should have been no real surprise, since the two of them had been friends since childhood, she had a feeling things were getting serious between Maggie and Jack Withers, and the thought of her daughter leaving home if they should decide to get married was a depressing one. Maggie was the one ray of sunshine in her drab existence, and she was so good with Billy, too. With a new baby on the way, Rose didn't know how she would manage without her.

But these feelings were, she told herself, just her being selfish. She should be glad for Maggie – and she was. Jack was a lovely lad. She'd known him all his life, as the Withers family lived just four doors up the rank at number ten. He was quiet, and as decent as they came, unlike his brother Josh, who had a terrible wild streak. When he was younger, you always knew that if there was trouble, Josh would be at the centre of it, and later on, the police were at his door so often that it seemed certain he'd end up in prison. In the end his long-suffering parents had sent him off to Florrie Withers's brother and his family in Wales in the hope that they could knock some sense into him, but he was back now, and as far as Rose could see, as wild as ever. What was more, she had noticed the way he looked at Maggie and been a little alarmed. She, more than anyone, should know how easy it was to be bowled over by roguish charm, and though the two boys were like peas in a pod, both dark and good-looking, she worried that the very things that made Josh unsuitable were the same ones that might well make him attractive to a girl.

No, all things considered, she should just be grateful that it was Jack and not Josh that Maggie had taken up with. But she couldn't help hoping it would be a while yet before they decided to get married.

Chapter Two

Though both had plans for later, the two Withers brothers were enjoying an early-evening pint in the public bar at the Prince of Wales.

The inn was crowded, as it always was on a Sunday night. Most weekday evenings the miners who frequented it were too tired to socialise – by the time they'd had their bath and their tea, all they wanted to do was collapse into an easy chair and 'snooge' till bedtime. And at this time of year, there were gardens and allotments to be tended, no matter how tired they were. But Sundays, when they'd had a day off, those that weren't out for a walk with the family or fussing with their racing pigeons liked to have a pint and a natter – 'chewing the fat', they called it.

And tonight there was plenty of fat to chew.

'You know they'm talking again about closing down the pit, don't you?' said Archie Russell, one of the older men, wiping the beer foam off his chin with the back of his hand.

'And about time too!' Josh said forcefully. 'The place is a death trap. Hasn't had any money spent on it in years.'

The other men sitting around the table glared at him indignantly. All very well for Josh Withers to talk; he didn't work at Shepton Fields as they did. Since coming home from

Wales, he'd got himself a job as a carpenter at Marston, one of the newest and best-equipped pits in the district – his uncle had taught him all about working with wood, apparently. Unlike the rest of them, Josh wouldn't find himself out of work if Shepton Fields closed, and many of them, Josh's own father included, would be lucky to get another job at their age.

'Let me tell you this, young 'un,' George Parfitt said. 'If we'd pressed for money to be spent on Shepton Fields, Sir Montague would have closed it down long ago. Not worth it, you see. Not for the coal that's left there.'

Josh rocked his chair back on to its back legs, and shrugged his broad shoulders.

'Well, it's your funeral. But the ventilation down there is a disgrace. And you haven't even got a proper cage. That hudge should have been condemned years ago, and would have been if the authorities knew about it. Just a rope, for goodness' sake! I wouldn't go down on the bloody thing if you paid me.'

'That's just it, though, in't it?' Archie Russell took another swig of beer. 'We'm being *paid*. So long as Shepton Fields is open, we'm being *paid*. And that be a lot better than finishing up over at Catcombe in the workhouse, however you'd-a look at it.'

'What have you got to say about it, my son?' George Parfitt swivelled on his stool to look at Jack, who was sitting quietly over his pint, not taking any part in the argument. 'Are you going to let yer brother get away wi' talking like that? Shepton Fields is good enough for you and your father, so why bain't it good enough for he?'

Jack Withers sighed inwardly. Privately he agreed with Josh. Shepton Fields was a death trap, and if the authorities knew the half of it they'd have come down like a ton of bricks on Sir Montague Fairley, the owner, long ago. But as Archie had said, it was a living for so many of them, his father included.

Jack wished with all his heart that he could leave and work in a better colliery, maybe even learn a trade as Josh had done. But he couldn't do that. Not while Gilby, his father, still needed work.

Although he was now almost twenty-two years old, Jack was still what was known as a carting boy. The seams here in the Somerset coalfield were too narrow and faulted for pit ponies, and so young men, crawling on their hands and knees, dragged the putts of coal from the face to the roadway, which was wide enough for tubs to run. It wasn't as easy nowadays to find lads willing to do that in an outdated pit like Shepton Fields, and Jack carted for Gilby. He'd once talked to Wilfred James, the manager, about leaving, and Wilfred had told him in no uncertain terms that if he went, he could take his father with him. So, against his will and better judgement, Jack stayed on. It would kill Gilby to lose his job at his age.

It wasn't in Jack's nature to get involved in arguments, though, and he didn't want to take Josh's part against men he had to work with. But neither did he want to pour scorn on his brother's assertions.

'I reckon our Josh is entitled to his opinion,' he said peaceably.

'You'm too bloody soft!' George Parfitt said vehemently.

'If you say so, George.'

Over Josh's shoulder, Jack could see through the open door to the snug beyond. Young Billy, Maggie's brother, was there, getting a jug filled up with beer – for his father, Jack guessed.

He shook his head, frowning. A pint with your mates was one thing; drinking alone as Paddy Donovan did was something else again. But at least seeing Billy there had given him an excuse to get away from the argument Josh had started, and he was keen to see Maggie anyway. He was madly in love with her, and the thought of being with her trumped a pint with his mates any day of the week.

'I'm going to love you and leave you.' He drained his glass and stood up.

'Ah well, you've got better fish to fry, I dare say.' George Parfitt winked at him. The other men guffawed. But none of them noticed that Josh wasn't laughing.

What was it, Josh wondered, that made him so soft when it came to Maggie? He'd known her all his life, from the time she'd been just a little girl in button-up boots and a smock, bowling a hoop along the rank, or pushing a rag doll in a crate on wheels that she pretended was a perambulator. Just another kid, and one of the Donovans at that, though Josh had never joined in the scornful jibes of his peers, who'd heard the disparaging remarks their parents made about the family and copied them in their own childish way. He hadn't even noticed her when he began taking an interest in girls. She was, after all, more than three years younger than he was, still no more than a skinny child, and there had been plenty of girls his own age coyly flicking their eyelashes at him and keen to show off their developing figures when he was around, a good-looking Jack the lad with a cheeky grin and an offhand manner that seemed to make them all the more eager to impress him.

But when he'd come home from Wales, where he'd been sent to live with his Uncle Fred and Aunt Eliza, it had been a different story. While he'd been away, Maggie had grown up. The first time he saw her, she'd taken his breath away, with her thick mane of chestnut hair, her wide laughing mouth and her sparkling blue eyes. He couldn't believe what a beauty that skinny little girl had become.

And it wasn't just the way she looked, either. There was something about Maggie that was special. Her soft voice, the way she carried herself, tall and proud, as if she was royalty, not a Donovan at all. And she was kind, yet not at all afraid to speak out when she thought it was called for – he'd heard her take the young toughs who lived in the rank to task more than once, such as when they'd been tormenting a mangy cat who'd come slinking along the terrace looking for scraps.

Maggie was special all right, but the trouble was, she was spoken for. She was walking out with Jack, his younger brother, and though Josh wouldn't have hesitated to try his luck if her beau had been anyone else, stealing his own brother's girlfriend was a step beyond the pale, even for a rascal like him. Even if he could have managed it – and he wasn't at all sure he could. She and Jack had been friends since childhood, and somewhere along the way that had developed into love. They seemed very close now. He'd seen the way she took his arm, smiling up at him so that they looked the perfect couple, and he knew Jack doted on her.

All the same . . . Josh still felt his heart miss a beat when he saw her. He couldn't help but regret that he hadn't been around when she'd blossomed from a skinny little waif into a lovely young woman – if he had been, he'd have made sure he beat Jack to it when it came to asking her out. And he'd never yet met any girl who could hold a candle to her in his opinion, though there was certainly no shortage of them lining up to vie for his attention.

And not just the single girls, either.

Josh checked his pocket watch. He'd said he'd see Peggy Bishop this evening if she could get away, and that was a welcome distraction from his feelings for Maggie.

He was playing with fire, of course. Peggy was a married

woman now, though he'd known her back in the old days when they were both young, free and single. She was the first girl he had kissed, and it had been a thirteen-year-old Peggy who had first initiated him into the mysteries of the female body, encouraging him to chase her round the haystacks or down to the river where the grass was long and sweet and a little wood met the meadow. He hadn't been the only one by a long chalk, he knew, but that hadn't mattered to him then, and it didn't matter now. Peggy was still as generous with her favours as she had always been, and that was a big attraction as far as Josh was concerned. Most of the girls he went out with turned coy when he tried to take things further than a kiss and a cuddle. They wanted a ring on their finger first, and a ring, and the commitment that went with it, was the last thing Josh wanted. He was nowhere near ready to settle down. No, much better to give Peggy a quick tumble, even though he suspected she'd begun to take their fun and games a little too seriously for his liking. He even enjoyed the thrill that came from living dangerously – Tom Bishop, the man Peggy had married, was known to have a filthy temper and wouldn't take kindly to being cuckolded. But that just added an extra frisson to the dalliance. And it took his mind off Maggie Donovan for a little while at least.

As the door swung shut after Jack, Josh stood up, jingling a handful of coins in his pocket.

'Right, lads,' he said cheerfully. 'I reckon I've got time to get another round in before I make tracks myself. Who's for another drink, courtesy of Marston, the best pit in the Somerset coalfield?'

As she finished polishing her boots, Maggie was keeping a sharp eye out for Billy. She didn't trust those louts not to waylay her brother on his way home, and if Dad's beer got spilled, there'd be hell to pay. He'd blame Billy, not his tormentors; might even take the strap to him.

They were in the alleyway behind the houses, kicking about a pig's bladder they'd got hold of to use as a football, not a bit ashamed of themselves. But they wouldn't be. For all that they were only carting boys themselves, they reckoned they were way above the Donovans in the pecking order.

Maggie sighed, and brushed a long strand of chestnut hair away from her face. It hadn't been easy growing up as a Donovan, but she reckoned she'd done pretty well for herself. She had a good job she enjoyed, and if she married Jack Withers – she had a feeling he was on the point of asking her – she would be joining a well-respected family. With any luck they would be able to get a little house well away from the Ten Houses and the folk who knew too much about the way her father carried on with his drinking and his gambling. And when her own children came along, at least they wouldn't have the cross of the Donovan name to bear.

Jack was a good man. They'd been friends since childhood, and she was very fond of him, though not as fond as he seemed to be of her. She just wished she felt a bit more excited at the idea of marrying him.

And a bit less worried about leaving her mother especially now, in her condition . . .

A worried frown creased Maggie's forehead and she glanced over her shoulder at Rose, who was cutting wedges of bread and cheese for the men's snap – with an early start in the morning, it was easier to prepare it overnight.

'Let me do that,' she offered, but Rose only gave a tight little shake of her head.

'It's all right. I've nearly finished.'

Maggie regarded her mother anxiously. 'You should be taking things easier.'

'Oh, don't talk silly. It's come to something if I can't cut up a bit of bread and cheese.' Rose flourished the bread knife. 'Go out and enjoy the sun while you can.'

Reluctantly Maggie returned to the doorway, but she was still worried about Rose. She shouldn't be having more babies at her age – Maggie couldn't forget poor Annie Tremlett, a one-time neighbour, who'd had twins in her forties and never walked again, and she prayed nothing like that would happen to her mother.

It wasn't long before she saw Billy turn into the alleyway. To her surprise, Jack was with him. She went out to meet them, swishing her skirts past her father, who was sitting on the low bench outside the back door, smoking and hawking up globules of phlegm.

'What are you doing back this early, Jack?' she greeted him. 'I wasn't expecting you for another half-hour.'

'I'll go again then, shall I?' Jack teased.

Maggie smiled at him. 'Get away with you!'

'I thought I'd better see young Billy home – make sure he didn't drink his father's beer on the way,' Jack said, giving Billy a playful clip round the ear. 'And it's a nice evening for a walk. Pity to waste it in the pub. I see you're making the most of it too, Mr Donovan.'

Paddy grunted and hawked again, stretching out a hand to take his jug of beer from Billy.

'If you're taking our Maggie for a walk, just you behave yourself, d'you hear me?'

Colour rose in Maggie's cheeks. 'Dad!'

'No, I know what it's like to be young. Don't you let him take advantage of you, my girl.'

'What do you think I am?' Maggie retorted sharply.

'Too pretty for your own good. Just like your mother used to be.' He wagged a finger at Jack. 'You remember what I said, my boyo, or you'll have me to answer to.'

Maggie turned away, embarrassed.

'I'll just fetch a shawl in case it gets cold later on.'

'It's not going to,' Jack said.

'All the same . . .' She flew into the house and emerged with a lacy white square. 'I just wanted to wear it,' she confessed to Jack as they walked along the alley. 'It's new – I only got it yesterday. Mrs Freeman let me put it on one side, and I've been saving up for it for weeks. Isn't it the prettiest thing you ever saw?'

Jack smiled. He wanted to say that Maggie was the prettiest thing he ever saw, but fine words didn't come easily to him.

'I shouldn't have bought it really,' Maggie confessed. 'There's all sorts of more important things to spend my money on.'

'If it makes you happy, then that is the most important thing,' Jack said fondly.

It was the closest he could come to expressing his feelings.

At the end of the rank, the track broadened into a lane, bordered by shoulder-high hedges that were thick with meadow-sweet and cow parsley. Beyond the hedge on the right was a cornfield overlooked by the fronts of the houses in the rank; beyond that again was the colliery, Shepton Fields, its headgear towering above the pit yards, and the black mound of coal waste that they called 'the batch' rising like a great dark carbuncle against the clear blue sky of the early summer evening. Maggie had never once stopped to think how odd it was that she could see both cornfields and coal dust from her bedroom window. She just accepted it for the way things were. Coal dust and cornfields, miners and farmhands, living and working side by side.

On the other side of the lane the hedges hid meadows that stretched all the way down the valley, steep and higgledy-piggledy, to a little wood with a river running through it. In winter it swelled to a torrent and sometimes flooded the lower reaches of the fields; at this time of year it was shallow and slow, muddied up by the herd of cows that trampled about in it to have a drink and cool themselves down when the sun was hot.

It had always been one of Maggie's favourite places. As a little girl she had often gone there, sitting on the bank with her knees drawn up to her chin, watching the darting dragonflies and the haze of gnats over the water, listening to the soft melodic gurgle as the brook ran over the stones and sucked at the bulrushes. Once she had seen a kingfisher, a flash of brilliant greeny blue. She'd gone back day after day looking for it, but she'd never seen it again.

At a gateway, Jack paused, 'Shall we go across the fields?'

'If you like.'

She knew why he wanted to go that way – he wanted a kiss and a cuddle, which was fine as long as it stopped there. When they'd first started walking out as a couple, rather than just the childhood friends they had always been, she'd quite enjoyed it. But lately he'd wanted to go further, and really she didn't like that at all. Of course, if he did ask her to marry him, and she accepted, as she probably would, she'd have to get used to that and more. But it wasn't something she wanted to think about, and when his hands strayed and she had to keep him in check, it made her horribly uncomfortable. A memory from long, long ago flashed unbidden to her mind. The kingfisher hadn't been the only thing she'd seen when she was daydreaming by the river as a child. Once, concealed in a hollow by the long grass and the overhanging branches of the trees, she'd seen Josh Withers and Peggy Bryant – Peggy Bishop as she was now – Peggy with the front of her blouse undone and her skirts rucked right up to her waist. Mortified as well as shocked, Maggie had curled herself into a ball, eyes tight shut, and stayed quiet as a mouse, praying they wouldn't notice her. If they did, she'd die of shame! But they hadn't seen her; when they'd gone again, she was able to creep home with no one the wiser, but the memory of it, of Peggy's giggles and Josh's low groans of appreciation that no amount of hiding could keep her from hearing, could still turn her cheeks scarlet and make her cringe with disgust. Silly, really. It was, after all, what men and women did, but they hadn't been men and women. They were Josh Withers and Peggy Bryant, just a few years older than her and nowhere near old enough to be behaving that way . . .

As soon as they were through the gateway and out of sight of the houses, Jack took Maggie's hand, and that felt so nice she wondered why she was so worried about other things It was nice when he pulled her into his arms and kissed her, too, but as his hand moved to her breast she felt the beginnings of the familiar panic. 'Jack! Stop it! It's too steep for that here! We'll fall over!'

He gave her a sideways grin. 'Doesn't matter, does it? The grass is nice and dry.'

'It does matter! I don't want to fall over!' She tried to keep her voice light and playful as she said it, and that obviously must have given him the wrong idea, because before she knew it, his arm had slipped behind her knees, lifting her off her feet and depositing her on the sloping bank before dropping down beside her.

'Jack!' she protested, laughing. 'What do you think you're doing?'

'I'll give you three guesses.' His face was very close to hers, and as he kissed her again, his hand went to the buttons of her blouse, opening them stealthily.

She pulled away a little. 'Jack – don't, please . . . !'

'Come on, Maggie, where's the harm? I'd never hurt you, you know that.' His breath was warm on her throat, just below her ear; his hand was inside her blouse now, his fingers slipping under her chemise.

She covered his hand with hers, holding it still. 'Stop it now.'

'There's nobody about.'

'I don't care. You mustn't! Goodness knows where it will lead, and you should know I'm not that kind of girl.'

'Oh, I know that well enough!' He rolled away, lying on his back beside her in the dry, scratchy grass, head turned to look at her. His eyes were dark with desire, but there was tenderness too in that look. 'Your dad needn't worry his head about you.'

'Whatever are you talking about?' Maggie asked teasingly. She knew very well, of course, and though she was relieved he was no longer trying to get her to do things she didn't want him to, she felt a little guilty, as if she were short-changing Jack, and also regretful that she didn't feel the way he did about taking their courtship a stage further.

She tucked her legs up beneath her skirts, plucking at a blade of grass, and Jack lay back against the bank, arms pillowed beneath his head. For a little while he was silent, then, out of the blue, he said: 'What would you say if I asked you to marry me?'

Maggie came out of her reverie with a jolt, glancing down at him. He wasn't looking at her, rather staring up into the darkening blue of the sky, and his tone was deceptively casual. A wave of tenderness suffused her, both for the boy who had been her childhood friend and champion, and the man he had become. Oh, maybe he didn't excite the sort of feelings in her that took her breath away, but she'd always known this moment would come and been content with it. Jack was good and kind, honest and hard-working. He'd take care of her, provide for her and any family they might have. She felt safe with him. And she did love him . . . she did. She was glowing with it right now.

She tilted her head, tickled his cheek with the blade of grass.

'I expect I'd say yes,' she said, echoing his light tone. 'We'll just have to wait and see, won't we?' She scrambled to her feet, brushing the bits of grass out of her skirt and twisting a lock of hair that had come loose back into its pins. 'Now, are we going for that walk or not?'

When he left the Prince of Wales, Josh cut across the fields, where herds of cows were grazing, making for the rickety wooden river bridge deep in the valley where he and Peggy had agreed to meet. It was a secluded spot, but within easy walking distance of the miners' cottages where Peggy and Tom lived. Just about safe, Josh reckoned.

There was no sign of Peggy when Josh arrived at the rendezvous, and after he'd been waiting for ten minutes or so, he began to doubt she was going to turn up. There had been a couple of occasions recently when she'd let him down because she couldn't get away, and Josh wondered if Tom might be getting suspicious. He hoped not. All very well for him to get a kick out of playing with fire, but it could turn nasty for Peggy. Josh didn't know Tom Bishop well – he worked at Northway, yet another of the rash of collieries that scarred the green Somerset valley – but from what he'd heard, the man was an evil-tempered devil. Perhaps it was time to call time on their clandestine meetings – no one could actually call it an affair – and look elsewhere for someone to take his mind off Maggie.

Just as he was thinking of giving up and heading for home, he saw Peggy coming down the path between the trees.

She'd put on a lot of weight in the last few years, he thought, but it rather suited her. Big breasts, big hips, the hint of a double chin . . . Maggie she wasn't, but what the hell? There was just all the more to get a hold of . . .

'You made it, then,' he said, as he went to meet her.

She giggled, a little out of breath from hurrying.

'I told Tom I was going over to my sister's.'

'And he believed you?'

'Didn't say a word. I've been a bit worried lately that he might have smelt a rat. He's been really funny with me whenever I've said I'm going out. But tonight he just said he was going down to the working men's club. I mustn't be too long, though. He might come home early, you never know.' She looked up at Josh coquettishly through fair, stubby lashes. He thought of Maggie's thick dark ones, then pushed the image away and grabbed Peggy round the waist.

'We'd better not waste any time then, had we?'

'Oh Josh, you are a one!' She wound her arms around his neck, eager, as always, for his kisses, and he drew her towards the bushes.

'I reckon I'd better do a Sir Walter Raleigh, don't you?' He took off his jacket and spread it out on the grass. Then he sat down, pulling her down beside him and scooping up her skirts.

Peggy giggled, then placed a hand over his to stop him going further.

'You do really think something of me, don't you, Josh?' she asked, coyly. 'I'm not just a bit of fun to you, am I?'

It was the same every time lately. She had to ask.

''Course you're not just a bit of fun,' he lied. 'If you didn't already have a husband—'

'Hey! What the bloody hell do you think you're doing?' The yell of fury made Josh jump as if he had been shot. A short, thickset man was on the path above them – Tom Bishop. 'You bloody bugger!' he roared. 'What are you doing with my missus?'

Peggy gave a gasp of horror, hastily trying to cover her bare legs, and Josh scrambled to his feet. For once in his life he was speechless. Tom charged down the bank, grabbed Peggy and yanked her up so roughly she lost her balance and stumbled against him.

'It's a good job I followed you, you bloody cheating cow!' he snarled at her. 'I knew you were up to something!'

'Calm down, mate,' Josh said ineffectually.

'Calm down?' Tom was practically apoplectic. 'I'll give her calm down when I get her home.'

'Leave her alone, you great bully. If you want to take it out on someone, take it out on me.'

Tom let go of Peggy's arm and whirled round. Expecting a punch to the jaw, Josh took a step backwards, readying himself. But Tom merely faced him furiously, his hands clenching and unclenching whilst a vein throbbed purple in his temple.

'Don't you worry, I bloody will!' he snarled between gritted teeth. 'I know who you are. You're that Withers, aren't you? Work over to Shepton Fields.'

It was clear Tom was confusing Josh with Jack, but Josh didn't bother to correct him. The first shock of being caught was wearing off, and with the rush of adrenalin when he'd thought Tom was going to start a fight hot in his blood, Josh was becoming aggressive himself, as he always did when he was up against it. Attack was the best means of defence in his book.

'If you were more of a man, your wife wouldn't have to go looking elsewhere,' he said pugnaciously. 'Look to yourself before you go blaming her.'

Once again he thought Tom was going to charge at him like Farmer Barton's bull – and who could blame him? The man's features contorted with rage, a dark purplish flush suffusing his face and neck, and he came right up to Josh. But to Josh's amazement, Tom merely shook his fist under his nose.

'I've got your number, chum!' His voice was low, and shaking with fury and cold determination. 'You'd better watch your back. Nobody messes about with my wife and gets away with it.'

There was something almost comical in his stance, and Josh laughed shortly.

'Oh, you really bloody scare me.'

'You'd do well to be bloody scared, mate. You can laugh now, but you don't know me. You better bloody watch out for yourself, that's all I'm saying.' He turned to the trembling Peggy, grabbing her again by the arm. 'Come on, you filthy bitch – home!'

'Hey – don't take it out on her!' Josh could feel his anger rising at the way Tom was manhandling Peggy up the bank. Goodness only knew what he would do when he got her on her own, and for a moment Josh almost went after them. But what good would that do? You didn't interfere between a husband and wife, and he couldn't protect Peggy when the front door closed after them. Anything he said or did might only make things worse for her.

But he didn't like the part he'd played in this. Yes, she'd thrown herself at him shamelessly, but he should have had the good sense to resist. Certainly he wasn't going to risk a repeat of this evening's fiasco. If Peggy came chasing after him again, he'd tell her so in no uncertain terms.

As he made his own way home, he wondered how she was faring. He hoped Tom wasn't giving her a hiding. But for all his nasty temper, that didn't really seem his style, unless, of course, he was more ready to use his fists on a woman than he had been on a grown man. Josh thought of the way he'd threatened him rather than punching him on the nose as he'd expected. It might just have been empty words, of course, but he could well imagine the man storing up his anger and resentment and waiting his chance to take his revenge in some cowardly way.

Oh well, if he did, Josh could deal with that. There wasn't much that worried him.

Except having to see his brother with Maggie Donovan. That was the one thing that really got to him, and he couldn't seem to do a thing about it.

Mam and Dad were arguing. Billy could hear their raised voices coming from the scullery, Dad growling, Mam shrill.

'It's the last thing I want! You should've been more careful, Paddy,' he heard Mam say.

Billy thought he knew what the argument was about. Mam was going to have another baby. He'd heard her and Maggie talking about it, but when he'd questioned Maggie, she'd gone very red and told him it didn't concern him. Billy had been upset. For one thing, he didn't like being excluded; it made him feel as unimportant at home as he felt everywhere else. For another, the thought of Dad doing such things to Mam disgusted him.

The argument was getting worse.

'Aw, Jesus, Mary and Joseph! Will you stop keeping on, woman!'

'It's all very well for you . . . you're not the one that has to go through it . . .'

'I have to put up with your nagging day and night.' Paddy was getting angrier by the minute – the beer was beginning to talk – and Billy decided to make himself scarce.

He picked up the dominoes he'd been idly shuffling through

and stacked them back in their wooden box. Then he went out through the scullery. Mam was leaning against the oilcloth-covered cupboard, arms wrapped around herself, head bent. He thought she might be crying.

'Where d'you think you're going?' Paddy demanded as Billy tried to slip past him.

Billy's eyes skittered nervously. 'Just out.'

'Haven't you been in enough trouble tonight?'

Billy shrugged. He was always in trouble one way or another. He sidled between Rose and Paddy and out of the door.

The brightness was fading from the day, but the air was still warm. There was no sign now of his tormentors, thank goodness, but Billy hurried past the Rogers house anyway, half expecting them to suddenly appear and pounce on him again.

Up the track he went, without any clear idea of where he was headed. Perhaps he'd go across the fields and look for birds' nests. It was a good time of year for that. He might see Maggie and Jack. That would be a bit of fun, just as long as they didn't see him first. He quite fancied spying on them – he was curious to know what they got up to when they were alone. But there was no sign of them anywhere, and Billy opted to take the path that led along the side of the cornfield in the direction of the pit.

It was no novelty; it was the way he went to work every morning with his father and the other men. What was different was that tonight he was alone, and the pit yard was silent and deserted. No chimneys belching steam, no winding gear creaking, and the screens where he had toiled every working day, sorting the coal that came up from the depths, were still. With no queue of hauliers' carts waiting to be loaded and no busy coal-blackened men milling about, the yard looked big and strangely ghostly.

Wouldn't it be funny, he thought, if they were all dead and he was the only one left alive in the world? No more big lads bullying him, no more Gaffer Hawkins yelling at him to work harder, no more Dad taking his belt to him, or doing unspeakable things to Mam. Perhaps one day there'd be an explosion underground and they'd all be killed. But that wasn't very likely. Explosions were almost unheard of here in Somerset. The seams might be faulted and topsy-turvy, so that floor was roof and roof floor, but there was no gas. Firedamp was the only danger in that respect.

He didn't fancy going underground, all the same. The thought of the narrow dark passages so far beneath ground, where the sun never shone, frightened him – he hated confined spaces, always had. The other lads said it was all right. They talked – when they talked to him at all – about the mice that came creeping out for crumbs when they were eating their cognockers of bread and cheese, and they didn't seem to mind the guss and crook, the length of rope that went around their waists and between their legs so that they could crawl along the passageways on hands and knees dragging the little putts of coal the colliers had hewed. He'd seen the ridges in the flesh of their backs where the rope cut into it. They said it didn't hurt once you got used to it, and the best way to harden the skin was to rub urine into it, but Billy thought it sounded awful.

No, working on the screens was bad enough; underground would be much, much worse. But he was going to have to face up to it soon. Some other young lad would be leaving school and taking his job, and he'd have to go down in that horrible hudge on the end of a long length of hemp rope with Frank Rogers and Charlie Oglethorpe and the others.

If it was still there.

He'd heard the men talking about it, saying it should have

been replaced by a proper cage years ago, and that if the authorities knew it was still in use it would be condemned and Shepton Fields would close down, as like as not.

The thought gave him hope. A length of hemp rope couldn't last for ever. Perhaps it would give up the ghost before he had to descend to the bowels of the earth on the end of it.

Billy kicked a piece of coal that lay at his feet, and followed it across the pit yard.

Chapter Three

Maggie had been awake for much of the night, wondering whether Jack had really asked her to marry him and whether it meant they were now engaged, or if it had been a rhetorical question. Nothing more had been said about it – they'd gone for their walk, returned home, and parted just as they always did with a kiss in the shadow of the outhouses, though there was an unaccustomed awkwardness in the air between them. It was odd, she thought, but she hadn't wanted to broach the subject again in case she'd mistaken his meaning, and she wasn't sure whether she'd be glad or sorry if she had. In a funny sort of way the half-proposal had quite shocked her, though it was only what she'd expected would come eventually, and she'd tossed and turned, dozing only to wake again, until with the pearly grey light of dawn she realised it was almost time to get up.

Cockerels were crowing now in their pens in the back gardens along the rank, the first birds had started their dawn chorus, and she heard the creak of the stairs as her mother went down to start her day. Maggie pushed the bedclothes aside and got up.

Mam wasn't too well in the mornings these days; she'd better go down and help her. The fire had to be lit to heat the water for the men's tea, and they'd want some breakfast, too, before they left for work. Only a bit of bread and dripping, but someone had to make it.

She pulled on her clothes, laced her feet into her freshly polished boots and went downstairs.

Rose was on her knees in front of the grate, trying to get the fire going. She looked grey and pinched, and Maggie saw her heave.

'Let me do that, Mam,' she said.

'No, you don't want to get yourself dirty. You've got to go to work.'

'I won't get dirty,' Maggie said, perhaps over-optimistically. She took the bellows from Rose, and Rose let her, covering her mouth with her hand to suppress the threatening nausea.

Maggie got the fire going and straightened up, looking at her mother anxiously.

'Have you seen the doctor, Mam?'

Rose managed a derisive snort. 'And where would I get the money to pay doctor's bills, I'd like to know? What can the doctor do anyway? There's nothing wrong with me that another few months won't take care of.'

'Well, have a word with Dolly Oglethorpe, anyway.'

Dolly Oglethorpe acted as midwife for all the women in the rank, as well as being called on to lay out the dead.

'All in good time.' Rose didn't add that she didn't want anyone knowing she was pregnant again until there was no hiding it. She was dreading being the subject of yet more gossip up and down the rank. Nothing was private here for long; the women talking outside their doors or over their washing lines made sure of that.

'We'd better get your dad and our Billy up,' she said, changing the subject.

'I'll do it.' Maggie clattered up the stairs and knocked loudly on the first door off the narrow landing. 'Dad! Time to get up!'

A grunt from within told her Paddy was awake. She went on along the landing and pushed open the door to Billy's room.

Once it had been Ewart and Walter's room too, the three lads sharing the big double bed that took up most of the floor space. Now Billy had it to himself, and he was making the most of it, spread-eagled corner to corner.

'Come on, our Billy.' Maggie went into the little room, squeezing past the bed to the window and drawing back the curtains to let in the first pale sunshine.

'Do I have to?' Billy groaned.

'Yes you do, if you don't want to be late for work.' She tweaked the sheet to reveal his ginger mop and fair-skinned face flushed pink with sleep.

'Don't want to go to work,' he mumbled.

'I don't suppose you do,' Maggie said tartly. 'But that's neither here nor there. If you can't keep time on the screens, they'll send you underground where our dad can keep an eye on you.'

That did the trick, just as she'd known it would. Billy was out of bed and reaching for his rushy duck trousers in a moment.

Maggie shook her head, filled suddenly with tenderness for her little brother. She wished with all her heart that he was tougher, better able to stand up for himself, or that he was still young enough for her to be able to take care of him. But he was just at that in-between age when he was neither a child nor a man, and he wasn't finding it easy.

A shout from downstairs startled her, and she pushed past Billy and ran out on to the landing.

'Mam! What's the matter?'

She ran down the stairs and through the living room into the scullery. The back door was open and Rose was on the step, gesticulating wildly.

'It's a blooming dog!' Rose said over her shoulder. 'A dog – come right into the house! Frightened the life of me, it did.' She waved her fist again. 'Go on – get away – go home!'

Maggie went to the door. The dog, squat and white, with a large head, small ears and one black-ringed eye, had retreated across the alley, but still stood there, tail wagging uncertainly.

'Go on home!' Rose shouted again, but the dog refused to move, looking at her with ears cocked, head on one side.

The bedroom window above them opened and Billy leaned out. 'Hey, boy!'

Rose craned her neck to scowl up at her son.

'Don't encourage him, our Billy!' She glowered at the dog and turned to go back inside. 'Make sure the door's shut, Maggie. We don't want him coming in again.'

In the busy morning round, both Maggie and Rose soon forgot the dog. But Billy did not. When he had swilled his face and neck at the stone scullery sink, he collected his slice of bread and dripping and took it over to the window.

'He's still there. That dog. Do you think he's lost?'

'I shouldn't think so,' Rose said shortly. 'I expect the Bridges' bitch is on heat. Dogs will go miles if they get the scent.'

'But he's not outside the Bridges' door,' Billy argued. 'He's outside ours. And he looks hungry. There's some old bacon rind, isn't there? Can't we give him that?'

'No we can't!' Rose snapped. 'If you feed him, we'll never get rid of him.'

Billy said nothing, but when he thought no one was looking, he slipped the remains of his bread and dripping into his pocket, wrapping it in his handkerchief. 'I need the lav,' he muttered, heading out of the back door.

The dog was still there. Billy took out the hunk of bread and dripping, and the dog's nose, cold and wet, nuzzled into his hand. Billy's heart swelled with pleasure. He'd be for it if his mam looked out of the window and saw that he had disobeyed her, but for once he didn't care.

He patted the dog, and it wagged its stumpy tail and licked his hand. Billy supposed it was because he could still smell lard on his palm. But he dared to hope not. For the first time in as long as he could remember, he felt as if he had found a friend.

Maggie was showing Cathy Small, the new apprentice, how to block a roll of cloth. Mondays were always quiet in the drapery shop, it being washing day, and the lack of customers provided a good opportunity for other things. Maggie had already changed the window display, a task she loved; she was very proud that Augusta had noticed her artistic streak and trusted her to arrange bonnets, gloves and silk floral sprays in a way that would attract the customers. Now she was engaged in training Cathy. But Cathy's attention wandered easily, especially if there were lads passing by outside, or if Horace, Mrs Freeman's husband, came into the shop. He was standing by the glass-fronted door now, thumbs tucked into the watch chain that stretched across his starched shirt front, casting surreptitious glances at the pretty new assistant, and Cathy was all fingers and thumbs.

'Oh Miss Donovan, I'll never get it right!' she groaned.

Maggie hid a secret smile. It amused her to be called Miss Donovan, something Mrs Freeman insisted on, since Cathy was her junior.

'Of course you will, Cathy. It's just a knack, that's all. But it's got to look neat, as if it's never been off the roll.' She unwound the cloth once more and spread it out along the counter. 'Now, try again.'

Cathy's efforts improved when Horace Freeman left the

shop to return to his own domain, the gents' outfitters next door. But it wasn't long before her concentration was wavering once more, this time due to a titbit of gossip her father had brought home with him from the working men's club the night before.

'It is Jack Withers you're walking out with, isn't it?' she said, a little hesitantly.

'Yes.' Maggie was puzzled. 'Why?'

Cathy caught her lip between her teeth, lowering her eyes as if wishing for once that she hadn't started this conversation. 'Oh . . . nothing.'

Then, as Maggie gazed at her questioningly, she went on, all of a rush: 'I don't know whether I ought to say or not, but my dad told us that Tom Bishop came into the club last night in a proper temper, saying that he'd caught Jack Withers fooling around with his wife.'

'What?' Maggie was astounded. 'That's ridiculous! Jack wouldn't fool around with a married woman, especially not Peggy Bishop.'

'I'm only repeating what he said.' Cathy had turned rather pink. 'That Jack Withers who works at Shepton Fields, that's what he said. And my dad reckoned he'd better watch out, because Tom Bishop can be really nasty, and he wouldn't want to be in Jack's shoes if Tom has got it in for him.'

'It's nothing but a load of nonsense,' Maggie said briskly, and at that moment Mrs Freeman came sweeping into the shop.

'There's a lot of chatter in here! Is any work being done?'

'We're just tidying the stock,' Maggie said.

She pulled the roll of cloth towards her, blocking it herself quickly and neatly, but to her annoyance, her hands were trembling a little.

Where in the world had Cathy's father got such a story from?

And men had the nerve to accuse the womenfolk of gossiping! Jack, carrying on with Peggy Bishop – ridiculous! Now if it had been Josh, she could have understood it . . .

Of course, that must be it, Maggie realised. People who didn't know them well often got Jack and Josh mixed up, and she supposed it was an easy enough mistake to make. They did look very alike, though there the resemblance ended, with Jack so quiet and Josh so wild. Trouble followed him around, her mother had always said. But for all that, there was something very attractive about him, with that breezy manner, the wicked twinkle in his eyes and the aura that might almost be danger that went with the hard muscles and the swagger. She could well imagine that Peggy Bishop might think it was a risk worth taking to go out with him on the sly. And for a moment she almost envied her – he'd put butterflies in *her* stomach the first time she'd seen him when he came home from Wales . . .

Maggie gave herself a little shake. All very well for Josh to get on the wrong side of Tom Bishop and not give a devil's cuss about it. But if Tom was mistaking Josh for Jack, then it was a different matter entirely. Suppose he got a gang of cronies together and waylaid Jack in some dark lane? They wouldn't give Jack the opportunity to tell them they'd got the wrong man before giving him a good hiding. She'd have to have a word with him, warn him.

Though what he could do to avert such a disaster, she really didn't know.

When Billy got home from work that evening, he was surprised and delighted to find the dog lying in the shade of the outhouses, his head between his paws. The moment he saw Billy, he got up and trotted towards the boy, pushing his eager wet nose into his hand.

Billy hurried into the house, where Rose was bailing hot water into the tin tub in front of the fire for Paddy's bath.

'Mam, that dog's still here. Let me have those bacon rinds for him . . . *please.*'

'Blinking thing!' Rose grumbled. Then she relented. 'Oh, go on, then. They're in the bin. No . . . I'll get them. You go back outside. You're getting coal dust all over my clean floor.'

Billy backed out hastily before she could change her mind, and a minute later she appeared in the doorway, with not only the bacon rinds but the knuckle bone from the piece of pork they would be finishing up cold for their tea.

'Here you are. Have this as well. I've cut the meat off of it, but I expect he'll find a few shreds if he's hungry enough.'

'Oh, thanks, Mam!' Billy's face was wreathed in smiles.

'Just make sure he doesn't come in the house again,' Rose admonished sternly.

She shouldn't be encouraging the darned dog, she thought. But it was good to see Billy happy and taking an interest in something. Just as long as he wasn't too upset when it wandered off again, as she was pretty sure it would.

A week later, however, the dog was still there, living on scraps and bones and sleeping on an old blanket in the corner of the outhouse. Though he disappeared a few times, once for a whole day and a night, he always came back.

Billy had given him a name – Bullseye, since he had a black patch around one eye in his otherwise snow-white face. It seemed to suit him. What was more, Billy felt they were two of a kind, both of them outcasts in their own way, and the thought was strangely comforting.

In that short space of time, Bullseye had become his dog, and the focus of his world.

Chapter Four

'I've got something to tell you, Maggie.'

Jack was trying very hard to keep his face straight, but there was no mistaking the smile that was trying to break out. It lifted the corners of his mouth and twinkled in his eyes.

It was another warm evening. Though it was still early in the year, summer had come early and the air was heavy with the scent of new-mown hay wafting across the terrace from the field beyond. The farmer and as many men as he could muster had been busy all day, harvesting the crop before the spell of good weather broke, and Maggie had been watching from her bedroom window as the heavy horse pulled the threshing machine up the field and back again and the sweating hands loaded the hay on to carts. Now she was at the back door, called down by Rose when Jack had come knocking.

'What's that, then?' she asked, curious to know what he was looking so pleased about.

'Come over here.' He drew her to the far side of the track, out of earshot of the houses, and the beam he had been trying to suppress escaped, lighting up his face. 'You know I asked you to marry me the other night? Well, I went to see the manager today, and we can have a house.' He hesitated, the smile wavering a little. 'That is . . . if you haven't changed your mind.'

Maggie was quite taken aback. Since that night nothing more had been said, and she'd come to the conclusion that she'd taken what was a casual question for a proposal. Now she was not only startled but a bit overwhelmed, and for a moment she was speechless.

Jack's face fell.

'You have thought better of it.'

'No . . . no . . . but when you didn't mention it again, I thought . . . Well, I thought you couldn't have meant it.'

Jack laughed self-consciously. 'I think I frightened myself, Maggie, and I shouldn't have asked before I had something to offer you. But I meant it all right. There's nothing in the world I want more. Suppose I were to ask you again, properly? I don't think I can go down on one knee here, right outside your back door, but . . . I hope you'd still say yes.'

'Oh Jack!' The little niggling doubts were still there, had never really gone away, but she'd gone mushy inside. She did love him – she did – even if the earth didn't move for her the way it did in fairy stories. And he'd gone so far as to approach the colliery manager about a house for them to live in; that showed how serious he was about this, and must have taken a good deal of courage.

'Of course I'd still say yes,' she said. 'But you should have talked to me again about it. You've given me quite a shock.'

'I know. I'm sorry. The thing is, I heard about this house coming vacant and I didn't want to lose the chance of it. Adge Scrivens is off to south Wales with his family – he's got a job in one of the pits down there. And it's a really nice house – one of those cottages down on the main road. Well, it's ours if we want it. It's only got the two rooms up and two down, but it'll suit us fine. We can go down and have a look at it any evening, Adge said . . .' He broke off. 'I'm sorry, Maggie, I'm rushing you. But

I was just over the moon when Wilfred James agreed that we could have it. You are pleased, aren't you?'

'Yes, of course I am,' Maggie said faintly, but her head was spinning.

'Oh Maggie, you've made me so proud and happy.' Jack was beaming from ear to ear. 'I can't wait to tell the world you're going to be my wife!'

'Hang on, we must tell my mam and dad first, and your parents too,' Maggie said sternly. 'We don't want them hearing about it from anybody but us, and Wilfred James already knows, by the sound of it.'

Jack grinned, a little shamefaced.

'I suppose by rights I should ask your dad for his permission. Shall I do that now?'

Once again Maggie experienced the scary feeling that she was riding in a carriage pulled by a runaway horse. Everything was happening so fast. But . . .

'You might as well, I suppose,' she said, swallowing her apprehension. 'He's in the kitchen.'

'Don't look so worried,' Jack urged her, but he looked apprehensive too. 'The worst he can do is throw me out on my ear.'

'Oh Jack, I'm sure he won't do that.' Maggie laughed, and immediately felt better. 'Come on, let's get it over with.'

She took his hand and led him into the house.

'Well that's lovely news!' Rose said, hugging Maggie.

Jack and Paddy had disappeared into the parlour, leaving the women in the kitchen, but, of course, the moment the door had closed after them, Maggie had told her mother what it was that Jack wanted to talk to Paddy about – as if Rose hadn't already guessed.

'I couldn't be more pleased,' Rose went on. 'Jack's a lovely lad, you couldn't wish for a better. And that's more than can be said for some you've looked at in the past.'

Maggie threw her a quizzical look, and Rose huffed.

'You know very well who I'm talking about. That Reuben Hillman that works in the gents' outfitters.'

'Oh, him!' Maggie laughed. 'There was never anything in that. Once was quite enough.'

'And I was very glad about that.' Rose sniffed loudly. 'I've never liked that lad. I couldn't say what it is, but there's something about him . . .'

'He's harmless enough,' Maggie said, but she knew what her mother meant. There was something about Reuben Hillman that made her cringe inwardly too.

Reuben worked as an assistant to Horace Freeman in his gents' outfitters next door, and when Maggie had started as an apprentice in the drapery, he'd taken a shine to her.

Truth to tell, in the beginning Maggie had been quite flattered. Reuben's father was a clerk at the office of the local solicitor, his mother was one of the most respected women in town, and his grandmother ran a dame school in a cottage in the high street. Though scarcely gentry, the family was certainly 'a cut above', as the saying went, thoroughly respectable, and not one of them a miner. When Reuben asked her to walk out with him she'd tried to put to one side the fact that she really didn't find him in the least attractive. It was uncharitable, she'd thought, to hold it against him that he was rather stout, with podgy hands, a soft mouth and beady little eyes. You couldn't judge a book by its cover, and he might turn out to be really nice.

But it wasn't long before she knew she'd made a terrible mistake. Nice or not, when he'd taken hold of her hand it was all she could do not to snatch it away; when he'd tried to kiss her, she'd curled up inside with revulsion.

'Reuben, behave yourself!' she'd reprimanded him, trying to pull away.

But he wasn't to be put off so easily.

'Come on, Maggie. Just a little kiss.'

'No – stop it this minute!'

One of his hands had been about her waist, holding her fast, the other . . . oh, she must have imagined it, surely! Not even Reuben Hillman would dare to touch her breast – would he?

She'd tensed, twisting away, wriggling out of his grasp, horrified, embarrassed and revolted by the imagined touch, the way his lips had felt, moist and flabby on hers, and the smell of him – carbolic soap on his skin, and something sweet and peppery in his breath. Even now Maggie couldn't smell carbolic soap without being reminded of that horrible encounter.

'It's time we went home,' she'd said, desperate to escape but not wanting to mention the fact that she thought he had tried to touch her breast. After all, she couldn't be sure she wasn't mistaken, and it would be terrible to accuse him of something that might have been an accident.

'When can I see you again, Maggie?' He'd been like an eager puppy.

'Oh . . . I don't know. I'm not sure it's a good idea. Working together . . .'

'We don't,' he'd argued. 'You're in the drapery, I'm in the gents' outfitters.'

'As good as.'

'But I really like you!' To Maggie's horror, Reuben had looked as if he was about to burst into tears. His blubbery face had turned very pink and there was a wobble in his lip.

'I'm sorry,' Maggie had said. 'I really don't want to.'

She'd thought that would be that, especially since she had started walking out with Jack not long afterwards, but she couldn't get rid of Reuben so easily. He came through to the drapery shop on the flimsiest of excuses, staring at her like a moonstruck calf and smiling a soppy smile that made her dreadfully uncomfortable. If the gents' outfitters closed before the drapery, he would hang about outside for as long as he dared, in the hope of walking her home, she supposed, and if the shops closed at more or less the same time, he'd materialise as if by magic, grinning and trying to strike up a conversation.

'I'm glad it's you he fancies and not me!' said Beat Clements, her fellow assistant. 'He's creepy!'

It was true, he was. There was something almost menacing about his obsession with her.

Well, now that she and Jack were going to be married, he'd surely realise there was no point in continuing with it, and leave her alone.

The front room door opened and Paddy and Jack emerged, Jack looking a little flushed and pleased with himself.

'Well, my girl, you can stop worrying yourself,' Paddy said heartily. 'Your chap here has asked me if he can marry you and I've said yes. Get the beer out, Rose, if there's any left. I reckon this calls for a drink, don't you?'

Maggie shook her head, smiling wryly.

What didn't call for a drink in her father's book? she would like to know.

Long after Paddy had finished the beer they had in the house and set out for the pub, Maggie and Jack sat outside in the warm evening air, making their plans. Whereas in the days since he had first asked her to marry him Jack had avoided the subject completely, now he couldn't stop talking about it. He'd even gone home to tell his own parents the news whilst Maggie was helping Rose with making the men's snap ready for the morning, returning to tell her that they were delighted. Maggie wasn't sure that was quite true; though Gilby Withers was an accepting sort, she rather thought that Florrie would be none too pleased that her son was marrying a Donovan. But if so, she had kept it well hidden, for Jack was still barely able to contain his delight that his dearest wish was becoming reality.

'They asked if we'd set a date,' he said now. 'I said I expected it would be as soon as I can sort out any work that needs doing on the house we've been offered – but it's up to you, of course.'

'That sounds fine,' Maggie said. She still felt a little dazed, but Jack's enthusiasm was infectious, and getting married and setting up home was, after all, a great adventure.

'And Mam wanted to know where the wedding will be,' he went on. 'I think she's hoping it will be at the Methodist, but you're a Catholic, aren't you?'

'Not really,' Maggie said. 'Dad is – or was. He only ever goes to Mass at Christmas and Easter. And Mam was never in agreement with it, though she had to say she was when she married Dad. That's why we don't really go anywhere regularly.' She considered. 'Yes, I think we should definitely be married at the Methodist, seeing as how your mam is such a stalwart there.'

'She'll be pleased about that,' Jack said, sounding relieved. 'And of course I shall ask our Josh to be my best man. He wasn't in when I told Mam and Dad or I'd have asked him already.'

He took her hand, holding it between his and stroking her ring finger as if imagining he was slipping on the wedding band.

'What about you? Who will you have for your bridesmaids? It's a pity you haven't got a sister . . .'

'I think that sometimes too,' Maggie said wistfully. It would

be so nice to have someone to share all the excitement with.
'But there you are, I haven't. Nor even any cousins. I suppose I
could ask Beat and Cathy from the shop. But getting dresses for
them would be an awful expense.'

'Don't worry about that,' Jack said. 'I'll take care of it. I want
you to have a day to remember.'

'Oh Jack, thank you!' Tenderness suffused Maggie again.
She *was* doing the right thing . . . she was! 'But how can you
afford it?'

'I'll find the money somehow,' Jack said determinedly. 'I've
been putting a bit aside for some time now, just waiting to get up
the courage to propose. It's not a lot, but I'm sure it can run to
dresses for your bridesmaids . . .' He broke off. 'Oh look, here's
our Josh now. He's going to be surprised to hear our news and
no mistake.'

Maggie turned her head and saw the familiar tall, dark figure
heading towards them along the track.

'Hey, Josh, come here!' Jack called as he neared. 'What do
you think? Maggie and I have just got engaged. How's that for a
cause for celebration?'

Quite suddenly Maggie felt dreadfully flustered. How stupid
was that? She'd have to get used to telling people about the
engagement, and to being the centre of attention for a little
while. But it wasn't just that. As she looked at Josh, she felt
herself blushing and experiencing the same strange flutter in
her stomach that she experienced whenever their paths crossed
– strange, and unwelcome. Unsettled, she thrust her hand
deeper into Jack's, taking comfort from the warm pressure of his
fingers on hers.

For just a moment, it seemed to her, Josh's eyes darkened.
Then he said heartily: 'Well, well, I suppose congratulations
are in order,' and offered his brother a firm handshake, and if

there was something forced in his smile, Maggie told herself afterwards that she'd imagined it.

'I was just saying to Maggie – I hope you'll be my best man when we tie the knot,' Jack said.

Once again that shadow hovered in Josh's eyes; once again it was almost instantly gone.

'Well, I'd be pretty upset if you asked anyone else,' he said lightly. 'You're a lucky man, our Jack. I hope you know that.'

'Oh, don't worry, I do!'

'Make her happy, all right?'

'If I don't, it won't be for the want of trying.'

'That's all right, then.'

And he was gone, walking along the track into the deepening evening shadows.

'I love you, Maggie,' Jack said softly.

'And I love you,' Maggie whispered back.

And almost managed to convince herself that it was the truth.

Next day, Bullseye followed Billy to work. The other boys threw stones, yelling at him to 'Bugger off!' and Billy simmered with hatred, afraid they would hurt the dog, or frighten him away for good. But Bullseye seemed to think it was just a new game. He picked up one of the stones and ran after the lads, right into the pit yard.

'What's that dog doing here?' Gaffer Hawkins snarled. 'He'd better keep out of the way or he'll end up in one of the coal sacks in the river.'

But the threat did no more to deter Bullseye than the stones had done.

Halfway through the morning, Gaffer Hawkins, a short, stout man who perspired a lot, decided it had not been a good idea to wear his long-sleeved vest to work today. He stripped off his shirt and vest, put his shirt back on again, and hung his vest over an empty tub. And there it would have stayed had Bullseye not caught sight of it and decided it would make a good plaything. After sniffing it and tossing it about a bit, he began dragging it round the yard, trailing it in the coal dust that lay everywhere.

'Hoi!' bellowed Gaffer, furious when he saw what was going on. 'That bloody dog's got my bloody vest!'

He began to chase it. Sensing even more fun to be had, Bullseye danced away from him and ran in a big excited circle.

'Billy Donovan! Get your bloody dog under control, can't you?' yelled Gaffer.

Billy called to Bullseye, who ignored him. He chased after him, to no avail. The more Billy tried to capture him, the more he was enjoying himself. And then, to add insult to injury, he retreated under a coal wagon, taking the vest with him.

Billy couldn't reach him; the only way he could think of to tempt him out was with food. Bullseye loved a bit of cheese more than anything. He untied the spotted kerchief that held his snap, got out the cheese and broke off a piece, holding it out to the dog.

'Here, Bullseye, see what I've got for you, boy!'

The dog inched forward on his belly, sensing a trap but unable to resist the aroma of good strong Cheddar. Billy caught him by the collar Jack had bought for him and dragged him out from beneath the wagon, then wriggled himself far enough under to reach the vest, which was now torn, filthy and wet from Bullseye's spittle.

'I got it, Mr Hawkins,' he ventured hopefully.

'And look at the state of it!' Gaffer was steaming mad. 'That was a bally good vest! Look at it!'

'I'm sorry,' Billy said miserably. 'He won't do it again.'

'Too right he won't! You're nothing but trouble, Donovan,

and you're big enough and ugly enough now to be underground with your father, where he can keep an eye on you. I'm going to see the manager right away and tell him to start you as a carting boy on Monday. Charlie Parfitt was telling me his boy Cliff is ready to leave school and looking for a job – I'll have him working here on the screens, and you can go bloody underground.'

Billy felt his stomach fall away.

'But Mr Hawkins—'

'Don't talk back at me, you young whippersnapper. You're going underground out of my way and that's the end of it.'

He stormed off in the direction of the manager's office and Billy could only stare after him, trembling, and helpless to do anything to change his mind.

'Oh Bullseye, look what you bin and gone and done now!' he muttered wretchedly.

He'd always known, of course, that it was only a matter of time before a new youngster was given his job on the screens and he was sent underground, but he hadn't thought it would come so soon, and the prospect terrified him. On Monday, barring a miracle, he was going to have to go down the pit in that horrible hudge.

In Billy's experience, miracles rarely happened.

When Josh left work at Marston Colliery the following evening, he was far from pleased to see Peggy Bishop waiting for him.

Josh had been in a black mood all day. The news that Jack and Maggie were to be married had come as a blow to him, and he'd realised that he'd been hoping all along that nothing would come of their romance. Now that hope had all but disappeared, and Josh had gone around as if the devil was in him, as his mother would say, snapping at everyone who spoke to him and letting out all his frustration and disappointment by attacking the wood so viciously that he had almost broken his saw. To see Peggy there, clearly set on waylaying him, was the last straw.

After the confrontation with Tom, he'd made up his mind that it had to be over, and he was sorely tempted to simply ignore her. But he owed her more than that, and in any case, he was still feeling guilty that she had probably had a hard time from Tom whilst he had escaped more or less scot free.

Josh slowed his step so he was lagging behind the other men, but there was no fooling them. He saw the nudges and winks and heard the low chuckles, and only hoped it wouldn't get back to Tom Bishop. But there was a pretty fair chance that it would. Though Tom worked at a different pit, everyone knew everyone else round here, and most were members of the working men's club.

'You all right, Peggy?' he greeted her.

She tossed her head and shrugged.

'What d'you think you're doing, waylaying me when I'm with my mates? I would have thought you'd have had more sense. We'll both be for it if Tom gets to hear about it.'

Peggy stuck her nose in the air.

'Oh, I'm past caring about him.'

'That's just bloody stupid,' Josh said. 'After what happened last time . . . He didn't give you a hiding, did he? If so . . .'

'What?' she asked, and he knew from the triumphant expression that crossed her face that she wanted to hear him say he'd give Tom a hiding back.

'I'm just asking. Did he?'

She pouted. 'Not a hiding. But he's been hell to live with, and I've had enough. Truth to tell, I'm sick to death of him, so I'm leaving. My bag's packed, and I'm going to my sister's.'

'You're *what*?' Josh was shocked. Plenty of couples had their ups and downs one way and another, but nobody actually left the family home. Nobody he knew, anyway.

Peggy smirked.

'That'll show him, won't it?'

Josh shook his head, bewildered and alarmed.

'He'll go crazy, Peg. You can't do that.'

'Why not? He's made my life a misery ever since he caught us. I'm not putting up with it any longer. That's why I wanted to see you, so you'd know where to find me.'

Josh swore inwardly. It would appear that Peggy thought that if she left Tom, the way would be clear for her to take up with him openly. And before long, she'd be expecting commitment from him just like every other single woman seemed to. The thought of being saddled with Peggy was not a pleasant one. What had seemed like a bit of fun was turning into a millstone round his neck, and he'd have to tell her in no uncertain terms that it was over.

The trouble was, he didn't feel up to the hassle here and now. She'd make a scene, he was fairly sure, and that was the last thing he wanted with his mates within earshot and no doubt taking note of everything that was going on. Better, perhaps, to let her down gently.

'OK, so now I know,' he said non-committally. 'I've got to go now, though.'

'But you will be in touch?' Peggy persisted.

'We'll see.'

'Josh!' She caught hold of his arm, her beady little eyes raking his face. 'You *will*, won't you?'

'Oh, I expect so. Come on now . . .' He shook his arm free. 'We're making a show of ourselves. Just give it time, Peggy, all right?'

He could see she was far from satisfied, but for the moment she nodded, and Josh broke into a trot to catch up with the other men.

Blimey, he'd had a narrow escape there! Or had he? He still found it hard to believe that Peggy would actually leave Tom, but if she did, there'd be hell to pay. Tom wouldn't take something like that lying down. His wounded pride would make him mad as a hatter. So far there had been no evidence of him carrying out the threats he'd made the night he'd caught them together, but if he thought Peggy had left him for Josh, then he really would be gunning for him.

Oh well, no use worrying about that now. He'd just have to deal with it if it ever happened. And the chances were it never would.

'Our Billy's starting as a carting boy next week,' Paddy said.

The family were having their tea – bacon, cabbage and potatoes moistened with the fat from the frying pan.

'He's what!' Rose was horrified. She dreaded the thought of her youngest son – her baby – going into the bowels of the earth and coming home with his waist rubbed raw by the rope that would be tied round it to drag the putts of coal. 'Oh my Lord, I hoped it would be a bit yet!'

'He got on the wrong side of the gaffer today,' Paddy said. 'Hawkins won't have him on the screens any more, and I can't say I blame him.'

He went on to relate the tale of Bullseye's prank.

'That darned dog!' Rose said. 'I knew we shouldn't have encouraged him. Couldn't you have a word with Hawkins, Paddy? Try to get him to change his mind?'

Paddy snorted derisively. 'As if he'd take notice of me! Anyway, it won't do the boy any harm to go underground. It might make a man of him. Now, are you going to eat that bacon, our Billy, or shall I finish it up?'

Without a word, Billy dumped the remains of his bacon on his father's plate. He had no appetite anyway. He felt sick with fright at the thought of what next week would bring. If he had to go down in that hudge, he'd just die. Oh, if only something would go wrong with it so they couldn't use it any more!

Terror exploded in Billy's heart, a terror so great it swamped him. He felt the chasm opening up beneath his feet as they tied him into the hudge, turning his stomach, making him dizzy, and the darkness closed in around him, the weight of all the tons of earth above him pressing down on his chest so he could scarcely breathe.

They couldn't make him do it! They couldn't!

But they would.

He grabbed the carving knife from the bread board in the middle of the table, brandishing it wildly.

'I won't go down the pit! Dad – please . . . don't make me!'

'Oh Billy!' Rose was alarmed by his white face and the crazed expression in his eyes. But Paddy merely tossed his head in disgust.

'Don't talk so daft, our Billy. And put that knife down before somebody gets hurt.'

Billy stared at him, his breath coming in quick, shallow sobs. If he had been able to string two thoughts together, they would have been all about hatred for the father who had never once spoken up for him, who belittled and beat him and did unspeakable things to Mam. But Billy was beyond thinking. He only knew he had to get out of here before the terror swallowed him alive.

With another wrenching sob, he pushed back his chair so roughly that it overturned, and ran from the house.

* * *

It was late when Maggie left the shop that evening. Closing time was never strictly observed – if there were customers to be served, then served they must be. Mrs Freeman even refused to allow them to lock the door if anyone was so much as looking in the window. And for some reason, the good people of High Compton seemed to have left it until the last moment to do their shopping today.

By the time Maggie was free to go, she was very tired. It had been a long day, and most of it spent on her feet, which felt hot and swollen inside her tightly laced boots. She'd be very glad to get home and take them off.

She and Beat Clements left together; Mrs Freeman had found a few more menial jobs to be done, and, as the new apprentice, they fell to Cathy, who was looking none too pleased about it. Maggie wondered, not for the first time, if she'd stay the course. She knew that Cathy had been hoping to get away in time to meet her latest admirer, Will Stevens, the baker's boy. She remembered only too well the days when she herself had been the one who had to stay behind tidying up so that shop and showroom reached Mrs Freeman's impeccable standards.

Maggie and Beat were so busy chatting that Maggie didn't see Reuben Hillman skulking in the doorway of the gents' outfitters, or notice him following as they made their way through the centre of town. It was only when she and Beat parted company at the crossroads that she heard hurrying footsteps and turned to see Reuben behind her.

'Are you following me?' she asked accusingly.

'Don't be angry, Maggie.' Reuben was a bit out of breath from the exertion of catching up with her; she was fit, and used to the walk, he was not. 'I just wanted to speak to you, that's all.'

'Surely if you had something to say you could have said it at work?' Maggie was feeling a little uneasy, for no reason that she could really explain except that she didn't like being alone on a quiet country lane with Reuben.

'Not really, no . . .' For a moment he seemed lost for words, then he launched into what sounded very much like a prepared speech.

'I've been wanting to ask you out again for ages. I shouldn't have tried to kiss you the first time, I know, and I'm sorry. I just couldn't help myself. But I won't do it again, I promise, if you don't want me to. Please, Maggie, won't you give me another chance?'

'Oh, Reuben . . .' Maggie groaned. *And are you sorry for trying to touch my breast too?* she wanted to say but didn't. She'd never mentioned it to a living soul and she wasn't going to now.

'Please, Maggie,' he begged again.

'Don't you know I have a sweetheart?' she asked, exasperated. 'In fact we're going to be married, Jack Withers and me.'

'Oh, him!' Reuben's face darkened and he pursed his flabby lips in an expression of distaste. 'You're far too good for him, Maggie. He's just a miner.'

'And what's wrong with that, I'd like to know?' Maggie demanded, annoyed. 'You're only a shop assistant yourself.'

'But I won't always be.' Reuben puffed himself up with importance. 'I've got plans for the future, I'll have you know, and when I come into my inheritance I shall be able to start my own business. I could give you plenty that a miner never could. I'd make sure you'd want for nothing.'

'For goodness' sake, Reuben, aren't you rather putting the cart before the horse?' Maggie snapped.

Reuben reached out suddenly and gripped her arm, pulling her round to face him.

'I mean it. I'd do anything for you, Maggie. Anything!' He

said it with an intensity that frightened her. Strange, she'd never thought of Reuben as frightening before – repulsive, yes, annoying, yes, but this . . . this persistence was bordering on obsession, and suddenly Maggie thought she glimpsed something almost sinister beneath that soft, chubby exterior.

'I'm very happy with Jack, thank you very much,' she retorted, shaking herself free and trying to hide the panic that was beginning to threaten her.

She began walking away from him, hoping against hope that he wouldn't follow, and then, to her relief, she saw a figure she recognised coming in the opposite direction.

Jack! He did come to meet her sometimes when she was late leaving work; thank goodness tonight was one of those occasions! She hurried towards him. 'Oh, am I pleased to see you!'

'What's wrong?' Jack asked. Maggie was visibly upset.

'That Reuben Hillman waylaid me and I just couldn't get rid of him.' Maggie slipped her hand into Jack's. 'Sometimes he really scares me.'

'What did he say? He didn't hurt you, did he?' Jack asked, concerned.

'Oh, he just keeps asking me out and won't take no for an answer. I've told him we're engaged, though, so I hope that'll be the end of it.' Now that she was with Jack, and Reuben was no longer a threat, Maggie thought it best to make light of the whole thing. She didn't want Jack confronting him; it would only make the situation more awkward than it already was.

'Well just let me know if he bothers you again, and I'll have a word with him,' Jack said grimly.

'Don't worry about it – he's harmless enough. Just really annoying,' Maggie said.

But as they set off up the road, she glanced apprehensively

over her shoulder. Reuben was still where she'd left him, just staring after them. Even when he saw Maggie looking back at him, he didn't turn away, and though it was still warm, Maggie shivered suddenly. There was something unnerving about the way he was simply standing there, watching them go.

He was obsessed with her, she knew, and she was beginning to wonder just how far that obsession would lead him. He'd followed her tonight; he might do it again. And would it stop there? *I'd do anything for you, Maggie. Anything!* It hadn't sounded like a simple declaration of love; it had sounded almost threatening. Perhaps she'd been wrong to make light of it; perhaps she should tell Jack just how bad this had become, and ask him to come and meet her more often. But Maggie had never been one to play the helpless female. She was more than a match for Reuben Hillman, she told herself, squaring her shoulders. She'd deal with him herself.

'Let's hurry, Jack,' she said, pushing her misgivings to one side. 'My boots are killing me, and the sooner I can get them off and give my toes a good stretch, the happier I shall be.'

It was dark before Billy came home. Rose – and Bullseye – were outside, looking for him.

'Oh, thank goodness, Billy! Where in the world have you been? I've been that worried!'

Billy's eyes were wide and staring. He did not even seem to notice when Bullseye pushed a wet nose into his hand.

Rose ushered him into the kitchen, where she poured strong stewed tea from the pot that stood on the hob.

'I suppose you've been off worrying yourself about having to go down the pit,' she said, stirring sugar into his cup and handing it to him.

Billy mumbled something unintelligible.

'You know if there was anything I could do about it, I would,' Rose said. 'But I can't. You've got to go to work, and it's either down the pit or see if you can get a job as a farm lad. We could ask Farmer Barton if he needs any help, I suppose. But take it from me, farm work's no picnic, either. At least down the pit you get Sundays off.'

Billy said nothing. He had placed his cup of tea on the mantelpiece and, for some reason known only to himself, picked up the clock key that lay there. Now he was repeatedly turning it over between his hands, putting it down, picking it up again, as if he was some kind of automaton.

'Is that what you'd like, then?' Rose asked. 'For me to go and have a word with Farmer Barton – see if there's any chance he'd take you on? You're still on the screens till next week, aren't you? You're not due to go underground till then? If you really are so set against it, we'll see what we can do.'

There was a long silence, then: 'It's too late, Mam,' Billy said flatly.

Rose sighed. She hated to see her youngest son so unhappy. But it was the way of the world. The Donovans were miners, like most of the folk who lived round here, and that was really all there was to it. She patted his hand.

'You'll get used to it, mark my words. This time next week you'll wonder what you were so worried about. Now, drink up your tea before it goes cold.'

Just saying it comforted her, if not Billy. And she had no way of knowing that by this time next week, their lives would have changed for ever.

Chapter Five

It began, that terrible, fateful day, like any other. Maggie and Rose were up with the dawn, working their way through their usual routine until it was time to rouse the men. When Maggie took out the ashes from the grate for riddling, the birds were singing and Bullseye, not yet ready to stir, regarded her lazily from his bed in the outhouse. It was going to be another fine, hot day.

When she went back indoors, Paddy was downstairs, a towel tucked around his neck as he attacked the day-old stubble on his chin with his cut-throat razor. He had been too tired last night to shave before going to bed as he usually did to save time in the morning. Of Billy there was no sign.

'You'd better give him another shout,' Rose said. 'He's gone back to sleep, I shouldn't be surprised. He had a late night.'

'Bloody little layabout,' Paddy muttered.

Maggie went upstairs. As she'd suspected, Billy was still in bed, the covers hiding all but a crest of bright ginger hair.

'Come on, our Billy, get up,' she said, shaking him.

'Oh Maggie, no – I feel awful.' He sounded awful too, his voice faint and slurred, and when she pulled the covers off him, she saw that his face was pale and puffy and he covered it with his hand to shut out the light. 'I'm not going to work,' he muttered.

'Don't talk so stupid, Billy! You've got to,' Maggie told him.

'What for? Gaffer doesn't want me on the screens, so he won't care if I'm there or not. He can't sack me for it, anyway – he's done that already.'

'They'll dock your wages.'

'I don't care. Just leave me alone. My head's aching like billy-o, and I feel really sick too.'

Billy pulled the bedspread back over his head and, defeated, Maggie went back downstairs.

'Billy says he's not going to work today. He's not well.'

'I'll give him not well!' Paddy wiped the last of the soap from his face and flung down the towel. 'He'll get up soon enough if I go up to him!'

'Leave him just for today, can't you?' Rose laid a restraining hand on her husband's arm. 'He was ever so upset last night.'

'He's always upset about something,' Paddy retorted, but he didn't go storming up the stairs as he had intended. 'Oh well, I suppose one day won't hurt. At least I won't have to look at his miserable face all the way to the pit. It's enough to turn the milk sour. Sure, I don't know what's the matter with the boy.'

'You do too,' Maggie said. 'He's frightened to death of going underground. You know he doesn't like the dark. He never has.'

'He'll just have to get used to it, then, won't he? Afraid of the bloody dark! He's just a big sissy.' Paddy picked up his bottle of tea and the kerchief containing his cognocker of bread and cheese. 'I'm off, then. Somebody from this house has to bring home a wage.'

He went to the door, and Maggie followed him out.

'Dad, I know you've got no time for our Billy, but couldn't you try and do something for him? Gaffer just lost his temper, I expect. He'll have calmed down now, and he might give our Billy another chance if you had a word with him.'

Paddy grunted impatiently. 'He's got to go down the pit sooner or later, so it might just as well be sooner. He'll earn better money as a carting boy than he does on the screens, and we can do with that, seeing as we'll soon be a wage short here.'

Maggie felt a flash of guilt. She knew what he was alluding to.

'I'm bound to get married sometime, Dad.'

'Ah sure, and don't I know it.' For just a moment there was regret on Paddy's florid features. Strange, a man always wanted sons, but Ewart and Walter had both left home as soon as they could, and as for Billy . . . well, the less said about Billy the better. But Maggie . . . he'd miss Maggie when she was no longer here.

The sound of a door banging up the rank, voices, and pit boots on the track, and Maggie looked round to see Jack swinging along, carrying his own cognocker and tea bottle, his father with him.

She flushed slightly, her hand flying to check that her hair was up neatly; she hadn't had time yet to tidy herself properly. But soon, she supposed, Jack really would see her as nature intended.

Gilby Withers, always a man of few words, nodded an acknowledgement, but Jack, full of the joys of spring, greeted them in cheerful imitation of Paddy's Irish brogue.

'Top o' the morning to you!'

He grabbed Maggie and stole a kiss so unashamedly it made her blush.

'Jack Withers! Will you behave yourself!'

'Not if I can help it.' Jack winked at her. 'See you tonight, sweetheart.'

'Where's your Billy?' Gilby enquired mildly.

'Skiving,' Paddy said shortly. 'Making out he's not well. He's a waste of space, that one. Come on, lads, we'd best get a move on, or we'll be late.'

The men walked off together along the rank. They were soon joined by Frank Rogers, running to catch them up, and, as they passed number three, by Charlie Oglethorpe and his father Ollie. The group would continue to grow as they neared the pit, all roads converging.

As she watched them go, a sudden sadness she could not explain twisted suddenly deep inside Maggie, so sharp that for a moment she felt she couldn't breathe. Then it was gone, leaving nothing but a small ache not unlike nostalgia or regret.

She gave herself a little shake. What on earth was wrong with her? She should be on top of the world too, just as Jack was. But the feeling of foreboding remained, nebulous but unmistakable, and all the brightness seemed to have gone out of the early-morning sunshine.

Peggy Bishop went to the back door of her little house and tried it for the dozenth time since Tom had left for work. No good. It still refused to budge.

She'd known it wouldn't, of course. She'd heard Tom turn his key in the lock when he left, and there was no way it could have miraculously undone itself. But she tried it again all the same, rattling it furiously as the panic and rage built up inside her. How dare he lock her in? She'd be stuck here all day in the stuffy, claustrophobic heat until he got home tonight. She had no key of her own; that had been lost long ago, and it had never worried her enough to go to all the trouble of getting another one cut. People didn't bother locking their doors until they went to bed at night, if then. Intruders were unheard of, and there was always someone about who would keep an eye open for dodgy pedlars or tramps.

Peggy knew she had no hope of climbing out of a window either. None of them opened wide enough. If she'd been ten years younger and a few stones lighter, it might have been a different story. As it was, she was very much afraid she'd get stuck, and even if she didn't, emerging head first into the peony bushes in full view of her neighbours was hardly dignified.

She attacked the door handle one last time, and exploded with frustration. How could Tom treat her like this, making a prisoner of her as if she was a common criminal? She wouldn't put up with it! She'd leave him the minute that door was opened, and go to her sister's. But of course, the reason he had locked her in was to stop her doing just that, though it was Josh he'd thought she intended running to. He'd locked her in last night, too, after the terrible row that must have been heard all the way to High Compton.

It was her own silly fault, of course. When she had got in after waylaying Josh, Tom had been waiting for her, his face like thunder. The bag she had packed earlier on in a fit of bravado had been dumped on the kitchen table – the evidence for the prosecution.

'What's this?' he had demanded, jabbing at it with a finger still black with coal dust.

Peggy had quailed inwardly, but managed to face him defiantly.

'What's it look like?'

'If you think you're going anywhere, my girl, you'm making a big mistake. I'm not having my wife make a fool out of me.'

Peggy turned away. 'You're a fool already,' she muttered.

He heard her. 'What did you say?'

She turned back. 'Oh, just leave it.'

'Leave it? And let you go off with that bloody Withers?' he spat. 'Not bloody likely!'

'At least he doesn't shout and swear at me,' Peggy said recklessly. 'At least he knows how to treat a woman.'

'Not by the time I've finished with him he won't!' Tom roared. 'By the time I've finished with him he'll be good for nothing but pushing up the daisies.'

Something in his face alarmed her, something cold and dangerous beneath the fury, but she wasn't going to let him see he was scaring her.

'Oh, don't talk so silly,' she said dismissively.

'Silly, is it? My wife going with another man, making herself and me a laughing stock? Oh no, you're the one that's silly, Peg. And that bloody Withers too if he thinks he can get away it. Gadding about with my wife! Talking her into running off with him!'

'He hasn't—'

'No? What's this, then?'

He picked up her bag and threw it across the kitchen. It slammed into the plant stand that supported her precious aspidistra. The whole lot came crashing down, the china pot smashing and dirt scattering across the floor.

'Tom! Now look what you've done!' she cried, distressed.

Tom grabbed his coat from the back of a kitchen chair and marched to the door.

'Where are you going?' she demanded.

'To sort out that bloody Withers once and for all.'

'Tom . . . wait! You've got it all wrong . . .'

He turned on her furiously. 'I don't think so. Not after what

I saw with me own eyes the other night. And you, my lady, can stay here. You won't be seeing him again.'

He had stormed out. The key had turned in the lock and Peggy had spent a miserable evening incarcerated in her own home.

It was late when Tom came in, smelling of drink. Peggy had tried to talk to him, but he would have none of it. She lay tearful and unable to sleep while he snored beside her, and this morning when he left for work he had locked her in again.

She paced the floor, desperate to know what Tom had done last night, whether he'd gone after Josh and picked a fight, or whether what he'd said had been just a lot of empty threats. She was desperate too to see Josh – who had somehow come to mean a great deal more to her than just a quick tumble – and simply to get out of the house.

But she couldn't. Peggy covered her face with her hands and burst into tears.

'Where's our Billy, Mam?' Maggie asked, coming downstairs, dressed now for work.

Rose, who was retching over the stone sink in the scullery, looked up, wiping her face on the towel Paddy had used for shaving.

'Well – in bed, isn't he?'

'No, he's not,' Maggie said. 'His bed's empty.'

'He must have come down while I was over in the privy,' Rose said. 'P'raps he's gone in the front room.'

But she didn't think he had. She'd been in there herself only a minute ago, pulling back the curtains that were drawn religiously every night when it got dark, even though their front room, like everyone else's, was used only for special occasions – and as a last resting place for the dead whilst awaiting their funeral.

Maggie went to look anyway, but Billy was not there.

'He must have gone off somewhere with that darned dog,' Rose said. 'But I certainly didn't see him go. Oh, dear Lord, he worries me to death. You never know what he's going to do next. And if he's poorly . . .'

'He didn't want to go to work, that's all,' Maggie said. 'He'll be back when it's too late for that.'

'Oh, you're probably right.' Rose was fighting another bout of nausea. When it began to pass, she looked fondly at her daughter, who was drying the last of the breakfast things and stacking them away in the cupboard.

'I'm ever so glad you and Jack have made up your minds to get married. He's a good man, Maggie. He'll treat you right, no doubt about that. Though if it was his brother you'd gone for, I wouldn't be so sure. He's a wild one, is Josh. Trouble follows him around like night follows day. Always has. Well, that's why he got sent off to Wales, isn't it? To get him away from that awful crowd he was in with. And to give his uncle the chance to knock some sense into him. But you'll never get a tiger to change his stripes.'

'A leopard to change his spots,' Maggie said, laughing.

'What?'

'It's a leopard, not a tiger. And I think Josh *has* changed. He was just young and silly, that's all. He's grown up now.'

'Hmm. If you say so.' Rose looked unconvinced. 'I still say you've got the best of it. I just hope it doesn't cause trouble between the two of them.'

Maggie raised an eyebrow.

'Whatever do you mean? Why should it cause trouble?'

'Because I reckon Josh is sweet on you,' Rose said shortly. 'I've seen the way he looks at you, my girl, if you haven't.'

Maggie huffed impatiently.

'Oh, get on with you, Mam! Don't talk so silly!' But she could feel faint pink colour rising in her cheeks.

It was nonsense, of course. Josh looked at every pretty girl that way. There was no denying he was a bit of a one. But all the same, she couldn't help remembering the shadow that had crossed his face when Jack had told him they were going to be married. And she couldn't forget the disconcerting tickle she felt deep inside whenever she saw him . . .

The unwelcome train of thought was interrupted suddenly. Something was going on outside along the rank, a man's voice shouting, doors banging.

'What on earth . . . ?'

She ran to the door, the first sharp twists of alarm stirring in her stomach. Women were out all along the rank, converging on the figure of a boy who looked like Charlie Oglethorpe. *Charlie?* What in the world was he doing home? He should be at work. What was going on?

The sweet morning air was suddenly overlaid with menace, as if the sun had been obscured by a thundercloud, or a pleasant dream had taken on the aura of a nightmare.

Maggie's stomach clenched with terror. Something terrible had happened. But what? What?

She started along the track, and Charlie broke away from the stunned group of women and came panting up to her. His eyes were bulging, his cheeks flushed, yet around the edges of the blotches of high colour his face was paper white, and he was visibly shaking.

'What is it, Charlie?' Maggie gasped. 'What's happened?'

At first he couldn't speak. His breath was coming hard. Then:

'Oh my God, Maggie,' he managed. 'It's the hudge. The hudge has gone down.'

Maggie felt as if a chasm had opened up within her. The blood drained from her face and her knees went weak, but for a moment she couldn't grasp what Charlie was saying. It was too enormous. *The hudge has gone down.* But it went down every morning, several times, until all the men were underground. That wasn't what Charlie meant. It couldn't be. *The hudge has gone down.* Oh, dear God, surely it couldn't be *that . . . The hudge has gone down . . .* There had been some kind of terrible accident.

The group of women who had been frozen with shock a few moments ago had broken up, some disappearing into their houses, others running to the end of the rank, where the track joined the road leading to the pit. Maggie grabbed Charlie's sleeve.

'Is it bad?' Charlie nodded wordlessly. 'Who?' she asked desperately, her voice little more than a whisper despite the clamour within her.

Charlie shook his head; whether in all the mayhem he really didn't know, or whether he didn't want to tell her, she couldn't be sure.

'I gotta let people know . . .' He shook his arm free of her grasp and ran on up the rank, knocking on the doors of those who had not come out to see what the commotion was all about.

For a stunned moment Maggie stood stock still, seeing in her mind's eye her father, Jack, and the others walking off along the track this morning, and feeling the icy waves of shock racing through her veins. Then she flew back into the house.

Rose was retching again over the scullery sink – the reason she had not followed Maggie outside to find out what was going on.

'Mam – there's been some kind of accident,' Maggie said, trying to keep the tremble out of her voice.

Rose jerked upright, hand covering her mouth, eyes wide and frightened above it.

'An accident? What . . . ? Who . . . ?'

'I don't know.' Maggie was desperate not to frighten Rose more than she could help. 'I'm going to the pit now to find out.'

'I'm coming too.' Rose was wiping her face.

'No, Mam, you stay here. I can run faster than you. I'll be back the minute I know anything.' Even as she said it, Maggie knew that her mother would follow her to the pit. Who could stay at home waiting for news at such a time? But she couldn't have borne to go at Rose's pace. She had to get there as fast as possible.

'Try not to worry, Mam,' she added. 'I don't expect it's any of ours involved.'

But that, too, she knew was wasted breath. How could anyone not worry until they knew their loved ones were safe? The sick dread inside her was like a cloud of doom. As she ran along the lane, feet flying, heart pounding, each step, each heartbeat, was an echo of their names – Dad . . . Jack . . . Jack . . . Dad – and her lips moved silently with a garbled prayer. *Please God, let them be all right. Oh please, let them be all right.* She overtook other women who were less young and fit than she was, but she didn't stop to speak. The only thing that mattered was getting to the pit head.

In the yard, men in their pit clothes, though not yet blackened with coal dust, were milling about everywhere. Some huddled in shocked groups; others had gathered around the winding engine house. The single pulley wheel was still, and there was something ominous about that stillness in the midst of all the chaos.

Maggie stopped short, looking around wildly from one group to another, her sweat-misted eyes searching vainly for Jack and her father, then started to run again towards the group that were gathered around the headgear. A figure she recognised detached itself from the others – Ollie Oglethorpe, Charlie's father – and came towards her. He, too, looked totally unlike himself, his normally ruddy face ravaged and white with shock.

'Maggie, love, you don't want to go over there,' he said awkwardly.

'But I've got to find Dad and Jack . . .' Her breath was coming in harsh, painful gasps.

Ollie went to put an arm round her heaving shoulders, then withdrew it awkwardly. Physical contact did not come easily to him, or any of these men.

'They bain't there, Maggie.' His voice was low and distressed.

'Where are they, then?'

'Maggie . . .' Somehow he overcame his reticence and touched her arm. 'Come over here, love, and sit down.' He tried to steer her towards the low wall that surrounded the engine house, but Maggie shook herself free. Panic was choking her now.

'No – I've got to find them! Where are they, Mr Oglethorpe? Where are they?'

Ollie shook his head slowly, glancing away from the distressed girl for a moment as if to draw on hidden reserves. Dear Lord, that he should have to be the one to break the news! But better him than the manager, or the gaffer. Better someone she'd known since she was a little girl . . .

'There's been a terrible accident,' he began awkwardly. 'The rope broke. When they were winding down the hudge, the rope broke.'

Although it was what she'd already gathered, she gasped, a short, sharp intake of breath, and her hand flew to her mouth as the full truth of it hit her. And yet she still couldn't take it in. Her thoughts were whirling like Ollie's racing pigeons when they were confined to their loft, a formless, ever-moving mass of fluttering feathers.

'Jack?' she whispered. 'Dad?'

Ollie nodded grimly.

'And ten others. Young Frank Rogers, Ben Bridges—'

Maggie cut him short. She didn't care about Frank Rogers, or Ben Bridges, or anyone else but Jack and her dad.

'You mean they're down there and nobody can reach them?'

'They'm down there all right,' Ollie muttered.

'But somebody must get to them! They'll be hurt!' she cried wildly. 'How can they get down to them if the rope on the hudge is broken?'

Ollie gesticulated helplessly, wondering how to tell her the awful truth: that the rope had given way so soon after the hudge had begun its descent that it was almost certain no one could have survived.

'They'll go down from New Grove,' he said awkwardly. New Grove, a mile and three-quarters away as the crow flew, was linked by its underground passages to Shepton Fields, providing ventilation of sorts, though the connecting tunnel was not big enough for regular traffic between the two pits. 'A party's gone over there now to try to make a way through to them.'

'That's where I should be, then!' Maggie was already turning away, urgency flooding her veins. 'I must be there when they bring them up!'

Ollie caught her arm, stopping her. 'Maggie . . . no.'

She tried to shake herself free, eyes blazing.

'They'll need me, Mr Oglethorpe! I have to get over there!'

Ollie's stomach turned as he thought of the mangled bodies that would be brought out when the cage returned to the surface at New Grove. He couldn't let Maggie go there and see that. No one should have to see it – certainly not this young lass.

'You don't understand, love . . .' he began.

She pulled again against his restraining hand on her arm.

'Let me go, Mr Oglethorpe. I've got to—'

She broke off as a figure she knew well emerged from one of the doorways in the pumping house. Gilby Withers – Jack's father.

'There's Mr Withers!' she cried, and Ollie let go of her arm, all too glad to relinquish responsibility.

Maggie ran towards Jack's father, calling his name, but when he turned and saw her, she was shocked by the look of him. This was a very different Gilby from the placid, upright man she knew. His face was ravaged, his eyes red and staring; he was bent and old suddenly, and he moved like a man in a dream.

'Oh Maggie, Maggie . . .' His voice, full of despair, chilled her all over again. 'I should have been on that damned hudge, not he!'

Tears of panic rose in Maggie's throat, almost choking her. She fought them down – and the dawning realisation of the awful truth along with them.

'I'm going over to New Grove,' she said desperately. 'Why don't you come too?'

Gilby shook his head slowly, unable for a moment to speak. Then, quite matter-of-factly, he said: ''Twouldn't do no good.'

Still Maggie shied away, refusing to acknowledge the finality of what had happened.

'But they'll need us!'

'No,' he said in the same almost unnaturally flat tone. 'They won't need us, Maggie. They won't ever need us again.'

And suddenly there was no escaping it, the terrible truth she had tried so hard to deny. They were dead. Jack and Dad and the others, whose names she hadn't even taken in. Twelve men and boys who had been on the hudge when it fell. But the others didn't matter. Only Jack and Dad mattered . . .

The sob broke in her throat and came out as a scream. 'No!'

The roaring in her ears deafened her to everything else around her, yet the scream was there, echoing inside her head. 'No! No! No!'

Maggie turned, fleeing she knew not where on legs that threatened to give way beneath her. Across the colliery yard she ran, dodging anyone in her way. Then, through the hot haze of tears, she saw Rose standing near the entrance with a knot of other women, arms wrapped around her thin frame, and still wearing her apron. The sight of her brought Maggie up short. She stopped, fighting to regain control of herself. Mam mustn't see her like this. Mam shouldn't be here at all in her condition.

For a moment panic threatened to overwhelm her at the prospect of having to break the news to Rose that Paddy was dead; then with almost startling suddenness she was the old, capable Maggie once more. Mam had to be looked after. Mam had to be told. And Maggie had to find the strength to do it.

Pushing her own grief aside, she went towards Rose and took her in her arms.

'Wherever has our Billy got to?' Rose asked distractedly. 'He doesn't know what's happened. You'd better go out and look for him, Maggie.'

It was mid afternoon and they were at home, drinking gallons of strong sweet tea, sitting in a daze at the kitchen table, trying to find things to do and then not being able to do them. Both were in such a state of shock that they had not yet been able to cry. The world had fallen in around them, yet in a way they were still in denial, discussing practicalities as if this were some minor domestic crisis, whilst their churning stomachs and shaking limbs told them it was much, much more.

'Don't worry about Billy, Mam,' Maggie said. 'He'll come home when he's ready.'

'But it's not right he doesn't know,' Rose insisted. 'His dad's dead, and he doesn't know.'

'Perhaps he does know,' Maggie said.

Rose's eyes skittered round. 'How do you mean?'

'Well . . . maybe he had a premonition. Maybe that's the reason he didn't want to go to work today.'

But *she* hadn't had a premonition. She'd always thought she was the intuitive one in the family, and she hadn't for a moment imagined anything like this . . .

Then, with a sickening jolt, she remembered the nightmare she'd had a few weeks ago, when she'd seemed to be plummeting into the depths of the earth, just as the hudge would have plummeted this morning. And just before she fell, Jack and her father and Frank Rogers had been with her. Now they were all gone.

She'd known something terrible was going to happen, and she'd said nothing to anyone. Instead she'd pushed it to the back of her mind. But this morning, when she'd watched the men go off along the rank to work, an echo of it had come back to haunt her. She remembered the feeling of sadness that had overcome her suddenly as she saw them go. And still she'd said nothing. She should have trusted her own instincts, and recognised the warning for what it was. But what could she have done? They would never have listened to her, even if she'd run after them and begged them not to go.

Tears welled in her eyes and she pressed a hand against her mouth, fighting to hide the terrible rush of guilt and despair.

'I just wish our Billy was here,' Rose said, desperately

needing what was left of her family around her. Another thought struck her. 'We'll have to let our Ewart and Walter know.'

With an effort, Maggie pulled herself together. 'Sir Montague said he'd take care of all that,' she reminded her mother gently.

Sir Montague Fairley had arrived at the pit head at some point during the morning, and when word had come back from New Grove that everyone who had been on the hudge had indeed perished, he had spoken with all the grieving womenfolk. He had expressed sympathy, which they were too numb yet to feel resentful of, given the years of underinvestment in Shepton Fields; he had promised that no widow would be turned unceremoniously out of her home, and he had offered to arrange for relatives in far-flung parts to be notified of what had happened. They had listened to all he said in stunned silence, deferential still to this man whose pit had taken the lives of their husbands, sons and fathers.

'Oh, do go and see if you can find our Billy,' Rose said. 'I expect he's down across the fields. Bring him home, there's a good girl. He ought to be here.'

Maggie got up, still moving as if in a dream, and went to the door. There was a deathly hush about the rank, and the day that had begun so brightly had clouded over, a thick grey canopy obscuring the sun. Dr Blackmore's horse and trap stood outside the door of number two – Frank Rogers' mother was in such a way that they'd called the doctor to her, Maggie guessed. She walked along the track in a fog of nightmarish unreality.

A small figure, running helter skelter, rounded the corner. Billy – with Bullseye at his heels. He pelted up to her, eyes wide, thin face tortured.

'Maggie! Maggie! Is it true? I met Charlie Oglethorpe, and he said . . .'

Maggie put an arm around the thin, shaking shoulders.

'Oh Billy! Yes, I'm afraid it is true. Dad's dead, and Jack, and a lot of others.'

A shuddering sob escaped him.

'Billy, you've got to be brave,' Maggie said. 'Try not to upset Mam.'

He stared at her as if all this was totally beyond his comprehension.

'Come on home,' she said.

They went back along the alleyway, Bullseye following at a distance, as if he too realised that something terrible had happened and wanted no part of it.

Rain was falling by the time the broken bodies were brought to the surface, and the men who carried out the grisly task would never, for the rest of their lives, talk about the things they had seen.

'I want your dad home,' Rose said. The years of ill-treatment were forgotten now; she remembered only the good times. She and Paddy had once been young and in love, and in spite of everything, she loved him still. 'I want him home. Where is he?'

The remains had all been taken to the mortuary. Maggie knew that the only way Paddy would come home was in a coffin with the lid securely screwed down. His injuries, and those of the other men, were too terrible for the eyes of their loved ones.

Night had fallen early because of the thick cloud base. Lamps burned at the windows of cottages for men who would never come home, and tea stewed in pots on fireside hobs, the only sustenance for people with no appetite for solid food.

'Oh, what a day!' Rose said, an understatement that was typical of the stoical breed that was miners and their families. And then: 'I'm so sorry, Maggie.'

Maggie glanced at her, puzzled.

'Jack,' Rose said. 'All I've been able to think about is your dad. But Jack's gone too. And just when everything was working out so well for you.'

Maggie turned away, unable to reply. All day she had refused to allow herself to think about Jack, for she knew that when she did, she would fall apart. She had tried to be strong for her mother, tried to be practical, but all the time the grief she was refusing to acknowledge had been there, gnawing at her insides, leaving her hollow, yet heavy as lead. Now it erupted, threatening to swamp her.

Jack was gone. She'd never again hear his voice, never touch him, never feel his hand, warm and sure, on hers. She would never stand beside him at the altar, never lie beside him, never make his tea and wash his pit clothes, never live with him in the little house he had been so delighted to be offered, never bear his children. Jack, her rock, her hope for the future, was no more, and she didn't know how she could bear it. And she certainly could not bear to think of what had happened today, or what it must have been like for him in those last moments as the hudge went crashing down into the bowels of the earth.

Why, oh why Jack? her heart wept. Why Jack, young, strong, honourable, kind? She hadn't deserved him. Now he had been taken from her and she had not even had the chance to say goodbye. Or to tell him that she loved him.

Guilt swamped her. She'd had her niggling little doubts about that. Had he known? Had she hurt him? Oh please, please no! The thought that she might have was unbearably painful. The tears that had been locked away inside all day spilled over, cascading in a hot tide down her crumpled face.

'Oh Mam,' she whispered.

Rose's face crumpled too. For a long moment they merely

looked at one another, sharing their grief and their loss. Then they went into each other's arms and clung together, weeping.

'I told you you wouldn't see that bloody Withers again, and I was right!' Tom Bishop said with something that might almost have been grim satisfaction. 'He got his comeuppance all right! Trouble is, a lot of others had to go along with him.'

'What are you on about?' Peggy asked distractedly. She had spent a terrible day locked in her cottage, but she had heard about the accident all the same. News of it had spread through the district like wildfire; when she had seen the neighbours gathered outside talking, she had opened the window as far as it would go and they had told her about it. But what Tom was saying made no sense at all.

'Your lover,' he sneered. 'He was one of them killed. And serve him bloody well right.'

'Josh doesn't work at Shepton Fields,' she said, puzzled

And then she realised: Tom had confused the two brothers.

'You bloody fool!' she shot at him. 'Josh works at Marston. It's Jack at Shepton Fields. He's the one who's been killed.'

It took a moment for Tom to take this in; he wasn't, and never would be, the sharpest knife in the box. Then his face changed, all manner of expressions she couldn't read distorting his puggy features before they were replaced by his usual belligerence.

'Well you'd better stay away from him then, hadn't you, if you don't want him to end up like his brother,' he snarled.

The bar at the Prince of Wales was crowded for a weekday evening, for the men had felt the need to come together and talk about the tragedy with others of their kind who understood. But the atmosphere was subdued, and the familiar faces that were missing brought the events of the day home to those who were there as nothing else had done. Archie Russell was amongst those who had gone down with the hudge; the chair he usually occupied was empty, for no one else could bring themselves to sit in it.

'What a thing,' George Parfitt said. 'And to think we was only saying t'other night as how Shepton Fields weren't safe. Josh Withers was on about how that hudge was a bloody death-trap, and we were all pooh-poohing him. Now his own brother's dead.'

'I don't understand it,' said Jim Parker, another of the men. 'That were a good thick rope, even if it were hemp and not wire. I can't understand how Hubie Britten didn't come to notice if it were getting frayed. He generally gives it a good check-over once a week or so.' Hubie drove the winding engine.

'Well, he's getting on, coming up for retirement. P'raps his eyes bain't as good as they were. Or he's getting forgetful.'

'Ah, p'raps that be it.'

As the men shook their heads and supped their pints, none of them had any way of knowing of the serious discussion that was taking place at this very moment between Wilfred James, the colliery manager, and Sir Montague Fairley, the owner.

Sir Montague, very red in the face from all the brandy he had consumed throughout a long and difficult day, was pacing his drawing room, yet another glass in his hand.

'This is shocking, James – shocking! Are you absolutely sure of your facts?'

Wilfred James's face was drawn and, for once, almost as dirty as any miner's.

'There's no doubt,' he said heavily. 'No doubt at all. That was no accident that happened today. The rope didn't give through wear and tear. It was cut. Somebody had severed it,

strand by strand. Then, as soon as it had to take the weight . . .'
He broke off, unable to finish.

'Good God! Then it's murder a dozen times over!' Sir
Montague exploded. 'But who would do such a thing? They
must have realised the consequences!'

'Well, that'll be for the police to find out,' Wilfred said. 'I
should have reported it to them straight away, but I thought it
best to speak to you first.'

'You did the right thing.' Sir Montague refilled his glass from
the crystal decanter that stood on a small pedestal table, then
belatedly raised the decanter in Wilfred's direction. 'Do you
want one, James?'

'No thanks, Sir Montague,' Wilfred said, though he could
certainly have done with one. 'In view of all I've still got to do,
I think it's best I stay sober.'

The implied criticism was lost on the pit owner, who was
only glad his best cognac was not going to be wasted on his
manager.

'Yes, I dare say you should.' He took another healthy gulp.
'Well, I suppose it's good news in a way.'

Wilfred stared at him, frowning. 'What do you mean? Twelve
of my men and boys are dead – hardly good news, Sir Montague.'

'No, no.' Fairley waved his glass impatiently. 'We could
have been for the jolly old high jump, James. When they get
over their shock, the men might well have been baying for our
blood, not to mention what the authorities could have had to
say about it. But if it was a deliberate act – well, we can hardly
be blamed, can we? No one could foresee a vandal or a
murderous madman severing the rope, now could they?'

'No, sir, I suppose they couldn't.'

Wilfred James turned away, shocked and disgusted by Sir
Montague's attitude. He wasn't going to say anything, though.

He had his own job to think of – if job there still was. Doubtless Shepton Fields would be closed down now. He knew that Sir Montague had been considering doing just that for some time, but had been afraid that if he did, the miners at the rest of the collieries he owned might go on strike in sympathy. Well, this had done the job for him. No wonder he was taking it so well. Good God, he wouldn't put it past Sir Montague to be behind the severed rope himself.

'Are you going to call the police, or am I?' he asked coldly.

Chapter Six

Maggie was dressed and ready for work. She wasn't sure how she was going to manage to go out and face the world, but she knew she had to try. For one thing, she couldn't afford to lose another day's wages, especially now that they were going to be without the money Paddy brought home each Saturday, and for another, she was desperate for some sort of normality. She'd go crazy, she thought, if she had to stay at home all day, just going over and over the terrible events of yesterday with Rose and the neighbours, all of whom were in such total shock they could talk of nothing else. It would probably be the same at the shop, but at least she could keep busy, even if it was only to dust fixtures, roll lace and sort pins. Anything would be better than being cooped up in the hot, airless kitchen where grief and shock hung in a suffocating cloud. But she couldn't help worrying about leaving Rose with only Billy for company.

'Are you sure you'll be all right, Mam?' she asked, looking anxiously at her mother.

'Of course I'll be all right.' Rose's voice was thin and shaky, but determined. 'What's going to happen to me? I'm in my own home – for now, anyway. Till Fairley decides he wants it for letting out to some other poor soul on his payroll.'

'Oh Mam . . .' Maggie didn't know what to say. She couldn't

yet begin to contemplate the consequences of what had happened. Dealing with the loss of Paddy, and Jack too, was more than enough. But Rose was right, of course. The pit owner was sure to want them out of his house before long.

'Go on, you get off or you'll be late,' Rose insisted.

'Well, if you're sure . . .'

Maggie tossed her shawl around her shoulders and felt tears catch in her throat. Was it really only a few days ago that she'd worn it to go for a walk with Jack? It seemed like a different lifetime.

She needed her shawl this morning, though. The sun that had seemed to shine endlessly these last few weeks had disappeared behind an ocean of lowering grey cloud, and it was quite chilly. Or perhaps that was just her. Maggie didn't think she'd felt properly warm, or stopped trembling, since the terrible events of the previous day.

She walked quickly, hoping no one would emerge from any of the other houses in the terrace. She really didn't want to have to speak to anybody. But as yet, the doors were all firmly closed and it was eerily quiet. Maggie supposed the other pits would be operating normally, but almost everyone who lived in the Ten Houses worked at Shepton Fields, and it would be a long time, if ever, before coal was mined there again.

Soon she was out on the main road that led to High Compton, and this too was quiet. A horse and cart passed her with milk churns rattling; she saw it most mornings as it made its way from farm to farm, but the dairyman never called a greeting. He was a surly fellow, Maggie always thought, but today she was glad of it. As she rounded a bend in the road, she saw Farmer Barton driving his herd of cows across it on the way back to their field from the milking parlour. She slowed her step until they all disappeared from view behind the high hedges and

Farmer Barton had closed the gate after them. Another encounter avoided. But it couldn't last much longer. As she approached the town, Maggie steeled herself and kept going at a brisk pace, hoping she wouldn't meet anyone she knew. To her relief, she managed it.

Freeman's, where she worked, was a big double-fronted shop on the corner of the high street, the drapery shop to one side of the main door and Horace Freeman's gentlemen's outfitters to the other. Maggie went around to the rear of the building as she always did and in through the back entrance, which opened directly into the showroom.

Augusta Freeman was there, unpacking hats from their boxes and selecting the ones that would go on the display stands. She looked up, surprised, as Maggie came in.

'Good gracious! Maggie! I didn't expect you to come to work today, my dear.' Her tone was much kindlier than the brusquely efficient one Maggie was used to.

'I didn't know what else to do, Mrs Freeman.' Maggie didn't take off her shawl; she just pulled it tighter around the high neck of the white blouse she wore for work, standing there in the doorway as if poised for flight.

'Oh Maggie, Maggie, I am so very sorry . . .' For once Augusta was lost for words.

'Thank you,' Maggie said stiffly. She looked dreadful, Augusta thought, deathly pale, with huge dark circles beneath her eyes, which seemed strangely dead.

'Really, you shouldn't be here.' Augusta set the bonnet she had been admiring on the counter. 'You're in no fit state . . .'

'I need to keep busy, Mrs Freeman.'

Augusta tried another tack. 'But what about your mother? Shouldn't you be with her? She's had a terrible shock. Will she be all right alone?'

'She's not alone. Our Billy's there.'

'Hmm.' Augusta's lips tightened. She didn't know Billy well, but from what she did know of him, she wasn't impressed. 'He's just a boy, though, isn't he? I'd have thought what your mother needs is another woman.'

Maggie bit her lip, which had begun to wobble at the unexpected show of sympathy.

'Don't send me home, please, Mrs Freeman,' she begged, and Augusta realised that what she needed most was a little normality, a respite from what must be the unrelenting atmosphere of doom and grief at home.

'Very well, Maggie. But I think it would be best if we found you something to do out here. You shouldn't be in the shop,' she said, and this time it wasn't just kindness that was motivating her. First and foremost, Augusta Freeman was a business-woman, and she couldn't imagine that Maggie in her present state would be capable of serving the customers with the efficiency she demanded. Just seeing her there, looking so obviously distressed, might well deter them from coming into the shop at all. Unless, of course, they wanted to gawp at one of those affected by the tragedy, and Augusta didn't want that either.

'Before we do anything else, why don't you make us a nice cup of tea?' she suggested.

It was a long, awkward morning. Cathy didn't know what to say to Maggie, and avoided her as much as possible, while Beat was overly sympathetic, squeezing Maggie's arm whenever she passed and gazing at her with great mournful eyes that looked ready to spill tears. Maggie busied herself with the tasks Augusta set her: unpacking parcels from the wholesaler, dusting fixtures, and even arranging the bonnets on their display stands – a huge privilege, since that was something Augusta normally liked to do herself. But still she couldn't stop the trembling in her stomach that was making her feel queasy, and her mind kept wandering to terrible visions of what it must have been like for Jack, her father and the others in their last moments.

Unbeknown to Maggie, rumours that the tragedy had been no accident were already spreading like wildfire around the town. More than one customer who came into the shop mentioned it, and Cathy and Beat talked about it in whispers when they were alone – gossip, even about something as momentous as this, was something Augusta would not tolerate.

'I can't believe anyone would do something so terrible!' Cathy said, shaking her head. 'It's just downright wicked!'

'I expect it's a tale got up by Sir Montague to save his own skin,' Beat opined. 'He knew that rope should have been replaced donkey's years ago, and was too busy pinching his pennies to do anything about it. If he can shift the blame, he will.'

But in the early afternoon, the rumour was confirmed.

Alice Love was married to the police sergeant in High Compton, and lived in the square, stone-built police station that had a small office at the front and three cells at the rear. The kitchen and living room were to one side of the building, but every sound carried up to the bedrooms, and nuisance though it was to be disturbed by the comings and goings of the two constables who shared the beat, or woken in the night by rowdy prisoners being brought in to be charged, or members of the public knocking on the door to report some crime or call for assistance, living on the premises had its advantages too. Alice was nosy by nature, and she also loved being the one in the know about what was going on. Even if Will, her long-suffering husband, had forbidden her to talk about what she'd seen or overheard, she was able to smile smugly when folk asked, tap her nose with a knowing look, and turn away revelling in her superior knowledge.

This time, though, there was no need for her to keep quiet. The police station had been a hive of activity all morning; Alfred Nicholls, the superintendent in charge of the division, had arrived from Bath, and investigations were already under way. Soon everyone would know that the rope on the hudge had been severed deliberately, and Alice was set on making sure that she was the one to pass on the news to as many people as possible.

The excuse she used for going into the drapery shop was that she needed a reel of black cotton to sew on a button that had come off Will's tunic, but Augusta was in no doubt it was just that – an excuse. She hovered like an avenging angel whilst Cathy served the obnoxious woman, her heart sinking as she listened with pretended indifference to what Alice was saying. Bad enough if the tragedy had been a terrible accident; this was even worse. How could the families of the victims cope with knowing their loved ones had been murdered? How could the town cope with it? The shadow of suspicion would turn neighbour against neighbour. Everyone would be looking over their shoulder for someone to blame. Augusta shuddered inwardly. She hoped Maggie had not overheard what was being said; she was in the showroom, but the door that separated it from the shop was far from soundproof. In any case, she would have to find out the truth sooner or later, and Augusta thought it would be better coming from her.

When Alice finally left with her reel of cotton and a self-satisfied smirk on her face, Augusta went into the showroom.

'Maggie, my dear, there's something I need to tell you,' she said gently.

* * *

Billy was sitting on the bank of the river, scrawny knees drawn up to his chin, arms wrapped around them. Bullseye lay beside him, nose between paws, but his eyes kept flicking to his young master, and every so often he got up and went to him, nudging him gently.

'Oh, Bullseye, leave me alone,' Billy snapped. For once he didn't want the dog's attention. He felt sick, his stomach turning over and over, and his mouth was so dry that he couldn't even moisten his lips.

It was his worst nightmare come true, the very thing he'd been so afraid of, hurtling down into the bowels of the earth with darkness all around. Helpless. Terrified. Being smashed to pieces . . . He pressed his hands into his eyes, but he couldn't shut out the awful pictures. He covered his ears, but he could still hear the screams in his head. And his heaving stomach felt the speed and the lurch of the fatal descent so vividly that he had to double over again, retching on to the bare earth between the tufts of lush grass.

Dead. All of them dead. It was too enormous a thing to take in. His dad . . . Jack Withers . . . Frank Rogers . . . He had hated Frank Rogers, and he had often thought he hated his father, too, but he would never have wished this on them. Not this. Never this. He didn't want to think about it, any of it, but he couldn't stop. Around and around it went until Billy thought he was going mad.

He covered his eyes with his hands again and began to cry, but no tears would come. It was as if every bit of moisture in his body had dried up. The sobs came all the same, racking his skinny body, tearing him apart. Billy thought they would never stop.

Bullseye was poking at him again with his nose, whining. He was restless, he wanted a game, and he didn't know what was wrong with his master. But something was, and Bullseye did what dogs do when they sense distress. He snuffled at Billy's face and began licking his ear and his neck.

At last Billy reached for him, grasping at the squat little body that had filled out now from all the scraps he was fed, and pulled him into the crook of his arm. There was comfort in the warm breath on his neck, the scratchy feel of the coarse hair under his fingers, and the steady beat of the dog's heart, and after a few minutes Billy's sobs quietened. But the ache was still there, deep inside him, and the blackness was still all around, closing in until he felt it had filled every corner of his mind and his body.

At least now he'd never now have to go down on the hudge, Billy thought. But given the enormity of what had happened, it was scant consolation.

It was Peggy Bishop's sister, Sarah, who told her the news about the rope having been cut deliberately. She lived on the other side of High Compton, but she had been into town shopping that afternoon, and made up her mind to go and see Peggy while she wasn't too far away. The last time they'd talked, Peggy had told her she was thinking of leaving Tom and asked if she could come and stay for a bit, but Sarah had heard nothing since, and she was worried about her sister and anxious to know what was going on.

Plenty of married couples had their ups and downs, of course, but leaving your husband was unheard of. Quite apart from the scandal it would cause, what would Peggy do? Sarah didn't want her sister staying with her for ever; though they got on well enough, Sarah's house was already overcrowded – she'd had five children so far, and given the ease with which she fell pregnant, there'd be more to follow before too long. (Funny, that, she sometimes thought: that she should have babies if she so much as *looked* at a man, whilst Peggy hadn't managed even one.) And how was Peggy going to live without Tom to support her? Sarah couldn't see her being able to contribute anything to the family budget, unless, of course, she found herself a job, but Peggy was lazy and always had been. She'd rather sit around all day than scrub floors for gentry or stitch gloves in the local factory. Really, Sarah couldn't afford another mouth to feed, even if that mouth was her own flesh and blood.

From what Peggy had told her, she'd gathered that her sister had ideas about setting up home with Josh Withers, but she couldn't see that happening in a hurry. Or even at all. Peggy was besotted with Josh, and Sarah could see the attraction – she'd fancied him herself when they'd all been young. But Josh was never going to be up for that. He was a Jack the lad, and he'd been taking advantage of Peggy, Sarah was sure. If she left Tom, she wouldn't see Josh for dust. Sarah had warned her that that would be the end of it, but she wasn't sure Peggy had taken any notice. She was too moonstruck to think straight.

Sarah was determined, though, to have one more try at getting her sister to see sense before she did something she'd regret – and descended on Sarah for what might turn out to be a very long time indeed.

She tried the back door of Peggy's little house, relieved to see when it opened that Tom was no longer locking her sister in. She called 'Coo-ee! It's only me!' but there was no response. Alarmed, Sarah called again – surely Peggy hadn't walked out already? She went through the scullery and into the living room, and there was her sister, fast asleep in one of the fireside chairs. She came to with a start, sitting up and wiping her mouth with the back of her hand.

'Sarah! Talk about frightening someone to death!'

'How can you go to sleep in the middle of the day?' Sarah

demanded. 'If you were Granny Dodds I could understand it, but at your age . . .'

'Oh, leave me be, our Sarah.' Peggy struggled upright. 'What are you doing here anyway? I don't usually see you in the middle of the week.'

'I was in town and I thought I'd pop round. I'll go again if you want me to.' But she sat down anyway in the chair opposite Peggy.

'I suppose you want a cup of tea now you're here,' Peggy grumbled.

'I wouldn't say no . . .'

Peggy swung the trivet so the kettle was over the fire, then eased back into her chair again.

'The truth of the matter is I've been wondering how things are between you and Tom,' Sarah said bluntly. 'I've been half expecting you to turn up on my doorstep these last few days. You're worrying me to death, our Peg.'

'There's no need for you to worry,' Peggy said breezily. 'I've been thinking things over, and I don't want to act too hastily.'

'Well, thank goodness for that! I'm glad you've seen sense. Tom's your husband. You made your bed, my girl, you have to lie in it.'

'Not for much longer, I hope.' Peggy smiled smugly. 'I just thought I'd let things quieten down for a bit. I don't want Tom chasing me over to your house – it's not fair on you. I reckon the best thing is to wait until I've got something fixed up with Josh. Tom'll think twice about knocking on our door and picking a fight. He knows Josh could beat him with one hand tied behind his back.'

Sarah sighed. 'If you want my opinion, it's never going to happen. Josh isn't interested in settling down with anyone, least of all you. You're living in cloud cuckoo land.'

Peggy pursed her lips mutinously, and Sarah went on: 'Besides, Tom might not pick a fight with Josh face to face, but he'd find a way of getting back at him. He's a dark horse, is Tom.'

With a stab of discomfort, Peggy remembered the things Tom had said last night, and the callous way he'd talked about the terrible tragedy at Shepton Fields.

'Can we change the subject?' she said shortly. 'What an awful thing that was, the accident at the pit yesterday. Twelve killed, they say. And all because Fairley wouldn't pay to put things right there, and the rope broke!'

'Oh Peg!' Sarah sat forward, hoisting her skirt clear of her ankles and resting her elbows on her knees. 'You'll never believe this! I just heard. They're saying it wasn't an accident at all. That rope were cut! Cut, strand by strand. Can you believe it? Who in the world would do such a terrible thing?'

Peggy froze.

'The rope was cut?' she repeated incredulously. 'You mean somebody did it on purpose so the hudge would go down?'

'That's what I heard. The police are on to it – the superintendent has come out from Bath to take charge of the investigation. They're questioning folk to try and find out if anybody saw anything suspicious, and if they know of anybody with a reason to want those poor blighters dead. I even heard talk that they might call in a detective from Scotland Yard . . .'

She chatted on, but Peggy was no longer listening. She had gone cold, as the most dreadful thought flashed unbidden into her mind.

Tom hadn't been just hard and callous last night when he'd talked about the tragedy. He'd seemed almost smug about it. Especially when he'd thought it was Josh who'd been killed. Busying herself with the kettle and teapot to cover the turmoil that was seething within her, she tried to remember exactly what he had said. *I told you you wouldn't see that bloody Withers again. He got his comeuppance all right. Trouble is, a lot of others had to go along with him.* She could hear his voice now, and she realised that he had sounded almost triumphant. Until he'd discovered it was Jack who had gone down with the hudge. That had put him out for a bit. *You'd better stay away from Josh if you don't want to end up like his brother.* That was what he'd said then. And it wasn't the first threat he'd made against Josh. What was it he'd said when he'd first found out for sure that she was seeing him? *He'll be fit for nothing but pushing up the daisies by the time I've finished with him.* Or something very like it.

Peggy's hand shook suddenly, and water splashed on to the hot trivet, where it sizzled and turned to steam.

'Hey, careful, our Peg!' Sarah warned. 'Don't go scalding yourself!'

'Oh, I'm fine, Sarah,' Peggy replied impatiently.

But she wasn't. She wasn't fine at all. She was suddenly very afraid that the person who had cut the rope and caused the hudge to go crashing down might have been a vengeful Tom.

As the day wore on, the anxiety Maggie had felt about leaving Rose alone with only Billy for company niggled more and more until she could think of nothing else.

By the time the hands on the showroom clock were showing five, she could stand it no longer.

'Mrs Freeman . . . do you think it would be all right if I went home?' she asked tentatively.

'My dear, you should never have come in today. I told you that this morning. Of course you can go.' Augusta was actually relieved; Maggie had completed all the jobs she had managed to find for her away from the shop floor, and having her here looking like a ghost was beginning to take its toll on her. 'Off you go. And I really think it might be best if you stayed at home tomorrow.'

'Thank you, Mrs Freeman,' Maggie said dutifully.

She collected her shawl and left by the rear door without saying goodbye to either of the other girls. Really, speaking at all was a tremendous effort.

As she reached the corner of the building, she caught sight of Reuben Hillman standing in the doorway of the gents' outfitters. It wasn't unusual for Horace or one of the assistants to step outside for a breath of fresh air if they had no customers, but she wished Reuben hadn't chosen this moment, and when he called her name she lowered her head and walked on, ignoring him. But just before crossing the road, she glanced over her shoulder and saw that he had taken a few steps along the pavement as if to follow her. Now he was staring after her with that sick puppy-dog expression that set her teeth on edge. Maggie turned her head quickly and crossed the road, but she had begun to shake, more upset than usual by his unwanted attention.

The pain of loss knifed through her again, bringing sudden tears to her eyes. She no longer had Jack to turn to if Reuben continued to be a nuisance. This was something she was going to have to handle on her own. She had never felt more alone, more vulnerable.

Anxious to get home and make sure Mam was all right, Maggie walked quickly and purposefully, and before long she had reached the turning that led to the Ten Houses terrace. Whereas this morning the narrow lane had been deserted and quiet as the grave, now there were signs of life. Three small boys were kneeling on the road playing marbles, and little Lucy Day was pushing a rag doll in a packing case set on trucks, her pretend perambulator. A couple of men squatted against the wall, smoking and talking about the disaster, no doubt. They fell silent as Maggie passed, giving her the briefest of nods before hastily dropping their gaze. But thankfully there were no womenfolk to be seen – they would be indoors preparing the evening meal at this time of day – and Maggie made it to number six without having to talk to anyone.

Though the day had been warm and muggy once the first chill of morning had passed, the door was closed. As Maggie walked in, the oppressive heat of the kitchen, where the fire burned winter and summer, rushed out to meet her.

'Mam?' she called. 'Mam, I'm home.'

There was no reply. Maggie pushed the door wide open, kicking the doorstop into place to prevent it closing again. Usually at this time of day there would be signs of the meal Rose would be preparing – potatoes peeled and in the pot ready to go on the trivet over the fire, vegetables from the garden in a basket on the worktop. Not today. It was hardly to be wondered at really, but Maggie's anxiety twisted up a notch anyway, and she hurried through into the living room.

Rose was sitting in one of the fireside chairs, and to Maggie's astonishment, Bullseye was beside her, his misshapen head on her lap whilst Rose stroked his neck in a compulsive rhythm.

'Mam?' she said anxiously. 'Are you all right?'

Rose seemed to come back from wherever it was she had been, snapping out of her trance.

'Oh, as right as I'll ever be, I expect,' she said, with a little snort that Maggie guessed was an attempt at a laugh. 'You're home early, Maggie. And I haven't even started on the tea.' She pushed Bullseye out of the way and got up.

'Don't worry about that, Mam, I'm not hungry anyway. We'll get something presently. And I'm early because Mrs Freeman let me go. I think I've been more hindrance than help to her today.' Maggie folded her shawl and put it over the back of one of the upright chairs. 'Where's our Billy?'

'I don't know. I haven't seen him since dinner time. He's gone off somewhere, but he left the dog here – why, I don't know. He usually takes him everywhere.' She sighed, shaking her head. 'I'm worried about him, Maggie. He's taken this terrible hard.'

'I expect he's all right, Mam,' Maggie said. 'He shouldn't have left you on your own, though.'

Rose laughed shortly again. 'Oh, I haven't been on my own. Folk have been popping in and out all day. Not that I want them to. I haven't felt like talking.' She wrapped her thin arms around herself as if to ward off unwelcome visitors, and the swelling mound of her stomach was clearly visible beneath her apron.

'All the same . . .' Maggie was wondering now how she was going to break the news about the rope of the hudge being cut deliberately. It was bound to upset her mother all over again. Unless she'd already been told, of course . . .

'Mam, I've heard something shocking,' she began tentatively, but Rose wasn't listening.

'And it's not only the neighbours who've been here either,' she went on as if Maggie hadn't spoken. 'I've had Wilfred James here too.'

'Wilfred James?' For a moment Maggie couldn't think who she meant.

'Wilfred James,' Rose repeated with emphasis. 'Manager at Shepton Fields. Came here to talk about burying your father, if you please. The cheek of it! And him one of the ones to blame for what's happened! I sent him away with a flea in his ear, I can tell you.'

Maggie frowned, puzzled. They hadn't discussed Paddy's funeral yet, though it would have to be arranged sometime. But there was no rush; there would have to be an inquest before he could be buried, they'd been told.

'What's it got to do with Wilfred James?' she asked.

'Hmm!' Rose snorted. 'That's what I'd like to know. Trying to soft-soap us, if you ask me. Fairley will arrange and pay for everything – that's what James said. If that's not his way of trying to keep us quiet, I don't know what is. He should have spent his money on keeping his pit in good order before something like this happened. A fat lot of use it is now they've all gone.'

Maggie hesitated, then took a deep breath.

'Mam – I heard today . . . the rope didn't give way on its own . . .' she said tentatively.

But to her surprise, Rose huffed with impatience.

'So they say. I don't know whether there's any truth in it or not. But if they'd put in a proper cable like they should have done, nobody could have cut it through like they're saying, could they?'

'That's true, I suppose,' Maggie agreed.

'And now, to add insult to injury, they think they can walk in and take over the funeral,' Rose went on indignantly.

Though it stuck in her craw too that someone other than the family should pay for Paddy's funeral, Maggie couldn't help thinking it wouldn't be such a bad thing. It had been one of the worries that had tormented her in the dark hours of the night. A funeral cost money – money they didn't have.

'Mam, I'm not sure we can afford to be proud,' she said gently.

Rose turned on her furiously, the rage that had been simmering in her all day bubbling to the surface in a rush. 'It's an insult and a disgrace. I can't have it! I won't!'

'Mam . . . I don't think you should be so hasty. If Sir Montague is willing to pay, then—'

'I haven't told you yet what he's suggested.' Rose was trembling with anger. 'A mass grave, in the churchyard at St Peter's. All of them in there together. And just the one burial service. Your father was a Catholic, Maggie. He should have a Mass and a proper Catholic burial. He should be in the part of the churchyard that's reserved for Catholics, not stuck in a grave with all the others!'

'Oh Mam . . .' Maggie felt the ready tears pricking behind her eyes. Apart from Christmas and Easter, Paddy hadn't been near a church in years, but she supposed her mother thought it was what was required when it came down to it, the one last thing she could do for him. 'Look, let's talk about this later. I don't suppose Dad would have minded very much one way or the other, but if it's what you want . . . we'll find the money somehow . . .'

She broke off. Someone was standing in the doorway that she had left open, a slight figure silhouetted against the light, late-afternoon sun turning the reddish hair the colour of burnished copper.

'Ewart?' she said wonderingly, hardly daring to believe it really was the brother she hadn't seen in several years.

'Maggie . . . Mam . . .' He came into the scullery, dumping his carpet bag on the floor beside the cupboard. And as Rose ran to him, taking him in her arms, Maggie felt as if an enormous weight was lifting from her shoulders.

Ewart was, and had always been, Mam's favourite. He would know what to do.

Chapter Seven

'I'm going to go and have a word with Josh, see what the Withers family think about it,' Ewart said, pushing back his chair.

Tea was over; when she'd got over the shock of seeing her beloved eldest son walking unannounced into her kitchen, Rose's first instinct was to feed him. 'You must be famished, coming all that way,' she'd said. 'I don't suppose you've had anything proper to eat since you left Yorkshire.'

'Don't worry about me, Mam. I had a pasty and a pint when the train got in, and the cart I got a lift on out of Bath was carrying a load of apples.' Ewart was loosening the scarf tied around his neck and undoing the top button of his shirt.

'Apples? They won't be ripe yet, surely?'

'I reckon they were fallers, bound for feeding to the pigs,' Ewart said ruefully.

Rose tutted, almost her old self.

'You'll get the belly ache, and you'll have nobody but yourself to blame. Give me a hand, Maggie, there's a good girl, and we'll get the tea on the go.'

Between them, Maggie and Rose prepared potatoes and cabbage and fried bacon with the added luxury of an egg on the side – Lottie Weeks from next door, who kept hens in a pen in her garden, had brought half a dozen, still warm from the straw, when she'd looked in to commiserate earlier in the day.

By the time the meal was ready, Billy had put in an appearance – much to Rose's relief – but he looked every bit as wretched as he had when he'd gone out this morning. He ignored Bullseye, who was waiting hopefully for the rinds off the bacon, and barely spoke even to Ewart, though he hero-worshipped his older brother. As soon as he'd finished picking at his meal, he threw the scraps to Bullseye and clattered off upstairs.

'He's in an awful way about what's happened,' Rose said, stacking the plates together. 'Still, at least you're here now, Ewart. I reckon that'll help take his mind off losing his father.'

'I didn't think they got on that well,' Ewart, who sometimes spoke without thinking, said bluntly.

'He was still his father,' Rose said, bristling. 'Yours too. And Walter's. Is he going to be able to come down for the funeral?'

'He'll do his best.' Ewart was drinking yet another cup of his mother's strong stewed tea, holding the mug between hands that were black-veined with coal dust that no amount of scrubbing could wash away. 'It's not so easy for him, though, with a family to think of.'

Though Ewart was the older of the two brothers, he was still free and single, whilst Walter had a wife, two children, and another on the way. He had met and married a Yorkshire lass soon after moving north; Rose, doing her sums, suspected the wedding had been what she would call 'a rush job' – unless of course little Jimmy had come early, which she doubted. She'd seen her grandson only the once, when Walter had brought Connie and the baby to visit, and she'd never seen the newborn, Edie, at all. She wished with all her heart they were not so far away. But Walter seemed happy enough with his little family; he'd always been the quieter of her two elder sons, not given to racketing around as Ewart did.

There'd been a time when she'd worried about Ewart – he'd been a sight too friendly with Josh Withers and the rest of his wild crowd, and had earned a reputation as something of a scallywag himself. As a boy, he'd always been up to something; she wished she had a silver sovereign for every time a neighbour had come knocking on the door to complain that he had been scrumping apples, or playing that stupid game of leaving a parcel in the road with a long string attached, hiding nearby, and then jerking the string to make the parcel move when a passer-by tried to pick it up. Later, he and the crowd he'd picked up with were forever getting involved in fights, or coming home very late, or not until next morning, because they'd walked all the way in to Bath for a night out.

No, it was no small wonder to her that whilst Walter had settled down to family life, Ewart was still footloose and fancy free. But at least with him now living so far away, she didn't have to know about his carryings-on, and for all that she wished he'd meet a nice girl and settle down too, it was the rascal in Ewart that made him so lovable.

'So, we've got to talk about this funeral,' he said, putting down his mug and pushing it back across the table.

It had been mentioned over tea, but since Rose was still so clearly upset at Sir Montague Fairley's suggestion, Maggie had insisted that any discussion should wait until they'd finished eating. Now Rose pushed back her chair and got up abruptly, heading for the teapot that was keeping the brew warm on the trivet over the fire.

'There's nothing to talk about. It's not right, Ewart. We've got to do things proper. A Catholic burial, and a grave that I can keep nice. I won't hear of anything else, so you might as well save your breath.'

'But Mam . . .' Ewart sighed and bit his lip. He didn't want to say what he was thinking – that there might well be a grisly reason for the suggestion that all the victims should be buried in a mass grave. From his own experience, he knew only too well how far the hudge would have fallen, and what the terrible results of that might be.

'I know what you're going to say – that funerals cost money. Well, it's a bad job if we can't find it from somewhere so we can do the right thing by your father.' Rose spun round, pointing the teapot at Ewart as if it were a weapon. 'To tell the truth, I'd have thought you'd offer to chip in, our Ewart. You're earning good money now. I'd have thought you'd want to!'

'Well, of course I will, if that's what you're set on, Mam. But it might not be as simple as that . . .' Ewart broke off, still avoiding saying what was in his mind. Tact might not be his strongest point, but even he shrank from enlightening Rose about the possibility of bodies so mangled and broken it was impossible to separate one from another.

Rose, however, was not to be so easily put off.

'What do you mean, not that simple?' she demanded.

That was when Ewart pushed back his chair and got up. 'I'm going to have a word with Josh, see what the Withers family think about it.'

'I couldn't care less what the Withers family are going to do,' Rose said disparagingly. 'That's up to them. But I wouldn't have thought they'd want Jack stuck in with all the rest of them any more than I want it for your father. And I wouldn't have thought you'd want it either, Maggie.'

'Well, I'm going to talk to them anyway,' Ewart said, heading for the door.

Maggie got up.

'I'll come with you.' She picked up the stack of dirty plates. 'I'll put these in the scullery. Leave the washing-up until I got back, Mam.'

There was a clatter of boots on the stairs and Billy appeared, his ginger hair sticking up in tufts as if he had been pulled through a bush backwards, as Rose might say, and his eyes red. He lowered his chin to his thin chest as he pushed past the others.

'Where are you going, our Billy?' Rose asked.

'Out.' He disappeared, Bullseye at his heels.

'You see what I mean?' Rose said. 'He's in an awful way.'

'Leave him be, Mam,' Ewart said. 'Come on then, Maggie, if you're coming. Let's go and talk to Josh, and Mr and Mrs Withers.'

It was Josh who answered the door of number ten, his wary expression turning to one of surprise when he saw his old friend on the doorstep.

'Ewart!'

'Josh.' The two men shook hands, the double clasp the only indication of how close they had once been. 'Look, mate, I don't know if this is a good time, but . . .' Ewart broke off; there was really no need to explain. There was no doubt why he and Maggie were here.

Josh stepped outside, pulling the door closed behind him.

'You want to have a word about Jack, and your father.'

Ewart nodded.

'Will I do? I'm not sure Mam and Dad are up to it.'

The door of the adjoining house opened and Hester Dallimore's head poked out.

'Oh, sorry, I thought that was somebody at my door . . .'

Josh glared at her; Hester was known for her nosiness, and he knew she hadn't thought any such thing. Seeing she was going to get short shrift, Hester withdrew, but left her door wide open. She'd be hiding behind it and listening, Josh guessed.

'Let's go down the garden,' he suggested. 'We can have a bit of privacy there.'

He led the way across the track and around the corner of the block of privies and outhouses. Behind them, the gardens belonging to the Ten Houses stretched away at right angles to the terrace. Long and narrow, they boasted rows of potato haulms, cabbages, parsnips, carrots, and runner beans, with their pretty vermilion flowers growing up tall frameworks of long sticks harvested from the local thickets. Several of the gardens had runs where hens strutted and pecked at the dry soil; one had a pig pen, though it was thankfully right at the far end, so that the unpleasant smells that came from it didn't reach the houses unless the wind was in the wrong direction.

A tiny square of the Witherses' garden, just inside the entrance, had been laid to grass and bordered with hollyhocks, sweet William, and snapdragons. Florrie Withers loved her flowers, even though using the precious space for them was a luxury her neighbours thought she could ill afford, and Gilby had made a wooden bench out of an old piece of fallen tree so she could sit there on fine evenings and enjoy the blooms she tended so carefully. There was room for three on the bench, but Josh indicated that Ewart and Maggie should sit on it, and he squatted down on the grass in front of them. It would be easier to talk that way.

'Well, it's good to see you after all this time, but I wish it hadn't taken this to get you home,' he said, rasping his fingers across his chin, where a dark shadow of stubble was beginning to show itself.

Ewart nodded, grimacing.

'It's a bugger.'

'You're right there.'

It was typical of the way the menfolk talked, hiding their true feelings, Maggie thought,. She could see from the set of Josh's jaw and the bleakness in his eyes that he was feeling the loss of his brother as much as any of them, but he would never put his grief into words, and it was the same with Ewart. They put on a front that was as hard as the coal they hewed.

It wasn't so easy for her, though, and the fact that Josh looked so like his dead brother didn't help. Seen through a blur of tears, it might almost have been Jack sitting there on the grass. Maggie bit down hard on her lip and glanced away, unable to bear it.

But things were about to get even worse. As the men talked about the terrible events of the previous day, Maggie couldn't help but relive it in every nightmarish detail. So long as she'd kept busy she'd been able to banish the darkest of her thoughts to the corners of her mind, though they hung there in a thick, impenetrable fog through which no chink of light could find its way, but now she could no longer escape them.

The men's voices seemed to be coming from a long way off, and she heard only snippets of what they were saying. But when they got around to the subject of the funeral, she pulled herself back from the nightmarish no-man's-land where she had been wandering. This was important. She needed to hear what was being decided.

'Well, we're going to go along with what Fairley suggested,' Josh was saying. 'Truth to tell, Ewart, I don't think there's much option. It's going to have to be a mass grave, whether Fairley pays for it or not.'

'That's what I thought,' Ewart agreed. 'Our mam is saying

Dad's got to be buried as a Catholic, but she's not thinking straight. Trouble is, I don't fancy being the one to tell her why that's not going to happen.'

Maggie frowned, puzzled. What was Ewart talking about? Then the explanation came to her in a blinding flash and she felt the blood leave her face in a rush.

Oh, dear God, it didn't bear thinking about. She wouldn't think of it. She couldn't!

'I've been to see Harry Rogers,' Josh went on. 'Young Frank was another of them that went down. And John Day, too. But I haven't seen Annie yet. I went along and knocked at her door, but nobody answered.'

John Day, from number four. Maggie hadn't realised John was gone too. That made four dead from their rank of just ten houses. And John had a young family – two pretty little girls who always looked as if they'd just stepped out of a bandbox, in their freshly laundered smocks and with ribbons in their fair curly hair. Whatever would Annie do now? This wasn't just Maggie's tragedy. It had torn so many other lives apart too.

'I think I saw her brother going in as I was coming home,' Ewart said. 'If he's there with her, it might be a good chance to have a word. We've all got to stick together on this.'

Josh nodded. 'You're right there. And it's the inquest tomorrow – they're having it in the town hall. I'm going to go and see what they say. Why don't you come with me?'

'I'll do that. Knock the door on your way past.' He got up. 'Are you coming with me to see John's family, Maggie?'

Maggie didn't reply; she didn't even seem to have heard him. She was staring into space, tears misting her eyes. She was unaware of Josh shaking his head at Ewart, mouthing, 'Leave her.'

Ewart nodded, cottoning on.

'I'll come back and let you know what they say. And if they're going to the inquest too.' He touched his sister's shoulder, squeezing it gently. 'I'll be back in a minute, Maggie.'

She came out of her reverie with a start.

'Oh – I've got to get home, Ewart. I've got to help Mam with the washing-up.'

She started to get up, but Josh scrambled to his feet, taking Ewart's place on the bench and pulling her down again.

'I'm sure there's no rush, Maggie. You look as if you could do with a bit of time to yourself. Stay here with me and wait till Ewart comes back.'

For once in her life, Maggie did as she was told.

'Don't upset yourself, Maggie,' Josh said when Ewart had gone.

The minute the words were out, he realised it was a stupid thing to say, but in all honesty, he was at a total loss for words. It broke his heart to see Maggie like this, so white and drawn, as if all the life had been sucked out of her. But what did he expect? She'd lost her father and her fiancé in the most terrible way. Being Maggie, though, she would be steeling herself to be strong for her mother and Billy, pushing her own grief to one side for their sake whilst all the time it was tearing her apart.

'Now that your Ewart's home, he'll take care of everything,' he went on awkwardly.

'He can't bring them back, though, can he?' Maggie's voice was bleak and a little bitter.

'No, you're right there.' Again he thought it wasn't the right thing to say, but words weren't Josh's strong point any more than they had been Jack's.

'Oh Josh, I'm sorry.' Maggie drew her fingers across her cheeks, wiping away the traces of her tears, though he could see they were already seeping out again. 'How can I be so selfish? You've lost your brother too.'

A lump rose suddenly in Josh's throat. He glanced away for a moment, choking it down. When he turned back, only the hard set of his jaw revealed the momentary weakness.

'That's true enough. I wish to God it had been me, not him.'

Maggie reached out and covered his hand with hers.

'Don't say that, Josh. Don't even think it.'

'It's true, though. I do. Our Jack was a good man. Never did anybody a moment's harm. A good son, too, always looking out for Mam and Dad, while I've caused them nothing but trouble. The rotten apple, that's me. Always have been. Ask anybody. No, I should be the one that's gone, not him.'

He fumbled in his pocket for cigarettes and matches, lighting one and drawing on it hard, his eyes narrowed against the curling smoke.

'You and Jack were different, that's all,' Maggie said, her own grief forgotten for the moment. 'That doesn't make you worth any less, and you mustn't think for a moment that it does.'

Josh's lips curled round his cigarette in a wry smile. It was nice of Maggie to say so, but he couldn't believe she meant it.

'Well, it's no use wishing things were different,' he said at last. 'It won't bring our Jack back any more than your Ewart being here can. No, all I can do is make sure I look out for Mam and Dad like he would have done. It won't be the same, I'll never be him, but I'll do my best.'

'I know you will, Josh,' Maggie said. 'And so will I. They would have been my mam and dad too before long, remember.'

Josh took another hard pull on his cigarette, thinking that where Maggie was concerned, at least, Jack had been a very lucky man. Her beauty didn't just go skin-deep, like some.

'If it's any consolation to you, I can tell you that you made Jack very happy when you agreed to marry him,' he said awkwardly. 'Happy – and proud, too. He was over the moon to think you were going to be his wife. That's one thing I'm really glad about.' He grinned sadly. 'I told him he'd drive me mad if he didn't stop whistling "A Little of What You Fancy Does You Good". And he was full of the plans he had to do up that little house you'd been offered. It wasn't in that good a condition, according to what he'd heard – the Scrivens family weren't the fussiest, if you take my meaning. Not that he knew a thing about building work or carpentry, of course, but that wouldn't have stopped him. Nothing was too good for you, Maggie, nor for the family I know he hoped you'd have—'

He broke off, pinching out his cigarette and flicking the butt into a clump of Florrie's snapdragons.

A muffled sob; he turned to look at Maggie. Her hand was pressed over her mouth, her face screwed up and her eyes closed, but the tears were squeezing out again and running down her cheeks.

'Oh Maggie, I'm sorry . . . Now I've upset you again,' he groaned, wondering how he could have been so stupid as to talk about the future that Jack and Maggie had been looking forward to sharing.

'I've got to go.' Maggie got up, half running across the patch of lawn.

'Maggie . . .' He caught up with her as she reached the corner of the block of outbuildings. He had no clear idea of what he intended to say or do, just that he didn't want to let her go like this. 'Look, you're in an awful state . . .'

She stopped, turning back.

'It's all right. I'm all right, honestly.'

But any fool could see that she wasn't. Her voice was thick with tears.

He caught her hand. 'Look, why don't you stay here for a bit? At least until Ewart comes back. He'll look after you.'

Maggie hesitated, like a gazelle poised for flight. Then, without a word, she suddenly turned her face into his shoulder, her free hand clutching his arm as if it were a lifeline.

For a moment, Josh stood stiff and awkward. Taken by surprise and embarrassed, he was unsure what he should do. Like most men, he hated to see a woman cry, and to have Maggie weeping into his shirt front threw him into a panic. Tentatively, he put his arm around her, patting her shoulder gently – somehow it seemed the right thing to do.

'It's all right, Maggie. You cry,' he heard himself say.

And cry she did, her grief, bottled up for so long, bursting from her in a flood. For long minutes she wept, her whole body shaking, and he held her, no longer embarrassed, but only concerned for her. At last the racking sobs softened to hiccups, and she pulled away, looking up at him with eyes that were swollen and red but no longer oozing tears.

'I'm sorry.'

'What for?'

She didn't answer, just gave a little shake of her head, and he pulled a handkerchief out of his pocket.

'Here – dry your eyes.'

She took it, blowing her nose and then balling the square of spotted cotton into her hand.

'Look – you know where I am if you need me,' he said.

'Yes. Thank you.'

She looked up at him again, smiling a faint watery smile that did not reach her eyes, and then she was gone, disappearing round the corner of the outbuildings and lost to his sight.

But the scent of her hair was still in his nostrils, the sleeve of his shirt wet with her tears, and he could still feel the softness of her body pressed against his.

Josh rasped his hand over the stubble that shadowed his jaw, his breath coming out on a long sigh, his thoughts whirling. He could make no sense of the emotion that was churning in his stomach; he only knew it was like nothing he had ever experienced before. Oh, he'd wanted Maggie for a very long time, but he'd told himself it was just a passing fancy. This, though . . . this was different. A fierce, burning desire to protect her, cherish her, make her happy even.

The trouble was, it was all wrong. Maggie was Jack's sweetheart; it was his brother she was grieving for. She'd turned to him because he was the closest thing to the man she'd lost, and if he'd been of some comfort to her he was glad of it. But the way he'd felt when she was in his arms, the way he was feeling now . . . yes, it was just plain wrong.

Josh foraged for his cigarettes and lit another, blowing smoke into the clear evening air, but it didn't seem to help. Might as well admit it, he'd wanted to do more than comfort her. But the admission only made him ashamed and angry.

He'd make damn sure it didn't happen again.

Chapter Eight

Tom Bishop grunted bad-temperedly and pushed his plate away from him.

'I don't know what you'd call that, my girl, but I call it a load of rubbish. There's more gristle than meat on that steak, and you've burned the potatoes again.'

'Oh, what the hell's the matter with you?' Peggy exploded. 'You've been in a filthy mood ever since you got in from work. Nothing's right for you, is it? Your bathwater wasn't hot enough, your beer not cold enough, though I've had it on the marble slab in the larder all day, and now you're moaning about your dinner. You're a miserable bugger, Tom Bishop.'

'And don't you think I've got reason enough? You think I can bloody well forget that you were making a bloody fool of me with that Josh Withers?'

'It was just the once,' Peggy lied.

'You expect me to believe that? Well, like I said before, you'd better not try it again, or you'll be sorry, both of you. And your lover will end up the same as his brother – six feet under.'

A nerve jumped suddenly in Peggy's throat. He'd said it again – more or less the same words he'd used on the evening of the tragedy, when he'd thought it was Josh who had been killed and she'd put him right. It had been niggling away at her ever since Sarah's visit this afternoon. What if Tom was the one who was responsible? Oh, surely he would never do such a terrible thing. But someone had. Someone who had wanted one of the men on the hudge dead. And Tom had got Josh mixed up with Jack, thought it was Josh that had been killed, and had been upset when she'd put him right.

Besides this, she knew Tom – nobody could bear a grudge quite like him, and his ruthless streak was one of the things that had attracted her to him in the beginning, that thrilling feeling that if pushed to his limits, he could actually be quite dangerous.

But this . . . this was unthinkable. Twelve men and boys were dead. Surely – surely – not even Tom would be capable of such a terrible thing? Why, he couldn't even have known for certain that the object of his cold fury would be one of those on the hudge when it went crashing down.

It was young vandals, I expect, she'd told herself. They get up to all sorts these days.

But still the suspicion had lingered like a bad taste that wouldn't go away, and now he'd said more or less the same thing again. And could it be that he was in a bad mood because he'd got rid of the wrong brother?

Peggy glanced anxiously at her husband over her shoulder as she fetched him a slice of fruit cake and a cup of tea. Should she just ask him, straight out, and set her mind at rest? But he wouldn't take kindly to that, whether he was guilty or innocent – it was sure to set off the most terrible row. And in any case, she was apprehensive about what she might learn. What in the world would she do if he admitted it? Her none-too-sharp mind boggled. She'd have to tell somebody, wouldn't she? But oh, the shame of it! A husband who was a murderer a dozen times over!

He wouldn't admit it, of course, even if he was guilty. He'd deny everything, and she'd be none the wiser, still wondering whether or not he'd told her the truth. And if he thought she suspected him, and might turn him in, then perhaps he would do away with her too! A man who could cold-bloodedly send twelve men to their deaths wouldn't think twice about putting his hands around her throat if he thought she was going to send him to the gallows. No, she couldn't ask him outright. But perhaps it wouldn't hurt to mention what Sarah had told her? He couldn't read anything into that, and she'd try to judge his reaction.

'Our Sarah came to see me today,' she said as she put the plate and cup on the table in front of him.

'Oh yes? Wondering why you hadn't turned up on her doorstep with all your worldly goods, I suppose?' Tom said unpleasantly.

Peggy ignored the jibe.

'She told me something awful,' she went on. 'She reckoned they're saying somebody cut the rope on the hudge on purpose.'

Tom spluttered.

'What a load of rubbish! Folk will say anything,' he said dismissively.

'No, I think it's right.' Peggy was trembling inwardly, but she steeled herself to carry on. 'The police are asking a lot of questions, Sarah said. They wouldn't be wasting their time if there wasn't something in it.'

She slipped into the chair at right angles to him, hoping to be able to catch his expression as she spoke, but his head was bent over his plate as he poked critically at the slice of fruit cake.

'It's awful, isn't it?' she prompted him.

'What, this cake? Too right, it's bloody awful. I don't know why you can't make a decent bit of cake. This is as hard as bullets.'

'No, not the cake, you ungrateful beggar. Somebody cutting the rope.'

'Oh, for crying out loud, Peg, I'm fed up with hearing about that bloody hudge!' Tom exploded. 'Can't you shut up about it and let me have my tea, such as it is, in peace?'

'Please yourself.' Peggy got up and headed for the scullery.

Well, she'd done her best and she was still none the wiser. Just because Tom didn't want to talk about it didn't mean a thing. If he'd condemned the sabotage, she'd have felt a whole lot better, but what did she expect? His horrible, callous attitude didn't make him a murderer. He was just a nasty-tempered man who said things to make himself feel important. A nasty-tempered man she'd give anything to get away from. But she honestly couldn't see how. All very well to have planned it, and pretended she could carry it through in the heat of the moment a few days ago. Now she'd had time to think about it, she'd realised it wasn't that easy.

To begin with, she didn't have any money to call her own, nor anywhere to go to, not really. Sarah had made it pretty clear that she didn't want Peggy there – not surprising considering she had such a houseful already – and truth to tell, Peggy wasn't even sure she'd want to put up with all those children for long. There wouldn't be a minute's peace. She wouldn't have a room of her own; she'd have to fit in where she could. And she and Sarah would probably fall out before long – two women in one kitchen was a recipe for disaster. At least here she had this house to herself all day while Tom was at work, and besides . . .

A tiny frisson of excitement prickled in Peggy's stomach, an excitement she hadn't experienced in a long while.

If Tom had done this terrible thing, it must mean he thought ever such a lot of her.

But of course, he hadn't. More than likely it was a gang of

young hooligans, so drunk that they'd thought it would be funny. Or a disgruntled miner who wanted the pit closed. And none of them thinking for a moment that anyone would be killed as a result of their actions..

That had to be it. Didn't it?

As she emerged from behind the outhouses opposite the Withers home, Maggie saw a figure she recognised walking in the opposite direction.

Ewart. Her heart sank. She didn't feel ready to speak to anyone yet. Although she wasn't actually crying now, she still felt weak and shaky, and she knew her eyes must be red and swollen. Really, she didn't want anyone to see her like that, even her own brother; her pride simply wouldn't allow it. Already she was horrified that she'd made such an exhibition of herself in front of Josh.

It would never have happened, she thought, if he hadn't mentioned Jack and how happy she'd made him, and it had been the last straw when he'd talked about the little house that was to be their home, and the plans Jack had been making to make it nice for her and the family they would one day have. Until then, she'd managed to remain so strong. Funny how one little thing could open the floodgates to emotion you'd thought you had under control. It didn't stop her from feeling thoroughly ashamed of herself, but at the time it had been a relief to let go, and certainly Josh had been very kind. She'd never realised before what a gentle side he had hidden beneath that Jack the lad exterior. But what must he think of her? It would have shocked and embarrassed him too when she suddenly fell apart and collapsed in his arms like that.

Now Maggie was desperately afraid that Ewart might say something to set her off again. She wished she could have at least a few minutes to compose herself, but if she turned back, she would most likely run into Josh again, and in any case, Ewart had seen her. It looked as if he had been on the point of going into their house, but now he'd stopped and was waiting for her.

Maggie coughed the last of the tears out of her throat, scrubbed hastily at her cheeks with Josh's handkerchief, which she was still clutching in a damp ball in her fist, and ran a hand over her hair, strands of which were escaping from the pins that were supposed to hold it in place. Nothing out of the ordinary there – her unruly hair was always falling down – but after being mussed against Josh's shoulder, it must be even untidier than usual.

'Did you manage to see Annie Day?' she asked when she and Ewart met outside the door of number six.

Ewart nodded. 'I've talked to her and her brother. They're both in agreement with Josh – it's going to be best to let Sir Montague handle things.' He broke off, looking more closely at Maggie. 'Are you all right?'

'I'm fine,' she said impatiently. 'You'd better go and see Josh. He's expecting you.'

'I'll go in a minute,' Ewart said. 'I want to talk to Mam first, try to get her to see it's for the best. The sooner this is settled, the better.'

'Oh, perhaps you're right.' Maggie was glad that it was Ewart and not her who would have to be the one to explain to Rose that really there was no other option.

In the wee small hours, Maggie woke with a start.

It had taken her a very long time to get to sleep; everything had been going round and round in her head, and her mother's distress at Ewart's insistence that they must go along with the mass burial had upset her all over again. But when she finally did drop off, she'd slept deeply, and she couldn't understand why she was now suddenly wide awake again.

She lay for a moment listening; the house was quiet except for the occasional creak of a settling rafter. Maggie turned over, plumping the pillow beneath her head and pulling the sheet up under her chin, but she couldn't shake the feeling that something was wrong. She wouldn't be able to go back to sleep until she'd satisfied herself that everything was all right.

She pushed back the covers and got up, padding over the rag rug beside her bed on bare feet. Her bedroom door was ajar; it never would close properly, not that Maggie minded that now, though she certainly had in the days when she had been much younger and her brothers were still at home. Across the narrow landing she could hear Ewart snoring gently – whatever had woken her hadn't disturbed him. Oh, she was probably just imagining things. She half turned to go back to bed, but the feeling of misgiving was still there, nagging at her.

And then she heard it. A muffled groan that sounded as if it was coming from downstairs.

Maggie's heart came into her mouth. She hurried along the landing and down the steep stairs that led directly into the living room. The door at the foot was closed, so the staircase was in almost complete darkness, but Maggie knew it so well she didn't need to be able to see where she was going. When she tried the door, though, it wouldn't budge. From the other side came another groan.

'Mam? Mam – is that you?' Alarmed, Maggie pushed at the door again, and managed to get it open just far enough to slide her hand through the gap. She dropped to her knees, feeling along the floor; sure enough, her fingers encountered what felt like the thin cotton of Rose's nightgown.

'Mam!' she called urgently. 'Mam, can you hear me?'

'Maggie?' Rose's voice was weak, tremulous, but just hearing it was a huge relief.

'Yes, Mam, it's me. But I can't get in to you. Can you move at all?'

Rose grunted, then grunted again, but she'd managed to inch herself away from the door a little.

'Keep going, Mam,' Maggie urged, but now Rose was groaning again, a low animal sound that filled Maggie's heart with dread.

'Is it the baby, Mam?' she asked urgently.

For long minutes that seemed like a lifetime to Maggie, there was nothing but the sound of Rose's laboured breathing, building to a crescendo until it died away in a whimper.

'Don't worry, Mam,' Maggie said, forcing herself to sound calm. 'I'll get our Ewart. Just lie still now.'

She scrambled to her feet, but Ewart was already at the top of the stairs. All the commotion must have woken him at last.

'What's going on?' he asked, his voice bleary with sleep.

'It's Mam! She's fallen down – she's on the floor in the way of the door. I can't get in to her.'

'Fallen down?' Ewart repeated, stumbling down the stairs. 'But what . . . ?'

'Just come and help me!' Maggie lowered her voice and added: 'I think she's losing the baby.'

She slid her arm through the gap between door and jamb again; it was definitely wider now.

'Roll over, Mam,' she instructed. 'Can you do that?'

More grunts and breathy groans, then a soft thud, and between them Maggie and Ewart were able to open the door a little further.

'I think I might be able to manage now . . .' Maggie turned

sideways on to the gap – thank goodness she wasn't very big!
– and by pulling in her stomach and twisting her shoulders
was just about able to squeeze through, even as Rose began
gasping again as another pain gripped her.

She took a step inside the room, which was dimly lit by the
first grey light of dawn creeping in at the window. As she put
her foot down, it skidded on the tiled floor. She clutched at the
door to regain her balance, and, glancing down, saw that
the floor was dark with blood.

Her heart lurched. Oh dear God, she'd been right! Mam
was losing the baby.

Rose was lying on her side now, more blood pooling around
her prone frame. Maggie dropped to her knees, feeling the hot
stickiness on her own skin as it soaked through the thin cotton
of her nightgown, and paying it no heed.

'Mam, let's move you a little bit more so our Ewart can get
in . . .'

She waited until Rose's spasm of pain passed, then got behind
her, slotting her arms beneath Rose's and heaving her further
to one side.

Ewart pushed the door fully open and came into the room,
and the look of horror on his face as he took in the grisly scene
told Maggie that he was going to be of little help. This was a job
for a woman – men were useless when it came to anything to do
with childbirth; they always kept a safe distance. But Maggie
wasn't at all confident she could deal with it either. What did
she know? And a miscarriage wasn't even a normal birth.

But surely Mam shouldn't be losing this much blood, even if
she was losing the baby?

'Ewart – get our Billy to go for Dr Blackmore,' she instructed.

But how long would it take for Billy to run the couple
of miles to Dr Blackmore's house? Probably a good twenty

minutes. Then he'd still have to knock the doctor up, and Dr Blackmore would have to get dressed, harness up his pony and trap, and drive all the way over to the Ten Houses. Maggie wasn't sure Mam could wait that long before getting the medical attention she so clearly needed.

'We'd better fetch Dolly Oglethorpe too,' she said. Dolly acted as a midwife amongst other things. Please God she would know what to do.

Ewart dashed up the stairs, but a moment later came clattering down again.

'The little bugger's not there!'

'I could have told you that,' Rose managed between pains. 'It was because of him I fell down the stairs.'

Maggie didn't know what she meant. It made no sense – if Rose had fallen down the stairs, how come she had ended up on the other side of the door, jamming it closed? And where was Billy? But she couldn't waste time wondering about any of it just now. She had other, more pressing matters to attend to.

'Well, if Billy's not here, you'll have to go then, Ewart,' she said decisively. 'Get Dolly to come quick, and then fetch Dr Blackmore.'

'Not the doctor,' Rose mumbled weakly. 'We can't afford . . .'

'Go on, Ewart,' Maggie said, ignoring her. 'And for goodness' sake make haste.'

With a last horrified glance at his mother lying there in a pool of her own blood, Ewart squeezed past and hurried out. As the door closed after him, Maggie thought she had never felt more alone in her life. But somehow, once again, she had to be strong.

'Don't worry, Mam. Everything is going to be all right,' she said consolingly.

And wished she could believe that it would be.

* * *

It was full daylight, a pearly summer morning, before Billy came home.

He trudged along the lane, Bullseye at his heels, head lowered, kicking at small stones in his path. He'd been walking across the fields for hours, but he hadn't been able to escape the blackness in his head, or the ache in his stomach that had been there ever since the terrible tragedy of the hudge.

His dad, and all the others, dead. It was too much to take in. But his body seemed to understand what his mind could not, and wouldn't stop trembling. He couldn't sleep, either. Well, he could fall asleep from sheer exhaustion, but a couple of hours later he'd be wide awake again, with everything going round and round in his head and whirling him with it, a merry-go-round he couldn't get off.

He didn't want to go home, and he didn't want to face Mam. She must have heard him get up, though Ewart, snoring beside him, had not, and had called out of her bedroom window to him as he emerged from the back door. He'd ignored her, and he knew she wouldn't be best pleased about that. But he couldn't stay out for ever. He was hungry – he'd hardly touched his tea last night – and though he wasn't sure he'd be able to eat much now, he had to try. And maybe Mam wouldn't go on at him too much. She had Ewart home now, and Ewart had always been her favourite.

He turned into the track at the back of the rank and was dismayed to see Charlie Oglethorpe sitting on the bench outside number three. He lowered his head, hoping to get past without some sort of confrontation, but as he drew level, Charlie called out to him.

'Where have you been then, Billy the rag man?'

'Nowhere,' Billy muttered.

'Well, wherever it was, you've missed all the fun. Don't you know your mam's been taken bad?'

Billy, who had been trying to sidle past, drew up short.

'What are you talking about?'

'Your mam. Your Ewart came knocking on our door in the middle of the night, and our mam's been up with her ever since. And we've had the doctor here an' all, though he's gone now. But it's something pretty bad if you ask me.'

Every bit of colour drained from Billy's face and for a moment he stared at Charlie in shock. Then, without another word, he turned and began to run homewards along the track.

The back door of the house was ajar; he pushed it open and ran in. There was no one in the scullery, but he could hear voices coming from the living room. He froze, fear rushing through his skinny body in a cold wave, then he crept nervously across the kitchen and put his head round the living room door.

Maggie and Ewart were there, talking in low voices. Of Mam there was no sign.

'What's going on?' he asked timorously.

Ewart looked up and saw him. He rose from the chair, his face like thunder. 'Where the devil have you been, you little blighter?'

'What's happening?' Billy asked again, ignoring the question. 'Where's Mam?'

'What do you care?' Ewart raged. 'This is all your fault, our Billy. What were you thinking, running out like that in the middle of the night?'

'Hush, Ewart. You're only making things worse.' Maggie got up too, crossing to Billy and putting an arm round his trembling shoulders. 'Come and sit down, Billy. I'll make you a nice cup of tea.'

'I'll give him a cup of tea!' Ewart muttered. 'And a bloody sight more besides!'

Maggie shot him a warning look.

'Come on, Billy. Ewart doesn't mean it. You're not to blame.'

'What for?' Billy wailed. 'What have I done?'

Maggie eased him into a chair, and while she fetched him a cup of tea from the pot that was seldom off the hob, she and Ewart told him.

Rose, it seemed, had heard Billy going downstairs and out of the back door at some unearthly hour. She'd opened her bedroom window and called to him, but he'd taken no notice and she'd tried to go after him. In her haste, she'd lost her footing on the stairs and fallen from top to bottom. Somehow she'd picked herself up and staggered into the living room, where she must have fainted, or collapsed, against the door. From the angry swelling on her head, Dr Blackmore had come to the conclusion that she'd cracked it on the tiled floor as she fell, and lost consciousness for a little while. Presumably it had been the racket as she tumbled down the stairs and the banging of the living room door as she fell against it that had woken Maggie.

And thank goodness it had, because of course that had been only the start of it. The bleeding had begun as she lay unconscious, and the labour pains – far too early – had quickly followed.

Ewart had run for Dolly Oglethorpe and Dr Blackmore. Dolly was quickly on the scene, but there was little she could do, and by the time Dr Blackmore arrived, it was all over. Rose had lost her baby, along with a great deal of blood, though thankfully the bleeding seemed to have stopped now.

'She's in a bad way, though,' Maggie said. 'We've got her up to bed, and Dolly is with her.'

Billy's eyes were huge and haunted.

'She will be all right, won't she?' he asked, almost pleading.

'It's touch and go,' Maggie said gently.

She reached out and took her brother's hand. In spite of the warmth in the kitchen, it felt stone cold.

'You mustn't blame yourself, Billy,' she said. 'I know you've taken Dad's death really hard, and you just want to be by yourself sometimes. I feel the same myself. But you weren't to know Mam would come running after you. A fall like that – it could have happened any time. It was just bad luck.'

Billy said nothing.

All very well for Maggie to tell him it wasn't his fault – he knew it was. And if his mother died too, he'd never forgive himself.

Chapter Nine

For the next few days, Rose hovered between life and death. Maggie stayed at home to look after her – although Ewart would be here at least until after the funeral and Billy, ashamed and frightened, was hanging around the house like a wraith instead of wandering off for hours on end, a woman was needed to nurse the desperately ill Rose. She wasn't to put a foot to the ground, Dr Blackmore had said; if she did, he wouldn't be responsible for the consequences, and Maggie made sure his instructions were carried out to the letter.

Her days were filled with emptying chamber pots and washing bedlinen, with making nourishing meals – soups and broths, pies and custards – and running up and downstairs to check on her mother, taking her cups of milk and mugs of locally brewed ale for good measure; Dr Blackmore had said the beer would help her regain her strength and replenish some of the blood she had lost. Maggie was glad of the activity. Exhausted though she was, at least keeping so busy left her little time for thinking, and lent a purpose to her life, filling the awful chasm left by the loss of Jack.

And Rose's incapacity meant that Maggie and Ewart were able to make the decision that Paddy would be buried along with the others in the mass funeral Sir Montague Fairley was arranging. Rose was in no fit state to argue; in fact she seemed to have resigned herself to the fact that that was the way it was going to be.

Clement Firkins, Sir Montague's agent, wearing a black bowler hat, a black tie and a lugubrious expression, had come to discuss the arrangements, but Ewart had taken care of that. Maggie didn't think she could have brought herself to be civil to him. If the hudge had been replaced by a proper cage, none of this would have happened. It was all down to Sir Montague's penny-pinching, and as his agent, Firkins was tarred with the same brush as far as she was concerned.

He had, though, delivered some welcome news. The families of the dead men would be allowed to stay in their cottages, for the time being at least.

'Sir Montague doesn't want to see anyone put out on the street when they are so recently bereaved,' he said, as if that somehow made up for what had happened.

Neighbours called to ask after Rose, and Maggie fielded their enquiries, though she was surprised by the sudden show of kindness. The Donovans had been ostracised and looked down on for so long; now it was as if, with Paddy gone, they were accepted into the community. Whilst she was grateful for the concern, and for the little gifts – a tureen of chicken soup, a basket of loganberries, half a dozen fresh eggs – Maggie, who knew nothing of the beatings Paddy had once inflicted on Rose, was hurt to think that their neighbours had had such a low opinion of her father. He hadn't been a bad man, just a profligate one – already she was forgetting Paddy's numerous faults and remembering only his good points. Not only didn't you speak ill of the dead, you didn't think it either, in Maggie's book, and to her, at least, he hadn't been a bad father.

Once, through the window of her mother's room, Maggie

caught sight of Josh passing the house on the track below, and drew back hastily. The memory of how she'd broken down and wept into his shoulder could still make her blush, a heat that suffused not just her cheeks but her whole body too. Seeing him reminded her that she still had his handkerchief – it was under her pillow. She'd taken it to bed with her the night he'd given it to her. It smelled of him and his tobacco, and she found it enormously comforting. She really must wash it soon and return it to him, but she kept putting it off.

Apart from that one glimpse of him, Maggie hadn't seen Josh at all since that night, and she was surprised he hadn't called in on Ewart. The two had been such close friends; they'd always been in and out of one another's houses in the old days. But she supposed that with Rose so ill, he might feel he was intruding.

He and Ewart had gone to the inquest together, though. It had been held in the town hall the day after Rose's miscarriage, and both men were anxious to hear what the coroner had to say. They hadn't been able to get inside; the hall was so packed with townsfolk, there was no room for them and they'd had to make do with standing on the steps outside and learning what was going on at second hand as reports were passed back through the crowd.

By all accounts they hadn't missed a great deal. Wilfred James, the colliery manager, and Hubie Britten, who had been in charge of the hudge, had both taken the stand and stated that the rope had been in good condition – 'What would you expect them to say?' Ewart snorted derisively – and a detective inspector who had been sent out from Bath to head the investigation testified that it had been severed 'by a sharp instrument'. No evidence had been discovered at the scene as to what that instrument was, no suspect had yet been detained, and enquiries were continuing.

'And much luck they'll have with that,' Josh said disgustedly when word was passed back to them through the crowd. 'We ought to make a few enquiries of our own, if you ask me. Somebody must know something.'

'I wouldn't like to be in the shoes of whoever did it if we do find out,' Ewart said darkly.

'Too true. He'd never live to get before a court of law,' Josh agreed, and some of the crowd around them muttered their agreement. Every last man of them would have liked to have half an hour in a dark alley with the perpetrator of the terrible crime.

Next day Walter turned up as unexpectedly as Ewart had done, and the little house that had seemed so empty when they had both left was suddenly full again, though the mood was sombre, with none of the raucous horseplay Maggie remembered. But having both her boys home seemed to do Rose the world of good – she kept Walter so long at her bedside, wanting to hear all about his wife and children, that Maggie was afraid she'd overtire herself and take a turn for the worse.

On the evening before the funeral was due to take place, Walter was once more sitting with Rose, and Maggie was taking the opportunity to run a mop and duster over the other bedrooms when she heard voices downstairs – Ewart, and a woman's voice, though she couldn't quite make out who it was.

Tucking her cleaning cloth into the pocket of her apron, she went down to investigate.

The door at the foot of the stairs was closed; she pushed it open and had the surprise of her life.

'Cathy!' she exclaimed. 'What are you doing here?'

Cathy was dressed in the black skirt and high-necked white blouse that Mrs Freeman insisted on, but also a stylish little bonnet that Maggie recognised as one of the new stock she'd unpacked the day after the tragedy. The girl must have taken a fancy to it and bought it for herself, Maggie supposed, and she could well understand why she'd been tempted. The bonnet sat well on Cathy's dark curls and framed her pretty face, which was slightly flushed – from the exertion of the walk out to the Ten Houses, presumably.

'Miss Donovan! Oh, Miss Donovan.' Even away from the shop, Cathy couldn't quite bring herself to use Maggie's Christian name. 'Mrs Freeman let me leave early. She wanted either me or Beat to come and see how you are, and I volunteered.'

'And you've walked all this way?' Cathy lived on the other side of town – it would take her a good hour to get home from here.

'Oh, it's nothing,' Cathy said. 'Mrs Freeman's worried about you. We all are. And we miss you too.' She delved into the bag that dangled from her wrist, pulled out a small white box tied with a blue ribbon, and held it out to Maggie. 'These are for you.'

'Oh my goodness!' Maggie recognised the box – it was one of those that Mr Rawlings, the confectioner, used for his finest sweets and chocolates, the ones that were displayed beneath the glass-topped counter. She'd often looked at them longingly when she'd gone into the shop for a quarter of peppermint candy or Everton toffee, but even if she could have afforded it, she'd never have bought them. Expensive bonbons were the sort of luxury reserved for rich folk, or perhaps a special gift for a sweetheart on Valentine's Day. 'Oh Cathy, you shouldn't have!'

'They're from all of us,' Cathy said. 'We thought they might cheer you up a bit . . .' She broke off, blushing. 'Oh, that's a silly thing to say. Nothing is going to cheer you up. But we thought . . . oh, you know what I mean.'

'That is so kind!' Maggie said, overwhelmed.

She untied the blue ribbon and opened the box to reveal the hand-decorated chocolates nestling inside – truffle balls rolled in vermicelli, rose and violet creams topped with scented sugar, fragile fluted chocolate cases filled with something pale and creamy.

'Would you like to try one, Cathy?' she asked.

'Oh no!' Cathy exclaimed, horrified. 'They're for you.'

'I hope I'm allowed one,' Ewart said, his hand hovering over the box.

Maggie slapped it away.

'Certainly not! You heard Cathy – they're for me.'

She put the box down on the table. Of course she'd share the chocolates with Ewart and Walter later, and Rose too if she fancied one, but she wasn't going to let her brother guzzle them now, in front of Cathy. In fact, truth to tell, they were so pretty it would be a crime to guzzle them at all!

'You'll have a cup of tea while you're here, won't you, Cathy?' she offered. 'I'll make some fresh. I expect what's in the pot is all stewed.'

She went off to the scullery, leaving Cathy and Ewart alone, and as she spooned tea into the pot, she could hear them chatting. Cathy even giggled once – at something Ewart had said, presumably. Maggie shook her head, actually smiling herself for the first time in days.

They made a good pair, those two. Ewart was a ladies' man, and Cathy was an incorrigible flirt. She'd do well not to leave the two of them alone for too long.

She put biscuits on a plate, and got out the best china tea set that only ever saw the light of day on special occasions – she didn't want Cathy to think they lived like paupers – then tipped sugar into a bowl and poured milk into the little rose-sprigged jug that matched the cups and saucers. When she carried it all into the living room, Ewart raised his eyebrows and winked at Cathy.

'My, you are honoured!'

'Ewart!' Maggie chastised him.

'I can't drink my tea out of those fiddly little things!' he protested. 'Can't I have my mug like I always do?'

'No, you cannot!' Maggie poured the tea, noticing as she did so that Cathy was looking at Ewart from beneath demurely lowered lids, the exact same way she tempted Horace Freeman when Augusta wasn't looking. Whether it was deliberate where Horace was concerned or whether she did it from habit, Maggie was never quite sure, but she was in no doubt it was deliberate now. And from experience, she knew that the ploy worked without fail; Cathy could twist any man round her little finger, and Maggie didn't suppose Ewart would be any exception.

'I hope you're not getting ideas about my apprentice,' she said when Cathy finally left. 'I should warn you, she's very flighty and she looks at all the men like that.'

'Spoilsport!' Ewart retorted. 'Anyway, surely you know I can look after myself where girls are concerned.'

'Look after the girls, more like!'

'And why not?' Ewart grinned wickedly. 'She's a cracker, I must say. You've kept her well hidden.'

'I've done no such thing! You haven't been here, have you? And she's my apprentice, remember. So just behave yourself where she's concerned,' Maggie said sternly.

'I'm making no promises.' Ewart's hand was straying towards the box of chocolates. 'Can I have one of these now she's gone?'

Maggie sighed theatrically.

'Oh, go on then.'

It was, she thought, the closest things had been to normality since her world had turned upside down. But the darkness was lurking, never far away.

Tomorrow she'd have to stand in the churchyard and watch as Jack and her father were laid to rest.

She didn't know how she would bear it.

Chapter Ten

It was a blur, nothing but a blur of people whose faces she couldn't see. Maggie was aware only of the gravelled path that cut across an expanse of lush grass dotted with centuries-old tombs and gravestones, some ivy-covered and leaning at perilous angles, and a mound of freshly dug earth at the far side of the churchyard marking the spot that had been chosen for the mass grave. She walked as if in a dream, Ewart on one side, Walter and Billy on the other, intent only on holding her head high and her tears at bay. Her pride was, after all, all she had left, and she was grimly determined to hold on to it.

As they reached the graveside, Ewart touched her elbow, urging her to step forward. Rose had not been well enough to attend, and the family had decided that Maggie would take her place as principal mourner.

'It should be you, Ewart,' she had protested. 'You're the oldest.'

But Ewart would have none of it.

'You were his favourite, Maggie. He worshipped the ground you walked on.'

Eventually Maggie had concurred, though she was less than happy to be taking her mother's place. The responsibility of it was daunting, and besides, she would have liked to be in a position to comfort Billy, who hadn't wanted to come at all. But Ewart and Walter had given him a stern talking-to, telling him he must, that not to attend his own father's funeral would be not only disrespectful but downright scandalous.

'If we can come all the way down from Yorkshire, you can walk just down the road, and we'm going to make damn sure you do,' Walter had told him.

So Billy was here, and so, almost, was Bullseye. When they'd set out, the dog had tried to follow and they'd had to tie him with a length of rope to a hook on the wall outside one of the outhouses. Maggie hoped he wouldn't get free; he was something of an escape artist, and the thought of the mayhem he would cause if he came running into the churchyard was just another thread in the nightmare that was clouding her brain and pervading her senses.

The service began – the entire ceremony was to take place at the graveside, since the church, though sizeable, would never have been able to hold so many coffins, so many mourners – and to Maggie that too was a blur. She scarcely heard the time-honoured words and phrases; they seemed to be coming from a very long way off, and the cawing of the rooks in the trees seemed more real than the voices of the vicar, the Methodist minister and the parish priest, who were officiating jointly. But she was glad Father O'Brien was here; at least she would be able to reassure Rose that Paddy had been afforded the ministrations of a Catholic priest.

Sir Montague Fairley said a few words too, though for the life of her Maggie couldn't recall afterwards what they had been. His tribute to the men who had died in his service flowed over her like a fast-moving stream over the stones in its path.

Then, one by one, the coffins were lowered into the gaping hole that had been dug in the green sward. Maggie pressed her hand to her mouth and closed her eyes. *Oh, Dad . . . Oh, Jack . . .* They had spent all their working lives in the dark passages and caverns below the Somerset countryside, but this time there would be no return. This time they wouldn't be coming home for their bath and their tea. This time the darkness would close in on them for ever . . .

A muffled sob, followed by a small commotion behind her, wrenched Maggie out of her reverie. She glanced over her shoulder and saw Billy pushing his way through the mourners gathered three deep around the grave. Walter was making a grab for him, but it was too late. To go after him would have caused even more of a commotion; in the end, Walter had no choice but to simply let him go.

Maggie, usually protective of Billy to a fault, felt a flash of irritation with her younger brother. She knew that in spite of their differences, Billy had taken the loss of his father very hard, but it wasn't easy for any of them. Billy might be only just thirteen years old, but that was no excuse. Sometime he was going to have to begin to grow up; stop behaving like a child and become a man. If only Ewart or Walter could stay to help the transition along! But in a few more days they'd be gone, back to Yorkshire. It would fall to her, Maggie, to steer Billy towards manhood.

'Ashes to ashes, dust to dust . . .'

Maggie forgot all about Billy and forced herself to watch as handfuls of crumbling soil pattered down on a dozen identical coffins.

'Let's move before the mourners start leaving.' Peggy's sister Sarah lifted up her toddler and sat him on the end of the perambulator in which her youngest was fast asleep so that his chubby legs dangled over the side and he could hold on to the handlebars.

The two women, along with a knot of others, had watched the funeral from the path that sloped down into the churchyard from the road above; the service was over now, people were beginning to disperse, and many of them would be heading up this path.

Peggy didn't move. She was craning her neck, trying to catch a glimpse of Josh. She hadn't seen him since the day she'd waylaid him on his way home from work; not surprising, really, given that he'd just lost his brother in the most terrible way. But even if it hadn't been for that, she wouldn't have dared go looking for him; she was too afraid of Tom and what he might do if he found out she'd so much as spoken to Josh. Things had been a little easier at home, and the last thing she wanted was to upset the apple cart again. But if Josh left the churchyard by way of the path where she and Sarah were standing, she could at least offer her condolences – surely no one, not even Tom, should he get to hear of it, could read anything into that.

'Can you give me a hand turning this pram, our Peg? It's awful heavy.' Sarah was struggling, the wheels sticking on the rough ground.

Sighing, Peggy added her strength to Sarah's, and between them they managed to manoeuvre the heavy baby carriage so that it was facing the other way.

Much as she wanted to speak to Josh, it was going to have to wait for another day.

A Wednesday had been chosen for the funeral because all the shops closed at lunchtime, and from a high point in the churchyard where he could easily see and be seen, Reuben Hillman was also watching the burial. He'd chosen the spot for that very reason. It was important to him that the town should know he'd come to pay his respects to those who had died, but he also wanted to be able to see Maggie, and perhaps intercept her when the service was over to let her know that he was thinking of her, and would be only too ready to do anything he could to help.

She hadn't been at work the last few days and her absence had left him bereft. Though of course they weren't in the same shop, just knowing she was on the other side of the dividing wall was a constant excitement to him, and thinking of ways he could get to see her filled his days with a sense of purpose. When he found an excuse to go into the shop next door, her smile was like the sun coming out from behind a dark cloud, lifting his spirits, and even if she glared at him disparagingly, it was better than not seeing her at all. At least it meant she'd noticed him; at least it was communication of a sort. He wished desperately that she would come to realise how happy he could make her if only she would give him the chance. But all that would change now, he felt sure. With Jack Withers gone, the last stumbling block between them would have gone too. As he watched the under-taker's men lower Jack's coffin into the ground, Reuben felt a surge of satisfaction. He felt genuinely sorry for all those other men and boys who had died, but Jack Withers was another matter entirely. No, he couldn't regret Jack's death for an instant. Surely now Maggie would turn to him and the comfort he could offer her?

He looked at her now, standing tall and straight, not shedding so much as a tear. Surely if she'd really loved Jack she'd be weeping now? But she wasn't. It was a very good sign. She'd probably only pretended to care for Jack in order to make Reuben jealous, just as she treated him coolly for the same reason. Girls were known to have some very funny ways, or so he'd heard – he had no real personal experience of them. Yes, that was very likely it.

Suddenly there was something of a commotion at the grave-side – young Billy Donovan was darting between the assembled mourners and making a run for the churchyard gate. For a moment Reuben thought Maggie or one of her brothers would go after him, but they didn't, and the boy disappeared behind the old stone wall that bordered the road beyond. But a man he didn't know did follow as far as the gateway before turning and rejoining another stranger in the shadow of the church porch.

Reuben stiffened, looking at them for the first time. The one who had made to follow Billy was quite tall and lanky. He wore a trilby hat and was clean-shaven, whilst the other, shorter and stout, had a full set of mutton-chop whiskers and sideburns.

Police. Reuben knew it instinctively. He'd heard they had arrived from Bath to investigate, an inspector and a sergeant apparently; several customers who had been into the shop in recent days had said so, and he'd been half expecting them to call in asking questions, though as yet they had not.

'I see the detectives are here,' he said conversationally to two women who were standing nearby.

'Looks like it.' The older of the two women, whom he recognised as the stationmaster's wife, nodded sagely. 'They've come to see who shows up at the funeral, I wouldn't be surprised. They've been round the pits, I hear, asking a whole lot of questions. Even talked to Sir Montague himself!' she added in a reverential tone, as if scarcely able to credit that a mere policeman, even a detective inspector, would dare to question his lordship.

The younger woman – her daughter, Reuben rather thought – was less respectful.

'Well they would, wouldn't they? Seeing as how it's his pit where it happened.'

'Oh, I know, but still . . . They can't think Sir Montague had anything to do with it, can they?'

'You never know. It was common knowledge he wanted the pit closed.'

'No, I reckon it was somebody with a grudge against one of them poor souls . . .'

The two women were talking to each other now, ignoring Reuben.

'Let's just hope they catch the devil who did it,' he said, trying to inveigle his way back into the conversation and make it clear where his sympathies lay. But the women turned their backs, shutting him out.

Reuben moved away a little, pretending not to mind that they didn't want anything to do with him. He should be used to being ostracised; he *was* used to it, but that didn't mean it didn't still hurt. Because it did. It did!

Except that when Maggie was his, he thought, it really wouldn't matter at all.

In many ways, Reuben Hillman was as much of an outcast as Billy Donovan, though the two could scarcely have been more different.

Where Billy was small and skinny, Reuben was plump and podgy; where Billy was red-headed, Reuben's dark hair flopped over a face that never, ever caught the sun and burned scarlet as Billy's did. But the differences ran far deeper than just the physical.

Whilst Billy had often felt the sting of his father's belt or the thwack across his buttocks of the stick used for stirring the washing in the copper, Reuben had been pampered and spoiled. The only child of elderly parents, he was the apple of their eye. He had only to express a desire for something and it was his, whether it be a toy, a sweet treat, or a trip on the train to the seaside. When he was small, his mother always ensured he was dressed in the finest silks and linens in all the latest styles – a large photograph of him, aged about two or three, hung above the mantelpiece in the sitting room of the family home, Fosse Villa. In it he was wearing a corduroy suit and a shirt with a ruffled Vandyke collar and sitting in a vast cane chair in the photographer's studio so that his plump little legs dangled over the edge of the seat. He was staring defiantly at the camera – or at any rate, at the black tent beneath which the photographer had disappeared – and his lips were pursed into a petulant pout. Anyone looking at the picture now could have been forgiven for thinking that Reuben had changed very little in the twenty or so years since.

When he was four years old, Reuben had begun attending his grandmother's dame school, and here too he was singled out for special treatment. Though his grandmother ruled with a rod of iron, and good behaviour was expected of Reuben every bit as much as of the other pupils, it was only natural that she favoured him. When there was talking in class, it was always the boy who sat next to him on the little bench seat behind the double desks who was blamed, even if Reuben had started it. He was chosen more often than anyone else to be ink monitor, and when visitors came to the school he was primed to answer the questions they might ask so that his hand would be the first to shoot up. Had he not been primed, the answers he gave might well have been the wrong ones, and sometimes still were in spite of it, for Reuben was not the cleverest of boys.

All this did nothing for his popularity, but even without it, the other children disliked him instinctively. Spoiled as he was, he was given to temper tantrums when things didn't go his way, turning red in the face and even sometimes throwing himself to the floor, squirming and kicking and punching anything or anyone within reach.

He also had a cruel streak. He liked nothing better than giving one of the other children a sly pinch and making them cry, though if they told on him, he denied it, looking so much the picture of innocence that he was always believed. He kept a beetle in a jar, delighting in its futile efforts to escape, until he tired of it, when he pulled its wings and legs off, one by one, and left the remains in the desk of one of the little girls, sending her into a fit of hysteria when she opened her exercise book and found the black fragments inside. He stole birds' eggs and smashed them, and even tormented a baby sparrow that had fallen out of its nest.

He was no more popular at big school when he started there at the age of nine, though he had grown even more sly and was better able to escape blame for the meanest of his tricks. And when he left to begin an apprenticeship at Horace Freeman's gents' outfitters, Stanley Stone, the assistant assigned to train him, made it abundantly clear that he didn't like Reuben either. Girls spurned his advances, and he squirmed inwardly as he saw them sniggering behind his back. But he told himself they didn't matter. One day he'd have Maggie, and she was the only one who mattered. When Maggie was on his arm, they'd all realise just what they were missing.

He looked at her now, the blind adoration that consumed him welling up in a hot tide. More than anything, he wanted to go over and speak to her, but there were too many people crowded around the grave and he thought perhaps this was not the right moment.

Reuben straightened his jacket, nodded to the two women who were standing beside him, and slipped away. He'd waited long enough; he could wait a little longer. Now that Jack Withers was gone, he had all the time in the world.

* * *

As Maggie turned away from the grave, one face materialised, clear and strong through the blur of her tears.

Josh. He had been standing just a few feet away from her all the time and she had not noticed him, but then Queen Victoria herself could have been there and she wouldn't have noticed. Now her heart leapt into her throat, and with it an overwhelming need that she couldn't explain and didn't try to. Behind her, Ewart was touching her shoulder, urging her to go with him, but she ignored him, taking a step or two towards Josh, as if drawn by a magnet. He didn't seem any more aware of her presence than she had been of his – he was talking to the Rogers family – but as the heel of her boot dug into the soft graveyard turf and she pitched forward, almost cannoning into him, his arm shot out to save her.

Maggie gasped, clutching for a moment at Josh's forearm, rock-hard muscle beneath the sleeve of his dark jacket. All she wanted was to bury her face in his shoulder as she had the night she had broken down in the garden, as if he could somehow miraculously take away all the raw pain that was twisting inside her and the black despair that surrounded her like an impenetrable fog. But of course she couldn't. She mustn't. With an enormous effort she regained control of herself, pulling the heel of her boot out from the turf and straightening up.

'I'm sorry . . . how stupid . . .'

'Are you all right, Maggie?' His hand was still beneath her elbow, steadying her, and his voice was low but urgent.

'Yes. It was just . . . my heel . . .'

For a long moment he looked at her, his eyes dark and narrowed with concern. Then, abruptly, his face hardened and he released her arm.

'Ewart!' he called. 'Can you come and look after your sister?'

Then, without another word, he turned and walked away.

* * *

As Billy came flying round the corner of the rank, Bullseye leapt up, barking excitedly and straining at the length of rope tying him to the outhouse wall. For once, Billy ignored him, running past on legs that were shaking with exertion, so that he thought they would give way beneath him. The dog's barks turned to bewildered and disappointed yelps as Billy ran indoors, and he dropped down on to his belly, his ugly head between his paws on the dirt track, and lay there whining miserably.

Billy ran through the kitchen. His breath was coming in huge painful gasps that racked his thin chest, his lungs burned, and his face felt as if it were on fire. He had run the whole of the way home, eyes blinded by tears but unable to escape the terrible pictures that still danced before his eyes. He thought that he would see the vast open grave and the simple coffins being lowered into it for the rest of his days.

His boots clattered noisily on the stairs, alerting Rose, who had been lying in her darkened room, tormented by the fact that she hadn't been able to attend her own husband's funeral.

'Who's that?' she called sharply.

Billy had been making for the sanctuary of his own room; now he hesitated, pushed open the door of his mother's room and stood there hanging on to the handle for support.

'Billy?' Rose said anxiously. 'What is it?'

Billy didn't answer. He had no breath left, and in any case there was nothing to say.

'Oh, our Billy, come here!'

Rose raised herself on the pillows, holding out her hand to him. With a sob, Billy stumbled across the room and threw himself on to the bed beside her. Her arms went round him, and he buried his head in her breast, knees drawn up, boots depositing bits of churchyard mud and blades of grass on the coverlet. As he sobbed wordlessly, Rose lowered her face to his ginger mop and wept with him.

They would still be there, clinging together, when the others came home.

On the pavement outside the churchyard, a knot of angry men was growing steadily to a rabble. They'd just witnessed an event more shocking than they could ever have imagined, and they wanted someone to blame.

'I vote we get Fairley!' one man yelled, his voice carrying over the general hubbub, and others took up the cry.

'He's to blame, the bugger!'

'Let's set fire to his bloody house!'

'Lynch the bastard!'

The commotion grew, the angry shouts shattering what had been, minutes before, a respectful silence.

Maggie, heading along the path towards the church gateway, felt a prickle of alarm, sharp and uncomfortable, as she approached the swelling band of men. The tide of fury hung menacingly in the air. Never in her life had she seen anything quite like it, and for a moment she hesitated, looking around for Ewart and Walter, but they were nowhere to be seen. Father O'Brien had buttonholed her when the service was over, and they'd gone on ahead, a little ashamed, both of them, that they no longer attended Mass and hadn't made a confession in years.

Maggie didn't often go to Mass either, but Father O'Brien always stopped for a few words if she saw him in the town, and sometimes she wished she was a better Catholic. There was something comforting about the priest, a fatherly demeanour that loved and forgave, and she liked the perfume of incense that clung to his soutane. It stirred memories of childhood, of the little church that had once been a tithe barn, and that had felt to her like a magical place, all glowing candles and ornate statuettes, a warm, welcoming sanctuary where she whispered prayers of her own as well as the ones whose words, though familiar, she didn't understand.

Today she'd wanted to rail at him; to demand to know how his God could let something so dreadful happen. She hadn't, of course – speaking to a priest in that way was something she'd never dare do – and locked in her daze of grief, she'd barely heard what he was saying to her either. But as he squeezed her hand, his grip firm and cool, she'd been surprised to feel a moment's peace amidst the turmoil that was raging inside her, and seemed to see a chink of light in the nightmarish fog that suffocated her.

'I hope we'll see you in church soon, Maggie,' he'd said, and she'd nodded.

'I will come, Father, I promise.'

'I hope so, Maggie. Your faith will sustain you. We'll pray together for the souls of the departed.'

And the doubts and the anger were back. What good would that do? God should have been there for Paddy, and for Jack, and for all the others when the hudge went down. If He was the loving father He was supposed to be, He'd never have let it happen.

Now, though, Maggie forgot the conversation in her anxiety about what was going on in the road outside the churchyard. A mob. It was the only word to describe the angry gathering. She couldn't hear what was being said, but she didn't need to to know that it was serious.

As she reached the gate, she saw to her horror that Ewart and Walter were amongst the ever-growing crowd. Ewart was punching the air with his fist, his lips curled in an uncharacteristic snarl, and Walter's head was thrown back as he added his voice to the swelling chorus.

Idiots! Something very nasty was brewing, and her brothers were part of it.

Maggie's anxiety flared to something close to panic.

'Ewart!' she called urgently. 'Walter!'

They didn't hear her above the furore, but when she began waving frantically, she managed to catch Walter's eye, and he shouldered his way back through the crowd to reach her.

'You go on home, Maggie. We've got business to attend to here.'

'And what business is that?' she demanded.

Walter's jaw was set, his usually mild expression now dark and determined.

'Never you mind. This is man's work.'

His words were almost drowned out by another roar from the mob.

'Are we going to get the bugger, then?' the ringleader shouted.

'We are . . . we are . . .'

'We'll tear him limb from limb . . . bloody Fairley . . .'

'Serve 'un right!'

'Walter!' cried Maggie, horrified, as it dawned on her where this was leading. 'They're not going after Sir Montague, surely?'

'He's got to be taught a lesson he won't forget in a hurry,' Walter grated.

'Oh don't be so stupid! This is asking for trouble!' Maggie had begun to tremble. 'Where's it going to end? You can't get mixed up with this, Walter!'

'We are mixed up, though, aren't we? That bugger killed our dad! And he's going to pay for it.'

'For goodness' sake!' Maggie caught at his sleeve. 'Just stop and think! Do you want to end up in prison – or worse? What about Connie and the children? What would they do then?'

The crowd was growing ever more restless and Maggie's anxiety gave way to sheer blind panic. Men she'd known all her life, peaceable men, had changed beyond recognition so that they were more like a herd of wild animals, and her brothers were amongst them. And Josh, too! Where were the police? Surely it was up to them to put a stop to this? But the only uniform in sight belonged to Will Love, the local sergeant, and he was skulking on the pavement on the opposite side of the road, unwilling, she supposed, to take on thirty or more opponents who were all fighting mad. And who could blame him? He wouldn't stand a chance on his own. If he tried to stop them, mad as they were, they'd most likely turn on him. They'd see him as the enemy, part of the same conspiracy as Sir Montague himself. The only person who could persuade them was one of their own, someone who'd shared their loss . . .

It came to her in a flash. She'd lost her father and her sweetheart, the two most important men in her life. Would they listen to her? She wasn't at all sure they would; they appeared to be beyond reason, and the thought of trying to make them see sense terrified her. But someone had to stop them from doing something most of them would later bitterly regret, and which could only end badly. She must at least try.

Maggie turned and ran back into the churchyard, up a grassy bank to a spot directly above the mob on the pavement below.

'Listen to me!' she cried. 'Listen, will you?'

At first she didn't hold out much hope of being heard, but when the men saw her there on the wall above them, arms outstretched like an avenging angel, they fell silent one by one, gawping at her in amazement.

'What do you think you're doing?' she cried, taking advantage of the moment's stunned silence. 'You've gone crazy, all of you!'

'We'm going to give Fairley what he deserves!' a voice yelled back from the crowd. 'He's killed twelve men and boys, and he's going to pay.'

'He didn't kill them!' Maggie shouted back. 'He wasn't the one that cut the rope. And even if he had, this isn't the way to get justice. If you do this, you're no better than him.'

'No, but we'll feel better!' someone called, and another voice, one that Maggie recognised, shouted: 'He killed your pa, Maggie. Just remember that! And he killed our Frank too. I'll swing for him, so help me.'

It was Harry Rogers, usually one of the gentlest of men, mad now with grief and rage.

'You want your wife to lose you as well as Frank?' Maggie cried. 'She will if they hang you. What good would that do anybody? You can't take the law into your own hands. You've got to leave it to the police to catch whoever did this terrible thing.'

'They'm as useless as a chocolate fire dog!' one wag yelled. 'If we wait for them, we'll be waiting till kingdom come.'

'But at least they won't lynch the wrong man!' Maggie was shaking from head to foot, her hands balled to fists in the folds of her skirt, but somehow she managed to keep her voice steady. 'I want to see someone punished as much as you do, Mr Rogers, but this isn't the way. Your Frank wouldn't want it any more than my dad or Jack would. And neither will you when you've calmed down. Look, we've only just laid them to rest. Let's show them some respect, at least for today.'

She paused for breath, not sure whether she was doing any good or not. To her, the men looked as angry and dangerous as ever, all snarling faces and bunched fists. A ripple was passing through the mob as they looked from her to one another and back again, and their muttering made a low growl, like the tide filling a cliff cavern.

Then one voice rose above the rest. 'She's right, lads.'

It was Josh who spoke, Josh who was elbowing his way out of the crush, running through the church gateway and up the bank beside her. The men fell silent as he leaned forward, one foot on the stone wall.

'She's right. It's no good going after Fairley. He's a bastard, yes, I know that, but he's not the one who did this. We should be trying to find out who did, not ending up in a prison cell for arson or murder. That'll do no one any good. Let's all calm down and talk about this another time, when we're thinking straight.'

The muttering was quieter now, and some of the men were nodding, their faces still transfigured with emotion, but no longer the crazed fury of a few moments before. A few dropped their chins to their chests, beginning to feel a little ashamed, perhaps, that they had been carried along on the wave of madness.

'Prince of Wales tonight, lads,' someone shouted.

'Tomorrow,' Josh called back. 'We should be with our families tonight.'

To Maggie's enormous relief, the worst seemed to be over. Already the crowd was thinning out, and at long last Sergeant Love came strutting across the road, standing there ramrod straight with his hands behind his back as the men broke away in twos and threes and dispersed.

'Oh Josh, thank you!' she whispered. Her knees felt weak now, as if they would no longer support her, and the tremble she'd managed to keep out of her voice when she had been addressing the mob refused to be controlled any longer. 'They'd never have listened to me.'

'They *were* listening to you. You were marvellous, Maggie,' he said.

She shook her head, still unable to believe she had dared address a mob of men baying for blood. 'I had to do something! If you and Ewart and Walter had ended up in prison, or worse . . . Oh, it doesn't bear thinking about.'

'It's time to get you home now,' Josh said gently.

'Maggie, my dear . . .' Father O'Brien was approaching; presumably he'd seen what was happening from the far side of the churchyard and was now coming to offer his support. 'That was a very brave thing you did. Your father would have been proud of you.'

'Oh, I don't know about that . . .'

'He *was* proud of you,' Father O'Brien insisted. 'Very proud. Do you know what he said to me once? "I've done a lot of wrong things in my life, Father, but there's one thing I hope will help to balance the books, and that's our Maggie. I can't be all bad, can I, if I can get a daughter like Maggie."'

Maggie felt her eyes filling with tears.

'Thank you, Father.'

She turned away. Ewart and Walter were standing awkwardly on the path, waiting for her.

But of Josh there was no sign.

Josh was heading for home as if the hounds of hell were on his heels. He overtook little groups walking on the pavement by keeping to the road, and spoke to no one. His head was bent against a stiff breeze that had blown up with a smattering of rain in it; his hands were balled to fists in the pockets of the dark coat, a size too small for him, that he'd borrowed so as to be suitably dressed for his brother's funeral. Anger and confusion were boiling inside him, fermenting into a potent mix that was driving him crazy – anger at the senseless deaths of a dozen men and boys, his own brother among them, that had made him join the mob baying for Fairley's blood, and confusion that was all down to Maggie.

What in the devil's name was she doing to him? He hadn't been able to get her out of his head since the night she'd wept in his arms, and when he'd seen her standing up there on the churchyard wall, daring to defy the furious gathering, the impulse to protect her had been overwhelming.

He could see her now through the red mist that clouded his eyes, her pretty face frightened but determined, her hands bunched in the folds of her skirt, that wayward curl escaping from its pins. Dear God, he wanted her, wanted her so badly it was a physical pain deep in his gut. But at the same time he felt heavy with guilt that he should feel this way about his dead brother's sweetheart when he'd just watched his remains laid to rest. Josh strode out along the road that would take him back to the Ten Houses in an attempt to exorcise the demons that tormented him. But the images of Maggie and of Jack were still there, and the turmoil inside him refused to be stilled.

Chapter Eleven

As the summer wore on, a certain degree of normality slowly returned to High Compton, or at least to those not directly affected by the tragedy. The Whitsun Fair, held each year in the Glebe Field, had been cancelled as a mark of respect, but the horticultural show, with a marquee provided by Farmer Barton and a new so-called 'Fur and Feathers' exhibition, went ahead – too much effort had gone into organising it to allow it to be cancelled. In July, a circus came to the town, and the same people who had watched the mass burial from a distance lined the High Street as the parade of horses, camels, jugglers and tumblers, led by a gilded coach, passed by. The annual competition for the best allotment went ahead, hotly contested as usual, and marred only by a spate of mysterious blight that ruined the cabbages and runner beans being grown by several of the favourites among the contenders. Suspicions ran high as to the identity of the culprit – weasly Sam Higgins, who was pipped at the post each year for the winner's trophy – but nothing could be proved, though there were many dark grumblings when Sam was awarded the cup for the first time ever.

There had been no more success in finding out who was responsible for severing the hudge rope either. At one time there had been rumours that Scotland Yard was being called in, but it

158

hadn't happened, and the detectives from Bath were seen less and less often going about their enquiries in the town and surrounding districts.

'What d'you expect? 'Twere only miners killed,' George Parfitt said bitterly when the regulars discussed it in the Prince of Wales. ''Twould have been a different story if 'twere one of the Fairleys in their grave,' and the others huffed their agreement into their ale. But there was no more talk of taking matters into their own hands. Even the hotheads amongst them had come to realise that mob action against the pit owner would do no good, and would only bring down more trouble on the stricken community.

Some of the younger generation, though, were less restrained – Frank Rogers and the other lads had been their pals – and there were one or two nasty incidents. Toady Griffin, the village idiot, was set upon one night as he walked his pet goat through the town, and there was a fracas when a gang of youths attacked a family of tinkers who had set up camp in a farmer's field. But no arrests were made, the perpetrators were given a dressing-down by Sergeant Love – who, truth be told, had every sympathy with them – the tinkers moved on, and Toady went home to nurse his bruises.

For a while at the end of July and the beginning of August, talk turned to the general election that was being held, but it wasn't of any great interest, as everyone knew the Tory candidate would get in again. Though the miners detested the Tories to a man, they held little hope of ousting him in favour of the Liberal candidate – their constituency, Somerset Northern, was a rural one, and everyone knew that the landowners would make sure their man was returned. And soon there was another topic of conversation to excite their interest – the FA Cup had been stolen from a shop window where it was being displayed by a victorious Aston Villa team. Who could have taken it, and whether it would ever be found, became the burning question of the moment – it seemed the Birmingham police were having no more luck in recovering it than the Somerset force were in discovering the identity of the murderer of twelve men and boys.

Slowly life was returning to normal, and it was only the families of those who had died who were still trapped by the consequences of that terrible day back in early summer.

Ewart and Walter had, of course, returned to Yorkshire after the funeral, but they came back, both of them, over the August bank holiday. Rose, Maggie and Billy had been too much on their minds for them to be able to even contemplate not making the long journey home when they had a precious day off, and Connie was very understanding; she'd lost her own father to the miners' lung disease, pneumoconiosis, a few years earlier, and remembered only too well how much emotional support her mother had needed – and her father's health had been failing for a very long time. Rose would have had no chance to prepare herself for her loss, and on top of that she'd suffered a miscarriage and was, according to Maggie's letters, still suffering from the after-effects.

'Of course you must go to Somerset,' she said to Walter. 'We'll be fine. There's an outing to Scarborough on the Monday. I can still go on that and take the children – there'll be plenty of folk I know going.'

'If you're sure . . .' Walter was torn; Connie was near her own time, with the new baby expected in just a few short weeks.

'I'm sure.' Connie was a capable Yorkshire lass, and her sunny, stoical nature meant that very little fazed her. 'Look, if your mam's still poorly, why don't you bring her back with you for a bit? The change might be just what she needs. Especially spending time with Jimmy and Edie. And another woman in the house . . . well, she'd be able to help out when the little one comes, if she's fit, wouldn't she? I wouldn't say no to that.'

Walter was surprised. Big-boned and wide-hipped, Connie sailed through pregnancy and childbirth, and generally declined all offers of help, even from her own mother. But he was pleased, too; he felt he'd neglected Rose since he'd uprooted to Yorkshire, and the offer was typical of Connie's generous heart.

When he found Rose as frail and poorly as Maggie's letters had suggested, he put the idea to her, and to everyone's surprise, she didn't take much persuading.

'It would be nice to see the children, and the new baby,' she said. 'But what about Billy? I've got to be sure he'll be all right.'

'Don't worry about Billy, Mam,' Maggie said swiftly. 'I can look after him. And he'll have a proper job soon anyway, I hope. That should be the making of him.'

She had managed to find Billy some casual labouring, helping Farmer Barton with the harvest, and she had high hopes of him being taken on permanently; she'd played the sympathy card for all she was worth when she'd gone to talk to the farmer, and he hadn't rejected the suggestion out of hand.

So it was decided. Rose would go to Yorkshire for a bit of a break, a couple of weeks, she said, but no date had been decided upon for her return.

Ewart, Maggie rather thought, had had a dual motive in coming home for the August bank holiday. She had the feeling that he was rather sweet on Cathy, her apprentice, and was in no doubt at all that Cathy was sweet on him. She often asked after him, and when she heard he was coming to visit, there was no mistaking the way her eyes lit up.

'Really?' she breathed excitedly.

Maggie bit back a smile. 'I suppose you'd like me to invite you for a cup of tea while he's here,' she said wryly.

A pink flush rose in Cathy's cheeks.

'Oh . . . I didn't mean . . .'

'Get away with you!' Maggie retorted. 'You know very well you did. I should warn you, though, our Ewart is a bit of a one with the girls, but he enjoys his freedom too much to take any of them seriously.'

'Well, I don't want to get serious about anybody either,' Cathy said quickly. 'I'm enjoying myself just as I am, thank you very much.'

That was certainly true, Maggie thought. Cathy's list of conquests was a long one, and she enjoyed keeping as many of them as possible on a string. But she seemed to be taking more interest in Ewart than in any of the others.

'So, are you going to come and see me over the holiday or not?' Maggie asked, and again saw that telltale sparkle in Cathy's eyes.

'I might. You never know.' Her enigmatically pursed lips curved into a broad smile. 'Thanks, Maggie.'

And of course, she did come, on the Sunday afternoon. Ewart was sitting on the bench outside the door, smoking, and the first Maggie knew of Cathy's arrival was when she heard voices. She'd been in the scullery, washing up the dinner things, and when she poked her head out, she could see that the two of them seemed to have picked up where they'd left off last time, flirting outrageously. She told Cathy she'd be with her in a minute, when she'd finished scouring the pans, and left them to it.

'Who's that our Ewart is talking to?' Rose had been upstairs packing some of the things she'd need for her visit to Yorkshire, and had heard the giggles floating in through the open door.

'It's Cathy, my apprentice. She's supposed to have come to see me, but . . .' Maggie lowered her voice, 'that's just an excuse. It's Ewart she's come to see really.'

'Oh, our Ewart!' Rose shook her head. 'He'll never change. Whatever are we going to do with him?'

There really was no answer to that. By the time Maggie ventured out to greet Cathy properly, it seemed arrangements had been made, and she and Ewart were going to meet that evening. There would only be the one occasion, though – Ewart and Walter had to head back to Yorkshire the next day so as to be ready for work on Tuesday morning. But they made the most of it, Maggie guessed – it was very late that night before Ewart came home, and when she arrived at the shop after the bank holiday, Cathy looked pleased with herself.

'I take it you enjoyed yourself with our Ewart,' Maggie said.

'Mind your own business!' Cathy returned pertly, and, turning away with a smile, Maggie did.

The house was quiet and empty again now with not only the two boys gone, but also Rose, but Maggie didn't mind that. She'd been so concerned about her mother, it was a relief to have only Billy to worry about, and he seemed to be much happier. Not that Billy was ever *happy* exactly, but at least he was behaving more normally, and seemed to be enjoying working on the farm.

At least the terrible tragedy had saved him from having to go underground as a carting boy, Maggie thought one day as she watched him go off along the rank with Bullseye at his heels, and was instantly horrified that she could have thought such a thing. But perhaps it was the only way to look at the blows life dealt you. To try and find a silver lining made the unbearable just that little bit more bearable, just as she believed you should always look for the good in folk, however bad they seemed to be.

It was Maggie's way. It was what helped her to survive.

The hot and often thundery purple days of August turned to the sapphire blue of September and the first yellows and ochres of October, and still Rose remained in Yorkshire. It was unlike her, Maggie thought, to stay away from home for so long – in all her life she couldn't remember a time when her mother had been absent for more than a day; perhaps to Weston-super-Mare or Weymouth. But she guessed that Rose, still weak and sickly, was dreading returning to the oppressive atmosphere of tragedy and loss, and was, hopefully, enjoying her grand-children. Connie had given birth, as easily as always, to a little girl they'd named Eva, and when she was well enough, Rose was able to help out with her and with the other two little ones. The new life must be a bright spot in the darkness for her, even though she had lost her own baby – which, sad as it was, could only be for the best in the long run, Maggie thought. Carrying a baby to full term, delivering it and then having to nurse and raise it would have been more than Rose's outworn body could have coped with.

Billy continued to seem much happier. Farmer Barton had taken him on now as a permanent hand, and much to Maggie's surprise, she hadn't had to rouse him one single morning so far to get out of bed and off to work; he was often out of the house before she woke herself, and didn't get home until darkness fell. She didn't even have to make him snap – the farmer's wife, who perhaps felt sorry for him, gave him a hunk of bread and cheese each day for his dinner, often accompanied by a spoonful of her spicy home-made pickle.

Maggie's days fell into an ordered routine. Sometimes the

grief caught up with her, a thick, suffocating cloud, and she would burst into tears for no apparent reason, crying simply because she wanted – needed – to cry. But for the most part she struggled on as she always had done, strong and stoical.

The anxiety that Sir Montague might at any time tell her she had to vacate the house was a constant niggle at the back of her mind, but with the closure of Shepton Fields, quite a few miners had left the district to find work further away, and consequently there were a number of houses empty or about to be vacated. Maggie paid the rent out of her meagre wages and hoped it would keep Sir Montague satisfied for the time being at least.

As for Josh, she had the feeling he was avoiding her, but that was all right by her. She was still embarrassed at having broken down on his shoulder that evening back in the early summer, and guilty at the treacherous feeling he had evoked in her. It was so disloyal to Jack, she thought. But that didn't stop the pang of longing when she caught a glimpse of him, a longing that quirked in her stomach and tingled in her veins before she was able to stamp on it with fierce determination – and shame. And she still hadn't returned his handkerchief either. The fact that it remained under her pillow was her guilty secret, the one little comfort she couldn't bring herself to give up.

She wasn't thinking of any of these things, though, when she left the shop one Saturday evening towards the beginning of October. Saturday was always the busiest day of the week; it was market day in nearby Hillsbridge, and people who had spent the day there often called into Augusta Freeman's drapery shop to make some small purchase on their way home. It wasn't unusual for it to be late before Maggie could escape, especially since everything had to be tidied away before she and the other assistants could leave.

The nights had begun to draw in, and it was already dark when Maggie, Cathy and Beat parted company in the centre of town. Light was spilling out from the doorway of the alehouse further up the street, but otherwise the windows were in darkness and had been for some time. Even the gents' outfitters had been closed for an hour or so – Horace Freeman was less dedicated than Augusta, and in any case not many men wanted to buy a shirt or a pair of socks on a Saturday evening – and Maggie was glad of it.

When the two shops closed at more or less the same time, Reuben had taken to waylaying her, walking with her, even, though he lived in quite the opposite direction. She had the uncomfortable feeling that he thought he stood a chance with her now Jack was gone, and she'd done her best to discourage him, but it wasn't easy without being outright rude, and outright rudeness didn't come easily to Maggie, especially since Reuben was, to all intents and purposes, being nothing but kind and solicitous. 'I'm just keeping an eye out for you, Maggie,' he would say when she told him she was perfectly safe walking home alone.

In any case, she actually felt a little sorry for him – he seemed to have no friends – and guilty, too, that he was so besotted with her, as if it was her fault.

As she walked up the street, the familiar noises of the alehouse floated out into the sharp chill of the evening air – the tinkling of the barroom piano belting out music hall favourites, and a cacophony of voices, some singing along to the piano, some trying to make themselves heard above the general hubbub within. To Maggie's dismay, a few people had spilled outside, and some kind of argument seemed to be going on. She hastened her step, anxious to get past as quickly as she could – the alehouse customers were known to be a rowdy crowd, who could become quarrelsome as well as merry, and neither would she put it past them to make a nuisance of themselves when they saw her, a girl out alone, at this time of night. Head held high, not so much as glancing in their direction, she marched past, and to her relief the men seemed too engrossed in their argument to notice her. But her heart was beating a little faster than usual, all the same, and when, just around the corner, an all-too-familiar figure emerged from one of the darkened doorways and planted himself directly in her path, Maggie's relief turned to annoyance.

Reuben Hillman. He should have been long gone. But no, here he was, waylaying her again.

'For goodness' sake, Reuben!' she snapped, her patience with his antics finally exhausted. 'What are you doing still here?'

Reuben smirked.

'Waiting for you, of course! I thought Mrs Freeman was never going to let you go.' He held out a little box, similar to the one Cathy had brought as a gift when Maggie had been off work nursing Rose, though smaller. 'I got these for you.'

'Chocolates.' Maggie's heart had sunk even further. 'Reuben, you shouldn't have. I don't want you buying me presents.'

'But I wanted to!' he protested. 'Cathy said you really like chocolates, and I thought they'd cheer you up. Take them, please!'

Maggie continued walking, refusing to so much as touch the box he was holding out to her.

'Thank you, but I can't accept them. This has got to stop, Reuben. It's getting beyond a joke. You must realise I'm just not interested in you, and a box of chocolates isn't going to change that.'

'But Maggie—'

'No!' She stopped, turning to face him. 'I'm sorry, but I don't want your chocolates, and I don't want you. Now, will you kindly stop bothering me?'

'But I just want to look after you, Maggie,' he said, sounding hurt. 'We're meant for each other, you and me. Don't you see? You're all alone now that Jack's gone, and so am I . . .'

'Haven't I made myself clear, Reuben?' Maggie exploded in exasperation. 'Just go away and leave me alone!'

For a moment he recoiled and froze, almost as if she had physically hit him. Then his hand shot out, grabbing her by the arm. His face had changed, the silly smile gone now, fleshy lips curled back from bared teeth in an expression that was almost feral.

'You can't treat me like this, Maggie,' he hissed. 'All I want is to make you happy. It's all I've ever wanted. You must know that.'

'I really don't care what you want, Reuben,' Maggie said staunchly, though she was beginning to be very frightened.

'Don't be like this!' Reuben's fingers bit into her arm. 'I can give you the sort of life you could only dream about before. Far more than that Jack Withers ever could. He's dead now, and good riddance. Don't you see, there's nothing now to stop us from being together.'

Maggie's fear began to turn into outright panic. She was seeing a side of Reuben she'd never seen before – in just a few short moments he had changed from a pathetic, grovelling creature into a monster who was capable of anything in the pursuit of his twisted desires.

Could it have been him who had cut the rope? To free her, as he seemed to see it, from her commitment to Jack? In that moment Maggie wouldn't have put anything past him.

'Let me go, Reuben!' She tried to snatch her arm away, but Reuben was holding her too tightly. He did drop the box of chocolates, though – it fell open as it landed on the pavement, and expensive bonbons rolled out into the gutter, but neither of them noticed.

'I love you, Maggie!' He was holding her fast now by both arms, pulling her towards him and at the same time pushing her back against the rough stone wall of the shuttered shop. She smelled sweat and carbolic soap and tried to twist away again, but his hands slid up so that they circled her throat and his moist, fleshy lips came down hard on hers, silencing her cry of protest. In vain she tried to push him away.

'I want you, Maggie! I've wanted you for so long!' he groaned, breathing hard. 'And now there's nothing to stop us being together. Nothing!'

His hand was on her breast now; this time she knew she was not imagining it. And he was trying to bunch up her skirts!

A burst of raucous laughter and raised voices carrying on the still night air reminded Maggie that they were only yards away from the alehouse and the men who'd been standing on the steps outside. She had been nervous about passing them; now anything, anyone, was less threatening than this horrible monster who was assaulting her. Gathering what little breath she had left, Maggie screamed, but if the men did hear her over the racket of the Saturday-night revelry, no one came to her aid.

Reuben was pressing himself against her now, and the horror of it galvanised Maggie. As he drove her back against the wall, his face close to hers, she lashed out with her teeth, catching his ear lobe and biting as hard as she could. Reuben sprang back, squealing in pain, and with a little more freedom of movement Maggie was able to deliver a hard kick to his shin before bringing her knee up to catch him between his legs – when a girl had three brothers, she knew exactly where it would hurt most.

Reuben doubled up, groaning and clutching at himself, and

Maggie shoved at him with both hands. He toppled over in a heap on the pavement, and she squeezed past him and began to run.

Along the road she fled, terrified that he might recover himself and come after her, out into the quiet dark countryside, running, running until her breath gave out and her legs were quivering with exhaustion. She slowed, gasping, looked over her shoulder, and then, although the road was deserted, forced herself to begin to run again. She was sobbing now, tears of fright and shame blurring her eyes, and a stitch throbbed in her side, but still she kept going, more slowly but just as frantically.

Oh Jack, Jack! Where are you? Jack, please, I need you . . .

He'd been there once before when Reuben had been bothering her, but he wasn't here now, and he never would be again.

Just when she thought she would never reach it, the lane that led to the Ten Houses was there on the left-hand side of the road. Staggering now, Maggie turned into it, and then on to the track between the rank and the outbuildings. The door of number six was closed but not locked. Maggie thrust it open and ran into the scullery, where she collapsed, weeping, against the stone sink.

'Maggie?' Billy appeared in the doorway, looking puzzled and concerned. 'Whatever is the matter, our Maggie?'

Maggie didn't answer. She sank slowly to the floor, knees drawn up, arms wrapped around them. The tears had begun to flow in earnest now. She buried her face in her skirts, and great shuddering sobs shook her body as she wept as she could never remember weeping before.

Billy stood staring helplessly down at his sister. He'd never seen her in such a state before. She was always so strong. The one who looked out for him. To see her like this frightened the life out of him – he felt as if the ground was shifting under his feet, everything solid in the world around him dissolving.

'Maggie! What's wrong with you?' he asked desperately.

Maggie didn't even seem to hear him, and her awful sobs filled the tiny scullery, making Billy want to cry too. He could feel his chest tightening with panic.

If only Mam were here! Or Ewart, or Walter. But they weren't. They were miles away, in Yorkshire, and he was on his own.

'Stop it, Maggie!' he begged tearfully.

Still Maggie took no notice, and Billy's panic rose until it was choking him. She wouldn't want anyone outside the family seeing her in such a state, he knew, but he couldn't leave her like this. He had to get help, or he didn't know where it would end.

Beside himself, Billy ran out on to the track behind the houses, looking wildly first one way then the other. Should he call Dolly Oglethorpe? But he hated going to the Oglethorpes', in case Charlie was there. He still avoided Charlie whenever he could.

It came to him in a flash. Josh Withers. Josh was the next best thing to Ewart and Walter. Josh would know what to do.

His breath coming in shallow little sobs, Billy ran up the track towards the Withers home.

Chapter Twelve

It was unusual for Josh to be at home on a Saturday evening; Saturday evenings were for a walk out with a young lady or a drink with your mates. These last months he'd done both, and enjoyed neither. Truth to tell, he was sick to death of the aimless small talk the men engaged in over a pint of ale, and sick to death of trying to pretend interest in a young lady. He'd romanced several – Edie Vranch, who worked in the glove factory; George Parfitt's niece, Polly, and a girl he'd met in Bath when he and some of the other lads had ventured further afield for a night out. But he couldn't work up any enthusiasm for any of them. He went through the motions, even enjoyed himself as far as it went, but afterwards there was nothing but emptiness and dissatisfaction and a restlessness that made him feel as if he'd sat down on an anthill. To make matters worse, it wasn't easy to get rid of them. Josh couldn't understand why it was he seemed to attract women like a jam jar attracts wasps – he didn't think he was that good-looking, and he certainly never went out of his way to charm the girls as some blokes did. And yet there always seemed to be one or another throwing herself at him and trying to cling on.

At least Peggy Bishop seemed to have realised he'd meant it when he said their fling was over, and he was very glad of that, but the others . . . he only had to walk out with them once or twice, maybe steal a kiss, and they acted as if the next step was a ring on their finger.

Josh felt bad about it. He didn't want to hurt or upset anyone and he certainly didn't want to lead them on. The fact of the matter was he just wasn't interested. He did wonder if the fact that he was still mourning Jack had something to do with it, but deep down he knew it was more than that. Josh had never been one of life's deep thinkers, but you didn't have to be to work out the reason.

Maggie.

He tried to avoid her whenever he could, but living in the same terrace of houses it was impossible not to catch sight of her from time to time, and every time he did, Josh felt the same kick in his stomach, the same stirring of his blood, the same quickening of his pulse. And afterwards . . . afterwards she was there in his head and in his heart and nothing he could do would banish her. Useless to tell himself to forget her, she wasn't for him. Not even the guilt that made him hate himself for envying the brother he was grieving for, and the unshakeable feeling that he was somehow betraying him, could stop the way he felt about Maggie. Love wasn't a word that figured in Josh's vocabulary, but he didn't have to put a name to it to know how he felt.

Nobody could hold a candle to Maggie, and he couldn't imagine they ever would. Perhaps eventually he'd meet a girl he liked well enough, settle down and raise a family, but she wouldn't be Maggie. Never Maggie. And for the moment, the very idea made his stomach clench and his hackles rise. One day, perhaps, he'd feel differently, but that day was a long way off.

That Saturday evening in October, Josh hadn't even thought

of going out. Instead, he'd got down to a few odd jobs that needed doing – a strut in the back of one of the kitchen chairs had come loose and needed repairing, and while he had his tools out, he'd fixed the larder door that had dropped so it dragged across the flagstone floor. Then he'd settled down to spend some time working on the candlesticks he was carving out of a nice piece of oak he'd picked up.

A carpenter by trade, Josh loved wood: the smell of it, the feel of it beneath his hands, the way he could whittle it and plane it and even polish or stain it if he wanted when he'd finished fashioning it. He'd made a small table with two shallow sliding drawers that he was secretly very proud of, and a little bookcase, but as the Withers family didn't own many books beyond the family Bible, the shelves were more or less empty. At least there would always be a use for candlesticks, and if nothing else, they could sit on the top shelf of the bookcase and fill the empty space.

Engrossed in what he was doing, Josh wasn't best pleased to be disturbed by the hammering on the back door. Gilby was out for a Saturday-night pint as usual, and Florrie had gone to bed with a sick headache, so there was nothing for it but for Josh to answer the door himself. He laid the candlestick and his tools carefully on the sheet of newspaper that was protecting the kitchen table and pushed back his chair, but before he got even as far as the scullery, the hammering began again.

'All right, all right! I'm coming!'

He opened the door, and was surprised to see Billy Donovan on the doorstep, his hand already raised to knock again.

'Billy! For goodness' sake! You'll bang the door down in a minute!'

'Oh Josh, can you come along to ours?' Billy appeared to be on the verge of tears.

'Why – what's happened?' Josh asked, alarmed.

'It's our Maggie. I don't know what's the matter with her, but she won't stop crying. Oh, please come, Josh, please!'

Just the mention of Maggie in trouble of some kind was enough for Josh. Without stopping for anything, he was out of the back door, leaving it open behind him, and heading down the track, Billy trailing behind him.

As he burst in through the door of number six, he almost fell over Maggie, still curled up against the scullery wall, still sobbing, though more softly now, in little trembling bursts.

'Maggie! Whatever is the matter?' He hunkered down beside her.

Maggie's shoulders convulsed, another sob catching in her throat.

'Maggie?' he said again, gently, reaching out to smooth a lock of hair back from her cheek where it had fallen. 'Come on, love, tell me what's wrong.'

Maggie raised her head for a moment, staring at Josh with eyes that were red and swollen from weeping, but also curiously blank and expressionless. She opened her mouth as if to say something, then abruptly closed it again, and her head sank to her knees once more.

For all that Billy had thought Josh would know what to do, truth to tell he felt as helpless as Billy had done, and he was seriously alarmed. But he had to do something.

'You can't stay down there, my love,' he said reasonably. 'Let's get you in the kitchen.'

He put an arm round her, and to his relief she raised her head again, wiping her nose with the back of her hand and looking at him with those anguished eyes.

'Oh, I'm sorry . . . I'm sorry . . .'

'Don't be silly! Sorry for what?'

'This! I'm sorry . . . I just . . .'

Her grief had caught up with her again, he thought. He'd seen it with his mother, how she could suddenly burst into tears for the loss of Jack, set off by the smallest thing, or sometimes nothing at all, even though she'd seemed perfectly composed moments before. He'd felt it himself, too, that sudden weight of sadness and disbelief that his brother was never coming back, coming out of nowhere like a thunderclap on a clear summer afternoon.

'Come on, let's get you up from there and we'll have a cup of tea,' he said encouragingly. 'Put the kettle on, Billy.'

Billy, who had been hanging back in the doorway, looking at his sister nervously, squeezed past them, and Josh helped Maggie to her feet and led her into the kitchen, where he sat her down in Rose's favourite armchair.

'I'm so sorry, Josh,' she apologised yet again. 'I'll be all right. Billy shouldn't have come bothering you.'

'No bother,' he said awkwardly. 'And do stop saying you're sorry. It's only natural you're upset, losing Jack like that.'

Maggie gulped, and her eyes filled, and for a moment he thought she was going to start crying again.

'It was just so horrible,' she managed between gasping breaths.

'You miss him. We all do.'

'I just couldn't . . . I've always dealt with him before, put him in his place, but tonight . . . it was all too much . . . I wanted Jack so badly . . . I really needed him . . .'

Josh frowned.

'What are you talking about, Maggie?'

'Reuben Hillman. He frightened the life out of me. He's done it before, but tonight . . .' She pressed her hands over her mouth, closing her eyes as if she could shut out the memory.

'Reuben Hillman?' Josh repeated, puzzled. 'What's he got to do with it?'

'He won't leave me alone. It's always been the same, but now that Jack's gone . . . oh Josh, he really frightened me to-night. There was nobody about, and he wouldn't let me go . . .'

Josh's face darkened.

'What did he do?'

Haltingly, she told him the whole story, and the anger grew and swelled in Josh's gut as he listened.

The little bugger! How dare he do that to Maggie? How dare he get her in a state like this! He needed to be taught a lesson, and he would be. Josh would make sure of that.

Billy, hunkered down beside the fireplace waiting for the kettle to boil, also listened in shocked silence to what Maggie was saying.

Josh got up. His hands were balling to fists, already itching to get to work on the miserable coward who had reduced Maggie to this state.

'Look after your sister, Billy,' he instructed harshly.

'Why? Aren't you . . . ? Where are you going, Josh?'

Josh's lips set in a hard line.

'Never you mind, Billy. Let's just say I've got business with that bloody Reuben Hillman.'

'Oh Josh – no!' Maggie protested. 'You mustn't!'

He ignored her, heading for the door.

'I'll look in and make sure you're all right when I get back,' was all he said.

Fury was boiling white hot in Josh's blood as he marched along the lane in the direction of High Compton. He didn't suppose Reuben would still be in the town – he wasn't one for frequenting the pubs and bars – but Josh knew the Hillmans' house, a villa within easy walking distance of the town centre, and he reckoned that was where he would find the little bugger, run home with his tail between his legs.

Well, his tail would certainly be between his legs by the time Josh had finished with him!

He carried on past the alehouse, which was getting rowdy now, down the street where Freeman's drapers occupied the corner premises, and up the hill beyond. A glow of light crept through the drawn curtains of the front room of the Hillman house; Josh harrumphed with satisfaction, opened the wicket gate, strode up the path and hammered on the front door. When nothing happened immediately, he knocked again, even more furiously than before, and called loudly: 'Come on out, you bastard! I know you're in there!'

He heard footsteps within, and the creak of a bolt being drawn, and bunched his fist in readiness. But when the door opened a crack, it was Clarence Hillman, Reuben's father, whose outraged face appeared in the gap.

'Who is this? How dare you—'

'I want to see your son,' Josh said between gritted teeth. 'I've got something to say to him.'

'Well, it will have to wait for another time, I'm afraid,' Clarence said coldly.

He went to close the door; Josh rammed it open with the toe of his boot.

'You'd better get him out here, or I'm coming in.' He gave the door a violent shove, and Clarence staggered backwards. Josh pushed past him. 'Where is he? I know he's here. Reuben, you bugger . . .'

The door to the left of the tiled hallway was ajar; Reuben himself appeared, looking alarmed.

'What . . . ? Who . . . ?'

When he saw Josh right there in the hallway, he shrank back, his podgy features melting into blubber, small eyes bright with fear.

In one stride Josh had him by the collar, bunching it up under his flabby chins so that he was lifted almost off his feet.

'I want a word with you, you miserable little rat!' he ground out. 'You lay a finger on Maggie Donovan again and you'll be bloody sorry.'

Reuben's eyes boggled.

'What are you talking about?' he burbled.

'Don't pretend you don't bloody know! She doesn't want anything to do with you. Understand that?'

'Let my boy go!' Clarence grabbed Josh's shoulder; he was quite a small man, and Josh shrugged him off easily.

'Understand?' he grated again into Reuben's quivering face.

Reuben's head nodded like a clockwork doll, and Josh glared into his eyes for a few more moments before releasing him.

'You'd better, or I swear I'll swing for you.'

He turned, pushing Clarence aside, and had almost reached the doorway when Reuben quivered defiantly: 'She's just a common tart anyway. You're welcome to her.'

Afterwards, Reuben didn't know what bravado had got into him to say such a dreadful thing about his beloved Maggie, and to a man of Josh Withers's size to boot. And at the time, he certainly didn't have the opportunity to wonder. Before he knew what was happening, Josh had swung round, the black rage that was bubbling inside him reaching boiling point. His fist shot out, connecting squarely with Reuben's jaw. Reuben staggered back, collided with an occasional table and went down like a felled tree. Josh aimed a furious kick, catching him between his plump legs.

Reuben squealed in pain, Clarence froze, momentarily too

shocked to do anything, and from the doorway Alexandra, Reuben's mother, gasped in horror and ran to her son.

'Get out! Get out!' Clarence yelled, recovering himself. 'I'll have the police on you, you thug!'

'Do what you bloody well like.' Josh stood threateningly over the stricken Reuben. 'But you . . . you leave Maggie alone, all right? Or you'll get more of the same, and that's a promise.'

With that, he turned and banged out of the house. He was still shaking with rage, but at least he'd done what he'd come for, and he was glad of it.

Nobody – nobody – was going to treat Maggie the way Reuben had, or call her filthy names, and get away with it. If it was the last thing he did, he'd make sure of that.

'Are you all right, Maggie?'

By the time he got back to number six, she certainly seemed to have recovered herself; she was in the scullery, washing up teacups.

'Yes . . . yes, I'm fine . . . Oh Josh, where have you been? What have you done?'

'Taught that little bugger Hillman a lesson he won't forget. I don't think he'll be bothering you again in a hurry.'

'Oh, you shouldn't have! Really you shouldn't!'

'He asked for everything he got,' Josh said flatly. 'If you have any more trouble from him, just let me know, all right?'

Maggie wiped her soapy hands on her apron.

'Josh, promise me – you haven't hurt him, have you? I don't want you doing anything silly on my account.

'He had to be shown he can't behave like that,' Josh said grimly. 'The state you were in . . .'

'I expect I made more of it than I should,' Maggie said. 'But he's got it into his head that now Jack's gone, he stands a chance with me, and he's . . . oh, I don't think he's all there. The things he was saying! It really frightened me, it was so peculiar. He was like a man possessed. You don't think, do you . . . ?' She drew a long, trembling breath. 'You don't think . . . no, no, of course not . . .'

'What?' Josh asked.

Maggie shook her head, unable to put into words the awful thought that had come into her head. That perhaps it was Reuben who had severed the rope on the hudge. He was so crazy for her, so persistent, and tonight she'd caught a glimpse of a man teetering on the edge of madness – not all there, as she'd put it. Supposing he had really believed that with Jack out of the way, she'd turn to him? Supposing he really thought that he could offer her things Jack never could, and in his twisted mind had excused the wicked act by pretending he was doing it for her, for her good?

But it made no sense. He couldn't have known for sure that Jack would be on the hudge when the rope gave way. And surely not even he could be responsible for something so terrible? She couldn't believe it. She didn't.

'Nothing,' she said. 'I'm just being silly.'

'Well . . .' Josh looked awkward suddenly. 'If you're all right now, I suppose I'd better be getting home. Mam and Dad will wonder where I am.'

'I'm fine, honestly. You go.'

He looked at her, at the rich chestnut hair curling about a face that was still paler than usual. Her eyes were still a bit swollen, too, and her mouth quivered a little before she caught her lower lip between her teeth, biting down hard on it. But in all the time he had known her, she had never looked more kissable, and it was all he could do not to give in to the urge to do just that.

'You know where I am if you need me.' He backed out of the door. 'Anything at all, don't hesitate.'

'Thanks, Josh.' She smiled tremulously. 'I just hope you don't get in any trouble over this.'

'It wouldn't be the first time, by a long chalk.'

'The first time on my account. And . . . oh, I don't know what you must think of me, forever bursting into tears on you. What a stupid woman I am!'

'Believe me, Maggie, that's the last thing you are,' he said with feeling.

And then, before the urge to take her in his arms could get the better of him, Josh left hurriedly.

Josh had been home about an hour when there was a knock at the door. His mother and father were both in bed, but Josh was far too wound up for sleep, and was sitting in the kitchen with a tot of whisky, thinking about Maggie, and the way he felt about her.

Was it so wrong to want her? Would it be so terrible for him to see if there was a chance she felt the same way? She didn't, of course. She was still mourning Jack. But she was a young woman, she couldn't go the whole of her life alone, could she? There were women who did just that, he knew, but he couldn't see Maggie as a bitter old maid. Surely one day she'd take up with someone else, and he knew that he wanted that someone to be him. However long it took, he'd wait for her. And in the meantime, he'd be there for her. She needed someone to protect her from the Reubens of this world.

Josh swallowed a glug of whisky and refilled his glass. Yes, that was what he'd do. He'd look out for her, if nothing else. Surely that would be what Jack would have wanted?

When the knock came, Josh's heart leaped. His first thought

was that it was Maggie, needing something, or Billy to say she'd become upset again. He hurried to answer it, but when he yanked it open it wasn't Maggie or Billy on the doorstep.

'Josh Withers, what have you been up to this time?'

It was a very irate Sergeant Love, red in the face from cycling over from High Compton and furious at being called out so late on a Saturday night.

Josh's heart sank. He'd had plenty of run-ins with the sergeant over the years, and though none of them were recent, he knew they wouldn't have been forgotten. Talk about giving a dog a bad name.

'Are you going to let me come in, or do I have to take you down to the station?' Sergeant Love snapped.

Josh sighed and stepped aside, and the policeman strode into the house, removing his helmet as he did so.

'I don't know, lad,' he said sorrowfully, as if he were talking to a young boy rather than a grown man. 'I thought you'd mended your ways. But you've really done it this time, haven't you? I've had a serious accusation made against you by a highly respected member of the community.'

Josh snorted.

'Respected, my eye! He asked for it, Sergeant. And while we're at it, I've got some accusations of my own. He attacked Maggie Donovan – I don't suppose he told you that. Frightened the life out of her, and other things besides.'

'Clarence Hillman attacked Maggie Donovan?' The sergeant's voice was scathing with disbelief. 'I can't see that happening in a month of Sundays.'

'Not Clarence. That useless lump of a son of his.' Josh ran a hand through his hair, leaving it standing on end. 'He waylaid her on her way home from work and . . . well, he did and said things no man should. He asked for all he got.'

'Still the hothead, I see.' Sergeant Love put his helmet down on the kitchen table and fished in his breast pocket for his notebook. 'You ought to keep that temper of yours under control, my son. You can't go barging into decent folk's houses, taking a swing at them and knocking them out cold.'

'He wasn't out cold,' Josh objected. 'He fell over, that's all.'

'That's not the way the Hillmans tell it. I'm going to have to arrest you, you know that, don't you? A complaint has been made, and all I can say is you're lucky not to be looking at very serious charges here.'

'I wish I bloody well was!' Josh flared. 'It would be no more than the little bugger deserved, and I might as well be hung for a sheep as a lamb.'

'You've been drinking, haven't you?' the policeman said disgustedly. 'Don't deny it – I can smell it on you. And you'd been drinking when you went terrorising the Hillman family as well, if I'm not mistaken. That's half the trouble with you, getting the drink in you.'

'You'd have had a drink too if you'd seen the state Maggie was in,' Josh retorted. 'And just for the record, when I lammed that little sod I was stone-cold sober. But charge me if you want to – I don't give a bugger. It was worth it just to see him go down like a ninepin. And I'd do it all over again. Come on then, are you taking me down the station or not?'

Sergeant Love sighed heavily. If he arrested Josh Withers and took him back to spend the night in the cells, they were going to have to walk the whole way, and the prospect, especially at this time of night, was far from appealing. The sergeant wanted his bed, and he wanted it soon, not in a couple of hours' time. Withers was home now, and no danger to anyone that he could see, and he wasn't likely to be going anywhere any time soon. In fact, the policeman was wishing he'd left the whole thing until the morning; he would have done, most likely, if the complainant had been anyone other than Clarence Hillman, the solicitor's clerk.

'If I leave you here tonight, I want you down at the station first thing in the morning,' he said.

'You can bet on it,' Jack said grimly. 'But you can tell that bloody Hillman that if he wants to press charges against me, he'll have a few of his own to answer. Assault on a lady! That's against the law too, isn't it? And a damn sight more shameful than giving a man the smack he deserves. Tell him that and see how he likes it before you run me in.'

Sergeant Love shook his head. This was getting worse by the minute.

'I still want to see you down that station tomorrow,' he said belligerently. 'You'll be there if you know what's good for you.'

Josh raised his hands in submission.

'All right, all right. But you'd best have another word with Hillman first. Tell him what I said.'

'Oh, I'll get to the bottom of it, never you fear.' Sergeant Love was trying desperately to reassert his authority. He picked up his helmet and headed for the door. With his hand on the latch, he turned. 'And you, my lad, had better learn to watch your temper, or you'll end up behind bars. I've got your card marked. I won't stand for any more goings-on like this on my patch. Understood?'

'Yes, Sergeant,' Josh said, mock-meekly.

But when the door closed after the policeman and he was alone again, he poured himself another slug of whisky.

Tonight had proved it to him – he was still too ready to use his fists, just as he always had been. When his temper was up, there was no telling what he was capable of. He might yet end up behind bars, just as Sergeant Love had predicted and as his long-suffering parents had feared when they'd sent him off to Wales to his aunt and uncle.

But whatever the consequences, he couldn't regret landing that punch on Reuben Hillman's fat, ugly nose. And if Hillman kept on bothering Maggie, he would do the same all over again.

He did report to the police station next morning as instructed, though not first thing – by the time he'd finally got to bed the previous night, he'd polished off the last of the whisky and slept like a log. Besides, he was counting on Sergeant Love speaking to Clarence Hillman before he got there, and telling him about Josh's counter-allegations. Josh couldn't see Maggie pressing charges, even if it would get him off the hook – she'd be mortified if the whole thing became public, and Josh wouldn't want to put her through that. But with any luck Reuben wouldn't want it made public either, and would have the grace to be thoroughly ashamed of what he'd done.

And it seemed that was the case.

After giving Josh another stern warning, Sergeant Love sent him on his way, and Josh found himself whistling all the way home.

It hadn't turned out so badly in the end. He had the satisfaction of having exacted revenge on Maggie's behalf and got away with it. He didn't think Reuben would bother her again. And he'd come to a decision.

He wasn't going to avoid Maggie any more. He was going to look out for her, and hope that one day he'd be more to her than just Jack's brother.

'You stupid, stupid boy!' Clarence Hillman said. 'Why in the world would you want anything to do with one of those Donovans? Have you been chasing after her? Is it true?'

Reuben, nursing a black eye and swollen cheek, avoided his father's eyes and said nothing.

'From your silence, I assume you were,' Clarence fumed. 'How could you place me in a position like this? It's intolerable! All I can hope for is that I can be assured that is the end of this foolishness. Well?'

'Yes, sir,' Reuben said sullenly.

But inwardly he was seething. His desire for Maggie was as strong as ever; he'd never let her go – never! But stronger even than his desire was the burning anger and his hatred for Josh Withers. Oh, he wouldn't forget this. The humiliation. The pain when Josh had landed his punch and kick. And worst of all, the suspicion that something was going on between him and Maggie, and that Josh was closer to her than he, Reuben, had ever managed to be.

Just you wait, Josh Withers! he thought bitterly. Just you wait!

Revenge was a dish best served cold, so the saying went. However long it took, Reuben was determined on one thing. When he got his revenge on Josh, it would be something he'd never forget. And Reuben would relish every moment of it.

Chapter Thirteen

'I'm a bit worried about Mam,' Maggie said.

She'd eaten her evening meal and was sitting at the kitchen table with a cup of tea when Josh called in, as he'd taken to doing most evenings since the night she'd been assaulted by Reuben Hillman – to make sure she was all right, he pretended to both of them, though in reality he knew it was much more than that.

If Billy was there he didn't stay too long, but tonight the lad wasn't yet home from work.

The moment he'd walked in he'd thought Maggie looked preoccupied, and she didn't get up to make him a cup of tea as she usually did. Now he pulled out a chair and sat down, and Maggie picked up an envelope lying on the table in front of her, pulled out a couple of sheets of writing paper and unfolded them.

'I got this letter from Walter today. He says Mam's not been at all well.'

'Oh, that's a shame.' Josh was typically nonchalant.

'He says she's off her food – well, she's been sick too a couple of times – and she's complaining of pains in her stomach.' Maggie ran her finger down the page, tracing Walter's neat, slanting handwriting. 'And the day he wrote this, she stayed in bed most of the morning. That's not like Mam. She likes to be up and doing.'

'I expect she ate something that upset her,' Josh said reasonably.

'Connie's a lovely cook,' Maggie argued. 'She wouldn't give Mam anything that was going off.'

'She's picked something up, then. You know how these things go round.'

Maggie sighed.

'I hope you're right. I just hope it isn't anything to do with . . .' She hesitated, fighting shy of mentioning Rose's miscarriage in so many words. 'What happened back in the summer,' she said instead.

Josh shifted in his chair, as uncomfortable with discussing women's problems as Maggie was.

'She's never been right since,' Maggie said. 'I reckon they ought to get the doctor to her, but whether they will . . . Walter's got a family to keep, and doctors cost money.'

'He'll find it if he thinks it's needed, or your Ewart will,' Josh said. 'But I wouldn't mind betting she's fine by now.'

Maggie chewed her lip, still staring down at Walter's letter as if she could change what it said by sheer willpower.

'She could be, I suppose. I certainly hope so. But I've got this really bad feeling . . .' She broke off as the dark dread filled her again, dragging her down to a place she really did not want to be. It had been hovering about her all day, even before she'd opened the letter, and it frightened her. Useless to tell herself she was simply still raw from the terrible things that had happened in the last months; she recognised that feeling of sick apprehension, and until she'd got home and read the letter there had been no reason whatever for her to be feeling that way. It was as if, deep inside, she knew something was terribly wrong, even when she hadn't the first idea what it was. But now here it was in black and white: Mam was poorly again, and Maggie was horribly afraid that what she was feeling wasn't just ordinary anxiety but an instinctive knowledge that was somehow compellingly different.

'I don't know what I'd do if anything happened to Mam,' she said, folding both hands tightly over the letter and lowering her eyes. 'I just couldn't bear it on top of everything else.'

'Nothing is going to happen to your mam, Maggie, trust me.' Josh reached across the table, covering her hands with his own.

Such a gentle touch, the smallest comforting squeeze, but it made Maggie quiver inwardly, and warmth ran through her veins in a glowing tide from the place where his fingers lay, making her almost forget the awful foreboding that had been suffocating her.

'Try not to worry,' he said comfortingly. 'Your mam is a strong woman. She'll be fine, you'll see.'

Maggie nodded. She didn't trust herself to speak.

'You're just looking on the black side,' he went on. 'It's not surprising, with all that's happened, but it's not like you. You're the one who generally keeps everybody else's spirits up.'

She smiled faintly. 'Am I?'

'You certainly are. And I've got to take my hat off to you, the way you've held things together since . . . you know . . . There's plenty who'd have gone under, with all you've had to deal with.'

'I just do what I have to do,' she said simply. It was no more than the truth.

'Well . . .' his fingers tightened on hers, 'you're not on your own, Maggie. You know that, don't you? Whatever you need, I'm here for you.'

Her skin was even more sensitised now, the little tingles that ran from his hands into hers sharper and more compelling, and she experienced a moment's panic and almost snatched her hand away. But somehow she didn't. For one thing, she didn't want to. She wanted him to go on holding her hand for ever. It felt so good and so safe, as well as exciting in that darkly dangerous way. And what would he think if she did? He didn't mean anything by it; he was just trying to comfort her, the most natural thing in the world. He was Jack's brother, after all, and she'd known him all her life. If she pulled away suddenly, it would give away her own treacherous thoughts and feelings, and make things horribly awkward.

Oh, what in the world was the matter with her? How was it he could make her feel like this? It was something she'd never experienced in her life before, and the longings it aroused in her shocked her and filled her with shame. She'd relived those longings often, lying in bed at night with Josh's handkerchief pressed to her face so she could smell the familiar scent of soap and tobacco, and wondered what on earth was happening to her. Jack had never made her feel this way, and she had been going to marry him. The thought of going beyond kisses had been repellent to her. Now . . . Maggie was aghast to realise she actually wanted – craved – the very things the thought of which had made her cringe where Jack had been concerned. What sort of a woman did that make her? One who was no better than she should be, that was for sure!

Besides that – even worse, perhaps – was the way she couldn't stop thinking about Josh. He was there, somehow, in everything she did. As she cooked a meal for herself and Billy, she imagined she was cooking it for Josh too. As she sorted boxes of haberdashery, she thought how nice it would be to sew buttons on his shirt and darn his socks. As she walked home along the lane in the falling dusk and heard a nightingale sing or an owl hoot, she wanted him there, sharing the moment with her. It was madness, utter madness, and though it made her feel horribly guilty that she should harbour such thoughts about Jack's brother when Jack was scarcely cold in his grave, she couldn't help feeling her heart soar and her imagination take flight.

This was the man who'd taken up cudgels on her behalf, gone after Reuben Hillman and punched him on the nose in his own front room; the man who'd climbed on the churchyard wall beside her when she'd been trying to dissuade the mob of angry miners from marching on Sir Montague's house after the funeral. It lent him an aura of romance, as if he were a knight in a fairy tale, and the dangerous edge of his wild youth, still there, though well hidden these days, added a little thrill of excitement that made the chemistry that existed between them even more potent.

It was there now, tingling in the place where his fingers touched, spreading warmth through her veins, twisting in her gut. And with it the familiar feelings of guilt and confusion.

'You wouldn't hesitate to come to me, would you, if there's anything you need, anything at all?' Josh went on.

'Thank you,' she said quietly. 'But I'm all right, really I am. It's just that sometimes I get this awful feeling that something else dreadful is going to happen. I expect I'm just being silly, though.'

'Like I said, hardly surprising.'

'I suppose.'

She raised her head, looking at him, trying to smile, and as their eyes met, something quite extraordinary happened.

The potent attraction was there again, sparking like an electric storm, but this time it felt to Maggie that it wasn't only she who was experiencing it. In that moment it seemed to her that her own tumultuous emotions were reflected in Josh's narrowed dark eyes. The breath caught in her throat as they gazed at one another, and for a long hiatus in time they remained perfectly motionless, frozen in a white-hot bubble of ice. Then Josh's hands closed more tightly over hers and he leaned towards her across the table, at the same time drawing her towards him. She offered no resistance. It was, she thought afterwards, as if she were nothing but an iron filing being sucked up by a magnet. His features were no longer in focus and she couldn't see him clearly, but the scent of him was sharp in her nostrils: soap and tobacco smoke, and something else, something so unmistakably male it took her breath away.

His breath kissed the soft skin of her cheek and she could almost taste his mouth on hers. She parted her lips, closing her eyes, floating in a universe that had become unreal as a dream.

And the dream shattered.

Neither of them had heard the back door open, but there was no missing the bang as it shut. Maggie jumped, startled out of her trance, panic rushing through her in a flood tide. She snatched her hands away from Josh's, half rising from her chair just as her brother came into the kitchen.

'Billy! You're home, then! Farmer kept you late tonight . . .' She was gabbling, she knew, but she couldn't help it. 'You must be tired out. Sit down . . . I'll get you something to eat.'

Billy slumped down in the easy chair.

'I'm all right. Farmer's wife cooked us bacon and egg.'

'Well, I'll get you a cup of tea anyway. You're bound to be thirsty.'

She couldn't look at Josh, couldn't meet his eyes.

He stood up too.

'I'd better be going. Try not to worry about your mam. She'll be fine, I'm sure of it.'

'What's wrong with our mam?' Billy asked sharply.

'Oh, it's something and nothing, I expect,' Maggie said. 'She hasn't been too well, but our Walter will look after her.'

'Oh . . . well . . .' was all Billy said, but there was still a pinched, anxious look on his pale little face. Billy missed his mother a lot, Maggie knew; apart from herself, Rose was the only one who was always there for him, and she hoped desperately for his sake as well as her own that it really was something and nothing, and that Rose would soon recover from whatever it was that was ailing her.

In the doorway, Josh paused and turned.

'Just remember – you know where I am if you want me.'

Hot colour flooded Maggie's cheeks. *If you want me . . .* He didn't mean it like that, of course, but all the same, the words were a bit too close to home for comfort.

She nodded, but for the life of her couldn't bring herself to say anything.

And then he was gone, and Maggie was left alone with Billy, and with the confusion that now raged in her more fiercely than ever.

As he walked back up the track to his own home, Josh burned with pent-up frustration. Why the hell had Billy chosen that very moment to come bursting in?

But for all that, he was elated. There was no mistaking what had so nearly happened between him and Maggie.

He'd been taking a hell of a chance there, of course, making a move like that this soon. If she didn't feel anything for him, it could well have been the end of his hopes. But she hadn't drawn back. She hadn't given him a slap, which would probably have been no more than he deserved. She'd been ready to let him kiss her. More than ready, he reckoned . . .

He could see her face now, close to his, lips parted, eyes

closed, and the fire in his belly flared like a burning hay barn. But he could wait. If he thought he stood a chance with her, he could wait a bit longer. And just at this moment, he thought he definitely stood a chance.

Josh kicked at a small stone in his path, sending it scudding merrily ahead of him, and whistled a music hall tune as he headed for home and a much-needed tot of whisky.

That same evening, Peggy Bishop was visiting her sister Sarah. She'd given up calling on her in the day; there was never a chance to talk properly when all the children were running around – a noisier, more demanding brood Peggy couldn't imagine, and she was only glad she'd never had any of her own. What sort of a life was that? Washing filthy nappies, wiping runny noses, bathing scraped knees, making piles of jam or dripping sandwiches, cleaning muddy floors, and all to the endless whines and cries and unintelligible chatter. Oh, she could do without all that, thank you very much!

They were sitting now in Sarah's cramped little kitchen, Sarah busy darning the toes and heels of much-worn socks that had been passed down from one growing child to the next, Peggy nursing the last dregs of a cup of sugary tea. So far, to Peggy's annoyance, they'd talked about nothing but the children – or at least, Sarah had talked and Peggy had been forced to listen to tedious accounts of teething problems and growing pains, bilious attacks and temper tantrums until she found herself wondering why she'd bothered to visit at all. The warmth of the fire was making her drowsy and she was, in fact, half asleep when Sarah unexpectedly changed the subject.

'Do you ever see anything of Josh Withers these days?'

Peggy roused herself.

'Not for ages,' she said. 'Why? What made you think of him?'

'Oh, nothing really, but I heard he was in trouble with the police again a couple of weeks ago.'

Peggy pricked up her ears.

'Whatever for?'

'Fighting. Well, worse really. He went to Clarence Hillman's house, forced his way in, and let into his son. Knocked him out cold, I heard. He's lucky not to be up before the court by the sounds of it. I don't know – there's some as will never learn.'

'Why ever would he go picking on Reuben Hillman?' Peggy wondered. 'I wouldn't have thought he even knew him.'

'Well, according to Tilly Yates, young Cathy Small, what works at Freeman's along with him and Maggie Donovan, reckoned he'd been making unwelcome advances to Maggie. I wouldn't like to say for sure, of course, but it sounds about right. When blokes start knocking twelve bells out of one another there's usually a girl involved, and I don't suppose Josh Withers is any different.'

Peggy snorted in disgust. The thought of Josh picking a fight with Reuben Hillman on behalf of Maggie Donovan was very hurtful to her, especially since he'd given her such an uncompromising brush-off. But she wasn't going to let Sarah know she cared a hoot.

'Silly sod,' she said contemptuously.

Sarah snipped through her wool and jammed the darning needle between her lips while she paired the sock she had been working on and dropped the roll into a basket at her side.

'To think that not so long ago you were thinking of running off with him!' she said. 'You've changed your tune.'

'Maybe I have and maybe I haven't,' Peggy said evasively.

Sarah gave her a sharp look as she cut another length of grey darning wool.

'You and Tom getting on better, then?'

'We're all right at the moment,' Peggy said, wishing Sarah would go back to talking about her children, boring as it was. She had no desire to tell her sister about the strange change in her relationship with her husband, and the peculiar shift in her own feelings towards him. Truth to tell, she couldn't quite understand it herself, and it certainly wasn't something to be shared, not even with Sarah, who'd known most of her secrets since they were girls. For over the past weeks, her awful suspicion that Tom might have been the one who severed the rope and caused the terrible disaster at Shepton Fields had given rise to something that was close to excitement. It wasn't something she was proud of – she barely wanted to admit it, even to herself – but it crackled and buzzed inside her all the same.

If she was right, if Tom had done something so unspeakably awful in order to punish the man who had been her lover, then he must care far more about her than he ever let on. That in itself was gratifying, but it was more than that. A dangerous man was also an attractive one, and the very idea of it titillated her. Oh, she'd always known Tom could be dangerous, of course, but in a mean, sly way that belittled him rather than enhancing his image in her eyes. This, though . . .

Somehow it had failed to occur to Peggy that cutting through a rope under cover of darkness was just as sly and cowardly as anything Tom had ever done – she saw only a man who could commit murder, and although on one level it shocked her, she was too exhilarated by the spice it added to their relationship to care.

Tom seemed to be behaving differently too, perhaps because of the change in her attitude towards him. Oh, he could still be surly and unpleasant and controlling but he sometimes surprised her with little generosities, and certainly he was very appreciative of her warm response in bed. And when he did say nasty things, she didn't feel as resentful as she used to; she just saw it as further evidence of the hard man he was, and even found satisfaction in allowing herself to be dominated, whereas before she had rebelled. It was almost as if she was falling in love with him all over again, but with the real Tom and not some idol she'd placed on a pedestal only to knock down in the cold, hard light of day. Others might regard him as a monster if they knew what she thought she knew, but the secret she was hugging to herself was strangely erotic.

Yes, at the moment she was more than satisfied with Tom, and with the surprising fillip all this had given to their love life.

'We're all right now,' she reiterated, and thought that she might just decide to leave Sarah and her tedious chit-chat and go home in the hope of an early night with her husband.

'There's nothing for it, Firkins. We shall have to raise the rent on all the tied cottages.'

Sir Montague Fairley stood, swaying slightly on his bow legs, a brandy glass in one hand, decanter in the other, in the centre of the Persian rug that covered his drawing room floor.

He'd already had a bad day. Alfred Nicholls, the police superintendent from Bath, had called to see him this morning and informed him that the enquiry into the pit accident was being scaled down. Every avenue had been explored, no progress was being made, and the manpower they had expended could no longer be sustained.

Sir Montague had been incensed; he was aware that there was talk in the town that he was to blame, and he wanted a culprit brought to book. But the superintendent refused to be moved with regard to the number of officers assigned to ask questions around the town, though he did attempt to appease the coal owner by promising that the case would remain open and that he personally, along with one of his best detectives, would continue the investigation.

Sir Montague was having none of it.

'You should have called in Scotland Yard at the outset,' he growled.

'They couldn't have done any more than we have done,' Nicholls asserted. 'Less, in fact. They don't know the locals as we do. I'm sorry, Sir Montague, that we have had no success so far, but I can assure you I still regard the case with the utmost seriousness, and it's my sincere hope that there will be a satisfactory outcome.'

'There had better be, or I shall see about calling in Scotland Yard myself,' Sir Montague threatened.

'I'm not sure that's within your power.' The superintendent sounded confident enough, but he was fiddling nervously with his collar stud as he said it.

'We'll see about that,' Sir Montague barked, his blood pressure rising dangerously. 'I want this matter laid to rest and I shall ensure that it is, whatever it takes. Now, are you willing to reconsider this so-called scaling-down?'

But the superintendent remained adamant.

'I'm sorry, I can't do that. We'll speak again when, and if, I have anything further to report.'

The unsatisfactory interview had made Sir Montague's hearty lunch lie heavily in his stomach, while his gout was playing him up too. So when Clement Firkins, his agent, had arrived with the news that two more families were leaving the area for work elsewhere and their houses would be falling vacant, his temper had reached boiling point.

'Good God, at this rate I'll be bankrupted!' he exploded. 'Rents will have to rise to compensate. With immediate effect.'

Clement Firkins stirred uneasily, and his highly polished boots squeaked on the varnished boards that surrounded the Persian rug.

'I'm not sure they'll be able to afford to pay, Sir Montague. Especially those who lost their breadwinner in the accident.'

Sir Montague juggled the brandy decanter and glass.

'They'll find it somehow. They will have to, if they want to keep a roof over their heads. I've been more than generous so far, but I'm afraid all good things must come to an end. They can remain in their homes until I have need of them, but they'll have to pay for the privilege. Do I make myself clear?'

'Perfectly, Sir Montague.' The agent knew better than to argue if he wanted to keep his job.

'Very well, see to it.' Sir Montague poured himself the refill he was craving. 'Close the door on your way out, Firkins. It's the maid's evening off, blast her.'

'I'll do that, Sir Montague,' Clement Firkins replied, with all the dignity he could muster.

'Bloody business!' muttered Sir Montague as the door closed after the agent.

And took a healthy gulp of the fine cognac, which he needed, he'd convinced himself, for medicinal purposes.

Chapter Fourteen

'Are you going out tonight, our Billy?' Maggie asked.

It was Sunday evening; Billy knew without questioning her why she was asking. Maggie liked to have a bath on a Sunday evening, ready for the week ahead, and in any case, he could hear the water simmering in the copper.

'It's all right,' he said. 'I think I'm just going to go to bed. I'm as knackered as Barney's bull.'

It was no more than the truth; as Rose had warned him long ago, farm work was no easy ride. As always, he had been up before dawn, toiled away all day in the pouring rain, and only got home when darkness had fallen. No days off for him. He didn't mind, though – he liked it on the farm, and since he had no real friends to go out with, he was happy enough just to catch up on some sleep before it was time to begin all over again.

'Do you want me to fetch the bath in for you?' he asked.

'No, you get off to bed if you're that tired.'

The rain was still falling heavily. Maggie scooted across the track to fetch the tin bath from the outhouse, and by the time she returned, little rivers of water running down her face, there was no sign of Billy. Bullseye was still there, though, sitting on the rug in front of the fire, the exact place where she wanted to put the bath. She ought to push him outside where he belonged, but she didn't have the heart. Instead she made him go and sit in the corner, then, using the metal dipper, ladled scalding water from the copper into the bath. She fetched soap and a towel and got undressed, folding her clothes neatly and piling them up on a chair.

She winced as she stepped into the hot water, wiggling about from foot to foot, then eased herself down to a sitting position and relaxed, enjoying the luxury as she always did. There was something so cosy about a bath in front of the fire at this time of year, with the glow of the embers the only light in the room and the warmth flushing her face as well as her body.

Maggie slid down so that the water covered her head and washed her hair with soap shavings. Then she scrubbed herself all over and settled back again to make the most of her weekly treat before the water cooled.

She was feeling much happier than she had done recently; she'd had a letter from Walter yesterday in which he said Rose seemed to be picking up, and that was a weight off her mind. But she did have another concern: Clement Firkins, Sir Montague's agent, had been to see all the families in the Ten Houses and informed them that their rents were to be raised.

It wouldn't be easy to find the extra; money was already tight. Whereas before Paddy had died she'd been able to keep a bit back for herself when she handed Mam her wage packet at the end of the week, now it was all eaten up on paying for the essentials. But she'd just have to cut her coat according to the cloth, Maggie thought. And she should be due a small rise in her wage at the end of the month – another whole year she'd been at the draper's. She'd manage somehow; really, she had no choice.

The warmth was making her drowsy, but a tin bath was no place to go to sleep, even if she rested her head on her knees. Maggie levered herself up and got out, shivering a little now as she towelled herself dry. Then she slipped into Rose's old dressing gown, which she'd laid out ready – Rose hadn't taken it with her, arguing that it would take up too much room in her suitcase, and Walter had promised to buy her a new one; not before time, he'd said.

Maggie put milk for a cup of cocoa to warm in a pan on the trivet and was just towelling her hair dry when there was a knock at the door, followed almost immediately by the creak of someone trying to turn the handle.

'Oh my goodness!' Maggie flew into the scullery. 'Who is it? Who's there?'

'It's me, Josh. Can I come in?'

'No! No, you can't . . . I'm . . .'

'I'm getting soaked to the skin out here!'

'No, you can't! I'm not decent.'

'Have a heart! It's pouring down.'

'Oh . . . wait a minute, then.' Relenting, Maggie undid the dressing gown sash and retied it tightly, then, with one hand holding the edges closely together around her throat, she unlocked the door.

'I wasn't expecting anyone at this time of night,' she said defensively as Josh came into the scullery, shaking himself like a rat. 'I've just had a bath.'

'I could do with a nice bath myself,' he said jokingly. 'Is the water still hot?'

'No, it's not! You go back to your own home if you want a bath, Josh Withers, 'cos you're not getting one here!' Maggie retorted, flustered but not wanting to show it.

He pulled a wry face. 'You're a hard woman, Maggie. If you

aren't going to be nice to me, I might just change my mind about what I've come to say.'

He was struggling to keep his voice light, struggling not to gaze at her. Her hair still damp and mussed up, falling in an untidy curtain to her shoulders. Her face flushed and rosy from the bath. The clean, soapy smell of her, sweet in his nostrils, lighting a fire in his blood. He'd never wanted her more; it was almost too much for a man to stand. Especially with her so close here in the cramped scullery, where there was scarcely room to swing a cat.

'So, what did you come to say?' she asked, her tone still short with embarrassment.

'Let's go in the kitchen and I'll tell you. You'll catch your death out here.'

It was no more than the truth – away from the warmth of the fire, the cold air of the October evening had invaded the scullery, and in spite of the dressing gown, Maggie could feel chilly shivers running over her skin.

'Oh, come on then, if you must.'

She led the way into the kitchen and he followed. The milk on the trivet was beginning to skim over and bubble up; she bent to pull it to one side.

'I'm just making a cup of cocoa. Do you want one?'

'I wouldn't say no.'

'I'll get some more milk, then.'

She eased past him back into the scullery, where the jug of milk lived on a cold slab, and his eyes followed her. God, she was beautiful! It was all he could do not to grab hold of her, untie that stupid sash, and—

'How's your mam?' he asked to distract himself.

'A bit better, thank goodness. I got another letter from Walter yesterday.'

She was bustling back and forth, pouring more milk into the saucepan and returning it to the trivet, setting out cups and spooning sugar and cocoa into them.

'There you are, what did I tell you? Didn't I say she'd be fine?'

'I don't know that she's *fine* exactly.'

'But she will be. She's tough, your mam.'

'Like me, you mean.' There was a hint of teasing in her voice now.

'I didn't say you were tough, Maggie. I said you were hard,' he responded, taking up the teasing.

'That's even worse! You make me sound like a walnut!'

'Could be! Hard shell, but sweet inside. Well worth cracking . . .'

'Josh Withers, stop it this instant!'

She was flirting, she realised! She could hardly believe it.

'So tell me why you're here, interrupting my bathtime.'

'And enjoying myself, too. But if you insist . . .'

'I do! I want to get to bed before I catch my death, as you so nicely put it.'

'To bed, eh?'

Colour flamed in her already rosy cheeks.

'Josh Withers! I've never heard the like!'

'Then perhaps it's time you did . . .'

She drew herself up.

'Stop it! You're as bad as Reuben Hillman!'

'Oh, him! That's a nice compliment to pay me, I must say.'

'I swear you are. And if you don't stop this right now and tell me why you've come bothering me . . .'

'Yes, what?' he challenged.

'Well . . .' Her eyes were wide with pretended indignation, her lips pursed. 'You'll just have to punch yourself on the nose, won't you?' she said, a giggle escaping even before she finished the sentence, and both of them dissolved into laughter.

'Come on, then.' With an effort, Maggie recovered herself. 'What did you come to say? Something nice?'

'Well, I hope you'll think so . . . Hey, watch that milk, it's going to boil over.'

Maggie swooped on it, poured scalding milk into the cups and then returned the lot to the saucepan.

'All right, I won't keep you in suspense any longer,' Josh said as she stirred the pan vigorously. 'I found out today that they're having a dance at the Miners' Welfare next Saturday. There's a band coming out from Bath, and it sounds as if it might be a bit of fun. I wondered if you fancied going.'

'Oh Josh, I don't know . . .' Maggie stopped stirring and glanced over her shoulder, serious again suddenly. 'Don't you think . . . ? Well, isn't it a bit soon?'

'How do you mean?' he asked, though he knew.

'Well . . .' She bit her lip. 'Dad . . . and Jack . . .'

'You've had a tough time, Maggie. We all have. I reckon we deserve a bit of fun. We can't shut ourselves away for ever. That's what the organising committee thought, I expect. That's why they're putting it on, so we can enjoy ourselves for a change. Hey, come on . . . I know I'd like to go. But not on my own.'

'You'd have plenty of partners, Josh Withers. Half the girls in the district would be lined up and waiting for you.'

Josh took a deep breath.

'Maybe. But not the one I want.'

For a moment he thought he'd gone too far. Maggie stood stock still; he could almost hear the beating of her heart. Then she moved abruptly, pouring the steaming cocoa into the cups and pushing one across the table towards him.

'Well, if it's an act of charity, I suppose I'd better say yes,' she said drily. 'Now, drink your cocoa and go on home. We've had quite enough of this nonsense for one night.'

Tired as he was, Billy couldn't get to sleep. It was too often like this nowadays; whereas once it was waking up that had been the problem, since the tragedy at Shepton Fields there hadn't been a single night when he'd been able to drop off and sleep right through to dawn. Every time he closed his eyes, it seemed, the horror of what had happened was there, chasing around and around inside his head until he thought it would drive him crazy. And when he did manage to sleep, there were the nightmares, not always about the accident, often making no sense at all, but dark and suffocating, awful, nebulous scenarios from which he couldn't escape when he woke, sweating and trembling. He was afraid then to go back to sleep in case the horror was still there waiting for him.

Tonight he'd lain with the sheet pulled up to his chin, staring into the darkness and listening to the rain gusting against the window but hearing only screams and cries inside his head. When he could stand it no longer, he pushed aside the covers and got up. He'd fetch Bullseye. Maggie would be cross with him for having the dog on the bed – it wasn't hygienic, she said, and it wasn't him who had to wash the sheets and pillow-cases either – but there was comfort in feeling the dog's weight on his feet, or pressed alongside him, and hearing the little snorts and snuffles the dog made when he was asleep. Sometimes he even barked softly and his feet made little scrabbling movements – dreaming that he was chasing rabbits, Mam said; no nightmares for him. And if Billy was feeling really scared, he could reach out and stroke the wiry hair, tweak one of the dog's misshapen ears, and Bullseye might stir enough to lick his hand, or even his face. That always made Billy feel better.

At the top of the stairs, though, he hesitated. He could hear voices in the kitchen below – Maggie's, and a man. It sounded like Josh Withers. Billy frowned. Maggie had been going to have a bath – in fact, he'd heard her bring the tub in, and the scent of her soap had filtered under the gap around the door and up the stairs.

So what was Josh Withers doing here? Billy's mind boggled. She wouldn't have let him in, surely, if she wasn't decent? Unless . . .

Suddenly it was another unpleasant memory that was uppermost in Billy's mind – the sounds he'd heard sometimes coming from his mam and dad's room. Oh, surely Maggie wouldn't . . . would she? He knew from talk he'd overheard amongst the men and boys that it wasn't only married folk that did *that thing* – like the cows humping in the farm fields. But Maggie . . . Maggie would never think of doing anything like that, would she? Why, he'd never even seen her not properly dressed; she'd shout at him to stay out of the room even when she was wearing her camisole and bloomers.

A kind of shocked curiosity overcame Billy. Hardly daring to breathe, he crept down the stairs, keeping as close to the side of the treads as he could to stop them from creaking. The occasional one still did, though, and each time he froze, waiting. But the door didn't fly open, with Maggie yelling at him and demanding to know what he thought he was doing, and when he reached it, he could still hear the rise and fall of voices coming from the other side.

Ah – there was Josh, perched against the kitchen table. And Maggie . . . as he peeped round the door and saw her bending over the trivet and doing something with a saucepan, his first reaction was one of relief. She wasn't naked. She wasn't even in her underwear. She was all wrapped up in Mam's old dressing gown.

But hot on the heels of the relief came a wash of something that was almost disappointment.

He hadn't wanted to catch Maggie and Josh doing *that thing* – he hadn't! But the very thought of it fascinated him, teased at him, in a way he couldn't really understand.

As he watched, Maggie straightened up, turning, and Billy withdrew hastily, pulling the door closed and holding his breath. A moment later a scratch at it made him almost jump out of his skin. But it was only Bullseye. He'd seen his young master, even if Maggie and Josh hadn't. Billy opened the door again, keeping well back to allow Bullseye through unnoticed. Then, the dog at his heels, he crept back up the stairs and into his room.

He slipped into bed and Bullseye jumped up and settled down beside him. Well, at least now he had his pal for company. But Billy thought it would still be a long while before he would be able to get to sleep.

Except that this time it wasn't the terrible tragedy on his mind, but something quite different.

The rain was still coming down in sheets. Josh pulled up his coat collar and tucked his chin into it as he jogged back up the track. With his head bent, he didn't notice Hester Dallimore emerging from the privy in the block on the opposite side to the houses. He cannoned into her, and one of the spokes of the umbrella she was holding over herself struck his cheek a sharp, painful blow.

'Hey, look out!' Hester exclaimed shrilly. 'You trying to knock a body over?'

'Sorry, Mrs Dallimore.'

'You want to watch where you're going. You could have done me an injury, and broke my umbrella into the bargain.'

'Sorry,' he said again.

He was in no mood to argue, or give her cheek as he might sometimes have done. He was elated. He'd done it! He'd bloody done it! He'd invited Maggie to the dance, and she'd accepted! Why, he felt like dancing right now! What would Hester Dallimore say if he caught hold of her and whirled her round, out here in the middle of the track in the pouring rain?

The very idea made him chuckle. Hester, hearing, called after him in annoyance.

'It's no laughing matter, Josh Withers! You're nothing but a young hooligan.'

'You're right there, Mrs Dallimore,' he called back over his shoulder. 'But let's look on the bright side. At least you didn't manage to put my eye out with that brolly of yours.'

He didn't catch her reply, just the angry slam of her door, and he laughed again from sheer exhilaration. He wasn't going to let a miserable old biddy like her upset him. Not even his stinging cheek bothered him, though he thought there might be blood trickling down his face along with the rain.

He was going to take Maggie to the dance. There was a long way to go yet, but it was a start. And Josh couldn't have been happier.

Maggie was really looking forward to going to the dance on Saturday. Josh was right, she could hardly remember when she'd last had any fun. The whole of the summer had been lost in a black morass of grief, worry and work. She hadn't been to a single social event, not the fetes, not the circus, and certainly not a dance.

Not that she'd ever been to many dances, and usually they had been the ones that followed one of the summer galas, when folk gathered on the recreation field or in the town square, and the Salvation Army band, more often than not, played. Jack had taken her once or twice, but since neither of them knew more than a few steps, it was more a case of jiggling about in time to the music than really dancing, and it had usually ended up as an excuse for a cuddle – well, if Jack got his way, anyway. Maggie was always too conscious of making a show in public and had tried her best to keep him at arm's length. It had been fun, though; the music always set her feet tapping and she wished she could learn to do it properly, as the gentry did.

But it wasn't just going to the dance that was exciting her. It was the prospect of a whole evening with Josh. Try as she might, Maggie couldn't forget the sparks that had crackled and fizzed between them that night when he had so very nearly kissed her, couldn't forget the heady euphoria and the longing that had rushed through her in a flood tide. Though she knew she shouldn't, she couldn't help imagining how it would be to dance with him, his arm around her, or at least his hand on her waist, and when she did, she felt dizzy with pleasurable anticipation. And the best part was that no one would think anything of it. It was what you were supposed to do when you were dancing, and there was no danger of things getting out of control when you were surrounded by other people.

Just as long as they didn't think she had no business being out enjoying herself, with her father and Jack dead only a few months . . . Just as long as they didn't think that she didn't care . . . The ever-present anxiety cast a shadow over her eager anticipation, but she tried to tell herself that surely no one could begrudge her one evening when she could forget about her troubles, and that the other revellers would know that Josh was simply escorting her because he was Jack's brother, and was looking after her for him.

But did she believe that any more? Was it just wishful thinking on her part, or had something really changed between them?

Josh had called in almost every evening over the last week, and though nothing untoward had happened, she was sure she'd felt that chemistry sizzling between them. The slightest of accidental touches set her skin shivering, the shared smiles filled her with joy, and when their eyes met, there was something in his gaze that made her almost believe he felt the same way she did. You've taken leave of your senses, she told herself. But daring to think he might made her feel good, so good that she didn't want to put an end to it.

Saturday came at last. All day, butterflies fluttered in Maggie's stomach, and she could barely concentrate on her work – she gave customers the wrong change twice, and then managed to spill a paper twist of pins all over the counter.

'What's up with you today, Miss Donovan?' Cathy asked, helping her to scoop them up again. 'You're like a cat on hot bricks.'

Maggie, down on her knees looking to see if any of the pins had fallen on to the floor, hesitated. She was reluctant to tell Cathy, who wouldn't be able to keep it to herself for a moment, but then after tonight, everyone else who attended the event would know anyway, wouldn't they?

She rescued some stray pins and got up.

'I'm going to a dance,' she confided. 'Josh is taking me. But I'm still not really sure whether I should go or not. What do you think?'

Cathy's face was a picture.

'Of course you should go! Why ever not?'

'It's not that long, though, is it, since Dad and Jack . . . You don't think I should still be in mourning?'

'You *are* in mourning!' Cathy said. 'But you need something to cheer you up. And I should think Josh Withers is just the right person to do it. He's quite a one, isn't he?'

Maggie bit her lip. *Quite a one.* He certainly was. At the unbidden thought, colour flooded her cheeks, and Cathy's eyes widened.

'Miss Donovan!' She pursed her lips as if trying to suppress a giggle. 'I do believe you fancy him!'

'Don't be silly!' Maggie snapped, but Cathy was still looking at her in that knowing way, and she relented.

'I do like him,' she admitted. 'That's the trouble, really. It makes me feel so guilty.'

'Now you're the one that's being silly,' Cathy said pertly. 'You've nothing to feel guilty about. It's only a dance, isn't it? Whatever is wrong with that? Jack would want you to have some fun. He wouldn't want you turning into a dried-up old maid.'

'I suppose not, but . . .'

'You just go and enjoy yourself. I wish I was going myself. Now if your Ewart was here . . .'

Maggie smiled. She'd wondered how long it would be before Cathy got around to mentioning Ewart.

'He was asking after you the last letter I had,' she said. 'But Yorkshire is an awful long way away, Cathy. You'd be far better off with a local lad.'

'Mm.' Cathy looked regretful.

The doorbell jangled; a customer was coming in.

'Just you stop worrying, Miss Donovan, and go out and have a lovely time,' Cathy whispered as the two girls lined up behind the counter, ready to serve. 'And let's just hope Mrs Freeman doesn't keep you too late tonight.'

'Let's hope not,' Maggie whispered back.

It was something else that had been worrying her a little; by the time she got home and changed into the fresh blouse and skirt she'd put out ready, they were bound to be late arriving at the dance. She'd warned Josh that she couldn't be sure what time she'd be able to get away, and he had said it didn't matter.

'Just as long as we get there before the beer's sold out, and in time for the refreshments,' he'd joked. 'We don't want to miss out on those.'

'Speak for yourself, Josh Withers!' she'd retorted. 'I don't know as I want dried-up sandwiches, and I certainly don't want any beer!'

But she knew Josh would be both hungry and thirsty, and she wasn't even sure whether they would make it in time for the interval refreshments if there was a stream of late customers coming into the shop.

She was watching the door anxiously when, just before seven, Augusta Freeman called her into the back room. Maggie's heart sank – she was in for a rollicking, she thought, over all the silly mistakes she'd been making today. But to her surprise, Augusta regarded her benignly.

'I'm quite happy for you to get off now, Maggie. I'm sure we can manage without you until closing time.'

Maggie's jaw dropped, and Augusta smiled – a fairly rare occurrence.

'You have a social evening to attend, I understand.'

'Well, yes, but . . .'

'Off you go, then. You don't want to be late.'

'Thank you, Mrs Freeman.' Maggie felt quite flustered, the butterflies skittering again.

'Don't thank me, my dear. Thank Cathy. She's offered to do all the jobs you generally do when we close for the weekend.'

'Oh, that's really nice of her!' Maggie was quite overwhelmed.

Fancy Cathy taking it upon herself to go to Mrs Freeman and beg time off for her!

'Let's not waste any more time, then.' Augusta resumed her usual stern manner, but Maggie thought she saw a twinkle in her employer's eye. 'And do try to enjoy yourself, Maggie, and forget all your troubles for a little while at least.'

'Thank you, Mrs Freeman,' Maggie said again.

And as the nervous excitement swelled inside her, she almost ran from the shop.

Reuben Hillman, standing by the glass-panelled door of the gents' outfitters next door so as to watch out for potential customers, saw Maggie leave and burned with the rage of frustrated desire and injustice.

He'd kept away from her since the night Josh had come after him and punched him in his own front room, because he was scared of what might happen if he didn't. Like all bullies, Reuben was a coward. He didn't want Josh going for him again, and neither did he want to incur his father's wrath. Clarence had been furious with him, as if the whole sorry incident had been his fault, and the atmosphere at home had been horrible for days afterwards, with his father glowering at him over the breakfast and dinner table, and his mother looking ready to burst into tears. They were disappointed in him, he knew, and their opinion meant a great deal to him. They were the ones, after all, who made him feel good about himself when nobody else seemed to like or admire him, and he couldn't bear it when even they seemed to turn against him.

But none of this changed the way he felt about Maggie. He couldn't shed his obsession with her like a snake shedding its skin. He wanted her as badly as ever, and he was just as determined that one day he'd have her. He just had to let this blow over. At least Jack Withers was out of the picture now, and though Josh had taken up cudgels on her behalf, he couldn't believe she'd look twice at a thug like him, not his lovely Maggie. He'd find a way to make her see that they were meant for each other, and when his parents got to know her, they'd love her too and welcome her into the family.

As the days had gone by, Reuben had talked himself into believing that this was the way it would be, curbing his impatience with the promise of what was to come – soon, very soon.

And then today, when he'd gone into the draper's side of the business to get change for the outfitter's till, he'd overheard Cathy Small asking Augusta Freeman if she'd let Maggie go early that evening as Josh Withers was taking her to a dance at the Miners' Welfare.

Reuben had scarcely been able to believe his ears. What in the world was Maggie thinking of? How could she turn him down and yet agree to go out with that varmint?

In that moment he hated her almost as much as he hated Josh Withers, and as he watched her hurry away across the street long before the shop closed, it boiled up in him again.

Who do you think you are, to treat me like this? he fumed. *I put you on a pedestal, and you're as bad as him!*

Until today, he'd never had a single bad thought about Maggie. Even when she'd spurned him, he'd made excuses for her. But this . . . this was a step too far.

As she disappeared into the darkness, Reuben moved away from the door. His hands were balled to fists, his flabby mouth pursed, and tears of anger and disappointment were gathering in his throat.

'Damn you, Josh Withers!' he muttered. 'And damn you too, Maggie.'

For the first time he was realising what a fine dividing line lay between love and hatred. For the first time he was thinking that if he could put his hands around Maggie's throat again, he'd strangle the life out of her. She wouldn't spurn him then! She'd be begging, pleading – and he'd be the one in control. Oh, that would feel good, so good. And she would be his at last, for ever.

Reuben's anger was suddenly superseded by a strange, wild elation. Maggie might be going to meet Josh Withers tonight, but his turn would come. He'd make sure of that.

Chapter Fifteen

Maggie flew along the track behind the Ten Houses and rapped on the door of the Withers house.

It was answered by Florrie, still wearing the big wraparound apron that womenfolk had usually taken off by this time of day. A delicious smell of baking wafted out around her.

Maggie felt a moment's nostalgia for the times when she'd come home from work to find their own kitchen full of the same appetising smell – Rose's fruit cakes were legendary, and they'd never lasted long when there was a hungry horde to demolish them, but Maggie thought those days had gone for good. Even if Rose was ever fit enough to make a cake again, she likely wouldn't bother, with only Maggie and Billy to eat it before it went stale.

But she was too excited tonight to dwell on times past.

'Oh, Mrs Withers, can you tell Josh I'm home? Mrs Freeman let me go early. I've just got to get changed now, that's all. If he gives me ten minutes, I'll be ready.'

'All right, Maggie, I'll tell him.' There was a certain reserve in Florrie's tone. She wasn't sure what she thought of Josh taking Maggie to a dance so soon after Jack . . . But she wasn't going to say so to either of them. Maggie had had a hard time lately, what with one thing and the other. She could do with something to take her out of herself. And if Josh had ideas about taking his brother's place, well, Maggie was a lovely girl whom anyone would be glad to have as a daughter-in-law. She just wished the thought of it didn't stick in her throat, but there it was. Maggie was bound to take up with another lad sometime, and what would be would be.

Maggie rushed home. Billy was in the kitchen, tucking into a plate of cold meat and bread, Bullseye sitting expectantly at his side.

'Oh good, you've got yourself something to eat, then,' she said. 'I got it ready before I went to work this morning because I knew I'd be in a rush when I got home. I'm going out.'

'Yes, so you said.'

'I'm sorry, Billy, but I can't stop to talk now. Josh will be here for me in a minute. You'll be all right, won't you?'

'I 'spect so,' Billy said, chewing on a mouthful of ham.

'I might be late home.'

'I'll be fine, our Maggie. I'm not a baby any more.'

'No, of course you're not.'

She hurried upstairs, slipped out of her working clothes and into her best blouse and skirt. The blouse had leg-of-mutton sleeves, and fastened at the cuff with a row of tiny pearl buttons; Maggie's fingers were shaking so much it seemed to take forever to do them up. Then she pinned a small silk rose on to the high collar band at the base of her throat – she'd experimented with it yesterday, and decided this was the best place for a touch of colour. And she'd been right. Now it seemed to reflect the pink glow of her cheeks that came partly from hurrying home and partly from excitement.

As she tidied her hair at the mirror on top of the chest of drawers, and slid a pretty comb into the knot at the nape of her neck, she heard voices downstairs. Josh was here! No time for anything else but to pinch some colour into her lips and check her image one last time before grabbing her shawl and running downstairs.

'Ready! How's that for a quick turnaround?'

His eyes were running over her appreciatively. The colour flamed in her cheeks again, and something sweet and sharp twisted inside her.

'You look lovely, Maggie,' he said. 'But are you going to be warm enough? Didn't you ought to wear a coat?'

'Oh, I don't want a coat!' It was the literal truth; she didn't want to spoil the effect of her best blouse and skirt by covering them with her old everyday coat, the only one she possessed. And she wasn't going to wear a hat either and risk dislodging the comb, which had cost her quite a lot of money in the days when she had had some of her wages to spare. 'It's a lovely night out now the rain has stopped, and I expect I shall be more than warm after all the dancing I'm going to be doing.'

'You reckon you're going to be dancing, then?' Josh said with a wicked twinkle.

'I certainly hope so! I thought that was the whole idea.'

'Like I told you, it's the supper and the beer I'm interested in.'

'Oh – men!' Maggie raised her eyes heavenward, knowing she was flirting again, and really not caring. When she lowered them, she encountered Josh's gaze, and there was another of those moments when their eyes held and time seemed to stand still. Then Josh crooked his arm, tucking her hand into it.

'Come on then.'

Maggie giggled.

At the door, she stopped, looking back over her shoulder.

'You will be all right, Billy, won't you?'

'Oh, for goodness' sake, Maggie!'

'We'll see you later, then.'

'I expect I'll be in bed by the time you get home.'

There was an expression on his face that she couldn't read. But then that was Billy all over. When did you ever really know what he was thinking? She remembered Mam once saying that Billy was different, and it was true, he was. Sometimes it felt as if he didn't belong on this planet, never mind in this family.

She wasn't going to worry about that now, though.

Josh opened the door and they stepped out into the cold, clear night.

By the time they arrived at the Miners' Welfare hall, the dance was already in full swing, the music floating out of the half-opened windows. It wasn't quite what Maggie had been expecting – a couple of fiddles and a squeeze box, by the sound of it – but it sounded jolly, and when they climbed the flight of steps and went into the hall, they were greeted by the sight of dozens of people lined up in the centre of the floor, clapping as they executed something that looked like a grown-up version of 'Oranges and Lemons'. The couple at the end had their arms raised to form an arch, and another couple, holding hands, were scooting down the space between the lines, ducking beneath the arch and taking up their new position.

'Whatever are they doing?' Maggie asked.

'Looks like a country dance,' Josh said.

'What's that? I've never seen anything like it!'

'Then you haven't lived.' He laughed. 'Come on, get rid of that shawl and we'll join in.'

'No!' Maggie was horrified. 'I wouldn't know what to do!'

'You don't need to. That bloke's calling out the moves. All you have to do is what he tells you.'

A short, fat, bewhiskered man was indeed shouting

instructions, his voice just about audible over the wheeze of the accordion. But even so . . .

'Let's watch for a minute,' Maggie begged. 'We can't just barge in anyway.'

'Fair enough.' Josh grinned at her. 'But don't think you can get away with it for ever. Next dance – we're in. Now, let's see if we can get a drink before the thirsty crowds hit the bar. What would you like?'

'Oh, I don't know . . .' Maggie wasn't a drinker. In her book, drinking was for the menfolk. There were women, she knew, who liked a drop of gin, but she didn't think it was very seemly. She associated it with those who were no better than they should be, like Aggie Weeks, who lived in a hovel in the court-yard behind the Prince of Wales, and was known to entertain gentlemen visitors in exchange for money to pay for her habit. Not that they were gentlemen, of course, far from it, but at least the expression described what was going on there without sounding vulgar.

'Leave it to me.' Josh escorted her to a vacant seat on the edge of the dance floor and made for the bar.

As Maggie sat watching the dancers, she began to feel a little less intimidated. At least there was a pattern emerging – they seemed to be doing the same routine over and over again.

Josh still hadn't returned when the dance ended; there was quite a crush in the bar, Maggie supposed, with a lot of people waiting to be served.

'Hey! That's my seat you're sitting in!'

A buxom woman was standing right in front of Maggie, glaring at her belligerently. It was Peggy Bishop.

'Oh, I'm sorry . . .' Maggie rose quickly, feeling flustered again.

'Didn't know these chairs were booked out, Peg.'

Maggie hadn't seen Josh returning amongst the crowd of

dancers who were now leaving the floor. But here he was, a glass in each hand.

'Josh!' Peggy looked startled. 'I didn't expect to see you here.'

'Well there you are, life's full of surprises,' he said easily.

Peggy backed off a little.

'It was our seats, though.'

'We weren't to know that, were we?'

'Come on, Peg. There's room over there.' Tom Bishop appeared at Peggy's shoulder, looking rather uncomfortable.

That wasn't like Tom Bishop, Maggie thought. He had a reputation for being nasty-tempered. But she was relieved, all the same, as he gave Peggy a little prod and led her off. She'd have willingly vacated the seat rather than cause trouble, but she had a feeling Josh intended to stand his ground. In spite of his affable tone, there had been a determined set to his face. He wasn't going to see her pushed around, and knowing it more than made up for the awkward moment.

'Here we are, then. I got you a sweet cider.' Josh handed her a mug brimming with amber liquid and sat down beside her. 'See what you think of that.'

Maggie took a tentative sip, then another.

'It's quite nice.'

'Haven't you ever had cider before?'

She shook her head.

'Take it steady, then. I don't want to have to carry you home.' he warned her.

Maggie thought secretly that she would quite enjoy that. But of course she didn't say so.

From the opposite side of the room, where they'd found fresh seats, Peggy Bishop was glaring surreptitiously at Maggie.

What was she doing here with Josh? What was Josh doing

here at all, come to that? She'd never have expected to see him at the dance – but then she was quite surprised to find herself and Tom here. When she'd heard about it, and mentioned that she quite fancied going, she'd expected him to pooh-pooh the idea. He hadn't taken her to a dance since their courting days. But to her surprise he'd come around. 'Well, we could go if you like, I suppose,' he'd said. She'd still expected him to change his mind at the last minute, but tonight, after they'd had their tea, he'd spruced himself up and here they were. He was even dancing instead of propping up the bar as she'd expected. He was acting differently lately, not a doubt of it. Ever since the accident at the pit, really.

The twist of strange dark excitement stirred in Peggy, the same excitement she felt every time she wondered if Tom might have had something to do with it. Strange as it seemed, things were better between them than they had been for years, as if fires that had all but gone out had been rekindled.

The band was getting ready to start up again, the caller inviting couples to take to the floor. Peggy saw Josh put his beer beneath his seat and get up, taking Maggie's hand.

In spite of her revived feelings for Tom, a little bolt of jealousy she couldn't contain shot through her, making her eyes narrow and her mouth tighten. She still fancied Josh, always had, always would. But perhaps it was all to the good that he was here tonight with Maggie Donovan and Tom had seen them together. He'd know that if Josh was courting Maggie, he wouldn't be sneaking off to meet Peggy. She thought again about what Tom had said after the terrible tragedy of the hudge. *He'd better leave you alone if he doesn't want to end up like his brother.* Yes, much as it stuck in her craw to see Josh with Maggie, perhaps it was for the best. She didn't want any more deaths on her conscience.

* * *

Though the windows had all been left partly open to the cold autumn air, it was hot and muggy in the hall from the sheer number of folk and their exertions, and Maggie's skin felt quite sticky under her blouse.

They'd been dancing almost non-stop, and she was really enjoying herself. Josh had been right, it wasn't difficult to follow the instructions of the caller, just as long as you could hear him over the band, and if you did make a mistake it didn't really matter; everyone was getting things wrong, and just laughing about it as the set descended into chaos.

The great 'grand chain' was fun, going hand-over-hand round a circle of dancers and never knowing who you would end up with as your partner, though Maggie was always glad to get back to Josh. She watched as he came nearer and nearer, her heart beating expectantly, and groaned inwardly if they had to pass and go on again. But best of all she loved the dances where he was required to whirl her round and round, his hands on her waist to steady her – and she certainly needed steadying! She'd had two glasses of cider now, drinking the last one down almost as if it were water in spite of Josh's warnings, and the spins were making her quite giddy. Then there were the exhilarating moments when she, Josh and another couple had to form a tight knot, arms around each other, and circle so fast that she and the other girl were lifted clean off their feet. Maggie screamed as her boots left the floor and her legs swung out behind her. But she was perfectly safe, supported by two strong men and hanging on to them herself for dear life, and when she was lowered again she collapsed against Josh, laughing and resting her head on his chest as the room spun around her.

'I think I need some fresh air,' she admitted.

'Get your shawl, then. It'll be cold outside.'

'That's exactly what I need!' Maggie said recklessly. 'I don't want to bother with a shawl – I just want to cool off! Come on!'

She pulled Josh towards the door and down the steps. The night air was cold on her hot cheeks and she breathed it in, crisp and clean after the heat and the tobacco fug inside the hall.

'Oh, this is such fun!'

'Glad you're enjoying it.'

'I am! Oh, I am!'

He caught her hand, pulling her in close with his arm around her, and she didn't resist. Her head nestled against his shoulder, and it felt so good, and at the same time just a little unreal, as if she were in a dream. They walked along the pavement to where an alleyway ran along the side of the hall. Josh turned into it, and before she knew it, Maggie was in his arms.

It was dark here; only the faintest glow from the gas lamp on the main street reached the alcove in which they were standing, so she couldn't see his face. But the scent of him was in her nostrils, intoxicating her – that familiar masculine scent of tobacco and beer and just the slightest hint of fresh sweat – and the nearness of him was making her skin prickle and her pulses race. She raised her head from the solid wall of his chest, and as his mouth came down on hers, something sharp and sweet twisted deep inside her.

His kiss was gentle at first, then, as her lips moved and parted beneath his, it became deeper, more urgent, and Maggie felt her own excitement rising with his. She'd never experienced anything like it in her life before; she'd quite enjoyed Jack's kisses, just as long as he didn't try to go any further, but this . . . this was something quite different. She felt as if she were floating outside her own body, and yet she was more aware of every nerve ending, every inch of skin, every bit of the deepest parts of her than she could ever have imagined possible. Except that she wasn't imagining, or even thinking. There was no room for thought. Only feeling. Ecstasy. Desire. A pressing need to be closer, closer still . . .

Suddenly Josh held her away.

'I think it's time we were going.' His voice was rough. 'You wait here and I'll get your shawl.'

Without waiting for a reply, he walked away from her, back towards the entrance of the hall, leaving her there in a state of shock. She felt bereft, suddenly, disappointed and frustrated. One minute he had been kissing her as if he wanted it every bit as much as she did; the next . . . Why had he walked off like that? Had she done something wrong? She was hope-lessly inexperienced in such matters, she knew. Josh was probably used to kissing girls who knew what to do much better than she did. And yet every fibre of her body ached with longing, and more than anything she wanted to experience that exhilarating madness again.

After just a few minutes he was back with her shawl. As he went to put it round her shoulders, she shivered.

'You're cold,' he said. His voice still sounded rough. 'I told you you would be.'

'I'm all right.'

'No you're not.'

It was true. The perspiration soaking her blouse had cooled, and the fabric now felt unpleasantly cold and damp against her skin.

'Here, have my coat, at least until you warm up.' He shrugged out of the jacket he'd retrieved from the hall along with her shawl, and draped it around her shoulders. She shivered again at his touch.

'Josh?' she said in a small voice. 'Don't you want to kiss me again?'

He snorted.

'You know damn well I do!'

She turned to him, shamelessly placing her hands on his chest, raising her face to his.

'Why don't you, then?'

'Because if I do, I can't guarantee what will happen, Maggie. Don't you know you're driving me crazy?'

'Oh!' The warmth was seeping back into her veins, even if it hadn't yet reached her chilled skin, and recklessness overcame her. 'I just really, really want you to kiss me again . . .'

'And I want a lot more. So I think we ought to get going before I do something I'll regret.'

'What if I want it too?' She couldn't believe she'd said that, but the madness was spiralling out of control and she could think of nothing but how much she wanted him, needed him. Really, nothing else in the whole world mattered.

'Maggie, you don't know what you're saying,' he said, sounding agonised.

'I do, Josh! I really, really want you.'

'Come on,' he said shortly. 'I'm going to take you home.'

His good intentions didn't last long, with Maggie snuggling beneath his arm, her head resting on his shoulder, stumbling a little as she walked. Her hair smelled sweet and soapy; he lowered his chin to drink it in, and when she turned her face up to his, he couldn't resist kissing her again.

The attraction between them was a force field, showering them with sparks even as it magnetised and drew them together; they were lost in it. The walk home took much longer than usual because clinging together slowed their steps and they stopped frequently to kiss again, kisses that only ratcheted up the intensity of the desire that was consuming them. They scarcely spoke; there was no need for words.

The terrace was in darkness, but for a lamp burning in an upstairs window of number four. Annie Day, unable to sleep again, no doubt. She was still in a terrible way at the loss of John.

When they reached Maggie's door, they kissed again. It was beginning to feel right now, comfortable as well as exciting.

'You want me to come in?' Josh asked softly.

'I don't want you to go.'

She opened the door and Josh followed her into the deserted kitchen. Good as his word, Billy must have gone to bed and taken Bullseye with him; there was neither sight nor sound of either of them.

Almost before the door had closed behind them, they were in each other's arms again, kissing, clinging, touching. And this time, neither of them had the will to stop.

Chapter Sixteen

Once during the night Maggie woke. She had no idea what time it might be, and she cared less. Cocooned in the darkness, she lay quite still for a few moments, drowsily basking in the rosy glow of contentment that suffused her. Her whole body felt replete and languorous, but she gradually became aware of little aches niggling in the pit of her stomach, and the place between her legs burned a bit too.

She slid her hands beneath her nightgown, wriggling it up over her thighs, and ran them over her stomach. The skin felt moist and slightly sticky, and as her fingers explored, a little echo of the sensations that had overwhelmed her earlier stirred deep within her.

As she relished it, the memory of all that had happened floated through her mind, precious, exciting, and yet hazy, as if it had all been a dream.

Josh's hands caressing every inch of her body, his mouth on her lips, her throat, her breasts. The sharp but somehow wonderful shock as his teeth closed over her nipple. The desperate ache of longing deep inside her as she raised her hips to his. The moment's fierce, searing pain as his body entered hers. The glory of feeling him moving inside her. His shout of triumph. And then, when it was over, the wonderful contentment that came from lying in his arms, his heart beating next to hers, their legs entwined, breathing synchronised.

And yet still she had wanted him, still the need yawned deep within her, still every inch of her flesh tingled, sensitised, drawn to his as if by an invisible magnet. It wasn't over yet; she was still yearning for him with every nerve ending, every tiny muscle, every breath.

And he seemed to know it. He took her again, there on the rug in front of the last faintly glowing embers of the fire, slowly this time, slowly and gently until the frantic need was screaming within her. His tongue was where his fingers and body had been and she'd writhed in delight, shameless with desire.

Oh Josh, oh Josh!

Nothing mattered, nothing, but to have him inside her again.

And he was. Moving rhythmically, deeper and deeper. Withdrawing so that she arched her back to find him, then thrusting deep within her once more. She'd thought she was going to die with the intensity of the sensations she was experiencing. Her nails raked his bare back as they grew more and more powerful, and she was swept up to a plateau of ecstasy that seemed to last for ever.

She gasped, then screamed, and Josh's hand covered her mouth, quietening her. Afterwards, lying once more in his arms, she was terrified that she might have woken Billy, but the house was quiet, the only sounds her own uneven breathing and Josh's voice, soft in her ear.

'All right, my love?'

'Yes . . . oh yes . . . oh Josh . . .'

She didn't want him to go, she wanted him to stay here for ever, holding her in his arms until the end of time. But he couldn't, of course. She watched as he got dressed, the faint glow of the firelight making planes and shadows of the long, hard muscles and the hollows that lay between them. She slipped into her blouse and stepped into her skirt with a reluctance she knew he shared, because as she did up her blouse, he took her in his arms again, kissing the valley between her breasts before fastening the tiny pearl buttons himself. He kissed her again, then kissed his fingers and pressed them to her lips, and on his fingers she could taste and smell her own self.

She followed him to the door, wanting to watch him walk up the track, to drink in every last moment of him, but he shook his head.

'Go back inside, Maggie. I want to know you're safe. I'd put you to bed myself, but . . .'

But with Billy asleep in the room across the landing, that wasn't an option.

Maggie tossed her head, regaining a little of the pertness that seemed to come naturally with Josh these days.

'I'm perfectly capable of putting myself to bed, thank you very much!'

'Mind you do. No falling asleep in the chair or you'll catch your death. Night night, my love.'

'Night night.'

And he was gone.

Now, half asleep, Maggie had very little recollection of getting ready for bed. She must have undressed again and put on her nightdress, since she was wearing it now, and she must have pulled the curtains and climbed into bed. But it was all something of a blur.

I do believe that cider made me tipsy! she thought, and giggled softly. For the moment, nothing mattered but that she and Josh had shared something utterly wonderful, and for the first time in her life she felt complete.

* * *

It was still dark when Maggie woke again, but she knew it must be almost morning because she could hear Billy up and about, getting ready for work, and guessed it must have been him who'd disturbed her.

The niggles were still there in her stomach, but now they felt more uncomfortable than pleasurable; her head was thick and muzzy, her mouth horribly dry and her throat parched, and a dull ache throbbed beneath one eyebrow. And it wasn't just the aches and pains that were bothering her now, either. Conscience had begun to prick her too, and the first barbs of shame.

What in the world had she done? The memory of it was no longer warm and exciting, but horrifying.

Oh! Maggie thought, beginning to tremble. How could I have let something like that happen? How could I have behaved so shamelessly?

She knew, of course. It must have been the cider, two whole glasses when she wasn't used to so much as a single sip. She had a sudden vision of her father tumbling up the stairs after he'd had too much beer and maybe a whisky chaser or two, and a memory of one long-ago night when a young Ewart had been found asleep in the grassy bank at the turning to the rank after a wild night out with some of his friends. But she couldn't understand how she could have been so stupid. Drunk! No better than her father. No better than the gangs of youths fighting and roistering outside the alehouses. No better than Aggie Weeks, tippling away at her gin and then going with men to get the money to buy more.

Oh, the shame of it!

And worse, far worse, allowing Josh liberties such as she'd never imagined in her wildest dreams, and enjoying every moment of it! Josh, of all people! Jack's own brother! How could she ever face him again? How could she face anyone, knowing what she'd done?

Maggie pressed her hands over her mouth, closing her eyes as if she could somehow erase the memory of it, make it all go away.

Oh Jack, Jack, I am so sorry! Oh, what have I done? How could I? How could I?

Shame, regret, disgust with herself, anger with Josh for taking advantage of her when she'd been in that awful, inebriated state, all welled up inside her, and, shaking, Maggie buried her throbbing head in the pillow and wished she could die.

The morning was half gone before Maggie felt well enough to get up and go downstairs. She didn't know when she'd last stayed so late in bed, but each time she'd tried to get up she'd become nauseous and dizzy and her head felt as if Walter Browning, the blacksmith, was hammering on his anvil inside it. There was a certain safety to be had in the blankets bunched around her. She could, if she wanted, pull them right over her head and shut out the world.

The very thought of having to face a single living soul was a sickening one. They'd know, they must do, what a terrible thing she'd done, what a terrible woman she was. To behave like a common floozy, and not only that, to betray Jack's memory so flagrantly with his own brother! As if she hadn't been betraying it for weeks with her feelings for Josh. That had been bad enough – but this . . . !

Every time she thought of it, Maggie cringed and her cheeks flamed scarlet. But eventually there was nothing for it but to struggle downstairs and make herself a cup of strong tea.

When a knock came at the door at about midday, she didn't want to answer it. She hung back, hoping that whoever it was would think there was no one home and go away. But the door clicked open, and a moment later the last voice on earth she wanted to hear was calling her name.

'Maggie? It's me!'

Josh. Panic filled her.

'What do you want?' she demanded as he came into the scullery.

'That's a nice welcome, I must say!' He brushed drops of moisture from his shoulders; it must be raining again. She hadn't noticed, she'd not so much as glanced out since coming downstairs.

'Are you all right?' he asked, giving her a concerned look.

'I've got a terrible headache, and I don't feel very well.'

'Ah.' He pulled a sympathetic face. 'A hangover. Bit of a bugger, aren't they? That's what it will be.'

'If you say so. I wouldn't know. I've never had one before.'

He grinned. 'No, I don't suppose you have. But you were certainly letting into that cider last night.'

The confusion she was feeling was making her angry; anger was far preferable to the awful combination of embarrassment and shame.

'You shouldn't have bought it for me. You know I don't drink.'

He raised an eyebrow.

'Maggie, you're a grown woman. You didn't have to drink it. Anyway, I thought it was doing you good. It was nice to see you enjoying yourself for once. Forgetting all the bad stuff for a bit.'

The bad stuff. The accident. Mam's miscarriage. Dad. Jack. Most of all, Jack.

'That's what was behind it, I suppose – you getting me drunk. It was *myself* you wanted me to forget. And I did. Oh, I'm so ashamed! I'll never forgive myself, never!'

'Hey, wait a minute, Maggie, I did not get you drunk, at least not on purpose. Oh, come here, you silly girl . . .' He took a step towards her, and she backed off as if facing a rabid dog.

'Stay away from me, Josh!'

He raised both hands in submission, frowning now.

'All right, all right! What in the world has got into you? Last night—'

'Don't mention last night!' She was trembling now, and the colour was hot in her cheeks. 'Don't ever mention it! I don't know what got into me! Well, I do . . . the drink . . . but to do what I did . . . Oh!' She broke off, covering her mouth with her hands. 'What must you think of me?' she whispered from behind her splayed fingers. 'And Jack. What would Jack think if he knew? Letting myself down like that? Letting you . . . What if he does know? What if he was watching us?'

'Oh Maggie, love . . .'

'No, what if he was?'

'Maggie, Jack is dead,' he said gently.

'But his spirit's still alive. He could be here, right now, looking down . . . What would he *think?* He'd be so hurt, Josh. So hurt!'

The tears were coming now; her throat was thick with them.

'Oh Maggie, don't torture yourself like this,' Josh groaned.

'Why not? Isn't it what I deserve? And you? Don't you feel the least bit guilty? Betraying him like that? Taking advantage of me?'

Something of what she said struck a nerve.

'Dammit, you wanted it as much as I did,' Josh growled, thrown suddenly on the defensive.

'Don't try to put the blame on me!' Maggie flashed. The tears were flowing now, running down her cheeks and trickling between her fingers, tears of guilt and grief and shame.

'Oh Maggie, don't cry!' Josh said helplessly. 'All right . . . it was my fault. I should have realised you didn't know what you were doing. But you can only push a man so far, and the way I feel about you . . . you're more than flesh and blood can stand, Maggie. These last few weeks – well, I thought you felt the same way. Seems I was mistaken, and if it wasn't what you wanted, then I'm sorry.'

For a long moment she stood motionless as his words sank in, then slowly she raised her eyes, still sparkling with tears, looking at him over the tips of her fingers.

'Oh Josh . . .'

She didn't need to say any more; it was there, written all over her face. Josh experienced a jolt of elation. He hadn't been mistaken. She did feel as he did. Then she started sobbing again.

'But it's wrong! So wrong! How can I want you so much when Jack's scarcely cold in his grave? How can I feel like that? We were going to be married. Married! And yet I never . . .' She broke off, unable to say those final words of betrayal: that for all their closeness, she had never wanted Jack as she had wanted Josh last night – as, in spite of everything, she still wanted him. Even now, mortified as she was at what had happened, her treacherous heart was aching for Josh, her body crying out for the comfort of his touch.

'I am a wicked, wicked woman,' she whispered, and the tears began again.

'Maggie, don't, please!' He came towards her again, and this time she didn't back away. He put his arms around her and she laid her head against his chest, sobbing softly, not really knowing any more why she was crying except that the weight within her was too great to bear.

At last her sobs quietened to hiccups and the tears slowed

and stopped. As she lifted her face, he scrabbled in his pocket for his handkerchief.

'Here . . .'

She dried her eyes, blew her nose, thrust the handkerchief back at him.

'You'd better take it this time, or you won't have any left.'

He gave her a puzzled look, and she sniffed a wry half-laugh.

'The one you lent me before. I've still got it. Under my pillow. How stupid is that? I just . . . like it being there.'

He smiled. 'You can have every handkerchief I own if that's what you want.'

'Oh – just one's enough.'

He brushed that stray lock that never would behave away from her cheek, let his fingers caress the lobe of her ear, slide down to stroke her neck.

'Better now?'

She nodded. 'Mm. My head's still pounding a bit, though.'

'I'm not surprised. It will go soon, I promise. Come and sit down, sweetheart.'

He sat down himself in Rose's armchair and pulled her on to his lap.

'So – what are we going to do?'

'What do you mean?' Maggie asked, puzzled.

'About us. I want you, Maggie, and I think you want me.'

At his words it all came rushing back: the guilt, the shame – and the despair.

'There's nothing we can do, is there? Not with things the way they are. It would be an insult to Jack's memory if we . . .' Her voice tailed off miserably.

Josh was silent, not knowing how to counter her argument. He wanted to say that Jack wouldn't want Maggie to mourn him for ever. That he'd want her to find happiness – the happiness that Josh believed they could share. But he couldn't find the words. It would simply sound as if he was chasing his own selfish ends.

'What would people say?' Maggie went on distractedly. 'Oh, I don't care about myself. I've learned not to take much notice, although it isn't always easy. But I do care that they don't think Jack can be forgotten so easily. Because he can't. He never will be.'

'Of course he won't be forgotten. But—'

'But it would look to other people as if he had been. As if we didn't care. You must see that, surely? I can't just take up with someone else, not now, not yet. And especially not his own brother. It makes a mockery of what we had. Besides . . .' Maggie hesitated, biting her lip, 'to be honest, I'm not sure I'm ready. It's too soon. This morning I felt so guilty, not just about what we did, but about the way I feel. I just hated myself. I can't live like that, Josh. Do you understand?'

He shrugged helplessly. This was all getting too complicated for him. Josh was a simple man who didn't go into things too deeply.

'All I know is that I want you, Maggie, and I think you want me. That's what really matters.'

'But it wouldn't be right. And I don't just mean what other people would think. If I feel this guilty now, how much worse would it be if we were openly courting? What if every time we . . . well, you know . . . did what we did last night, all I can think about is that I'm betraying Jack? You'll get angry with me, and I'll hate myself, and it would spoil everything. You must see – I just can't do it, Josh. Not yet, not for a long while yet.'

Josh felt deflated, but he could see that pressurising Maggie just now would do no good.

'All right, we'll take it slowly,' he said.

'No.' Maggie wriggled out of his arms and stood up, crossing the kitchen, then turning to face him. Her lips were a tight, determined line. 'That won't work either. We've got to stop seeing each other. It's the only way.'

'For goodness' sake, Maggie, this is ridiculous!' he exploded.

'Look, to begin with, however discreet we might be, people will find out. They will! They're not stupid. They saw us at the dance together last night. They'll see you coming here; they'll put two and two together. Your mam and dad especially, and that would be bound to upset them. And being secretive about it somehow makes it all the worse. It just goes to prove we have something to be ashamed of. We'd be the talk of the town before long, just as much as if we were open about it.'

'Oh Maggie . . .'

'And then there's the other thing.' Hot colour flooded her cheeks. 'What we did last night. That can't happen again. It mustn't.'

'What if I promise to make sure it doesn't?'

Even as he said it, Josh was wondering if he'd be able to find the strength to control himself when they were alone, and Maggie, clearly, was thinking the same thing.

'That's easier said than done.' She wiped her damp palms on her skirt. 'If we're here, on our own – what was it you said just now? "More than flesh and blood can stand"? No, the only way is to stop seeing one another altogether until . . . well, at least until there's a decent interval and I don't feel I'm being unfaithful to Jack just being with you, let alone anything else.'

Josh's dismay came out on a snort.

'And will you ever feel that?'

Maggie bowed her head.

'I honestly don't know. I'm sorry. All I can tell you is how I feel right now.'

'Well if that's how you feel, I suppose there's nothing more to be said.' His tone was aggressive; he wasn't going to let her see how much her rejection was hurting him.

He strode to the door, looked back just once, perhaps hoping that she might relent even now. But her mouth was set in a firm line though he could see tears glistening again on her lashes.

'I'm sorry, Josh,' was all she said.

There had to be a way. Dammit, there had to be!

Josh had thought of nothing else for days, and it was driving him crazy. He'd drunk too much and slept too little, he was in the foulest of tempers, and each time he caught sight of Maggie, his gut wrenched and the blood raced in his veins.

All very well to have salvaged his dignity by walking away from her as if he'd accepted her decision and didn't care too much about it. The truth was, he couldn't stand being so close to her and yet so distant. If she was going to refuse to see him, he had to get away. But where? Not that it really mattered, just as long as he wasn't confronted daily with a tantalising glimpse of the woman who'd stolen his heart, his senses, his every waking thought.

He'd leave High Compton. He'd worry about her constantly, he knew, but it was the only way he could hold on to his pride and his sanity. He had a trade – surely he'd be able to find work as a carpenter pretty well anywhere? Wales, perhaps? He knew folk there, and could stay with his aunt and uncle until he found permanent lodgings. But their farm was in a remote spot, and besides, he could imagine his aunt asking too many questions that he didn't want to answer. Explaining to his mother and father why he was going away would be bad enough; there was no way he was going to admit to the truth.

Josh turned the possibilities over endlessly, and eventually came to a decision. He'd go to Bristol; Bristol was a busy port and he was confident he'd be able to find work there. It also had the advantage of being only fifteen or sixteen miles from High Compton, far enough to be well out of Maggie's way, but not so far that he couldn't get back if there was a family crisis – or if she needed him. And who knew? Maybe when he'd got a job and sorted out somewhere to live, she'd join him. She might feel less guilty about marrying him if they weren't under the noses of the people who knew she'd been engaged to Jack.

Marry him! Josh smiled to himself. He'd never so much as considered marriage before; now the thought of it came as easily to him as breathing. He wanted to marry her – nothing less would do. And the best way to achieve that was a fresh start for both of them, far from the scene of the tragedy and the people who mourned, out of sight of the black batches that were a constant reminder of the sacrifices of those who toiled far beneath the green fields.

Perhaps he'd ask her before he left. He couldn't see her accepting here and now, but at least she'd be left in no doubt about his feelings for her, and time might change her mind where he could not.

On the Sunday morning exactly two weeks after their last encounter, he decided to take the bull by the horns. Sunday was the one day he could be sure of finding her at home and Billy at work, the one day he could talk to her without fear of interruption. If she'd talk to him at all. She might well slam the door in his face . . .

Tension was a tight knot in his chest as he walked down the track. Josh, who took most things in his stride, admitted to himself that he had never felt more nervous in his life.

* * *

Maggie was making a stew. Cold and murky weather had set in and comfort food was called for A good big pot of scrag end beef and vegetables would last for days, ready to be warmed up when she got home, chilled to the marrow and perhaps wet through, after a hard day's work, and ready for Billy too if Farmer Barton's wife hadn't already fed him.

She'd found planning meals a chore these last two weeks; she seemed to have no energy or enthusiasm for anything, really. A shroud of depression had settled around her, thick and persistent as the fog that descended each evening – so dense it was difficult to see even the outhouses on the other side of the track, never mind the end of the rank – and sometimes lingered, grey and moist, most of the day. Maggie, usually sunny-natured and optimistic, felt trapped and miserable. After all the terrible things that had happened, she'd glimpsed joy and fulfilment beyond her wildest dreams, but that was all it could be, a glimpse, and even that had been spoiled by the feelings of guilt she couldn't ignore. What hope was there for her, torn between that guilt and her longing for Josh? None whatever, really. She was trapped between her conscience and her heart; she could see no way out, and it was a bad place to be.

It had been all she could do to summon the energy to begin making the stew, but now the beef was beginning to come to a simmer on the trivet over the fire, the carrots were peeled and cut up ready to pop in, and she was skinning the onions, which were already beginning to make her eyes sting. She blinked hard in an effort to keep them from running, but she knew she was fighting a losing battle. Before long, tears would be streaming down her cheeks and she'd barely be able to see what she was doing.

She tutted when she heard the knock at the door; she just

wanted to get the job in hand over and done with. She put down her knife, and with the onion still in her hand went to see who was there and what they wanted.

As she opened the door and saw Josh standing on the step, her heart lurched, and her hand tightened over the half-peeled onion.

'Oh!' For the moment, no other words would come.

'Maggie, I have to talk to you,' Josh said. 'Can I come in?'

'No! No, you can't!' Conflicting joy and dismay made her begin to tremble; really these days her nerves were so dreadfully on edge. 'You know . . . we agreed.'

'I didn't agree to anything,' Josh stated baldly.

'You shouldn't be here.' Maggie tried to close the door, but his foot was in the way. 'Josh, please . . .'

'Would you rather I said what I've come to say out here, where all the world can get an earful?'

'Oh – you are impossible!'

Beaten, Maggie opened the door. She didn't want anyone seeing him coming into the house when she was alone, but neither did she want to have an argument with him on the door-step. In a close-knit terrace like this one, there was little privacy, and though not everyone was as nosy as Hester Dallimore, they didn't miss much.

Josh came into the scullery and closed the door behind him. Suddenly she was aware of him with every fibre of her being. It was exactly what she was afraid of, that the nearness of him would make her weaken; lure her, before she could save herself, into doing something she'd very quickly come to regret.

She put the onion down on the cupboard top, wiping her hands on her long wraparound apron.

'Let's go in the kitchen.'

There was more room in the kitchen; she wouldn't be forced into such close proximity to him as in the cramped scullery. But it was also the very place where they'd—

Maggie cut off the memory. It horrified her, and yet it could still make her glow with remembered warmth. She and Josh on the rug in front of the fire, limbs entwined, bodies united. The glory of it. The contentment. And the shame.

'Just say what you've come to say and go,' she said shortly.

'Oh, for goodness' sake, Maggie!' Josh exploded. 'I'm not about to ravish you again, much as I might want to.'

The hot colour rushed to her cheeks. *I want it too! Oh, you have no idea how much!*

'That's all right then,' she heard herself say instead. 'Just as long as—'

'What do you take me for?' he demanded. Though he'd intended to keep his cool whatever her response, his defences were coming up and making him sound aggressive again. 'The only reason I'm here is because I've decided to go away. I thought I ought to tell you, and make sure you're all right before I leave.'

It was something else that had been preying on his mind; he didn't think it was likely Maggie would have fallen pregnant as a result of that one night of passion, but you never could be sure. His meaning was lost on Maggie, though; she'd heard only one thing, and her heart seemed to have stopped beating.

'You're going away? Where?'

'Bristol, I thought. I'm sure I can get a job there, better paid, too. I just thought you ought to know.'

'But why, Josh?' Maggie felt as if her world was falling apart around her.

'I can't stay here with things as they are. It's driving me crazy.'

'But I don't want you to go!' she said before she could stop herself.

He shook his head ruefully.

'You can't have it both ways, Maggie. You've made it pretty clear that there's no hope for us for the foreseeable future, and it seems to me it would be a darned sight easier for both of us if I was out of the way.'

'But . . . *Bristol*!' To Maggie, it felt as if he was proposing to fly to the moon.

Distractedly she rubbed her eyes, and instantly the onion juice on her fingers was stinging, making her wince and squeeze them tight. 'Oh, blooming onions!'

Josh didn't know whether to be grateful for the distraction. He was confused by the mixed messages Maggie was sending him. In one breath she was telling him she didn't want to so much as speak to him; in the next she was seemingly horrified by the idea of him moving away.

It was now or never, he decided.

'You could always come with me,' he said, quite flippantly.

Her squinting eyes appeared over the top of the back of her wrist.

'What are you talking about?'

'Come to Bristol with me. Nobody there knows us. It would be a fresh start. Oh, for goodness' sake, don't look so shocked, Maggie. I'm not trying to turn you into a scarlet woman. I'm asking you to marry me.' There. He'd said it.

All the breath seemed to leave Maggie's body in a rush and her mouth dropped open.

'Marry you!'

'Is it such a daft idea?'

Maggie's pulses were racing. She could not imagine anything more wonderful. But she was totally stunned by Josh's proposal.

It wasn't as if they'd been courting properly; he'd taken her out only the once. In any case, Josh had never seemed to her to be the marrying type – quite the opposite. What could have brought it on? Was he feeling guilty because of what had happened between them?

'A daft idea? Well, yes, it is really,' she said, more curtly than she meant to. 'Given the way things are.'

His ready defences were up.

'In that case, I'm sorry I asked.' His tone, too, was short, belying what this meant to him. 'But seeing as I'm going away, I thought . . .' He turned for the door.

'You thought what? That you'd better offer to make an honest woman of me?' she shot after him. 'That's very commendable of you, but it's really not necessary.'

'That's all right then.' He was in the scullery now, his hand on the door latch. 'I won't bother you again, don't worry.'

Maggie's heart was pounding in her throat. This was all happening too fast.

'Josh, please don't go, please . . . not like this.'

He turned back, and beneath the hard lines of his face she could see the hurt, clearly written. This wasn't just a proposal to save her honour; he'd asked her to marry him because it was what he wanted. He wasn't a man for flowery sentiments. They came no more easily to him than they had to Jack; perhaps even less so. But that didn't mean they didn't come from the heart.

'There's nothing I'd like better than to marry you, Josh,' she said. 'But I can't, don't you see? Not now. Not like this. We've been through it all before. You know how I feel. It's all very well to say that no one in Bristol would know about me and Jack, but people here would find out, they'd be bound to. Your mam and dad for a start. You can't keep something like that quiet. Besides,

I'd know, and I can't do it yet, I just can't. It feels all wrong, and it's no way to start a life together.'

He grimaced.

'Fair enough. I more or less knew what you'd say, but I thought it was worth a try. I know it's still Jack with you.'

'You're wrong. You couldn't be more wrong!' *I love you*! she wanted to say, but she couldn't bring herself to.

'Well that's how it seems from here,' he said ruefully. 'We look alike pretty much, so I'm the closest you could get to having him back.'

'No!' But how could she explain that she had never felt this way about Jack without doing the very thing she was trying so hard not to do – denigrate his memory? 'It's not that at all!'

'Then come with me. Marry me.' It was one last desperate throw of the dice.

'Oh Josh . . .' Maggie felt as if she was being torn in two. 'I've tried to explain that I can't, not yet, and if you don't understand, I don't know what else I can say. In any case, I couldn't just up sticks and leave. There's Billy to think of. I can't abandon him – you know what he's like.'

'Your mam will be coming home soon, surely?'

'I don't know . . . it hasn't been mentioned yet. But even if she did, she's still not a well woman. She'd need a lot of looking after herself.'

'Seems to me,' he said, 'you're looking for excuses.'

'They're not excuses – they're reasons!'

'Well, call it what you like. It comes to the same thing in the end. You don't want to come to Bristol with me.'

Maggie was tired of arguing, of saying the same thing over and over again.

'I can't, Josh,' she said simply.

He nodded.

All The Dark Secrets

'That's that, then.' He opened the door, turned back. 'When I've sorted out somewhere to stay, I'll write and let you have an address so you know where to find me if you want to.'

And he was gone. Maggie felt that her heart was breaking, but what choice did she have? She covered her face with her hands, and this time it was not just the onion juice on her fingers that brought the ready tears.

Chapter Seventeen

Later, much later, when there was no escaping the reality of what was happening, Maggie couldn't understand how she had managed to avoid it for so long. Hadn't Josh hinted at the possibility that last Sunday morning when he'd come to tell her he was going to Bristol? But she'd been so confused that day, desperate to tell him how much she wanted him, how much she'd love to marry him, but unable to find the words; torn apart by her longing for him and her loyalty to Jack. She'd been overwhelmed by her emotions and by the responsibility she felt to her own family, and the possible consequences of their night of passion had passed her by.

She had been a little anxious a few weeks later when she realised she hadn't had a period for a while, although she wasn't sure just when it was due – she had too many other things on her mind to remember exact dates, and certainly no time to make a note of them. She had niggly little pains in her stomach, which she hoped meant her period was about to start, and she felt a bit queasy, but she put that down to getting herself in a bit of a stew, as her mother would have described her state of constant anxiety. And then she had a little bleed, lighter and for a shorter time than normal, but undoubtedly fresh blood, and, relieved, she'd thought that everything was going to be all right.

She had made a note of the date this time, but there were few spare minutes to think about it. With Christmas fast approaching, Freeman's was very busy, and it was often late in the evening before she could leave. Besides this, Ewart had written to say that he was bringing Rose home for Christmas. She still really wasn't well, but she was insistent that it was what she wanted. They would travel down the day before Christmas Eve and he'd stay over for the festivities.

Though she was looking forward to seeing her mother again, Maggie couldn't help worrying as to how she'd manage if Rose needed a lot of looking after. She was concerned too that Rose might think she'd let things slide in her absence, and when she got home from work each evening, dog tired, she set herself the task of giving every room in the house a thorough clean. She made the beds up with clean sheets, and even bought dried fruit to make two Christmas puddings and set them to boil in the copper.

No wonder she was feeling under the weather, she thought when she got up one morning vaguely nauseous and a little faint. And still it didn't occur to her, until she was having a good strip wash at the scullery sink – much easier than carrying hot water upstairs to the jug and basin in her bedroom when Billy was at work and she had the house to herself – and realised her breasts felt tender. Strange! She didn't ever remember them being tender before. She glanced down and was shocked to see the nipples standing out like soldiers at attention and the areolas around them dark against her pale skin.

It must be the poor light here in the scullery, she thought; on these dark December mornings, very little filtered in through the small window. But when she went upstairs to dress, she looked again, carrying the free-standing mirror from her chest of drawers to the window, and this time there was no mistaking it.

251

They *were* different, the usual rosy pink darkened to a dark reddish brown.

The first flutters of alarm stirred in Maggie. No! It couldn't be, surely? She'd had the curse last month, hadn't she? But it had been very light, only a couple of soiled towels rather than the outpouring she usually experienced . . .

Panicked, she searched for the old envelope she'd used to note down the date, failed to find it, and instead tried to remember something that would peg the date the bleed had begun. She'd still been anxiously awaiting it on Bonfire Night – she remembered the smoke hanging heavy in the foggy air as she crossed the track to the privy hoping to find that she'd started. But she'd thought everything was all right by her birthday, which she always celebrated on 12 November, though no one was exactly sure whether that was the correct day or not, and of course, with only Billy for company, there had been no celebration at all this year.

So – Maggie consulted her mother's Old Moore's Almanac – that meant she was late again.

Her stomach seemed to fall away, and though she tried to persuade herself otherwise, Maggie knew the truth with a conviction that refused to be denied. The evidence was all there; she could ignore it no longer.

Pregnant. A hot tide of horror suffused her. This couldn't be happening! But it was. In all her life, she didn't think she'd ever felt more frightened or alone.

It was a nightmare she couldn't wake up from, the last thing she thought of at night and the first thing in the morning, and it hung over her in a dark cloud every minute of the day.

Though she still clung desperately to the hope that the curse would come as it had last month, in her heart she knew it would not. That little bleed had just been some sort of hiccup in the scheme of things, perhaps the start of a miscarriage that hadn't, in the end, happened. Maggie took a bath, as hot as she could stand it, in the hope of setting things off again; she drank gin and swallowed syrup of figs, but the gin only made her violently sick and the syrup of figs kept her running to the privy all the next day, and still there was no sign of a bleed.

In a strange sort of way she was almost glad. The baby growing inside her was Josh's baby, and the thought of losing it through her own actions was something that made her shrink inwardly. As for seeking out someone who could use more certain methods to get rid of it, she never considered such a thing for a moment. It was against all the tenets of the Catholic church, which were ingrained in her though it was a long time since she'd attended Mass regularly, and besides, she'd heard it could be very dangerous.

But what was she going to do? Oh, if only Josh were still here! If only she'd agreed to go with him as he'd asked, at least she wouldn't have to flaunt the evidence of her betrayal of Jack in front of all the folk who'd known him. But now . . . was it too late? Did Josh still want her? Or had he moved on, building a new life that didn't include her? Maggie had the most awful feeling that that might be the case.

She'd received just one letter from him since he had left, giving the address of the house in Bristol where he'd found lodgings, and since then nothing. Unsurprising, really, since she'd decided not to reply, but she'd kept the letter, folded neatly beneath a stack of handkerchiefs in the top drawer of her tallboy. She got it out now, though she knew it almost by heart, spread it out on the kitchen table and fetched writing paper and pen.

For a long while she pondered what she should say, and even then it took three attempts before she was satisfied.

Dear Josh.

I hope this finds you well. Something awful has happened and I really need to talk to you. Are you coming home for Christmas? Do you think you could, even if you weren't planning to? It's really important.

Please write soon.

I remain, your ever-loving Maggie.

She posted the letter and waited impatiently for Josh's reply.

None came.

Rose and Ewart arrived as planned on the day before Christmas Eve. Maggie was unable to meet them, as the drapery shop was open until late, but she arranged for Fred Carson to be there with his pony and trap – Rose would be far too tired after the long journey to walk all the way from the station to the Ten Houses, she knew. But Billy, finishing work earlier now that it was dark by four o'clock, was able to make it, and rode home sitting beside Fred, with Rose and Ewart and their luggage piled in behind.

Maggie had left a plate of cold cuts and a pan of potatoes peeled and ready to be boiled, and by the time she got home, the others had eaten. But Rose had a plate of mash and cabbage keeping warm for her over a saucepan of simmering water on the trivet, and the table was laid with pickles and chutney, just as it would have been when she was late home from work in the old days.

'Mam!' Maggie hugged her mother, realising with a shock just how thin Rose had become. Why, she was little more than skin and bone! 'Oh Mam, I've missed you so much! It's so lovely to have you home! But you haven't been eating properly, have you? What have you done with her, Ewart? She's as skinny as a rake!'

'Oh, I've no appetite these days,' Rose said. 'It's not Ewart's fault, or Walter's. They've been looking after me very well. Though I must say it's nice to be back in my own kitchen.'

She held Maggie away, regarding her critically.

'You don't look so good yourself, my girl. Have you been overdoing things?'

Maggie's stomach contracted. She was dreading having to admit the truth to Rose, and this was not the moment.

'I'm fine, Mam,' she said. 'I've just been really busy, that's all.'

'Well, you've kept everything nice, I must say. Now, come and have your tea before it spoils.'

Bullseye was standing beside the table, nose raised and twitching expectantly.

'You've still got that darned dog, I see,' she added tartly, lifting the lid from the plate and setting it down in the place that was laid ready for Maggie.

'And you're still as stubborn as ever when it comes to taking things easy,' Maggie returned.

'Yes, well. Eat up now.'

The trouble was, Maggie had no appetite whatsoever; hadn't had since she'd realised the awful truth about her condition. But she made a heroic effort anyway. She didn't want Mam or Ewart to suspect anything was wrong – not yet, anyway.

'Is Cathy still working at the shop with you?' Ewart asked as Maggie cut ham into small, manageable pieces and forked up mashed potato.

Maggie managed a smile.

'Oh yes, and she's very excited that you're home. I suppose you'll be seeing her while you're here?'

'I certainly hope so. She's a little cracker, your apprentice.' Ewart, who had been sprawled in the chair in front of the fire, got up. 'Well, now that you're home, our Maggie, I think I'll go up and catch up with Josh.'

Maggie's heart lurched.

'I don't think you'll find him at home, Ewart. He's gone to Bristol to live.'

'Gone to Bristol?' Ewart repeated, staggered. 'What do you mean?'

The potato was going round and round in Maggie's mouth; she simply couldn't swallow it.

'He left – oh, it must be a couple of months ago. He wanted a change, I suppose.'

'You *have* taken me by surprise!' Ewart scratched his head. 'Well, I think I'll go up anyway, see if he's coming home for Christmas. If not, they're sure to have an address for him. I wouldn't want to lose touch.'

Maggie lowered her eyes and said nothing. She didn't want to admit that she had an address – Ewart would wonder how she came by it, and why. Besides, Josh's family might have more up-to-date news, and she too was anxious to know whether he was coming home for Christmas. It could be that he was, and that was the reason he hadn't replied to her letter. She couldn't imagine he was much of a letter-writer, and if he'd thought he'd see her in person, he might well have put it off.

But she knew she was clutching at straws. Really it didn't bode well that he hadn't put pen to paper, and Maggie couldn't avoid the horrible feeling that he'd guessed exactly what it was she wanted to talk to him about and had decided he'd rather not know.

Ewart was back almost before she'd finished her tea, and she steeled herself not to appear too eager to find out what he'd learned, leaving it to Rose to ask.

'Well, he's not coming for Christmas as far as they know,'

Ewart told her. 'But at least I've got an address for him – in Totterdown, wherever that is.'

'Totterdown! That doesn't sound like much of a place,' Rose commented, but Maggie found a small crumb in the fact that the address she had was in Totterdown too. At least Josh hadn't moved on and failed to let her know. But the news that he wasn't expected home for Christmas made her heart sink. She so desperately needed to talk to him; she didn't know how she could cope with the situation on her own.

She felt the now-familiar stirrings of panic, and tried to ignore them. She'd just have to get through the festive season, and then decide what to do. But it wasn't going to be easy. Oh, it wasn't going to be easy at all.

In houses all over High Compton, families were preparing for Christmas. Kitchens and parlours were decorated with freshly cut holly – 'The blooming birds have had most of the berries this year!' Peggy Bishop complained as she stuck the best sprigs she'd been able to find behind the pictures that hung on her kitchen walls – and bunches of mistletoe were suspended in doorways. The Hillmans had a Christmas tree in their parlour that reached almost to the ceiling, and a goose in the larder on the cold slab. Maggie unwrapped the cloth that she'd tied over one of her puddings so that her mother could poke it with a skewer and make sure it was done in the middle – Rose didn't totally trust her to have boiled it for long enough – but the skewer came out clean except for a few soggy raisins. And Rose sniffed the pudding and pronounced it a job well done.

'I know it won't be like yours, Mam,' Maggie said apologetically as she tied a fresh piece of string around the cloth her mother was holding in place over the top of the basin. 'It wasn't made early enough, for one thing.'

'We had other things to think about when we should have been making puddings,' Rose said. 'We'll have one for Christmas Day and put the other one in the larder for next year. It'll be all the better for keeping.'

Then her eyes misted as she looked at the chair Paddy had used to occupy, empty now.

'Who'd have thought it?' she said sadly. 'Who'd have ever thought last Christmas that it was going to be your father's last? And all those others too . . . However must they all be feeling? I can't understand how Josh Withers could have gone off and left his mam and dad like that when he's the only one they've got now, and not so much as come home to see them on the day. And what about all those little children without a father this year? It doesn't bear thinking about.'

Maggie said nothing. She'd seen little Lucy Day staring forlornly out of the window of number four when she'd passed on her way home from work, and could only guess at what a miserable Christmas she would have with her father gone and her mother barely holding herself together. There wouldn't be any spare money for little presents or good things to eat either, with the breadwinner gone and Sir Montague pressing for increased rent on the house. Maggie had managed to find the extra, though it had meant she'd had to buy a boiling fowl for Christmas dinner instead of the cockerel she'd planned on, and the fruit and nuts they usually treated themselves to had had to stay in the shop. But at least she was in work – for the moment, anyway, though what would happen when she started to show, she didn't dare think about.

'Well, we'll just have to make the best of it,' Rose went on, pulling herself together. 'At least our Ewart's here, and that'll be nice, and I've got you and our Billy too. And that blooming dog!' she added.

Bullseye was lurking beneath the kitchen table, and Maggie knew the reason why. She'd taken to feeding him covertly, bits from her plate that she just couldn't stomach but didn't want to leave to invite comment from her mother. Even now Rose was studying her closely and frowning.

'Are you all right, Maggie? You look a bit peaky to me.'

'I'm just tired, I expect,' Maggie said. 'You know what it's like in the shop at this time of year.'

'And you've had everything to do here too,' Rose said. 'Well, I'm home now, and you'll be able to take it a bit easier.'

'Mam, you're not well yourself, remember.'

'There's nothing wrong with me,' Rose said shortly, and Maggie thought ruefully that they were both good liars.

Christmas Day passed in a haze of unreality. Ewart had brought presents for them all: a brooch for Maggie, slippers for Rose – 'to go with that new dressing gown,' he said – and a bright spotted neckerchief for Billy.

'Oh Ewart, you shouldn't have!' Maggie said, unwrapping the delicate porcelain oval set in a make-believe gold surround. 'I haven't got anything for you. I just haven't had time to go to the shops.'

But to her surprise, Billy went upstairs to his room and returned with small packages that he handed round – tobacco for Ewart, who had taken to smoking a pipe, and sweets for Maggie and Rose, all bought from his meagre wages. He also had a marrowbone for Bullseye, who fell on it eagerly and had to be pushed outside where he could gnaw on it to his heart's content without leaving grease and bone splinters all over the kitchen floor.

There was an extra parcel in Ewart's bag, Maggie noticed, which he'd made no attempt to give to any of them.

'Who's that for then, Ewart?' she asked, though she had a pretty fair idea.

Ewart flushed a little and folded the bag over the little parcel. 'Never you mind, Miss Nosy-Poke.'

'I can guess. You can't fool me. You'll be going out later to see a certain young lady, if I'm not much mistaken.'

'I might be,' Ewart admitted, and grinned. 'Don't suppose she'll want to come out tonight, but there's always tomorrow.' He sighed. 'And then I suppose I shall have to be heading home.'

Home. It still jarred with Maggie that he referred to Yorkshire now as home instead of Somerset.

'Why don't you move back here?' she suggested.

It was a vain hope, she knew, but she couldn't help the irrational feeling that somehow, if Ewart was here instead of miles away, things wouldn't seem quite so bad.

That hope was quickly dashed.

'Back to Somerset and the conditions here?' Ewart said scathingly. 'I wouldn't want to do that. No, I'm far better off in Yorkshire. Our Walter would tell you the same. Oh, Cathy's a nice girl. I like her a lot. But not so much that I'd come back to this hellhole.'

'And I wouldn't want you to,' Rose said. 'Look what happened to your father and all the others.'

'Accidents can happen anywhere.' Maggie was clutching at straws, and she knew it.

'That's true enough,' Ewart conceded, 'but there's nothing here but faulted seams, and buggers like Fairley. Look at Josh: he's gone off further afield, and he wasn't even down the bloody pit.'

Maggie lowered her eyes. Without blurting out the truth, there was no way she could tell Ewart that Josh's leaving had nothing whatever to do with the work to be found in High Compton, and she was nowhere near ready to do that.

Ewart left the day after Boxing Day.

'Are you sure you're not coming with me, Mam?' he asked, and Rose assured him she was perfectly sure.

'I couldn't be doing with a long journey like that again so soon,' she said, and it was true, she did look very tired.

To Maggie's knowledge, Ewart had seen Cathy twice, and had been very late coming home the previous evening. Under normal circumstances she would have been looking forward to seeing her assistant when she returned to work the following day to find out her side of the story, but as things were, she had far too much on her mind to give it a second thought.

She absolutely had to decide what she was going to do. Though she thought her waist looked a little thicker and her breasts a little fuller when she checked her reflection in the mirror, that might be just her imagination; certainly the casual observer wouldn't notice any difference. But it wouldn't be long, certainly not more than another couple of months, before she would no longer be able to hide it, however tightly she laced her corset.

Her mind ran in frantic circles, but always it came back to the same thing.

Josh. She had to talk things over with Josh. Had to know whether he would be prepared to stand by her. She could write again and be more explicit this time, she supposed, but she couldn't abide the thought of more weeks of waiting for a letter that didn't come.

In desperation, she came to a momentous decision that both scared and excited her.

She would go to Bristol in person, find the address he'd sent her, which must be correct seeing as he'd given his parents exactly the same one, and speak to him face to face.

Daunting though the prospect was for a girl who had scarcely set foot outside of High Compton, for the first time in weeks Maggie felt that at least she was taking control of her dire situation.

Chapter Eighteen

The house was tall and narrow, one of a terrace, but totally unlike the terrace that was the Ten Houses.

Maggie paused to catch her breath. After the steep climb up the hill from the railway station, it had taken her forever to find the right place, asking passers-by and even a rag-and-bone man for directions. But this was it. Now all she had to do was walk along the street and look at the numbers on the doors.

Her heart pounded, and not just from her exertions. Would Josh be at home? She'd chosen a Sunday as the most likely day to find him in, but there was no guarantee. And if he was, how would he react to seeing her on the doorstep, and to what she had to tell him? *How* was she going to tell him, even? On the train journey to Bristol, she'd run over and over it in her head, but still she wasn't sure it would come out right. And however she put it, the news was bound to come as a dreadful shock to him. Maggie shrank from the dismay she could imagine seeing on his face, and worse . . . Supposing he turned her away without even discussing it? What would she do then? She'd have to go home, admit to Mam that the excuse she'd made about spending the day with Cathy was a lie, and tell her the truth that she wasn't going to be able to conceal for much longer.

Pull yourself together, she told herself. *You've come this far, you can't give up now.*

But her heart was still pounding, and the nerves fluttering in her stomach were making her feel far more sick than the nausea she sometimes experienced in the mornings.

She started along the street, checking house numbers as she went. It was far from deserted: a lad bowling a hoop almost cannoned into her, and on the pavement, children, well wrapped up against the cold winds of early January, played hopscotch in squares they had marked out with a chalky stone. Outside one house an old man squatted collier-style smoking a pipe; from an upstairs window a woman called to one of the children that dinner was ready.

Maggie found the house she was looking for, swallowed hard at the nervous lump that had formed in her throat, and knocked at the door.

It was less well kept than its neighbours, she noticed, green paint peeling away to reveal a muddy brown beneath; the knocker and doorknob didn't look as if they'd been polished in a while, and the curtains at the window were greyish and grubby rather than the white lace they had once been.

Maggie waited a moment, then knocked again, desperately hoping she hadn't come all this way only to find no one at home, and anxiously listening for some sound of life within.

'He's probably down the boozer, love.' She turned quickly to see a short, rotund woman in the doorway of the house next door. 'He's always down the boozer of a Sunday dinner time. That's if it's Albie you want. Or if it's Cissie, you're out of luck there too.'

So – the neighbours here could be just as nosy as they were in High Compton.

'No, I was looking for—' Maggie got no further, for she

heard a bolt being drawn on the inside of the door she'd been knocking at.

'It's all right, there is someone home,' she said quickly, and the rotund woman retreated a little, though Maggie was sure she'd keep her own door ajar so as to listen and satisfy her curiosity.

The door scraped open and Maggie found herself face to face with a giant of a man, so tall and broad he filled the narrow doorway. A head of unkempt hair and a full beard obscured much of his face; a calico shirt was open to the waist revealing a none-too-clean undershirt, which was, mercifully, buttoned to the neck. Braces dangled from their fastenings, allowing his trousers to hang low beneath an ample belly.

Albie, she assumed. Not the sort of man you'd want to meet in an alleyway on a dark night!

'Mr . . . um . . .' she began nervously, though she had no idea of what his second name might be.

'Who wants him?' The tone was belligerent, and he was squinting at her as if the pale January sun was hurting his eyes.

'Actually, I'm looking for Josh Withers,' Maggie said, taking her courage in both hands. 'He lodges here, I think.'

The man grunted and swore – a word Maggie had never heard before, but which she knew instinctively was incredibly vulgar.

She bit her lip, striving to maintain her dignity.

'I have got the right house, have I?'

'Ah, you've got the right house, but you won't find 'im here no more,' the man said shortly. 'He's gone – and my missus too – and good riddance to the pair of them.'

Maggie's mouth fell open.

'What do you mean?'

'What d'you bloody well think I mean? They run off together, didn't they? And don't ask me where, 'cos I don't know and don't care. So you might as well get on back to where you come from. All right?'

These statements were all peppered with expletives, and before she'd had time to take in what he was saying, let alone ask more, the door slammed shut in Maggie's face.

She stood staring at it stupidly, too shocked to move.

'Oh, he's a bad-tempered bugger, that one.'

Maggie had been right: the woman next door had been listening to every word. Now her door was fully open again and she was leaning against the frame, arms folded across her ample bosom.

'What he said's right, though,' she went on. 'If you're looking for that young chap that was lodging with them, you won't find him here. He's been gone now . . . oh, a couple of weeks before Christmas it must have been.'

'And . . . that man's *wife*?' Maggie could barely string two words together.

'Seems that way. I couldn't tell you the ins and outs of it,' the woman said regretfully. 'All I know is Albie was working away – he's a ganger on the railway – and when he came home, he found them both gone. He's in a bit of a way about it, but I can't say as I blame Cissie. She's far too good for the likes of him, and that Josh is a handsome fellow.'

She paused to take a wheezing breath, and then went on: 'He'll have his work cut out with her, though. She's a bit of a one, is Cissie. He isn't the first lodger she's carried on with. There was another one a year or so back. Albie came home and caught them red-handed. Well – the to-do! You could hear it right through these walls. I thought they was going to end up killing one another. So I was real surprised, I can tell you, when he let one as young and good-looking as that Josh into the house. He should have known it was asking for trouble.' She squinted at Maggie, mean little eyes bright in her doughy face like currants in a steamed suet duff. 'You a friend of his, are you?'

Maggie didn't reply. She was still reeling in shock; all she wanted to do was get away from this dirty-looking house – how could Josh have lived here? – away from the belligerent cuckolded husband, and most of all, away from this horrible woman who was glorying in every detail of the scandal.

Grasping her bag tightly between both hands to keep them from trembling, she turned away and started back down the street. The view of the city from here was breathtaking, the river cutting a broad swathe through the valley, wooded hills rising beyond and the majestic sweep of the suspension bridge spanning it. But Maggie scarcely noticed.

Josh had run off with another man's wife. Though he'd never made any promises to her, it still hurt dreadfully. She could scarcely believe it, and yet it must be true. These people had no reason to lie to her.

In some ways, though, it wasn't so unbelievable. Josh had always been a rascal, in scrapes of one kind or another, and he'd always been irresistible to women. She'd dared to think that he had feelings for her, and perhaps he had, for a little while. But when she'd turned him down, it hadn't taken him long to look for pastures new. She'd had her chance and she'd thrown it away, and Josh had wasted no time in finding someone to take her place.

Hot tears stung Maggie's eyes as she made her way back down the steep hill to the railway station. What would she do now? She hadn't the faintest idea. But even so, frightened as she was at facing her problems alone, it was the thought of Josh with another woman that hurt the most.

Oh Josh, Josh!

The loss of his love – if love it had ever been – was a pain in her chest so sharp that she thought her heart was breaking.

'Is there something wrong, Maggie?' Augusta Freeman asked. 'Something you'd like to share with me, perhaps?'

It was late February, cold, dark and wet, and business was slow, as it always was at this time of year. There'd been plenty of quiet moments for Augusta to observe Maggie, and she'd seen the change in her. Whereas usually Maggie was industrious, efficient and sociable, these last weeks she'd seemed preoccupied and withdrawn. And with her sharp eyes, used to assessing measurements as accurately as any tape, Augusta had noticed that Maggie's wasp waist had thickened, so that the waistband of her skirt strained around it, puckering into tiny pleats.

Augusta found it hard to believe that Maggie was the sort of girl to let herself down, but of course these things sometimes happened, and to the ones you'd least expect it of, whilst the tramps and trollops often got away with it. What really shocked her was that it was a good nine months since Jack had been killed, and if Maggie had behaved foolishly with him, the evidence would be far more obvious than this by now. That she should have gone with someone else was almost unthinkable – to Augusta's knowledge, she'd been mourning the loss of her fiancé and not so much as looked at another man. But as the days passed, her suspicions grew, and today she had decided it was time to say something about it.

Now, one look at the girl's face was enough to confirm her worst fears. Guilt and panic were written all over it, and her hands flew to that too-tight waistband.

'Oh Maggie!' Augusta said heavily. 'We'd better go somewhere quiet and have that talk.'

Maggie's shoulders slumped and her chin quivered, and Augusta sighed. This wasn't something she wanted to do; quite the opposite. But first and foremost she was a businesswoman, and fond as she was of Maggie, she couldn't let that make any difference.

As she led the way through the back of the shop into the living room of the house beyond, her mind was already made up. If Maggie confirmed what Augusta was certain she already knew, she would be left with no choice.

'You leave me no choice, Maggie,' she said. 'I have to give you notice, with immediate effect. I'll pay your wages up to the end of the week, but I'd prefer it if you didn't come in again.

'But I'm not showing yet.' Maggie was close to tears. 'I won't be for ages.'

'I noticed, didn't I?' Augusta said tartly.

'If I was to tighten my corset . . .'

'And have you fainting in the shop? I don't think so, Maggie. And besides, there is the moral aspect to consider. How do you think Cathy's mother, or even Beat's, would feel about me allowing her to work with you?'

'They wouldn't catch it from me like the measles,' Maggie blurted with a flash of her old spirit.

Augusta's lips tightened. 'Cathy, especially, is a young and impressionable girl. Whilst you, I am afraid . . .' She closed her eyes and gave a sharp shake of the head, indicating her reluctance to put a name to the kind of woman Maggie had shown herself to be. 'I have to think of the customers too,' she went on. 'And the good name of this establishment. I can't – won't – be seen to be condoning immoral behaviour. I'm sorry, Maggie, but I have to let you go.'

It was, of course, no more than Maggie had expected. She'd

only hoped she could delay the inevitable for as long as possible. How on earth they were going to manage for money without her wage, she had no idea – the pittance Billy earned would be nowhere near enough to provide what they needed to live on. He could barely afford to keep himself, let alone Rose, and herself and a baby, especially now that Sir Montague was demanding more rent.

'But you'll be short-staffed,' she said in one last desperate attempt to achieve a reprieve.

The faint hope was quickly dashed.

'We're very quiet at this time of year, Maggie. Beattie is quite capable of taking over as chief assistant, Cathy is coming along nicely, and I shall take on a new apprentice.'

She's got it all thought out, Maggie thought wretchedly.

'How in the world did it come to this, Maggie?' Augusta was shaking her head sadly. 'I would have thought you were the last girl to get herself into this sort of trouble, and so soon after the death of your fiancé, too. Will the father stand by you?'

Maggie couldn't bring herself to reply.

'Who is he?' Augusta asked. 'Perhaps if Horace was to speak to him, remind him of his responsibilities . . .'

Still Maggie was silent.

'Well, if you won't tell me who it is, there's nothing I can do to help you,' Augusta said shortly. 'This really is a most regrettable business. I've been more than satisfied with your work, and I had great hopes of you. To see you come to this . . . Wait here and I'll go and make up your wages. Then I would like you to go home without further ado.'

'Can't I even go and say goodbye to the girls?' Maggie asked miserably.

'I think it would be best all round if you just leave quietly,' Augusta said firmly. 'Anything else would only cause a great deal of distress and embarrassment. I'll explain the situation to them in my own good time.'

She disappeared back into the shop, closing the door after her.

In all the time Maggie had worked at the drapery, she'd only ever been into this room once before, and then she'd marvelled at the beautiful furniture – a green velvet-covered chaise longue, a highly polished table, a glass-fronted display cabinet filled with ruby cut glass and highly decorated bone china, and the carved case clock, gleaming brass candlesticks and figurines of a shepherd and shepherdess on the mantel above the fireplace. Now she stared at it all and saw nothing but a swirl of darkness so thick she felt as if she were falling into it.

A few minutes later Augusta was back with a brown envelope in her hand and Maggie's coat over her arm.

'I've put in a little extra,' she said, handing Maggie the envelope. 'Now, I'd like you to leave by the back door. We don't want to cause an upset in the shop.'

'Thank you, Mrs Freeman,' Maggie managed.

She slipped on her coat and pushed the envelope containing her wages deep into the pocket. Then Augusta led her through to the private side entrance and opened the door.

'I hope you are able to find some way of resolving this, Maggie,' she said, sounding genuinely regretful. But her ramrod back and the tight lines of her face were as unyielding as before.

Augusta could not, would not, allow the slightest smear of scandal to threaten the business she had built up through hard work and acumen, even though it meant turning her most valued employee out on the street to manage as best she could. And if she felt the slightest sympathy for Maggie's plight, it was far outweighed by her disappointment and disgust.

* * *

A biting wind whipped at Maggie's thin coat as the door closed behind her, funnelled by the corner of the building, but she noticed it no more than she had noticed Augusta's fine furniture and ornaments. She felt dazed now, unable to gather her thoughts, lost in the dreadful fog of fear and anxiety that seemed not only to weigh her down but to have crept right inside her.

She crossed the road and began walking in the direction of home, dreading having to explain herself to Rose when she got there. But she could see no way of avoiding it. And very soon it wouldn't be just Rose who knew the truth, but the whole of High Compton.

What had she done? How could she have been so stupid as to get herself into this terrible predicament?

She knew, of course. The drink was to blame – that and her crazy passion for Josh. A wave of longing for him engulfed her. Even now, she still wanted him with every fibre of her being, wanted to see him, to speak to him, to have him put his arms around her and tell her that everything was going to be all right. But that wasn't going to happen. Josh had left her and run off with another woman. She was alone in this dreadful nightmare.

Just out of the centre of town, a break in the footpath made way for a narrow road leading off to the right. As she reached it, Maggie's steps slowed to a halt. At the end of the road was St Christopher's, the Catholic church. She hadn't set foot inside it for years, Easter and Christmas excepted, and this year she hadn't even gone at Christmas. But now, for some reason she couldn't explain, she felt drawn towards it. A reluctance to go home – or something more? Maggie didn't know, and didn't even pause to wonder. Without making any conscious decision, she turned up the rough track.

The church had once been a tithe barn. It sat in an oasis of lawn and garden, bare now, but vibrant with roses and fuchsia in the summer. Maggie approached the heavy oak door, grasped the iron ring that served as a handle and turned it. The door opened with a loud creak, and as she stepped inside, the scent of incense enveloped her, heady and oddly comforting.

She stood for a moment breathing it in as her eyes roamed around the once familiar interior. The vast beams supporting the low ceiling – when she was a child she'd been afraid one might come crashing down, and the roof with it, but Paddy had said God would never allow such a thing to happen. The rustic pews into which she and her brothers had crowded – Ewart would never sit still, he'd fidget and pull faces to try and make her laugh, and once a marble he'd got out of his pocket to play with had rolled away, right down the aisle to where Father O'Brien was consecrating the bread and wine for Mass, all in Latin, of course, of which Maggie didn't understand a word, and which seemed to drone on for ever. The brightly painted statues set in alcoves along the north and south wall – the Holy Mother in azure and white, St Martin, rich brown, St Theresa with her pink roses, St Agnes draped in a green shawl with a lamb in her arms. Often candles burned in the little votives set up before each shrine, but today there were only the blackened stubs – there had been no service this morning, and it was not a day when folk would leave the warmth of their homes unless they had good reason to. Even the candles on the altar were unlit, and the grey light filtering in through the small windows barely reached the magnificent tabernacle, yet still there was that aura of welcoming mystery.

Maggie dipped her fingers into the little bowl of holy water beside the door and dabbed it on her forehead, bobbed a genuflection towards the altar, and walked slowly down the aisle, her boots clicking on the paved stone. She paused there for a moment, then turned towards the narrow side aisle and the effigies in their little alcoves. She hesitated at that of the Holy Mother, then passed by, averting her eyes. How could she pray to the Blessed Virgin in her state of sinfulness? But when she reached St Theresa she stopped, took a little candle from the basket at the saint's feet, and fell to her knees on the wooden step that served as a prie-dieu. Of all the saints, it was St Theresa to whom she had always been drawn, though other children usually chose St Agnes, because of the lamb.

She had no way of lighting the candle, but she clutched it between her hands anyway, holding it close to her heart as she gazed up into the beautiful face of the saint. If she left it in the votive, someone would light it later, and whilst it burned it would waft her prayer towards heaven.

'Please help me, dearest St Theresa,' she whispered, and then no more words would come, though her heart was full of them.

'Help me, please,' she whispered again, crossing herself, before placing the candle in the votive and getting up to stand for a few more moments, unwilling to leave the delicately fashioned figure.

A thud, loud in the silence of the church, startled her and she swung round to see the black soutane-clad figure of Father O'Brien, who had emerged from the sacristy – the thud must have been made by the door closing after him.

Maggie's heart lurched and she felt as guilty as if she'd been caught stealing from the offertory box. Father O'Brien was bound to wonder what she was doing here in the middle of a working day. But he was coming towards her, and Maggie could see no way of avoiding him.

'Maggie, my dear.' He smiled at her warmly. 'It's not often we see you here these days.'

'I know, Father. I just . . .' She gestured towards the votive.

'Would you light my candle for me, please, when you have time?'

'Of course. It's a comfort to you, I hope, praying for their souls. And I am sure our heavenly Father will hear your prayer.'

Guilt suffused Maggie; she hadn't said a single word for the redemption of her father and Jack, who could well be languishing in purgatory waiting for enough Hail Marys to be said to speed them on to heaven.

'I know, my child, I know,' he went on comfortingly, mistaking her guilt for grief. 'It's hard, and beyond our understanding. But be sure they are in a better place.'

'Oh Father . . .' Quite suddenly it was all too much for Maggie. His sympathy was only making her feel worse – she didn't deserve it! The weight of the secrets she was keeping felt too heavy for her shoulders; she couldn't bear it a moment longer. 'Father . . . will you hear my confession?'

The priest's expression grew concerned, but he responded in the same gentle tone.

'Of course, my child.'

He indicated that she should make her way to the confessional, but when they reached it, Maggie hesitated. She'd always hated the tiny enclosed space, hated the musty smell and the darkness, the way the priest's voice filtered, disembodied, through the grille in the wooden wall that separated them, hated the feeling of being trapped in what had always seemed to her to resemble a coffin. Now, more than ever, the similarity frightened her.

'Couldn't we do it out here?' she asked. 'There's nobody but us.'

'If that's what you want . . .' Father O'Brien sounded reluctant, but Maggie was insistent.

'It is.'

'Very well. Shall we sit down, then?'

He led her to the front pew, right beside the figurine of the Holy Virgin, Maggie noticed uncomfortably.

'You're going to think I'm terrible,' she said in a small voice.

'My dear, we are all sinners. That's why Jesus died for us. So that, through him, we might be saved.'

'I think I'm beyond that,' Maggie said wretchedly.

'No one who repents is beyond the mercy of our heavenly Father.' The priest folded his hands together in his lap and waited.

Maggie swallowed hard, uncertain where to begin.

'I've done something so wrong. I've betrayed Jack, I've let myself down, and oh – I know I deserve what's happening, but Mam doesn't, and . . . oh, Father, it's awful, really awful, and I don't know what to do . . .'

The priest was starting to guess what it was that was troubling Maggie, but he said nothing, waiting for her to tell him in her own words. After a further brief hesitation, Maggie began.

'What am I going to do, Father?' she asked miserably.

The formal part of the confession was over, Father O'Brien had spoken the words of the absolution, and given Maggie a penance of five decades of the rosary to be said for five consecutive days. Now he looked at her sadly, seeing only a young woman who had fallen from grace as so many before her had done and would go on doing for as long as men and women lived and loved. A decent girl, even if her attendance at Mass was not what it should be, a girl who had slipped only the once if her confession was to be believed, and been caught out where so many, far more promiscuous than she, escaped retribution. And she had been through so much these last months! Small wonder she had sought comfort where she could find it.

She would be forgiven, of that he had no doubt, but that

wouldn't solve the terrible problems she faced, and the disgrace was the least of these. Her lapse would have been forgotten eventually if the father of her baby had been prepared to marry her, but that, it seemed, was not an option. Maggie would have to raise her child alone, with no means of support, and Rose, and Billy too, would suffer, since they were dependent on her. Already she'd been dismissed from her position at the drapery shop, and it was hard to see who would offer employment to a fallen woman. She'd be ostracised, penniless, homeless too, in all likelihood. She needed more than absolution – she needed practical help, and Father O'Brien felt not only obligated to do what he could, but found himself desperately wanting to.

As always when he felt helpless, the priest reached for the crucifix that dangled from his girdle, holding it between his palms and pressing his fingertips together in an attitude of prayer. And quite suddenly, as if his prayer had been answered, inspiration struck.

'Maggie.' He raised his eyes, looking at her over the tips of his fingers. 'I can make no promises, but there's just a possibility I may be able to help. Come back and see me in a day or so, and I'll be able to tell you if I've been successful.'

Hope and bewilderment in equal measure flickered in her eyes.

'What do you mean? How can you help?'

'No.' Father O'Brien shook his head. He didn't want to raise her hopes only to have them dashed. 'There's someone I need to speak to before I say more. But I shall be praying that God has provided an answer to our supplications.'

'Oh!' Tears sprang to Maggie's eyes. 'Oh, I'll pray too, Father! You don't know how hard I'll pray!'

'Just remember to say those rosaries, my child.'

As she left the church, the wind seemed to have dropped and

the cold was less biting. And to Maggie it felt miraculously as if a weight had been lifted from her shoulders and she was filled with a sense of peace as well as hope.

It seemed almost foolhardy to dare to think that Father O'Brien could really do anything to help her situation. Yet in that moment, anything seemed possible.

Chapter Nineteen

The house stood in the centre of a triangle of land, bordered on all three sides by roads – a main and two lanes – about six miles west of High Compton. Maggie, who had walked the whole way in driving rain, made her way around the perimeter until she found a gate in the high laurel hedge.

Oh, why couldn't it have been a fine day? She tucked a straggling end of wet hair back under the shawl she'd tied over her head and brushed moisture from her cheeks. She wasn't looking her best – in fact she felt like a drowned rat – and it was so important she should make a good impression. All very well for Father O'Brien to have recommended her to Lawrence Jacobs, the man she had come all this way to see; if she looked slovenly and unkempt, it wasn't likely he'd want to take her on as his housekeeper.

Housekeeper! It sounded very impressive, but Maggie had little idea of what such a position entailed, though Father O'Brien had assured her it would be well within her capabilities.

'Lawrence lives a simple life,' he'd told her when she'd gone back to see him and he was elaborating on the idea he'd mentioned the day he'd taken her confession. 'All he needs is someone to keep his house clean, his clothes laundered, and

279

food on his table. He rarely entertains, and mostly he's immersed in his work.'

'What does he do?' Maggie asked, though to be honest, it scarcely mattered if it meant an income to help support herself, her unborn child, Rose and Billy.

'He works in stained glass,' Father O'Brien told her. 'He's made windows for some of our finest churches. That's how I came to meet him – he restored a window for the abbey. I found the process fascinating, he allowed me to visit his workshop, and we've been friends ever since.'

'Goodness!' Maggie was impressed. She loved looking at stained-glass windows, the vivid colours glowing when the light shone through them, but she'd never really stopped to wonder about the process involved or the artist who had recreated saints and martyrs from a mosaic of glass shards. 'Like the window over the altar, you mean?'

'Exactly.' Father O'Brien smiled. 'Our own window is but a poor example, I'm afraid. Lawrence's work is far superior, and I understand he is very much in demand. The trouble is that when he is busy with a commission, he forgets to eat and sleep, let alone keep his home clean and tidy, and the woman who looked after him for many years has fallen into poor health and can no longer carry out her duties. I knew Lawrence needed someone to replace her, and it occurred to me you might suit him very well. I've spoken to him, and he seems to think so too. He would like to meet you. So, what do you say?'

The prospect of a lifeline was so overwhelming, Maggie was almost speechless.

'Oh, thank you so much!'

He patted her arm.

'Don't thank me yet, Maggie. I've secured an interview for you, nothing more. It will be Lawrence's decision as to whether you are the right person for him.'

'Does he know about . . .' Maggie felt the hot colour of shame rush to her cheeks.

Father O'Brien nodded. 'Of course. I wouldn't have recommended you under false pretences.

'And he doesn't mind?'

'Lawrence judges no one. He leaves that to God. As do I.'

Now, soaking wet, and with her heart hammering with nervousness as she unlatched the wicket gate, Maggie reminded herself of the priest's words, and hoped desperately that he was right and this opportunity would prove to be the answer to her prayers.

The house – a rambling cottage half covered in creeper – was all in darkness, no glimmer of the light of an oil lamp showing at the windows, though given the oppression of the lowering skies it must have been very dim inside, and when Maggie tugged on the bell rope outside the porch door, all was silence. She tugged again, harder, hoping against hope that she hadn't come all this way on a fool's errand. She had the right day and time, she was sure, but if Lawrence was as vague about practical matters as Father O'Brien had suggested, perhaps he had forgotten. Then a voice from behind her made her turn.

A man was emerging from an outbuilding set amongst shrubs and hawthorn trees to the left of the path, calling to her as he approached.

'It's all right, my dear, I'm coming!'

He hurried towards her, holding an old piece of sacking over his head to keep off the rain. He was, Maggie judged, well into his fifties, of medium height and wiry build, and his gait was uneven, as if one leg was considerably shorter than the other.

'Mr Jacobs?' she said tentatively.

'And you must be Maggie. I'm sorry, my dear, I was in my workshop.' He opened the front door and stood aside. 'Do go in. You're soaked to the skin.'

The door led directly into a living room, long, low and narrow. A fire burned in an open grate on the far wall, stairs led upwards from a corner. The room was comfortably furnished, but dreadfully untidy – open newspapers, a pile of books, used crockery and a bowler hat and cane left not an inch of space on the dining table; more books were stacked beside the chintz-covered sofa, and on the settle that stood in front of the little lead-paned window. Mud and leaves, trodden in from the garden, littered the stained board floor and a threadbare carpet. Lawrence Jacobs, however, seemed blissfully unaware of the chaos, even when his toe connected with yet another pile of books and sent it toppling.

'Let me take your coat. I'll put it by the fire, though I doubt it will dry much before you need it again. Can I offer you a cup of tea, or perhaps a nice hot chocolate?'

Maggie wasn't at all sure she fancied either. Judging by the state of the room, she could well imagine the cup and saucer would need a good wash in hot soapy water before it would be fit to drink out of – if, indeed, there was any unused crockery left in the house.

'Don't bother on my account, please,' she said.

'No bother at all! It will warm you up.'

'No – really – I'm fine.'

'As you wish. Do please sit down, Maggie. May I call you Maggie?'

'Yes, of course.'

Maggie perched in a space on the sofa, knees tightly drawn together, hands in lap, trying to appear demure. Somehow she had to override any preconception this man might have of her.

Lawrence took a seat himself opposite her, moving a pair of fire irons from an easy chair and stacking them untidily in the fireplace before he did so.

'So, Maggie, how is your mother?'

Maggie was quite taken aback – of all the questions she had expected him to ask, this was not one of them. Of course, Father O'Brien would have told him that Paddy had met his death in the terrible accident last spring, and perhaps Lawrence was simply trying to put her at her ease. But even so . . .

'She's bearing up,' Maggie said. 'She really isn't well, but she spent some time in Yorkshire with my brothers Walter and Ewart, and I think that helped.'

Lawrence shook his head sadly.

'A terrible business. Terrible. I'm sure it hit you all very hard.'

'Yes,' Maggie said. 'It did.'

For a moment there was silence, and Maggie shifted awkwardly in her seat.

'Father O'Brien says you're looking for someone to . . .'

'Look after me. Yes.' Lawrence smiled slightly, the narrow face between the mutton-chop whiskers taking on an expression of faint embarrassment – the first time he'd acknowledged the chaos that reigned in his home. 'As you can see, I'm not particularly good at doing it myself.'

Maggie tactfully refrained from agreeing.

'I've never worked as a housekeeper, Mr Jacobs, but I do know all about keeping house. Well – I can cook a little, and light a fire, and iron a sheet . . .'

'I'm sure you can.' He smiled again. It was a kind smile, Maggie thought; it reached his eyes and softened the lines etched deeply into his face. 'I'm sure you've been well schooled, and my needs are simple. As long as the house is kept tidy and I have clean clothes to put on and good, plain food on the table, I shall be more than satisfied. And I may need you to remind me to eat sometimes.' He chuckled. 'When I'm hard at work, I do tend to forget.'

'That's not good for you,' Maggie said.

'Indeed it is not. The sooner we can come to an arrangement, the better, don't you think?'

Maggie was surprised. Lawrence Jacobs was talking as if he had already decided to take her on, and he hadn't asked her a single pertinent question.

'Don't you want to know something about me?' she blurted.

Lawrence waved a hand airily. His fingers were long and fine, Maggie noticed, though they sprang from surprisingly broad palms.

'I think I know all I need to, my dear.'

Again, Maggie was surprised. Father O'Brien must have given a very thorough report on her – and a glowing reference. She really must begin going to church regularly so that he'd know how grateful she was.

'You're going to take me on as your housekeeper, then?' she asked before she could stop herself.

Lawrence hesitated, his long, thin fingers tracing invisible lines from his knees to mid thigh and back again.

'That is not quite what I had in mind. I'm afraid there would be all kinds of problems with such an arrangement.' He half rose from his chair. 'Are you sure you won't take a cup of tea?'

'I really don't want one, thank you.' Maggie was beginning to feel anxious as well as puzzled. 'I just want—'

'I know my dear. I'm prevaricating, I expect. I often do, when really it would be much better to get to the point. The thing is, I don't think it would be seemly to take you on as a housekeeper, for a number of reasons.'

'Oh,' Maggie said dully, wondering why had he brought her all this way if he had no intention of offering her the job. And why had he talked as if he was about to do just that?

'Let me explain,' Lawrence said as if he had read her mind. 'You live some distance on the far side of High Compton, don't you? It would be impractical for you to get here each day to carry out your duties and then have to go all the way home again.'

'I don't mind,' Maggie said swiftly. 'I walked it today and—'

'And got soaked through. Besides, before long I can't imagine such a long trek would be advisable, or even feasible.'

Maggie flushed; it was the first time any mention had been made of her condition, and having a gentleman allude to it, even obliquely, made her dreadfully uncomfortable. He was right, of course. How much longer would she be able to walk the six or so miles here and home again? By the time she was seven or eight months gone, it would exhaust her, especially as the weather might well have turned hot in those last weeks. And afterwards . . . what then? She'd assumed that once she'd finished nursing, she could leave the baby at home with Rose while she was at work, but by then it would be winter. Suppose it was a hard one? How could she plough all that way through deep snow?

Maggie bit her lip. How could she have been so stupid as to not think of it herself? She'd been so carried away with euphoria at the prospect of having her problems solved that she hadn't considered it sensibly, she supposed.

'It really would not be practical, would it, my dear?' Lawrence went on. 'A housekeeper has to live in if she's to carry out her duties. But in your case, I don't think that is the answer either. Can you imagine what people would have to say? A young lady, single, living alone under the same roof as an old bachelor?'

Maggie didn't know whether to laugh or cry. He was talking as if she was perfectly respectable, and had a reputation to maintain.

'I'm afraid they're going to be talking about me anyway,' she said with a small ironic laugh.

'Perhaps. But what I'm going to suggest might help to alleviate that – in time, anyway – and restore your good name. My offer is for you to come here not as my housekeeper, but as my wife.'

For a moment Maggie was too startled to speak, or even to think. This couldn't be right! She must have caught a chill and be hallucinating. This man, this stranger, asking her to marry him? It was beyond belief.

'I've shocked you,' Lawrence said. 'I don't expect you to give me an answer right away, of course. You'll need time to think it over. But let me state my case. I would ask nothing of you beyond the duties we've already discussed. I have been celibate for most of my life, and I'm content to remain in that state. What I'm offering is a completely platonic relationship, but one that would benefit both you and your child. You would gain the respectability that comes from being a married woman, and your child would escape the stigma of being known as what our cruel world calls a bastard. Tongues may wag for a little while, but it would soon be forgotten, and in any case you would be far enough away from High Compton for it not to bother you unduly.

'Then there's the financial aspect. You'd have no need to worry any more with regards to supporting yourself and your baby. Or, indeed, your immediate family. I'm not a wealthy man, perhaps I should make myself clear about that, but I'm comfortably off, enough to ensure you'd want for nothing. And when I die, everything I have would be yours. There should be enough to keep you free of worry in that regard for as long as you are in need, and perhaps a little longer – as long as the man you choose to marry after I'm gone isn't a gambler or a spendthrift.'

When I die . . . Dazed as she was, his choice of words leapt out at Maggie, and again he seemed to read her mind.

'It's unlikely I have more than a few years left,' he said, without the slightest hint of regret or self-pity. 'I was very sick as a child – infantile paralysis, they called it – and besides a withered leg, I was also left with a weak heart and chest. This winter I've been fortunate, and I have managed to avoid the chills and fevers, but that won't always be the case. If next winter is harsh and I succumb, there's no telling what might happen. I wouldn't like you to find yourself in the position of being without means of support again so quickly, and with a young baby to care for into the bargain.'

Maggie's thoughts were reeling.

'I don't understand,' she said faintly. 'Why would you . . . ?'

Lawrence smiled, and Maggie saw a twinkle in those kindly eyes.

'You're wondering what benefit there is in this for me? Well, it's obvious, surely? I gain a young and comely wife, which will considerably raise my standing in the eyes of all those who think of me as a dry old stick! No . . .' He became serious again. 'It's true that I'd much prefer to see a pretty face when I come in from my workshop. Mrs Hoskins was a wonderful cook, and a good soul, but beauty was never one of her attributes, even in her younger days. And of recent times, having her here puffing and wheezing over even the least onerous of tasks has, I confess, been something of a trial as well as a cause for anxiety. She's been good to me, and I shouldn't speak ill of her, I suppose, but there it is. If I became sick, she certainly couldn't have cared for me – she could barely care for herself.'

His eyes levelled with Maggie's.

'Perhaps I should lay a little more emphasis on my tendency to periods of ill health,' he said. 'It may well be that I am in need of a nurse as well as a housekeeper. So there you have it. If you agree to my suggestion, I shall be assured of someone I can depend on in time of need, and you will gain financial security and a degree of respectability. It's not such a bad bargain, is it?'

'No . . . no, but . . .' Maggie was still in a state of disbelief that something as life-changing as a proposal of marriage should have come out of the blue like this. 'You don't know me at all. I could be the sort of woman who—'

'Would rob me of all my money and run off and leave me in my hour of need?' he interrupted her, his eyes twinkling again. Serious as he might appear, at least Lawrence had a sense of humour, she thought later. 'Well, I don't know you, of course. But I have a mind to trust you, Maggie.'

'On Father O'Brien's word?'

'Not entirely.' His eyes narrowed, and he appeared to be staring intently yet unseeing at some point beyond Maggie's shoulder.

'Well, that's my offer to you,' he said, coming back abruptly from wherever he'd been wandering. 'It won't have been what you were expecting, I know, and I'm sure you will want some time to think it over. But I very much hope you'll come to see it as not entirely disagreeable to you.'

'No,' Maggie said, making up her mind.

She couldn't let an opportunity like this slip through her fingers, and it wasn't such a bad deal. Though she'd only just met him, Lawrence seemed kind, and she felt sure Father O'Brien would never have sent her to him if he knew different. She would, of course, be tying herself to a man she didn't love, for whom, in fact, she had no feelings whatsoever, but so long as he expected nothing from her but the same duties she'd been prepared to take on as his housekeeper, then she could hardly complain.

In any case, what was love? She'd thought she'd found it with Josh, and what had that got her? A disastrous situation and a broken heart. What Lawrence was offering her was far more than she could have dared hope for. Security. Respectability. A home for herself and her baby. Support for Rose and Billy.

'No,' she said, and Lawrence looked at her questioningly, thinking perhaps that she was turning down his proposal. She hastened to assure him otherwise.

'I don't need time to think,' she said swiftly. 'I'm not even sure I have it, before tongues start wagging. I'd like to accept your kind offer.'

'Only if you are sure, Maggie,' he said. His eyes levelled with hers.

'I'm sure,' she said with all the confidence she could muster.

And thought: in the last resort, what choice did she have?

The rain had eased a little by the time Maggie left, though with her thoughts whirling, she barely noticed. What in the world was Rose going to have to say about all this?

She'd been in a dreadful way, of course, when Maggie had confessed that she was pregnant and had been dismissed from her job because of it.

'Oh Maggie, you silly, silly girl!' she'd said, wringing her thin hands. 'What were you thinking of?'

'I wasn't thinking,' Maggie replied miserably.

But she'd refused to answer Rose's next question as to the identity of the father, just as she'd refused to tell Augusta. And she hadn't told her about the interview Father O'Brien had arranged for her either – she didn't want to raise her mother's hopes only to have them dashed. She'd made some excuse about going to Hillsbridge to look for work.

'On a day like this?' Rose had said. 'Why don't you leave it until the rain's stopped?'

'I can't just sit at home doing nothing,' Maggie had replied. 'A drop of rain won't hurt me.'

Now there could be no more prevaricating. As she walked, Maggie ran over all the options.

'Mam, I'm going to be married to a man I met this morning.'

'Mam, there's no need for you to worry any more about how I'm going to manage.'

'Mam, I expect you'll think I've gone funny in the head, but . . .'

She shrank inwardly as she imagined Rose's shocked reaction. Would she be relieved? Would she be horrified? Maggie had no idea. Both, probably.

In the event, the one reaction she didn't expect, hadn't considered for even a moment, was the one that actually happened.

Rose fainted clean away.

As Maggie told her haltingly about Lawrence Jacobs, she saw the colour drain from her mother's face, saw her clutch at the neck of her blouse and sway.

'Mam?' she said urgently. 'Are you all right?'

Rose didn't reply. Her knees were buckling, and though her eyes were still fixed on Maggie, they'd gone unfocused. She went down slowly, almost gracefully, though her head made a horrible thud as it connected with the tiled floor.

'Oh Mam!' Maggie wailed.

She rushed to fetch the smelling salts, wafting them under

Rose's nose, and after what seemed like an eternity, Rose's eyes opened and her head rolled from side to side.

'Have a sip of this, Mam,' Maggie held a cup of water to her mother's lips.

'I don't know what happened to me,' Rose said faintly. 'Oh dear, I feel ever so sick . . .'

Maggie hurried to the kitchen to fetch a bowl. Mercifully, Rose wasn't sick, but she was still paper white.

'What an old fool I am!' she groaned.

'No, you're not. I gave you an awful shock.' Maggie felt dreadfully guilty as well as anxious. 'Oh Mam, I am so sorry . . . about everything.'

Rose was recovering herself little by little.

'What's done's done. No use being sorry.'

'But . . . you think I'm wrong to agree to marry a man I don't really know at all?'

'Well, of course I wish things were different. But he's a good man and he'll take care of you.'

'How can you know that?' Maggie asked.

For a moment, Rose's mouth worked, though no words came. Then:

'Father O'Brien wouldn't have sent you to him if he wasn't. No, it's for the best, I expect.'

'I honestly don't think I have any choice,' Maggie said.

In the grey light of early morning, Billy was driving the herd of cows along the lane for milking. His head was bent, chin resting on chest, and rain dripped in a steady plop-plop from his hat on to the waterproof cape he wore over his coat, sometimes even finding its way inside his collar and trickling down his neck. He scarcely noticed. He could think of nothing but that Maggie was going to be married to a man he didn't even know, his mother was going to move to Yorkshire to live with Walter and Connie, and his own future was horribly uncertain.

It had been suggested he should go to Yorkshire too, and he had wondered if it might be a good idea to leave High Compton with all its terrible memories and start afresh. But he liked his job on the farm – Billy was always more comfortable around animals than people – and if he moved to Yorkshire, he might be expected to go down the pit like his brothers. The thought of it made his stomach clench with fear. The very idea of the descent into the bowels of the earth terrified him just as it always had. Besides, there was Bullseye to think of. Connie might not want a dog in the house, and leaving Bullseye behind to fend for himself was unthinkable.

But where would he live? He couldn't stay on in the family home; he couldn't have afforded the rent even before Sir Montague increased it, and he didn't suppose he'd be allowed to anyway. He'd have to find lodgings somewhere, but again Bullseye came into the equation. He'd sleep rough on the streets rather than be parted from his beloved dog.

Maggie had suggested he should ask Farmer Barton if he could have a room at the farm, or even a cottage, and that, he thought, was the best option. But he was pretty sure there were no cottages vacant, and Farmer might not want him in the farmhouse. There was nothing for it, of course, but to take the bull by the horns and ask, but Billy was still struggling to get up the courage. It wasn't so much that he was afraid to; rather that if Farmer refused, he didn't know what he'd do next.

One of the cows had stopped to feast on the lush grass that grew along the side of the road and the others were bunching up behind her. Billy swished his stick to move them on, then gave the culprit a smack on the rump and yelled at her to get going. He could hear the clip-clop of a horse's hooves coming along the lane behind him – it sounded like a pony and trap, Fred Carson maybe. Well, he'd just have to be patient; Billy couldn't make the cows go any faster and they didn't have much further to go now.

As he plodded stoically on, he found himself wondering yet again why Maggie was marrying this Lawrence Jacobs. No reason had been given for it, but he'd heard Mam and Maggie talking together in low whispers, and as far as he was aware, there was really only one reason for a rushed job like this. If it had been Josh, or Jack before he was killed, Billy would have been able to understand it. But why this Lawrence Jacobs? Surely Maggie hadn't been putting herself about with strangers to make ends meet? He huffed disgustedly at the thought and tried to block it out, just as he tried to block out all the other things that were too disturbing to think about. Sometimes he succeeded, and sometimes he didn't, but right now he had to concentrate on working out what he was going to say to Farmer about his future living arrangements. One thing at a time.

Billy shrugged deeper into his waterproofs and trudged the last few yards to the gate that led to the milking parlour.

Three weeks later, Maggie and Lawrence were married quietly by Father O'Brien at St Margaret's, the Catholic church in Hillsbridge. St Margaret's was the sister church to St Christopher's in High Compton, and Father O'Brien shared the ministry with a monk from the nearby abbey. The witnesses were Billy and Ewart, who had travelled down from Yorkshire and would be taking Rose back with him.

Rose did not attend the ceremony. She'd been very quiet ever since Maggie had told her the news, but though she looked pale and drawn, it hadn't occurred to Maggie that she was so ill she wouldn't be able to come to the church to see her daughter married. On the morning of the wedding, though, she told Maggie that she felt very poorly, and was afraid she was going to have to miss it.

'How can I get married without you there?' Maggie asked, distressed.

'You wouldn't want me fainting again in the church, would you?' Rose said. 'Think of the upset it would cause! No, it's best I stay at home.' She smiled weakly. 'And you know you have my blessing. That's all that matters.'

'If you're feeling that bad, perhaps you shouldn't be travelling all the way to Yorkshire,' Maggie said anxiously. 'Perhaps you should wait a few days until you feel a bit better.'

'I'll be all right,' Rose assured her. 'I'll have to be. Our Ewart can't lose more time off work.'

'Oh Mam . . .' Maggie put her arms round her mother's thin frame, hugging her. 'I should be here for you. It's all so wrong.'

Rose was silent for a moment, but the stiffness of her shoulders and the shallowness of her breathing told Maggie that she was struggling to keep from crying. Just one soft gulp escaped her, then she held Maggie away, trying to smile.

'It'll all work out for the best, Maggie, you'll see. The Lord alone knows I wish it could have been different, but like I said before, you've got a good man there, even if he's not the one you'd have picked, given the chance. And you'll come and visit me, won't you, after the baby is born? I'd like to see it – and I shall be dying to see you.'

'Of course I will, Mam,' Maggie said, tears pricking her own eyes.

Rose wiped her nose with the back of her hand.

'Get off with you now. You don't want to be late for your own wedding.'

Ewart was waiting for her, all spruced up in a white shirt with a wing collar.

'Don't worry about Mam,' he reassured Maggie. 'I'll take good care of her.'

'I know you will, Ewart,' Maggie said.

The pony and trap Lawrence had hired to take them to Hillsbridge would be waiting at the end of the lane – Maggie hadn't wanted the neighbours to see them go – but if it was there for much longer, someone was certain to walk past and start wondering about it.

Maggie hugged Rose one last time and walked out of the house that was the only home she had ever known. She knew it was unlikely she would ever return.

When the brief ceremony was over, another hired pony and trap took Maggie and Lawrence back to his house on the outskirts of town. There they celebrated with a small glass of sherry and a fruit cake Maggie had baked under her mother's instruction, and sat for a while talking.

'I don't suppose this is how you imagined your wedding day would be,' Lawrence said thoughtfully.

'Not really.' Maggie sighed wistfully. 'But then things don't very often work out the way you expect, do they? Dreams . . .' She bit her lip. 'Dreams are just that. For children.'

The minute she'd said it, she regretted it, afraid he would think her ungrateful.

'I mean, when I was little, all I wanted to do was draw pictures, or make clothes for my doll,' she went on hastily. 'I thought that when I grew up and didn't have to go to school, I could do that all the time. Sell my pictures, or design dresses for fine ladies.' She laughed shortly. 'Imagine it! That someone like me could do something like that! The closest I ever got was dressing the window at the shop, or putting ribbons and flowers together to trim a plain bonnet. Now I don't even have the chance to do that.'

'But life may yet have some pleasant surprises in store for you,' Lawrence said gently. 'You're far too young to give up on your dreams. One day, perhaps, some of them will come true in ways you could never imagine.'

'Perhaps,' Maggie said, anxious not to make the mistake again of saying anything that might give him the idea that she was ungrateful; not wanting to hurt his feelings, she realised. Rose had been right: he was a good man.

'I'll make some tea,' she said.

Lawrence nodded. 'That would be nice, my dear.'

Later, when the fire was burning low and the lamp flickering, Maggie went upstairs to the cosy room under the eaves that was to be hers, leaving Lawrence downstairs. As she was undressing, she heard the side door beneath her window open and close. She looked out; his shadowy figure was making its way along the path to his workshop, a storm lantern held aloft. Relieved that he was keeping to his side of the bargain, Maggie finished her toilet and slipped beneath the patchwork quilt.

The narrow bed was comfortable enough, and the sheets were freshly laundered – she knew, because she'd made up the bed herself. But homesickness was already beginning to gnaw at her, and a feeling of being trapped.

This was not, she thought, how she had imagined her wedding day would be. But Lawrence Jacobs had offered her a lifeline, and she must be grateful for it.

Chapter Twenty

Gossip and speculation was rife in High Compton, but not a single person, apart from Father O'Brien, knew the whole truth. All that was certain was that Maggie was no longer employed in the drapery, and number six Fairley Terrace was all shut up, with no one at home. Ewart had been there for a couple of days, the neighbours said, and they thought he'd taken Rose back to Yorkshire with him, but that didn't explain Maggie and Billy's absence, and no one had seen Bullseye either. He wasn't hanging about outside the locked-up house waiting for someone to come home; one or other of the Donovans must have taken him with them. But where had they gone without a word to anyone – and why?

Theories abounded. That the family owed money they couldn't repay and had done a moonlight flit was one of the favourites. Billy was in trouble with the police was another, but this had to be discounted when it was discovered that he was still working at the farm, and now living in, Bullseye with him. And of course, the one that was closest to the truth – that Maggie had got herself in a pickle and she too had gone to Yorkshire, where no one knew her, to hide her shame.

The bolder and more curious, Hester Dallimore among them, found excuses to go into Freeman's shop in the hope of learning something of interest, but got nowhere. The girls who worked there became nervous and uncomfortable at the mention of Maggie's name – unsurprising, really, since it elicited a warning glare from Augusta, who was known to be a strict disciplinarian, and who would come down hard on any employee who engaged in gossip about another. In fact, the girls knew little more than anyone else.

'Mrs Freeman wouldn't say why she gave Maggie the sack,' Cathy told her mother when she asked. 'And we never got the chance to ask Maggie herself. Mrs Freeman let her out the back way, and we haven't set eyes on her since.'

Cathy, of course, was unhappy that she'd lost her contact with Ewart, besides being concerned about Maggie.

Then a surprise snippet of information added spice to the mix. Hester Dallimore was discussing the mystery with a cousin who lived in Hillsbridge when she struck gold.

'Maggie Donovan, did you say?' the cousin asked. 'I'm sure someone of that name had their banns called in our church a few weeks back.'

Instantly Hester was all ears.

'Your church?'

'St Margaret's. Yes.'

'And Maggie Donovan had banns read there?' Hester probed eagerly.

'I couldn't say for sure, but I think that was the name. We were all saying to one another – "Who's that when she's at home?" And we didn't know the chap's name either. It was all double Dutch to us.'

'I thought you had to live in a parish to have your banns called,' Hester said.

'Well, strictly speaking, you do. But if you leave a suitcase with your clothes in for a couple of weeks, and the priest's on your side, you can get round it, or so I understand. It doesn't often happen, but it's not unheard of.'

'Well!' Hester was agog. 'So you reckon Maggie Donovan's got married on the QT!'

'I wouldn't know about that.' The cousin, knowing Hester's reputation as a gossip, was beginning to wish she'd kept quiet.

'And you don't know who it was she was marrying?'

'That's what I said.'

'It wasn't Josh Withers, was it?'

'I can't remember, our Hester. And that's the truth.'

'I'll bet that's who it was!' Hester was triumphant. 'He's gone off somewhere too. Well, well. Maggie and Josh Withers! And she was engaged to his brother, the one that got killed at Shepton Fields. No wonder they wanted to hush it up!'

It didn't take long, of course, for Hester to begin sharing her juicy news. When it reached the ears of Josh's mother she was quick to deny it, but Hester was not to be deterred.

'Florrie reckons he's away working, but that's her story,' she said smugly as she spread the gossip ever further. 'You should have seen her face! Scarlet, she was. Scarlet!'

'Well I never! There's a thing!'

'No wonder poor Rose's took bad and gone off out of the way . . .'

'Maggie Donovan and Josh Withers! You reckon they had to do it in a hurry?'

Oh, it was a juicy story right enough, and it spread like wildfire, gaining embellishments along the way.

For a few weeks it provided much-needed entertainment in a town that was still in mourning for its lost sons.

Just two weeks after Maggie O'Donovan married Lawrence

Jacobs, an envelope had dropped through the letter box of the Withers home.

When she saw it lying on the tiled floor, Florrie swooped on it eagerly. It was a good while now since Josh had written – he wasn't much of a letter-writer, she knew, and she couldn't expect weekly missives like the ones she got from her sister, who was married to a policeman and lived in Torquay, but she did like just a line or two so that she knew he was all right. Though he was a grown man, she still worried about him, especially since the awful thing that had happened to Jack.

She carried the envelope into the kitchen and sat down at the table, reaching for the magnifying glass. Her sight wasn't as good as it used to be, but there was no way she could afford to see an oculist and be fitted for spectacles. The writing on the envelope was certainly Josh's, but to her surprise Florrie saw that the postmark was Belfast, Ireland. Puzzled, she tore open the envelope and took out the two sheets of lined writing paper covered with Josh's hurried scrawl.

Dear Mam and Dad, she read. *I hope this finds you well.*

I expect you will be surprised to hear that I am in Ireland now, working at the Harland and Wolff shipyard. I couldn't get anything in Bristol, only casual labouring at the docks. It wasn't paying enough to keep body and soul together really, but then somebody told me they were looking for carpenters in the shipyard here in Belfast and I thought I'd try my luck. I came over to have a look at the place and see what was going, and they offered me a job.

There was a bit of a to-do when I got back to Bristol to pick up my belongings. Cissie, my landlady, had left her husband and run away, and he thought we'd gone off together. Fat chance of that! He was all ready to pick a fight over her, but I soon put him right. She was seeing a chap who used to lodge with them before me, I know. He came to the house once or twice when Albie was away working, and Cissie told me he was a Londoner who bummed around with a travelling funfair when he couldn't find work in the docks. I told Albie his missus was sitting in a caravan somewhere gazing in a crystal ball and getting her palm crossed with silver (she used to tell fortunes reading the tea leaves if anybody asked her to) and he said he'd give her crystal ball if she came back! Well, it was on those lines, but I don't want to shock you, Mam, with telling you what he really said.

Anyway, I packed up my stuff and left him to it, and now here I am in Ireland.

It's a great place, and I'm earning good money. I wanted to settle myself somewhere before I let you know as I thought you'd only worry, but now I've found nice lodgings with a couple of pals. So I'm writing to tell you I'm doing fine, and if you want to write back, you will find me at this address.

I will write again soon.

Your loving son

Josh

PS Do you see anything of Maggie? Is she all right?

'Well, well, well!' Florrie said wonderingly, and she read the letter again before going out into the garden, where Gilby was digging parsnips for dinner, to tell him the news.

She wished with all her heart that Josh hadn't gone away at all, especially not as far as Ireland. But at least it sounded as if he was doing well for himself, and perhaps one day he'd get tired of foreign places and come home. It was the best she could hope for.

On the same day, the postman pushed an envelope containing an almost identical letter through the letter box of number six.

It was addressed to Miss Maggie Donovan. The postman wondered idly who would be writing to both Maggie and the Withers family all the way from Ireland, but then he was forever asking himself questions about the mail he delivered to which he'd never get the answers. As long as the letters went to the right address, his job was done. It wasn't his concern that there was no one at home to receive them.

'I suppose you've heard – your boyfriend's got married.' Tom Bishop pushed back his empty dinner plate and belched loudly.

Peggy turned away, pretending to be clearing the table.

'Oh, is that right?' she said non-committally, though in fact she already knew – Sarah had told her yesterday when she'd visited with half her brood in tow. Peggy had pretended with her too – that it couldn't matter less – but in fact she'd been dismayed. Though it had been all over between them for a long time now, she still carried a torch for Josh that had been burning more brightly lately. Tom was slipping back into his bad old ways – surly, discontented – and the novelty of imagining he might have ruthlessly murdered a dozen men and boys for the love of her was wearing a little thin.

If Josh had finally settled down, it put an end to any hopes Peggy might have had of rekindling their affair, and she was surprised at how much that could still upset her.

'Done all right for himself, too,' Tom was going on. 'That Maggie Donovan's a little cracker. Though from what I hear of it, there'll be a nipper along soon to spoil their fun and games. Dipped his wick once too often if you ask me.'

'Don't talk so disgusting,' Peggy snapped.

Tom guffawed sarcastically.

'Don't like to think of him putting it about with anybody but you, is that it? Well let me tell you this, Peg, he wouldn't look twice at you now. Even if I hadn't scared the blighter off, he's got better fish to fry. And just as well he has, 'cos he knows if he came sniffing round after you again he'd get what was coming to him.'

He belched again, and something snapped in Peggy. She wheeled round, humiliation and disgust with Tom, his nasty tongue and his filthy habits, making her throw caution to the winds.

'It was you, wasn't it, you bugger!' she accused.

'What you talking about, woman?'

'The rope on the hudge. It was you cut it. You mixed Josh up with Jack, and you cut that bloody rope to get your own back on him.'

The light in the kitchen was too dim for her to be able to see his face clearly, but she heard his quick intake of breath.

'Have you took leave of your senses?' he snarled.

Peggy straightened up, hands on ample hips.

'You can't fool me, Tom Bishop. I know you, and I know your nasty temper. But you needn't worry. I haven't said anything to anybody else, and I won't. I don't want folk knowing I'm married to a murderer.'

'You bloody stupid woman,' Tom grunted.

Peggy half smiled. 'In any case, I quite like it that you care that much about me. So come on, you might as well own up. It was you, wasn't it? Tell the truth and shame the devil.'

Tom leaned back in his chair, his chest swelling, and patted his full belly.

'You'd like to know, wouldn't you? You fancy having something over me. Well, you can just go on wondering, m'dear. Now, I think I'm going out for a pint – unless there's something better on offer here.'

'And what would that be?' Peggy demanded, a little saucily.

Talking about what had happened was having that erotic effect on her again, making Tom seem more attractive, making her forget Josh and that stupid Donovan girl. Josh might be a bit of a stud, but he'd given her the brush-off long before he'd taken up with Maggie Donovan, and in any case, she couldn't imagine he'd ever have done what Tom had done, even if he'd been mad for her.

Tom caught hold of her arm, yanking her roughly towards him.

'Come here, Peg, and I'll show you.'

He pulled her down on to his lap, and Peggy smiled to herself as he rucked up her skirts.

Oh, Tom might be uncouth, he might be ill-tempered, but first and foremost he was what she thought of as a real man.

Peggy Bishop was not the only one dismayed to learn that Maggie Donovan was married.

Reuben was in the living room, sorting the latest acquisitions for his stamp collection and being hassled by his mother to pack it away so that she could lay for tea when his father came home from the office.

It was unusual for Reuben to be at home before Clarence, except, of course, on a Wednesday, which was early-closing day in High Compton, but he was suffering from a severe head cold and Horace had sent him home the previous day saying it was unhygienic for him to be sneezing all over the customers.

'We're not busy, nor likely to be,' he had said firmly. 'Have a hot toddy or two and come back when you're no danger to the rest of us.'

Reuben hadn't been sorry. He didn't feel at all well, and since Maggie had disappeared from the drapery shop, there was no incentive for him to struggle in to work. He couldn't understand what had happened to her; he didn't like to ask, and in any case he had a strong feeling that he would get no answer. When Stanley Stone, his fellow assistant, had asked if she was on holiday, Horace had simply replied that she was no longer an employee, and his expression had forbidden further discussion of the matter.

Reuben was puzzled – and wretched. Even though she had rejected his advances, even if she could barely bring herself to look at him, let alone speak to him these days, it was as if a light had gone out in his world. He'd even walked out to the lane leading to the Ten Houses one evening in the hope of seeing her, though he'd had no idea what he would say to her if he did. He'd stood on the road in the freezing cold, stamping his feet and blowing on his hands for a good half-hour before he'd given up and gone home.

In an effort to forget Maggie, he'd decided to ask Cathy if she would go out with him. He'd waited for her outside the shop one night, but Cathy had been rude and scornful.

'I wouldn't go out with you, Reuben Hillman, if you were the last man in England!' she'd said, with a toss of her hair. 'And you'd better not start mithering me the way you mithered Maggie, or my brothers will be after you. They won't just give you a punch on the nose like Josh did, either. They'll put you in the hospital!'

'Don't worry, I didn't really want to go out with you anyway,' Reuben had retorted before slinking away with his tail between his legs. But his pride was badly dented, not least for being reminded of the ignominy of being felled by a single blow from Josh Withers.

Now he was about to be reminded of it again.

'It would seem,' Clarence said, when he'd taken his coat off and draped it over the back of one of the dining chairs, 'that that hobbledehoy Withers, who came here and violated our home, has left the district. And he has taken the Donovan girl with him. In fact, if the story I heard today is to be believed, he has married her. So I think it unlikely that we will be troubled by either of them again.'

Reuben's stomach fell away and his already congested airways seemed to close completely so that he could hardly breathe.

Maggie – married! No! He couldn't believe it. Couldn't bear it!

'I'm very glad to hear it,' Alexandra said. 'Perhaps you'll forget about her now, Reuben, and find yourself a nice young lady.'

'He's forgotten her already, haven't you, son?' Clarence smoothed his hair, shiny and sleek with macassar oil. 'He was taken in by a pretty face, as young men often are. But common sense has prevailed, I'm glad to say. A girl like that was never good enough for him, and he knows that now. Isn't that right, Reuben?'

Reuben mumbled something unintelligible, found his handkerchief and blew his blocked-up nose.

'That's all right then,' Alexandra said, approaching the table with the cutlery box. 'Now, if you could just pack up what you're doing, Reuben, I can get this table laid.'

Reuben stuffed his handkerchief back into his pocket, somehow managing to brush his carefully sorted stamps so that they were all over the place again. Some had even fluttered to the floor. Normally he would have been annoyed, but right now he was past caring.

Nothing seemed of the slightest importance by comparison with the fact that Maggie was now out of his reach for ever. Misery overwhelmed him, and with it a wave of hatred for Josh

Withers. The man who had humiliated him in front of his father. The man who had stolen the love of his life.

I'll get back at him if it's the last thing I do! Reuben vowed silently as he scrabbled around under the table for the last stray stamp.

Revenge. Planning it really was the only consolation left to him.

In the isolation of her new home, Maggie was blissfully unaware of all the furore her marriage had caused in High Compton, though, truth be told, even if she had known about it, she would have spared it little thought. There were far too many other things on her mind.

Rose for one. Her failing health was a constant worry, and the long journey to Yorkshire wouldn't have done her any good. Walter, Connie and Ewart would take good care of her, Maggie knew, but they weren't miracle-workers, and the way Rose had fainted the day Maggie had told her she was getting married, and the fact that she had felt too unwell to attend the wedding ceremony, didn't bode well. Ever since she'd suffered the miscarriage, it had seemed to be one thing after the other. Until then, although she'd always looked as if a puff of wind would blow her away, she'd had an iron constitution, but now it seemed to Maggie that her mother was slipping away, little by little, and there was nothing she could do to stop the relentless deterioration.

It could be it had started even earlier, with the accident and Paddy's death, of course, and Maggie had been too distraught herself to notice. But whatever, the decline could no longer be denied, and it was a constant weight on Maggie's mind.

Then there was Billy. Farmer Barton had agreed to let him have a room over the stables, and Billy had seemed happy enough with that – at least it meant an extra half-hour in bed for him in the mornings. Farmer's wife was feeding him, too, and Maggie had no doubt that it would be good, wholesome food. But she wasn't so sure about the accommodation, which would be cold and damp at this time of year, she felt sure. And good as Farmer's wife might be, she wasn't family. Billy was such a loner, so difficult to communicate with, and though he'd always been one to go off on his own when something upset him, he'd always had her and Mam to come home to, comforting him simply with their presence even if there was nothing they could say to help.

Well, at least he had Bullseye with him, Maggie comforted herself. And he seemed to think more of that dog than he did of any human.

Last but not least, Maggie worried about being a good wife to Lawrence. As he'd told her the very first time she met him, his needs were simple enough, but Maggie felt duty-bound to go above and beyond the bare essentials. Lawrence had given her so much – a home, respectability, financial security – and soon there would be a baby in the house, which was bound to disrupt his way of life, however bound up he was in his work and however much Maggie tried not to let it. She cooked the meals she thought he'd enjoy – roast meats and hearty soups, bread and butter puddings, fresh custards, and Victoria buns, a recipe from a cookbook by Mrs Beeton that she discovered in a cupboard in the living room, and which was proving a godsend.

She washed and scrubbed, dusted and ironed, spreading a thick blanket over the kitchen table and heating the flatirons over the fire. She opened the windows to air the upstairs rooms when the weather was good enough, and tidied Lawrence's numerous books on to shelves that had previously been filled with clutter. She polished the brass and swept last year's dead leaves away from the doorstep; she went to market in Hillsbridge once a week to buy butter, cheese and fresh vegetables, thankful that no one in the town knew her and that she did not know them. And still she felt it was not enough.

What company was she for him? They had no shared experiences or interests, no friends in common apart, she supposed, from Father O'Brien. Confined to the house most of the day, she had nothing of interest to relate. And Lawrence was not, by nature, a talkative man. Too many years of his own company had made him quietly introspective, and Maggie felt obliged to fill the silence over the meal table, or when they sat down in the evenings in the chintz-covered chairs one each side of the open fire, even though she worried that her chatter was either boring or annoying him, and perhaps both.

He did sometimes ask her questions about her family and her past, it was true, but then he would retreat into himself so that she wasn't sure whether or not he was listening, and, uncomfortable, she would force herself to bite her tongue.

But what had she expected? Lawrence was fifty-six – more than ten years older than her father had been. He was an educated man; the books she tidied away bore witness to that – volumes of poetry and plays, works of philosophy and history. Some of them weren't even in English but Latin, which she recognised though she didn't understand it, and other languages she didn't recognise at all. There was evidence amidst the clutter that he'd travelled, too. Programmes from the opera in Paris, musical recitals in Berlin and Rome, a well-thumbed map of London. Small artefacts that looked as if they'd been picked up along the way – a piece of crystal, a phial containing what looked like red sand, a wallet whose cover depicted a scene of warriors in a mosaic of multicoloured leather. And the inevitable religious icons too, rosaries and medallions and tiny statuettes, none of which looked English.

They stirred something in Maggie, a thirst for experiences beyond her mundane existence that had always lurked at the edges of her consciousness but which she had put to one side as silly and fanciful. But they also emphasised the huge gulf of experience that yawned between her and Lawrence.

How could she ever hope to connect with such a man? Maggie wondered, without any real hope of finding an answer.

As for his work, which occupied almost every moment of his day, she knew next to nothing. He rarely talked about it, and she'd never so much as set foot in his workshop – he'd told her it was the one place she didn't need to keep clean and tidy and she'd thought that he was afraid she might damage something or interfere with a delicate stage of the process, whatever that might entail. All she knew was that he was engaged on an important project that he'd been working on for a year or more, and which would continue to occupy him for some months to come.

'But what is it?' she'd asked, and he'd told her that he had been commissioned to make a triptych window for a cathedral in New York.

Maggie's eyes had widened in amazement and awe. New York! Why, that was half a world away!

'How did you come to get a job like that?' she'd asked.

'Through a friend I made when I was training in London, many years ago,' he said, looking a little embarrassed at her open admiration. 'Jacob was an American, and a master craftsman, over here to carry out some highly specialised restoration work. He taught me all I know. But he's too old now to do the things he used to, his sight is failing and his hands are too stiff, and when he was approached he suggested I should be commissioned in his place. There have been times, I confess, when I've wondered whether my health would allow such a thing, but I've carried on with the making of the windows just hoping I would be able to oversee their installation for myself, and I think that hope has proved to be justified.' He smiled at her. 'Since I've had you to take care of me, my dear, I've never felt better.'

'I do my best,' Maggie teased. 'But how will you get the windows all the way to America when they're finished?'

'They will be crated up and sent by sea,' Lawrence told her. 'Then, God willing, they will be mounted in the lady chapel they are intended for. But that's a good way off yet, and will continue to be unless I get to work. I'll leave you to whatever you need to do, my dear.'

He had gone out to his workshop and Maggie had been left with a thousand unanswered questions and a tickle of excitement bubbling deep inside that felt in some strange way as if she were almost within reach of her childhood dreams, something precious and secret.

There were numerous examples of Lawrence's craftsmanship scattered about the house – a lampshade that glowed, jewel-like, when the candle it covered was alight, a circular plate hung by a length of wire over one of the window panes, and many more, and she had often marvelled at them as she dusted and cleaned, wondering how the facets had been shaped and fitted together into the lead strips that held them in place, but she had not asked. It seemed to her that Lawrence's art went beyond the skilful; there was a mystique about it that bordered on the sacred, and to question him about it would somehow be irreverent.

After a while, however, her curiosity began to overcome her reluctance to pry into his private world, the world that existed within the tumbledown walls of the workshop, and one day when she'd finished her chores and he was still missing, she wondered if she dared pay a visit to his mysterious domain. There could be no harm in showing an interest, surely? She was, after all, his wife! But still her heart was beating a nervous tattoo at the very thought of it.

Rain was falling, thick and steady, as it had seemed to do incessantly these last weeks. Maggie pulled a shawl over her head and ran down the unevenly paved path to the workshop, tucked between shrubs that were beginning to sprout new growth for a spring that still seemed a long way off. As she tapped at the door, rainwater dripped from the overhanging branches of the sycamore tree, splashing on to her face and hands, and she turned the iron handle and opened the door a crack.

Lawrence was at a vast bench, his back towards her.

'I just wondered if you'd like a cup of tea,' she said hesitantly.

'Oh, my dear, come inside, do!' Lawrence said without turning round.

'Are you sure?' Maggie felt once again that she was trespassing in a holy of holies.

'Well of course!' He glanced over his shoulder and smiled at her before bending to his work once more.

Maggie stepped inside. It was surprisingly warm in the workshop, the heat emanating from a kiln, inside which a heap of coke glowed fiery red. Various tools and brushes lay on side tables or were affixed to wall racks, and long, thin strips of what she assumed was lead hung over a bracket. But it was the panel spread out on the workbench that drew, and held, her attention. Some five feet in length, and half as wide, it took up almost all of the bench, and Maggie could see it was nearing completion.

'Oh, that's beautiful!' she gasped before she could stop herself – and so it was.

The panel depicted a woman, almost life-size. Her flowing

robes were sapphire blue, and a halo, white and gold, shimmered around her head. Her hands were clasped in prayer, her feet bare against emerald grass, and above her, in an azure sky, a tiny cherub emerged from a fluffy cloud, blowing on a silver trumpet.

'The Holy Mother,' Maggie whispered reverently.

'Indeed.' Lawrence nodded. 'She is one of the three windows that make up the triptych – her place will be to left of the central, which will be of our Lord Jesus Christ on the cross. I haven't begun work on that yet, but the right-hand panel, depicting St Joseph, is already complete.'

'May I see it?' Maggie asked eagerly.

'You may, but not just yet. I have it stored for safe keeping, and for you to fully appreciate it would mean unwrapping it and bringing it into the light.'

'Oh, I don't want to cause you any trouble,' Maggie said hastily. 'This . . .' she nodded towards the Blessed Virgin, 'is more than enough for me. But however do you do it? Those little pieces – how do you get them to be the right shape; how do you know where each of them goes, and stick them together? I can't begin to understand!'

'It's a long process, my dear,' Lawrence told her. 'There are many stages, and it takes years to learn them all. Most craftsmen concentrate on one or the other – the design, the cutting and painting, the lead work, the firing. I couldn't be satisfied with that – I was fortunate to be able to learn them all. The only thing I don't do myself is the painting of the cartoon. I make a rough drawing of the design required and call on the help of a friend who is a much more talented artist than I. When the picture is finished, and has my approval and that of whoever has commissioned the work, I make a tracing to work from and continue from there.'

Already Maggie was quite lost in the explanation. Drawing – tracing – cutting – painting – leadwork – she didn't understand any of it. Seeing the bewilderment on her face, Lawrence smiled.

'I know. It must seem unfathomable to you. Let me finish the Blessed Virgin, and when I begin working on the crucifixion, you can follow me through each stage. As you learn, you can perhaps make a small panel of your own, if you'd like to.'

'Oh, I'd love that!' Maggie said, delighted. 'But what about my usual duties? I can't neglect them.'

Lawrence shrugged.

'As long as we have a meal on the table and clean clothes to put on . . . there are better things in life, Maggie, than a continuous round of domestic tasks. I'd like to think I'd introduced you to some of them. Now, why don't you make us that cup of tea and you can watch me working . . . until, of course, you become bored.'

'Oh, I won't be bored for a moment!' Maggie protested.

She could imagine nothing more fascinating than watching as this beautiful window was made ready to go to the home for which it was destined. A home goodness only knew how many miles away, on the other side of an ocean. On the other side of the world!

Chapter Twenty-One

Winter softened into spring, spring blossomed into summer. The window portraying the Blessed Virgin was finished now and stored beneath its protective covering as the one of St Joseph had been. Now Lawrence had begun work on the central window, depicting the terrible beauty of the crucifixion, and Maggie had fallen into the habit of hurrying through her daily chores so that she could join him in his workshop and watch as he worked, talking her through each stage of the process with a patience that was typical of him. She now knew the names of the tools, each of which had its proper place, and something of the different types of glass, though remembering them all was still beyond her. She had helped Lawrence carefully unroll the drawing of Christ on the cross, and he had allowed her to trace some of the outlines, and even make some of the bolder cuts, though he had executed the more intricate pieces himself, running the diamond over the glass, then holding the sheet between finger and thumb as he teased out the required shape. She'd seen him make the square-cornered framework, and stretch lengths of lead, with one end firmly under his foot whilst he pulled with all his strength on the other. She'd even tried her hand at painting, using first the camel-hair matting brush, then the badger, laying down a wash with vertical strokes as he showed her. She had learned how to fire the kiln with coke and charcoal, and she had drawn a simple design of her own, a pit wheel in the centre, a Davy lamp, a helmet, a slag heap and a pickaxe arranged in sections around it, and traced it as she had seen Lawrence do on to a small piece of glass.

'You have a talent for drawing,' Lawrence had said. 'I can see that I'll be able to dispense with the services of my artist friend before long.'

Maggie had flushed with pleasure and pride.

'I've always loved to draw,' she said shyly. 'When I was a little girl, I was forever doing pictures with coloured pencils on every bit of scrap paper I could get my hands on. But I haven't done anything like that for years now. I've never had the time.'

'Well, you have the time now,' he said kindly. 'Practice is what you need, and lots of it, and then I think we might make an artist of you.'

'Oh, I'm not so sure of that!' Maggie knew that whatever talent she possessed was raw and undeveloped, and it would be a long time before she could hope to produce anything good enough to form the basis of one of Lawrence's beautiful windows.

She was, though, happier than she had ever believed possible. There was a purpose now to her days that she'd never experienced before; the moment she woke in the mornings, she was filled with a sense of anticipation and eagerness that bubbled inside her like a fine wine – though Maggie, who had never so much as tasted a fine wine, was unable to make the comparison. All the pressures of her previous life seemed to have melted away; it was as if she inhabited a different world. Lawrence made no demands on her, the news from Yorkshire was encouraging – the warmer weather was suiting Rose, it seemed – and even Billy worried her less. He seemed to have settled in well to the life of a farmhand, and though when he first came to visit he was awkward and sullen, Lawrence treated him with enormous kindness and patience, and slowly Billy began to respond.

'I'm sorry – our Billy can be very difficult,' she'd said after that first time, when he'd lowered his eyes and shuffled his feet whenever Lawrence spoke to him. But Lawrence had only smiled, that kind, gentle smile that seemed to belong more to one of the saints in his stained-glass creations than to a flesh-and-blood man.

'He's young and shy,' he said. 'I was much the same myself once.'

Maggie found it hard to believe that Lawrence had ever been as awkward as Billy, but she was grateful to him for his understanding. She didn't argue that Ewart and Walter had never behaved the way Billy did; that seemed unwarranted and cruel. He was just different, as Mam had always said, and that far she did go one day when Billy had been particularly rude to Lawrence. 'Different, yes.' Lawrence nodded. 'But one day he'll find his metier, just as we all do.'

Maggie didn't recognise the word, or really know what it meant, but she got the gist of it. She was learning all the time, she thought, simply from being in Lawrence's company: new words, new manners, new customs, and of course, most of all, new skills.

And she was learning, too, that love came in many forms, not simply the blind passion she had felt for Josh, or the fierce loyalty of blood ties. She was coming to love Lawrence, she realised – his kindness, his gentleness, his modesty, his enduring faith in a God to whom he had dedicated his life in his own way. This love was a seed planted in gratitude, and it grew and deepened with each passing day, fed and watered by the interest they now shared, he as the teacher, she as his student. Josh seemed now more like a distant dream, an ache in her heart with which she had learned to live, and though she still woke sometimes in the night with tears on her cheeks and the longing for him strong as ever, she had trained herself to put it away.

Josh had left her. He was with someone else. He had never loved her as she loved him. But a part of him was with her still. As her stomach swelled to a baby-shaped mound, as she felt the child move within her, as she traced her fingers over small protruding lumps that she knew were either a fist or a tiny foot, she experienced something close to a sense of triumph.

This child was Josh's child, and that fact alone made it very special, the last thing she had, would ever have, of the man she had loved with all her heart. Yet it was also her child and hers alone, and no one and nothing but God or a cruel fate could take it away from her. Thanks to Lawrence, the baby had a future that was secure, holding far more than he could otherwise have hoped for. He wouldn't be branded a bastard; he wouldn't have to fight bigger boys who called him names; he wouldn't have to wear hand-me-down clothes that were shabby, threadbare or too big for him. He wouldn't have to give up his education and toil in the darkness far beneath the green fields. And if he turned out to be a she, she wouldn't have to go into the drudgery of service – though Maggie felt quite certain that the unborn baby was a boy.

Caressing her swollen stomach, she reflected on all this, and vowed that she would never do anything to jeopardise her baby's assured future. Even if that meant devoting herself to Lawrence and forgetting that Josh ever existed.

This was her life now; she would be content with it.

And she was, she was.

* * *

The telegram was delivered one morning in early July.

Maggie had been up since dawn. She'd had a restless night, and the old feeling of foreboding she'd learned to dread had been nagging at her, indeterminate but too strong to ignore. Besides this, the niggling ache low in her back that had kept her from settling was growing more intense. She'd been trying to ignore it and get through her daily chores so that she could join Lawrence in his workshop; today she was due to begin the delicate task of cutting the tiny fragments of glass that would make up the sections of sky that peeped between the spokes of the pit wheel in the plate she was making, and she was eager to begin. The concentration required would soon make her forget this stupid ache, she told herself.

When the doorbell jangled she was upstairs, debating whether or not to change the bedlinen. It was a fine, warm day; if she washed the sheets and pillowcases they'd dry quickly on the line that ran the length of the garden outside the kitchen window. But the thought of carrying buckets of hot water from the copper, heaving the wet fabric up and down in the sink, rinsing, and then, worst of all, running the lot through the mangle was not an appealing one, so the sound of the bell was a welcome distraction. She was puzzled as to who could be calling, though; visitors were a rarity, and it was too early for the baker, who came twice weekly. Sometimes a gypsy would come to the door with a basket of clothes pegs to sell, or a bunch of lucky white heather – if they had set up camp in the nearby countryside, their route into Hillsbridge took them past Lawrence's home. Perhaps it was a gypsy; well, she'd just have to send them on their way. She didn't need clothes pegs and she wasn't sure Lawrence would approve of the lucky heather, being a devout Catholic and scathing with regard to superstition. Then again, he might give them a few pennies or a silver threepenny bit out of sympathy. But it wasn't her place to raid his purse, and she had no intention of interrupting him to find out if he was feeling charitable today.

She glanced out of the window and saw a bicycle propped up against the gate. Not gypsies, then. Maggie descended the stairs slowly, her bulk making her feel a little unsafe, and the doorbell jangled again.

'All right, I'm coming!' she muttered, crossing the living room and rubbing her aching back as she did so.

As she unlatched the door and saw the uniformed boy on the doorstep, holding out a small buff envelope, her heart missed a beat. A telegram! Though she'd never received one in her life, she knew what it was, all right. And she knew too that telegrams rarely brought good news.

'Mrs Jacobs?' The boy thrust the envelope towards her. 'For you.'

'For my husband,' she corrected him automatically.

'No, missus, for you.' The boy had a cheeky little face, red from the exertion of pedalling out from Hillsbridge as fast as his legs would take him, and a voice to match, a reedy voice that had not yet broken.

Maggie took the envelope, and her heart thudded again as she saw that it was indeed her name emblazoned on the front of it.

'Thank you,' she said faintly.

The boy made no effort to leave.

'Do you need paying?' she asked. She had no idea of the protocol involved.

'Sixpence wouldn't come amiss,' the boy replied. 'It's a long way out here, you know.'

'Very well. Wait a minute.'

Maggie went back into the house; Lawrence's purse was, she

knew, in a dresser drawer. She opened it and found a sixpence. Though she wouldn't have done it for the gypsies, this was different. This was official.

She returned to the door, gave the sixpence to the boy, and he went whistling down the path. Only when he had retrieved his bicycle and pedalled away did she go back into the house and tear open the envelope.

The ache in her back was forgotten now, but she felt sick with dread, and as she unfolded the sheet of paper and read the message it contained, her worst fears were realised.

It was brutally brief and to the point – not a single word beyond what was necessary – as telegrams, she supposed, always were.

Mam passed in the night. Will write. Walter.

Her stomach fell away and the ground seemed to be dissolving beneath her feet.

It shouldn't have been a shock, though recently Mam had apparently been better; wasn't this exactly what Maggie had been fearing for the last year and more? And yet it was.

Mam, dead? No! Oh, please, no!

Mam dead, so far from home, and Maggie hadn't been with her. She would never see her again; Mam would never see her new grandchild. The thought was almost more than she could bear.

For long moments she stood, swaying on her feet, her mind racing in wild circles. What should she do? What *could* she do? Should she go to Yorkshire? She so wanted to be there, with Ewart and Walter – oh, how she wanted that. But with the baby due at any time, it didn't seem possible. And Billy – how was she going to tell Billy? He was going to be so upset. The thought of his distress only added to her own.

Lawrence. She must tell Lawrence. He would know what to

do. But her feet seemed welded to the floor and she shrank from the thought of making all this real by putting it into words.

'Maggie?' Lawrence's voice from the doorway. 'Maggie, my dear, whatever is wrong?'

He must have heard the clang of the bell and come to see who was calling.

'Oh . . .' Maggie whispered, and still the words would not come. 'Oh . . .'

Lawrence took the telegram from her, reading it with one quick glance.

'My dear . . . I'm so sorry . . .' His distress was genuine. 'She was a good woman . . . such a good woman . . .'

Maggie was briefly puzzled by his words. As far as she knew, Lawrence had never met her mother. But as he reached for her hands, squeezing them tight between his own, the shock and grief came rushing in, and she could think of nothing else. Tears gathered in her eyes and ran down her cheeks unchecked.

And not only her cheeks. Moisture was running down her legs in a hot rush. For a horrified moment Maggie thought her bladder had released, but it wasn't that.

'Oh dear God!' she gasped. 'I think . . .'

But she was unable to articulate that either. How could she find the words to tell a man – even her husband – what was happening?

Her waters had broken, Maggie knew. Her baby was coming.

One in, one out. The old adage popped into Maggie's head more than once in the hours that followed, in between the spasms that were now gripping her. At first they weren't much worse than the ache that had been troubling her since the middle of the night, but gradually they increased in strength so that when they came she could no longer think of anything at all beyond riding out each excruciating wave and waiting for the next. Only the despair remained, an overwhelming wretchedness that needed no coherent thought but lent an aura of nightmare to the contractions that racked her.

Lawrence had arranged for a midwife and a doctor from Hillsbridge to attend her, a luxury Maggie would never have been afforded in her former life. As soon as it became evident that she had begun her labour, the midwife was sent for, a big-boned, capable-looking woman named Mrs Harvey. She came bustling in, divesting herself of her cape and looking around critically at the small, cluttered living room.

'Let's get you upstairs then, missy, and I can have a good look at you.'

Maggie, who had been walking the length of the room and back again, over and over, went, obedient as a child, leaving an anxious Lawrence downstairs.

In the bedroom – which warranted more critical looks – Mrs Harvey tied a voluminous apron around her ample frame and examined first the bed – 'Are these clean sheets? Best put some old ones on if you don't want them all mucked up' – and then Maggie. Maggie hated that; it was both humiliating and painful. Mrs Harvey seemed unnecessarily rough, and Maggie had to grit her teeth against the prodding fingers.

'You'll be a good while yet,' the midwife pronounced.

'Oh, I was hoping it wouldn't be too long,' Maggie said, before catching her breath as another pain racked her, and Mrs Harvey snorted derisively.

'You'll have a lot more than that to put up with before this is over,' she said, and it seemed to Maggie that she was taking pleasure in the prospect.

Oh Mam, she thought, tears pricking her eyes. *Where are you? I need you! Where have you gone?*

But Rose wasn't here, and never would be again, no matter how much Maggie wanted her. There was only Mrs Harvey, bossy and unsympathetic, and Maggie could only hope she was as good at her job as her reputation suggested. It was she the Hillsbridge doctor had recommended when Lawrence had taken her to see him, and she had been booked on the strength of his advice.

The doctor, at least, had seemed nice, though much younger than Dr Blackmore in High Compton. But he was a Scot, with a strong Highland accent, and Maggie had had trouble under-standing a word he said. Everything and everyone was alien to what she was used to, and although she was only a few miles from home, she felt lost and frightened, cut off from the comfortable and familiar.

It would be some time, anyway, before the doctor arrived. He had better things to do than sit by the bedside of a woman in labour, and would only be sent for when the redoubtable Mrs Harvey deemed it necessary.

As the day wore on, it seemed that moment would never come. The room was stiflingly hot, the windows all closed and the fire in the grate burning fiercely as Mrs Harvey kept it well stoked up from the coal bucket that stood beside it. Maggie tossed and turned, wriggled and writhed, tugging on the old pillowcase that the midwife had tied around the bedhead for her to hang on to when the pain became unbearable. Sweat poured down her face, gathered in the hollow between her breasts and soaked her nightgown. She wanted to get up and try to walk about – anything, she thought, would be better than lying on the bed with sheets that were rumpled and untidy no matter how often Mrs Harvey smoothed them out, and damp with Maggie's perspiration – but the midwife wouldn't hear of it. She wiped Maggie's forehead occasionally with a cool wet flannel and allowed her sips of water, but neither seemed to help.

The pain was almost continuous now, one long agony from which Maggie could not escape, and still Mrs Harvey, after more painful prodding and poking, maintained she wasn't anywhere near ready to deliver her baby. Eventually, though, Lawrence took matters into his own hands.

Dimly Maggie was aware of his uneven gait on the stairs and a tap at the door. Mrs Harvey harrumphed impatiently – husbands were most definitely not welcome in what had become her domain – but she opened it a crack and there was a whispered conversation.

'Mr Jacobs wants to get the doctor,' she said, disapproval evident in her tone. 'I've told him it'll be hours yet, but he thinks he knows best.'

Maggie was past caring and certainly past arguing, but she felt a wave of relief all the same. Surely the doctor would do something? This couldn't go on for much longer. She couldn't stand it! She stuffed her fist into her mouth to keep herself from crying out as another pain built to a crescendo – even now her pride wouldn't allow her to let herself down, as she thought of it, in front of this hatchet-faced woman whom she was coming to dislike more with every passing hour. But she couldn't help herself from whispering, 'Oh God, dear God, please help me!' only to evoke the sharp retort: 'He is helping you, my girl.'

The light outside the window was fading, and Mrs Harvey had fetched an oil lamp and placed it on the chest of drawers beside the bed by the time the doctor arrived. He came into the room, dumped his medical bag on the chair Mrs Harvey had been sitting in between her ministrations and crossed to Maggie. His tall, lanky form seemed to tower over her, and she still couldn't understand a word he said, but his thin, angular face was kindly, and when he examined her, he was far gentler than Mrs Harvey had been.

'Och aye, you're doing fine.'

Miracle of miracles, she understood that! And miracle of miracles, now that he was here, nothing seemed quite so bad.

'Oh Doctor, is it going to be much longer?' she whispered.

And was quite suddenly overcome with a powerful need to push. Though it was what she had been waiting for all day, she was still startled by the strength of the compulsion.

'Ah, that's the way, hinny.' The lilting accent was soothing, and for all that the pain had reached new dimensions, Maggie felt safe with him. Even in those panic-stricken moments when she thought her body was being torn in two, that lilting voice and kind eyes had the power to calm her.

More lamps were brought, fetched from every corner of the house at Dr Mackay's request, even the candle lamp with the stained-glass shade, and it was on that that Maggie focused as she strained and pushed with each contraction. Darkness fell and the candle flame glowed, an oasis of light in the darkness that seemed to surround her.

And at last – at last! – Maggie felt a soft rush as her baby slipped from her into Mrs Harvey's waiting hands and uttered his first mewling cry.

'A little boy! You've got a beautiful little boy!' the midwife told her, triumphant as if she herself was solely responsible for the new life.

Maggie fell back against the rumpled pillows, too exhausted to even try to peek at her baby. But a little while later, when the midwife placed the small, tightly swaddled bundle in her arms, she gazed in awe at the little red face, puckered into creases around a perfect pursed mouth, as if he was angry at having been kept waiting so long to be delivered; at the mass of fine dark hair covering a pointed head, and at shell-like ears that lay flat against his skull, and a wave of love stronger than any she had experienced before in her life swept through her.

But oh! Her heart twisted. He was so like Josh!

Not possible. Surely it was far too early for him to look like anyone. Yet that first impression was too strong to be denied, and Maggie didn't know whether to be angry or glad.

'What is the bairn to be called?' asked Dr Mackay, washing his hands in the china bowl on the washstand. How was it she could now understand him, though his accent was as thick as ever? The shared experience, perhaps?

Maggie looked at Lawrence, who had at last been allowed into the bedroom and was standing beside the bed gazing at the baby with much the same awe as Maggie was feeling.

They hadn't talked about a name. Though Maggie had run over a few, testing them on her tongue to see how they sounded, she'd never asked Lawrence's opinion and he hadn't offered it. But now the baby was here, flesh and blood, a real, living human being, not just a swelling beneath her petticoats. He deserved a name, and Lawrence, who had given her refuge and the baby a future, deserved to be consulted.

'Lawrence?' she said softly.

'You're calling him after your husband?' Dr Mackay asked, misunderstanding, and then, after just a moment's hesitation, Maggie said:

'We could, yes.'

'Oh, I think not!' Lawrence shook his head, smiling. 'That would be far too confusing. And besides, a baby doesn't want to be named for an old duffer like me.'

'You are not an old duffer,' Maggie said stoutly. 'And we could always call him Laurie to make the distinction. Laurie . . . I

327

like that . . .' She paused for a moment. 'And perhaps Patrick besides, after my father.'

'Patrick Lawrence, then,' Lawrence said. 'We'll decide later.' But Maggie thought he looked pleased and as proud as if he was the baby's real father.

'Patrick,' she whispered, and smoothed one peachy cheek with her thumb. 'Patrick Lawrence . . .'

But her eyes were drooping. With her baby nestled against her breast, Maggie fell asleep.

Chapter Twenty-Two

September 1897

The little house on the outskirts of Hillsbridge was a flurry of activity. The three tall stained-glass windows were finished at last, crated securely and ready to be shipped across the Atlantic, and Lawrence was to go to New York to see them safely fitted in the lady chapel of the cathedral. His passage was booked – he was to sail from Liverpool on the steam ship *Campania* in just a few days' time, and Maggie was helping him to pack a trunk with all he would need and a suitcase with sufficient to see him through the voyage.

As she folded shirts and undergarments, Patrick waddled around behind her on plump little legs, which sometimes collapsed beneath him so that he landed in a heap on his bottom, lost patience with the business of walking and scrambled after her at a rapid crawl.

He was growing fast, no longer a baby but a little boy. His hair, thick and dark even when he was born, was now a mass of curls and ringlets falling around cheeks rosy with health. His nose had grown straight, and his eyes turned from that first clear blue to hazel, the exact same colour as his father's, and Maggie could not look at him without thinking how like Josh he was. She found it hard to believe, in fact, that no one else could see it, but of course no one in Hillsbridge knew Josh, and when Ewart had come to visit, in early summer, if he'd seen the likeness he didn't comment on it, and for that she was grateful. No one beyond her immediate family knew the truth; as far as the outside world was concerned, Lawrence was Patrick's father, and if they questioned it in private, she never knew it.

In the first months after Patrick was born, she'd walked into Hillsbridge often, pushing him in his perambulator, and the people she met in the shops and the market would coo over him. Maggie was glad they thought he was Lawrence's, even if perhaps they wondered in private how an old man like him could have fathered such a beautiful child. It wasn't just that she wanted to keep her secret; it seemed to her to be a little tribute to the man who had given her a whole new life.

And what a life! Scarcely a day passed but Maggie counted her blessings. She never had to worry for a moment as to where the next penny was coming from; Lawrence gave her a generous allowance for housekeeping and paid without questioning for everything she needed for herself and Lawrence. She had a nice home, she had the most beautiful son, and a husband who demanded nothing of her that she was unprepared to give. Though Lawrence had insisted the laundry be sent once a week to a washerwoman, and brought in a girl to help with the spring cleaning after the chimney sweep had been, her days were full, and they were for the most part happy.

There had been dark ones, of course, in the months following Rose's death, days when she had been ready to burst into tears, and times when she had railed at the heavens that Rose had been taken without seeing her grandchild. There were times when she worried about Billy, as much the loner as ever, perhaps even more so, for his beloved Bullseye had died, too, in the long, hard winter – he'd gone missing for a few days before Billy had found him lying in a corner of the barn, curled up and half hidden behind the threshing machine. And there were times when she still ached for Josh, longed for him with a fervour that was, she told herself, far more than he deserved. But she had little time for such thoughts. When she wasn't engaged in domestic duties, her every waking moment was occupied with helping Lawrence work on the precious stained-glass window.

She had a talent for it, Lawrence had said, and that filled her with pride, though she was all too aware of her limitations. The plate she'd made to her own design looked clumsy and amateurish compared to Lawrence's fine work, so intricate and precise, but it would come with practice, he assured her, and she could almost believe him, for she was beginning to be able to see exactly what needed to be done, even if her fingers were not yet nimble enough to always follow suit.

'Try your hand at a new piece of your own whilst I'm away,' Lawrence encouraged her, and she promised she would, though she wasn't sure how she'd manage it now that Patrick was walking. She wouldn't be able to take him into the workshop with her with only one pair of eyes to watch what he was up to; there were far too many dangers there, from the kiln to the cutting tools and the collection of sheets of glass. Even if she took some of his toys with him, he'd most likely find the unfamiliar attractions far more interesting, and she couldn't risk him cutting or burning himself. But perhaps she would be able to snatch a little time while he was asleep. The evening hours would be long and lonely while Lawrence was away.

She was going to miss him, Maggie realised. The man who

had once been no more than a kind stranger had become her closest friend, and where she had once felt shy and awkward with him, now she told him everything. Though he was as quiet as ever, Maggie more than made up for it, filling what could have been long silences with her chatter, relating every detail of her day and reporting on Patrick's latest development.

It was because of Patrick that the bond between them had grown and strengthened, she thought – Lawrence doted on the little boy. But he was also unfailingly kind and caring towards her, and surprisingly fond of Billy, whom he encouraged to come to the house whenever he had a day off. He'd been especially good when Bullseye had died, spending time with Billy and seemingly comforting him, not so much with words as simply by being there. Perhaps it was because neither of them were outgoing that they were able to communicate with few words spoken, Maggie thought. They understood one another. And now that he was about to leave for America, Lawrence had asked if Billy could come and see him off.

Maggie hadn't been sure if it would be possible, or even if Billy would want to. But when the day came, and the pony and trap deposited her, Patrick and Lawrence at the Hillsbridge railway station, Billy was there, leaning against the fence beside the entrance, the bicycle that he'd borrowed from Farmer propped up beside him.

They all trooped on to the platform, the elderly porter, who had appeared as if by magic, wheeling Lawrence's trunk on a set of trucks. The stationmaster himself emerged from his office to speak to Lawrence, and Maggie realised yet again how well regarded he was in the town. It wasn't long before a signal clanked and the level-crossing gates closed across the main road, then the train was pulling into the station. Patrick squealed excitedly, his little face animated as he pointed with chubby fingers at the clouds of steam coming from the engine. Lawrence's trunk was manhandled into the guard's van and the porter held a door open for Lawrence to climb into the carriage.

He turned, chucking Patrick under the chin, and squeezed Billy's shoulder.

'Look after your sister while I'm gone.'

Billy nodded. 'I will, sir,' and Maggie thought how odd that was – she'd always been the one to look after him.

Last but not least, Lawrence embraced Maggie, and then there was nothing for it but to get into the carriage, though he wound down the window and stood looking out as the porter slammed doors up and down the train. The guard blew his whistle and raised a green flag, then with another hiss of steam the train pulled away, Lawrence still at the open window.

Maggie waved her handkerchief until the train rounded a bend in the line and was lost to sight. She felt utterly bereft.

'I suppose I'd better get home,' she said to Billy.

'I've got to go too,' Billy said. 'Farmer will dock my wages if I'm gone too long.'

'Will you come over and see me when you get some time off?' she asked.

'If you like.'

The pony and trap were waiting for her. The driver lifted Patrick up, then handed her in. As the pony trotted off, she looked back over her shoulder; Billy was still standing beside his bicycle watching her go and looking as small and lost as ever.

'It's going to be funny without your daddy, isn't it, my love?' she said to Patrick, but his eyelids were drooping, long lashes fanning out across his soft, plump cheeks. Maggie cradled him to her, burying her chin in his curls, and long before they left the town behind, he was fast asleep.

* * *

She'd been right – she did miss him. There was suddenly a Lawrence-shaped space in the little house, and even with Patrick tumbling about, it felt strangely empty and silent. Patrick's attempts at speaking were mostly unintelligible garbles, with the occasional 'Ma-ma' or 'birdie' thrown in, and when she talked to him it tended to be about the mundane and the infantile.

Loneliness crept up on her unawares; she wished she could venture into High Compton to meet up with Beat and Cathy, and one day she pushed Patrick in his perambulator almost to the outskirts of the town. But there she stopped, before turning around to go back the way she'd come. It was too far, she told herself; by the time she made it all the way home again, it would be well past Patrick's tea time. And it was too hot – one of those scorching days of Indian summer; her back and armpits were moist with a sheen of perspiration beneath the leg-of-mutton sleeves of her blouse, and her feet felt swollen inside her laced boots. But in reality she knew she'd turned back for quite another reason – how could she simply walk into the drapery shop and face Augusta and the girls after all this time? She had nothing to be ashamed of now – she was a respectable married woman, after all – but Mrs Freeman knew the truth even if the girls did not, and she simply couldn't bring herself to do it.

'Let's go and listen to the echo, Patrick,' she said – there was a spot in the woods only a little off the beaten track where a shouted 'Hello!' would reverberate off the railway arches across the valley, and she thought it would amuse him.

But when she began calling out, a terrible feeling of sadness overcame her. For Mam, for Jack, for Paddy . . . all dead and gone. And then for Josh, the father Patrick would never know, and also for Lawrence, who was by now half a world away.

'Be safe, Lawrence,' she whispered, tears misting her eyes.

'Ma-ma?' Patrick was staring up at her, his clear hazel eyes puzzled, as if he'd picked up on her change of mood and he too might begin to cry.

'It's all right, my love,' Maggie said, swallowing her tears and managing to call out again to the echo, making him smile.

Then she bumped the perambulator over the rough ground until they were back on the road, and walked briskly off in the direction of the place she now called home.

Lawrence had been gone for more than two weeks when Maggie took Patrick to market in Hillsbridge one Saturday morning.

The market was a huge affair, as much a social event as a commercial enterprise. There was a vast purpose-built hall with entrances on three sides, which was always filled with stalls, and even then there wasn't space for them all. They spilled out on to the cobbled square outside, which also formed the forecourt of the George Hotel: fruiterers, butchers, fishmongers, grocers, a stall selling butter, cream and cheese, though this one was of course inside in the shade. Smasher the chinaware man was there, tossing plates and cups into the air and letting them crash into a thousand pieces on the cobbles to attract attention to his wares; a pair of Indian doctors were selling pills and potions they claimed would cure all ills, and there was even a wagon where a swarthy man with what looked like an enormous pair of pliers would pull aching teeth in full view of the watching crowd.

The market would continue well into the evening, and sometimes the Salvation Army band would play and people would dance while a tiny woman went around with a hat, collecting money to go to good causes. Maggie had never been there in the evening, of course – before she was married, she'd always been at work herself for late-night opening, and now she had Patrick to think of. Besides which, she had heard, things could turn rowdy later on. The miners would have divided up their week's wages earlier on in the bar of the Miners' Arms, just across the street from the George, and some of them would have whiled away the day spending too much of it on a few drinks.

When Maggie arrived soon after ten in the morning, however, all was respectable hustle and bustle. She bought butter, bacon, and a small wedge of cheese from the dairy stall, apples and vegetables from the greengrocer, and half a pound of biscuits from the grocer, loading it all into the well of the perambulator. On the way back down the aisle between the stalls she made a detour to one that sold novelties, and treated Patrick to a little paper windmill on a stick. Outside, she was showing him how it turned by blowing on it, for there was not enough wind to do it for him, when she heard someone call her name.

'Maggie!'

She looked round, startled – who in Hillsbridge would call her by her given name instead of Mrs Jacobs?

Then her stomach fell away and her heart seemed to stop beating.

Pushing his way towards her through the crowd was the tall figure of the man she'd tried so hard to forget.

It was Josh Withers.

She couldn't move, couldn't speak. If she hadn't been holding on to the handle of the perambulator, she thought her legs might have given way beneath her.

'Maggie! Thank goodness!'

From somewhere she found her voice.

'What are you doing here?'

'Looking for you, of course! Hester Dallimore said she thought she'd seen you at the market last week, so I came on the off chance you'd be here again.'

'You came specially looking for me?' There was no containing that spurt of fierce joy.

'I've been trying to find you ever since I got home and found you gone. Nobody at home seemed to know what had become of you, not even Mam and Dad. You certainly know how to give a man the runaround!'

'Really!' Quite suddenly that joy was soured with anger. 'I've given you the runaround! Well, that's rich coming from you, I must say! And it's a bit late to be looking for me, isn't it?'

'Oh Maggie!' Josh's eyes went to Patrick, who was staring up, round-eyed, from the perambulator, his new windmill forgotten. 'It was right, then, what people are saying. Why didn't you tell me?'

She raised her chin, remembering all too clearly the despair she'd felt that day she'd made the trip into Bristol looking for Josh. Oh, he had a nerve, all right!

'And how was I supposed to do that when you disappeared from the only address you gave anybody and ran off with somebody else, I'd like to know?'

'Maggie, I didn't! And I wrote, soon as I was settled . . .'

'Oh, don't lie to me, Josh!' she snapped. 'You didn't give a fig about me. Well, I'm all right now, so just leave me alone.'

She turned away, manoeuvring the perambulator through a gap in the shoppers. Josh followed.

'Maggie! Wait! We need to talk . . .'

'I've got nothing to say to you, Josh.' A red mist flaring in front of her eyes, she forged a path towards the road, thinking of nothing but escaping from her churning emotions and the man who was responsible for them. The railway delivery wagon was approaching, the horse at a fast trot, but she didn't even notice it until Josh grabbed the handle of the perambulator, stopping her abruptly.

'For goodness' sake, Maggie! Are you trying to get yourself and the baby killed?'

She was trembling violently now, realisation that she had very nearly pushed Patrick into the path of the oncoming wagon piling in on the shock of meeting Josh so unexpectedly.

'Please, just go away!' she begged.

'I'm not going anywhere until we've had the chance to talk.'

He had never sounded more determined, his voice a low growl, and quite suddenly the fight drained out of her.

She was all too aware of the nearness of him, his hand brushing hers on the handle of the perambulator; all too aware of the maelstrom of emotion churning inside her. No matter that he'd let her down, no matter what he'd done or not done, she loved him still.

'Oh Josh,' she whispered, and all the despair, all the longing was there in her voice. He was here, right beside her, but he might as well have been a million miles away. 'It's too late.'

'I can see that.' His eyes went to her hand, and her wedding ring. 'I'd still like to sort things out.'

'Not here. I don't want the whole town knowing my business. We'd better find somewhere quiet. We could go in the churchyard, there's a bench there . . .'

'Churchyard, eh?'

'It's on my way home. I can't be too long, Patrick has his dinner at midday.'

It wasn't what he'd hoped for when he'd come to Hillsbridge this morning in search of her, but he reckoned it was more than he had a right to expect. He was cursing himself, as he had cursed himself every day since he had come home and found Maggie gone, that he hadn't made more of an effort to check with her that she wasn't pregnant before he went off to Ireland. But she'd made it crystal clear that she couldn't allow them to be together, for a long while at least. He'd written to her from Bristol and she hadn't even replied, and when he planned to go to Belfast in search of work in the Harland and Wolff shipyard, he'd written again, to both her and his parents. He'd asked Cissie to post the letters for him, and assumed she had, but now he knew she'd had other things on her mind – namely running off with her fairground lover. By the time he wrote again, with the address of his new lodgings in Belfast, it was, of course, too late. Number six was all shut up and the Donovans were gone, his mother had told him.

How much had she known? he wondered now. She'd been very evasive, and wouldn't speculate beyond the rumours that had been circulating, one of which was that Maggie had got herself into trouble.

'If that's what's behind it, I hope it wasn't anything to do with you, my lad,' she'd said, giving him a dark look. 'I hope that isn't why you went off to Ireland, to get out of doing the right thing by her.'

'What do you think I am?' Josh had growled, and Florrie had merely said: 'Well, that's all right then,' and let the subject drop. But Josh couldn't forget it, any more than he could forget Maggie.

There was a job going for a colliery carpenter at Northway pit; Josh had gone to see the manager, secured it, and returned to Belfast only to pick up his belongings. Back in High Compton, he'd tried every which way to find out what had become of Maggie, and got nowhere. Not even Beat or Cathy could tell him anything, though Cathy had promised to write to Ewart and ask for information – a good excuse to get in touch with him, Josh suspected; her face had turned very pink when she mentioned his name. But both girls seemed seemed genuinely concerned to know what had become of their friend.

And then, as he'd told Maggie, the gossip of the rank, Hester Dallimore, had spotted her at the market one Saturday.

'And she was pushing a pram with a nipper in it, about a year old, I'd say!' she added triumphantly as she spread the news far and wide.

Josh's stomach had turned over when he heard it. If Maggie had a child about a year old, there was no doubt in his mind that it must be his. It was no more than he'd feared, but he couldn't stop castigating himself for not having been here for her when she needed him. His stupid pride was to blame, he thought – when she'd told him she wouldn't go with him to Bristol, didn't know if she'd ever be able to be with him, he'd thought it was because he was just a poor second to Jack. He'd been badly hurt and had gone on the defensive, and when she hadn't replied to his letter he'd taken it as further evidence that she didn't want him. Why the hell hadn't he been more assertive? Or more dogged? Why the hell had he assumed that if she wanted, or needed, him, she would come to him?

And where did they go from here?

Josh had never before been in the Hillsbridge churchyard. A path led around the old grey-stone building, opening up into a vast expanse of grass, dotted with headstones so old they were beginning to totter and crumble, but beyond the church door the ground sloped upwards and the graves there were clearly newer and well tended. Near the path a bench had been set under a tree – a magnolia, Josh thought, but he wasn't that good at identifying flora, and just at the moment couldn't have cared less.

Maggie parked the perambulator next to it, lifted Patrick out and set him down on the dry grass with a soft knitted toy and his new windmill.

'Play with this like a good boy,' she said. 'And don't poke the sails like that or you'll break it.'

But still the little boy couldn't resist – sticking a chubby finger into the gap in the paper and wriggling it round.

An unfamiliar emotion twisted within Josh. He'd barely ever taken notice of a baby before, but this one, he knew, was his, and the tenderness mixed with warmth and pride he was experiencing now took him completely by surprise.

'Well,' Maggie said, sitting down on the bench, 'what's happened to this woman you ran off with, then?'

Josh sighed. So many misunderstandings, and yet in the end it all came back to one thing.

'I never ran off with any woman, Maggie,' he said. 'You've got to believe me when I say there's never been anyone for me but you.'

'So where were you?' she demanded. 'Where were you when I came to Bristol to find you? And why did her husband tell me you had? That's what I'd like to know!'

'If you'll just hush up for a minute I'll tell you,' Josh said.

'What are we going to do, then?' Josh asked when he had finished.

'There's nothing we can do.' Maggie's eyes were full of tears. She had a feeling of déjà vu. First the ghost of Jack had stood between her and Josh; now it was Lawrence, a living, breathing man who had been so kind to her, who had offered her a refuge when she had desperately needed it. He was her husband, she loved him, though in a quite different way to the way she loved Josh, and she wouldn't, couldn't, hurt or betray him.

Patrick, who had been playing quietly all the time they had been talking, was becoming restless. She'd had to get up a few times now to go after him when he toddled or crawled too far away, and now he was pulling at her skirts, his small face twisting into an expression of discontent that she knew was the precursor to tears. He was getting hungry, she guessed, as well as being bored.

'I'm going to have to go,' she said.

'I want to see you again. You – and Patrick.'

Oh, how she wanted to see him too! But . . . She shook her head.

'That wouldn't be a good idea.'

'I let you go once . . . I'm not going to let you go again,' he said fiercely.

'Oh Josh, don't make this harder for me, please!' She lifted Patrick, holding him between them.

'But if your husband is away . . . I could come and see you both . . .'

'And where would that end? You know as well as I do. No, I'm sorry, Josh, but it has to stop here. When Patrick is older, perhaps he can come and visit you – if Lawrence doesn't mind, and always provided you still want to see him, of course. But you've got to forget about me. I took marriage vows to Lawrence, and I intend to keep them.'

'I see. He matters more to you than I do, then.'

'Oh, don't do this to me, please!' she begged.

'What am I supposed to think? If you loved me . . .'

Maggie set Patrick down in the perambulator and turned to face him.

'Oh Josh, believe me, I love you. I've always loved you, and I always will. But . . .'

The tears were pricking her eyes again, Patrick had begun to grizzle and bounce restlessly so that the perambulator rocked on the uneven ground. Holding on to the handle to steady it, Maggie leaned towards Josh and kissed him briefly on the cheek.

Then, before she could weaken, she turned the perambulator, steadied it back down the slope to the path and walked away without a backward glance.

Chapter Twenty-Three

Lawrence arrived home two weeks later, the pony and trap that had brought him from the railway station pulling up outside the cottage just as dusk was falling on a blustery autumnal day.

Maggie ran to the door to greet him, Patrick in her arms.

'Oh Lawrence, it's so good to have you back!' she exclaimed, and it was. She'd been feeling really down since her encounter with Josh, with too much time on her hands to think about what might have been. Now, as Lawrence hugged her and Patrick, taking the little boy from her and swinging him round to make him laugh, she knew that for all her regrets, she had done the right thing. Though he'd probably hide it behind a patient smile, he would be so terribly hurt if she left him to be with Josh. And she didn't like to think of him left alone either. He was such a solitary soul, but she knew he was glad of what she and Patrick had brought into his life, and would miss them dreadfully.

'How have you been, my dear?' he asked when he'd taken off his coat and was sitting in the wing chair with Patrick on his knee.

'We've been fine, haven't we, Patrick?' Maggie still hadn't decided whether to tell him that Josh was back in the area – she'd hate him to hear about it from anyone but her – but this wasn't the moment.

'That's good.' Lawrence jiggled Patrick on to his good leg so that he could reach for the cup of tea Maggie had placed on an occasional table beside him. 'Because I'm afraid I'm going to have to go back again, and soon.'

'Go back? But why?' Maggie was astounded.

'Unfortunately, one of the windows was damaged in the transportation,' Lawrence said.

'Oh no! Which one?'

'The Blessed Virgin. How it happened, I don't know. It was so securely crated and went with clear instructions that it should be handled with care. But somehow the damage has occurred, and I have agreed to go back to New York to make the necessary repairs there rather than risk it on yet another Atlantic crossing.'

'Why didn't you do it while you were there?' Maggie asked.

'Well, for one thing I wanted to ensure that the glass is the same as I used originally – the blue of the Virgin's robe is a very particular shade, and I wasn't sure I'd be able to match it. Besides which, I'd much prefer to use my own tools; foolish, I suppose – one badger brush is much like another – but there you are.' Lawrence took a sip of his tea. 'But the main reason is that the damage is really quite extensive and the repairs are likely to be rather a long job. I didn't feel I could stay to complete them without coming home first to make sure you were all right. And I have to confess, I was rather hoping that perhaps you might come back with me.'

'To New York?' Maggie was staggered.

'Why not? I think you'd enjoy it. It's a wonderful city. And with your new-found skills, you could help me with the repairs.'

'Oh my goodness!' Maggie shook her head, overwhelmed by the enormity of the suggestion. 'But I couldn't take a baby all that way on a steamship!'

'The voyage took only six days, and the *Campania* is a

marvellous vessel. The public rooms are all panelled in oak and satinwood, with thick carpets and velvet curtains and richly upholstered furniture. There is even an open fireplace in the smoking room, and the dining salon . . . my dear, you should see it! It must be ten feet high, and in the centre a well rises up through three decks to a skylight. When I unpack, I'll show you the handbook each passenger was given. The crossing alone would be a tremendous experience for you.'

'It sounds . . . amazing . . .' Maggie was lost for words.

'You'd enjoy working with me in the cathedral, too,' Lawrence went on. 'And I could do with your assistance. Sometimes I think my eyesight isn't what it was, and you could help me so much when the light is failing.'

'You've almost persuaded me,' Maggie said, laughing.

'Good. Because I have taken the liberty of booking passages for all of us on a sailing at the end of November,' Lawrence said with a twinkle. 'I know, I shouldn't have done it before I'd discussed it with you, but truth be told, I was missing you and this little fellow.' He smiled at Patrick, who was trying to pull on his whiskers. 'I don't want to miss any more of your growing up, my lad. Goodness knows, I've missed enough already! Where has that little baby gone, I'd like to know?'

A sharp pang gnawed at Maggie. Lawrence wasn't the only one missing the precious stages of Patrick's development. Josh was missing them too, not just a month or so, but all of them. But she mustn't think about Josh. Lawrence was her husband, he was a good man and she had promised to love and to cherish him until death did them part.

If it was the last thing she did, Maggie would see to it that she kept her marriage vows. And if that meant going to New York with Lawrence, then that was what she would do.

* * *

'Are you seeing that bugger again?' Tom Bishop demanded.

'No, I'm bloody not!' Peggy, poking a fork into the potatoes that were boiling on the trivet to see if they were done, wheeled round. 'I haven't so much as set eyes on him since he got back.'

That wasn't the whole truth; she had caught sight of Josh a couple of times in High Compton and her heart had given the same little flutter it always did. Once, they'd come face to face on the pavement outside the ironmonger's, but Josh had merely nodded at her and crossed the road – to get out of her way, she'd thought, hurt and disappointed.

'You'd bloody well better not be,' Tom growled.

'Leave it be, can't you?' Peggy grabbed the handle of the saucepan and lifted it off the trivet with a vicious jerk. Boiling water splashed on to her wrist and she squealed, almost dropping the pan. 'Oh – now I've burned myself! You and your stupid fancies!'

'You should be more careful, you clumsy mare.'

Although it was the first time Josh's name had been mentioned since Tom had come home from work one day and told her that he was back, spats like this one happened pretty well every day now. Tom had reverted to his old surly ways and things had gone back to being as bad as they'd ever been, perhaps worse. These past weeks, since he'd turned up at work one day and spotted Josh walking across the colliery yard, he'd been in a foul mood most of the time.

'Was that Josh Withers I just saw out there?' he'd asked as the men collected their helmets and lamps from the lamp room.

A couple of the men shrugged, but Hughie Saunders, who knew everything, confirmed it.

'Oh ah, he be working in the carpenter's shop. Started last week. They've been one short since Skiffy Small took bad, and Gaffer took 'im on. He's a bloody good carpenter, so they do say.'

'Bloody good for nothing!' Tom retorted, jamming his lamp into place.

'He been working in Ireland, I do hear,' Hughie went on, keen to share his superior knowledge. 'Now he's come home, living with his mam and dad again. They be glad to have him back, I shouldn't wonder. His brother was one of them got killed over at Shepton Fields when they had that terrible do.'

'We all know that, Hughie,' Tom snapped, and strode out of the lamp room seething.

Of all the pits in High Compton and Hillsbridge, why in the world had Josh Withers had to get a job here, at Northway? Right under his nose? It was the bloody limit!

Every time Tom caught a glimpse of Josh striding across the yard or squatting collier-style under the wall outside the carpenters' shop, his blood boiled. Arrogant sod! The picture of Peggy rolling around in the grass with him that long-ago night was burned into his brain. He'd never forgotten it, never would. And he'd never trust Peggy again either. She'd been acting funny lately, miserable as sin and telling him to leave her alone when all he wanted was his husband's rights. Well, she'd better not be messing about with Josh again or he'd teach the pair of them a lesson they wouldn't forget in a hurry.

Tom simmered with a fury that was just waiting to boil over. Josh Withers had made a fool of him once; he would make sure it didn't happen again.

'Did 'ee know they'm asking questions again about the accident over at Shepton Fields?' one of the Northway miners asked.

The men had finished their shift and, in a group, Tom amongst them, were smoking and sharing a chinwag before going their separate ways.

Instantly he had everyone's attention. Though time had

passed, feelings about the terrible tragedy still ran high, and always would. Something like that would never be forgotten, even by those who had been fortunate enough not to lose a friend or family member.

'Oh ah, they were down the club last night,' Hughie Saunders supplied, nodding his head sagely. He always had to be in the know, though several of the others had been there too. 'Fairley's stirred things up, from what I hear.'

This last, at least, was something of a revelation, but it was in fact not far from the truth. Hughie had got it from his niece, who was in service at Fairley Hall, and, being as nosy as her uncle, was given to eavesdropping whenever the opportunity arose.

A new superintendent had recently taken charge of the police division; Sir Montague had been in his company at a pheasant shoot and expressed his displeasure that no one had ever been brought to book for the cutting of the rope on the hudge, and the new superintendent, keen to make his mark and show that he was far superior and more efficient than his predecessor, had reopened the case. He'd visited the Hall himself, along with a sharp young detective he was nurturing, and when Nellie, Hughie's niece, had been instructed to serve them tea, she'd managed to listen at the door long enough to overhear the gist of their conversation.

'They'm never going to find out who did it after all this time,' one of the men said now, and the others muttered their agreement.

All but Tom. As they were talking, he'd seen Josh Withers leave the carpenters' shop and stride across the yard, cocky as ever, and the loathing and desire for revenge had boiled up in him, potent as ever.

'I reckon I've got a pretty good idea who did it,' he said darkly. 'That Josh Withers. I wouldn't put anything past him.'

'Josh Withers? Never!'

'His own brother were killed.'

'Why would he do a thing like that?'

'Well, he were after his brother's girl, weren't he?' Tom said. 'I seen them together with me own eyes at that dance in the Miners' Welfare not long after the accident. He'd set his cap at her all right, and he wanted his brother out of the way so he could step in.'

'Never!'

'But she bain't here now. He's living back home, and I don't know where she be.'

'He were gone, though, weren't he, and her too. My missus reckoned there was some funny business there. 'Twouldn't surprise me if they didn't get off out of the way 'cos they had something to hide.'

'An' then she found out what he done and they fell out . . .'

'You never do know.'

'Josh Withers! Well, I'll be damned . . .'

The story had started, and it would grow and spread, embellished a bit here and a bit there. Josh was unaware of it, barely even noticed the suspicious looks, the whispers behind cupped hands. Until, eventually and inevitably, it reached the ears of the bright young detective who had been assigned to the case.

At twenty-nine years old, Alfred Turner was already making his mark in the force, with a promotion to inspector and a move out of uniform and into the criminal investigation department, but he was ambitious, and impatient to climb the ladder. If he could make an arrest in the Shepton Fields case, it would be a real feather in his cap that he'd succeeded where others before him had failed, but so far he'd run into just as many dead ends as the officers who had conducted the first investigation.

Now, for the first time, he had the name of a suspect, and when he made enquiries of the local officers, he was elated to learn that this Josh Withers had a record stretching back to his youth. What was more, not so long ago he'd burst into a house and assaulted a young man for no other reason than that the boy had shown an interest in Maggie Donovan – the very same young lady who'd been engaged to Withers's brother, one of the victims of the tragedy. He was clearly a violent man who had no control over his temper, and if he could punch a lad on the nose for merely looking at the girl he was besotted with, then it was certainly possible that he would go much further if he thought he was about to lose her for ever.

'Bring him in,' he instructed a shocked Sergeant Love.

'Oh, I don't think Josh would do anything like that,' the sergeant protested. 'He's been a hothead and a rascal in his time, but—'

'That is the trouble with this case,' Alfred stated pompously. 'You all find it impossible to credit that someone you've known all their life could be responsible. But it was a local, I'm convinced of it. And I am determined to clear up the matter once and for all. So if you'd kindly do as I say and get the man in, we'll say no more about it.'

Sergeant Love was bristling with anger at being spoken to in such a way, but he knew he had to bite his tongue and bide his time. With any luck, this cocky young upstart would fall flat on his face, but for the moment he had no choice but to bring Josh Withers in as instructed.

'Where in the world have you been?' Florrie Withers demanded when Josh eventually got home close to nine o'clock that evening. 'Not in the pub, I hope! Well, your dinner's ruined. I threw it in the bin an hour ago.'

Josh sank down into the chair and buried his head in his hands.

'It doesn't matter about my dinner, Mam. I couldn't have eaten it anyway. I just want a bloody drink.'

'But whatever . . . ?' Florrie couldn't understand it. Josh hadn't been himself since he'd come home and found Maggie Donovan married, but this was something else. 'What's happened, Josh?' she asked.

For a moment he didn't move or speak, then he straightened, stretching his neck and massaging it with the tips of his fingers.

'I've been down the police station most of the day,' he said flatly. 'They've only just let me go, and they'll be hauling me in again tomorrow, I shouldn't wonder.'

'What!' Florrie gasped. 'But why . . . ? Oh Josh, what have you been up to now? Not fighting again, I hope.'

Josh snorted a hollow laugh.

'I wish that's all it was, Mam.'

'Then what is it?'

Again he was silent, not knowing how to tell her.

'Josh, what have you done?' Florrie asked again.

He looked up, his face showing the strain of the terrible day he'd endured since Sergeant Love had arrived at the carpenters' shop this morning and told him he was wanted at the police station for questioning.

'It's not what I've done, Mam, it's what they think I did. They've got it into their heads that it was me cut the rope on the hudge. They reckon I wanted our Jack out of the way so I could have Maggie.'

'What!' Florrie had turned white; she sank into the chair on the opposite side of the fireplace. 'But that's ridiculous! I've never heard such a thing . . .'

'That's what they're saying. And how can I prove otherwise?

I can't remember for sure where I was the night before the accident, and even if I could, it's no help. I could have crept out of my bed in the middle of the night and gone across the fields with no one any the wiser – that's what they're saying.'

'Oh, I'm not having this!' Florrie's shock was turning to anger. 'Let me get my coat and I'll go down to that police station and have a word myself – tell that Sergeant Love what I think of him!'

'It's not him, Mam – it's some jumped-up detective from Bath. Sergeant Love couldn't do anything even if he wanted to.'

'But they've let you go . . .' Florrie was looking for any crumb of comfort.

'For now. But like I said, we haven't heard the last of it. This Inspector Turner's made up his mind it was me, and truth to tell, who can blame him? He's desperate to find the culprit, and I fit the bill, don't I? With my record, and what he thinks is a motive . . . Oh, they'll be having me in again all right, and I wouldn't be surprised if I didn't end up on a charge of murder.'

'We've got to do something,' Florrie said determinedly. 'What you need is a solicitor. I reckon we ought to go and see Mr Beaven first thing in the morning. He'll be able to tell us what to do.'

'Oh Mam, I don't know . . .'

'When your dad gets home from the Prince of Wales we'll talk about it again. But that's what I reckon. First thing in the morning, we'll see Mr Beaven.'

Josh was too drained, too weary and too upset to argue.

'I've got the right man, I'm sure of it.' Alfred Turner, looking smug, was reporting back to the superintendent before returning to High Compton the next morning. 'He had motive, he had means, and he had opportunity. He has no alibi – how could he have? The rope could have been cut at any time between the pit closing in the evening and the miners turning up for work next morning. And he has a history of violence. His record alone will be enough to convince a jury of his guilt.'

The superintendent looked doubtful.

'You may well be right. But I'd prefer it if you could come up with something concrete before we charge him. We don't want this falling apart when it gets to court. Hard evidence is what we need, Turner. A credible witness, perhaps. Go back and do a bit more digging and we'll talk again. But well done anyway. This is more promising than anything has been so far.'

'Thank you, sir,' Turner said, as he knew was expected of him.

He didn't actually hold out much hope of finding either; the trail of hard evidence had had too long to go cold, and the community was too tight-knit to produce a credible witness. If no one had been prepared to speak out at the time, he couldn't imagine that they would now.

Little did he know that exactly what he wanted was about to fall into his lap.

Reuben Hillman's excitement knew no bounds. At last his chance to wreak revenge had come! His father had arrived home that evening with the news that Josh Withers had been to see Jeremiah Beaven, the solicitor for whom he worked, seeking legal advice, as he thought he was about to be charged with the murder of twelve men and boys at Shepton Fields.

Clarence Hillman should not, of course have been discussing it at all – what was said within the bounds of the solicitor's office should have remained there and been treated with strict confidentiality. But he was quite unable to keep the news to himself.

'That dreadful man who came here and assaulted you is suspected of being the one who cut the rope on the hudge,' he said, failing to hide the triumph he was feeling. 'As far as I can make out, an arrest is imminent. But Mr Beaven is of the opinion that what the police have against him is not enough on its own. I hope and pray it is, but we shall see, we shall see. The man should have been charged with assaulting you, Reuben. Sergeant Love should never have let him get away with it. He's a danger to the community. I can only hope they find further evidence so that he doesn't get away with this – the most dreadful crime imaginable. A witness, someone who saw him that night where he shouldn't have been, that's what's needed.'

Reuben's cheeks had turned pink with excitement, and his thoughts were racing. All the police needed was for someone to say they'd seen Josh that night . . . someone who would be believed. Well, *he* would be believed, wouldn't he? He held a responsible post – why, only a month ago he'd been promoted to chief assistant to Horace Freeman. He'd never been in any sort of trouble. His father was clerk to a solicitor, his mother was forever doing good works in the town, his grandmother had run the dame school, which everyone knew was where the best families sent their children to learn their letters, their numbers, and good manners too.

It was the perfect opportunity to get back at Josh Withers.

'I saw him, Father,' he said eagerly.

'*You* saw him? Where?' Clarence asked, astonished.

'Going across the fields that night,' Reuben blurted.

'But how could you have seen him?' Alexandra asked, puzzled. 'Shepton Fields is a good two miles from here.'

'I'd walked out that way in the hope of seeing Maggie,' Reuben said. His mother and father wouldn't be best pleased at the admission, but what did that matter compared to the satisfaction he'd get from seeing Josh Withers charged with murder? 'I was standing by the gate, and I saw him.'

'What time was this?' Clarence asked.

'Oh, I'm not sure, but it was beginning to get dark,' Reuben said.

'But you saw him clearly enough to know it was him?'

'Oh, it was him all right,' Reuben confirmed. 'And he had a knife in his hand,' he went on, embellishing the story enthusiastically. 'I thought it was peculiar, but—'

'Why did you not say something at the time?' Clarence demanded. 'Why wait until now?'

Reuben thought furiously. His father wouldn't be the only one to ask that question if he took his story to the police.

'I was afraid to,' he said. It wasn't a very flattering thing to confess to, but it sounded quite plausible. 'You know what he's like, Father. How nasty and violent he can be. I thought if I said anything and the police didn't believe me, he'd come after me, give me a good hiding, or worse. A man who could do something like that . . . well, he might do anything. But if the police have got him, they'll make sure he doesn't hurt me, won't they? Won't they?' he repeated pitifully.

'Oh Clarence . . .' Alexandra was looking extremely worried. 'Reuben's right! What if this Josh Withers should come after him? He'd be no match . . .'

'I'm quite sure Reuben would be afforded protection,' Clarence said confidently. 'You must speak out, Reuben; be a man and tell the police what you know. In fact, I think we should go down to the police station right away. I don't suppose the detective will be there now, but you'll find it easier speaking to someone you know. Sergeant Love will pass it on to the appropriate quarter.'

'Let him have his tea first,' Alexandra begged. 'The poor boy needs to keep his strength up.'

Clarence's own stomach was rumbling, and the lamb that

had been roasting half the afternoon smelled good.

'Very well,' he said. 'But when we've eaten – well, we must do what we must do.'

'I will, Father,' Reuben promised.

But he thought he would have difficulty swallowing so much as a single mouthful.

It was two days later when Maggie and Lawrence were startled by the bell jangling fiercely, followed by a frenzied knocking at the door. Patrick was upstairs sleeping soundly and they had been enjoying a nightcap by the fire before retiring themselves.

'What in the world . . . ?' Maggie made to get up and answer it, but Lawrence raised a cautionary finger.

'Stay there, my dear. I'll see who it is.'

He crossed to the door, Maggie following anxiously in spite of his admonition. She couldn't think who could be hammering so urgently at this time of night. Lawrence drew back the bolt and opened the door, and Billy tumbled into the living room, dishevelled, wild-eyed.

'Billy! Whatever is the matter?'

Billy's face crumpled, and for a moment he couldn't speak.

'Billy!' Maggie said again.

At last the words burst from him.

'It's Josh!' he gasped, still breathless. 'They've arrested Josh! They think he's the one who cut the rope on the hudge!'

Chapter Twenty-Four

Time seemed to stand still. Maggie felt as if the ground were dissolving beneath her feet.

'Josh?' she repeated in a disbelieving whisper. 'But that's ridiculous! Where did you get this from, Billy?'

'Farmer. He went to bank this afternoon. Everybody in town is talking about it. They say Josh was the one cut the rope. They say he'll hang for it.' Billy's face crumpled, and tears rolled down his flushed cheeks.

'He's been arrested, you say?' Lawrence asked. 'You're sure you're not mistaken?'

'No. They came for him at work. Took him off – in handcuffs!' Billy was beside himself.

'It's ridiculous!' Maggie said again. 'There must be some mistake. Why would they think it was Josh cut the rope?'

'It was that Reuben, the one you used to work with.' Billy's teeth were chattering so violently he could scarcely get the words out. 'He says he saw Josh going across the fields to the pit that night with a knife.'

'What? He's lying! He has to be! Surely no one would believe him!'

'But they do!' Billy gasped. 'I told you – why won't you listen to me? They've taken Josh off to prison! Oh Maggie, what are we going to do?'

Maggie was still too shocked, too stunned, to reply. It was Lawrence who went to Billy, putting an arm around his thin, shaking shoulders.

'Come on, my lad, sit down. You look all in. Maggie will make us a nice cup of tea and then you'll feel a lot better.'

He urged Billy towards the sofa and the boy's legs seemed to collapse beneath him as he sank down, but almost at once he was up again like a jack-in-the-box on the end of a spring.

'We've got to do something, Maggie!' He shook off Lawrence's soothing hand, running after his sister. 'Maggie, please! Maggie . . .'

'For goodness' sake, Billy!' Maggie said impatiently, unable to understand just why Billy was so distressed. It was most peculiar. She was upset, of course she was. Josh was the love of her life, the father of her child. But Billy . . . Josh had never been anything to him beyond a neighbour and a friend of his brothers. She'd always looked after Billy, tried to comfort him when his funny moods dragged him low, but just at the moment it was more than she could cope with.

'Never mind the tea, Maggie. I think we could all do with something a bit stronger.' Lawrence was at the dresser, opening the cupboard door and taking out a bottle of cognac and some glasses. He poured a little into one and folded it into Billy's shaking hands. 'Here you are, my lad. Take it steady, though. It's strong stuff.'

Billy sipped it and coughed.

'He'll be sick,' Maggie said. 'Mam always used to give us a drop of brandy to make us sick if we had an upset stomach.'

Lawrence ignored her comment, passing a second glass to her.

'This is the best cognac money can buy. Have a little drop yourself. It'll do you good.'

The smell was enough to turn Maggie's stomach, but she took a sip anyway, and didn't dislike it. It was much smoother than the rough, cheap brand Mam used to dispense, and as it trickled down her throat, the warmth seemed to spread into her veins. She'd been shaking too, she realised, chilled by the shock of Billy's news.

The brandy didn't seem to be doing anything to calm Billy, though. He was still jerking like a marionette on a string, still crying, his mouth working as he tried to control the sobs. His nose was running, a trail of slime reaching his upper lip. He looked, Maggie thought, exactly as he had looked when he was ten or eleven years old and being bullied by the older boys.

'Pull yourself together, Billy, do,' she said.

'But what if they hang Josh?'

'They won't hang Josh.' She said it firmly, as much to convince herself as to comfort Billy. 'There's been a terrible mistake. Josh didn't cut that rope.'

Billy's lip trembled. 'I know.'

'Of course he didn't. Reuben Hillman is just making up a story to get back at Josh. I'll go and see Sergeant Love in the morning, tell him how Reuben used to follow me around, how he used to frighten me until Josh put a stop to it. I'll tell them what a nasty piece of work he is, and . . .'

She broke off, realising the futility of what she was saying. Would anyone take the slightest notice of her? Somehow she doubted it. The police had wanted to arrest a culprit, Sir Montague Fairley wanted it. If they had someone to pin the blame on at last, they weren't likely to let it go so easily, and her testimony would be brushed aside, especially if it came out that Josh was the father of her child.

Even worse, if the case came to court, as it almost certainly would, and it was Reuben Hillman's word against Josh's, it was going to be Reuben a jury would believe – Reuben who, in spite of being a horrible little toad, had not a stain on his character, whilst Josh . . .

'Oh my God,' she whispered, as the horror of it washed over her in an icy tide.

Billy was right. If the jury believed Reuben Hillman, Josh could be sent to the gallows for a crime he didn't commit. For he hadn't done that terrible thing, of that she was perfectly certain.

'What can we do, Lawrence?' she asked pleadingly, unconsciously echoing Billy's words of a few moments ago.

Lawrence laid a hand on her arm.

'My dear, I'm not sure there's anything we can do.'

'But he's Patrick's father!' It was the first time she'd ever said it out loud. In her anguish, she'd almost forgotten Billy was there, but in any case, though she'd never told him who the father of her child was, she thought he would have guessed. He'd seen them together, after all.

'I can't see him hanged! I can't!' she wailed. 'Whoever did that terrible thing, I know it wasn't Josh.'

'Oh Maggie.' Lawrence put his arms around her and she laid her head against his shoulder, her whole body contorting with the waves of panic that were sweeping through her.

A sudden crash made her jump, and she jerked round to see the occasional table overturned, the books that had been heaped on it scattered across the floor, and Billy darting towards the door.

Lawrence released her and made to go after the boy, but his limp slowed him down, and Maggie reached the door first, running after Billy into the garden.

'Billy!' she called. 'Billy – wait!'

Down the path he ran, disappearing into the shadows. She'd never catch him, she thought, and almost abandoned the chase. But as she reached the gate, she heard the sound of sobs coming from the other side of the hedge, and when she rounded the corner, she saw the dark bulk of a figure crouched against the darker foliage.

'Billy! Whatever is it?' she asked.

For long moments he didn't answer. He was bent double, arms wrapped around himself, shoulders shaking, breath coming in long, tearing gasps between the sobs.

'Oh Billy, don't, please!' Maggie begged helplessly. 'You mustn't take it so hard. None of this is your fault.'

His head jerked up. By the light of the moon, which had emerged from behind a cloud, she could see his tear-stained face, his mouth working as he mumbled something unintelligible.

'What?' she asked.

'I can't . . . I can't . . .'

'Can't what, Billy?'

'Tell you . . .'

'Tell me what? For goodness' sake, Billy . . .'

Another gasp. Another sob. More garbled muttering. And then, on a heart-rending wail, the words she would never forget as long as she lived.

'It was me, Maggie. It was me!'

Maggie froze, and the world seemed to have frozen around her too.

'You mean . . . ?' She couldn't bring herself to put into words the awful suspicion that was assailing her. 'You mean it was you who . . .'

Billy couldn't answer; his only reply was the sound of his sobs.

'Oh Billy! Oh Billy!' Maggie, too, was lost for words. She just pulled her brother to her, wrapping him in her arms and burying her face in the spiky red hair while tears of her own rolled down her cheeks.

'Whatever possessed you to do such a thing?' Maggie asked.

They were back in the living room, Maggie sitting on the sofa beside Billy, holding both his hands in hers and gently rubbing his nails, bitten to the quick, with the tips of her fingers. His frenzied weeping had quietened now to intermittent gasps and sobs. Lawrence crouched beside him, a gentle hand laid on the boy's bony knee. Every line of his face reflected the shock and horror he'd felt when Maggie and Billy had returned to the house and Maggie told him of Billy's confession; every small pouch between sagged with anxiety.

'I never meant for anybody to be hurt,' Billy said in a tearful whisper. 'I didn't want to go down the pit, and I thought if the hudge was broken they wouldn't be able to make me.'

'He was terrified,' Maggie said to Lawrence, needing to make some excuse for the terrible thing Billy had done, wanting desperately to make Lawrence understand. 'They said he had to go underground, as a carting boy, and he was terrified.'

'So you sawed through the rope?' Lawrence said.

Billy nodded. 'With Mam's kitchen knife.'

With something of a shock Maggie suddenly found herself remembering how she had been unable to find it when she was preparing a meal in the days following the accident, and Mam saying: 'Oh, blame our Billy. He went off with it when he was in a state about having to go underground. You'll have to ask him what he did with it.'

She hadn't asked; she'd used another old knife, and forgotten all about the missing one. Now she wondered why it had never occurred to her that Billy might have used it to sever the rope in a desperate attempt to avoid going underground the next day. But she hadn't. Not for a moment. They'd been so fixated on trying to think who could have had a motive for deliberate murder that such an explanation had never occurred to any of them.

'I thought the hudge would just fall down when I did it,' Billy whispered. 'I never knew . . .' He began crying again, more softly this time.

'But it didn't,' Lawrence said. 'You didn't cut the rope right through.'

'No, but I didn't know . . . honest, I didn't know . . .'

'It's all right, Billy,' Maggie said gently.

It wasn't, of course, it would never be all right. Maggie felt she was being torn in two, witnessing his obvious distress, knowing how he must have suffered this last couple of years. No wonder he'd become ever more withdrawn. No wonder he'd turned and fled from the graveside when the victims of the disaster were being laid to rest. It had been so much more than grief that had driven him. The guilt, the regret must have been unbearable.

Now, however, it was time for Billy to face up to the consequences of what he had done. Josh had been accused of the crime and might well suffer the ultimate penalty for it. Even if it had been anyone but the love of her life whose freedom was at stake, she'd have felt the same. Billy couldn't allow someone else to pay for what he'd done; he couldn't have that on his conscience too.

As if reading her mind, Lawrence patted the boy's knee gently.

'You know what you have to do, don't you, lad?' he said quietly.

Billy nodded wordlessly.

'Would you like me to write down a confession for you? That might be the easiest way.'

Billy nodded again. He could write; in spite of his withdrawn ways, he'd learned at school as easily as the others. But Lawrence was an educated man; he'd know how to put the confession together in a way that would be easily understood, he'd know how to spell the long and awkward words, and hopefully he would be able to show exactly Billy's terrified state of mind when he'd done what he'd done – the fact that he had never meant anyone to come to harm – and present the mitigating circumstances in such a way that the judge would show some mercy when the case was heard.

Lawrence rose with some difficulty from his cramped position on the floor beside Billy, fetched a pen and writing paper and drew up a chair so he was facing the boy.

'Tell me everything, Billy,' he said. 'In your own words. I'll write it down for you.'

It was a long and laborious process. Billy spoke haltingly; Lawrence asked him questions from time to time, considering the answers carefully before incorporating them in the statement. The police would do it all again, of course, but Lawrence believed this first confession could also be introduced as evidence, and might help to sway the outcome in Billy's favour.

At one point Maggie said she thought she heard Patrick crying, and excused herself to go to him, but Patrick was sleeping soundly and Maggie knew that she'd used him as an excuse to escape the relentless retelling of every detail of that fateful night. By the time she returned, they were almost done. Lawrence was reading the statement back to Billy, and when the boy nodded his agreement, Lawrence passed him the paper and pen and Billy signed in his round, childish hand.

'Will they hang me?' he asked fearfully, and Maggie's heart contracted painfully. Until a few hours ago, she'd willingly have assisted the hangman herself in fastening the noose around the neck of the perpetrator of the terrible crime, and triggered the trapdoor that would send him to his death. Now she looked at the pathetic little figure of her brother, guilt-ridden and tormented, and prayed only for mercy for him.

'I don't know, Billy.' Lawrence answered him with honesty. 'I do think at the very least you will go to prison for rather a long time.'

Maggie saw the terror in his eyes again, the terror of confined spaces that had always plagued him, and wanted to cry.

'All I can promise,' Lawrence said, 'is that you will have the very best legal representation that money can buy. I'll see to that, have no fear. And now I think it would be best if we all try to get some rest. We have a long and trying day to get through tomorrow.'

'You can have my bed, Billy,' Maggie said at once. 'I'll sleep down here on the sofa.'

Lawrence spoke quietly in her ear.

'If you can bear it, my dear, we could always share my bed.'

For all the closeness that had developed between them in the time they had been man and wife, never once had Lawrence made the suggestion, and neither had Maggie. The intimacy had always seemed a step too far. Now, however, she realised she wanted nothing more than the comfort of another body close to hers.

'We'll do that, Lawrence,' she said softly.

Maggie took Billy upstairs to her room, drew the curtains and turned back the covers on the narrow bed. Then she kissed him on the forehead as she hadn't done since he was a child, whispered: 'Try to get some sleep, Billy,' and left him.

Lawrence was already in his nightshirt when she went into his room. He climbed into bed, and Maggie undressed as quickly and modestly as she could and slipped in beside him.

'God moves in mysterious ways, Maggie,' he said softly. 'Try not to worry, my dear. This has been a dreadful shock for you, I know, but I'm sure everything will work out in the end.'

Maggie wished she shared his confidence. She lay for a while carefully keeping the distance between them, then slowly she crept closer, curling herself around the curve of his back. Then and only then did her eyes grow heavy, and for a little while she slept.

A sound somewhere in the house wakened her. Her eyes flew open and she lay motionless, listening, as the dreadful disclosures of the previous hours came rushing in on her like a cloud of dark-winged ravens, fluttering, suffocating. All was silent, though, and she was beginning to think she'd imagined the sound when she heard another coming from downstairs, a scraping, followed by a thud.

Maggie slid away from the sleeping Lawrence, pushed aside the covers and rolled out of bed. The boards were cold against her bare feet as she crept out of the bedroom, silvered by moonlight, and the night air chilled her warm skin. Across the landing she went, pushing open the door to her own room. Just as she had suspected, there was no human-shaped mound beneath the covers, no ginger mop on the pillow. Anxious, but still reluctant to disturb Lawrence, she crept downstairs.

The living room and kitchen were empty, not a sign of Billy. Maggie went to the front door, which was unlatched, opened it and looked out, but he was nowhere to be seen. He'd gone out, she was sure of it, but where? Back to the farm, or just for a walk to clear his head? She couldn't go after him in her nightgown and with nothing on her feet, and she wasn't sure whether she should in any case. Perhaps he needed some time alone. But she'd wait up for him – there was no way she'd be able to go back to sleep now. She'd make herself a hot drink if there was enough warmth left in the fire to heat the milk; her mouth felt dry from the after-effects of the cognac she'd drunk a few hours earlier.

The moon had disappeared again in cloud and the room was in darkness. Maggie lit a candle, found a lamp and lit that too. It was when she set it down on the table that she saw it – a single sheet of paper placed centrally. A sheet of paper covered not with Lawrence's neat, sloping script but by Billy's s round, childish hand.

Apprehensive suddenly, she picked up the paper, tilting it towards the light so she could read it, and felt her stomach fall away.

I am so sorry, Maggie. I am gone to Newby Pond. I won't bother you any more. Please tell them all I'm sorry. I never knew wot would happen. I can't stand it any more.
   Your loving brother
   Billy

Newby Pond! Billy had gone to Newby Pond! Men went there to fish sometimes in summer, children went to pan in the shallows for tadpoles. But Maggie knew several people who'd gone there for quite another reason – well, she didn't actually know anyone who'd done it, but she'd heard all right. 'He went to Newby Pond' was a euphemism for 'he killed himself'. And the wording of Billy's note left her in no doubt. He hadn't gone there in the middle of the night to admire the scenery or take a dip – he couldn't even swim. Billy had gone there to end his torment in the dark, muddy waters.

Her heart racing with terror, Maggie rushed upstairs.

'Lawrence! Lawrence! Wake up! Something terrible has happened!'

'What . . . ? What in the world . . . ?' Lawrence sounded confused, bleary.

'It's Billy! He's gone to Newby Pond! I've got to go after him . . .' She was shedding her nightgown, all pretence of modesty forgotten now, dragging on the clothes she'd stacked neatly last night on the bedside chair.

Lawrence was shaking off sleep, barely able to comprehend what Maggie was saying.

'He's left a note. He's gone to Newby Pond!'

'Oh no!' Fully awake now, Lawrence thrust aside the bed covers. 'Leave this to me, Maggie. I'll go after him. You stay here.'

'I must come too!'

'And leave Patrick alone in the house?'

'I can run faster than you. I've more chance of catching him.'

'And if you don't? He has a head start. Our best hope is that he has second thoughts and delays doing anything stupid. But if not . . . I don't suppose you can swim, can you?'

'No, of course I can't . . .'

'But I can.' Lawrence was more or less dressed now. 'Look after Patrick, and pray God I'm in time to save Billy.'

Maggie followed him downstairs, and stood in the doorway watching as he went, at a surprisingly fast pace, down the path and disappeared into the darkness.

Her heart was pounding and terror was making her sob, but Lawrence was right, there was nothing she could do now.

Nothing but wait, and pray.

It was a mile or so from the cottage to Newby Pond. Lawrence hastened as fast as his gammy leg would allow along the road, then turned down an uneven track that grew ever narrower between overhanging trees and dense thicket. Sometimes the moon emerged from behind the scudding clouds, but he saw no sign of Billy ahead of him. A stitch pricked painfully in his ribs, and his leg ached horribly, sending sharp jolts into his hip, but he pressed on, driven by desperate anxiety and black dread.

'Oh, the silly boy! The silly boy!' He kept hearing his own voice, but knew it was only in his head – he had no breath left to speak aloud.

After a few hundred yards the path forked to left and to right, skirting the perimeter of the pond, a dark expanse before him. Lawrence paused, casting his eyes about in the hope of catching sight of Billy, but there was no one to be seen and no sound but for the mournful hooting of an owl and the rustle of a creature of the night in the undergrowth.

Fearful that he might be too late, Lawrence paused for a moment, scanning the murky water. He thought he saw a dark shape breaking the surface close to the bank a little further along and hurried towards it in an agony of suspense. But it was just a thick fallen branch that had snagged in the mud. Again he looked to left and to right, calling Billy's name, and heard the rustling in the thicket again and twigs snapping, louder this time. Could it be a fox or a badger? But it wasn't likely that either would come so close to the water's edge – the open fields would be their hunting ground.

'Billy!' he called again. 'I know you're there! Come out, there's a good lad, so we can talk.'

For a moment the silence was complete, then, with a suddenness that startled him, a flurry of disturbance, and the thin figure of Billy emerged from the thicket just yards from him. He stood unmoving, like a terrified deer at bay, then, as Lawrence moved towards him, he turned and darted away.

'Billy! Come back! Please . . .' Lawrence knew he had no hope of catching the boy, but Billy stopped again, looking over his shoulder.

'Don't try and stop me.' His voice was reedy and thin, shaky but determined.

'This isn't the answer, Billy,' Lawrence said. 'It's a mortal sin, you know that.'

'I don't know nuffin' any more,' Billy wailed. 'Only I can't stand it, that's all.'

'We'll sort something out. Just come home with me. Maggie is going out of her mind with worry.'

'Maggie hates me.'

'That's not true, and you know it.'

''Tis. She's bound to hate me. Everybody will.'

'They'll understand you didn't mean for it to happen. You've owned up to us now, that was the hardest part, and we don't judge you, I promise.' He took a step towards Billy, but at once the boy retreated further.

'Don't come any closer!'

'All right, all right.' Lawrence raised his hands in submission. 'But stop and think. This is no answer. What would your mother say if she was here?'

'But she's not here! She never will be again!'

'It's true she's in a better place, but she is with you in spirit, watching over you. And what would it do to Maggie? Don't you think she's suffered enough?'

Billy clapped his hands over his ears, crumpling in torment.

'Let's go home to her, Billy.'

Lawrence took a tentative step towards the boy, then another, holding his breath. He had almost reached him when Billy suddenly let out an agonised wail and turned and fled once more. Lawrence started after him, calling to him again, but Billy ran on. The path was higher above the water here; a muddy bank fell steeply away from the edge to the deepest part of the lake. Lawrence felt his feet losing purchase on the carpet of wet leaves that covered it and had to slow his pace, but Billy raced on.

'Be careful, Billy!' Lawrence shouted.

Too late. To his horror, he saw Billy slip and lose his balance. Over the edge of the rise he went, and there was a loud splash as he hit the water.

'Oh dear God!'

Disregarding his own safety now, Lawrence half ran towards the spot where Billy had been. As he did so, Billy surfaced, flailing wildly, coughing and screaming for help. Whatever his intentions when he had come to the lake, now that it was a reality, all his instincts for self-preservation had taken over. Lawrence didn't hesitate. Stripping off his coat and boots, he jumped.

The icy-cold water closed over his head, and he fought his way back to the surface. He had hoped that he would be near enough to Billy to grab him, but he was still feet away, and the boy's struggles were taking him further out into the lake. Lawrence swam towards him, the cold of the water making him breathless, the weight of his sodden clothes slowing him down. He reached Billy and tried to get a hold of him, but Billy, totally panicked and still struggling wildly, grabbed him around the neck, dragging him down so that the water closed over the pair of them. 'Don't fight me, lad!' Lawrence managed to say as they surfaced once more, gasping and spluttering, before once again Billy dragged him down.

How long the dance of death went on, Lawrence had no idea; he only knew that if Billy kept struggling, he would drown them both. He had swallowed a lot of foul-tasting water and he was weakening fast when suddenly Billy went limp and the terrifying battle ceased. Lawrence knew nothing of life-saving techniques; he simply grabbed a handful of Billy's hair and with the last of his strength made for the bank, towing the unconscious boy behind him.

He had forgotten, though, how far above the water the bank was at this point. There was no way he could even climb out himself, much less get Billy out. Driven on by willpower alone, he made for a spot where the bank was shallower, scrambled out and dragged Billy on to the rough path. Though he was of slight build, Billy's waterlogged clothing made him heavy, but somehow Lawrence managed it. He turned the boy on to his stomach, head to one side, and began to pump as hard as he could between Billy's shoulder blades. Water came out of him in a rush and, daring to hope that he would begin breathing again, Lawrence redoubled his efforts.

To no avail. Again Lawrence lost all count of time as he worked to try and save Billy, but at last, shivering and exhausted, he realised it would do no good.

'Oh lad, lad, what have you done?' he groaned, sitting back on his heels and surveying the sodden, lifeless body. And then, as his religion had taught him, he began to pray.

After a few minutes, he got up and went to retrieve his coat. He had trouble forcing his feet into his boots, and his hands were shaking so much he was unable to tie the laces properly.

He had failed. There was nothing more he could do for Billy now but ensure he was given a proper Catholic burial. Heavy of heart, dreading telling Maggie what had happened, and shivering uncontrollably, Lawrence set out for home.

Chapter Twenty-Five

All of High Compton was buzzing with the news. Billy Donovan was the one who had cut the rope on the hudge. He'd confessed, and then he'd drowned himself in Newby Lake. The town had rarely known such excitement. There were some who had the story correct, that in the end Billy's death had been an accident, but not many folk believed this version – it was far more satisfying to think that, overcome by guilt, he'd taken his own life.

'Just as well, if you ask me,' Sarah said to Peggy. 'If he was still alive and kicking, he'd be lynched and that's a fact,'

'I expect you're right,' Peggy said. She didn't know whether to feel regretful or relieved to discover that it wasn't Tom who'd cut the rope after all.

'I can't understand it,' Reuben Hillman blustered. He was worried that there might be repercussions with regard to the statement he'd made to the police that had led to Josh's arrest. 'It was definitely Josh Withers I saw going across the fields with a knife that night.'

'Nobody doubts you, my boy,' his father replied. 'He was setting snares to catch rabbits, I expect. But whatever he was doing, he was up to no good, of that you can be sure. You did the right thing in speaking out.'

'But what if he comes after me?' Reuben snivelled. 'If he knows it was me told on him, goodness knows what he'll do.'

Clarence paled. He did not want a repeat of the night Josh had forced his way into the house. But he put a brave face on it.

'He won't do any such thing unless he wants to end up back in prison. Don't worry, son, I'll seek advice from Mr Beaven first thing in the morning, and speak to Sergeant Love, too, if needs be. But I think you'll find that Josh Withers has learned his lesson.'

'Oh, poor Maggie!' Cathy Small said when she heard the news. 'First her father and Jack, then her mother, and now Billy! It's her whole family gone, all but Ewart and Walter. Whatever will she do?'

But she was unable to suppress a spark of quite inappropriate hope that Ewart would come home for the funeral. He'd been writing to her from time to time – that was how she'd learned of Rose's death – and though she'd walked out with a few boys in the last year, none of them measured up to Ewart in her eyes.

But it was for Billy that Florrie Withers's heart was breaking once Josh was released from prison and was home again, the terrible charges against him dropped.

'That poor little boy,' she said, shaking her head. 'Oh, it's too awful to think about.'

'That poor little boy killed twelve men and boys, including your own son, and damn nearly got the other one hanged for it,' Gilby said grimly. 'Don't you go wasting your tears on him, our Florrie.'

'But he owned up in the end, didn't he?' Florrie argued stoutly. 'When he heard our Josh was being blamed. And he never meant for it to happen, any of it. All he wanted was not to have to go underground, and he just didn't think. You know what he was like, Gilby. Scared of his own shadow. Always bullied by them as was bigger and bolder than him. The state he must have been in ever since the accident . . . well, it doesn't bear thinking about. And then to go and drown . . . dear, dear, dear. It fair breaks my heart.'

'Well, perhaps we'll find out at last what became of Maggie Donovan,' Hester Dallimore said to Dolly Oglethorpe. 'The funeral's going to be here, or so I hear. Will she come, do you think?'

'I don't know, Hester, and to tell you the truth I don't care much,' Dolly said. 'I wouldn't think there'd be many that'd go to the church or the cemetery anyway. Not for the funeral of a lad who did what he did. And if you ask me, those as do go are just plain nosy!'

And that, she thought, had put Hester in her place, and about time someone did it too.

Around and around went the gossip and the comment, and perhaps the only person who remained silent on the subject was Josh.

He was relieved, of course he was, to have been cleared – he'd thought Reuben Hillman's testimony might well put a noose around his neck, and almost as bad was knowing that all the people he knew and respected would believe that he had been responsible for the terrible accident, so jealous of his brother that he'd been prepared to end the lives of twelve men and boys in the most dreadful way. But, like Cathy Small, it was Maggie of whom he was thinking. He wished with all his heart that he could go to her and comfort her, but he knew he couldn't. If she hadn't been prepared to leave her husband for him before, then she would be even more determined not to do anything to hurt him now that he had apparently made such a heroic attempt to rescue Billy from the lake.

He loved her, he knew that now; she would always be in

his heart and his mind. But there was not a thing he could do about it.

As Dolly Oglethorpe had predicted, few folk attended Billy's funeral. Most stayed away to show their disgust at what Billy had done; others, though bursting with curiosity, didn't want to be seen as ghouls. But those who did come were treated to their first glimpse of the man Maggie had married, and it caused quite a stir as she walked up the aisle behind the coffin holding tightly to his arm. There were nudges and exchanged glances and whispers that were drowned out by the organ before they all remembered themselves and lowered their eyes in respectful silence. There would be plenty of time later for discussing the sensation – Maggie Donovan married to a man old enough to be her father.

Cathy was amongst the congregation – it was a Wednesday afternoon, so early closing at the shop – but she managed to stop herself from looking at Ewart, who was sitting with Walter and Maggie in the front pew. It wasn't seemly to be having romantic thoughts at such a time.

The Withers family were there too, and similarly, Josh managed to avoid looking too long at Maggie, though he had noticed how deathly pale she was beneath her black veil as she followed the coffin past the pew where he was sitting. A small group of other neighbours had filed in self-consciously and taken seats at the back of the church.

Farmer Barton and his wife arrived late, after the service had started, causing a few raised eyebrows as Farmer's boots clumped noisily on the flagged floor for all his best efforts to move stealthily. He hadn't wanted to come, but his wife had insisted, and he stood staring glumly at the hymn book as she sang lustily, glad only that it wasn't to be a full requiem Mass. If it had been, he'd have clumped out again long before it was finished, on the excuse that it would be milking time and he was a hand short.

But Maggie was almost unaware that the church was half empty and that those who were there were goggling at her and her husband. She was lost in a horrible fog, too upset – and too worried about Lawrence – to notice anything. He'd taken a chill after his heroic exploits of a few days ago, and she had tried to persuade him to stay at home. But poorly as he was, he had insisted. He was all right; nothing would persuade him to stay at home in the warm.

She glanced at him now, sitting beside her, as Father O'Brien recited the prayers. She could hear the rattle in his breathing, and try as he might, he was unable to suppress the persistent cough that had kept her awake most of last night. He was flushed, too, but shivering, so she was sure he had a temperature. And no wonder! When he'd arrived home on the night of Billy's death, he'd been exhausted, chilled to the marrow and in a state of shock. She'd got him into clean, dry clothes, relit the fire and made him a hot toddy – though she was in shock herself, she'd done what had to be done as mechanically as if she'd been one of the automatons in a glass case on the pier that went through jerky actions when you put a penny in the slot. But it didn't seem to have helped. Lawrence was going to suffer for his selfless actions, and the unfairness of it was just another cross she had to bear.

At last the service was over, and the mourners filed out behind the coffin. There wasn't a graveyard at the church; instead, a part of the town cemetery had been dedicated for Catholics, and as Maggie and the other family members set off up the road, friends and neighbours followed at a discreet distance; all but Farmer and Mrs Barton, who headed for home.

The committal was as brief as the service had seemed inter-
minable – Maggie bowed her head, fighting back tears as the
clods of earth thudded down on to the dark oak coffin that
Lawrence had insisted was the only kind good enough for Billy.

'Oh Maggie, you've had trials enough these last couple of
years to last you a lifetime,' Father O'Brien said, squeezing
her hand when the official part of his business was over. 'But
remember, God never sends us more than we are able to
bear, and you have a good man here.' He smiled briefly at
Lawrence.

'I'll take care of her, Father, never fear,' Lawrence said, but
as he began coughing again, Maggie was overcome with concern
for him. It was going to be the other way around if she was not
much mistaken.

'I think we should get you home and into the warm,
Lawrence,' she said firmly.

As they approached the cemetery gate, Maggie was startled
to see Josh there, standing on the path outside. For a brief
moment their eyes locked and she felt the familiar wrench in
her gut. Then, with just the briefest nod of acknowledgement,
he turned and was gone, and there was nothing left for her to
do but help Lawrence into the trap that was waiting for them,
the pony pawing the ground impatiently. She mustn't think
about Josh. All that mattered was getting Lawrence home. They
wouldn't have the peace that she would have liked when
they got there – Connie was there with her brood, looking after
Patrick while Maggie attended the funeral, and with Ewart
staying too, the house would be overflowing. But tomorrow
they'd be heading back to Yorkshire – the men couldn't afford
to lose another day's work – though Ewart had hinted he might
be back soon, looking for work back in Somerset.

Much as she loved them all, under the circumstances Maggie

thought she would be glad to see the back of them. Just now, all she wanted was to be alone with her husband and son.

Lawrence had taken a turn for the worse, and Maggie was desperately worried about him. His temperature was raging, and he had fits of shivering so violent that he couldn't even hold a cup of water to his lips; he also coughed constantly, a tight, chest-racking bark that took his breath away and wouldn't loosen, despite the doses of the linctus Dr Mackay had prescribed and the tar rope she had tied around his neck, an old remedy of her mother's.

'There's nothing more to be done,' the doctor had said the last time he came to see Lawrence. 'All we can hope for is that the infection runs its course quickly and his heart is strong enough to withstand the strain this is putting on it.'

Maggie nodded wordlessly. The black dread was hanging over her in a thick cloud. Would all this never end? Surely, surely Lawrence wouldn't be taken from her too?

Just to make matters worse, she thought she was coming down with a cold or influenza herself. Her throat and mouth were dry and tickly, her eyes itchy, and she felt drained and distant, as if she were a million miles away. She couldn't be ill, she told herself firmly. If she was, who would look after Lawrence and Patrick? She was exhausted, that was all, from running up and down the stairs and trying to keep Patrick from disturbing Lawrence. But her determination was not enough. Her nose began to stream and she started coughing herself, a chesty cough which though not tight and painful like Lawrence's still left her feeling weak and ill.

On the Sunday, to her surprise and, she had to admit, relief, Cathy arrived unannounced at the door.

'Tell me to go if I'm not welcome, but I've been worried about you,' she said.

On the point of asking how Cathy had known where she lived, Maggie realised – Ewart must have told her. He'd gone out the evening following the funeral, no doubt to meet Cathy, and if she wasn't mistaken, that was what was behind his statement that he was going to look for work back here in Somerset. He must be as keen on Cathy as she was on him if he was prepared to return to the narrow, faulted seams here when he'd got used to better conditions in Yorkshire.

'You know you're always welcome, Cathy,' Maggie said now. 'I'd have got in touch ages ago if it hadn't meant coming into the shop and making things awkward for you with Mrs Freeman. And I have to admit I'm pleased to see you now. I've got my hands full here, and I don't feel too good myself.'

'You look awful,' Cathy stated bluntly. She set her basket down on the table and took out a jug covered with a clean muslin cloth. 'I brought some of my mam's chicken soup and what a good thing I did. It's just what you need if I'm not much mistaken.'

Maggie made a cup of tea for them both and the two girls sat chatting for a while, Cathy filling Maggie in on all the gossip from the shop, Maggie content to just listen. She really didn't feel up to talking, and she guessed Ewart would have acquainted Cathy with all the details of what had happened to Billy, for which she was very grateful. Having to go over it all again was the last thing she wanted just now.

The one subject she couldn't avoid was Patrick, who was scooting round their feet chasing a wooden horse on wheels that Lawrence had bought for him.

'What a lovely little chap he is!' Cathy said. 'There's no mistaking who his father is, though. I am right, aren't I?'

Maggie swallowed hard at the lump that had risen in her throat.

'Lawrence is his father,' she said stoically.

Cathy raised an eyebrow.

'If you say so.'

'He is, in every way that counts.' Maggie had to pause to blow her nose. 'Really, Cathy, I can never repay him for everything he's done for us, and he adores Patrick, every bit as much as if he were his own. Josh . . .' She bit her lip, turning her head so that Cathy would not see the tears in her eyes. 'I don't want to talk about it really.'

'Look, Maggie,' Cathy said after a moment. 'Why don't I take Patrick out for a bit of a walk and you can have a rest?'

Maggie hesitated. She could scarcely bear to let Patrick out of her sight, and she lived in fear that he would catch the same bug that was affecting her and Lawrence.

'It's a bit of a cold wind . . .'

'But it's nice in the sun. If he's well wrapped up, the fresh air will do him good and he'll be out of your hair for a bit.'

Maggie relented. 'All right. If you're sure you don't mind . . .'

'I wouldn't have offered if I minded,' Cathy said smartly. 'You put your feet up for half an hour. You look done in, honest you do.'

When they were ready, Cathy manoeuvred the perambulator down the path a little awkwardly. She paused at the gate for Patrick to wave to Maggie, and called a goodbye. Still feeling a little apprehensive, Maggie went back indoors. It was nice of Cathy to give her a little time to herself, but much as she would have liked to, she wouldn't feel comfortable sinking into a chair and perhaps dozing off when Lawrence was upstairs alone. She made another cup of tea for herself and one for him and carried them up to the bedroom.

'How are you feeling?' she asked anxiously; she'd been able

to hear the angry rasp of his breathing from halfway up the stairs.

'Never mind me. What about you?' It was typical of Lawrence to be more concerned with Maggie than with himself.

'I'm all right. Cathy's come to visit and she's taken Patrick out for a walk, so there's nothing to stop me sitting with you for a bit.'

She pulled the chair up to the bedside and sat down, close enough to be able to take the cup if Lawrence should get one of his shaking fits. But he didn't seem to want the tea; he set it down on the bedside table and took her hand in his.

'I've been wanting to talk to you, Maggie. You know, don't you, that if anything happens to me, you are well taken care of.'

'Nothing is going to happen to you!' Maggie protested.

'I hope not, but you heard the doctor. My heart . . .'

'Don't even think such things!' But she admitted to herself that it was hard not to when just talking was making him horribly breathless.

'Listen, Maggie.' Lawrence turned his head on the pillow so that he could look at her. 'The stained-glass window. If I'm not able to do it, I want you to.'

Maggie frowned. Her head felt thick and muzzy and Lawrence wasn't making any sense. Was he delirious? she wondered.

'What stained-glass window?' she asked.

'The Blessed Virgin. The one that was damaged. If I'm not able to, I want you to go to New York and repair it.'

'Me!' she exclaimed. 'I couldn't . . .'

'You could. You've learned so much and you have a talent. Everything you'd need to do the job is put together ready in my workshop. All you have to do is pack it safely.'

'But . . . I couldn't go all the way to New York without you!' Maggie gasped, horrified.

A small smile lifted the corners of Lawrence's mouth.

'Oh, you underestimate yourself, my dear. You are the most independent and resourceful woman I have ever met. Going to New York would be nothing compared with all you've endured. The passages are booked, as I told you. You'd need only to get yourself and Patrick to Liverpool, and on to the ship, and my old friend will take care of you when you arrive in America. You'd enjoy it, I'm sure. And experience and travel broaden the mind. You'll come back a different woman, Maggie.'

'Oh, I don't know . . .'

Lawrence's fingers tightened over Maggie's hand; glancing down at them, she thought that they were nothing but skin and bone, like the talons of a bird.

'Please, Maggie. It's very important to me that I keep my promise to restore the window and see it safely installed. If I am not able to do it, I want you to do it for me. Is that so much to ask?'

'Oh Lawrence . . .' What Lawrence had done for her was, as she had told Cathy, a debt she could never repay, and this was the first thing he had ever asked of her. Of course it wasn't too much.

'Please, Maggie,' he said again.

'Very well.' She sighed. 'If it comes to that, I'll do it. But it won't. You're going to get better and you'll be able to do the job yourself.'

'I don't know that I am, Maggie,' he said quietly, and indeed he looked dreadfully drained as he sank back again into the pillows. 'Thank you, my dear.' It was no more than a whisper, and when his breathing had quietened again he drifted off into an exhausted doze. Maggie could do nothing but sit beside him, still holding his hand in hers.

* * *

The next day the fever flared again. Out of her mind with worry, and still full of a cold herself, Maggie ran up and downstairs in between making food for Patrick and doing the necessary chores, dabbing Lawrence's forehead with a cool flannel and urging him to take tiny sips of boiled water, which she left in a carafe beside his bed. She desperately wanted to call the doctor again, but she couldn't leave Lawrence and there was no one she could get to relay a message.

As if an angel had answered her prayers, the doorbell rang at around midday, and when she answered it, there on the doorstep was Dr Mackay himself.

'I'm out on my rounds and thought I'd call in,' he said in the lilting accent she still found quite difficult to understand. 'How is Lawrence?'

'Awful, Doctor. I'm so glad you're here.'

'Hmm. I'll have a look at him, but as I told you, there's little I can do, I'm afraid.' The dreadful sound of rasping breathing could be heard now throughout the house, and Dr Mackay stood for a moment listening to it before making for the stairs.

Maggie followed, Patrick in her arms, and stood by the window as the doctor approached the bed and examined Lawrence.

Sweat was pouring from him and he seemed almost unaware that anyone was in the room. He was mumbling something, but Maggie couldn't make out the words, and the ones she did hear seemed to make no sense.

'He's delirious,' Dr Mackay said by way of explanation. 'I don't think the crisis can be far off.'

'The crisis?' She knew what he meant, but asked automatically.

'The moment when either the fever will break or . . .' His lips set in a tight line and he gave a small shake of his head. 'I have seen him like this before and he's pulled through, but I don't think he has ever been quite this bad. His lungs are dreadfully congested, and his heart . . . To be honest, I'm not sure how much more strain it will take.'

Maggie nodded dumbly. The doctor was really only telling her what she already knew.

'You are a silly fellow, Lawrence,' Dr Mackay said. 'Jumping into an icy lake in the middle of October in your state of health. What on earth were you thinking of?'

'Billy.'

Out of it as Lawrence had seemed a moment ago, that word came out loud and clear.

'Yes, yes, I know. And very commendable too. But you should never have done it. You had no hope of saving him from what I hear; he almost drowned you both, and look where it's landed you.'

'Had to!' Lawrence was becoming agitated. 'Had to save him! My son!'

'Not your son, old boy. But never mind . . .'

'My son!' Lawrence insisted.

The doctor moved away from the bed, shaking his head.

'He's confused. It's not unusual. The Lord alone knows where his poor troubled mind is wandering. He's imagining, I expect, that it was Patrick he went into the water to save.'

'Not Patrick! Billy!' Lawrence's agitation was increasing, and the doctor returned to his medical bag.

'I'll give him something to quieten him down. You need to save your strength,' he said to Lawrence. 'If you don't, I won't be answerable for the consequences.'

With difficulty, since Lawrence was still protesting, he managed to get a spoonful of tincture into the sick man's mouth, and almost immediately he fell back on the pillows, his head rolling from side to side for a few minutes before his eyes closed and there was nothing but the tortured breathing.

'Is there someone I can call to help you out with your husband's care?' Dr Mackay asked as he repacked and closed his medical bag. 'It really is too much for you to manage alone.'

Maggie shook her head. 'There's no one.'

'Would you consider getting in a nurse, then? I'm sure Mrs Harvey would be willing to assist you.'

Maggie's heart sank at the thought of having the horrible woman under her roof again at such a time, but Dr Mackay was right, she didn't think she could manage alone.

'Isn't there anyone else?' she asked.

'I don't know of anyone better qualified.'

Maggie was thinking furiously. Dolly Oglethorpe had attended Billy's funeral; there was no longer any need for secrecy. And she'd always got on well with Dolly. Suddenly she was yearning for a familiar face.

'There's someone who used to be a neighbour of mine, a Mrs Oglethorpe,' she said. 'It's a long way for her to come, I know, but if I sent a pony and trap for her . . . Would you be able to ask her, at least? I don't care what it costs, and I'm sure Lawrence wouldn't mind either.'

'I'll see what I can do,' the doctor promised. 'And I'll call by again tomorrow, though I should warn you . . .'

'I know.' Maggie didn't want to hear him say the words she was dreading; that it was very possible Lawrence would not live to see tomorrow.

Dr Mackay touched her arm briefly.

'Take care of yourself, Mrs Jacobs. You're doing a fine job.'

'Thank you, Doctor.'

But Maggie was not at all sure that what she was doing would be enough.

Dr Mackay must have gone straight to High Compton and spoken to Dolly, for by mid afternoon, Fred Carson's pony and trap was drawing up outside the gate and Dolly came bustling in.

'Oh, thank you so much for coming!' Maggie said.

'Just doing my job, dear.' She cocked her head, listening to the dreadful rasping breathing coming from upstairs. 'I don't like the sound of that. Pneumonia, is it?'

'I think so. And his heart is very weak, too.'

'Well, at least I'm here now and you won't be on your own.' She smiled at Patrick, who was peeping from behind Maggie's skirts. 'He's a bonny one, and no mistake.'

'Yes, he is, isn't he?' Maggie was wondering if Dolly had noticed the likeness to Josh, but she had too much on her mind to worry about that.

'You take care of him and I'll sit with your husband,' Dolly said, taking off her coat. 'Just you get on with whatever you've got to do and I'll call you if there's any change.'

'I am so grateful,' Maggie said, and meant it with all her heart.

As day wore on and night fell, Maggie had ever more reason to be grateful to Dolly. They took turns at sitting beside Lawrence's bed, which Maggie found almost unbearably distressing. But even that was preferable to trying to do what she had to do elsewhere with that terrible breathing invading every corner of the house.

'You try to get a couple of hours' rest or you'll be good for nothing tomorrow,' Dolly said as the clock chimed eleven. 'I'll wake you, don't worry, if he gets any worse.'

Maggie couldn't see how Lawrence could possibly be worse. He was tossing and turning, obviously delirious, but he was quite unaware of her presence, and Dolly was right: she was exhausted and needed at least a catnap in order to be fit to deal with whatever tomorrow might bring. She sponged him down one last time, then made a hot drink for herself and Dolly and went to her room. She'd thought sleep would be impossible, but almost the moment her head hit the pillow, black oblivion closed in.

The dream, when it came, was muddled but vivid. She was by the lake, except that it was a much vaster expanse of water than Newby Pond and the wind was whipping the surface into huge waves. A feeling of nightmarish dread was making her shiver, though at first she couldn't understand why. And then she saw them, Billy and Lawrence, out there in the water, splashing, struggling.

There was a small boat pulled up on the bank nearby; almost choking on panic, she managed to get it afloat and climbed in. But the oars were on the bank; she couldn't reach them. Somehow she began to paddle with her hands, but she was making no progress. She couldn't see Billy now, but Lawrence was still there, waving to her, calling for help. She paddled more desperately, but still she could not reach him. The waves were so high they kept hiding him from her view, and Maggie was desperately afraid that the next time they subsided, Lawrence would be gone like Billy. She redoubled her efforts, but the boat was rocking now, rocking so violently she was sure it would capsize—

'Maggie! Maggie, wake up!'

Maggie came abruptly through the layers of sleep and realised that the rocking boat in her dream was in fact Dolly shaking her hard. In an instant she was up, her heart beating so fast it seemed to jar the whole of her chest.

'What is it? Lawrence . . . ?'

'I think you should come, Maggie.' Dolly's voice was low and urgent.

Stopping only to grab Mam's dressing gown, which she had left on the bedside chair for just such an emergency, Maggie flew across the landing and into Lawrence's room.

He was gasping now, long, shuddering, painful gasps with ominous silences between them. Maggie dropped to her knees beside the bed, taking his hand in hers.

'I think he's going, Maggie,' Dolly said quietly, and retreated to the doorway so as to afford them some privacy.

'Oh Lawrence, I do love you so much, and I'm going to miss you so,' Maggie whispered. 'But don't worry, my love, I'll be all right, and I'll do as you asked. I'll go to New York and I'll do my very best with the window. It'll be the finest in the whole cathedral, I promise.'

Lawrence didn't answer; Maggie didn't know if he even realised she was there. But suddenly a faint smile lifted the corners of his mouth. One last shuddering gasp, and all was silence.

With a sob, Maggie laid her head against his chest, listening for a heartbeat, or a whisper of breath in his lungs. There was nothing.

'He's gone, Mrs Oglethorpe,' she said, and her voice was surprisingly steady. She kissed Lawrence on the lips, and laid her face on his chest again. Then the tears began, hot and bitter, tears for the man who had rescued her when she had been in the depths of despair, and who had shown her a life she could never have dreamed of.

Chapter Twenty-Six

Another death. Another funeral. Would it never end? Maggie felt as if she were living in a nightmare from which she could not escape. Even Patrick, who usually brightened her days, was subdued, picking up on the atmosphere that pervaded the little house.

She had to keep going for his sake, of course, and at least she was not alone. Ewart had dropped everything and come down from Yorkshire, and Cathy was there for her too, taking a few days off from work with Mrs Freeman's blessing.

Removed as she felt from everything around her, Maggie was pleased to see the two of them together. They were so well suited, comfortable in one another's company, and clearly in love. It gladdened her heart to think that at last Ewart seemed to have found a girl to make his life complete, and she liked the idea of having Cathy for a sister-in-law.

But nothing could ease her grief for long. It hung over her, dark and heavy, clouding her every thought and making every action an effort; grief not only for Lawrence, but for all those she had loved and lost. Maggie wondered if she would ever be happy again.

'Well that's it, then, I've got myself a job at Northway pit,' Ewart said.

It was a few days after the funeral. He and Maggie had finished their evening meal and were lingering over a cup of tea.

'Oh Ewart, that's wonderful,' Maggie said. 'Northway is so much better than any of Fairley's pits. Josh . . .' She broke off.

'It was through Josh I got the job,' Ewart admitted. 'And it's also the reason I didn't mention it before. I know he's a touchy subject as far as you're concerned.'

Maggie ignored that.

'I suppose you and Cathy will be getting married, then?'

Ewart flushed.

'I haven't asked her yet . . .'

'Well you'd better – and quickly!'

'I've got to find somewhere for us to live first.'

'That's no problem. You can live here.'

'There's not a lot of room,' Ewart said doubtfully. 'We wouldn't want to put you out.'

'You wouldn't be. You see, there's something I haven't told you. I'm going to America in a few weeks.'

She laughed at Ewart's amazed expression, the first time, it seemed, that she had laughed in a long time.

'I'd better explain.'

'You certainly had!'

She told him the story from the beginning, and Ewart listened, amazed and a little awed.

'Well, I suppose nothing you do should surprise me, our Maggie. But this time you've got me beat!' he said when she'd finished. 'How long will you be gone?'

'Judging by the time it took Lawrence in the first place, and given that I'm nowhere near the craftsman he was, I'd say a year at least,' Maggie said. 'So you see, there's no need for you to be in any hurry to find a place of your own. I'll be glad to know someone is looking after this house, keeping it warm and aired for when I come back. If I do come back,' she added after a moment.

'What do you mean?' Ewart asked, alarmed.

'I mean I might just decide to stay in America. It's a wonderful land of opportunity, so they say. What a start in life it would give Patrick! And . . . well, there's nothing to keep me here now.'

'That's not quite true, though, is it?' Ewart broke off, unwilling to admit he'd been discussing Maggie with Josh. 'Think about this, Maggie, for goodness' sake, before you do anything silly. This is your home. You'd miss it, though you might not think so at the moment. *I* missed it, and I was only in Yorkshire. America – well, that's a whole different kettle of fish.'

'There's nothing to think about,' Maggie said flatly. 'I promised Lawrence I'd do this, and I'm going to keep my word. It's the last thing he asked of me, about the only thing that made any sense in those last few days. Most of the time he was talking nonsense.'

'Well there you are!' Ewart argued. 'He wasn't thinking straight. He wouldn't expect you to go all the way to America on your own with a baby.'

Maggie shook her head. 'No, he knew what he was saying all right. He was desperate to make me understand what he wanted and get me to promise to do this one last thing for him. It was different from all the other stuff, when he was wandering goodness knows where. Why, at one time he was even trying to say that Billy was his son. Where he got that from, I don't know. He was very fond of Billy, of course, really good with him, but still . . .' She trailed off, fighting back tears.

'He said Billy was his son?' Ewart said wonderingly.

'Yes. That's the sort of nonsense he was talking.'

Ewart was silent. He'd gone very thoughtful suddenly, his face creased in concentration, his eyes distant.

'What?' Maggie asked.

'Oh, it's nothing . . .'

'Come on, what are you thinking?' Maggie pressed him.

Ewart blew breath over his top lip.

'I'm being stupid, I expect, but you've just made me think,' he said reluctantly. 'When we were little, Mam used to go out charring a couple of days a week. I don't know where it was, but I know it was quite a long way from home. Dad used to go on at her to give it up because the long walk tired her out.'

'I don't remember that,' Maggie said.

'I don't suppose you would; you were only little, but I was old enough to know there was something going on. I heard rows that really frightened me.'

'There were always rows.'

'True enough. Like I say, I'm just being stupid. Forget it.'

'No, wait a minute.' The hairs on the back of Maggie's neck were prickling. She sat forward, elbows on the table. 'Are you saying you think it might have been Lawrence Mam was charring for, and they . . . had an affair? That Lawrence was speaking the truth when he said he was Billy's father?'

'I don't know what I was saying, Maggie. I was talking even more rubbish than Lawrence when he was delirious.' Ewart scraped back his chair. 'I'm going to see Cathy, tell her the news.'

'And ask her to marry you?' Maggie was trying to push aside the thoughts that were assailing her and introduce some levity.

'Maybe.' Ewart grinned at her, his old self once more. 'If I do, I promise you'll be the first to know.'

Left alone in the house, and with Patrick tucked up and fast asleep, Maggie found her thoughts returning to what Ewart had said. It was preposterous, of course. Ewart hadn't believed it for a moment, and neither did she. But all the same . . .

Now that the seed had been planted in her mind, she couldn't forget about it. The thought of the aesthetic Lawrence having an affair with anyone, especially her mother, was almost beyond belief. Yet he had been young once – was it such a stretch of the imagination to think that perhaps he had known lust and love? Priests swore celibacy, but some had been known to stray, and Lawrence hadn't been a priest. As for Rose, she had been a pretty woman before hardship and toil had worn her down. Was it possible that she had worked for Lawrence in those days? And that the two of them . . . Was that the reason why Rose had fainted clean away when Maggie had told her she was going to marry Lawrence? And why she had excused herself from attending the wedding? She'd claimed she was ill, yet she had been fit to travel to Yorkshire the very next day. Had the real reason been that she didn't want to come face to face with Lawrence?

Try as she might to push such thoughts out of her head, Maggie couldn't. She kept returning to them, as compulsively as picking at a scab. In some ways it would explain so much – how different Billy was to the other Donovan boys, for one thing. He'd never been rough-and-tumble like them; he was shy and sensitive, a target for bullies. It would also explain why Lawrence had been so ready to help her when she had been in trouble, offering her not just a job but a home and respectability. He had been so kind to her, making sure she wanted for nothing, even teaching her the art that was his life. He had adored Patrick. And he had taken Billy under his wing, showed him endless patience and understanding, and in the end given his life for him.

And something else . . . the memory flashed unbidden into Maggie's head. 'She was a good woman,' Lawrence had said. Maggie had thought it strange at the time that he should speak of Rose as if he had known her, but had then forgotten all about it. Now she remembered, and remembered too how sad he had seemed. She had thought his sadness was for her, that she had lost her mother. But might it have been something quite different?

And now that she came to think about it, Rose had said something similar about Lawrence. Though to Maggie's knowledge she had never met him, she had seemed convinced that he was a good man who would treat Maggie well.

Maggie sighed, shaking her head. She really didn't know, and she supposed she never would now. All those who would have known the truth were dead. The rest was nothing but a little boy's imperfect memory and a whole lot of conjecture. But strangely enough, Maggie found comfort in the idea.

Rose and Lawrence. It would be nice to think they had shared some happiness, however fleeting.

Smiling wistfully, she went upstairs to check on the sleeping Patrick.

'I have some exciting news, Reuben,' Clarence Hillman said.

Reuben, who had just arrived home from work, had barely had time to take his coat off before his father approached him. His eyes narrowed in his pudgy face. The only exciting news he could imagine his father bringing home would be that the police believed they had got things all wrong and Josh Withers had been arrested after all for the severing of the rope. The debacle of his accusation still stung badly. Though his mother and father insisted he had done the right thing in reporting what he had seen, he couldn't help feeling embarrassed every time he thought of it. He wasn't ashamed, or sorry for what Josh had been put through – in Reuben's book it was no more nor less than a bounder like him deserved. But he thought that he'd been made to look a fool. It was that that really hurt.

'Josh Withers is in trouble again?' he said hopefully.

'No – well, not so far as I am aware.' Clarence stroked his whiskers, a small satisfied smile playing about his face. 'This has nothing to do with that unfortunate business. It's your future we are talking about, my boy.'

'Oh!' Reuben was startled.

'Mr Beaven is looking to take on a junior clerk,' Clarence went on. 'I've taken the liberty of putting your name forward for the post, and Mr Beaven responded very favourably to the suggestion. He'd like to see you as soon as possible to discuss it, but I think we can be reasonably confident the job is yours. Now isn't that good news?'

'I suppose it is, yes,' Reuben said, a little uncertainly. His first thought was that his father wanted him where he could keep an eye on him, and that rankled. They'd go to work together and come home together; there would be no minute of Reuben's day when he wasn't under supervision, no opportunity to pursue some secret fantasy of his own, no real freedom.

But on the other hand, it would certainly be a step up in the world. He was becoming a little tired of working in a gents' outfitter's. The attraction had been Maggie working just next door, and of course she was no longer there. And there was a certain prestige about being a solicitor's clerk, even if he would only be a junior to begin with.

'Well, what do you say, my boy? It's a wonderful opportunity, isn't it?'

Reuben considered. If he could tell the young ladies that he had such a job, perhaps they would be more inclined to take a second look at him. Maybe even Maggie. She was, after all, a widow now. The thought lifted his spirits and he nodded vigorously.

'Yes, Father. I'm sure you're right,' he said.

* * *

The date for her departure to America was fast approaching. Maggie had sorted out all the things she would need for the restoration of the damaged window and they had already been dispatched. Now all she had to do was pack a trunk for herself and Patrick.

She was upstairs putting clothes in neat piles on the bed when there was a ring at the doorbell. She scooped Patrick up and went to answer it – if she left him up here alone, he would very likely pull all the things she was laying out into a jumbled heap on the floor, or he might attempt to come down the stairs by himself and take a tumble.

With Patrick still in her arms, she opened the door, expecting to see the baker's boy with his basket full of pound loaves and currant buns. But it wasn't the baker's boy.

'Josh!' Maggie said, taken completely by surprise.

'Maggie.'

'What are you doing here?'

'What do you think? Ewart tells me you're going to America.'

'Well, yes, I am.'

She should have known, of course, that Ewart would at least mention her departure to Josh. But it hadn't occurred to her that he would turn up on the doorstep. She'd thought that after their last encounter he would find someone else; forget her and all the heartache she had caused him. If, of course, she had caused him heartbreak. Maggie still found it difficult to believe that Josh cared for her as deeply as she cared for him; that it wasn't just the fact that she was out of his reach that made her attractive to him.

'It's madness, Maggie!'

'No, it's something I have to do.'

'Ewart says you might not come back. That you might stay in America.'

'I don't know. I don't know anything at the moment. It's too early to be making decisions that affect my whole future.'

'And my son's future!' Josh rammed his fist into the door frame. 'Oh, I know you don't give a damn about me, Maggie. I know you'll always find some excuse why we shouldn't be together. But this is beyond the pale.'

How was it that when they were not in one another's arms, they always seemed to end up yelling at one another? Maggie sighed.

'Josh, I am not deliberately doing this to hurt you.'

'That's how it looks from where I'm standing.'

'Well, it's not.' The wind was whipping waves of fallen leaves around Josh's feet and gusting through the open door. 'You'd better come in.'

In the living room, she set Patrick down on the floor amongst the toys she'd scattered earlier to amuse him.

'I owe this to Lawrence. Please try to understand.'

Josh's face was set and grim.

'All I know is you're running away again.'

'I am not running away!'

'Last time we talked, you told me you wouldn't leave Lawrence because you didn't want to hurt him. Well, he's not here now, is he? He's dead. And still you're using him as an excuse.'

'How can you be so callous?' Maggie flared.

'There's always some reason why you say we can't be together. First it was Jack, then this husband of yours, now some stupid promise you made him. It's hardly surprising that I'm fed up with it.'

'I'm sorry,' Maggie said wretchedly. 'I suppose it must seem that way. It's not what I want, honestly it's not, but I have to do this. I owe him so much and I must do as I promised. When I come back . . .'

'*If* you come back. You said yourself that you might not. And even if you do, what makes you think I'll still be here waiting?'

Maggie bit her lip.

'That's a chance I have to take. I do love you, Josh. I'll never love anyone the way I love you, but you must see I have to do this.'

He shook his head.

'You and your conscience.'

'I can't change the way I am,' Maggie said defiantly.

'Oh Maggie . . .' He looked so defeated suddenly, all the fight gone out of him. Maggie had always seen him as being so strong, but in that moment she caught a glimpse of the vulnerability that lay beneath the rugged exterior.

'I'm sorry,' she said again, helplessly.

'I know. And I suppose I wouldn't have you any other way. I love you just the way you are.'

Had she heard aright? He'd said he loved her?

'Oh Josh . . .' She had no words left. She bit hard down on her lip, overcome with conflicting emotions. If only things had been different, if only they'd somehow managed to discover one another at the right time, when they would have been free to explore a relationship. If only . . . but things were as they were. She couldn't go back on her promise to Lawrence, however much she might want to, any more than she had been able to desecrate Jack's memory. And for all the strength of their feelings, it was creating an impossible gulf between them.

'I'd better go, hadn't I?' Josh said.

She nodded. 'I think you had.'

If she had had her way, she would have put her arms around him, kissed him, loved him, but from bitter experience she knew where that would lead. And she couldn't find herself pregnant again now. She couldn't go to New York and do what she'd promised if she was carrying a child.

Josh knew it too. He pulled her toward him briefly, kissed her on the lips, then let her go while he still could. Maggie felt as if her heart were breaking.

'I almost forgot.' He fished in his coat pocket and pulled out a toy railway engine. 'I made this for Patrick.'

Through a haze of tears, Maggie looked at it. Perfectly carved in what looked like light oak, varnished to a high sheen, the toy must have been many hours in the making. And Josh had attached a string to the front fender, so that Patrick would be able to pull it along behind him as well as pushing it on its sturdy wheels.

'Oh Josh, it's beautiful.'

'It's OK. I was going to make some trucks or carriages to go behind, but . . .' He left the sentence unfinished. *If you're not going to be here, there's no point.*

'Here you are, little man. This is for you.'

He crouched down beside Patrick, offering him the toy in the palm of his hand; then, as Patrick took it wonderingly and tried to stuff it into his mouth, he eased it out of the chubby fingers, set it on its wheels and pushed it back and forth in front of the little boy. Patrick gurgled in delight, reached out to do the same, then picked it up and once again tried to stuff it into his mouth.

'Patrick – no! It's not a cake.' Maggie bent to retrieve the engine, and for a moment she and Josh were but inches apart, heads almost touching. Then Josh rose abruptly.

'It's all right, I didn't use anything that would harm him if he does try to eat it. But he'll soon discover he doesn't care for the taste, I expect.'

He smiled, but his eyes were moist. He ruffled Patrick's hair, dropped a kiss on the top of Maggie's head and moved towards the door.

Maggie followed him with tear-filled eyes. *Please don't go!* she wanted to implore him, but she bit back the words. Her last promise to Lawrence must be kept.

As the door closed after him, she bent her chin to her chest, covered her face with her hands, and let the tears come.

Peggy Bishop could scarcely believe it. She'd come to see Dr Blackmore because she'd been feeling poorly for a while now; well, not exactly poorly, maybe, but certainly more tired than usual, and her stomach was swollen. At first it was hardly noticeable beneath the rolls of fat that came from too many helpings of rice pudding and fruit cake, and she'd made a half-hearted effort to eat less and take more exercise, but it hadn't made any difference. In fact she'd had to loosen the waistband of her skirt yet again. But it was when she started to experience niggling aches and shooting pains that she'd become seriously worried. Did she have a growth? She had gone cold at the thought. Tom, almost as worried as she was when she told him, had suggested she go to the doctor on a Saturday morning so that he could accompany her to the surgery.

He hadn't come into the consulting room, though – that wouldn't have been seemly. Instead she'd left him sitting on a hard bench in the waiting room along with the other patients awaiting their turn.

Now she gazed open-mouthed at Dr Blackmore.

'That can't be right, Doctor!'

The doctor smiled thinly.

'There's no mistake, Mrs Bishop. You are going to be a mother in about – oh, three months, I'd say. Had you no idea?'

'No . . . none . . .' It sounded stupid, she thought, but it was no more than the truth. All these years she'd been married, all the times she'd allowed favours in the past, and never so much as had a scare, so that she'd come to believe she never would. The possibility of it now simply hadn't crossed her mind.

'It is good news, I hope?' the doctor said, looking at her over the wire-framed spectacles that perched on the end of his nose.

'Well . . . I don't know, Doctor. You've given me that much of a shock . . . You are sure?'

'No doubt about it, Mrs Bishop. None at all. You'd better start getting used to the idea. I can see you're surprised, but sometimes these things happen just when you think they never will.'

'You can say that again, Doctor,' Peggy said.

'Don't worry, I'm confident you will carry this baby and bear it with no problems.' Dr Blackmore hitched his glasses up his nose again. 'You're young and strong – healthy, too. Eat well, have a glass or two of good strong ale when you fancy it, and rest if you're tired, and you'll sail through. And you know you can call me when the time comes. Would you like me to make a booking for your confinement?'

'Oh not now, Doctor. I shall have to talk to Tom about that.'

She left the surgery in a daze, and nodded briefly at Tom, who got up and followed her on to the street.

'What did the doctor say, Peg?' he asked anxiously.

Peggy gave a small shake of her head.

'Not here, Tom. Let's wait until we get home.'

'Is it bad news, then?' For the first time in years, Tom was seriously concerned for his wife. If it was a growth . . . the thought of losing her made him feel sick to the stomach. Oh, she got on his nerves sometimes, and she hadn't been the most faithful of wives, but then maybe he hadn't been the best of husbands. He caught her arm.

'For God's sake, Peg, tell me the worst.'

'I'll tell you when we get home. I can't talk about it here in the street.'

She stepped out determinedly and he took her hand and tucked it through the crook of his arm, all manner of unwelcome thoughts flashing through his head. The minute the front door closed after them, he sat her down on a chair and stood facing her.

'Come on, Peg, I can't stand this any longer. You're not going to die on me, are you?'

Peggy started to laugh, covering her mouth with her hands.

'No, I'm not going to die on you. But by the time this is over, you might be wishing I had. I'm going to have a baby, Tom. In about three months' time, Dr Blackmore says.'

'What!' Tom was almost as flabbergasted as Peggy had been.

'It's true. I know – I couldn't believe it either. I'm going to be a mother. And you are going to be a father.'

'Well, well, well!' Tom huffed breath over his top lip. 'That is a turn-up for the books.'

Peggy looked at him anxiously.

'You aren't cross?'

She'd half expected an explosion from Tom. They'd agreed long ago when no children had come along that they didn't really want them anyway, but now, quite suddenly, Peggy was feeling differently about it, as if just by carrying a baby, albeit unknowingly, she was developing maternal feelings and fulfilling a need she hadn't realised she had. Now she was hoping desperately that Tom wouldn't object too strenuously.

'Cross? No!' Tom huffed again. 'Taken aback, more like. And all this time I've thought I was firing blanks . . .' His eyes narrowed suddenly with suspicion. 'You haven't . . . have you?'

'Of course not!' Peggy snapped, ludicrously indignant given

her past history. 'I never did really. I only liked a bit of fun, that's all.'

Tom's brow cleared, all too ready now to believe her.

'Well, well, well!' he said again, shaking his head. Then a beam split his face from ear to ear, replacing his usual surly expression. 'Me a father! Who'd have thought it! There's one or two that'll be surprised at that! Wait till I tell 'em there's life in the old dog yet!'

'Oh, get on with you! You're not old!'

'Old to be a father for the first time. Well, I'll show the young 'uns they bain't the only ones with fire in their bellies!' He glanced at her solicitously. 'Do you want a cup of tea? I'll make one for you if you like. You'd better start taking things a bit easy, my girl.'

Consideration of this kind was the very last thing Peggy had expected. She watched Tom setting the kettle on the trivet over the fire with almost the same disbelief with which she had received the news of her pregnancy. He actually seemed pleased with the news. Could it be that some of his bad temper had come from believing he was less of a man than his mates? Had it been eating away at him secretly, making him sour and snappy?

Well, only time would tell, but for the moment he was a changed man, and Peggy was determined she would make the most of it.

Chapter Twenty-Seven

Liverpool docks. Maggie had never seen anything like it in her life. The sprawling warehouses and the containers piled high, the small ships darting amongst the big ones, the hustle and bustle, the dirt and the noise. And amidst it all, the splendid liner that was the *Campania*, towering majestically above the wharf, dwarfing everything around her. How in the world could such an enormous vessel stay afloat? Maggie wondered, trembling with nervousness as she approached the gangplank. Surely the sheer weight of her would take her straight to the bottom of the ocean! But she made the crossing regularly, Lawrence had said, and since he'd sailed on her twice, Maggie's common sense told her she must believe it. And really, there was no time for doubts and worries. A steward was waiting to show her to her cabin. Carrying Patrick, she followed him.

On the way, the steward pointed out some of the public rooms, and Maggie saw that they were every bit as impressive as Lawrence had described them, all panelled oak and thick carpet, with rich velvet drapes and carved pilasters. The thought of entering one of them was even more daunting than that of being on the ocean – Maggie wondered how she would ever be able to hold her own with the sort of people who would be her fellow passengers. But she wasn't the ignorant shop girl and miner's daughter she had once been, she reminded herself. Lawrence had taught her so much and broadened her mind. He would tell her she was their equal, and she must begin to believe it. Why, who else amongst them would be able to create a stained-glass window for a cathedral in America's largest city?

That, too, was a daunting prospect, but Maggie wasn't going to start worrying about it yet.

Her trunk had already been delivered to her cabin, which was larger than she'd imagined it would be, and a cot had been provided for Patrick beside her bunk bed. She plumped him down in it while she unpacked her skirts and a dress so that the creases would fall out before she needed to wear them. She didn't want Patrick getting into some sort of mischief that she hadn't foreseen; she would make a thorough inspection of the cabin before letting him loose.

A loud honking attracted her attention. She peeped out of the porthole to see a tug coming alongside the *Campania*, and as she realised they were about to sail, her heart thudded in her chest like the pendulum of a grandfather clock swinging against its casing. So far today she'd had little time to think about the enormity of what she was doing; now, suddenly, it rushed over her in a crushing wave. For a moment she steadied herself against the bunk, breathing deeply and trying to get the better of the sudden rush of apprehension; then, anxious not to miss the moment of departure, she rescued Patrick from the cot and went back on deck with him in her arms.

The dock was a flurry of activity and Maggie lifted Patrick up so he could watch proceedings. But it did nothing to alleviate the panic she was feeling

Everything and everyone she knew and loved was here in England. Though today the weather was overcast, the skies grey and lowering and a cold wind gusting across the deck, she thought of the sights and smells and sounds of a summer morning – the swifts and swallows floating in the pale sunshine over green fields, the fresh scent of new-mown hay vying with the pungent, slightly acrid smell of coal dust, the clip-clop of a horse or pony ebbing and rising as it trotted around the bends in the road, coming ever closer. She'd miss all that; she couldn't imagine any of it in a great city like New York.

And then there were the people she was leaving behind. True, she'd lost many of those closest to her in recent times, but the ones that were left were very dear to her. And there was always someone familiar to turn to, something she'd have to forgo in New York. She'd never forget how kind Dolly Oglethorpe, her old neighbour, had been when she'd needed help nursing Lawrence, or Father O'Brien, who had put her in touch with him, or Cathy, who was soon to become her sister-in-law. Ewart had finally asked her to marry him; he'd come home cock-a-hoop one evening to tell Maggie the news.

'And about time too!' Maggie had chided him. 'You should have made up your mind to come home and make an honest woman of her long ago.'

'I expect you're right, Maggie,' was all he had said, but he couldn't seem to stop smiling.

Maggie had been sorry she would miss the wedding, which was to take place at Christmas, but she didn't suppose they'd miss her. They would have eyes only for each other.

But most of all, of course, she was aching for Josh. She wanted him here, beside her, more than she'd ever wanted him. To feel his arm about her, strong and comforting, to rest her head against his shoulder as the ship departed, to know that he was here for her, now and always. Would he be waiting for her when – if – she came back from America? Given that she always seemed to be turning him away, it was a big ask. Really she couldn't blame him if he looked elsewhere, found himself a woman who would always put him first instead of way down her list of commitments. At the very thought, something seemed to close up inside Maggie, pinching painfully at her heart.

Was she turning her back on a chance of happiness for ever? Depriving Patrick of his real father? She'd promised Lawrence that she would make this trip, and she intended to keep her promise. But at what cost? The enormity of the sacrifice she was making threatened to undo her, and all she wanted was to rush to the gangplank with Patrick in her arms and disembark before it was too late.

But she wouldn't, of course. All she needed to do was steel herself for a few more minutes and then there could be no turning back.

'Look, Patrick!' In an effort to distract herself from her disturbing thoughts and emotions, she drew Patrick's attention to the activity on the quayside below them.

Seamen swarmed about amid coiled ropes and hawsers, and there were quite a few people lined up on the dock, waving or peering eagerly to catch sight of the relative or friend they had come to see off.

Copying, as he was apt to do, Patrick was waving too.

'That's right, my love, you wave!' she said, trying to smile. 'It's exciting, isn't it?' Patrick ignored her. He wasn't looking at the assembled crowd, she realised; instead his attention was focused on someone approaching along the dockside. A tall, dark figure who was waving back. To Maggie's disbelieving eyes, it looked for all the world like Josh. For goodness' sake! she chided herself. Thinking about him was driving her a little crazy. Wishful thinking couldn't make him materialise like a genie from a bottle, however much she wanted it. But she couldn't take her eyes off the figure all the same. The men working on the gangway had almost completed their job and were about to move it away when the figure broke into a run.

'Wait! Wait!'

He was no longer waving to Patrick, but shouting to the dock workers, who paused, looking towards him and making no effort to disguise their impatience.

'Wait!'

Maggie's heart gave a gigantic leap.

She wasn't going crazy. It was Josh! He must have come to see her off.

'Josh!' she called, waving frantically herself with her free arm as she tried to attract his attention.

He looked up, still running along the dock far beneath her, but made no reply. To her astonishment, she saw that he was carrying a large carpet bag, and he was making for the gangway. Then he was on it, disappearing out of her sight, and the men were wheeling it away, ready for departure.

Totally confused, Maggie turned to the companionway just as Josh emerged.

'What are you doing?' she demanded, unable to think of anything else to say.

'What do you think? Coming with you.'

'Oh Josh! I don't believe this . . .'

'You'd better. And you'd better not think of an excuse to send me home again either, because it's too late for that.'

And then she was in his arms, a startled Patrick sandwiched between them, and his mouth was on hers, devouring her with an intensity that seemed to draw their very souls together.

The ship's siren honked loudly again, bringing them back to reality.

'We're moving!' Maggie said, her voice trembling a little from both excitement and the power of that kiss. 'We're sailing!'

'For once, I timed it just right then, didn't I?' Josh said.

He took Patrick out of her arms, settling him comfortably on his shoulders. Then he put an arm round Maggie's waist, and together they watched as the *Campania* moved slowly away from the dock.

Postscript

A year later

Winter sunshine fractured through the jewel-coloured glass, so that it seemed to glow with a depth and vitality that was almost ethereal. The blue of the Madonna's gown was deeper and richer than a September sky; the halo of light encircling her head shone brighter and more luminous than the evening star. She sat there now in her proper place on one side of her beloved son, the Lord Jesus Christ, completing the triptych with St Joseph. As Maggie gazed up at her, she felt she would burst with pride. She'd done it. She'd done what Lawrence had asked of her and she'd done it unaided. Never in all her life before had she felt so fulfilled as she did now, gazing up at her achievement.

'What do you think then, Lawrence?' she asked silently. 'Does it look as you intended?'

She often talked to him still, and she had sometimes felt he was there at her shoulder as she worked painstakingly to repair the damaged window. Though her life was so different now, she would never forget him, and the things he had taught her would never cease to matter. If she had a guardian angel, it might very well be him, she thought.

But in truth, of course, he had been all too human, and she was certain now that he had indeed been Billy's father. In the pocket of her coat her fingers closed over the letter from Ewart that had arrived many months ago now telling her of the will he had found in the drawer of Lawrence's desk. He'd been surprised that Maggie had not known it was there, or found it herself, but there hadn't been time for her to turn out every drawer and cubbyhole before leaving for America. And Ewart had been even more surprised by what the will contained.

It was dated a few days before he and Maggie had been married, witnessed by Father O'Brien and the monk with whom he shared the ministry of the two churches. The bulk of his estate was to go to Maggie in the event of his death, but there was another provision: 'As stated in my previous will, I bequeath to William Donovan the sum of five hundred pounds, which I hope will allow him to pursue whatever course he wishes to follow in life.'

Five hundred pounds! A fortune! Of course, poor Billy would never now inherit; he had already died before Lawrence breathed his last, but there had been no opportunity for the will to be changed. But the implications of the bequest were crystal clear. The will had been written before Lawrence had taken Billy under his wing, and even referred to a previous will that had also included Billy as a beneficiary. Both Ewart and Maggie had come to the same conclusion. Lawrence was making provision for his son, even though he hadn't specifically owned him as such.

Maggie wished with all her heart that he had been able to tell her himself, but she could understand that it wasn't a subject Lawrence had felt inclined to broach, and neither, of course, had Mam. But although she was slightly shocked at the thought of her mother being unfaithful to her father, she couldn't find it in herself to blame her. Dad hadn't been the most attentive of husbands, he'd seemed to care more about his gambling and drinking than he did about Mam, and all in all she'd had a hard life. If she had found some joy with a good man such as Lawrence, then Maggie could only be glad for her.

She folded her hands and bowed her head, whispering a prayer for all of them, and might almost have been back in the converted barn that was St Christopher's instead of this great cathedral on the other side of the world. The scent of incense mingled with the slight mustiness of old stone was familiar, the candles glowed on the high altar and in the votives, and though everything here was so much grander, the feeling of reverence was just the same. The window that Lawrence had created was a part of that grandeur now, part of that offering, and would be for generations to come. And she had played a small part in its completion, which made her feel humble as well as proud.

Footsteps echoing on the tiled aisle made her turn, and she saw her husband and son approaching her. Josh was holding Patrick by the hand, but the little boy was walking well now; no more waddling – he looked ready to skip and run. He was growing tall; Maggie felt a moment's regret as she thought that soon it would be time to take him out of his baby dresses and put him in a proper pair of trousers, and cut the curls that tumbled to his shoulders. But, God willing, there would be other children. Whilst she had been working on the window, she and Josh had taken care that she didn't fall pregnant again, but now that it was finished, they might well decide it was time for Patrick to have a little brother or sister.

And there were other decisions to be made, too, important ones. Would they go home, or would they stay in this wonderful land of opportunity? They hadn't yet made up their minds. But whatever happened, they would be together, that much was certain. Both Maggie and Josh were determined that nothing would keep them apart again.

Maggie bent now, opening her arms, and Patrick let go of Josh's hand and scooted down the aisle towards her. She lifted him up, pointing at the window.

'What do you think, Patrick? Isn't it splendid? And Mammy did a little bit of it, though most of the work was Lawrence's.' She wanted to keep Lawrence alive in the little boy's memory; he had, after all, played such an enormous part in his early years.

'Pretty!' Patrick stretched out his hands as if he could touch the glowing shards far above his head.

'Yes, pretty,' she agreed, smiling.

'Beautiful,' Josh corrected her, gazing up in awe. 'Do you think you'll ever do another?'

'I'd be hard pressed to do something like this from scratch,' Maggie said. 'Lawrence taught me a lot, but it will take years and years – if ever – before I'm able to even think of something on this scale. But I would like to do some smaller projects. If I can.'

'We'll make sure of it,' Josh said, putting an arm around her waist. 'It would be a shame to let a talent like yours go to waste.'

'I'd like that.' Maggie rested her head against Josh's shoulder, thinking how lucky she was. None of what she had been through seemed important now. She would never forget those she had loved and lost, never stop loving them. But here and now, she felt she held the world in her arms.

A shaft of sunlight touched her face with the golden glow that came from the shining stained-glass halos, and Maggie knew she was truly blessed.

All the Dark Secrets

Bonus material

Get to know Jennie Felton . . .

The inspiration for Jennie's Families of Fairley Terrace sagas...

I grew up in what was the Somerset Coalfield, and a very close-knit community. In 1839 a terrible 'accident' occurred at Wellsway Pit when the hemp rope bearing the 'hudge', a sort of man-riding cage, gave way and twelve men and boys lost their lives as it plunged down the shaft. It was thought the rope had been severed deliberately.

This dreadful tragedy was the starting point for me, as I imagined the impact it must have had on the community. I envisaged a rank of miners' cottages where several families lost a loved one, a husband, a son, a brother, a breadwinner, and decided to tell the stories of some of those directly affected.

I took the liberty of setting the accident some sixty years later. *All the Dark Secrets* begins with the tragedy; the second book, *The Miner's Daughter*, is set later, but tells how the loss of a beloved husband and father is still affecting the lives of his widow and daughters. I have plans to follow the lives of the families who lived in the 'Ten Houses' of Fairley Terrace, their children and grandchildren. I hope you come to love them and care for them as much as I do!

Starting to write...

I have been writing for as long as I can remember. My first readers were my classmates at Grammar school – I wrote serials on exercise book paper which were passed hand to hand. This came to an abrupt end when I was caught writing under the desk in a chemistry lesson!

For a while I wrote just for my own pleasure, then began selling short stories and serials to magazines, and from there moved on to novels. I've written under several names – Janet Tanner, Amelia Carr and now Jennie Felton – and I simply can't imagine a life that didn't include writing.

If I need motivation, though, I read. Much as I love reading, it invariably stirs my desire to be writing myself.

Favourite things...

One of the nicest parts of being a writer is having the excuse to travel to places I probably wouldn't have otherwise visited. Take Darwin, in the Northern Territory of Australia. I went there to research for *Women and War* (written as Janet Tanner) and loved the feel of the outback – it reminded me somehow of the old Wild West. I loved Hong Kong, too, and Singapore, where I absolutely had to have a Singapore Gin Sling in the bar where it was invented, in Raffles Hotel. These both made appearances in *Oriental Hotel*, another of my Janet Tanner titles.

Top of the fictional character list...

I'm going to pick one of my own – Brit, the ex-RAF pilot turned intelligence agent in *Oriental Hotel*. I based a lot of his looks and character on my husband, Terry – who actually also provided some of his one-liners. If I was getting too carried away by fantasy I would ask Terry what he would have said or done in that situation and he could always bring me back to earth. Sadly, I lost Terry last year, so there's no contest as to which character I would like to spend time with.

Favourite book...

I think my all-time favourite is *Gone with the Wind*. I love the great sweeping background, the characters, the drama and pathos, even the ending . . .

Greatest achievement...

I count gaining my private pilot's licence as my greatest achievement. Terry gave me a trial lesson for my 50th birthday and both he and I went on to learn to fly. It was a huge adventure for me, and while I really enjoyed the actual flying, I did find navigation a huge challenge, so my solo cross-countries were done with my heart in my mouth! I was also certain I'd never pass the navigation part of my final exams, but miraculously I did!

A dream dinner party guest list...

That's a difficult one, as the people I'd like to meet probably wouldn't have anything to say to one another or would end up arguing! Tony Wedgewood Benn and Enoch Powell . . . that would be interesting! Authors Wilbur Smith and Diane Chamberlain . . . and definitely a young Elvis Presley!

Realistically, though, I can't imagine anything nicer than being surrounded by my family and close friends – they know who they are!

Sharing guilty pleasures...

Oh no, sorry! I'm keeping them to myself! Though I will admit to Cadbury's Bourneville dark chocolate and butter icing. If I make some to top a cake I always end up scraping the bowl.

Best piece of advice...

The more you put into something the more you get out of it.

Never leave the house without...

My keys! House and car are on the same ring. And I don't like going out without just a touch of eye shadow and liner.

A prized possession...

My engagement ring. A few years ago I hid it while I was away on holiday, and when I got home I couldn't find it. I thought maybe I'd hidden it in a tissue in a pocket and thrown it away by mistake. Then, months later, when I was dusting, a candlestick fell off the mantel-piece, the candle fell out – and out rolled my ring! I'd convinced myself I wasn't too worried about losing it, that what mattered was that Terry and I were still together and the ring was just a symbol. But I was so happy to find it again it's scarcely been off my finger since, and means even more now that Terry is no longer with us.

A motto for life...

Do unto others as you would be done unto. And whenever possible spread a little happiness.

Introducing the Families of Fairley Terrace...

The Withers at No. 10

Gilby and Florrie Withers are devastated to lose their beloved son Jack in the mining disaster. Luckily their other son Josh wasn't working at Shepton Fields. But will they be able to keep him close by when his feelings for his late brother's fiancée become too strong to ignore?

The Donovans at No. 6

When the hudge goes down, the Donovans lose their patriarch Paddy. With her elder brothers Ewart and Walter working away, it's up to daughter Maggie to help her mother Rose keep the roof over their heads and look after younger son Billy, whilst dealing with the loss of her fiancé Jack Withers too.

The Days at No. 4

Twenty-eight-year-old Annie Day loses her loving husband John, leaving her two little girls, Kitty and Lucy, without their beloved father. Surely it's only a matter of time before they are turned out of Fairley Terrace – how will they survive?

The Oglethorpes at No. 3

Dolly and Ollie Oglethorpe are well known in the community, with Dolly serving as midwife for the Ten Houses. They are one of the lucky families as both Ollie and their son Charlie escape the disaster.

The Rogers at No. 2

Queenie and Harry are not so fortunate – they lose their young son Frank in the accident and things are never the same for them again.

To find out more about the fate of the Day family,
and to see what happens to rest of the Families
of Fairley Terrace, look out for the other titles
in Jennie Felton's powerful series.

*The Families of Fairley Terrace Sagas
will continue!*

Look for

THE
MINER'S DAUGHTER

Coming soon.

Stay in touch with Jennie!

Visit her on Facebook at

www.facebook.com/JennieFeltonAuthor

for her latest news.

Or follow her on Twitter @Jennie_Felton,

and join the #FamiliesofFairley

conversation!